# THE COMPLETE **EARLY POIROT**

*This portrait of Agatha Christie appeared in* The Sketch *on February 28, 1923.*

# THE COMPLETE EARLY POIROT OMNIBUS

*The Mysterious Affair at Styles*
*The Murder on the Links*
*The Man who Was Number Four*
*... And 25 Others*

BY **AGATHA CHRISTIE**

*With Introduction by Finn J.D. John*

Bankshott
BOOKS

Dustjacket art by Katherine Greymour.

First edition, softcover

ISBN: 978-1-63591-662-1

Bankshott Books
An imprint of Pulp-Lit Productions
Corvallis, Oregon

http://bankshott.pulp-lit.com

# TABLE OF CONTENTS.

*Third series of short stories (a serial novel):*

# The Maker of "The Grey Cells of M. Poirot."

With her daughter, Rosalind: Agatha Christie, the great detective-story writer.

At the telephone.

At her writing table.

At work with her type-writer.

In her drawing-room: the author of the series of detective stories we begin this week.

With "Tutankhamen cushions: Agatha Christie and her little girl.

**CREATOR OF THE MOST INTERESTING DETECTIVE SINCE SHERLOCK HOLMES: AGATHA CHRISTIE.**

Agatha Christie (who is in private life Mrs. Archibald Christie, the mother of a charming little daughter, Rosalind) is the brilliant writer of detective fiction, and creator of Hercule Poirot, the most fascinating character any novel-reader could wish to meet. Her first book, "The Mysterious Affair at Styles," introduced Poirot, the detective who, by the aid of what he calls "those brave little grey cells" of his brain, unravels the strangest tangles of crime. A series of stories dealing with Poirot's further exploits has been written for "The Sketch," and opens this week—on the page opposite. The tales are a thrilling set of detective yarns which equal anything ever published in that style.

Photograph by Alfieri, specially taken for "The Sketch."

*This photo spread on Agatha Christie was published in* The Sketch *in 1923.*

# INTRODUCTION.

## HERCULE POIROT: THE EARLY YEARS.

Hercule Poirot made his first public appearance in 1920 at the age, one guesses, of about 60. He finally breathed his metaphorical last in 1975 at the age of maybe 75 or 80. And in that short span of time — either 55 years or about 20, depending on how you count it — Poirot became one of England's most profitable and ubiquitous export commodities.

But it's very clear that his creator, Agatha Christie, did not at first intend for it to go that way. She made a very definite attempt to end the Hercule Poirot saga in the mid-1920s, when his story consisted simply of three novels and 25 short stories.

It is that first Hercule Poirot bibliography, the one Christie clearly intended to leave for posterity when she typed up the last few words of "The Crag in the Dolomites" sometime in 1924, that is presented in this collection.

Hercule Poirot and his author both burst upon the literary scene at the same time in 1920, when Christie found a publisher for the novel she'd written four years earlier during the Great War. She had been working as a nurse at a hospital near her home in Devon, and drew her inspiration for the character from a group of Belgian refugees who were housed nearby. What has become known as "the rape of Belgium" — Imperial Germany's invasion and brutal suppression of that tiny neutral kingdom in its attempt to conquer France — was, of course, the main *causus belli* of the war for England. The Germans, who had somehow expected the Belgians to just let them roll through unmolested, reacted to the spirited resistance they encountered there with almost comical outrage and with not-at-all comical vengefulness; and the plight of "plucky little Belgium" was much in the English mind as the war ground painfully on. Poirot, who was literally a plucky little Belgian, was a fantastic analog for his home country.

We first meet Poirot as an older man — old enough to be retired from the police service, but young enough to consider that he might yet "marry and range myself," as he puts it at the very end of the last story in this collection.

In his first story, *The Mysterious Affair at Styles*, he just happens to be around and handy to solve the mysterious murder of a prominent-but-not-much-loved club woman, Emily Inglethorp, mistress of Styles, a country estate in Essex. In the course of solving this case, Poirot strikes up a strong friendship with our narrator, Arthur Hastings. And it's through the eyes of Hastings — fundamentally impulsive, incurably romantic, remarkably brave, a bit supercilious, unimaginatively conservative, not very intelligent but not stupid either, a bit of a snob but not without humility — that we meet and get to know Poirot.

Upon this first novel's release in 1920, it proceeded to take the country by storm, effectively launching the Golden Age of Detective Fiction. As its popularity grew, Bruce Ingram, the editor of *The Sketch: A Journal of Art and Actuality*, a popular (and positively gorgeous) slick weekly society magazine, reached out to her. Impressed by the characters he'd met in the pages of *Styles*, and wanting, like many other English readers, to spend a little more time with them, he invited her to write a series of twelve short stories featuring Poirot and Hastings, for publication in his magazine.

*The Sketch* had a standing section for short fiction, which it published regularly. It was called "Tales with a Sting." And it was under this header that the first twelve Hercule Poirot short stories were published, one per week, every week, throughout the second quarter of 1923.

By the time this happened, the reading public had already had a crack at the second Poirot novel, *The Murder on the Links*. It was published in serial form, in four parts, in *Grand Magazine*, a high-end British pulp that was on the literary level of *Argosy* or *Blue Book* in the U.S., starting in December of 1922. The series was assembled into a complete novel and published in mid-1923.

This sequence of stories truly made Agatha Christie a household name. *The Sketch* promptly commissioned a second series, this time to run under its own section header, "The Grey Cells of Monsieur Poirot" — "Tales with a Sting" being deemed too generic.

*Hercule Poirot as he was depicted in The Sketch in 1923.*

Finally, in early 1924, The Sketch published a third series of Poirot stories — a serial novel broken up into twelve parts, and collectively titled *The Man Who Was Number Four.* When it finished, to all appearance, so was the story of Hercule Poirot.

Actually, Christie seems to have initially intended for *The Murder on the Links* to be the end of it. Its ending feels very conclusive; Hastings is off to South America with his new bride to start a new life; Poirot is still at loose ends, of course, but he's already sounding a bit like a man going into retirement for real; and, anyway, how can Poirot be Poirot without Hastings to admire and interpret him?

These plans, if such they were, got disrupted by Bruce Ingram's timely proposal. *The Sketch* was more or less the top of the pecking order of British magazines, a glossy, gorgeous, thick thing, heavy in the hand, and so full of gorgeous portrait prints of people and works of art that many public libraries had to hide their copies away in the archives room to protect them from marauders with razor knives. Ingram's was surely an offer Christie wouldn't refuse. So, out came our hero for an encore performance … and another … and, early the following year, yet another.

The last of these, *The Man Who Was Number Four*, leaves no question in the reader's mind as to whether Christie was finished writing Poirot stories. At the end of it, Poirot has shaved off his moustaches, pledged himself to the retirement and the cultivation of vegetable marrows (summer squashes and decorative gourds), and is on the brink of proposing marriage to his great criminal opponent, the Countess Vera Rossakoff — who plays Catwoman to Poirot's Batman, if you'll pardon the anachronism. And Hastings, of course, is off back home to South America, where his way-too-young-for-him wife awaits his return.

End of story, right? Certainly Christie seemed to think so. And why wouldn't she be eager to move on? Her second novel, *The Secret Adversary*, was much more to her taste. In reading it, it's hard to escape the impression that Christie strongly identified with its heroine, Tuppence Cowley. And why wouldn't she? A novel about two bright young things, just back from the war but somehow unscarred by it, setting out with cheeky optimism and youthful energy to conquer the world, one unsolved crime at a time — this was definitely a story far better calculated to appeal to a slightly-repressed-but-still-high-spirited bright young thing like the young Mrs. Christie.

"To all those who lead monotonous lives, in the hope that they experience at second hand the delights and dangers of adventure," Christie wrote, in the dedication to *The Secret Adversary*. It's easy to see that she numbered herself amongst that cohort, particularly in light of later events in her life (her famous nervous breakdown and temporary disappearance after her unfaithful husband surprised her with a demand for a divorce).

And so the next Agatha Christie series to appear in *The Sketch*, later in 1924, ran under the header, "Tommy and Tuppence: A Detective Series by Agatha Christie." And into the archives went the old-people story — the story of the elderly detective and his stodgy protégé, with their country-estate murders and jewel thefts and bond robberies — and into more youthful pastures with adventure stories featuring bright young things like Tuppence and Tommy and Anne Beddingfield (in *The Man in the Brown Suit*).

Fortunately for all of us, Christie brought the old duffer out of retirement and put him back in action two years later, in 1926, with *The Murder of Roger Ackroyd*, one of the best and most famous novels of her career; and after that, she never really looked back. Fifty-five years and nearly three dozen Poirot novels later, she finally retired him for good with *Curtain*, which she'd actually written many years earlier with the idea that it would be published after her death; but she changed her mind, and it ended up being the last novel she published before her own death, at the age of 85, on January 12, 1976.

It's an unmistakable irony that Agatha Christie's career began and ended with Hercule Poirot. There must have been something of the spirit of that spunky Belgian, somehow simultaneously preening and humble, comfortable in his brilliance, kindhearted but merciless in the pursuit of his duty, in the spirit of his creator — that English national treasure, the one and only Bard of

Winterbrook, Dame Agatha Mary Clarissa (Miller) Christie.

— FINN J.D. JOHN

*Corvallis, Oregon*
*March 15, 2020*

# THE MYSTERIOUS AFFAIR AT STYLES.

*The First Hercule Poirot Novel*
*Written 1916; Published 1920.*

# I.

## I GO TO STYLES.

The intense interest aroused in the public by what was known at the time as "The Styles Case" has now somewhat subsided. Nevertheless, in view of the world-wide notoriety which attended it, I have been asked, both by my friend Poirot and the family themselves, to write an account of the whole story. This, we trust, will effectually silence the sensational rumours which still persist.

I will therefore briefly set down the circumstances which led to my being connected with the affair.

I had been invalided home from the Front; and, after spending some months in a rather depressing Convalescent Home, was given a month's sick leave. Having no near relations or friends, I was trying to make up my mind what to do, when I ran across John Cavendish. I had seen very little of him for some years. Indeed, I had never known him particularly well. He was a good fifteen years my senior, for one thing, though he hardly looked his forty-five years. As a boy, though, I had often stayed at Styles, his mother's place in Essex.

We had a good yarn about old times, and it ended in his inviting me down to Styles to spend my leave there.

"The mater will be delighted to see you again — after all those years," he added.

"Your mother keeps well?" I asked.

"Oh, yes. I suppose you know that she has married again?"

I am afraid I showed my surprise rather plainly. Mrs. Cavendish, who had married John's father when he was a widower with two sons, had been a handsome woman of middle-age as I remembered her. She certainly could not be a day less than seventy now. I recalled her as an energetic, autocratic personality, somewhat inclined to charitable and social notoriety, with a fondness for opening bazaars and playing the Lady Bountiful. She was a most generous woman, and possessed a considerable fortune of her own.

Their country-place, Styles Court, had been purchased by Mr. Cavendish early in their married life. He had been completely under his wife's ascendancy, so much so that, on dying, he left the place to her for her lifetime, as well as the larger part of his income; an arrangement that was distinctly unfair to his two sons. Their step-mother, however, had always been most generous to them; indeed, they were so young at the time of their father's remarriage that they always thought of her as their own mother.

Lawrence, the younger, had been a delicate youth. He had qualified as a doctor but early relinquished the profession of medicine, and lived at home while pursuing literary ambitions; though his verses never had any marked success.

John practised for some time as a barrister, but had finally settled down to the more congenial life of a country squire. He had married two years ago, and had taken his wife to live at Styles, though I entertained a shrewd suspicion that he would have preferred his mother to increase his allowance, which would have enabled him to have a home of his own. Mrs. Cavendish, however, was a lady who liked to make her own plans, and expected other people to fall in with them, and in this case she certainly had the whip hand, namely: the purse strings.

John noticed my surprise at the news of his mother's remarriage and smiled rather ruefully.

"Rotten little bounder too!" he said savagely. "I can tell you, Hastings, it's making life jolly difficult for us. As for Evie — you remember Evie?"

"No."

"Oh, I suppose she was after your time. She's the mater's factotum, companion, Jack of all trades! A great sport — old Evie! Not precisely young and beautiful, but as game as they make them."

"You were going to say — ?"

"Oh, this fellow! He turned up from nowhere, on the pretext of being a second cousin or something of Evie's, though she didn't seem particularly keen to acknowledge the relationship. The fellow is an absolute outsider, anyone can see that. He's got a great black beard, and wears patent leather boots in all weathers! But the mater cottoned to him at once, took him on as secretary — you know how she's always running a hundred societies?"

I nodded.

"Well, of course the war has turned the hundreds into thousands. No doubt the fellow was very useful to her. But you could have knocked us all down with a feather when, three months ago, she suddenly announced that she and Alfred were engaged! The fellow must be at least twenty years younger than she is! It's simply bare-faced fortune hunting; but there you are — she is her own mistress, and she's married him."

"It must be a difficult situation for you all."

"Difficult! It's damnable!"

Thus it came about that, three days later, I descended from the train at Styles St. Mary, an absurd little station, with no apparent reason for existence, perched up in the midst of green fields and country lanes. John Cavendish was waiting on the platform, and piloted me out to the car.

"Got a drop or two of petrol still, you see," he remarked. "Mainly owing to the mater's activities."

The village of Styles St. Mary was situated about two miles from the little station, and Styles Court lay a mile the other side of it. It was a still, warm day in early July. As one looked out over the flat Essex country, lying so green and peaceful under the afternoon sun, it seemed almost impossible to believe that, not so very far away, a great war was running its appointed course. I felt I had suddenly strayed into another world. As we turned in at the lodge gates, John said:

"I'm afraid you'll find it very quiet down here, Hastings."

"My dear fellow, that's just what I want."

"Oh, it's pleasant enough if you want to lead the idle life. I drill with the volunteers twice a week, and lend a hand at the farms. My wife works regularly 'on the land.' She is up at five every morning to milk, and keeps at it steadily until lunchtime. It's a jolly good life taking it all round — if it weren't for that fellow Alfred Inglethorp!" He checked the car suddenly, and glanced at his watch. "I wonder if we've time to pick up Cynthia. No, she'll have started from the hospital by now."

"Cynthia! That's not your wife?"

"No, Cynthia is a protégée of my mother's, the daughter of an old schoolfellow of hers, who married a rascally solicitor. He came a cropper, and the girl was left an orphan and penniless. My mother came to the rescue, and Cynthia has been with us nearly two years now. She works in the Red Cross Hospital at Tadminster, seven miles away."

As he spoke the last words, we drew up in front of the fine old house. A lady in a stout tweed skirt, who was bending over a flower bed, straightened herself at our approach.

"Hullo, Evie, here's our wounded hero! Mr. Hastings — Miss Howard."

Miss Howard shook hands with a hearty, almost painful, grip. I had an impression of very blue eyes in a sunburnt face. She was a pleasant-looking woman of about forty, with a deep voice, almost manly in its stentorian tones, and had a large sensible square body, with feet to match — these last encased in good thick boots. Her conversation, I soon found, was couched in the telegraphic style.

"Weeds grow like house afire. Can't keep even with 'em. Shall press you in. Better be careful."

"I'm sure I shall be only too delighted to make myself useful," I responded.

"Don't say it. Never does. Wish you hadn't later."

"You're a cynic, Evie," said John, laughing. "Where's tea to-day — inside or out?"

"Out. Too fine a day to be cooped up in the house."

"Come on then, you've done enough gardening for to-day. 'The labourer is worthy of his hire,' you know. Come and be refreshed."

"Well," said Miss Howard, drawing off her gardening gloves, "I'm inclined to agree with you."

She led the way round the house to where tea was spread under the shade of a large sycamore.

A figure rose from one of the basket chairs, and came a few steps to meet us.

"My wife, Hastings," said John.

I shall never forget my first sight of Mary Cavendish. Her tall, slender form, outlined against the bright light; the vivid sense of slumbering fire that seemed to find expression only in those wonderful tawny eyes of hers, remarkable eyes, different from any other woman's that I have ever known; the intense power of stillness she possessed, which nevertheless conveyed the impression of a wild untamed spirit in an exquisitely civilised body — all these things are burnt into my memory. I shall never forget them.

She greeted me with a few words of pleasant welcome in a low clear voice, and I sank into a basket chair feeling distinctly glad that I had accepted John's invitation. Mrs. Cavendish gave me some tea, and her few quiet remarks heightened my first impression of her as a thoroughly fascinating woman. An appreciative listener is always stimulating, and I described, in a humorous manner, certain incidents of my Convalescent Home, in a way which, I flatter myself, greatly amused my hostess. John, of course, good fellow though he is, could hardly be called a brilliant conversationalist.

At that moment a well-remembered voice floated through the open French window near at hand:

"Then you'll write to the Princess after tea, Alfred? I'll write to Lady Tadminster for the second day, myself. Or shall we wait until we hear from the Princess? In case of a refusal, Lady Tadminster might open it the first day, and Mrs. Crosbie the second. Then there's the Duchess — about the school fête."

There was the murmur of a man's voice, and then Mrs. Inglethorp's rose in reply:

"Yes, certainly. After tea will do quite well. You are so thoughtful, Alfred dear."

The French window swung open a little wider, and a handsome white-haired old lady, with a somewhat masterful cast of features, stepped out of it on to the lawn. A man followed her, a suggestion of deference in his manner.

Mrs. Inglethorp greeted me with effusion.

"Why, if it isn't too delightful to see you again, Mr. Hastings, after all these years. Alfred, darling, Mr. Hastings — my husband."

I looked with some curiosity at "Alfred darling." He certainly struck a rather alien note. I did not wonder at John objecting to his beard. It was one of the longest and blackest I have ever seen. He wore gold-rimmed pince-nez, and had a curious impassivity of feature. It struck me that he might look natural on a stage, but was strangely out of place in real life. His voice was rather deep and unctuous. He placed a wooden hand in mine and said:

"This is a pleasure, Mr. Hastings." Then, turning to his wife: "Emily dearest, I think that cushion is a little damp."

She beamed fondly on him, as he substituted another with every demonstration of the tenderest care. Strange infatuation of an otherwise sensible woman!

With the presence of Mr. Inglethorp, a sense of constraint and veiled hostility seemed to settle down upon the company. Miss Howard, in particular, took no pains to conceal her feelings. Mrs. Inglethorp, however, seemed to notice nothing unusual. Her volubility, which I remembered of old, had lost nothing in the intervening years, and she poured out a steady flood of conversation, mainly on the subject of the forthcoming bazaar which she was organizing and which was to take place shortly. Occasionally she referred to her husband over a question of days or dates. His watchful and attentive manner never varied. From the very first I took a firm and rooted dislike to him, and I flatter myself that my first judgments are usually fairly shrewd.

Presently Mrs. Inglethorp turned to give some instructions about letters to Evelyn Howard, and her husband addressed me in his painstaking voice:

"Is soldiering your regular profession, Mr. Hastings?"

"No, before the war I was in Lloyd's."

"And you will return there after it is over?"

"Perhaps. Either that or a fresh start altogether."

Mary Cavendish leant forward.

"What would you really choose as a profession, if you could just consult your inclination?"

"Well, that depends."

"No secret hobby?" she asked. "Tell me — you're drawn to something? Everyone is — usually something absurd."

"You'll laugh at me."

She smiled.

"Perhaps."

"Well, I've always had a secret hankering to be a detective!"

"The real thing — Scotland Yard? Or Sherlock Holmes?"

"Oh, Sherlock Holmes by all means. But really, seriously, I am awfully drawn to it. I came across a man in Belgium once, a very famous detective, and he quite inflamed me. He was a marvellous little fellow. He used to say that all good detective work was a mere matter of method. My system is based on his — though of course I have progressed rather further. He was a funny little man, a great dandy, but wonderfully clever."

"Like a good detective story myself," remarked Miss Howard. "Lots of nonsense written, though. Criminal discovered in last chapter. Everyone dumbfounded. Real crime — you'd know at once."

"There have been a great number of undiscovered crimes," I argued.

"Don't mean the police, but the people that are right in it. The family. You couldn't really hoodwink them. They'd know."

"Then," I said, much amused, "you think that if you were mixed up in a crime, say a murder, you'd be able to spot the murderer right off?"

"Of course I should. Mightn't be able to prove it to a pack of lawyers. But I'm certain I'd know. I'd feel it in my fingertips if he came near me."

"It might be a 'she'," I suggested.

"Might. But murder's a violent crime. Associate it more with a man."

"Not in a case of poisoning." Mrs. Cavendish's clear voice startled me. "Dr. Bauerstein was saying yesterday that, owing to the general ignorance of the more uncommon poisons among the medical profession, there were probably countless cases of poisoning quite unsuspected."

"Why, Mary, what a gruesome conversation!" cried Mrs. Inglethorp. "It makes me feel as if a goose were walking over my grave. Oh, there's Cynthia!"

A young girl in V.A.D. uniform ran lightly across the lawn.

"Why, Cynthia, you are late to-day. This is Mr. Hastings — Miss Murdoch."

Cynthia Murdoch was a fresh-looking young creature, full of life and vigour. She tossed off her little V.A.D. cap, and I admired the great loose waves of her auburn hair, and the smallness and whiteness of the hand she held out to claim her tea. With dark eyes and eyelashes she would have been a beauty.

She flung herself down on the ground beside John, and as I handed her a plate of sandwiches she smiled up at me.

"Sit down here on the grass, do. It's ever so much nicer."

I dropped down obediently.

"You work at Tadminster, don't you, Miss Murdoch?"

She nodded.

"For my sins."

"Do they bully you, then?" I asked, smiling.

"I should like to see them!" cried Cynthia with dignity.

"I have got a cousin who is nursing," I remarked. "And she is terrified of 'Sisters.'"

"I don't wonder. Sisters *are*, you know, Mr. Hastings. They simply *are!* You've no idea! But I'm not a nurse, thank heaven, I work in the dispensary."

"How many people do you poison?" I asked, smiling.

Cynthia smiled too.

"Oh, hundreds!" she said.

"Cynthia," called Mrs. Inglethorp, "do you think you could write a few notes for me?"

"Certainly, Aunt Emily."

She jumped up promptly, and something in her manner reminded me that her position was a dependent one, and that Mrs. Inglethorp, kind as she might be in the main, did not allow her to forget it.

My hostess turned to me.

"John will show you your room. Supper is at half-past seven. We have given up late dinner for some time now. Lady Tadminster, our Member's wife — she was the late Lord Abbotsbury's daughter — does the same. She agrees with me that one must set an example of economy. We are quite a war household; nothing is wasted here — every scrap of waste paper, even, is saved and sent away in sacks."

I expressed my appreciation, and John took me into the house and up the broad staircase, which forked right and left half-way to different wings of the building. My room was in the left wing, and looked out over the park.

John left me, and a few minutes later I saw him from my window walking slowly across the grass arm in arm with Cynthia Murdoch. I heard Mrs. Inglethorp call "Cynthia" impatiently, and the girl started and ran back to the house. At the same moment, a man stepped out from the shadow of a tree and walked slowly in the same direction. He looked about forty, very dark with a melancholy clean-shaven face. Some violent emotion seemed to be mastering him. He looked up at my window as he passed, and I recognized him, though he had changed much in the fifteen years that had elapsed since we last met. It was John's younger brother, Lawrence Cavendish. I wondered what it was that had brought that singular expression to his face.

Then I dismissed him from my mind, and returned to the contemplation of my own affairs.

The evening passed pleasantly enough; and I dreamed that night of that enigmatical woman, Mary Cavendish.

The next morning dawned bright and sunny, and I was full of the anticipation of a delightful visit.

I did not see Mrs. Cavendish until lunch-time, when she volunteered to take me for a walk, and we spent a charming afternoon roaming in the woods, returning to the house about five.

As we entered the large hall, John beckoned us both into the smoking-room. I saw at once by his face that something disturbing had occurred. We followed him in, and he shut the door after us.

"Look here, Mary, there's the deuce of a mess. Evie's had a row with Alfred Inglethorp, and she's off."

"Evie? Off?"

John nodded gloomily.

"Yes; you see she went to the mater, and—Oh,—here's Evie herself."

Miss Howard entered. Her lips were set grimly together, and she carried a small suit-case. She looked excited and determined, and slightly on the defensive.

"At any rate," she burst out, "I've spoken my mind!"

"My dear Evelyn," cried Mrs. Cavendish, "this can't be true!"

Miss Howard nodded grimly.

"True enough! Afraid I said some things to Emily she won't forget or forgive in a hurry. Don't mind if they've only sunk in a bit. Probably water off a duck's back, though. I said right out: 'You're an old woman, Emily, and there's no fool like an old fool. The man's twenty years younger than you, and don't you fool yourself as to what he married you for. Money! Well, don't let him have too much of it. Farmer Raikes has got a very pretty young wife. Just ask your Alfred how much time he spends over there.' She was very angry. Natural! I went on, 'I'm going to warn you, whether you like it or not. That man would as soon murder you in your bed as look at you. He's a bad lot. You can say what you like to me, but remember what I've told you. He's a bad lot!'"

"What did she say?"

Miss Howard made an extremely expressive grimace.

"'Darling Alfred'—'dearest Alfred'—'wicked calumnies'—'wicked lies'—'wicked woman'—to accuse her 'dear husband!' The sooner I left her house the better. So I'm off."

"But not now?"

"This minute!"

For a moment we sat and stared at her. Finally John Cavendish, finding his persuasions of no avail, went off to look up the trains. His wife followed him, murmuring something about persuading Mrs. Inglethorp to think better of it.

As she left the room, Miss Howard's face changed. She leant towards me eagerly.

"Mr. Hastings, you're honest. I can trust you?"

I was a little startled. She laid her hand on my arm, and sank her voice to a whisper.

"Look after her, Mr. Hastings. My poor Emily. They're a lot of sharks — all of them. Oh, I know what I'm talking about. There isn't one of them that's not hard up and trying to get money out of her. I've protected her as much as I could. Now I'm out of the way, they'll impose upon her."

"Of course, Miss Howard," I said, "I'll do everything I can, but I'm sure you're excited and overwrought."

She interrupted me by slowly shaking her forefinger.

"Young man, trust me. I've lived in the world rather longer than you have. All I ask you is to keep your eyes open. You'll see what I mean."

The throb of the motor came through the open window, and Miss Howard rose and moved to the door. John's voice sounded outside. With her hand on the handle, she turned her head over her shoulder, and beckoned to me.

"Above all, Mr. Hastings, watch that devil — her husband!"

There was no time for more. Miss Howard was swallowed up in an eager chorus of protests and good-byes. The Inglethorps did not appear.

As the motor drove away, Mrs. Cavendish suddenly detached herself from the group, and moved across the drive to the lawn to meet a tall bearded man who had been evidently making for the house. The colour rose in her cheeks as she held out her hand to him.

"Who is that?" I asked sharply, for instinctively I distrusted the man.

"That's Dr. Bauerstein," said John shortly.

"And who is Dr. Bauerstein?"

"He's staying in the village doing a rest cure, after a bad nervous breakdown. He's a London specialist; a very clever man — one of the greatest living experts on poisons, I believe."

"And he's a great friend of Mary's," put in Cynthia, the irrepressible.

John Cavendish frowned and changed the subject.

"Come for a stroll, Hastings. This has been a most rotten business. She always had a rough tongue, but there is no stauncher friend in England than Evelyn Howard."

He took the path through the plantation, and we walked down to the village through the woods which bordered one side of the estate.

As we passed through one of the gates on our way home again, a pretty young woman of gypsy type coming in the opposite direction bowed and smiled.

"That's a pretty girl," I remarked appreciatively.

John's face hardened.

"That is Mrs. Raikes."

"The one that Miss Howard —"

"Exactly," said John, with rather unnecessary abruptness.

I thought of the white-haired old lady in the big house, and that vivid wicked little face that had just smiled into ours, and a vague chill of foreboding crept over me. I brushed it aside.

"Styles is really a glorious old place," I said to John.

He nodded rather gloomily.

"Yes, it's a fine property. It'll be mine some day — should be mine now by rights, if my father had only made a decent will. And then I shouldn't be so damned hard up as I am now."

"Hard up, are you?"

"My dear Hastings, I don't mind telling you that I'm at my wits' end for money."

"Couldn't your brother help you?"

"Lawrence? He's gone through every penny he ever had, publishing rotten verses in fancy bindings. No, we're an impecunious lot. My mother's always been awfully good to us, I must say. That is, up to now. Since her marriage, of course —" He broke off, frowning.

For the first time I felt that, with Evelyn Howard, something indefinable had gone from the atmosphere. Her presence had spelt security. Now that security was removed — and the air seemed rife with suspicion. The sinister face of Dr. Bauerstein recurred to me unpleasantly. A vague suspicion of everyone and everything filled my mind. Just for a moment I had a premonition of approaching evil.

# II.

## THE 16TH AND 17TH OF JULY.

I had arrived at Styles on the 5th of July. I come now to the events of the 16th and 17th of that month. For the convenience of the reader I will recapitulate the incidents of those days in as exact a manner as possible. They were elicited subsequently at the trial by a process of long and tedious cross-examinations.

I received a letter from Evelyn Howard a couple of days after her departure, telling me she was working as a nurse at the big hospital in Middlingham, a manufacturing town some fifteen miles away, and begging me to let her know if Mrs. Inglethorp should show any wish to be reconciled.

The only fly in the ointment of my peaceful days was Mrs. Cavendish's extraordinary, and, for my part, unaccountable preference for the society of Dr. Bauerstein. What she saw in the man I cannot imagine, but she was always asking him up to the house, and often went off for long expeditions with him. I must confess that I was quite unable to see his attraction.

The 16th of July fell on a Monday. It was a day of turmoil. The famous bazaar had taken place on Saturday, and an entertainment, in connection with the same charity, at which Mrs. Inglethorp was to recite a War poem, was to be held that night. We were all busy during the morning arranging and decorating the Hall in the village where it was to take place. We had a late luncheon and spent the afternoon resting in the garden. I noticed that John's manner was somewhat unusual. He seemed very excited and restless.

After tea, Mrs. Inglethorp went to lie down to rest before her efforts in the evening and I challenged Mary Cavendish to a single at tennis.

About a quarter to seven, Mrs. Inglethorp called us that we should be late as supper was early that night. We had rather a scramble to get ready in time; and before the meal was over the motor was waiting at the door.

The entertainment was a great success, Mrs. Inglethorp's recitation receiving tremendous applause. There were also some tableaux in which Cynthia took part. She did not return with us, having been asked to a supper party, and to remain the night with some friends who had been acting with her in the tableaux.

The following morning, Mrs. Inglethorp stayed in bed to breakfast, as she was rather overtired; but she appeared in her briskest mood about 12:30, and swept Lawrence and myself off to a luncheon party.

"Such a charming invitation from Mrs. Rolleston. Lady Tadminster's sister, you know. The Rollestons came over with the Conqueror — one of our oldest families."

Mary had excused herself on the plea of an engagement with Dr. Bauerstein.

We had a pleasant luncheon, and as we drove away Lawrence suggested that we should return by Tadminster, which was barely a mile out of our way, and pay a visit to Cynthia in her dispensary. Mrs. Inglethorp replied that this was an excellent idea, but as she had several letters to write she would drop us there, and we could come back with Cynthia in the pony-trap.

We were detained under suspicion by the hospital porter, until Cynthia appeared to vouch for us, looking very cool and sweet in her long white overall. She took us up to her sanctum, and introduced us to her fellow dispenser, a rather awe-inspiring individual, whom Cynthia cheerily addressed as "Nibs."

"What a lot of bottles!" I exclaimed, as my eye travelled round the small room. "Do you really know what's in them all?"

"Say something original," groaned Cynthia. "Every single person who comes up here says that. We are really thinking of bestowing a prize on the first individual who does *not* say: 'What a lot of bottles!' And I know the next thing you're going to say is: 'How many people have you poisoned?'"

I pleaded guilty with a laugh.

"If you people only knew how fatally easy it is to poison someone by mistake, you wouldn't joke about it. Come on, let's have tea. We've got all sorts of secret stories in that cupboard. No, Lawrence — that's the poison cupboard. The big cupboard — that's right."

We had a very cheery tea, and assisted Cynthia to wash up afterwards. We had just put away the last tea-spoon when a knock came at the door. The countenances of Cynthia and Nibs were suddenly petrified into a stern and forbidding expression.

"Come in," said Cynthia, in a sharp professional tone.

A young and rather scared looking nurse appeared with a bottle which she proffered to Nibs, who waved her towards Cynthia with the somewhat enigmatical remark:

"I'm not really here to-day."

Cynthia took the bottle and examined it with the severity of a judge.

"This should have been sent up this morning."

"Sister is very sorry. She forgot."

"Sister should read the rules outside the door."

I gathered from the little nurse's expression that there was not the least likelihood of her having the hardihood to retell this message to the dreaded "Sister."

"So now it can't be done until to-morrow," finished Cynthia.

"Don't you think you could possibly let us have it to-night?"

"Well," said Cynthia graciously, "we are very busy, but if we have time it shall be done."

The little nurse withdrew, and Cynthia promptly took a jar from the shelf, refilled the bottle, and placed it on the table outside the door.

I laughed.

"Discipline must be maintained?"

"Exactly. Come out on our little balcony. You can see all the outside wards there."

I followed Cynthia and her friend and they pointed out the different wards to me. Lawrence remained behind, but after a few moments Cynthia called to him over her shoulder to come and join us. Then she looked at her watch.

"Nothing more to do, Nibs?"

"No."

"All right. Then we can lock up and go."

I had seen Lawrence in quite a different light that afternoon. Compared to John, he was an astoundingly difficult person to get to know. He was the opposite of his brother in almost every respect, being unusually shy and reserved. Yet he had a certain charm of manner, and I fancied that, if one really knew him well, one could have a deep affection for him. I had always fancied that his manner to Cynthia was rather constrained, and that she on her side was inclined to be shy of him. But they were both gay enough this afternoon, and chatted together like a couple of children.

As we drove through the village, I remembered that I wanted some stamps, so accordingly we pulled up at the post office.

As I came out again, I cannoned into a little man who was just entering. I drew aside and apologised, when suddenly, with a loud exclamation, he clasped me in his arms and kissed me warmly.

"*Mon ami* Hastings!" he cried. "It is indeed *mon ami* Hastings!"

"Poirot!" I exclaimed.

I turned to the pony-trap.

"This is a very pleasant meeting for me, Miss Cynthia. This is my old friend, Monsieur Poirot, whom I have not seen for years."

"Oh, we know Monsieur Poirot," said Cynthia gaily. "But I had no idea he was a friend of yours."

"Yes, indeed," said Poirot seriously. "I know Mademoiselle Cynthia. It is by the charity of that good Mrs. Inglethorp that I am here." Then, as I looked at him inquiringly: "Yes, my friend, she had kindly extended hospitality to seven of my countrypeople who, alas, are refugees from their native land. We Belgians will always remember her with gratitude."

Poirot was an extraordinary looking little man. He was hardly more than five feet, four inches, but carried himself with great dignity. His head was exactly the shape of an egg, and he always perched it a little on one side. His moustache was very stiff and military. The neatness of his attire was almost incredible. I believe a speck of dust would have caused him more pain than a bullet wound. Yet this quaint dandified little man who, I was sorry to see, now limped badly, had been in his time one of the most celebrated members of the Belgian police. As a detective, his *flair* had been extraordinary, and he had achieved triumphs by unravelling some of the most baffling cases of the day.

He pointed out to me the little house inhabited by him and his fellow Belgians, and I promised to go and see him at an early date. Then he raised his hat with a flourish to Cynthia, and we drove away.

"He's a dear little man," said Cynthia. "I'd no idea you knew him."

"You've been entertaining a celebrity unawares," I replied.

And, for the rest of the way home, I recited to them the various exploits and triumphs of Hercule Poirot.

We arrived back in a very cheerful mood. As we entered the hall, Mrs. Inglethorp came out of her boudoir. She looked flushed and upset.

"Oh, it's you," she said.

"Is there anything the matter, Aunt Emily?" asked Cynthia.

"Certainly not," said Mrs. Inglethorp sharply. "What should there be?" Then catching sight of Dorcas, the parlourmaid, going into the dining-room, she called to her to bring some stamps into the boudoir.

"Yes, m'm." The old servant hesitated, then added diffidently: "Don't you think, m'm, you'd better get to bed? You're looking very tired."

"Perhaps you're right, Dorcas — yes — no — not now. I've some letters I must finish by post-time. Have you lighted the fire in my room as I told you?"

"Yes, m'm."

"Then I'll go to bed directly after supper."

She went into the boudoir again, and Cynthia stared after her.

"Goodness gracious! I wonder what's up?" she said to Lawrence.

He did not seem to have heard her, for without a word he turned on his heel and went out of the house.

I suggested a quick game of tennis before supper and, Cynthia agreeing, I ran upstairs to fetch my racquet.

Mrs. Cavendish was coming down the stairs. It may have been my fancy, but she, too, was looking odd and disturbed.

"Had a good walk with Dr. Bauerstein?" I asked, trying to appear as indifferent as I could.

"I didn't go," she replied abruptly. "Where is Mrs. Inglethorp?"

"In the boudoir."

Her hand clenched itself on the banisters, then she seemed to nerve herself for some encounter, and went rapidly past me down the stairs across the hall to the boudoir, the door of which she shut behind her.

As I ran out to the tennis court a few moments later, I had to pass the open boudoir window, and was unable to help overhearing the following scrap of dialogue. Mary Cavendish was saying in the voice of a woman desperately controlling herself:

"Then you won't show it to me?"

To which Mrs. Inglethorp replied:

"My dear Mary, it has nothing to do with that matter."

"Then show it to me."

"I tell you it is not what you imagine. It does not concern you in the least."

To which Mary Cavendish replied, with a rising bitterness:

"Of course, I might have known you would shield him."

Cynthia was waiting for me, and greeted me eagerly with:

"I say! There's been the most awful row! I've got it all out of Dorcas."

"What kind of a row?"

"Between Aunt Emily and *him*. I do hope she's found him out at last!"

"Was Dorcas there, then?"

"Of course not. She 'happened to be near the door.' It was a real old bust-up. I do wish I knew what it was all about."

I thought of Mrs. Raikes's gipsy face, and Evelyn Howard's warnings, but wisely decided to hold my peace, whilst Cynthia exhausted every possible hypothesis, and cheerfully hoped, "Aunt Emily will send him away, and will never speak to him again."

I was anxious to get hold of John, but he was nowhere to be seen. Evidently something very momentous had occurred that afternoon. I tried to forget the few words I had overheard; but, do what I would, I could not dismiss them altogether from my mind. What was Mary Cavendish's concern in the matter?

Mr. Inglethorp was in the drawing-room when I came down to supper. His face was impassive as ever, and the strange unreality of the man struck me afresh.

Mrs. Inglethorp came down last. She still looked agitated, and during the meal there was a somewhat constrained silence. Inglethorp was unusually quiet. As a rule, he surrounded his wife with little attentions, placing a cushion at her back, and altogether playing the part of the devoted husband. Immediately after supper, Mrs. Inglethorp retired to her boudoir again.

"Send my coffee in here, Mary," she called. "I've just five minutes to catch the post."

Cynthia and I went and sat by the open window in the drawing-room. Mary Cavendish brought our coffee to us. She seemed excited.

"Do you young people want lights, or do you enjoy the twilight?" she asked. "Will you take Mrs. Inglethorp her coffee, Cynthia? I will pour it out."

"Do not trouble, Mary," said Inglethorp. "I will take it to Emily." He poured it out, and went out of the room carrying it carefully.

Lawrence followed him, and Mrs. Cavendish sat down by us.

We three sat for some time in silence. It was a glorious night, hot and still. Mrs. Cavendish fanned herself gently with a palm leaf.

"It's almost too hot," she murmured. "We shall have a thunderstorm."

Alas, that these harmonious moments can never endure! My paradise was rudely shattered by the sound of a well known, and heartily disliked, voice in the hall.

"Dr. Bauerstein!" exclaimed Cynthia. "What a funny time to come."

I glanced jealously at Mary Cavendish, but she seemed quite undisturbed, the delicate pallor of her cheeks did not vary.

In a few moments, Alfred Inglethorp had ushered the doctor in, the latter laughing, and protesting that he was in no fit state for a drawing-room. In truth, he presented a sorry spectacle, being literally plastered with mud.

"What have you been doing, doctor?" cried Mrs. Cavendish.

"I must make my apologies," said the doctor. "I did not really mean to come in, but Mr. Inglethorp insisted."

"Well, Bauerstein, you are in a plight," said John, strolling in from the hall. "Have some coffee, and tell us what you have been up to."

"Thank you, I will." He laughed rather ruefully, as he described how he had discovered a very rare species of fern in an inaccessible place, and in his efforts to obtain it had lost his footing, and slipped ignominiously into a neighbouring pond.

"The sun soon dried me off," he added, "but I'm afraid my appearance is very disreputable."

At this juncture, Mrs. Inglethorp called to Cynthia from the hall, and the girl ran out.

"Just carry up my despatch-case, will you, dear? I'm going to bed."

The door into the hall was a wide one. I had risen when Cynthia did, John was close by me. There were therefore three witnesses who could swear that Mrs. Inglethorp was carrying her coffee, as yet untasted, in her hand.

My evening was utterly and entirely spoilt by the presence of Dr. Bauerstein. It seemed to me the man would never go. He rose at last, however, and I breathed a sigh of relief.

"I'll walk down to the village with you," said Mr. Inglethorp. "I must see our agent over those estate accounts." He turned to John. "No one need sit up. I will take the latch-key."

# III.

## THE NIGHT OF THE TRAGEDY.

To make this part of my story clear, I append the following plan of the first floor of Styles.

*(See next page.)*

It seemed to be the middle of the night when I was awakened by Lawrence Cavendish. He had a candle in his hand, and the agitation of his face told me at once that something was seriously wrong.

"What's the matter?" I asked, sitting up in bed, and trying to collect my scattered thoughts.

"We are afraid my mother is very ill. She seems to be having some kind of fit. Unfortunately she has locked herself in."

"I'll come at once."

I sprang out of bed; and, pulling on a dressing-gown, followed Lawrence along the passage and the gallery to the right wing of the house.

John Cavendish joined us, and one or two of the servants were standing round in a state of

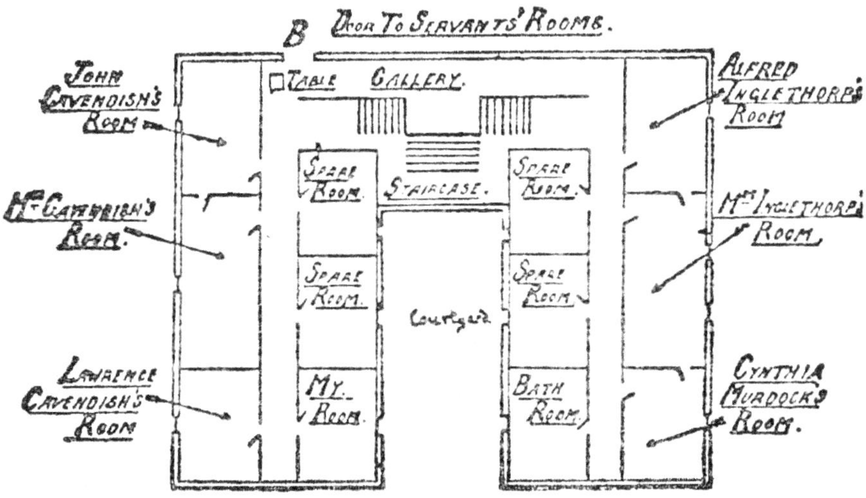


*The servants' rooms are reached through the door B. They have no communication with the right wing, where the Inglethorps' rooms were situated.*

awe-stricken excitement. Lawrence turned to his brother.

"What do you think we had better do?"

Never, I thought, had his indecision of character been more apparent.

John rattled the handle of Mrs. Inglethorp's door violently, but with no effect. It was obviously locked or bolted on the inside. The whole household was aroused by now. The most alarming sounds were audible from the interior of the room. Clearly something must be done.

"Try going through Mr. Inglethorp's room, sir," cried Dorcas. "Oh, the poor mistress!"

Suddenly I realized that Alfred Inglethorp was not with us — that he alone had given no sign of his presence. John opened the door of his room. It was pitch dark, but Lawrence was following with the candle, and by its feeble light we saw that the bed had not been slept in, and that there was no sign of the room having been occupied.

We went straight to the connecting door. That, too, was locked or bolted on the inside. What was to be done?

"Oh, dear, sir," cried Dorcas, wringing her hands, "what ever shall we do?"

"We must try and break the door in, I suppose. It'll be a tough job, though. Here, let one of the maids go down and wake Baily and tell him to go for Dr. Wilkins at once. Now then, we'll have a try at the door. Half a moment, though, isn't there a door into Miss Cynthia's rooms?"

"Yes, sir, but that's always bolted. It's never been undone."

"Well, we might just see."

He ran rapidly down the corridor to Cynthia's room. Mary Cavendish was there, shaking the girl — who must have been an unusually sound sleeper — and trying to wake her.

In a moment or two he was back.

"No good. That's bolted too. We must break in the door. I think this one is a shade less solid than the one in the passage."

We strained and heaved together. The framework of the door was solid, and for a long time it resisted our efforts, but at last we felt it give beneath our weight, and finally, with a resounding crash, it was burst open.

We stumbled in together, Lawrence still holding his candle. Mrs. Inglethorp was lying on the bed, her whole form agitated by violent convulsions, in one of which she must have overturned the table beside her. As we entered, however, her limbs relaxed, and she fell back upon the pillows.

John strode across the room, and lit the gas. Turning to Annie, one of the housemaids, he sent her downstairs to the dining-room for brandy. Then he went across to his mother whilst I unbolted the door that gave on the corridor.

I turned to Lawrence, to suggest that I had better leave them now that there was no further need of my services, but the words were frozen on my lips. Never have I seen such a ghastly look on any man's face. He was white as chalk, the candle he held in his shaking hand was sputtering onto the carpet, and his eyes, petrified with terror, or some such kindred emotion, stared fixedly over my head at a point on the further wall. It was as though he had seen something that turned him to stone. I instinctively followed the direction of his eyes, but I could see nothing unusual. The still feebly flickering ashes in the grate, and the row of prim ornaments on the mantelpiece, were surely harmless enough.

The violence of Mrs. Inglethorp's attack seemed to be passing. She was able to speak in short gasps.

"Better now — very sudden — stupid of me — to lock myself in."

A shadow fell on the bed and, looking up, I saw Mary Cavendish standing near the door with her arm around Cynthia. She seemed to be supporting the girl, who looked utterly dazed and unlike herself. Her face was heavily flushed, and she yawned repeatedly.

"Poor Cynthia is quite frightened," said Mrs. Cavendish in a low clear voice. She herself, I noticed, was dressed in her white land smock. Then it must be later than I thought. I saw that a faint streak of daylight was showing through the curtains of the windows, and that the clock on the mantelpiece pointed to close upon five o'clock.

A strangled cry from the bed startled me. A fresh access of pain seized the unfortunate old lady. The convulsions were of a violence terrible to behold. Everything was confusion. We thronged round her, powerless to help or alleviate. A final convulsion lifted her from the bed, until she appeared to rest upon her head and her heels, with her body arched in an extraordinary manner. In vain Mary and John tried to administer more brandy. The moments flew. Again the body arched itself in that peculiar fashion.

At that moment, Dr. Bauerstein pushed his way authoritatively into the room. For one instant he stopped dead, staring at the figure on the bed, and, at the same instant, Mrs. Inglethorp cried out in a strangled voice, her eyes fixed on the doctor:

"Alfred — Alfred —" Then she fell back motionless on the pillows.

With a stride, the doctor reached the bed, and seizing her arms worked them energetically, applying what I knew to be artificial respiration. He issued a few short sharp orders to the servants. An imperious wave of his hand drove us all to the door. We watched him, fascinated, though I think we all knew in our hearts that it was too late, and that nothing could be done now. I could see by the expression on his face that he himself had little hope.

Finally he abandoned his task, shaking his head gravely. At that moment, we heard footsteps outside, and Dr. Wilkins, Mrs. Inglethorp's own doctor, a portly, fussy little man, came bustling in.

In a few words Dr. Bauerstein explained how he had happened to be passing the lodge gates as the car came out, and had run up to the house as fast as he could, whilst the car went on to fetch Dr. Wilkins. With a faint gesture of the hand, he indicated the figure on the bed.

"Ve-ry sad. Ve-ry sad," murmured Dr. Wilkins. "Poor dear lady. Always did far too much — far too much — against my advice. I warned her. Her heart was far from strong. 'Take it easy,' I said to her, 'Take — it — easy.' But no — her zeal for good works was too great. Nature rebelled. Na-ture re-belled."

Dr. Bauerstein, I noticed, was watching the local doctor narrowly. He still kept his eyes fixed on him as he spoke.

"The convulsions were of a peculiar violence, Dr. Wilkins. I am sorry you were not here in time to witness them. They were quite titanic in character."

"Ah!" said Dr. Wilkins wisely.

"I should like to speak to you in private," said Dr. Bauerstein. He turned to John. "You do not object?"

"Certainly not."

We all trooped out into the corridor, leaving the two doctors alone, and I heard the key turned in the lock behind us.

We went slowly down the stairs. I was violently excited. I have a certain talent for deduction, and Dr. Bauerstein's manner had started a flock of wild surmises in my mind. Mary Cavendish laid her hand upon my arm.

"What is it? Why did Dr. Bauerstein seem so — peculiar?"

I looked at her.

"Do you know what I think?"

"What?"

"Listen!" I looked round, the others were out of earshot. I lowered my voice to a whisper. "I believe she has been poisoned! I'm certain Dr. Bauerstein suspects it."

"*What?*" She shrank against the wall, the pupils of her eyes dilating wildly. Then, with a sudden cry that startled me, she cried out: "No, no — not that — not that!" And breaking from me, fled up the stairs. I followed her, afraid that she was going to faint. I found her leaning against the bannisters, deadly pale. She waved me away impatiently.

"No, no — leave me. I'd rather be alone. Let me just be quiet for a minute or two. Go down to the others."

I obeyed her reluctantly. John and Lawrence were in the dining-room. I joined them. We were all silent, but I suppose I voiced the thoughts of us all when I at last broke it by saying:

"Where is Mr. Inglethorp?"

John shook his head.

"He's not in the house."

Our eyes met. Where *was* Alfred Inglethorp? His absence was strange and inexplicable. I remembered Mrs. Inglethorp's dying words. What lay beneath them? What more could she have told us, if she had had time?

At last we heard the doctors descending the stairs. Dr. Wilkins was looking important and excited, and trying to conceal an inward exultation under a manner of decorous calm. Dr. Bauerstein remained in the background, his grave bearded face unchanged. Dr. Wilkins was the spokesman for the two. He addressed himself to John:

"Mr. Cavendish, I should like your consent to a post-mortem."

"Is that necessary?" asked John gravely. A spasm of pain crossed his face.

"Absolutely," said Dr. Bauerstein.

"You mean by that — ?"

"That neither Dr. Wilkins nor myself could give a death certificate under the circumstances."

John bent his head.

"In that case, I have no alternative but to agree."

"Thank you," said Dr. Wilkins briskly. "We propose that it should take place to-morrow night — or rather to-night." And he glanced at the daylight. "Under the circumstances, I am afraid an inquest can hardly be avoided — these formalities are necessary, but I beg that you won't distress yourselves."

There was a pause, and then Dr. Bauerstein drew two keys from his pocket, and handed them to John.

"These are the keys of the two rooms. I have locked them and, in my opinion, they would be better kept locked for the present."

The doctors then departed.

I had been turning over an idea in my head, and I felt that the moment had now come to broach it. Yet I was a little chary of doing so. John, I knew, had a horror of any kind of publicity, and was an easy-going optimist, who preferred never to meet trouble half-way. It might be difficult to convince him of the soundness of my plan. Lawrence, on the other hand, being less conventional, and having more imagination, I felt I might count upon as an ally. There was no doubt that the moment had come for me to take the lead.

"John," I said, "I am going to ask you something."

"Well?"

"You remember my speaking of my friend Poirot? The Belgian who is here? He has been a most famous detective."

"Yes."

"I want you to let me call him in — to investigate this matter."

"What — now? Before the post-mortem?"

"Yes, time is an advantage if — if — there has been foul play."

"Rubbish!" cried Lawrence angrily. "In my opinion the whole thing is a mare's nest of Bauerstein's! Wilkins hadn't an idea of such a thing, until Bauerstein put it into his head. But, like all specialists, Bauerstein's got a bee in his bonnet. Poisons are his hobby, so of course he sees them everywhere."

I confess that I was surprised by Lawrence's attitude. He was so seldom vehement about anything.

John hesitated.

"I can't feel as you do, Lawrence," he said at last. "I'm inclined to give Hastings a free hand, though I should prefer to wait a bit. We don't want any unnecessary scandal."

"No, no," I cried eagerly, "you need have no fear of that. Poirot is discretion itself."

"Very well, then, have it your own way. I leave it in your hands. Though, if it is as we suspect, it seems a clear enough case. God forgive me if I am wronging him!"

I looked at my watch. It was six o'clock. I determined to lose no time.

Five minutes' delay, however, I allowed myself. I spent it in ransacking the library until I discovered a medical book which gave a description of strychnine poisoning.

# IV.

## POIROT INVESTIGATES.

The house which the Belgians occupied in the village was quite close to the park gates. One could save time by taking a narrow path through the long grass, which cut off the detours of the winding drive. So I, accordingly, went that way. I had nearly reached the lodge, when my attention was arrested by the running figure of a man approaching me. It was Mr. Inglethorp. Where had he been? How did he intend to explain his absence?

He accosted me eagerly.

"My God! This is terrible! My poor wife! I have only just heard."

"Where have you been?" I asked.

"Denby kept me late last night. It was one o'clock before we'd finished. Then I found that I'd forgotten the latch-key after all. I didn't want to arouse the household, so Denby gave me a bed."

"How did you hear the news?" I asked.

"Wilkins knocked Denby up to tell him. My poor Emily! She was so self-sacrificing — such a noble character. She over-taxed her strength."

A wave of revulsion swept over me. What a consummate hypocrite the man was!

"I must hurry on," I said, thankful that he did not ask me whither I was bound.

In a few minutes I was knocking at the door of Leastways Cottage.

Getting no answer, I repeated my summons impatiently. A window above me was cautiously opened, and Poirot himself looked out.

He gave an exclamation of surprise at seeing me. In a few brief words, I explained the tragedy that had occurred, and that I wanted his help.

"Wait, my friend, I will let you in, and you shall recount to me the affair whilst I dress."

In a few moments he had unbarred the door, and I followed him up to his room. There he installed me in a chair, and I related the whole story, keeping back nothing, and omitting no circumstance, however insignificant, whilst he himself made a careful and deliberate toilet.

I told him of my awakening, of Mrs. Inglethorp's dying words, of her husband's absence, of the quarrel the day before, of the scrap of conversation between Mary and her mother-in-law that I had overheard, of the former quarrel between Mrs. Inglethorp and Evelyn Howard, and of the latter's innuendoes.

I was hardly as clear as I could wish. I repeated myself several times, and occasionally had to go back to some detail that I had forgotten. Poirot smiled kindly on me.

"The mind is confused? Is it not so? Take time, *mon ami*. You are agitated; you are excited — it is but natural. Presently, when we are calmer, we will arrange the facts, neatly, each in his proper place. We will examine — and reject. Those of importance we will put on one side; those of no importance, pouf!" — he screwed up his cherub-like face, and puffed comically enough — "blow them away!"

"That's all very well," I objected, "but how are you going to decide what is important, and what isn't? That always seems the difficulty to me."

Poirot shook his head energetically. He was now arranging his moustache with exquisite care.

"Not so. *Voyons!* One fact leads to another — so we continue. Does the next fit in with that? *A merveille!* Good! We can proceed. This next little fact — no! Ah, that is curious! There is something missing — a link in the chain that is not there. We examine. We search. And that little curious fact, that possibly paltry little detail that will not tally, we put it here!" He made an extravagant gesture with his hand. "It is significant! It is tremendous!"

"Y — es —"

"Ah!" Poirot shook his forefinger so fiercely at me that I quailed before it. "Beware! Peril to the detective who says: 'It is so small — it does not matter. It will not agree. I will forget it.' That way lies confusion! Everything matters."

"I know. You always told me that. That's why I have gone into all the details of this thing whether they seemed to me relevant or not."

"And I am pleased with you. You have a good memory, and you have given me the facts faithfully. Of the order in which you present them, I say nothing — truly, it is deplorable! But I make allowances — you are upset. To that I attribute the circumstance that you have omitted one fact of paramount importance."

"What is that?" I asked.

"You have not told me if Mrs. Inglethorp ate well last night."

I stared at him. Surely the war had affected the little man's brain. He was carefully engaged in brushing his coat before putting it on, and seemed wholly engrossed in the task.

"I don't remember," I said. "And, anyway, I don't see —"

"You do not see? But it is of the first importance."

"I can't see why," I said, rather nettled. "As far as I can remember, she didn't eat much. She was obviously upset, and it had taken her appetite away. That was only natural."

"Yes," said Poirot thoughtfully, "it was only natural."

He opened a drawer, and took out a small despatch-case, then turned to me.

"Now I am ready. We will proceed to the *château*, and study matters on the spot. Excuse me, *mon ami*, you dressed in haste, and your tie is on one side. Permit me." With a deft gesture, he rearranged it.

"*Ça y est!* Now, shall we start?"

We hurried up the village, and turned in at the lodge gates. Poirot stopped for a moment, and gazed sorrowfully over the beautiful expanse of park, still glittering with morning dew.

"So beautiful, so beautiful, and yet, the poor family, plunged in sorrow, prostrated with grief."

He looked at me keenly as he spoke, and I was aware that I reddened under his prolonged gaze.

*Was* the family prostrated by grief? Was the sorrow at Mrs. Inglethorp's death so great? I realized that there was an emotional lack in the atmosphere. The dead woman had not the gift of commanding love. Her death was a shock and a distress, but she would not be passionately regretted.

Poirot seemed to follow my thoughts. He nodded his head gravely.

"No, you are right," he said, "it is not as though there was a blood tie. She has been kind and generous to these Cavendishes, but she was not their own mother. Blood tells — always remember that — blood tells."

"Poirot," I said, "I wish you would tell me why you wanted to know if Mrs. Inglethorp ate well last night? I have been turning it over in my mind, but I can't see how it has anything to do with the matter?"

He was silent for a minute or two as we walked along, but finally he said:

"I do not mind telling you — though, as you know, it is not my habit to explain until the end is reached. The present contention is that Mrs. Inglethorp died of strychnine poisoning, presumably administered in her coffee."

"Yes?"

"Well, what time was the coffee served?"

"About eight o'clock."

"Therefore she drank it between then and half-past eight — certainly not much later. Well, strychnine is a fairly rapid poison. Its effects would be felt very soon, probably in about an hour. Yet, in Mrs. Inglethorp's case, the symptoms do not manifest themselves until five o'clock the next morning: nine hours! But a heavy meal, taken at about the same time as the poison, might retard its effects, though hardly to that extent. Still, it is a possibility to be taken into account. But, according to you, she ate very little for supper, and yet the symptoms do not develop until early the next morning! Now that is a curious circumstance, my friend. Something may arise at the autopsy to explain it. In the meantime, remember it."

As we neared the house, John came out and met us. His face looked weary and haggard.

"This is a very dreadful business, Monsieur Poirot," he said. "Hastings has explained to you that we are anxious for no publicity?"

"I comprehend perfectly."

"You see, it is only suspicion so far. We have nothing to go upon."

"Precisely. It is a matter of precaution only."

John turned to me, taking out his cigarette-case, and lighting a cigarette as he did so.

"You know that fellow Inglethorp is back?"

"Yes. I met him."

John flung the match into an adjacent flower bed, a proceeding which was too much for Poirot's feelings. He retrieved it, and buried it neatly.

"It's jolly difficult to know how to treat him."

"That difficulty will not exist long," pronounced Poirot quietly.

John looked puzzled, not quite understanding the portent of this cryptic saying. He handed the two keys which Dr. Bauerstein had given him to me.

"Show Monsieur Poirot everything he wants to see."

"The rooms are locked?" asked Poirot.

"Dr. Bauerstein considered it advisable."

Poirot nodded thoughtfully.

"Then he is very sure. Well, that simplifies matters for us."

We went up together to the room of the tragedy. For convenience I append a plan of the room and the principal articles of furniture in it:

*(See facing page)*

Poirot locked the door on the inside, and proceeded to a minute inspection of the room. He darted from one object to the other with the agility of a grasshopper. I remained by the

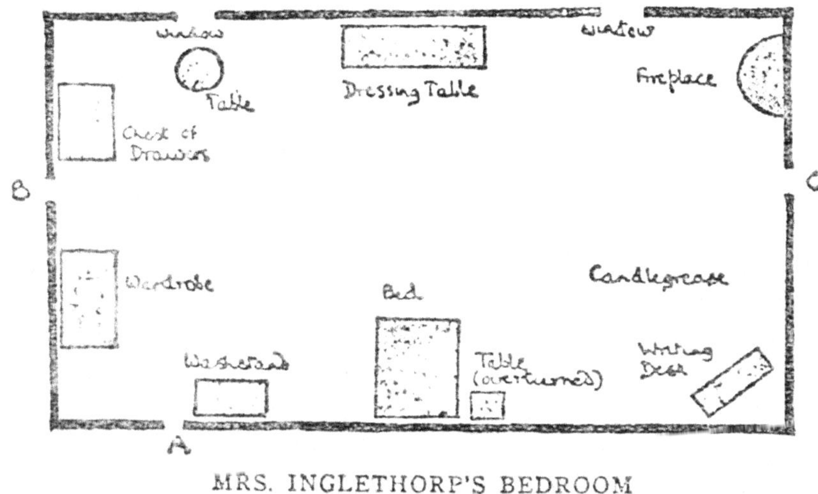


MRS. INGLETHORP'S BEDROOM
A.—Door into Passage
B.—Door into Mr. Inglethorp's Room.
C.—Door into Cynthia's Room

door, fearing to obliterate any clues. Poirot, however, did not seem grateful to me for my forbearance.

"What have you, my friend," he cried, "that you remain there like — how do you say it? — ah, yes, the stuck pig?"

I explained that I was afraid of obliterating any foot-marks.

"Foot-marks? But what an idea! There has already been practically an army in the room! What foot-marks are we likely to find? No, come here and aid me in my search. I will put down my little case until I need it."

He did so, on the round table by the window, but it was an ill-advised proceeding; for, the top of it being loose, it tilted up, and precipitated the despatch-case on the floor.

"*Eh voilà une table!*" cried Poirot. "Ah, my friend, one may live in a big house and yet have no comfort."

After which piece of moralising, he resumed his search.

A small purple despatch-case, with a key in the lock, on the writing-table, engaged his attention for some time. He took out the key from the lock, and passed it to me to inspect. I saw nothing peculiar, however. It was an ordinary key of the Yale type, with a bit of twisted wire through the handle.

Next, he examined the framework of the door we had broken in, assuring himself that the bolt had really been shot. Then he went to the door opposite leading into Cynthia's room. That door was also bolted, as I had stated. However, he went to the length of unbolting it, and opening and shutting it several times; this he did with the utmost precaution against making any noise.

Suddenly something in the bolt itself seemed to rivet his attention. He examined it carefully, and then, nimbly whipping out a pair of small forceps from his case, he drew out some minute particle which he carefully sealed up in a tiny envelope.

On the chest of drawers there was a tray with a spirit lamp and a small saucepan on it. A small quantity of a dark fluid remained in the saucepan, and an empty cup and saucer that had been drunk out of stood near it.

I wondered how I could have been so unobservant as to overlook this. Here was a clue worth having. Poirot delicately dipped his finger into liquid, and tasted it gingerly. He made a grimace.

"Cocoa — with — I think — rum in it."

He passed on to the debris on the floor, where the table by the bed had been overturned. A reading-lamp, some books, matches, a bunch of keys, and the crushed fragments of a coffee-cup lay scattered about.

"Ah, this is curious," said Poirot.

"I must confess that I see nothing particularly curious about it."

"You do not? Observe the lamp — the chimney is broken in two places; they lie there as they fell. But see, the coffee-cup is absolutely smashed to powder."

"Well," I said wearily, "I suppose someone must have stepped on it."

"Exactly," said Poirot, in an odd voice. "Someone stepped on it."

He rose from his knees, and walked slowly across to the mantelpiece, where he stood abstractedly fingering the ornaments, and straightening them — a trick of his when he was agitated.

"*Mon ami,*" he said, turning to me, "somebody stepped on that cup, grinding it to powder, and the reason they did so was either because it contained strychnine or — which is far more serious — because it did *not* contain strychnine!"

I made no reply. I was bewildered, but I knew that it was no good asking him to explain. In a moment or two he roused himself, and went on with his investigations. He picked up the bunch of keys from the floor, and twirling them round in his fingers finally selected one, very bright and shining, which he tried in the lock of the purple despatch-case. It fitted, and he opened the box, but after a moment's hesitation, closed and relocked it, and slipped the bunch of keys, as well as the key that had originally stood in the lock, into his own pocket.

"I have no authority to go through these papers. But it should be done — at once!"

He then made a very careful examination of the drawers of the wash-stand. Crossing the room to the left-hand window, a round stain, hardly visible on the dark brown carpet, seemed to interest him particularly. He went down on his knees, examining it minutely — even going so far as to smell it.

Finally, he poured a few drops of the cocoa into a test tube, sealing it up carefully. His next proceeding was to take out a little notebook.

"We have found in this room," he said, writing busily, "six points of interest. Shall I enumerate them, or will you?"

"Oh, you," I replied hastily.

"Very well, then. One, a coffee-cup that has been ground into powder; two, a despatch-case with a key in the lock; three, a stain on the floor."

"That may have been done some time ago," I interrupted.

"No, for it is still perceptibly damp and smells of coffee. Four, a fragment of some dark green fabric — only a thread or two, but recognizable."

"Ah!" I cried. "That was what you sealed up in the envelope."

"Yes. It may turn out to be a piece of one of Mrs. Inglethorp's own dresses, and quite unimportant. We shall see. Five, *this!*" With a dramatic gesture, he pointed to a large splash of candle grease on the floor by the writing-table. "It must have been done since yesterday, otherwise a good housemaid would have at once removed it with blotting-paper and a hot iron. One of my best hats once — but that is not to the point."

"It was very likely done last night. We were very agitated. Or perhaps Mrs. Inglethorp herself dropped her candle."

"You brought only one candle into the room?"

"Yes. Lawrence Cavendish was carrying it. But he was very upset. He seemed to see something over here" — I indicated the mantelpiece — "that absolutely paralysed him."

"That is interesting," said Poirot quickly. "Yes, it is suggestive" — his eye sweeping the whole length of the wall — "but it was not his candle that made this great patch, for you perceive that this is white grease; whereas Monsieur Lawrence's candle, which is still on the dressing-table, is pink. On the other hand, Mrs. Inglethorp had no candlestick in the room, only a reading-lamp."

"Then," I said, "what do you deduce?"

To which my friend only made a rather irritating reply, urging me to use my own natural faculties.

"And the sixth point?" I asked. "I suppose it is the sample of cocoa."

"No," said Poirot thoughtfully. "I might have included that in the six, but I did not. No, the sixth point I will keep to myself for the present."

He looked quickly round the room. "There is nothing more to be done here, I think, unless" — he stared earnestly and long at the dead ashes in the grate. "The fire burns — and it destroys. But by chance — there might be — let us see!"

Deftly, on hands and knees, he began to sort the ashes from the grate into the fender, handling them with the greatest caution. Suddenly, he gave a faint exclamation.

"The forceps, Hastings!"

I quickly handed them to him, and with skill he extracted a small piece of half charred paper.

"There, *mon ami!*" he cried. "What do you think of that?"

I scrutinized the fragment. This is an exact reproduction of it:—

I was puzzled. It was unusually thick, quite unlike ordinary notepaper. Suddenly an idea struck me.

"Poirot!" I cried. "This is a fragment of a will!"

"Exactly."

I looked up at him sharply.

"You are not surprised?"

"No," he said gravely, "I expected it."

I relinquished the piece of paper, and watched him put it away in his case, with the same methodical care that he bestowed on everything. My brain was in a whirl. What was this complication of a will? Who had destroyed it? The person who had left the candle grease on the floor? Obviously. But how had anyone gained admission? All the doors had been bolted on the inside.

"Now, my friend," said Poirot briskly, "we will go. I should like to ask a few questions of the parlourmaid—Dorcas, her name is, is it not?"

We passed through Alfred Inglethorp's room, and Poirot delayed long enough to make a brief but fairly comprehensive examination of it. We went out through that door, locking both it and that of Mrs. Inglethorp's room as before.

I took him down to the boudoir which he had expressed a wish to see, and went myself in search of Dorcas.

When I returned with her, however, the boudoir was empty.

"Poirot," I cried, "where are you?"

"I am here, my friend."

He had stepped outside the French window, and was standing, apparently lost in admiration, before the various shaped flower beds.

"Admirable!" he murmured. "Admirable! What symmetry! Observe that crescent; and those diamonds—their neatness rejoices the eye. The spacing of the plants, also, is perfect. It has been recently done; is it not so?"

"Yes, I believe they were at it yesterday afternoon. But come in—Dorcas is here."

"*Eh bien, eh bien!* Do not grudge me a moment's satisfaction of the eye."

"Yes, but this affair is more important."

"And how do you know that

these fine begonias are not of equal importance?"

I shrugged my shoulders. There was really no arguing with him if he chose to take that line.

"You do not agree? But such things have been. Well, we will come in and interview the brave Dorcas."

Dorcas was standing in the boudoir, her hands folded in front of her, and her grey hair rose in stiff waves under her white cap. She was the very model and picture of a good old-fashioned servant.

In her attitude towards Poirot, she was inclined to be suspicious, but he soon broke down her defences. He drew forward a chair.

"Pray be seated, mademoiselle."

"Thank you, sir."

"You have been with your mistress many years, is it not so?"

"Ten years, sir."

"That is a long time, and very faithful service. You were much attached to her, were you not?"

"She was a very good mistress to me, sir."

"Then you will not object to answering a few questions. I put them to you with Mr. Cavendish's full approval."

"Oh, certainly, sir."

"Then I will begin by asking you about the events of yesterday afternoon. Your mistress had a quarrel?"

"Yes, sir. But I don't know that I ought—" Dorcas hesitated.

Poirot looked at her keenly.

"My good Dorcas, it is necessary that I should know every detail of that quarrel as fully as possible. Do not think that you are betraying your mistress's secrets. Your mistress lies dead, and it is necessary that we should know all—if we are to avenge her. Nothing can bring her back to life, but we do hope, if there has been foul play, to bring the murderer to justice."

"Amen to that," said Dorcas fiercely. "And, naming no names, there's *one* in this house that none of us could ever abide! And an ill day it was when first *he* darkened the threshold."

Poirot waited for her indignation to subside, and then, resuming his business-like tone, he asked:

"Now, as to this quarrel? What is the first you heard of it?"

"Well, sir, I happened to be going along the hall outside yesterday—"

"What time was that?"

"I couldn't say exactly, sir, but it wasn't tea-time by a long way. Perhaps four o'clock—or it may have been a bit later. Well, sir, as I said, I happened to be passing along, when I heard voices very loud and angry in here. I didn't exactly mean to listen, but—well, there it is. I stopped. The door was shut, but the mistress was speaking very sharp and clear, and I heard what she said quite plainly. 'You have lied to me, and deceived me,' she said. I didn't hear what Mr. Inglethorp replied. He spoke a good bit lower than she did—but she answered: 'How dare you? I have kept you and clothed you and fed you! You owe everything to me! And this is how you repay me! By bringing disgrace upon our name!' Again I didn't hear what he said, but she went on: 'Nothing that you can say will make any difference. I see my duty clearly. My mind is made up. You need not think that any fear of publicity, or scandal between husband and wife will deter me.' Then I thought I heard them coming out, so I went off quickly."

"You are sure it was Mr. Inglethorp's voice you heard?"

"Oh, yes, sir, whose else's could it be?"

"Well, what happened next?"

"Later, I came back to the hall; but it was all quiet. At five o'clock, Mrs. Inglethorp rang the bell and told me to bring her a cup of tea — nothing to eat — to the boudoir. She was looking dreadful — so white and upset. 'Dorcas,' she says, 'I've had a great shock.' 'I'm sorry for that, m'm,' I says. 'You'll feel better after a nice hot cup of tea, m'm.' She had something in her hand. I don't know if it was a letter, or just a piece of paper, but it had writing on it, and she kept staring at it, almost as if she couldn't believe what was written there. She whispered to herself, as though she had forgotten I was there: 'These few words — and everything's changed.' And then she says to me: 'Never trust a man, Dorcas, they're not worth it!' I hurried off, and got her a good strong cup of tea, and she thanked me, and said she'd feel better when she'd drunk it. 'I don't know what to do,' she says. 'Scandal between husband and wife is a dreadful thing, Dorcas. I'd rather hush it up if I could.' Mrs. Cavendish came in just then, so she didn't say any more."

"She still had the letter, or whatever it was, in her hand?"

"Yes, sir."

"What would she be likely to do with it afterwards?"

"Well, I don't know, sir, I expect she would lock it up in that purple case of hers."

"Is that where she usually kept important papers?"

"Yes, sir. She brought it down with her every morning, and took it up every night."

"When did she lose the key of it?"

"She missed it yesterday at lunch-time, sir, and told me to look carefully for it. She was very much put out about it."

"But she had a duplicate key?"

"Oh, yes, sir."

Dorcas was looking very curiously at him and, to tell the truth, so was I. What was all this about a lost key? Poirot smiled.

"Never mind, Dorcas, it is my business to know things. Is this the key that was lost?" He drew from his pocket the key that he had found in the lock of the despatch-case upstairs.

Dorcas's eyes looked as though they would pop out of her head.

"That's it, sir, right enough. But where did you find it? I looked everywhere for it."

"Ah, but you see it was not in the same place yesterday as it was to-day. Now, to pass to another subject, had your mistress a dark green dress in her wardrobe?"

Dorcas was rather startled by the unexpected question.

"No, sir."

"Are you quite sure?"

"Oh, yes, sir."

"Has anyone else in the house got a green dress?"

Dorcas reflected.

"Miss Cynthia has a green evening dress."

"Light or dark green?"

"A light green, sir; a sort of chiffon, they call it."

"Ah, that is not what I want. And nobody else has anything green?"

"No, sir — not that I know of."

Poirot's face did not betray a trace of whether he was disappointed or otherwise. He merely remarked:

"Good, we will leave that and pass on. Have you any reason to believe that your mistress was likely to take a sleeping powder last night?"

"Not *last* night, sir, I know she didn't."

"Why do you know so positively?"

"Because the box was empty. She took the last one two days ago, and she didn't have any more made up."

"You are quite sure of that?"

"Positive, sir."

"Then that is cleared up! By the way, your mistress didn't ask you to sign any paper yesterday?"

"To sign a paper? No, sir."

"When Mr. Hastings and Mr. Lawrence came in yesterday evening, they found your mistress busy writing letters. I suppose you can give me no idea to whom these letters were addressed?"

"I'm afraid I couldn't, sir. I was out in the evening. Perhaps Annie could tell you, though she's a careless girl. Never cleared the coffee-cups away last night. That's what happens when I'm not here to look after things."

Poirot lifted his hand.

"Since they have been left, Dorcas, leave them a little longer, I pray you. I should like to examine them."

"Very well, sir."

"What time did you go out last evening?"

"About six o'clock, sir."

"Thank you, Dorcas, that is all I have to ask you." He rose and strolled to the window. "I have been admiring these flower beds. How many gardeners are employed here, by the way?"

"Only three now, sir. Five, we had, before the war, when it was kept as a gentleman's place should be. I wish you could have seen it then, sir. A fair sight it was. But now there's only old Manning, and young William, and a new-fashioned woman gardener in breeches and such-like. Ah, these are dreadful times!"

"The good times will come again, Dorcas. At least, we hope so. Now, will you send Annie to me here?"

"Yes, sir. Thank you, sir."

"How did you know that Mrs. Inglethorp took sleeping powders?" I asked, in lively curiosity, as Dorcas left the room. "And about the lost key and the duplicate?"

"One thing at a time. As to the sleeping powders, I knew by this." He suddenly produced a small cardboard box, such as chemists use for powders.

"Where did you find it?"

"In the wash-stand drawer in Mrs. Inglethorp's bedroom. It was Number Six of my catalogue."

"But I suppose, as the last powder was taken two days ago, it is not of much importance?"

"Probably not, but do you notice anything that strikes you as peculiar about this box?"

I examined it closely.

"No, I can't say that I do."

"Look at the label."

I read the label carefully: "'One powder to be taken at bedtime, if required. Mrs. Inglethorp.' No, I see nothing unusual."

"Not the fact that there is no chemist's name?"

"Ah!" I exclaimed. "To be sure, that is odd!"

"Have you ever known a chemist to send out a box like that, without his printed name?"

"No, I can't say that I have."

I was becoming quite excited, but Poirot damped my ardour by remarking:

"Yet the explanation is quite simple. So do not intrigue yourself, my friend."

An audible creaking proclaimed the approach of Annie, so I had no time to reply.

Annie was a fine, strapping girl, and was evidently labouring under intense excitement, mingled with a certain ghoulish enjoyment of the tragedy.

Poirot came to the point at once, with a business-like briskness.

"I sent for you, Annie, because I thought you might be able to tell me something about the letters Mrs. Inglethorp wrote last night. How many were there? And can you tell me any of the names and addresses?"

Annie considered.

"There were four letters, sir. One was to Miss Howard, and one was to Mr. Wells, the lawyer, and the other two I don't think I remember, sir — oh, yes, one was to Ross's, the caterers in Tadminster. The other one, I don't remember."

"Think," urged Poirot.

Annie racked her brains in vain.

"I'm sorry, sir, but it's clean gone. I don't think I can have noticed it."

"It does not matter," said Poirot, not betraying any sign of disappointment. "Now I want to ask you about something else. There is a saucepan in Mrs. Inglethorp's room with some cocoa in it. Did she have that every night?"

"Yes, sir, it was put in her room every evening, and she warmed it up in the night — whenever she fancied it."

"What was it? Plain cocoa?"

"Yes, sir, made with milk, with a teaspoonful of sugar, and two teaspoonfuls of rum in it."

"Who took it to her room?"

"I did, sir."

"Always?"

"Yes, sir."

"At what time?"

"When I went to draw the curtains, as a rule, sir."

"Did you bring it straight up from the kitchen then?"

"No, sir, you see there's not much room on the gas stove, so cook used to make it early, before putting the vegetables on for supper. Then I used to bring it up, and put it on the table by the swing door, and take it into her room later."

"The swing door is in the left wing, is it not?"

"Yes, sir."

"And the table, is it on this side of the door, or on the farther — servants' side?"

"It's this side, sir."

"What time did you bring it up last night?"

"About quarter-past seven, I should say, sir."

"And when did you take it into Mrs. Inglethorp's room?"

"When I went to shut up, sir. About eight o'clock. Mrs. Inglethorp came up to bed before I'd finished."

"Then, between seven-fifteen and eight o'clock, the cocoa was standing on the table in the left wing?"

"Yes, sir." Annie had been growing redder and redder in the face, and now she blurted out unexpectedly:

"And if there *was* salt in it, sir, it wasn't me. I never took the salt near it."

"What makes you think there was salt in it?" asked Poirot.

"Seeing it on the tray, sir."

"You saw some salt on the tray?"

"Yes. Coarse kitchen salt, it looked. I never noticed it when I took the tray up, but when I came to take it into the mistress's room I saw it at once, and I suppose I ought to have taken it down again, and asked cook to make some fresh. But I was in a hurry, because Dorcas was out, and I thought maybe the cocoa itself was all right, and the salt had only gone on the tray. So I dusted it off with my apron, and took it in."

I had the utmost difficulty in controlling my excitement. Unknown to herself, Annie had provided us with an important piece of evidence. How she would have gaped if she had realized that her "coarse kitchen salt" was strychnine, one of the most deadly poisons known to mankind. I marvelled at Poirot's calm. His self-control was astonishing. I awaited his next question with impatience, but it disappointed me.

"When you went into Mrs.

Inglethorp's room, was the door leading into Miss Cynthia's room bolted?"

"Oh! Yes, sir; it always was. It had never been opened."

"And the door into Mr. Inglethorp's room? Did you notice if that was bolted too?"

Annie hesitated.

"I couldn't rightly say, sir; it was shut but I couldn't say whether it was bolted or not."

"When you finally left the room, did Mrs. Inglethorp bolt the door after you?"

"No, sir, not then, but I expect she did later. She usually did lock it at night. The door into the passage, that is."

"Did you notice any candle grease on the floor when you did the room yesterday?"

"Candle grease? Oh, no, sir. Mrs. Inglethorp didn't have a candle, only a reading-lamp."

"Then, if there had been a large patch of candle grease on the floor, you think you would have been sure to have seen it?"

"Yes, sir, and I would have taken it out with a piece of blotting-paper and a hot iron."

Then Poirot repeated the question he had put to Dorcas:

"Did your mistress ever have a green dress?"

"No, sir."

"Nor a mantle, nor a cape, nor a—how do you call it?—a sports coat?"

"Not green, sir."

"Nor anyone else in the house?"

Annie reflected.

"No, sir."

"You are sure of that?"

"Quite sure."

"*Bien!* That is all I want to know. Thank you very much."

With a nervous giggle, Annie took herself creakingly out of the room. My pent-up excitement burst forth.

"Poirot," I cried, "I congratulate you! This is a great discovery."

"What is a great discovery?"

"Why, that it was the cocoa and not the coffee that was poisoned. That explains everything! Of course it did not take effect until the early morning, since the cocoa was only drunk in the middle of the night."

"So you think that the cocoa—mark well what I say, Hastings, the *cocoa*—contained strychnine?"

"Of course! That salt on the tray, what else could it have been?"

"It might have been salt," replied Poirot placidly.

I shrugged my shoulders. If he was going to take the matter that way, it was no good arguing with him. The idea crossed my mind, not for the first time, that poor old Poirot was growing old. Privately I thought it lucky that he had associated with him someone of a more receptive type of mind.

Poirot was surveying me with quietly twinkling eyes.

"You are not pleased with me, *mon ami?*"

"My dear Poirot," I said coldly, "it is not for me to dictate to you. You have a right to your own opinion, just as I have to mine."

"A most admirable sentiment," remarked Poirot, rising briskly to his feet. "Now I have finished with this room. By the way, whose is the smaller desk in the corner?"

"Mr. Inglethorp's."

"Ah!" He tried the roll top tentatively. "Locked. But perhaps one of Mrs. Inglethorp's keys would open it." He tried several, twisting and turning them with a practiced hand, and finally uttering an ejaculation of satisfaction. "*Voilà!* It is not the key, but it will open it at a pinch." He slid back the roll top, and ran a rapid eye over the neatly filed papers. To my surprise, he did not examine them, merely remarking approvingly as he relocked the desk: "Decidedly, he is a man of method, this Mr. Inglethorp!"

A "man of method" was, in Poirot's estimation, the highest praise that could be bestowed on any individual.

I felt that my friend was not what he had been as he rambled on disconnectedly:

"There were no stamps in his desk, but there might have been, eh, *mon ami?* There might have been? Yes"—his eyes wandered round the room — "this boudoir has nothing more to tell us. It did not yield much. Only this."

He pulled a crumpled envelope out of his pocket, and tossed it over to me. It was rather a curious document. A plain, dirty looking old envelope with a few words scrawled across it, apparently at random. The following is a facsimile of it:

possessed
I am possessed

He is possessed
I am possessed
possessed

# V.

## "IT ISN'T STRYCHNINE, IS IT?"

"Where did you find this?" I asked Poirot, in lively curiosity.

"In the waste-paper basket. You recognise the handwriting?"

"Yes, it is Mrs. Inglethorp's. But what does it mean?"

Poirot shrugged his shoulders.

"I cannot say—but it is suggestive."

A wild idea flashed across me. Was it possible that Mrs. Inglethorp's mind was deranged? Had she some fantastic idea of demoniacal possession? And, if that were so, was it not also possible that she might have taken her own life?

I was about to expound these theories to Poirot, when his own words distracted me.

"Come," he said, "now to examine the coffee-cups!"

"My dear Poirot! What on earth is the good of that, now that we know about the cocoa?"

"Oh, *là là!* That miserable cocoa!" cried Poirot flippantly.

He laughed with apparent enjoyment, raising his arms to heaven in mock despair, in what I could not but consider the worst possible taste.

"And, anyway," I said, with increasing coldness, "as Mrs. Inglethorp took her coffee upstairs with her, I do not see what you expect to find, unless you consider it likely that we shall discover a packet of strychnine on the coffee tray!"

Poirot was sobered at once.

"Come, come, my friend," he said, slipping his arm through mine. "*Ne vous fâchez pas!* Allow me to interest myself in my coffee-cups, and I will respect your cocoa. There! Is it a bargain?"

He was so quaintly humorous that I was forced to laugh; and we went together to the drawing-room, where the coffee-cups and tray remained undisturbed as we had left them.

Poirot made me recapitulate the scene of the night before, listening very carefully, and verifying the position of the various cups.

"So Mrs. Cavendish stood by the tray — and poured out. Yes. Then she came across to the window where you sat with Mademoiselle Cynthia. Yes. Here are the three cups. And the cup on the mantelpiece, half drunk, that would be Mr. Lawrence Cavendish's. And the one on the tray?"

"John Cavendish's. I saw him put it down there."

"Good. One, two, three, four, five — but where, then, is the cup of Mr. Inglethorp?"

"He does not take coffee."

"Then all are accounted for. One moment, my friend."

With infinite care, he took a drop or two from the grounds in each cup, sealing them up in separate test tubes, tasting each in turn as he did so. His physiognomy underwent a curious change. An expression gathered there that I can only describe as half puzzled, and half relieved.

"*Bien!*" he said at last. "It is evident! I had an idea — but clearly I was mistaken. Yes, altogether I was mistaken. Yet it is strange. But no matter!"

And, with a characteristic shrug, he dismissed whatever it was that was worrying him from his mind. I could have told him from the beginning that this obsession of his over the coffee was bound to end in a blind alley, but I restrained my tongue. After all, though he was old, Poirot had been a great man in his day.

"Breakfast is ready," said John Cavendish, coming in from the hall. "You will breakfast with us, Monsieur Poirot?"

Poirot acquiesced. I observed John. Already he was almost restored to his normal self. The shock of the events of the last night had upset him temporarily, but his equable poise soon swung back to the normal. He was a man of very little imagination, in sharp contrast with his brother, who had, perhaps, too much.

Ever since the early hours of the morning, John had been hard at work, sending telegrams — one of the first had gone to Evelyn Howard — writing notices for the papers, and generally occupying himself with the melancholy duties that a death entails.

"May I ask how things are proceeding?" he said. "Do your investigations point to my mother having died a natural death — or — or must we prepare ourselves for the worst?"

"I think, Mr. Cavendish," said Poirot gravely, "that you would do well not to buoy yourself up with any false hopes. Can you tell me the views of the other members of the family?"

"My brother Lawrence is convinced that we are making a fuss over nothing. He says that everything points to its being a simple case of heart failure."

"He does, does he? That is very interesting — very interesting," murmured Poirot softly. "And Mrs. Cavendish?"

A faint cloud passed over John's face.

"I have not the least idea what my wife's views on the subject are."

The answer brought a momentary stiffness in its train. John broke the rather awkward silence by saying with a slight effort:

"I told you, didn't I, that Mr. Inglethorp has returned?"

Poirot bent his head.

"It's an awkward position for all of us. Of course one has to treat him as usual — but, hang it all, one's gorge does rise at sitting down to eat with a possible murderer!"

Poirot nodded sympathetically.

"I quite understand. It is a very difficult situation for you, Mr. Cavendish. I would like to ask you one question. Mr. Inglethorp's reason for not returning last night was, I believe, that he had forgotten the latch-key. Is not that so?"

"Yes."

"I suppose you are quite sure that the latch-key *was* forgotten — that he did not take it after all?"

"I have no idea. I never thought of looking. We always keep it in the hall drawer. I'll go and see if it's there now."

Poirot held up his hand with a faint smile.

"No, no, Mr. Cavendish, it is too late now. I am certain that you would find it. If Mr. Inglethorp did take it, he has had ample time to replace it by now."

"But do you think—"

"I think nothing. If anyone had chanced to look this morning before his return, and seen it there, it would have been a valuable point in his favour. That is all."

John looked perplexed.

"Do not worry," said Poirot smoothly. "I assure you that you need not let it trouble you. Since you are so kind, let us go and have some breakfast."

Everyone was assembled in the dining-room. Under the circumstances, we were naturally not a cheerful party. The reaction after a shock is always trying, and I think we were all suffering from it. Decorum and good breeding naturally enjoined that our demeanour should be much as usual, yet I could not help wondering if this self-control were really a matter of great difficulty. There were no red eyes, no signs of secretly indulged grief. I felt that I was right in my opinion that Dorcas was the person most affected by the personal side of the tragedy.

I pass over Alfred Inglethorp, who acted the bereaved widower in a manner that I felt to be disgusting in its hypocrisy. Did he know that we suspected him, I wondered? Surely he could not be unaware of the fact, conceal it as we would. Did he feel some secret stirring of fear, or was he confident that his crime would go unpunished? Surely the suspicion in the atmosphere must warn him that he was already a marked man.

But *did* everyone suspect him? What about Mrs. Cavendish? I watched her as she sat at the head of the table, graceful, composed, enigmatic. In her soft grey frock, with white ruffles at the wrists falling over her slender hands, she looked very beautiful. When she chose, however, her face could be sphinx-like in its inscrutability. She was very silent, hardly opening her lips, and yet in some queer way I felt that the great strength of her personality was dominating us all.

And little Cynthia? Did she suspect? She looked very tired and ill, I thought. The heaviness and languor of her manner were very marked. I asked her if she were feeling ill, and she answered frankly:

"Yes, I've got the most beastly headache."

"Have another cup of coffee, mademoiselle?" said Poirot solicitously. "It will revive you. It is unparalleled for the *mal de tête*." He jumped up and took her cup.

"No sugar," said Cynthia, watching him, as he picked up the sugar-tongs.

"No sugar? You abandon it in the war-time, eh?"

"No, I never take it in coffee."

"*Sacré!*" murmured Poirot to himself, as he brought back the replenished cup.

Only I heard him, and glancing up curiously at the little man I saw that his face was working with suppressed excitement, and his eyes were as green as a cat's. He had heard or seen something that had affected him strongly—but what was it? I do not usually label myself as dense, but I must confess that nothing out of the ordinary had attracted *my* attention.

In another moment, the door opened and Dorcas appeared.

"Mr. Wells to see you, sir," she said to John.

I remembered the name as being that of the lawyer to whom Mrs. Inglethorp had written the night before.

John rose immediately.

"Show him into my study." Then he turned to us. "My mother's lawyer," he explained. And in a lower voice: "He is also Coroner—you understand. Perhaps you would like to come with me?"

We acquiesced and followed him

out of the room. John strode on ahead and I took the opportunity of whispering to Poirot:

"There will be an inquest then?"

Poirot nodded absently. He seemed absorbed in thought; so much so that my curiosity was aroused.

"What is it? You are not attending to what I say."

"It is true, my friend. I am much worried."

"Why?"

"Because Mademoiselle Cynthia does not take sugar in her coffee."

"What? You cannot be serious?"

"But I am most serious. Ah, there is something there that I do not understand. My instinct was right."

"What instinct?"

"The instinct that led me to insist on examining those coffee-cups. *Chut!* no more now!"

We followed John into his study, and he closed the door behind us.

Mr. Wells was a pleasant man of middle-age, with keen eyes, and the typical lawyer's mouth. John introduced us both, and explained the reason of our presence.

"You will understand, Wells," he added, "that this is all strictly private. We are still hoping that there will turn out to be no need for investigation of any kind."

"Quite so, quite so," said Mr. Wells soothingly. "I wish we could have spared you the pain and publicity of an inquest, but of course it's quite unavoidable in the absence of a doctor's certificate."

"Yes, I suppose so."

"Clever man, Bauerstein. Great authority on toxicology, I believe."

"Indeed," said John with a certain stiffness in his manner. Then he added rather hesitatingly: "Shall we have to appear as witnesses — all of us, I mean?"

"You, of course — and ah — er — Mr. — er — Inglethorp."

A slight pause ensued before the lawyer went on in his soothing manner:

"Any other evidence will be simply confirmatory, a mere matter of form."

"I see."

A faint expression of relief swept over John's face. It puzzled me, for I saw no occasion for it.

"If you know of nothing to the contrary," pursued Mr. Wells, "I had thought of Friday. That will give us plenty of time for the doctor's report. The post-mortem is to take place to-night, I believe?"

"Yes."

"Then that arrangement will suit you?"

"Perfectly."

"I need not tell you, my dear Cavendish, how distressed I am at this most tragic affair."

"Can you give us no help in solving it, monsieur?" interposed Poirot, speaking for the first time since we had entered the room.

"I?"

"Yes, we heard that Mrs. Inglethorp wrote to you last night.

You should have received the letter this morning."

"I did, but it contains no information. It is merely a note asking me to call upon her this morning, as she wanted my advice on a matter of great importance."

"She gave you no hint as to what that matter might be?"

"Unfortunately, no."

"That is a pity," said John.

"A great pity," agreed Poirot gravely.

There was silence. Poirot remained lost in thought for a few minutes. Finally he turned to the lawyer again.

"Mr. Wells, there is one thing I should like to ask you — that is, if it is not against professional etiquette. In the event of Mrs. Inglethorp's death, who would inherit her money?"

The lawyer hesitated a moment, and then replied:

"The knowledge will be public property very soon, so if Mr. Cavendish does not object —"

"Not at all," interpolated John.

"I do not see any reason why I should not answer your question. By her last will, dated August of last year, after various unimportant legacies to servants, etc., she gave her entire fortune to her stepson, Mr. John Cavendish."

"Was not that — pardon the question, Mr. Cavendish — rather unfair to her other stepson, Mr. Lawrence Cavendish?"

"No, I do not think so. You see, under the terms of their father's will, while John inherited the property, Lawrence, at his stepmother's death, would come into a considerable sum of money. Mrs. Inglethorp left her money to her elder stepson, knowing that he would have to keep up Styles. It was, to my mind, a very fair and equitable distribution."

Poirot nodded thoughtfully.

"I see. But I am right in saying, am I not, that by your English law that will was automatically revoked when Mrs. Inglethorp remarried?"

Mr. Wells bowed his head.

"As I was about to proceed, Monsieur Poirot, that document is now null and void."

"*Hein!*" said Poirot. He reflected for a moment, and then asked: "Was Mrs. Inglethorp herself aware of that fact?"

"I do not know. She may have been."

"She was," said John unexpectedly. "We were discussing the matter of wills being revoked by marriage only yesterday."

"Ah! One more question, Mr. Wells. You say 'her last will.' Had Mrs. Inglethorp, then, made several former wills?"

"On an average, she made a new will at least once a year," said Mr. Wells imperturbably. "She was given to changing her mind as to her testamentary dispositions, now benefiting one, now another member of her family."

"Suppose," suggested Poirot, "that, unknown to you, she had made a new will in favour of someone who was not, in any sense of the word, a member of the family — we will say Miss Howard, for instance — would you be surprised?"

"Not in the least."

"Ah!" Poirot seemed to have exhausted his questions.

I drew close to him, while John and the lawyer were debating the question of going through Mrs. Inglethorp's papers.

"Do you think Mrs. Inglethorp made a will leaving all her money to Miss Howard?" I asked in a low voice, with some curiosity.

Poirot smiled.

"No."

"Then why did you ask?"

"Hush!"

John Cavendish had turned to Poirot.

"Will you come with us, Monsieur Poirot? We are going through my mother's papers. Mr. Inglethorp is quite willing to leave it entirely to Mr. Wells and myself."

"Which simplifies matters very much," murmured the lawyer. "As technically, of course, he was entitled —" He did not finish the sentence.

"We will look through the desk in the boudoir first," explained John, "and go up to her bedroom afterwards. She kept her most important papers in a purple despatch-case, which we must look through carefully."

"Yes," said the lawyer, "it is quite possible that there may be a later will than the one in my possession."

"There *is* a later will." It was Poirot who spoke.

"What?" John and the lawyer looked at him startled.

"Or, rather," pursued my friend imperturbably, "there *was* one."

"What do you mean — there was one? Where is it now?"

"Burnt!"

"Burnt?"

"Yes. See here." He took out the charred fragment we had found in the grate in Mrs. Inglethorp's room, and handed it to the lawyer with a brief explanation of when and where he had found it.

"But possibly this is an old will?"

"I do not think so. In fact I am almost certain that it was made no earlier than yesterday afternoon."

"What?" "Impossible!" broke simultaneously from both men.

Poirot turned to John.

"If you will allow me to send for your gardener, I will prove it to you."

"Oh, of course — but I don't see —"

Poirot raised his hand.

"Do as I ask you. Afterwards you shall question as much as you please."

"Very well." He rang the bell.

Dorcas answered it in due course.

"Dorcas, will you tell Manning to come round and speak to me here."

"Yes, sir."

Dorcas withdrew.

We waited in a tense silence.

Poirot alone seemed perfectly at his ease, and dusted a forgotten corner of the bookcase.

The clumping of hobnailed boots on the gravel outside proclaimed the approach of Manning. John looked questioningly at Poirot. The latter nodded.

"Come inside, Manning," said John, "I want to speak to you."

Manning came slowly and hesitatingly through the French window, and stood as near it as he could. He held his cap in his hands, twisting it very carefully round and round. His back was much bent, though he was probably not as old as he looked, but his eyes were sharp and intelligent, and belied his slow and rather cautious speech.

"Manning," said John, "this gentleman will put some questions to you which I want you to answer."

"Yessir," mumbled Manning.

Poirot stepped forward briskly. Manning's eye swept over him with a faint contempt.

"You were planting a bed of begonias round by the south side of the house yesterday afternoon, were you not, Manning?"

"Yes, sir, me and Willum."

"And Mrs. Inglethorp came to the window and called you, did she not?"

"Yes, sir, she did."

"Tell me in your own words exactly what happened after that."

"Well, sir, nothing much. She just told Willum to go on his bicycle down to the village, and bring back a form of will, or such-like — I don't know what exactly — she wrote it down for him."

"Well?"

"Well, he did, sir."

"And what happened next?"

"We went on with the begonias, sir."

"Did not Mrs. Inglethorp call you again?"

"Yes, sir, both me and Willum, she called."

"And then?"

"She made us come right in, and sign our names at the bottom of a long paper — under where she'd signed."

"Did you see anything of what was written above her signature?" asked Poirot sharply.

"No, sir, there was a bit of blotting paper over that part."

"And you signed where she told you?"

"Yes, sir, first me and then Willum."

"What did she do with it afterwards?"

"Well, sir, she slipped it into a long envelope, and put it inside a sort of purple box that was standing on the desk."

"What time was it when she first called you?"

"About four, I should say, sir."

"Not earlier? Couldn't it have been about half-past three?"

"No, I shouldn't say so, sir. It would be more likely to be a bit after four — not before it."

"Thank you, Manning, that will

do," said Poirot pleasantly.

The gardener glanced at his master, who nodded, whereupon Manning lifted a finger to his forehead with a low mumble, and backed cautiously out of the window.

We all looked at each other.

"Good heavens!" murmured John. "What an extraordinary coincidence."

"How — a coincidence?"

"That my mother should have made a will on the very day of her death!"

Mr. Wells cleared his throat and remarked drily:

"Are you so sure it is a coincidence, Cavendish?"

"What do you mean?"

"Your mother, you tell me, had a violent quarrel with — someone yesterday afternoon —"

"What do you mean?" cried John again. There was a tremor in his voice, and he had gone very pale.

"In consequence of that quarrel, your mother very suddenly and hurriedly makes a new will. The contents of that will we shall never know. She told no one of its provisions. This morning, no doubt, she would have consulted me on the subject — but she had no chance. The will disappears, and she takes its secret with her to her grave. Cavendish, I much fear there is no coincidence there. Monsieur Poirot, I am sure you agree with me that the facts are very suggestive."

"Suggestive, or not," interrupted John, "we are most grateful to Monsieur Poirot for elucidating the matter. But for him, we should never have known of this will. I suppose, I may not ask you, monsieur, what first led you to suspect the fact?"

Poirot smiled and answered:

"A scribbled over old envelope, and a freshly planted bed of begonias."

John, I think, would have pressed his questions further, but at that moment the loud purr of a motor was audible, and we all turned to the window as it swept past.

"Evie!" cried John. "Excuse me, Wells." He went hurriedly out into the hall.

Poirot looked inquiringly at me.

"Miss Howard," I explained.

"Ah, I am glad she has come. There is a woman with a head and a heart too, Hastings. Though the good God gave her no beauty!"

I followed John's example, and went out into the hall, where Miss Howard was endeavouring to extricate herself from the voluminous mass of veils that enveloped her head. As her eyes fell on me, a sudden pang of guilt shot through me. This was the woman who had warned me so earnestly, and to whose warning I had, alas, paid no heed! How soon, and how contemptuously, I had dismissed it from my mind. Now that she had been proved justified in so tragic a manner, I felt ashamed. She had known Alfred Inglethorp only too well. I wondered whether, if she had remained at Styles, the tragedy would have taken place, or would the man have feared her watchful eyes?

I was relieved when she shook me by the hand, with her well-remembered painful grip. The eyes that met mine were sad, but not reproachful; that she had been crying bitterly, I could tell by the redness of her eyelids, but her manner was unchanged from its old gruffness.

"Started the moment I got the wire. Just come off night duty. Hired car. Quickest way to get here."

"Have you had anything to eat this morning, Evie?" asked John.

"No."

"I thought not. Come along, breakfast's not cleared away yet, and they'll make you some fresh tea." He turned to me. "Look after her, Hastings, will you? Wells is waiting for me. Oh, here's Monsieur Poirot. He's helping us, you know, Evie."

Miss Howard shook hands with Poirot, but glanced suspiciously over her shoulder at John.

"What do you mean — helping us?"

"Helping us to investigate."

"Nothing to investigate. Have they taken him to prison yet?"

"Taken who to prison?"

"Who? Alfred Inglethorp, of course!"

"My dear Evie, do be careful. Lawrence is of the opinion that my mother died from heart seizure."

"More fool, Lawrence!" retorted Miss Howard. "Of course Alfred Inglethorp murdered poor Emily — as I always told you he would."

"My dear Evie, don't shout so. Whatever we may think or suspect, it is better to say as little as possible for the present. The inquest isn't until Friday."

"Not until fiddlesticks!" The snort Miss Howard gave was truly magnificent. "You're all off your heads. The man will be out of the country by then. If he's any sense, he won't stay here tamely and wait to be hanged."

John Cavendish looked at her helplessly.

"I know what it is," she accused him, "you've been listening to the doctors. Never should. What do they know? Nothing at all — or just enough to make them dangerous. I ought to know — my own father was a doctor. That little Wilkins is about the greatest fool that even I have ever seen. Heart seizure! Sort of thing he would say. Anyone with any sense could see at once that her husband had poisoned her. I always said he'd murder her in her bed, poor soul. Now he's done it. And all you can do is to murmur silly things about 'heart seizure' and 'inquest on Friday.' You ought to be ashamed of yourself, John Cavendish."

"What do you want me to do?" asked John, unable to help a faint smile. "Dash it all, Evie, I can't haul him down to the local police station by the scruff of his neck."

"Well, you might do something. Find out how he did it. He's a crafty beggar. Dare say he soaked fly papers. Ask cook if she's missed any."

It occurred to me very forcibly at that moment that to harbour Miss Howard and Alfred Inglethorp under the same roof, and keep the peace between them, was likely to prove a Herculean task, and I did not envy John. I could see by the expression of his face that he fully appreciated the difficulty of the position. For the moment, he sought refuge in retreat, and left the room precipitately.

Dorcas brought in fresh tea. As she left the room, Poirot came over from the window where he had been standing, and sat down facing Miss Howard.

"Mademoiselle," he said gravely, "I want to ask you something."

"Ask away," said the lady, eyeing him with some disfavour.

"I want to be able to count upon your help."

"I'll help you to hang Alfred with pleasure," she replied gruffly. "Hanging's too good for him. Ought to be drawn and quartered, like in good old times."

"We are at one then," said Poirot, "for I, too, want to hang the criminal."

"Alfred Inglethorp?"

"Him, or another."

"No question of another. Poor Emily was never murdered until *he* came along. I don't say she wasn't surrounded by sharks — she was. But it was only her purse they were after. Her life was safe enough. But along comes Mr. Alfred Inglethorp — and within two months — hey presto!"

"Believe me, Miss Howard," said Poirot very earnestly, "if Mr. Inglethorp is the man, he shall not escape me. On my honour, I will hang him as high as Haman!"

"That's better," said Miss Howard more enthusiastically.

"But I must ask you to trust me. Now your help may be very valuable to me. I will tell you why. Because, in all this house of mourning, yours are the only eyes that have wept."

Miss Howard blinked, and a new note crept into the gruffness of her voice.

"If you mean that I was fond of her — yes, I was. You know, Emily was a selfish old woman in her way. She was very generous, but she always wanted a return. She never let people forget what she had done for them — and, that way she missed love. Don't think she ever realized it, though, or felt the lack of it. Hope not, anyway. I was on a different footing. I took my stand from the first. 'So many pounds a year I'm worth to you. Well and good. But not a penny piece besides — not a pair of gloves, nor a theatre ticket.' She didn't understand — was very offended sometimes. Said I was foolishly proud. It wasn't that — but I couldn't explain. Anyway, I kept my self-respect. And so, out of the whole bunch, I was the only one who could allow myself to be fond of her. I watched over her. I guarded her from the lot of them, and then a glib-tongued scoundrel comes along, and pooh! all my years of devotion go for nothing."

Poirot nodded sympathetically.

"I understand, mademoiselle, I understand all you feel. It is most natural. You think that we are lukewarm — that we lack fire and energy — but trust me, it is not so."

John stuck his head in at this juncture, and invited us both to come up to Mrs. Inglethorp's room, as he and Mr. Wells had finished looking through the desk in the boudoir.

As we went up the stairs, John looked back to the dining-room door, and lowered his voice confidentially:

"Look here, what's going to happen when these two meet?"

I shook my head helplessly.

"I've told Mary to keep them apart if she can."

"Will she be able to do so?"

"The Lord only knows. There's one thing, Inglethorp himself won't be too keen on meeting her."

"You've got the keys still, haven't you, Poirot?" I asked, as we reached the door of the locked room.

Taking the keys from Poirot, John unlocked it, and we all passed in. The lawyer went straight to the desk, and John followed him.

"My mother kept most of her important papers in this despatch-case, I believe," he said.

Poirot drew out the small bunch of keys.

"Permit me. I locked it, out of precaution, this morning."

"But it's not locked now."

"Impossible!"

"See." And John lifted the lid as he spoke.

"*Milles tonnerres!*" cried Poirot, dumbfounded. "And I — who have both the keys in my pocket!" He flung himself upon the case. Suddenly he stiffened. "*Eh voilà une affaire!* This lock has been forced."

"What?"

Poirot laid down the case again.

"But who forced it? Why should they? When? But the door was locked?" These exclamations burst from us disjointedly.

Poirot answered them categorically — almost mechanically.

"Who? That is the question. Why? Ah, if I only knew. When? Since I was here an hour ago. As to the door being locked, it is a very ordinary lock. Probably any other of the doorkeys in this passage would fit it."

We stared at one another blankly. Poirot had walked over to the mantelpiece. He was outwardly calm, but I noticed his hands, which from long force of habit were mechanically straightening the spill vases on the mantelpiece, were shaking violently.

"See here, it was like this," he said at last. "There was something in that case — some piece of evidence, slight in itself perhaps, but still enough of a clue to connect the murderer with the crime. It was vital to him that it should be destroyed before it was discovered and its significance appreciated. Therefore, he took the risk, the great risk, of coming in here. Finding the case locked, he was obliged to force it, thus betraying his presence. For him to take that risk, it must have been something of great importance."

"But what was it?"

"Ah!" cried Poirot, with a gesture of anger. "That, I do not know! A document of some kind, without doubt, possibly the scrap of paper Dorcas saw in her hand yesterday afternoon. And I—" his anger burst forth freely—"miserable animal that I am! I guessed nothing! I have behaved like an imbecile! I should never have left that case here. I should have carried it away with me. Ah, triple pig! And now it is gone. It is destroyed—but is it destroyed? Is there not yet a chance—we must leave no stone unturned—"

He rushed like a madman from the room, and I followed him as soon as I had sufficiently recovered my wits. But, by the time I had reached the top of the stairs, he was out of sight.

Mary Cavendish was standing where the staircase branched, staring down into the hall in the direction in which he had disappeared.

"What has happened to your extraordinary little friend, Mr. Hastings? He has just rushed past me like a mad bull."

"He's rather upset about something," I remarked feebly. I really did not know how much Poirot would wish me to disclose. As I saw a faint smile gather on Mrs. Cavendish's expressive mouth, I endeavoured to try and turn the conversation by saying: "They haven't met yet, have they?"

"Who?"

"Mr. Inglethorp and Miss Howard."

She looked at me in rather a disconcerting manner.

"Do you think it would be such a disaster if they did meet?"

"Well, don't you?" I said, rather taken aback.

"No." She was smiling in her quiet way. "I should like to see a good flare up. It would clear the air. At present we are all thinking so much, and saying so little."

"John doesn't think so," I remarked. "He's anxious to keep them apart."

"Oh, John!"

Something in her tone fired me, and I blurted out:

"Old John's an awfully good sort."

She studied me curiously for a minute or two, and then said, to my great surprise:

"You are loyal to your friend. I like you for that."

"Aren't you my friend too?"

"I am a very bad friend."

"Why do you say that?"

"Because it is true. I am charming to my friends one day, and forget all about them the next."

I don't know what impelled me, but I was nettled, and I said foolishly and not in the best of taste:

"Yet you seem to be invariably

charming to Dr. Bauerstein!"

Instantly I regretted my words. Her face stiffened. I had the impression of a steel curtain coming down and blotting out the real woman. Without a word, she turned and went swiftly up the stairs, whilst I stood like an idiot gaping after her.

I was recalled to other matters by a frightful row going on below. I could hear Poirot shouting and expounding. I was vexed to think that my diplomacy had been in vain. The little man appeared to be taking the whole house into his confidence, a proceeding of which I, for one, doubted the wisdom. Once again I could not help regretting that my friend was so prone to lose his head in moments of excitement. I stepped briskly down the stairs. The sight of me calmed Poirot almost immediately. I drew him aside.

"My dear fellow," I said, "is this wise? Surely you don't want the whole house to know of this occurrence? You are actually playing into the criminal's hands."

"You think so, Hastings?"

"I am sure of it."

"Well, well, my friend, I will be guided by you."

"Good. Although, unfortunately, it is a little too late now."

"Sure."

He looked so crestfallen and abashed that I felt quite sorry, though I still thought my rebuke a just and wise one.

"Well," he said at last, "let us go, *mon ami.*"

"You have finished here?"

"For the moment, yes. You will walk back with me to the village?"

"Willingly."

He picked up his little suit-case, and we went out through the open window in the drawing-room. Cynthia Murdoch was just coming in, and Poirot stood aside to let her pass.

"Excuse me, mademoiselle, one minute."

"Yes?" she turned inquiringly.

"Did you ever make up Mrs. Inglethorp's medicines?"

A slight flush rose in her face, as she answered rather constrainedly:

"No."

"Only her powders?"

The flush deepened as Cynthia replied:

"Oh, yes, I did make up some sleeping powders for her once."

"These?"

Poirot produced the empty box which had contained powders.

She nodded.

"Can you tell me what they were? Sulphonal? Veronal?"

"No, they were bromide powders."

"Ah! Thank you, mademoiselle; good morning."

As we walked briskly away from the house, I glanced at him more than once. I had often before noticed that, if anything excited him, his eyes turned green like a cat's. They were shining like emeralds now.

"My friend," he broke out at last, "I have a little idea, a very strange, and probably utterly impossible idea. And yet — it fits in."

I shrugged my shoulders. I privately thought that Poirot was rather too much given to these fantastic ideas. In this case, surely, the truth was only too plain and apparent.

"So that is the explanation of the blank label on the box," I remarked. "Very simple, as you said. I really wonder that I did not think of it myself."

Poirot did not appear to be listening to me.

"They have made one more discovery, *là-bas*," he observed, jerking his thumb over his shoulder in the direction of Styles. "Mr. Wells told me as we were going upstairs."

"What was it?"

"Locked up in the desk in the boudoir, they found a will of Mrs. Inglethorp's, dated before her marriage, leaving her fortune to Alfred Inglethorp. It must have been made just at the time they were engaged. It came quite as a surprise to Wells — and to John Cavendish also. It was written on one of those printed will forms, and witnessed by two of the servants — not Dorcas."

"Did Mr. Inglethorp know of it?"

"He says not."

"One might take that with a grain of salt," I remarked sceptically. "All these wills are very confusing. Tell me, how did those scribbled words on the envelope help you to discover that a will was made yesterday afternoon?"

Poirot smiled.

"*Mon ami*, have you ever, when writing a letter, been arrested by the fact that you did not know how to spell a certain word?"

"Yes, often. I suppose everyone has."

"Exactly. And have you not, in such a case, tried the word once or twice on the edge of the blot ting-paper, or a spare scrap of paper, to see if it looked right? Well, that is what Mrs. Inglethorp did. You will notice that the word 'possessed' is spelt first with one 's' and subsequently with two — correctly. To make sure, she had further tried it in a sentence, thus: 'I am possessed.' Now, what did that tell me? It told me that Mrs. Inglethorp had been writing the word 'possessed' that afternoon, and, having the fragment of paper found in the grate fresh in my mind, the possibility of a will — (a document almost certain to contain that word) — occurred to me at once. This possibility was confirmed by a further circumstance. In the general confusion, the boudoir had not been swept that morning, and near the desk were several traces of brown mould and earth. The weather had been perfectly fine for some days, and no ordinary boots would have left such a heavy deposit.

"I strolled to the window, and saw at once that the begonia beds had been newly planted. The mould in the beds was exactly similar to that on the floor of the boudoir, and also I learnt from you that they *had* been planted yesterday afternoon. I was now sure that one, or possibly both of the gardeners — for there were two sets of footprints in the bed — had entered the boudoir, for if Mrs. Inglethorp had merely wished to speak to them she would in all probability have stood at the window, and they would not have come into the room at all. I was now quite convinced that she had made a fresh will, and had called the two gardeners in to witness her signature. Events proved that I was right in my supposition."

"That was very ingenious," I could not help admitting. "I must confess that the conclusions I drew from those few scribbled words were quite erroneous."

He smiled.

"You gave too much rein to your imagination. Imagination is a good servant, and a bad master. The simplest explanation is always the most likely."

"Another point — how did you know that the key of the despatch-case had been lost?"

"I did not know it. It was a guess that turned out to be correct. You observed that it had a piece of twisted wire through the handle. That suggested to me at once that it had possibly been wrenched off a flimsy key-ring. Now, if it had been lost and recovered, Mrs. Inglethorp would at once have replaced it on her bunch; but on her bunch I found what was obviously the duplicate key, very new and bright, which led me to the hypothesis that somebody else had inserted the original key in the lock of the despatch-case."

"Yes," I said, "Alfred Inglethorp, without doubt."

Poirot looked at me curiously.

"You are very sure of his guilt?"

"Well, naturally. Every fresh circumstance seems to establish it more clearly."

"On the contrary," said Poirot quietly, "there are several points in his favour."

"Oh, come now!"

"Yes."

"I see only one."

"And that?"

"That he was not in the house last night."

"'Bad shot!' as you English say! You have chosen the one point that to my mind tells against him."

"How is that?"

"Because if Mr. Inglethorp knew that his wife would be poisoned last night, he would certainly have arranged to be away from the house. His excuse was an obviously trumped up one. That leaves us two possibilities: either he knew what was going to happen or he had a reason of his own for his absence."

"And that reason?" I asked sceptically.

Poirot shrugged his shoulders.

"How should I know? Discreditable, without doubt. This Mr. Inglethorp, I should say, is somewhat of a scoundrel — but that does not of necessity make him a murderer."

I shook my head, unconvinced.

"We do not agree, eh?" said Poirot. "Well, let us leave it. Time will show which of us is right. Now let us turn to other aspects of the case. What do you make of the fact that all the doors of the bedroom were bolted on the inside?"

"Well—" I considered. "One must look at it logically."

"True."

"I should put it this way. The doors *were* bolted—our own eyes have told us that—yet the presence of the candle grease on the floor, and the destruction of the will, prove that during the night someone entered the room. You agree so far?"

"Perfectly. Put with admirable clearness. Proceed."

"Well," I said, encouraged, "as the person who entered did not do so by the window, nor by miraculous means, it follows that the door must have been opened from inside by Mrs. Inglethorp herself. That strengthens the conviction that the person in question was her husband. She would naturally open the door to her own husband."

Poirot shook his head.

"Why should she? She had bolted the door leading into his room—a most unusual proceeding on her part—she had had a most violent quarrel with him that very afternoon. No, he was the last person she would admit."

"But you agree with me that the door must have been opened by Mrs. Inglethorp herself?"

"There is another possibility. She may have forgotten to bolt the door into the passage when she went to bed, and have got up later, towards morning, and bolted it then."

"Poirot, is that seriously your opinion?"

"No, I do not say it is so, but it might be. Now, to turn to another feature, what do you make of the scrap of conversation you overheard between Mrs. Cavendish and her mother-in-law?"

"I had forgotten that," I said thoughtfully. "That is as enigmatical as ever. It seems incredible that a woman like Mrs. Cavendish, proud and reticent to the last degree, should interfere so violently in what was certainly not her affair."

"Precisely. It was an astonishing thing for a woman of her breeding to do."

"It is certainly curious," I agreed. "Still, it is unimportant, and need not be taken into account."

A groan burst from Poirot.

"What have I always told you? Everything must be taken into account. If the fact will not fit the theory—let the theory go."

"Well, we shall see," I said, nettled.

"Yes, we shall see."

We had reached Leastways Cottage, and Poirot ushered me upstairs to his own room. He offered me one of the tiny Russian cigarettes he himself occasionally smoked. I was amused to notice that he stowed away the used matches most carefully in a little china pot. My momentary annoyance vanished.

Poirot had placed our two chairs in front of the open window which commanded a view of the village street. The fresh air blew in warm and pleasant. It was going to be a hot day.

Suddenly my attention was arrested by a weedy looking young man rushing down the street at a great pace. It was the expression on his face that was extraordinary — a curious mingling of terror and agitation.

"Look, Poirot!" I said.

He leant forward.

"*Tiens!*" he said. "It is Mr. Mace, from the chemist's shop. He is coming here."

The young man came to a halt before Leastways Cottage, and, after hesitating a moment, pounded vigorously at the door.

"A little minute," cried Poirot from the window. "I come."

Motioning to me to follow him, he ran swiftly down the stairs and opened the door. Mr. Mace began at once.

"Oh, Mr. Poirot, I'm sorry for the inconvenience, but I heard that you'd just come back from the Hall?"

"Yes, we have."

The young man moistened his dry lips. His face was working curiously.

"It's all over the village about old Mrs. Inglethorp dying so suddenly. They do say —" he lowered his voice cautiously — "that it's poison?"

Poirot's face remained quite impassive.

"Only the doctors can tell us that, Mr. Mace."

"Yes, exactly — of course —" The young man hesitated, and then his agitation was too much for him. He clutched Poirot by the arm, and sank his voice to a whisper: "Just tell me this, Mr. Poirot, it isn't — it isn't strychnine, is it?"

I hardly heard what Poirot replied. Something evidently of a non-committal nature. The young man departed, and as he closed the door Poirot's eyes met mine.

"Yes," he said, nodding gravely. "He will have evidence to give at the inquest."

We went slowly upstairs again. I was opening my lips, when Poirot stopped me with a gesture of his hand.

"Not now, not now, *mon ami*. I have need of reflection. My mind is in some disorder — which is not well."

For about ten minutes he sat in dead silence, perfectly still, except for several expressive motions of his eyebrows, and all the time his eyes grew steadily greener. At last he heaved a deep sigh.

"It is well. The bad moment has passed. Now all is arranged and classified. One must never permit confusion. The case is not clear yet — no. For it is of the most complicated! It puzzles *me*. *Me*, Hercule Poirot!

There are two facts of significance."

"And what are they?"

"The first is the state of the weather yesterday. That is very important."

"But it was a glorious day!" I interrupted. "Poirot, you're pulling my leg!"

"Not at all. The thermometer registered 80 degrees in the shade. Do not forget that, my friend. It is the key to the whole riddle!"

"And the second point?" I asked.

"The important fact that Monsieur Inglethorp wears very peculiar clothes, has a black beard, and uses glasses."

"Poirot, I cannot believe you are serious."

"I am absolutely serious, my friend."

"But this is childish!"

"No, it is very momentous."

"And supposing the Coroner's jury returns a verdict of Willful Murder against Alfred Inglethorp. What becomes of your theories, then?"

"They would not be shaken because twelve stupid men had happened to make a mistake! But that will not occur. For one thing, a country jury is not anxious to take responsibility upon itself, and Mr. Inglethorp stands practically in the position of local squire. Also," he added placidly, "*I* should not allow it!"

"*You* would not allow it?"

"No."

I looked at the extraordinary little man, divided between annoyance and amusement. He was so tremendously sure of himself. As though he read my thoughts, he nodded gently.

"Oh, yes, *mon ami*, I would do what I say." He got up and laid his hand on my shoulder. His physiognomy underwent a complete change. Tears came into his eyes. "In all this, you see, I think of that poor Mrs. Inglethorp who is dead. She was not extravagantly loved — no. But she was very good to us Belgians — I owe her a debt."

I endeavoured to interrupt, but Poirot swept on.

"Let me tell you this, Hastings. She would never forgive me if I let Alfred Inglethorp, her husband, be arrested *now* — when a word from me could save him!"

# VI.

## THE INQUEST.

In the interval before the inquest, Poirot was unfailing in his activity. Twice he was closeted with Mr. Wells. He also took long walks into the country. I rather resented his not taking me into his confidence, the more so as I could not in the least guess what he was driving at.

It occurred to me that he might have been making inquiries at Raikes's farm; so, finding him out when I called at Leastways Cottage on Wednesday evening, I walked over there by the fields, hoping to meet him. But there was no sign of him, and I hesitated to go right up to the farm itself. As I walked away, I met an aged rustic, who leered at me cunningly.

"You'm from the Hall, hain't you?" he asked.

"Yes. I'm looking for a friend of mine whom I thought might have walked this way."

"A little chap? As waves his hands when he talks? One of them Belgies from the village?"

"Yes," I said eagerly. "He has been here, then?"

"Oh, ay, he's been here, right enough. More'n once too. Friend of yours, is he? Ah, you gentlemen from the Hall—you'm a pretty lot!" And he leered more jocosely than ever.

"Why, do the gentlemen from the Hall come here often?" I asked, as carelessly as I could.

He winked at me knowingly.

"*One* does, mister. Naming no

names, mind. And a very liberal gentleman too! Oh, thank you, sir, I'm sure."

I walked on sharply. Evelyn Howard had been right then, and I experienced a sharp twinge of disgust, as I thought of Alfred Inglethorp's liberality with another woman's money. Had that piquant gypsy face been at the bottom of the crime, or was it the baser mainspring of money? Probably a judicious mixture of both.

On one point, Poirot seemed to have a curious obsession. He once or twice observed to me that he thought Dorcas must have made an error in fixing the time of the quarrel. He suggested to her repeatedly that it was four-thirty, and not four o'clock when she had heard the voices.

But Dorcas was unshaken. Quite an hour, or even more, had elapsed between the time when she had heard the voices and five o'clock, when she had taken tea to her mistress.

The inquest was held on Friday at the Stylites Arms in the village. Poirot and I sat together, not being required to give evidence.

The preliminaries were gone through. The jury viewed the body, and John Cavendish gave evidence of identification.

Further questioned, he described his awakening in the early hours of the morning, and the circumstances of his mother's death.

The medical evidence was next taken. There was a breathless hush, and every eye was fixed on the famous London specialist, who was known to be one of the greatest authorities of the day on the subject of toxicology.

In a few brief words, he summed up the result of the post-mortem. Shorn of its medical phraseology and technicalities, it amounted to the fact that Mrs. Inglethorp had met her death as the result of strychnine poisoning. Judging from the quantity recovered, she must have taken not less than three-quarters of a grain of strychnine, but probably one grain or slightly over.

"Is it possible that she could have swallowed the poison by accident?" asked the Coroner.

"I should consider it very unlikely. Strychnine is not used for domestic purposes, as some poisons are, and there are restrictions placed on its sale."

"Does anything in your examination lead you to determine how the poison was administered?"

"No."

"You arrived at Styles before Dr. Wilkins, I believe?"

"That is so. The motor met me just outside the lodge gates, and I hurried there as fast as I could."

"Will you relate to us exactly what happened next?"

"I entered Mrs. Inglethorp's room. She was at that moment in a typical tetanic convulsion. She turned towards me, and gasped out: 'Alfred — Alfred — '"

"Could the strychnine have been administered in Mrs. Inglethorp's after-dinner coffee which was taken to her by her husband?"

"Possibly, but strychnine is a fairly rapid drug in its action. The symptoms appear from one to two hours after it has been swallowed. It is retarded under certain conditions, none of which, however, appear to have been present in this case. I presume Mrs. Inglethorp took the coffee after dinner about eight o'clock, whereas the symptoms did not manifest themselves until the early hours of the morning, which, on the face of it, points to the drug having been taken much later in the evening."

"Mrs. Inglethorp was in the habit of drinking a cup of cocoa in the middle of the night. Could the strychnine have been administered in that?"

"No, I myself took a sample of the cocoa remaining in the saucepan and had it analysed. There was no strychnine present."

I heard Poirot chuckle softly beside me.

"How did you know?" I whispered.

"Listen."

"I should say"— the doctor was continuing — "that I would have been considerably surprised at any other result."

"Why?"

"Simply because strychnine has an unusually bitter taste. It can be detected in a solution of one in seventy thousand, and can only be disguised by some strongly flavoured substance. Cocoa would be quite powerless to mask it."

One of the jury wanted to know if the same objection applied to coffee.

"No. Coffee has a bitter taste of its own which would probably cover the taste of strychnine."

"Then you consider it more likely that the drug was administered in the coffee, but that for some unknown reason its action was delayed."

"Yes, but, the cup being completely smashed, there is no possibility of analyzing its contents."

This concluded Dr. Bauerstein's evidence. Dr. Wilkins corroborated it on all points. Sounded as to the possibility of suicide, he repudiated it utterly. The deceased, he said, suffered from a weak heart, but otherwise enjoyed perfect health, and was of a cheerful and well-balanced disposition. She would be one of the last people to take her own life.

Lawrence Cavendish was next called. His evidence was quite unimportant, being a mere repetition of that of his brother. Just as he was about to step down, he paused, and said rather hesitatingly:

"I should like to make a suggestion if I may?"

He glanced deprecatingly at the Coroner, who replied briskly:

"Certainly, Mr. Cavendish, we

are here to arrive at the truth of this matter, and welcome anything that may lead to further elucidation."

"It is just an idea of mine," explained Lawrence. "Of course I may be quite wrong, but it still seems to me that my mother's death might be accounted for by natural means."

"How do you make that out, Mr. Cavendish?"

"My mother, at the time of her death, and for some time before it, was taking a tonic containing strychnine."

"Ah!" said the Coroner.

The jury looked up, interested.

"I believe," continued Lawrence, "that there have been cases where the cumulative effect of a drug, administered for some time, has ended by causing death. Also, is it not possible that she may have taken an overdose of her medicine by accident?"

"This is the first we have heard of the deceased taking strychnine at the time of her death. We are much obliged to you, Mr. Cavendish."

Dr. Wilkins was recalled and ridiculed the idea.

"What Mr. Cavendish suggests is quite impossible. Any doctor would tell you the same. Strychnine is, in a certain sense, a cumulative poison, but it would be quite impossible for it to result in sudden death in this way. There would have to be a long period of chronic symptoms which would at once have attracted my attention. The whole thing is absurd."

"And the second suggestion? That Mrs. Inglethorp may have inadvertently taken an overdose?"

"Three, or even four doses, would not have resulted in death. Mrs. Inglethorp always had an extra large amount of medicine made up at a time, as she dealt with Coot's, the Cash Chemists in Tadminster. She would have had to take very nearly the whole bottle to account for the amount of strychnine found at the post-mortem."

"Then you consider that we may dismiss the tonic as not being in any way instrumental in causing her death?"

"Certainly. The supposition is ridiculous."

The same juryman who had interrupted before here suggested that the chemist who made up the medicine might have committed an error.

"That, of course, is always possible," replied the doctor.

But Dorcas, who was the next witness called, dispelled even that possibility. The medicine had not been newly made up. On the contrary, Mrs. Inglethorp had taken the last dose on the day of her death.

So the question of the tonic was finally abandoned, and the Coroner proceeded with his task. Having elicited from Dorcas how she had been awakened by the violent ringing of her mistress's bell, and had subsequently roused the household, he passed to the subject of the quarrel on the preceding afternoon.

Dorcas's evidence on this point

was substantially what Poirot and I had already heard, so I will not repeat it here.

The next witness was Mary Cavendish. She stood very upright, and spoke in a low, clear, and perfectly composed voice. In answer to the Coroner's question, she told how, her alarm clock having aroused her at four-thirty as usual, she was dressing, when she was startled by the sound of something heavy falling.

"That would have been the table by the bed?" commented the Coroner.

"I opened my door," continued Mary, "and listened. In a few minutes a bell rang violently. Dorcas came running down and woke my husband, and we all went to my mother-in-law's room, but it was locked—"

The Coroner interrupted her.

"I really do not think we need trouble you further on that point. We know all that can be known of the subsequent happenings. But I should be obliged if you would tell us all you overheard of the quarrel the day before."

"I?"

There was a faint insolence in her voice. She raised her hand and adjusted the ruffle of lace at her neck, turning her head a little as she did so. And quite spontaneously the thought flashed across my mind: "She is gaining time!"

"Yes. I understand," continued the Coroner deliberately, "that you were sitting reading on the bench just outside the long window of the boudoir. That is so, is it not?"

This was news to me and glancing sideways at Poirot, I fancied that it was news to him as well.

There was the faintest pause, the mere hesitation of a moment, before she answered:

"Yes, that is so."

"And the boudoir window was open, was it not?"

Surely her face grew a little paler as she answered:

"Yes."

"Then you cannot have failed to hear the voices inside, especially as they were raised in anger. In fact, they would be more audible where you were than in the hall."

"Possibly."

"Will you repeat to us what you overheard of the quarrel?"

"I really do not remember hearing anything."

"Do you mean to say you did not hear voices?"

"Oh, yes, I heard the voices, but I did not hear what they said." A faint spot of colour came into her cheek. "I am not in the habit of listening to private conversations."

The Coroner persisted.

"And you remember nothing at all? *Nothing*, Mrs. Cavendish? Not one stray word or phrase to make you realize that it *was* a private conversation?"

She paused, and seemed to reflect, still outwardly as calm as ever.

"Yes; I remember. Mrs. Inglethorp said something—I do not remember exactly what—about causing scandal between husband and wife."

"Ah!" the Coroner leant back satisfied. "That corresponds with what Dorcas heard. But excuse me, Mrs. Cavendish, although you realized it was a private conversation, you did not move away? You remained where you were?"

I caught the momentary gleam of her tawny eyes as she raised them. I felt certain that at that moment she would willingly have torn the little lawyer, with his insinuations, into pieces, but she replied quietly enough:

"No. I was very comfortable where I was. I fixed my mind on my book."

"And that is all you can tell us?"

"That is all."

The examination was over, though I doubted if the Coroner was entirely satisfied with it. I think he suspected that Mary Cavendish could tell more if she chose.

Amy Hill, shop assistant, was next called, and deposed to having sold a will form on the afternoon of the 17th to William Earl, under-gardener at Styles.

William Earl and Manning succeeded her, and testified to witnessing a document. Manning fixed the time at about four-thirty, William was of the opinion that it was rather earlier.

Cynthia Murdoch came next. She had, however, little to tell. She had known nothing of the tragedy, until awakened by Mrs. Cavendish.

"You did not hear the table fall?"

"No. I was fast asleep."

The Coroner smiled.

"A good conscience makes a sound sleeper," he observed. "Thank you, Miss Murdoch, that is all."

"Miss Howard."

Miss Howard produced the letter written to her by Mrs. Inglethorp on the evening of the 17th. Poirot and I had, of course already seen it. It added nothing to our knowledge of the tragedy. The following is a facsimile:

July 17th

Styles Court
Essex

My dear Evelyn
Can we not bury the hatchet? I have found it hard to forget the things you said against my dear husband but I am an old woman & very fond of you
yours affectionately
Emily Inglethorp

It was handed to the jury who scrutinized it attentively.

"I fear it does not help us much," said the Coroner, with a sigh. "There is no mention of any of the events of that afternoon."

"Plain as a pikestaff to me," said Miss Howard shortly. "It shows clearly enough that my poor old friend had just found out she'd been made a fool of!"

"It says nothing of the kind in the letter," the Coroner pointed out.

"No, because Emily never could bear to put herself in the wrong. But *I* know her. She wanted me back. But she wasn't going to own that I'd been right. She went round about. Most people do. Don't believe in it myself."

Mr. Wells smiled faintly. So, I noticed, did several of the jury. Miss Howard was obviously quite a public character.

"Anyway, all this tomfoolery is a great waste of time," continued the lady, glancing up and down the jury disparagingly. "Talk — talk — talk! When all the time we know perfectly well —"

The Coroner interrupted her in an agony of apprehension:

"Thank you, Miss Howard, that is all."

I fancy he breathed a sigh of relief when she complied.

Then came the sensation of the day. The Coroner called Albert Mace, chemist's assistant.

It was our agitated young man of the pale face. In answer to the Coroner's questions, he explained that he was a qualified pharmacist, but had only recently come to this particular shop, as the assistant formerly there had just been called up for the army.

These preliminaries completed, the Coroner proceeded to business.

"Mr. Mace, have you lately sold strychnine to any unauthorized person?"

"Yes, sir."

"When was this?"

"Last Monday night."

"Monday? Not Tuesday?"

"No, sir, Monday, the 16th."

"Will you tell us to whom you sold it?"

You could have heard a pin drop.

"Yes, sir. It was to Mr. Inglethorp."

Every eye turned simultaneously to where Alfred Inglethorp was sitting, impassive and wooden. He started slightly, as the damning words fell from the young man's lips. I half thought he was going to rise from his chair, but he remained seated, although a remarkably well acted expression of astonishment rose on his face.

"You are sure of what you say?" asked the Coroner sternly.

"Quite sure, sir."

"Are you in the habit of selling strychnine indiscriminately over the counter?"

The wretched young man wilted visibly under the Coroner's frown.

"Oh, no, sir — of course not. But, seeing it was Mr. Inglethorp of the Hall, I thought there was no harm in it. He said it was to poison a dog."

Inwardly I sympathized. It was only human nature to endeavour to please "The Hall" — especially when it might result in custom being transferred from Coot's to the local establishment.

"Is it not customary for anyone

purchasing poison to sign a book?"

"Yes, sir, Mr. Inglethorp did so."

"Have you got the book here?"

"Yes, sir."

It was produced; and, with a few words of stern censure, the Coroner dismissed the wretched Mr. Mace.

Then, amidst a breathless silence, Alfred Inglethorp was called. Did he realize, I wondered, how closely the halter was being drawn around his neck?

The Coroner went straight to the point.

"On Monday evening last, did you purchase strychnine for the purpose of poisoning a dog?"

Inglethorp replied with perfect calmness:

"No, I did not. There is no dog at Styles, except an outdoor sheepdog, which is in perfect health."

"You deny absolutely having purchased strychnine from Albert Mace on Monday last?"

"I do."

"Do you also deny *this*?"

The Coroner handed him the register in which his signature was inscribed.

"Certainly I do. The handwriting is quite different from mine. I will show you."

He took an old envelope out of his pocket, and wrote his name on it, handing it to the jury. It was certainly utterly dissimilar.

"Then what is your explanation of Mr. Mace's statement?"

Alfred Inglethorp replied imperturbably:

"Mr. Mace must have been mistaken."

The Coroner hesitated for a moment, and then said:

"Mr. Inglethorp, as a mere matter of form, would you mind telling us where you were on the evening of Monday, July 16th?"

"Really — I cannot remember."

"That is absurd, Mr. Inglethorp," said the Coroner sharply. "Think again."

Inglethorp shook his head.

"I cannot tell you. I have an idea that I was out walking."

"In what direction?"

"I really can't remember."

The Coroner's face grew graver.

"Were you in company with anyone?"

"No."

"Did you meet anyone on your walk?"

"No."

"That is a pity," said the Coroner dryly. "I am to take it then that you decline to say where you were at the time that Mr. Mace positively recognized you as entering the shop to purchase strychnine?"

"If you like to take it that way, yes."

"Be careful, Mr. Inglethorp."

Poirot was fidgeting nervously.

"*Sacré!*" he murmured. "Does this imbecile of a man *want* to be arrested?"

Inglethorp was indeed creating a bad impression. His futile denials would not have convinced a child. The Coroner, however, passed briskly to the next point, and Poirot drew a deep breath of relief.

"You had a discussion with your wife on Tuesday afternoon?"

"Pardon me," interrupted Alfred Inglethorp, "you have been misinformed. I had no quarrel with my dear wife. The whole story is absolutely untrue. I was absent from the house the entire afternoon."

"Have you anyone who can testify to that?"

"You have my word," said Inglethorp haughtily.

The Coroner did not trouble to reply.

"There are two witnesses who will swear to having heard your disagreement with Mrs. Inglethorp."

"Those witnesses were mistaken."

I was puzzled. The man spoke with such quiet assurance that I was staggered. I looked at Poirot. There was an expression of exultation on his face which I could not understand. Was he at last convinced of Alfred Inglethorp's guilt?

"Mr. Inglethorp," said the Coroner, "you have heard your wife's dying words repeated here. Can you explain them in any way?"

"Certainly I can."

"You can?"

"It seems to me very simple. The room was dimly lighted. Dr. Bauerstein is much of my height and build, and, like me, wears a beard. In the dim light, and suffering as she was, my poor wife mistook him for me."

"Ah!" murmured Poirot to himself. "But it is an idea, that!"

"You think it is true?" I whispered.

"I do not say that. But it is truly an ingenious supposition."

"You read my wife's last words as an accusation"—Inglethorp was continuing—"they were, on the contrary, an appeal to me."

The Coroner reflected a moment, then he said:

"I believe, Mr. Inglethorp, that you yourself poured out the coffee, and took it to your wife that evening?"

"I poured it out, yes. But I did not take it to her. I meant to do so, but I was told that a friend was at the hall door, so I laid down the coffee on the hall table. When I came through the hall again a few minutes later, it was gone."

This statement might, or might not, be true, but it did not seem to me to improve matters much for Inglethorp. In any case, he had had ample time to introduce the poison.

At that point, Poirot nudged me gently, indicating two men who were sitting together near the door. One was a little, sharp, dark, ferret-faced man, the other was tall and fair.

I questioned Poirot mutely. He put his lips to my ear.

"Do you know who that little man is?"

I shook my head.

"That is Detective Inspector James Japp of Scotland Yard—Jimmy Japp. The other man is from Scotland Yard too. Things are moving quickly, my friend."

I stared at the two men intently. There was certainly nothing of the policeman about them. I should never have suspected them of being official personages.

I was still staring, when I was startled and recalled by the verdict being given:

"Willful Murder against some person or persons unknown."

# VII.

## POIROT PAYS HIS DEBTS.

As we came out of the Stylites Arms, Poirot drew me aside by a gentle pressure of the arm. I understood his object. He was waiting for the Scotland Yard men.

In a few moments, they emerged, and Poirot at once stepped forward, and accosted the shorter of the two.

"I fear you do not remember me, Inspector Japp."

"Why, if it isn't Mr. Poirot!" cried the Inspector. He turned to the other man. "You've heard me speak of Mr. Poirot? It was in 1904 he and I worked together — the Abercrombie forgery case — you remember, he was run down in Brussels. Ah, those were great days, Moosier. Then, do you remember 'Baron' Altara? There was a pretty rogue for you! He eluded the clutches of half the police in Europe. But we nailed him in Antwerp — thanks to Mr. Poirot here."

As these friendly reminiscences were being indulged in, I drew nearer, and was introduced to Detective-Inspector Japp, who, in his turn, introduced us both to his companion, Superintendent Summerhaye.

"I need hardly ask what you are doing here, gentlemen," remarked Poirot.

Japp closed one eye knowingly.

"No, indeed. Pretty clear case I should say."

But Poirot answered gravely:

"There I differ from you."

"Oh, come!" said Summerhaye, opening his lips for the first time. "Surely the whole thing is clear as daylight. The man's caught red-handed. How he could be such a fool beats me!"

But Japp was looking attentively at Poirot.

"Hold your fire, Summerhaye," he remarked jocularly. "Me and Moosier here have met before — and there's no man's judgment I'd sooner take than his. If I'm not greatly mistaken, he's got something up his sleeve. Isn't that so, Moosier?"

Poirot smiled.

"I have drawn certain conclusions — yes."

Summerhaye was still looking rather sceptical, but Japp continued his scrutiny of Poirot.

"It's this way," he said, "so far, we've only seen the case from the outside. That's where the Yard's at a disadvantage in a case of this kind, where the murder's only out, so to speak, after the inquest. A lot depends on being on the spot first thing, and that's where Mr. Poirot's had the start of us. We shouldn't have been here as soon as this even, if it hadn't been for the fact that there was a smart doctor on the spot, who gave us the tip through the Coroner. But you've been on the spot from the first, and you may have picked up some little hints. From the evidence at the inquest, Mr. Inglethorp murdered his wife as sure as I stand here, and if anyone but you hinted the contrary I'd laugh in his face. I must say I was surprised the jury didn't bring it in Wilful Murder against him right off. I think they would have, if it hadn't been for the Coroner — he seemed to be holding them back."

"Perhaps, though, you have a warrant for his arrest in your pocket now," suggested Poirot.

A kind of wooden shutter of officialdom came down from Japp's expressive countenance.

"Perhaps I have, and perhaps I haven't," he remarked dryly.

Poirot looked at him thoughtfully.

"I am very anxious, Messieurs, that he should not be arrested."

"I dare say," observed Summerhaye sarcastically.

Japp was regarding Poirot with comical perplexity.

"Can't you go a little further, Mr. Poirot? A wink's as good as a nod — from you. You've been on the spot — and the Yard doesn't want to make any mistakes, you know."

Poirot nodded gravely.

"That is exactly what I thought. Well, I will tell you this. Use your warrant: Arrest Mr. Inglethorp. But it will bring you no kudos — the case against him will be dismissed at once! *Comme ça!*" And he snapped his fingers expressively.

Japp's face grew grave, though Summerhaye gave an incredulous snort.

As for me, I was literally dumb with astonishment. I could only conclude that Poirot was mad.

Japp had taken out a handkerchief, and was gently dabbing his brow.

"I daren't do it, Mr. Poirot. *I'd* take your word, but there's others over me who'll be asking what the devil I mean by it. Can't you give me a little more to go on?"

Poirot reflected a moment.

"It can be done," he said at last. "I admit I do not wish it. It forces my hand. I would have preferred to work in the dark just for the present, but what you say is very just — the word of a Belgian policeman, whose day is past, is not enough! And Alfred Inglethorp must not be arrested. That I have sworn, as my friend Hastings here knows. See, then, my good Japp, you go at once to Styles?"

"Well, in about half an hour. We're seeing the Coroner and the doctor first."

"Good. Call for me in passing — the last house in the village. I will go with you. At Styles, Mr. Inglethorp will give you, or if he refuses — as is probable — I will give you such proofs that shall satisfy you that the case against him could not possibly be sustained. Is that a bargain?"

"That's a bargain," said Japp heartily. "And, on behalf of the Yard, I'm much obliged to you, though I'm bound to confess I can't at present see the faintest possible loop-hole in the evidence, but you always were a marvel! So long, then, Moosier."

The two detectives strode away, Summerhaye with an incredulous grin on his face.

"Well, my friend," cried Poirot, before I could get in a word, "what do you think? *Mon Dieu!* I had some warm moments in that court; I did not figure to myself that the man would be so pig-headed as to refuse to say anything at all. Decidedly, it was the policy of an imbecile."

"H'm! There are other explanations besides that of imbecility," I remarked. "For, if the case against him is true, how could he defend himself except by silence?"

"Why, in a thousand ingenious ways," cried Poirot. "See; say that it is I who have committed this murder, I can think of seven most plausible stories! Far more convincing than Mr. Inglethorp's stony denials!"

I could not help laughing.

"My dear Poirot, I am sure you are capable of thinking of seventy! But, seriously, in spite of what I heard you say to the detectives, you surely cannot still believe in the possibility of Alfred Inglethorp's innocence?"

"Why not now as much as before? Nothing has changed."

"But the evidence is so conclusive."

"Yes, too conclusive."

We turned in at the gate of Leastways Cottage, and proceeded up the now familiar stairs.

"Yes, yes, too conclusive," continued Poirot, almost to himself. "Real evidence is usually vague and unsatisfactory. It has to be examined — sifted. But here the whole thing is cut and dried. No, my friend, this evidence has been very cleverly manufactured — so cleverly that it has defeated its own ends."

"How do you make that out?"

"Because, so long as the evidence against him was vague and intangible, it was very hard to disprove. But, in his anxiety, the criminal has drawn the net so closely that one cut will set Inglethorp free."

I was silent. And in a minute or two, Poirot continued:

"Let us look at the matter like this. Here is a man, let us say, who sets out to poison his wife. He has lived by his wits as the saying goes. Presumably, therefore, he has some wits. He is not altogether a fool. Well, how does he set about it? He goes boldly to the village chemist's and purchases strychnine under his own name, with a trumped up story about a dog which is bound to be proved absurd. He does not employ the poison that night. No, he waits until he has had a violent quarrel with her, of which the whole household is cognisant, and which naturally directs their suspicions upon him. He prepares no defence — no shadow of an alibi, yet he knows the chemist's assistant must necessarily come forward with the facts. Bah! Do not ask me to believe that any man could be so idiotic! Only a lunatic, who wished to commit suicide by causing himself to be hanged, would act so!"

"Still — I do not see —" I began.

"Neither do I see. I tell you, *mon ami*, it puzzles me. *Me* — Hercule Poirot!"

"But if you believe him innocent, how do you explain his buying the strychnine?"

"Very simply. He did *not* buy it."

"But Mace recognized him!"

"I beg your pardon, he saw a man with a black beard like Mr. Inglethorp's, and wearing glasses like Mr. Inglethorp, and dressed in Mr. Inglethorp's rather noticeable clothes. He could not recognize a man whom he had probably only seen in the distance, since, you remember, he himself had only been in the village a fortnight, and Mrs. Inglethorp dealt principally with Coot's in Tadminster."

"Then you think —"

"*Mon ami*, do you remember the two points I laid stress upon? Leave the first one for the moment, what was the second?"

"The important fact that Alfred Inglethorp wears peculiar clothes, has a black beard, and uses glasses," I quoted.

"Exactly. Now suppose anyone wished to pass himself off as John or Lawrence Cavendish. Would it be easy?"

"No," I said thoughtfully. "Of course an actor —"

But Poirot cut me short ruthlessly.

"And why would it not be easy? I will tell you, my friend: Because they are both clean-shaven men. To make up successfully as one of these two in broad daylight, it would need an actor of genius, and a certain initial facial resemblance. But in the case of Alfred Inglethorp, all that is changed. His clothes, his beard, the glasses which hide his eyes — those are the salient points about his personal appearance. Now, what is the first instinct of the criminal? To divert suspicion from himself, is it not so? And how can he best do that? By throwing it on someone else. In this instance, there was a man ready to his hand. Everybody was predisposed to believe in Mr. Inglethorp's guilt. It was a foregone conclusion that he would be suspected; but, to make it a sure thing there must be tangible proof — such as the actual buying of the poison, and that, with a man of the peculiar appearance of Mr. Inglethorp, was not difficult. Remember, this young Mace had never actually spoken to Mr. Inglethorp. How should he doubt that the man in his clothes, with his beard and his glasses, was not Alfred Inglethorp?"

"It may be so," I said, fascinated by Poirot's eloquence. "But, if that was the case, why does he not say where he was at six o'clock on Monday evening?"

"Ah, why indeed?" said Poirot, calming down. "If he were arrested, he probably would speak, but I do not want it to come to that. I must make him see the gravity of his position. There is, of course, something discreditable behind his silence. If he did not murder his wife, he is, nevertheless, a scoundrel, and has something of his own to conceal, quite apart from the murder."

"What can it be?" I mused, won over to Poirot's views for the moment, although still retaining a faint conviction that the obvious deduction was the correct one.

"Can you not guess?" asked Poirot, smiling.

"No, can you?"

"Oh, yes, I had a little idea sometime ago — and it has turned out to be correct."

"You never told me," I said reproachfully.

Poirot spread out his hands apologetically.

"Pardon me, *mon ami*, you were not precisely *sympathique*." He turned to me earnestly. "Tell me — you see now that he must not be arrested?"

"Perhaps," I said doubtfully, for I was really quite indifferent to the fate of Alfred Inglethorp, and thought that a good fright would do him no harm.

Poirot, who was watching me intently, gave a sigh.

"Come, my friend," he said, changing the subject, "apart from Mr. Inglethorp, how did the evidence at the inquest strike you?"

"Oh, pretty much what I expected."

"Did nothing strike you as peculiar about it?"

My thoughts flew to Mary Cavendish, and I hedged:

"In what way?"

"Well, Mr. Lawrence Cavendish's evidence for instance?"

I was relieved.

"Oh, Lawrence! No, I don't think so. He's always a nervous chap."

"His suggestion that his mother might have been poisoned accidentally by means of the tonic she was taking, that did not strike you as strange — *hein?*"

"No, I can't say it did. The doctors ridiculed it of course. But it was quite a natural suggestion for a layman to make."

"But Monsieur Lawrence is not a layman. You told me yourself that he had started by studying medicine, and that he had taken his degree."

"Yes, that's true. I never thought of that." I was rather startled. "It *is* odd."

Poirot nodded.

"From the first, his behaviour has been peculiar. Of all the household, he alone would be likely to recognize the symptoms of strychnine poisoning, and yet we find him the only member of the family to uphold strenuously the theory of death from natural causes. If it had been Monsieur John, I could have understood it. He has no technical knowledge, and is by nature unimaginative. But Monsieur Lawrence — no! And now, to-day, he puts forward a suggestion that he himself must have known was ridiculous. There is food for thought in this, *mon ami!*"

"It's very confusing," I agreed.

"Then there is Mrs. Cavendish," continued Poirot. "That's another who is not telling all she knows! What do you make of her attitude?"

"I don't know what to make of it. It seems inconceivable that she should be shielding Alfred Inglethorp. Yet that is what it looks like."

Poirot nodded reflectively.

"Yes, it is queer. One thing is certain, she overheard a good deal more of that 'private conversation' than she was willing to admit."

"And yet she is the last person one would accuse of stooping to eavesdrop!"

"Exactly. One thing her evidence *has* shown me. I made a mistake. Dorcas was quite right. The quarrel did take place earlier in the afternoon, about four o'clock, as she said."

I looked at him curiously. I had never understood his insistence on that point.

"Yes, a good deal that was peculiar came out to-day," continued Poirot. "Dr. Bauerstein, now, what was *he* doing up and dressed at that hour in the morning? It is astonishing to me that no one commented on the fact."

"He has insomnia, I believe," I said doubtfully.

"Which is a very good, or a very bad explanation," remarked Poirot. "It covers everything, and explains nothing. I shall keep my eye on our clever Dr. Bauerstein."

"Any more faults to find with the evidence?" I inquired satirically.

"*Mon ami*," replied Poirot gravely, "when you find that people are not telling you the truth — look out! Now, unless I am much mistaken, at the inquest to-day only one — at most, two persons were speaking the truth without reservation or subterfuge."

"Oh, come now, Poirot! I won't cite Lawrence, or Mrs. Cavendish. But there's John — and Miss Howard, surely they were speaking the truth?"

"Both of them, my friend? One, I grant you, but both — !"

His words gave me an unpleasant shock. Miss Howard's evidence, unimportant as it was, had been given in such a downright straightforward manner that it had never occurred to me to doubt her sincerity. Still, I had a great respect for Poirot's sagacity — except on the occasions when he was what I described to myself as "foolishly pig-headed."

"Do you really think so?" I asked. "Miss Howard had always seemed to me so essentially honest — almost uncomfortably so."

Poirot gave me a curious look, which I could not quite fathom. He seemed to speak, and then checked himself.

"Miss Murdoch too," I continued, "there's nothing untruthful about *her*."

"No. But it was strange that she never heard a sound, sleeping next door; whereas Mrs. Cavendish, in the other wing of the building, distinctly heard the table fall."

"Well, she's young. And she sleeps soundly."

"Ah, yes, indeed! She must be a famous sleeper, that one!"

I did not quite like the tone of his voice, but at that moment a smart knock reached our ears, and looking out of the window we perceived the two detectives waiting for us below.

Poirot seized his hat, gave a ferocious twist to his moustache, and, carefully brushing an imaginary speck of dust from his sleeve, motioned me to precede him down the stairs; there we joined the detectives and set out for Styles.

I think the appearance of the two Scotland Yard men was rather a shock — especially to John, though of course after the verdict, he had realized that it was only a matter of time. Still, the presence of the detectives brought the truth home to him more than anything else could have done.

Poirot had conferred with Japp in a low tone on the way up, and it was the latter functionary who requested that the household, with the exception of the servants, should be assembled together in the drawing-room. I realized the significance of this. It was up to Poirot to make his boast good.

Personally, I was not sanguine. Poirot might have excellent reasons for his belief in Inglethorp's innocence, but a man of the type of Summerhaye would require tangible proofs, and these I doubted if Poirot could supply.

Before very long we had all trooped into the drawing-room, the door of which Japp closed. Poirot politely set chairs for everyone. The Scotland Yard men were the cynosure of all eyes. I think that for the first time we realized that the thing was not a bad dream, but a tangible reality. We had read of such things — now we ourselves were actors in the drama. To-morrow the daily papers, all over England, would blazon out the news in staring headlines:

"MYSTERIOUS TRAGEDY IN ESSEX," "WEALTHY LADY POISONED."

There would be pictures of Styles, snap-shots of "The family leaving the Inquest" — the village photographer had not been idle! All the things that one had read a hundred times — things that happen to other people, not to oneself. And now, in this house, a murder had been committed. In front of us were "the detectives in charge of the case." The well-known glib phraseology passed rapidly through my mind in the interval before Poirot opened the proceedings.

I think everyone was a little surprised that it should be he and not one of the official detectives who took the initiative.

"*Mesdames* and *messieurs*," said Poirot, bowing as though he were a celebrity about to deliver a lecture, "I have asked you to come here all together, for a certain object. That object, it concerns Mr. Alfred Inglethorp."

Inglethorp was sitting a little by himself — I think, unconsciously, everyone had drawn his chair slightly away from him — and he gave a faint start as Poirot pronounced his name.

"Mr. Inglethorp," said Poirot, addressing him directly, "a very dark shadow is resting on this house — the shadow of murder."

Inglethorp shook his head sadly.

"My poor wife," he murmured. "Poor Emily! It is terrible."

"I do not think, monsieur," said Poirot pointedly, "that you quite realize how terrible it may be — for you." And as Inglethorp did not appear to understand, he added: "Mr. Inglethorp, you are standing in very grave danger."

The two detectives fidgeted. I saw the official caution "Anything you say will be used in evidence against you," actually hovering on Summerhaye's lips. Poirot went on.

"Do you understand now, monsieur?"

"No. What do you mean?"

"I mean," said Poirot deliberately, "that you are suspected of poisoning your wife."

A little gasp ran round the circle at this plain speaking.

"Good heavens!" cried Inglethorp, starting up. "What a monstrous idea! *I* — poison my dearest Emily!"

"I do not think" — Poirot watched him narrowly — "that you quite realize the unfavourable nature of your evidence at the inquest. Mr. Inglethorp, knowing what I have now told you, do you still refuse to say where you were at six o'clock on Monday afternoon?"

With a groan, Alfred Inglethorp sank down again and buried his face in his hands. Poirot approached and stood over him.

"Speak!" he cried menacingly.

With an effort, Inglethorp raised his face from his hands. Then, slowly and deliberately, he shook his head.

"You will not speak?"

"No. I do not believe that anyone could be so monstrous as to accuse me of what you say."

Poirot nodded thoughtfully, like a man whose mind is made up.

"*Soit!*" he said. "Then I must speak for you."

Alfred Inglethorp sprang up again.

"You? How can you speak? You do not know—" he broke off abruptly.

Poirot turned to face us. "*Mesdames* and *messieurs*! I speak! Listen! I, Hercule Poirot, affirm that the man who entered the chemist's shop, and purchased strychnine at six o'clock on Monday last was not Mr. Inglethorp, for at six o'clock on that day Mr. Inglethorp was escorting Mrs. Raikes back to her home from a neighbouring farm. I can produce no less than five witnesses to swear to having seen them together, either at six or just after and, as you may know, the Abbey Farm, Mrs. Raikes's home, is at least two and a half miles distant from the village. There is absolutely no question as to the alibi!"

# VIII.

## FRESH SUSPICIONS.

There was a moment's stupefied silence. Japp, who was the least surprised of any of us, was the first to speak.

"My word," he cried, "you're the goods! And no mistake, Mr. Poirot! These witnesses of yours are all right, I suppose?"

"*Voilà!* I have prepared a list of them—names and addresses. You must see them, of course. But you will find it all right."

"I'm sure of that." Japp lowered his voice. "I'm much obliged to you. A pretty mare's nest arresting him would have been." He turned to Inglethorp. "But, if you'll excuse me, sir, why couldn't you say all this at the inquest?"

"I will tell you why," interrupted Poirot. "There was a certain rumour—"

"A most malicious and utterly untrue one," interrupted Alfred Inglethorp in an agitated voice.

"And Mr. Inglethorp was anxious to have no scandal revived just at present. Am I right?"

"Quite right." Inglethorp nodded. "With my poor Emily not yet buried, can you wonder I was anxious that no more lying rumours should be started."

"Between you and me, sir," remarked Japp, "I'd sooner have any amount of rumours than be arrested for murder. And I venture to think your poor lady would have felt the same. And, if it hadn't been for Mr. Poirot here, arrested you would have been, as sure as eggs is eggs!"

"I was foolish, no doubt," murmured Inglethorp. "But you do not know, inspector, how I have been persecuted and maligned." And he shot a baleful glance at Evelyn Howard.

"Now, sir," said Japp, turning briskly to John, "I should like to see the lady's bedroom, please, and after that I'll have a little chat with the servants. Don't you bother about anything. Mr. Poirot, here, will show me the way."

As they all went out of the room, Poirot turned and made me a sign to follow him upstairs. There he caught me by the arm, and drew me aside.

"Quick, go to the other wing. Stand there—just this side of the baize door. Do not move till I come." Then, turning rapidly, he rejoined the two detectives.

I followed his instructions, taking up my position by the baize door, and wondering what on earth lay behind the request. Why was I to stand in this particular spot on guard? I looked thoughtfully down the corridor in front of me. An idea struck me. With the exception of Cynthia Murdoch's, everyone's room was in this left wing. Had that anything to do with it? Was I to report who came or went? I stood faithfully at my post. The minutes passed. Nobody came. Nothing happened.

It must have been quite twenty minutes before Poirot rejoined me.

"You have not stirred?"

"No, I've stuck here like a rock. Nothing's happened."

"Ah!" Was he pleased, or disappointed? "You've seen nothing at all?"

"No."

"But you have probably heard something? A big bump—eh, *mon ami?*"

"No."

"Is it possible? Ah, but I am vexed with myself! I am not usually clumsy. I made but a slight gesture"—I know Poirot's gestures—"with the left hand, and over went the table by the bed!"

He looked so childishly vexed and crest-fallen that I hastened to console him.

"Never mind, old chap. What does it matter? Your triumph downstairs excited you. I can tell you, that was a surprise to us all. There must be more in this affair of Inglethorp's with Mrs. Raikes than we thought, to make him hold his tongue so persistently. What are you going to do now? Where are the Scotland Yard fellows?"

"Gone down to interview the servants. I showed them all our exhibits. I am disappointed in Japp. He has no method!"

"Hullo!" I said, looking out of the window. "Here's Dr. Bauerstein. I believe you're right about that man, Poirot. I don't like him."

"He is clever," observed Poirot meditatively.

"Oh, clever as the devil! I must say I was overjoyed to see him in the plight he was in on Tuesday. You never saw such a spectacle!" And I described the doctor's adventure. "He looked a regular scarecrow! Plastered with mud from head to foot."

"You saw him, then?"

"Yes. Of course, he didn't want to come in — it was just after dinner — but Mr. Inglethorp insisted."

"What?" Poirot caught me violently by the shoulders. "Was Dr. Bauerstein here on Tuesday evening? Here? And you never told me? Why did you not tell me? Why? Why?"

He appeared to be in an absolute frenzy.

"My dear Poirot," I expostulated, "I never thought it would interest you. I didn't know it was of any importance."

"Importance? It is of the first importance! So Dr. Bauerstein was here on Tuesday night — the night of the murder. Hastings, do you not see? That alters everything — everything!"

I had never seen him so upset. Loosening his hold of me, he mechanically straightened a pair of candlesticks, still murmuring to himself: "Yes, that alters everything — everything."

Suddenly he seemed to come to a decision.

"*Allons!*" he said. "We must act at once. Where is Mr. Cavendish?"

John was in the smoking-room. Poirot went straight to him.

"Mr. Cavendish, I have some important business in Tadminster. A new clue. May I take your motor?"

"Why, of course. Do you mean at once?"

"If you please."

John rang the bell, and ordered round the car. In another ten minutes, we were racing down the park and along the high road to Tadminster.

"Now, Poirot," I remarked resignedly, "perhaps you will tell me what all this is about?"

"Well, *mon ami*, a good deal you can guess for yourself. Of course you realize that, now Mr. Inglethorp is out of it, the whole position is greatly changed. We are face to face with an entirely new problem. We know now that there is one person who did not buy the poison. We have cleared away the manufactured clues. Now for the real ones. I have ascertained that anyone in the household, with the exception of Mrs. Cavendish, who was playing tennis with you, could have personated Mr. Inglethorp on Monday evening. In the same way, we have his statement that he put the coffee down in the hall. No one took much notice of that at the inquest — but now it has a very different significance. We must find out who did take that coffee to Mrs. Inglethorp eventually, or who passed through the hall whilst it was standing there. From your account, there are only two people whom we can positively say did not go near the coffee — Mrs. Cavendish, and Mademoiselle Cynthia."

"Yes, that is so." I felt an inexpressible lightening of the heart.

Mary Cavendish could certainly not rest under suspicion.

"In clearing Alfred Inglethorp," continued Poirot, "I have been obliged to show my hand sooner than I intended. As long as I might be thought to be pursuing him, the criminal would be off his guard. Now, he will be doubly careful. Yes — doubly careful." He turned to me abruptly. "Tell me, Hastings, you yourself — have you no suspicions of anybody?"

I hesitated. To tell the truth, an idea, wild and extravagant in itself, had once or twice that morning flashed through my brain. I had rejected it as absurd, nevertheless it persisted.

"You couldn't call it a suspicion," I murmured. "It's so utterly foolish."

"Come now," urged Poirot encouragingly. "Do not fear. Speak your mind. You should always pay attention to your instincts."

"Well then," I blurted out, "it's absurd — but I suspect Miss Howard of not telling all she knows!"

"Miss Howard?"

"Yes — you'll laugh at me —"

"Not at all. Why should I?"

"I can't help feeling," I continued blunderingly; "that we've rather left her out of the possible suspects, simply on the strength of her having been away from the place. But, after all, she was only fifteen miles away. A car would do it in half an hour. Can we say positively that she was away from Styles on the night of the murder?"

"Yes, my friend," said Poirot unexpectedly, "we can. One of my first actions was to ring up the hospital where she was working."

"Well?"

"Well, I learnt that Miss Howard had been on afternoon duty on Tuesday, and that — a convoy coming in unexpectedly — she had kindly offered to remain on night duty, which offer was gratefully accepted. That disposes of that."

"Oh!" I said, rather nonplussed. "Really," I continued, "it's her extraordinary vehemence against Inglethorp that started me off suspecting her. I can't help feeling she'd do anything against him. And I had an idea she might know something about the destroying of the will. She might have burnt the new one, mistaking it for the earlier one in his favour. She is so terribly bitter against him."

"You consider her vehemence unnatural?"

"Y — es. She is so very violent. I wondered really whether she is quite sane on that point."

Poirot shook his head energetically.

"No, no, you are on a wrong tack there. There is nothing weak-minded or degenerate about Miss Howard. She is an excellent specimen of well-balanced English beef and brawn. She is sanity itself."

"Yet her hatred of Inglethorp seems almost a mania. My idea was — a very ridiculous one, no doubt — that she had intended to poison him — and that, in some way, Mrs. Inglethorp got hold of it by mistake. But I don't at all see how it could have been done. The whole thing is absurd and ridiculous to the last degree."

"Still you are right in one thing. It is always wise to suspect everybody until you can prove logically, and to your own satisfaction, that they are innocent. Now, what reasons are there against Miss Howard's having deliberately poisoned Mrs. Inglethorp?"

"Why, she was devoted to her!" I exclaimed.

"*Tcha! Tcha!*" cried Poirot irritably. "You argue like a child. If Miss Howard were capable of poisoning the old lady, she would be quite equally capable of simulating devotion. No, we must look elsewhere. You are perfectly correct in your assumption that her vehemence against Alfred Inglethorp is too violent to be natural; but you are quite wrong in the deduction you draw from it. I have drawn my own deductions, which I believe to be correct, but I will not speak of them at present." He paused a minute, then went on. "Now, to my way of thinking, there is one insuperable objection to Miss Howard's being the murderess."

"And that is?"

"That in no possible way could Mrs. Inglethorp's death benefit Miss Howard. Now there is no murder without a motive."

I reflected.

"Could not Mrs. Inglethorp have made a will in her favour?"

Poirot shook his head.

"But you yourself suggested that possibility to Mr. Wells?"

Poirot smiled.

"That was for a reason. I did not want to mention the name of the person who was actually in my mind. Miss Howard occupied very much the same position, so I used her name instead."

"Still, Mrs. Inglethorp might have done so. Why, that will, made on the afternoon of her death may —"

But Poirot's shake of the head was so energetic that I stopped.

"No, my friend. I have certain little ideas of my own about that will. But I can tell you this much — it was not in Miss Howard's favour."

I accepted his assurance, though I did not really see how he could be so positive about the matter.

"Well," I said, with a sigh, "we will acquit Miss Howard, then. It is partly your fault that I ever came to suspect her. It was what you said about her evidence at the inquest that set me off."

Poirot looked puzzled.

"What did I say about her evidence at the inquest?"

"Don't you remember? When I cited her and John Cavendish as being above suspicion?"

"Oh — ah — yes." He seemed a little confused, but recovered himself. "By the way, Hastings, there is something I want you to do for me."

"Certainly. What is it?"

"Next time you happen to be alone with Lawrence Cavendish, I want you to say this to him. 'I have a message for you, from Poirot. He says: "Find the extra coffee-cup, and you can rest in peace!" Nothing more. Nothing less."

"'Find the extra coffee-cup, and you can rest in peace.' Is that right?" I asked, much mystified.

"Excellent."

"But what does it mean?"

"Ah, that I will leave you to find out. You have access to the facts. Just say that to him, and see what he says."

"Very well—but it's all extremely mysterious."

We were running into Tadminster now, and Poirot directed the car to the "Analytical Chemist."

Poirot hopped down briskly, and went inside. In a few minutes he was back again.

"There," he said. "That is all my business."

"What were you doing there?" I asked, in lively curiosity.

"I left something to be analysed."

"Yes, but what?"

"The sample of cocoa I took from the saucepan in the bedroom."

"But that has already been tested!" I cried, stupefied. "Dr. Bauerstein had it tested, and you yourself laughed at the possibility of there being strychnine in it."

"I know Dr. Bauerstein had it tested," replied Poirot quietly.

"Well, then?"

"Well, I have a fancy for having it analysed again, that is all."

And not another word on the subject could I drag out of him.

This proceeding of Poirot's, in respect of the cocoa, puzzled me intensely. I could see neither rhyme nor reason in it. However, my confidence in him, which at one time had rather waned, was fully restored since his belief in Alfred Inglethorp's innocence had been so triumphantly vindicated.

The funeral of Mrs. Inglethorp took place the following day, and on Monday, as I came down to a late breakfast, John drew me aside, and informed me that Mr. Inglethorp was leaving that morning, to take up his quarters at the Stylites Arms until he should have completed his plans.

"And really it's a great relief to think he's going, Hastings," continued my honest friend. "It was bad enough before, when we thought he'd done it, but I'm hanged if it isn't worse now, when we all feel guilty for having been so down on the fellow. The fact is, we've treated him abominably. Of course, things did look black against him. I don't see how anyone could blame us for jumping to the conclusions we did. Still, there it is, we were in the wrong, and now there's a beastly feeling that one ought to make amends; which is difficult, when one doesn't like the fellow a bit better than one did before. The whole thing's damned awkward! And I'm thankful he's had the tact to take himself off. It's a good thing Styles wasn't the mater's to leave to him. Couldn't bear to think of the fellow lording it here. He's welcome to her money."

"You'll be able to keep up the place all right?" I asked.

"Oh, yes. There are the death duties, of course, but half my father's money goes with the place, and Lawrence will stay with us for the present, so there is his share as well. We shall be pinched at first, of course, because, as I once told you, I am in a bit of a hole financially myself. Still, the Johnnies will wait now."

In the general relief at Inglethorp's approaching departure, we had the most genial breakfast we had experienced since the tragedy. Cynthia, whose young spirits were naturally buoyant, was looking quite her pretty self again, and we all, with the exception of Lawrence, who seemed unalterably gloomy and nervous, were quietly cheerful, at the opening of a new and hopeful future.

The papers, of course, had been full of the tragedy. Glaring headlines, sandwiched biographies of every member of the household, subtle innuendoes, the usual familiar tag about the police having a clue. Nothing was spared us. It was a slack time. The war was momentarily inactive, and the newspapers seized with avidity on this crime in fashionable life: "The Mysterious Affair at Styles" was the topic of the moment.

Naturally it was very annoying for the Cavendishes. The house was constantly besieged by reporters, who were consistently denied admission, but who continued to haunt the village and the grounds, where they lay in wait with cameras, for any unwary members of the household. We all lived in a blast of publicity. The Scotland Yard men came and went, examining, questioning, lynx-eyed and reserved of tongue. Towards what end they were working, we did not know. Had they any clue, or would the whole thing remain in the category of undiscovered crimes?

After breakfast, Dorcas came up to me rather mysteriously, and asked if she might have a few words with me.

"Certainly. What is it, Dorcas?"

"Well, it's just this, sir. You'll be seeing the Belgian gentleman to-day perhaps?" I nodded. "Well, sir, you know how he asked me so particular if the mistress, or anyone else, had a green dress?"

"Yes, yes. You have found one?" My interest was aroused.

"No, not that, sir. But since then I've remembered what the young gentlemen"—John and Lawrence were still the "young gentlemen" to Dorcas—"call the 'dressing-up box.' It's up in the front attic, sir. A great chest, full of old clothes and fancy dresses, and what not. And it came to me sudden like that there might be a green dress amongst them. So, if you'd tell the Belgian gentleman—"

"I will tell him, Dorcas," I promised.

"Thank you very much, sir. A very nice gentleman he is, sir. And quite a different class from them two detectives from London, what goes prying about, and asking questions. I don't hold with foreigners as a rule, but from what the newspapers say I make out as how these brave Belgies isn't the ordinary run of foreigners, and certainly he's a most polite spoken gentleman."

Dear old Dorcas! As she stood there, with her honest face upturned to mine, I thought what a fine specimen she was of the old-fashioned servant that is so fast dying out.

I thought I might as well go down to the village at once, and look up Poirot; but I met him half-way, coming up to the house, and at once gave him Dorcas's message.

"Ah, the brave Dorcas! We will look at the chest, although — but no matter — we will examine it all the same."

We entered the house by one of the windows. There was no one in the hall, and we went straight up to the attic.

Sure enough, there was the chest, a fine old piece, all studded with brass nails, and full to overflowing with every imaginable type of garment.

Poirot bundled everything out on the floor with scant ceremony. There were one or two green fabrics of varying shades; but Poirot shook his head over them all. He seemed somewhat apathetic in the search, as though he expected no great results from it. Suddenly he gave an exclamation.

"What is it?"

"Look!"

The chest was nearly empty, and there, reposing right at the bottom, was a magnificent black beard.

"*Ohó!*" said Poirot. "*Ohó!*" He turned it over in his hands, examining it closely. "New," he remarked. "Yes, quite new."

After a moment's hesitation, he replaced it in the chest, heaped all the other things on top of it as before, and made his way briskly downstairs. He went straight to the pantry, where we found Dorcas busily polishing her silver.

Poirot wished her good morning with Gallic politeness, and went on:

"We have been looking through that chest, Dorcas. I am much obliged to you for mentioning it. There is, indeed, a fine collection there. Are they often used, may I ask?"

"Well, sir, not very often nowadays, though from time to time we do have what the young gentlemen call 'a dress-up night.' And very funny it is sometimes, sir. Mr. Lawrence, he's wonderful. Most comic! I shall never forget the night he came down as the Char of Persia, I think he called it — a sort of Eastern King it was. He had the big paper knife in his hand, and 'Mind, Dorcas,' he says, 'you'll have to be very respectful. This is my specially sharpened scimitar, and it's off with your head if I'm at all displeased with you!' Miss Cynthia, she was what they call an Apache, or some such name — a Frenchified sort of cut-throat, I take it to be. A real sight she looked. You'd never have believed a pretty young lady like that could have made herself into such a ruffian. Nobody would have known her."

"These evenings must have been great fun," said Poirot genially. "I suppose Mr. Lawrence wore that fine black beard in the chest upstairs, when he was Shah of Persia?"

"He did have a beard, sir," replied Dorcas, smiling. "And well I know it, for he borrowed two skeins of my black wool to make it with! And I'm sure it looked wonderfully natural at a distance. I didn't know as there was a beard up there at all. It must have been got quite lately, I think. There was a red wig, I know, but nothing else in the way of hair. Burnt corks they use mostly — though 'tis messy getting it off again. Miss Cynthia was a nigger once, and, oh, the trouble she had."

"So Dorcas knows nothing about that black beard," said Poirot thoughtfully, as we walked out into the hall again.

"Do you think it is *the* one?" I whispered eagerly.

Poirot nodded.

"I do. You notice it had been trimmed?"

"No."

"Yes. It was cut exactly the shape of Mr. Inglethorp's, and I found one or two snipped hairs. Hastings, this affair is very deep."

"Who put it in the chest, I wonder?"

"Someone with a good deal of intelligence," remarked Poirot dryly. "You realize that he chose the one place in the house to hide it where its presence would not be remarked? Yes, he is intelligent. But we must be more intelligent. We must be so intelligent that he does not suspect us of being intelligent at all."

I acquiesced.

"There, *mon ami*, you will be of great assistance to me."

I was pleased with the compliment. There had been times when I hardly thought that Poirot appreciated me at my true worth.

"Yes," he continued, staring at me thoughtfully, "you will be invaluable."

This was naturally gratifying, but Poirot's next words were not so welcome.

"I must have an ally in the house," he observed reflectively.

"You have me," I protested.

"True, but you are not sufficient."

I was hurt, and showed it. Poirot hurried to explain himself.

"You do not quite take my meaning. You are known to be working with me. I want somebody who is not associated with us in any way."

"Oh, I see. How about John?"

"No, I think not."

"The dear fellow isn't perhaps

very bright," I said thoughtfully.

"Here comes Miss Howard," said Poirot suddenly. "She is the very person. But I am in her black books, since I cleared Mr. Inglethorp. Still, we can but try."

With a nod that was barely civil, Miss Howard assented to Poirot's request for a few minutes' conversation.

We went into the little morning-room, and Poirot closed the door.

"Well, Monsieur Poirot," said Miss Howard impatiently, "what is it? Out with it. I'm busy."

"Do you remember, mademoiselle, that I once asked you to help me?"

"Yes, I do." The lady nodded. "And I told you I'd help you with pleasure — to hang Alfred Inglethorp."

"Ah!" Poirot studied her seriously. "Miss Howard, I will ask you one question. I beg of you to reply to it truthfully."

"Never tell lies," replied Miss Howard.

"It is this. Do you still believe that Mrs. Inglethorp was poisoned by her husband?"

"What do you mean?" she asked sharply. "You needn't think your pretty explanations influence me in the slightest. I'll admit that it wasn't he who bought strychnine at the chemist's shop. What of that? I dare say he soaked fly paper, as I told you at the beginning."

"That is arsenic — not strychnine," said Poirot mildly.

"What does that matter? Arsenic would put poor Emily out of the way just as well as strychnine. If I'm convinced he did it, it doesn't matter a jot to me *how* he did it."

"Exactly. *If* you are convinced he did it," said Poirot quietly. "I will put my question in another form. Did you ever in your heart of hearts believe that Mrs. Inglethorp was poisoned by her husband?"

"Good heavens!" cried Miss Howard. "Haven't I always told you the man is a villain? Haven't I always told you he would murder her in her bed? Haven't I always hated him like poison?"

"Exactly," said Poirot. "That bears out my little idea entirely."

"What little idea?"

"Miss Howard, do you remember a conversation that took place on the day of my friend's arrival here? He repeated it to me, and there is a sentence of yours that has impressed me very much. Do you remember affirming that if a crime had been committed, and anyone you loved had been murdered, you felt certain that you would know by instinct who the criminal was, even if you were quite unable to prove it?"

"Yes, I remember saying that. I believe it too. I suppose you think it nonsense?"

"Not at all."

"And yet you will pay no attention to my instinct against Alfred Inglethorp."

"No," said Poirot curtly. "Because

your instinct is not against Mr. Inglethorp."

"What?"

"No. You wish to believe he committed the crime. You believe him capable of committing it. But your instinct tells you he did not commit it. It tells you more — shall I go on?"

She was staring at him, fascinated, and made a slight affirmative movement of the hand.

"Shall I tell you why you have been so vehement against Mr. Inglethorp? It is because you have been trying to believe what you wish to believe. It is because you are trying to drown and stifle your instinct, which tells you another name —"

"No, no, no!" cried Miss Howard wildly, flinging up her hands. "Don't say it! Oh, don't say it! It isn't true! It can't be true. I don't know what put such a wild — such a dreadful — idea into my head!"

"I am right, am I not?" asked Poirot.

"Yes, yes; you must be a wizard to have guessed. But it can't be so — it's too monstrous, too impossible. It *must* be Alfred Inglethorp."

Poirot shook his head gravely.

"Don't ask me about it," continued Miss Howard, "because I shan't tell you. I won't admit it, even to myself. I must be mad to think of such a thing."

Poirot nodded, as if satisfied.

"I will ask you nothing. It is enough for me that it is as I thought. And I — I, too, have an instinct. We are working together towards a common end."

"Don't ask me to help you, because I won't. I wouldn't lift a finger to — to —" She faltered.

"You will help me in spite of yourself. I ask you nothing — but you will be my ally. You will not be able to help yourself. You will do the only thing that I want of you."

"And that is?"

"You will watch!"

Evelyn Howard bowed her head.

"Yes, I can't help doing that. I am always watching — always hoping I shall be proved wrong."

"If we are wrong, well and good," said Poirot. "No one will be more pleased than I shall. But, if we are right? If we are right, Miss Howard, on whose side are you then?"

"I don't know, I don't know —"

"Come now."

"It could be hushed up."

"There must be no hushing up."

"But Emily herself —" She broke off.

"Miss Howard," said Poirot gravely, "this is unworthy of you."

Suddenly she took her face from her hands.

"Yes," she said quietly, "that was not Evelyn Howard who spoke!" She flung her head up proudly. "*This* is Evelyn Howard! And she is on the side of Justice! Let the cost be what it may." And with these words, she walked firmly out of the room.

"There," said Poirot, looking after her, "goes a very valuable ally. That woman, Hastings, has got brains as well as a heart."

I did not reply.

"Instinct is a marvellous thing," mused Poirot. "It can neither be explained nor ignored."

"You and Miss Howard seem to know what you are talking about," I observed coldly. "Perhaps you don't realize that *I* am still in the dark."

"Really? Is that so, *mon ami?*"

"Yes. Enlighten me, will you?"

Poirot studied me attentively for a moment or two. Then, to my intense surprise, he shook his head decidedly.

"No, my friend."

"Oh, look here, why not?"

"Two is enough for a secret."

"Well, I think it is very unfair to keep back facts from me."

"I am not keeping back facts. Every fact that I know is in your possession. You can draw your own deductions from them. This time it is a question of ideas."

"Still, it would be interesting to know."

Poirot looked at me very earnestly, and again shook his head.

"You see," he said sadly, "*you* have no instincts."

"It was intelligence you were requiring just now," I pointed out.

"The two often go together," said Poirot enigmatically.

The remark seemed so utterly irrelevant that I did not even take the trouble to answer it. But I decided that if I made any interesting and important discoveries — as no doubt I should — I would keep them to myself, and surprise Poirot with the ultimate result.

There are times when it is one's duty to assert oneself.

# IX.

## DR. BAUERSTEIN.

I had had no opportunity as yet of passing on Poirot's message to Lawrence. But now, as I strolled out on the lawn, still nursing a grudge against my friend's high-handedness, I saw Lawrence on the croquet lawn, aimlessly knocking a couple of very ancient balls about, with a still more ancient mallet.

It struck me that it would be a good opportunity to deliver my message. Otherwise, Poirot himself might relieve me of it. It was true that I did not quite gather its purport, but I flattered myself that by Lawrence's reply, and perhaps a little skillful cross-examination on my part, I should soon perceive its significance. Accordingly I accosted him.

"I've been looking for you," I remarked untruthfully.

"Have you?"

"Yes. The truth is, I've got a message for you — from Poirot."

"Yes?"

"He told me to wait until I was alone with you," I said, dropping my voice significantly, and watching him intently out of the corner of my eye. I have always been rather good at what is called, I believe, creating an atmosphere.

"Well?"

There was no change of expression in the dark melancholic face. Had he any idea of what I was about to say?

"This is the message." I dropped my voice still lower. "'Find the extra coffee-cup, and you can rest in peace.'"

"What on earth does he mean?" Lawrence stared at me in quite unaffected astonishment.

"Don't you know?"

"Not in the least. Do you?"

I was compelled to shake my head.

"What extra coffee-cup?"

"I don't know."

"He'd better ask Dorcas, or one of the maids, if he wants to know about coffee-cups. It's their business, not mine. I don't know anything about the coffee-cups, except that we've got some that are never used, which are a perfect dream! Old Worcester. You're not a connoisseur, are you, Hastings?"

I shook my head.

"You miss a lot. A really perfect bit of old china — it's pure delight to handle it, or even to look at it."

"Well, what am I to tell Poirot?"

"Tell him I don't know what he's talking about. It's double Dutch to me."

"All right."

I was moving off towards the house again when he suddenly called me back.

"I say, what was the end of that message? Say it over again, will you?"

"'Find the extra coffee-cup, and you can rest in peace.' Are you sure you don't know what it means?" I asked him earnestly.

He shook his head.

"No," he said musingly, "I don't. I — I wish I did."

The boom of the gong sounded from the house, and we went in together. Poirot had been asked by John to remain to lunch, and was already seated at the table.

By tacit consent, all mention of the tragedy was barred. We conversed on the war, and other outside topics. But after the cheese and biscuits had been handed round, and Dorcas had left the room, Poirot suddenly leant forward to Mrs. Cavendish.

"Pardon me, madame, for recalling unpleasant memories, but I have a little idea" — Poirot's "little ideas" were becoming a perfect byword — "and would like to ask one or two questions."

"Of me? Certainly."

"You are too amiable, madame. What I want to ask is this: the door leading into Mrs. Inglethorp's room from that of Mademoiselle Cynthia, it was bolted, you say?"

"Certainly it was bolted," replied Mary Cavendish, rather surprised. "I said so at the inquest."

"Bolted?"

"Yes." She looked perplexed.

"I mean," explained Poirot, "you are sure it was bolted, and not merely locked?"

"Oh, I see what you mean. No, I don't know. I said bolted, meaning that it was fastened, and I could not open it, but I believe all the doors were found bolted on the inside."

"Still, as far as you are concerned,

the door might equally well have been locked?"

"Oh, yes."

"You yourself did not happen to notice, madame, when you entered Mrs. Inglethorp's room, whether that door was bolted or not?"

"I — I believe it was."

"But you did not see it?"

"No. I — never looked."

"But *I* did," interrupted Lawrence suddenly. "I happened to notice that it *was* bolted."

"Ah, that settles it." And Poirot looked crestfallen.

I could not help rejoicing that, for once, one of his "little ideas" had come to naught.

After lunch Poirot begged me to accompany him home. I consented rather stiffly.

"You are annoyed, is it not so?" he asked anxiously, as we walked through the park.

"Not at all," I said coldly.

"That is well. That lifts a great load from my mind."

This was not quite what I had intended. I had hoped that he would have observed the stiffness of my manner. Still, the fervour of his words went towards the appeasing of my just displeasure. I thawed.

"I gave Lawrence your message," I said.

"And what did he say? He was entirely puzzled?"

"Yes. I am quite sure he had no idea of what you meant."

I had expected Poirot to be disappointed; but, to my surprise, he replied that that was as he had thought, and that he was very glad. My pride forbade me to ask any questions.

Poirot switched off on another tack.

"Mademoiselle Cynthia was not at lunch to-day? How was that?"

"She is at the hospital again. She resumed work to-day."

"Ah, she is an industrious little *demoiselle*. And pretty too. She is like pictures I have seen in Italy. I would rather like to see that dispensary of hers. Do you think she would show it to me?"

"I am sure she would be delighted. It's an interesting little place."

"Does she go there every day?"

"She has all Wednesdays off, and comes back to lunch on Saturdays. Those are her only times off."

"I will remember. Women are doing great work nowadays, and Mademoiselle Cynthia is clever — oh, yes, she has brains, that little one."

"Yes. I believe she has passed quite a stiff exam."

"Without doubt. After all, it is very responsible work. I suppose they have very strong poisons there?"

"Yes, she showed them to us. They are kept locked up in a little cupboard. I believe they have to be very careful. They always take out the key before leaving the room."

"Indeed. It is near the window, this cupboard?"

"No, right the other side of the room. Why?"

Poirot shrugged his shoulders.

"I wondered. That is all. Will you come in?"

We had reached the cottage.

"No. I think I'll be getting back. I shall go round the long way through the woods."

The woods round Styles were very beautiful. After the walk across the open park, it was pleasant to saunter lazily through the cool glades. There was hardly a breath of wind, the very chirp of the birds was faint and subdued. I strolled on a little way, and finally flung myself down at the foot of a grand old beech-tree. My thoughts of mankind were kindly and charitable. I even forgave Poirot for his absurd secrecy. In fact, I was at peace with the world. Then I yawned.

I thought about the crime, and it struck me as being very unreal and far off.

I yawned again.

Probably, I thought, it really never happened. Of course, it was all a bad dream. The truth of the matter was that it was Lawrence who had murdered Alfred Inglethorp with a croquet mallet. But it was absurd of John to make such a fuss about it, and to go shouting out: "I tell you I won't have it!"

I woke up with a start.

At once I realized that I was in a very awkward predicament. For, about twelve feet away from me, John and Mary Cavendish were standing facing each other, and they were evidently quarrelling. And, quite as evidently, they were unaware of my vicinity, for before I could move or speak John repeated the words which had aroused me from my dream.

"I tell you, Mary, I won't have it."

Mary's voice came, cool and liquid:

"Have *you* any right to criticize my actions?"

"It will be the talk of the village! My mother was only buried on Saturday, and here you are gadding about with the fellow."

"Oh," she shrugged her shoulders, "if it is only village gossip that you mind!"

"But it isn't. I've had enough of the fellow hanging about. He's a Polish Jew, anyway."

"A tinge of Jewish blood is not a bad thing. It leavens the—" she looked at him—"stolid stupidity of the ordinary Englishman."

Fire in her eyes, ice in her voice. I did not wonder that the blood rose to John's face in a crimson tide.

"Mary!"

"Well?" Her tone did not change.

The pleading died out of his voice.

"Am I to understand that you will continue to see Bauerstein against my express wishes?"

"If I choose."

"You defy me?"

"No, but I deny your right to criticize my actions. Have *you* no friends of whom I should disapprove?"

John fell back a pace. The colour ebbed slowly from his face.

"What do you mean?" he said, in an unsteady voice.

"You see!" said Mary quietly. "You *do* see, don't you, that *you* have no right to dictate to *me* as to the choice of my friends?"

John glanced at her pleadingly, a stricken look on his face.

"No right? Have I *no* right, Mary?" he said unsteadily. He stretched out his hands. "Mary—"

For a moment, I thought she wavered. A softer expression came over her face, then suddenly she turned almost fiercely away.

"None!"

She was walking away when John sprang after her, and caught her by the arm.

"Mary"—his voice was very quiet now—"are you in love with this fellow Bauerstein?"

She hesitated, and suddenly there swept across her face a strange expression, old as the hills, yet with something eternally young about it. So might some Egyptian sphinx have smiled.

She freed herself quietly from his arm, and spoke over her shoulder.

"Perhaps," she said; and then swiftly passed out of the little glade, leaving John standing there as though he had been turned to stone.

Rather ostentatiously, I stepped forward, crackling some dead branches with my feet as I did so. John turned. Luckily, he took it for granted that I had only just come upon the scene.

"Hullo, Hastings. Have you seen the little fellow safely back to his cottage? Quaint little chap! Is he any good, though, really?"

"He was considered one of the finest detectives of his day."

"Oh, well, I suppose there must be something in it, then. What a rotten world it is, though!"

"You find it so?" I asked.

"Good Lord, yes! There's this terrible business to start with. Scotland Yard men in and out of the house like a jack-in-the-box! Never know where they won't turn up next. Screaming headlines in every paper in the country—damn all journalists, I say! Do you know there was a whole crowd staring in at the lodge gates this morning. Sort of Madame Tussaud's chamber of horrors business that can be seen for nothing. Pretty thick, isn't it?"

"Cheer up, John!" I said soothingly. "It can't last for ever."

"Can't it, though? It can last long enough for us never to be able to hold up our heads again."

"No, no, you're getting morbid on the subject."

"Enough to make a man morbid, to be stalked by beastly journalists and stared at by gaping moon-faced idiots, wherever he goes! But there's worse than that."

"What?"

John lowered his voice:

"Have you ever thought, Hastings — it's a nightmare to me — who did it? I can't help feeling sometimes it must have been an accident. Because — because — who could have done it? Now Inglethorp's out of the way, there's no one else; no one, I mean, except — one of us."

Yes, indeed, that was nightmare enough for any man! One of us? Yes, surely it must be so, unless —

A new idea suggested itself to my mind. Rapidly, I considered it. The light increased. Poirot's mysterious doings, his hints — they all fitted in. Fool that I was not to have thought of this possibility before, and what a relief for us all.

"No, John," I said, "it isn't one of us. How could it be?"

"I know, but, still, who else is there?"

"Can't you guess?"

"No."

I looked cautiously round, and lowered my voice.

"Dr. Bauerstein!" I whispered.

"Impossible!"

"Not at all."

"But what earthly interest could he have in my mother's death?"

"That I don't see," I confessed, "but I'll tell you this: Poirot thinks so."

"Poirot? Does he? How do you know?"

I told him of Poirot's intense excitement on hearing that Dr. Bauerstein had been at Styles on the fatal night, and added:

"He said twice: 'That alters everything.' And I've been thinking. You know Inglethorp said he had put down the coffee in the hall? Well, it was just then that Bauerstein arrived. Isn't it possible that, as Inglethorp brought him through the hall, the doctor dropped something into the coffee in passing?"

"H'm," said John. "It would have been very risky."

"Yes, but it was possible."

"And then, how could he know it was her coffee? No, old fellow, I don't think that will wash."

But I had remembered something else.

"You're quite right. That wasn't how it was done. Listen." And I then told him of the cocoa sample which Poirot had taken to be analysed.

John interrupted just as I had done.

"But, look here, Bauerstein had had it analysed already?"

"Yes, yes, that's the point. I didn't see it either until now. Don't you understand? Bauerstein had it analysed — that's just it! If Bauerstein's the murderer, nothing could be simpler than for him to substitute some ordinary cocoa for his sample, and send that to be tested. And of course they would find no strychnine! But no one would dream of suspecting Bauerstein, or think of taking another sample — except Poirot," I added, with belated recognition.

"Yes, but what about the bitter taste that cocoa won't disguise?"

"Well, we've only his word for that. And there are other possibilities. He's admittedly one of the world's greatest toxicologists—"

"One of the world's greatest what? Say it again."

"He knows more about poisons than almost anybody," I explained. "Well, my idea is, that perhaps he's found some way of making strychnine tasteless. Or it may not have been strychnine at all, but some obscure drug no one has ever heard of, which produces much the same symptoms."

"H'm, yes, that might be," said John. "But look here, how could he have got at the cocoa? That wasn't downstairs?"

"No, it wasn't," I admitted reluctantly.

And then, suddenly, a dreadful possibility flashed through my mind. I hoped and prayed it would not occur to John also. I glanced sideways at him. He was frowning perplexedly, and I drew a deep breath of relief, for the terrible thought that had flashed across my mind was this: that Dr. Bauerstein might have had an accomplice.

Yet surely it could not be! Surely no woman as beautiful as Mary Cavendish could be a murderess. Yet beautiful women had been known to poison.

And suddenly I remembered that first conversation at tea on the day of my arrival, and the gleam in her eyes as she had said that poison was a woman's weapon. How agitated she had been on that fatal Tuesday evening! Had Mrs. Inglethorp discovered something between her and Bauerstein, and threatened to tell her husband? Was it to stop that denunciation that the crime had been committed?

Then I remembered that enigmatical conversation between Poirot and Evelyn Howard. Was this what they had meant? Was this the monstrous possibility that Evelyn had tried not to believe?

Yes, it all fitted in.

No wonder Miss Howard had suggested "hushing it up." Now I understood that unfinished sentence of hers: "Emily herself—" And in my heart I agreed with her. Would not Mrs. Inglethorp have preferred to go unavenged rather than have such terrible dishonour fall upon the name of Cavendish?

"There's another thing," said John suddenly, and the unexpected sound of his voice made me start guiltily. "Something which makes me doubt if what you say can be true."

"What's that?" I asked, thankful that he had gone away from the subject of how the poison could have been introduced into the cocoa.

"Why, the fact that Bauerstein demanded a post-mortem. He needn't have done so. Little Wilkins would have been quite content to let it go at heart disease."

"Yes," I said doubtfully. "But we don't know. Perhaps he thought it safer in the long run. Someone might have talked afterwards. Then the Home Office might have ordered exhumation. The whole thing would have come out, then, and he would have been in an awkward position, for no one would have believed that a man of his reputation could have been deceived into calling it heart disease."

"Yes, that's possible," admitted John. "Still," he added, "I'm blest if I can see what his motive could have been."

I trembled.

"Look here," I said, "I may be altogether wrong. And, remember, all this is in confidence."

"Oh, of course — that goes without saying."

We had walked, as we talked, and now we passed through the little gate into the garden. Voices rose near at hand, for tea was spread out under the sycamore-tree, as it had been on the day of my arrival.

Cynthia was back from the hospital, and I placed my chair beside her, and told her of Poirot's wish to visit the dispensary.

"Of course! I'd love him to see it. He'd better come to tea there one day. I must fix it up with him. He's such a dear little man! But he *is* funny. He made me take the brooch out of my tie the other day, and put it in again, because he said it wasn't straight."

I laughed.

"It's quite a mania with him."

"Yes, isn't it?"

We were silent for a minute or two, and then, glancing in the direction of Mary Cavendish, and dropping her voice, Cynthia said:

"Mr. Hastings."

"Yes?"

"After tea, I want to talk to you."

Her glance at Mary had set me thinking. I fancied that between these two there existed very little sympathy. For the first time, it occurred to me to wonder about the girl's future. Mrs. Inglethorp had made no provisions of any kind for her, but I imagined that John and Mary would probably insist on her making her home with them — at any rate until the end of the war. John, I knew, was very fond of her, and would be sorry to let her go.

John, who had gone into the house, now reappeared. His good-natured face wore an unaccustomed frown of anger.

"Confound those detectives! I can't think what they're after! They've been in every room in the house — turning things inside out, and upside down. It really is too bad! I suppose they took advantage of our all being out. I shall go for that fellow Japp, when I next see him!"

"Lot of Paul Prys," grunted Miss Howard.

Lawrence opined that they had to make a show of doing something.

Mary Cavendish said nothing.

After tea, I invited Cynthia to come for a walk, and we sauntered off into the woods together.

"Well?" I inquired, as soon as we

were protected from prying eyes by the leafy screen.

With a sigh, Cynthia flung herself down, and tossed off her hat. The sunlight, piercing through the branches, turned the auburn of her hair to quivering gold.

"Mr. Hastings — you are always so kind, and you know such a lot."

It struck me at this moment that Cynthia was really a very charming girl! Much more charming than Mary, who never said things of that kind.

"Well?" I asked benignantly, as she hesitated.

"I want to ask your advice. What shall I do?"

"Do?"

"Yes. You see, Aunt Emily always told me I should be provided for. I suppose she forgot, or didn't think she was likely to die — anyway, I am *not* provided for! And I don't know what to do. Do you think I ought to go away from here at once?"

"Good heavens, no! They don't want to part with you, I'm sure."

Cynthia hesitated a moment, plucking up the grass with her tiny hands. Then she said: "Mrs. Cavendish does. She hates me."

"Hates you?" I cried, astonished.

Cynthia nodded.

"Yes. I don't know why, but she can't bear me; and *he* can't, either."

"There I know you're wrong," I said warmly. "On the contrary, John is very fond of you."

"Oh, yes — *John*. I meant Lawrence. Not, of course, that I care whether Lawrence hates me or not. Still, it's rather horrid when no one loves you, isn't it?"

"But they do, Cynthia dear," I said earnestly. "I'm sure you are mistaken. Look, there is John — and Miss Howard —"

Cynthia nodded rather gloomily. "Yes, John likes me, I think, and of course Evie, for all her gruff ways, wouldn't be unkind to a fly. But Lawrence never speaks to me if he can help it, and Mary can hardly bring herself to be civil to me. She wants Evie to stay on, is begging her to, but she doesn't want me, and — and — I don't know what to do." Suddenly the poor child burst out crying.

I don't know what possessed me. Her beauty, perhaps, as she sat there, with the sunlight glinting down on her head; perhaps the sense of relief at encountering someone who so obviously could have no connection with the tragedy; perhaps honest pity for her youth and loneliness. Anyway, I leant forward, and taking her little hand, I said awkwardly:

"Marry me, Cynthia."

Unwittingly, I had hit upon a sovereign remedy for her tears. She sat up at once, drew her hand away, and said, with some asperity:

"Don't be silly!"

I was a little annoyed.

"I'm not being silly. I am asking you to do me the honour of becoming my wife."

To my intense surprise, Cynthia

burst out laughing, and called me a "funny dear."

"It's perfectly sweet of you," she said, "but you know you don't want to!"

"Yes, I do. I've got—"

"Never mind what you've got. You don't really want to—and I don't either."

"Well, of course, that settles it," I said stiffly. "But I don't see anything to laugh at. There's nothing funny about a proposal."

"No, indeed," said Cynthia. "Somebody might accept you next time. Good-bye, you've cheered me up *very* much."

And, with a final uncontrollable burst of merriment, she vanished through the trees.

Thinking over the interview, it struck me as being profoundly unsatisfactory.

It occurred to me suddenly that I would go down to the village, and look up Bauerstein. Somebody ought to be keeping an eye on the fellow. At the same time, it would be wise to allay any suspicions he might have as to his being suspected. I remembered how Poirot had relied on my diplomacy. Accordingly, I went to the little house with the "Apartments" card inserted in the window, where I knew he lodged, and tapped on the door.

An old woman came and opened it.

"Good afternoon," I said pleasantly. "Is Dr. Bauerstein in?"

She stared at me.

"Haven't you heard?"

"Heard what?"

"About him."

"What about him?"

"He's took."

"Took? Dead?"

"No, took by the perlice."

"By the police!" I gasped. "Do you mean they've arrested him?"

"Yes, that's it, and—"

I waited to hear no more, but tore up the village to find Poirot.

# X.

## THE ARREST.

To my extreme annoyance, Poirot was not in, and the old Belgian who answered my knock informed me that he believed he had gone to London.

I was dumbfounded. What on earth could Poirot be doing in London! Was it a sudden decision on his part, or had he already made up his mind when he parted from me a few hours earlier?

I retraced my steps to Styles in some annoyance. With Poirot away, I was uncertain how to act. Had he foreseen this arrest? Had he not, in all probability, been the cause of it? Those questions I could not resolve. But in the meantime what was I to do? Should I announce the arrest openly at Styles, or not? Though I did not acknowledge it to myself, the thought of Mary Cavendish was weighing on me. Would it not be a terrible shock to her? For the moment, I set aside utterly any suspicions of her. She could not be implicated — otherwise I should have heard some hint of it.

Of course, there was no possibility of being able permanently to conceal Dr. Bauerstein's arrest from her. It would be announced in every newspaper on the morrow. Still, I shrank from blurting it out. If only Poirot had been accessible, I could have asked his advice. What possessed him to go posting off to London in this unaccountable way?

In spite of myself, my opinion of his sagacity was immeasurably heightened. I would never have dreamt of suspecting the doctor, had not Poirot put it into my head. Yes, decidedly, the little man was clever.

After some reflecting, I decided to take John into my confidence, and leave him to make the matter public or not, as he thought fit.

He gave vent to a prodigious whistle, as I imparted the news.

"Great Scott! You *were* right, then. I couldn't believe it at the time."

"No, it is astonishing until you get used to the idea, and see how it makes everything fit in. Now, what are we to do? Of course, it will be generally known to-morrow."

John reflected.

"Never mind," he said at last, "we won't say anything at present. There is no need. As you say, it will be known soon enough."

But to my intense surprise, on getting down early the next morning, and eagerly opening the newspapers, there was not a word about the arrest! There was a column of mere padding about "The Styles Poisoning Case," but nothing further. It was rather inexplicable, but I supposed that, for some reason or other, Japp wished to keep it out of the papers. It worried me just a little, for it suggested the possibility that there might be further arrests to come.

After breakfast, I decided to go down to the village, and see if Poirot had returned yet; but, before I could start, a well-known face blocked one of the windows, and the well-known voice said:

*"Bonjour, mon ami!"*

"Poirot," I exclaimed, with relief, and seizing him by both hands, I dragged him into the room. "I was never so glad to see anyone. Listen, I have said nothing to anybody but John. Is that right?"

"My friend," replied Poirot, "I do not know what you are talking about."

"Dr. Bauerstein's arrest, of course," I answered impatiently.

"Is Bauerstein arrested, then?"

"Did you not know it?"

"Not the least in the world." But, pausing a moment, he added: "Still, it does not surprise me. After all, we are only four miles from the coast."

"The coast?" I asked, puzzled. "What has that got to do with it?"

Poirot shrugged his shoulders.

"Surely, it is obvious!"

"Not to me. No doubt I am very dense, but I cannot see what the proximity of the coast has got to do with the murder of Mrs. Inglethorp."

"Nothing at all, of course," replied Poirot, smiling. "But we were speaking of the arrest of Dr. Bauerstein."

"Well, he is arrested for the murder of Mrs. Inglethorp —"

"What?" cried Poirot, in apparently lively astonishment. "Dr. Bauerstein arrested for the murder of Mrs. Inglethorp?"

"Yes."

"Impossible! That would be too good a farce! Who told you that, my friend?"

"Well, no one exactly told me,"

I confessed. "But he is arrested."

"Oh, yes, very likely. But for espionage, *mon ami.*"

"Espionage?" I gasped.

"Precisely."

"Not for poisoning Mrs. Inglethorp?"

"Not unless our friend Japp has taken leave of his senses," replied Poirot placidly.

"But — but I thought you thought so too?"

Poirot gave me one look, which conveyed a wondering pity, and his full sense of the utter absurdity of such an idea.

"Do you mean to say," I asked, slowly adapting myself to the new idea, "that Dr. Bauerstein is a spy?"

Poirot nodded.

"Have you never suspected it?"

"It never entered my head."

"It did not strike you as peculiar that a famous London doctor should bury himself in a little village like this, and should be in the habit of walking about at all hours of the night, fully dressed?"

"No," I confessed, "I never thought of such a thing."

"He is, of course, a German by birth," said Poirot thoughtfully, "though he has practised so long in this country that nobody thinks of him as anything but an Englishman. He was naturalized about fifteen years ago. A very clever man — a Jew, of course."

"The blackguard!" I cried indignantly.

"Not at all. He is, on the contrary, a patriot. Think what he stands to lose. I admire the man myself."

But I could not look at it in Poirot's philosophical way.

"And this is the man with whom Mrs. Cavendish has been wandering about all over the country!" I cried indignantly.

"Yes. I should fancy he had found her very useful," remarked Poirot. "So long as gossip busied itself in coupling their names together, any other vagaries of the doctor's passed unobserved."

"Then you think he never really cared for her?" I asked eagerly — rather too eagerly, perhaps, under the circumstances.

"That, of course, I cannot say, but — shall I tell you my own private opinion, Hastings?"

"Yes."

"Well, it is this: that Mrs. Cavendish does not care, and never has cared one little jot about Dr. Bauerstein!"

"Do you really think so?" I could not disguise my pleasure.

"I am quite sure of it. And I will tell you why."

"Yes?"

"Because she cares for someone else, *mon ami.*"

"Oh!" What did he mean? In spite of myself, an agreeable warmth spread over me. I am not a vain man where women are concerned, but I remembered certain evidences, too lightly thought of at the time, perhaps, but which certainly seemed to indicate —

My pleasing thoughts were interrupted by the sudden entrance of Miss Howard. She glanced round hastily to make sure there was no one else in the room, and quickly produced an old sheet of brown paper. This she handed to Poirot, murmuring as she did so the cryptic words:

"On top of the wardrobe." Then she hurriedly left the room.

Poirot unfolded the sheet of paper eagerly, and uttered an exclamation of satisfaction. He spread it out on the table.

"Come here, Hastings. Now tell me, what is that initial — J. or L.?"

It was a medium sized sheet of paper, rather dusty, as though it had lain by for some time. But it was the label that was attracting Poirot's attention. At the top, it bore the printed stamp of Messrs. Parkson's, the well-known theatrical costumiers, and it was addressed to "— (the debatable initial) Cavendish, Esq., Styles Court, Styles St. Mary, Essex."

"It might be T., or it might be L.," I said, after studying the thing for a minute or two. "It certainly isn't a J."

"Good," replied Poirot, folding up the paper again. "I, also, am of your way of thinking. It is an L., depend upon it!"

"Where did it come from?" I asked curiously. "Is it important?"

"Moderately so. It confirms a surmise of mine. Having deduced its existence, I set Miss Howard to search for it, and, as you see, she has been successful."

"What did she mean by 'On the top of the wardrobe'?"

"She meant," replied Poirot promptly, "that she found it on top of a wardrobe."

"A funny place for a piece of brown paper," I mused.

"Not at all. The top of a wardrobe is an excellent place for brown paper and cardboard boxes. I have kept them there myself. Neatly arranged, there is nothing to offend the eye."

"Poirot," I asked earnestly, "have you made up your mind about this crime?"

"Yes — that is to say, I believe I know how it was committed."

"Ah!"

"Unfortunately, I have no proof beyond my surmise, unless —" With sudden energy, he caught me by the arm, and whirled me down the hall, calling out in French in his excitement: *"Mademoiselle Dorcas, Mademoiselle Dorcas, un moment, s'il vous plaît!"*

Dorcas, quite flurried by the noise, came hurrying out of the pantry.

"My good Dorcas, I have an idea — a little idea — if it should prove justified, what magnificent chance! Tell me, on Monday, not Tuesday, Dorcas, but Monday, the day before the tragedy, did anything go wrong with Mrs. Inglethorp's bell?"

Dorcas looked very surprised.

"Yes, sir, now you mention it, it did; though I don't know how you came to hear of it. A mouse, or some such, must have nibbled the wire through. The man came and put it right on Tuesday morning."

With a long drawn exclamation of ecstasy, Poirot led the way back to the morning-room.

"See you, one should not ask for outside proof — no, reason should be enough. But the flesh is weak, it is consolation to find that one is on the right track. Ah, my friend, I am like a giant refreshed. I run! I leap!"

And, in very truth, run and leap he did, gambolling wildly down the stretch of lawn outside the long window.

"What is your remarkable little friend doing?" asked a voice behind me, and I turned to find Mary Cavendish at my elbow. She smiled, and so did I. "What is it all about?"

"Really, I can't tell you. He asked Dorcas some question about a bell, and appeared so delighted with her answer that he is capering about as you see!"

Mary laughed.

"How ridiculous! He's going out of the gate. Isn't he coming back to-day?"

"I don't know. I've given up trying to guess what he'll do next."

"Is he quite mad, Mr. Hastings?"

"I honestly don't know. Sometimes, I feel sure he is as mad as a hatter; and then, just as he is at his maddest, I find there is method in his madness."

"I see."

In spite of her laugh, Mary was looking thoughtful this morning. She seemed grave, almost sad.

It occurred to me that it would be a good opportunity to tackle her on the subject of Cynthia. I began rather tactfully, I thought, but I had not gone far before she stopped me authoritatively.

"You are an excellent advocate, I have no doubt, Mr. Hastings, but in this case your talents are quite thrown away. Cynthia will run no risk of encountering any unkindness from me."

I began to stammer feebly that I hoped she hadn't thought — But again she stopped me, and her words were so unexpected that they quite drove Cynthia, and her troubles, out of my mind.

"Mr. Hastings," she said, "do you think I and my husband are happy together?"

I was considerably taken aback, and murmured something about it's not being my business to think anything of the sort.

"Well," she said quietly, "whether it is your business or not, I will tell you that we are not happy."

I said nothing, for I saw that she had not finished.

She began slowly, walking up and down the room, her head a little bent, and that slim, supple figure of hers swaying gently as she walked. She stopped suddenly, and looked up at me.

"You don't know anything about

me, do you?" she asked. "Where I come from, who I was before I married John — anything, in fact? Well, I will tell you. I will make a father confessor of you. You are kind, I think — yes, I am sure you are kind."

Somehow, I was not quite as elated as I might have been. I remembered that Cynthia had begun her confidences in much the same way. Besides, a father confessor should be elderly, it is not at all the role for a young man.

"My father was English," said Mrs. Cavendish, "but my mother was a Russian."

"Ah," I said, "now I understand —"

"Understand what?"

"A hint of something foreign — different — that there has always been about you."

"My mother was very beautiful, I believe. I don't know, because I never saw her. She died when I was quite a little child. I believe there was some tragedy connected with her death — she took an overdose of some sleeping draught by mistake. However that may be, my father was broken-hearted. Shortly afterwards, he went into the Consular Service. Everywhere he went, I went with him. When I was twenty-three, I had been nearly all over the world. It was a splendid life — I loved it."

There was a smile on her face, and her head was thrown back. She seemed living in the memory of those old glad days.

"Then my father died. He left me very badly off. I had to go and live with some old aunts in Yorkshire." She shuddered. "You will understand me when I say that it was a deadly life for a girl brought up as I had been. The narrowness, the deadly monotony of it, almost drove me mad." She paused a minute, and added in a different tone: "And then I met John Cavendish."

"Yes?"

"You can imagine that, from my aunts' point of view, it was a very good match for me. But I can honestly say it was not this fact which weighed with me. No, he was simply a way of escape from the insufferable monotony of my life."

I said nothing, and after a moment, she went on:

"Don't misunderstand me. I was quite honest with him. I told him, what was true, that I liked him very much, that I hoped to come to like him more, but that I was not in any way what the world calls 'in love' with him. He declared that that satisfied him, and so — we were married."

She waited a long time, a little frown had gathered on her forehead. She seemed to be looking back earnestly into those past days.

"I think — I am sure — he cared for me at first. But I suppose we were not well matched. Almost at once, we drifted apart. He — it is not a pleasing thing for my pride, but it is the truth — tired of me very soon." I must have made some murmur of dissent, for she went on quickly: "Oh, yes, he did! Not that it matters now — now that we've come to the parting of the ways."

"What do you mean?"

She answered quietly:

"I mean that I am not going to remain at Styles."

"You and John are not going to live here?"

"John may live here, but I shall not."

"You are going to leave him?"

"Yes."

"But why?"

She paused a long time, and said at last:

"Perhaps — because I want to be — free!"

And, as she spoke, I had a sudden vision of broad spaces, virgin tracts of forests, untrodden lands — and a realization of what freedom would mean to such a nature as Mary Cavendish. I seemed to see her for a moment as she was, a proud wild creature, as untamed by civilization as some shy bird of the hills. A little cry broke from her lips:

"You don't know, you don't know, how this hateful place has been prison to me!"

"I understand," I said, "but — but don't do anything rash."

"Oh, rash!" Her voice mocked at my prudence.

Then suddenly I said a thing I could have bitten out my tongue for:

"You know that Dr. Bauerstein has been arrested?"

An instant coldness passed like a mask over her face, blotting out all expression.

"John was so kind as to break that to me this morning."

"Well, what do you think?" I asked feebly.

"Of what?"

"Of the arrest?"

"What should I think? Apparently he is a German spy; so the gardener had told John."

Her face and voice were absolutely cold and expressionless. Did she care, or did she not?

She moved away a step or two, and fingered one of the flower vases.

"These are quite dead. I must do them again. Would you mind moving — thank you, Mr. Hastings." And she walked quietly past me out of the window, with a cool little nod of dismissal.

No, surely she could not care for Bauerstein. No woman could act her part with that icy unconcern.

Poirot did not make his appearance the following morning, and there was no sign of the Scotland Yard men.

But, at lunch-time, there arrived a new piece of evidence — or rather lack of evidence. We had vainly tried to trace the fourth letter, which Mrs. Inglethorp had written on the evening preceding her death. Our efforts having been in vain, we had abandoned the matter, hoping that it might turn up of itself one day. And this is just what did happen, in the shape of a communication, which arrived by the second post from a firm of French music publishers, acknowledging Mrs. Inglethorp's cheque, and regretting they had been unable to trace a certain series of Russian folksongs. So the last hope of solving the mystery, by means of Mrs. Inglethorp's correspondence on the fatal evening, had to be abandoned.

Just before tea, I strolled down to tell Poirot of the new disappointment, but found, to my annoyance, that he was once more out.

"Gone to London again?"

"Oh, no, monsieur, he has but taken the train to Tadminster. 'To see a young lady's dispensary,' he said."

"Silly ass!" I ejaculated. "I told him Wednesday was the one day she wasn't there! Well, tell him to look us up to-morrow morning, will you?"

"Certainly, monsieur."

But, on the following day, no sign of Poirot. I was getting angry. He was really treating us in the most cavalier fashion.

After lunch, Lawrence drew me aside, and asked if I was going down to see him.

"No, I don't think I shall. He can come up here if he wants to see us."

"Oh!" Lawrence looked indeterminate. Something unusually nervous and excited in his manner roused my curiosity.

"What is it?" I asked. "I could go if there's anything special."

"It's nothing much, but—well, if you are going, will you tell him—" he dropped his voice to a whisper—"I think I've found the extra coffee-cup!"

I had almost forgotten that enigmatical message of Poirot's, but now my curiosity was aroused afresh.

Lawrence would say no more, so I decided that I would descend from my high horse, and once more seek out Poirot at Leastways Cottage.

This time I was received with a smile. Monsieur Poirot was within. Would I mount? I mounted accordingly.

Poirot was sitting by the table, his head buried in his hands. He sprang up at my entrance.

"What is it?" I asked solicitously. "You are not ill, I trust?"

"No, no, not ill. But I decide an affair of great moment."

"Whether to catch the criminal or not?" I asked facetiously.

But, to my great surprise, Poirot nodded gravely.

" 'To speak or not to speak,' as your so great Shakespeare says, 'that is the question.' "

I did not trouble to correct the quotation.

"You are not serious, Poirot?"

"I am of the most serious. For the most serious of all things hangs in the balance."

"And that is?"

"A woman's happiness, *mon ami*," he said gravely.

I did not quite know what to say.

"The moment has come," said Poirot thoughtfully, "and I do not know what to do. For, see you, it is a big stake for which I play. No one but I, Hercule Poirot, would attempt it!" And he tapped himself proudly on the breast.

After pausing a few minutes respectfully, so as not to spoil his effect, I gave him Lawrence's message.

"Aha!" he cried. "So he has found the extra coffee-cup. That is good. He has more intelligence than would appear, this long-faced Monsieur Lawrence of yours!"

I did not myself think very highly of Lawrence's intelligence; but I forebore to contradict Poirot, and gently took him to task for forgetting my instructions as to which were Cynthia's days off.

"It is true. I have the head of a sieve. However, the other young lady was most kind. She was sorry for my disappointment, and showed me everything in the kindest way."

"Oh, well, that's all right, then, and you must go to tea with Cynthia another day."

I told him about the letter.

"I am sorry for that," he said. "I always had hopes of that letter. But no, it was not to be. This affair must all be unravelled from within." He tapped his forehead. "These little grey cells. It is 'up to them'—as you say over here." Then, suddenly, he asked: "Are you a judge of finger-marks, my friend?"

"No," I said, rather surprised, "I know that there are no two finger-marks alike, but that's as far as my science goes."

"Exactly."

He unlocked a little drawer, and took out some photographs which he laid on the table.

"I have numbered them, 1, 2, 3. Will you describe them to me?"

I studied the proofs attentively.

"All greatly magnified, I see. No. 1, I should say, are a man's finger-prints; thumb and first finger. No. 2 are a lady's; they are much smaller, and quite different in every way. No. 3"—I paused for some time—"there seem to be a lot of confused finger-marks, but here, very distinctly, are No. 1's."

"Overlapping the others?"

"Yes."

"You recognize them beyond fail?"

"Oh, yes; they are identical."

Poirot nodded, and gently taking the photographs from me locked them up again.

"I suppose," I said, "that as usual, you are not going to explain?"

"On the contrary. No. 1 were the finger-prints of Monsieur Lawrence. No. 2 were those of Mademoiselle Cynthia. They are not important. I merely obtained them for comparison. No. 3 is a little more complicated."

"Yes?"

"It is, as you see, highly magnified. You may have noticed a sort of blur extending all across the picture. I will not describe to you the special apparatus, dusting powder, etc., which I used. It is a well-known process to the police, and by means of it you can obtain a photograph of the finger-prints of any object in a very short space of time. Well, my friend, you have seen the finger-marks — it remains to tell you the particular object on which they had been left."

"Go on — I am really excited."

"*Eh bien*! Photo No. 3 represents the highly magnified surface of a tiny bottle in the top poison cupboard of the dispensary in the Red Cross Hospital at Tadminster — which sounds like the house that Jack built!"

"Good heavens!" I exclaimed. "But what were Lawrence Cavendish's finger-marks doing on it? He never went near the poison cupboard the day we were there!"

"Oh, yes, he did!"

"Impossible! We were all together the whole time."

Poirot shook his head.

"No, my friend, there was a moment when you were not all together. There was a moment when you could not have been all together, or it would not have been necessary to call to Monsieur Lawrence to come and join you on the balcony."

"I'd forgotten that," I admitted. "But it was only for a moment."

"Long enough."

"Long enough for what?"

Poirot's smile became rather enigmatical.

"Long enough for a gentleman who had once studied medicine to gratify a very natural interest and curiosity."

Our eyes met. Poirot's were pleasantly vague. He got up and hummed a little tune. I watched him suspiciously.

"Poirot," I said, "what was in this particular little bottle?"

Poirot looked out of the window.

"Hydro-chloride of strychnine," he said, over his shoulder, continuing to hum.

"Good heavens!" I said it quite quietly. I was not surprised. I had expected that answer.

"They use the pure hydro-chloride of strychnine very little — only occasionally for pills. It is the official solution, Liq. Strychnine Hydro-clor. that is used in most medicines. That is why the finger-marks have remained undisturbed since then."

"How did you manage to take this photograph?"

"I dropped my hat from the balcony," explained Poirot simply. "Visitors were not permitted below at that hour, so, in spite of my many apologies, Mademoiselle Cynthia's colleague had to go down and fetch it for me."

"Then you knew what you were going to find?"

"No, not at all. I merely realized that it was possible, from your story, for Monsieur Lawrence to go to the poison cupboard. The possibility had to be confirmed, or eliminated."

"Poirot," I said, "your gaiety does not deceive me. This is a very important discovery."

"I do not know," said Poirot. "But one thing does strike me. No doubt it has struck you too."

"What is that?"

"Why, that there is altogether too much strychnine about this case. This is the third time we run up against it. There was strychnine in Mrs. Inglethorp's tonic. There is the strychnine sold across the counter at Styles St. Mary by Mace. Now we have more strychnine, handled by one of the household. It is confusing; and, as you know, I do not like confusion."

Before I could reply, one of the other Belgians opened the door and stuck his head in.

"There is a lady below, asking for Mr. Hastings."

"A lady?"

I jumped up. Poirot followed me down the narrow stairs. Mary Cavendish was standing in the doorway.

"I have been visiting an old woman in the village," she explained, "and as Lawrence told me you were with Monsieur Poirot I thought I would call for you."

"Alas, madame," said Poirot, "I thought you had come to honour me with a visit!"

"I will some day, if you ask me," she promised him, smiling.

"That is well. If you should need a father confessor, madame"—she started ever so slightly—"remember, Papa Poirot is always at your service."

She stared at him for a few minutes, as though seeking to read some deeper meaning into his words. Then she turned abruptly away.

"Come, will you not walk back with us too, Monsieur Poirot?"

"Enchanted, madame."

All the way to Styles, Mary talked fast and feverishly. It struck me that in some way she was nervous of Poirot's eyes.

The weather had broken, and the sharp wind was almost autumnal in its shrewishness. Mary shivered a little, and buttoned her black sports coat closer. The wind through the trees made a mournful noise, like some great giant sighing.

We walked up to the great door of Styles, and at once the knowledge came to us that something was wrong.

Dorcas came running out to meet us. She was crying and wringing her hands. I was aware of other servants huddled together in the background, all eyes and ears.

"Oh, m'am! Oh, m'am! I don't know how to tell you—"

"What is it, Dorcas?" I asked impatiently. "Tell us at once."

"It's those wicked detectives. They've arrested him—they've arrested Mr. Cavendish!"

"Arrested Lawrence?" I gasped.

I saw a strange look come into Dorcas's eyes.

"No, sir. Not Mr. Lawrence—Mr. John."

Behind me, with a wild cry, Mary Cavendish fell heavily against me, and as I turned to catch her I met the quiet triumph in Poirot's eyes.

# XI.

## THE CASE FOR THE PROSECUTION.

The trial of John Cavendish for the murder of his stepmother took place two months later.

Of the intervening weeks I will say little, but my admiration and sympathy went out unfeignedly to Mary Cavendish. She ranged herself passionately on her husband's side, scorning the mere idea of his guilt, and fought for him tooth and nail.

I expressed my admiration to Poirot, and he nodded thoughtfully.

"Yes, she is of those women who show at their best in adversity. It brings out all that is sweetest and truest in them. Her pride and her jealousy have —"

"Jealousy?" I queried.

"Yes. Have you not realized that she is an unusually jealous woman? As I was saying, her pride and jealousy have been laid aside. She thinks of nothing but her husband, and the terrible fate that is hanging over him."

He spoke very feelingly, and I looked at him earnestly, remembering that last afternoon, when he had been deliberating whether or not to speak. With his tenderness for "a woman's happiness," I felt glad that the decision had been taken out of his hands.

"Even now," I said, "I can hardly believe it. You see, up to the very last minute, I thought it was Lawrence!"

Poirot grinned.

"I know you did."

"But John! My old friend John!"

"Every murderer is probably somebody's old friend," observed Poirot philosophically. "You cannot mix up sentiment and reason."

"I must say I think you might have given me a hint."

"Perhaps, *mon ami*, I did not do so, just because he *was* your old friend."

I was rather disconcerted by this, remembering how I had busily passed on to John what I believed to be Poirot's views concerning Bauerstein. He, by the way, had been acquitted of the charge brought against him. Nevertheless, although he had been too clever for them this time, and the charge of espionage could not be brought home to him, his wings were pretty well clipped for the future.

I asked Poirot whether he thought John would be condemned. To my intense surprise, he replied that, on the contrary, he was extremely likely to be acquitted.

"But, Poirot —" I protested.

"Oh, my friend, have I not said to you all along that I have no proofs. It is one thing to know that a man is guilty, it is quite another matter to prove him so. And, in this case, there is terribly little evidence. That is the whole trouble. I, Hercule Poirot, know, but I lack the last link in my chain. And unless I can find that missing link —" He shook his head gravely.

"When did you first suspect John Cavendish?" I asked, after a minute or two.

"Did you not suspect him at all?"

"No, indeed."

"Not after that fragment of conversation you overheard between Mrs. Cavendish and her mother-in-law, and her subsequent lack of frankness at the inquest?"

"No."

"Did you not put two and two together, and reflect that if it was not Alfred Inglethorp who was quarrelling with his wife — and you remember, he strenuously denied it at the inquest — it must be either Lawrence or John. Now, if it was Lawrence, Mary Cavendish's conduct was just as inexplicable. But if, on the other hand, it was John, the whole thing was explained quite naturally."

"So," I cried, a light breaking in upon me, "it was John who quarrelled with his mother that afternoon?"

"Exactly."

"And you have known this all along?"

"Certainly. Mrs. Cavendish's behaviour could only be explained that way."

"And yet you say he may be acquitted?"

Poirot shrugged his shoulders.

"Certainly I do. At the police court proceedings, we shall hear the case for the prosecution, but in all probability his solicitors will advise him to reserve his defence. That will be sprung upon us at the trial. And — ah, by the way, I have a word of caution to give you, my friend. I must not appear in the case."

"What?"

"No. Officially, I have nothing to do with it. Until I have found that last link in my chain, I must remain behind the scenes. Mrs. Cavendish must think I am working for her husband, not against him."

"I say, that's playing it a bit low down," I protested.

"Not at all. We have to deal with a most clever and unscrupulous man, and we must use any means in our power — otherwise he will slip through our fingers. That is why I have been careful to remain in the background. All the discoveries have been made by Japp, and Japp will take all the credit. If I am called upon to give evidence at all" — he smiled broadly — "it will probably be as a witness for the defence."

I could hardly believe my ears.

"It is quite *en règle*," continued Poirot. "Strangely enough, I can give evidence that will demolish one contention of the prosecution."

"Which one?"

"The one that relates to the destruction of the will. John Cavendish did not destroy that will."

Poirot was a true prophet. I will not go into the details of the police court proceedings, as it involves many tiresome repetitions. I will merely state baldly that John Cavendish reserved his defence, and was duly committed for trial.

September found us all in London. Mary took a house in Kensington, Poirot being included in the family party.

I myself had been given a job at the War Office, so was able to see them continually.

As the weeks went by, the state of Poirot's nerves grew worse and worse. That "last link" he talked about was still lacking. Privately, I hoped it might remain so, for what happiness could there be for Mary, if John were not acquitted?

On September 15th John Cavendish appeared in the dock at the Old Bailey, charged with "The Wilful Murder of Emily Agnes Inglethorp," and pleaded "Not Guilty."

Sir Ernest Heavywether, the famous K.C., had been engaged to defend him.

Mr. Philips, K.C., opened the case for the Crown.

The murder, he said, was a most premeditated and cold-blooded one. It was neither more nor less than the deliberate poisoning of a fond and trusting woman by the stepson to whom she had been more than a mother. Ever since his boyhood, she had supported him. He and his wife had lived at Styles Court in every luxury, surrounded by her care and attention. She had been their kind and generous benefactress.

He proposed to call witnesses to show how the prisoner, a profligate and spendthrift, had been at the end of his financial tether, and had also been carrying on an intrigue with a certain Mrs. Raikes, a neighbouring farmer's wife. This having come to his stepmother's ears, she taxed him with it on the afternoon before her death, and a quarrel ensued, part of which was overheard. On the previous day, the prisoner had purchased strychnine at the village chemist's shop, wearing a disguise by means of which he hoped to throw the onus of the crime upon another man — to wit, Mrs. Inglethorp's husband, of whom he had been bitterly jealous. Luckily for Mr. Inglethorp, he had been able to produce an unimpeachable alibi.

On the afternoon of July 17th, continued Counsel, immediately after the quarrel with her son, Mrs. Inglethorp made a new will. This will was found destroyed in the grate of her bedroom the following morning, but evidence had come to light which showed that it had been drawn up in favour of her husband. Deceased had already made a will in his favour before her marriage, but — and Mr. Philips wagged an expressive forefinger — the prisoner was not aware of that. What had induced the deceased to make a fresh will, with the old one still extant, he could not say. She was an old lady, and might possibly have forgotten the former one; or — this seemed to him more likely — she may have had an idea that it was revoked by her marriage, as there had been some conversation on the subject. Ladies were not always very well versed in legal knowledge. She had, about a year before, executed a will in favour of the prisoner. He would call evidence to show that it was the prisoner who ultimately handed his stepmother her coffee on the fatal night. Later in the evening, he had sought admission to her room, on which occasion, no doubt, he found an opportunity of destroying the will which, as far as he knew, would render the one in his favour valid.

The prisoner had been arrested in consequence of the discovery, in his room, by Detective Inspector Japp — a most brilliant officer — of the identical phial of strychnine which had been sold at the village chemist's to the supposed Mr. Inglethorp on the day before the murder. It would be for the jury to decide whether or not these damning facts constituted an overwhelming proof of the prisoner's guilt.

And, subtly implying that a jury which did not so decide, was quite unthinkable, Mr. Philips sat down and wiped his forehead.

The first witnesses for the prosecution were mostly those who had been called at the inquest, the medical evidence being again taken first.

Sir Ernest Heavywether, who was famous all over England for the unscrupulous manner in which he bullied witnesses, only asked two questions.

"I take it, Dr. Bauerstein, that strychnine, as a drug, acts quickly?"

"Yes."

"And that you are unable to

account for the delay in this case?"

"Yes."

"Thank you."

Mr. Mace identified the phial handed him by Counsel as that sold by him to "Mr. Inglethorp." Pressed, he admitted that he only knew Mr. Inglethorp by sight. He had never spoken to him. The witness was not cross-examined.

Alfred Inglethorp was called, and denied having purchased the poison. He also denied having quarrelled with his wife. Various witnesses testified to the accuracy of these statements.

The gardeners' evidence, as to the witnessing of the will was taken, and then Dorcas was called.

Dorcas, faithful to her "young gentlemen," denied strenuously that it could have been John's voice she heard, and resolutely declared, in the teeth of everything, that it was Mr. Inglethorp who had been in the boudoir with her mistress. A rather wistful smile passed across the face of the prisoner in the dock. He knew only too well how useless her gallant defiance was, since it was not the object of the defence to deny this point. Mrs. Cavendish, of course, could not be called upon to give evidence against her husband.

After various questions on other matters, Mr. Philips asked:

"In the month of June last, do you remember a parcel arriving for Mr. Lawrence Cavendish from Parkson's?"

Dorcas shook her head.

"I don't remember, sir. It may have done, but Mr. Lawrence was away from home part of June."

"In the event of a parcel arriving for him whilst he was away, what would be done with it?"

"It would either be put in his room or sent on after him."

"By you?"

"No, sir, I should leave it on the hall table. It would be Miss Howard who would attend to anything like that."

Evelyn Howard was called and, after being examined on other points, was questioned as to the parcel.

"Don't remember. Lots of parcels come. Can't remember one special one."

"You do not know if it was sent after Mr. Lawrence Cavendish to Wales, or whether it was put in his room?"

"Don't think it was sent after him. Should have remembered it if it was."

"Supposing a parcel arrived addressed to Mr. Lawrence Cavendish, and afterwards it disappeared, should you remark its absence?"

"No, don't think so. I should think someone had taken charge of it."

"I believe, Miss Howard, that it was you who found this sheet of brown paper?" He held up the same dusty piece which Poirot and I had examined in the morning-room at Styles.

"Yes, I did."

"How did you come to look for it?"

"The Belgian detective who was employed on the case asked me to search for it."

"Where did you eventually discover it?"

"On the top of—of—a wardrobe."

"On top of the prisoner's wardrobe?"

"I—I believe so."

"Did you not find it yourself?"

"Yes."

"Then you must know where you found it?"

"Yes, it was on the prisoner's wardrobe."

"That is better."

An assistant from Parkson's, Theatrical Costumiers, testified that on June 29th, they had supplied a black beard to Mr. L. Cavendish, as requested. It was ordered by letter, and a postal order was enclosed. No, they had not kept the letter. All transactions were entered in their books. They had sent the beard, as directed, to "L. Cavendish, Esq., Styles Court."

Sir Ernest Heavywether rose ponderously.

"Where was the letter written from?"

"From Styles Court."

"The same address to which you sent the parcel?"

"Yes."

"And the letter came from there?"

"Yes."

Like a beast of prey, Heavywether fell upon him:

"How do you know?"

"I—I don't understand."

"How do you know that letter came from Styles? Did you notice the postmark?"

"No—but—"

"Ah, you did *not* notice the postmark! And yet you affirm so confidently that it came from Styles. It might, in fact, have been any postmark?"

"Y—es."

"In fact, the letter, though written on stamped notepaper, might have been posted from anywhere? From Wales, for instance?"

The witness admitted that such might be the case, and Sir Ernest signified that he was satisfied.

Elizabeth Wells, second housemaid at Styles, stated that after she had gone to bed she remembered that she had bolted the front door, instead of leaving it on the latch as Mr. Inglethorp had requested. She had accordingly gone downstairs again to rectify her error. Hearing a slight noise in the West wing, she had peeped along the passage, and had seen Mr. John Cavendish knocking at Mrs. Inglethorp's door.

Sir Ernest Heavywether made short work of her, and under his unmerciful bullying she contradicted herself hopelessly, and Sir Ernest sat down again with a satisfied smile on his face.

With the evidence of Annie, as

to the candle grease on the floor, and as to seeing the prisoner take the coffee into the boudoir, the proceedings were adjourned until the following day.

As we went home, Mary Cavendish spoke bitterly against the prosecuting counsel.

"That hateful man! What a net he has drawn around my poor John! How he twisted every little fact until he made it seem what it wasn't!"

"Well," I said consolingly, "it will be the other way about to-morrow."

"Yes," she said meditatively; then suddenly dropped her voice. "Mr. Hastings, you do not think — surely it could not have been Lawrence — Oh, no, that could not be!"

But I myself was puzzled, and as soon as I was alone with Poirot I asked him what he thought Sir Ernest was driving at.

"Ah!" said Poirot appreciatively. "He is a clever man, that Sir Ernest."

"Do you think he believes Lawrence guilty?"

"I do not think he believes or cares anything! No, what he is trying for is to create such confusion in the minds of the jury that they are divided in their opinion as to which brother did it. He is endeavouring to make out that there is quite as much evidence against Lawrence as against John — and I am not at all sure that he will not succeed."

Detective-inspector Japp was the first witness called when the trial was reopened, and gave his evidence succinctly and briefly. After relating the earlier events, he proceeded:

"Acting on information received, Superintendent Summerhaye and myself searched the prisoner's room, during his temporary absence from the house. In his chest of drawers, hidden beneath some underclothing, we found: first, a pair of gold-rimmed pince-nez similar to those worn by Mr. Inglethorp" — these were exhibited — "secondly, this phial."

The phial was that already recognized by the chemist's assistant, a tiny bottle of blue glass, containing a few grains of a white crystalline powder, and labelled: "Strychnine Hydro-chloride. POISON."

A fresh piece of evidence discovered by the detectives since the police court proceedings was a long, almost new piece of blotting-paper. It had been found in Mrs. Inglethorp's cheque book, and on being reversed at a mirror, showed clearly the words: "... erything of which I die possessed I leave to my beloved husband Alfred Ing ..." This placed beyond question the fact that the destroyed will had been in favour of the deceased lady's husband. Japp then produced the charred fragment of paper recovered from the grate, and this, with the discovery of the beard in the attic, completed his evidence.

But Sir Ernest's cross-examination was yet to come.

"What day was it when you searched the prisoner's room?"

"Tuesday, the 24th of July."

"Exactly a week after the tragedy?"

"Yes."

"You found these two objects, you say, in the chest of drawers. Was the drawer unlocked?"

"Yes."

"Does it not strike you as unlikely that a man who had committed a crime should keep the evidence of it in an unlocked drawer for anyone to find?"

"He might have stowed them there in a hurry."

"But you have just said it was a whole week since the crime. He would have had ample time to remove them and destroy them."

"Perhaps."

"There is no perhaps about it. Would he, or would he not have had plenty of time to remove and destroy them?"

"Yes."

"Was the pile of underclothes under which the things were hidden heavy or light?"

"Heavyish."

"In other words, it was winter underclothing. Obviously, the prisoner would not be likely to go to that drawer?"

"Perhaps not."

"Kindly answer my question. Would the prisoner, in the hottest week of a hot summer, be likely to go to a drawer containing winter underclothing. Yes, or no?"

"No."

"In that case, is it not possible that the articles in question might have been put there by a third person, and that the prisoner was quite unaware of their presence?"

"I should not think it likely."

"But it is possible?"

"Yes."

"That is all."

More evidence followed. Evidence as to the financial difficulties in which the prisoner had found himself at the end of July. Evidence as to his intrigue with Mrs. Raikes — poor Mary, that must have been bitter hearing for a woman of her pride. Evelyn Howard had been right in her facts, though her animosity against Alfred Inglethorp had caused her to jump to the conclusion that he was the person concerned.

Lawrence Cavendish was then put into the box. In a low voice, in answer to Mr. Philips' questions, he denied having ordered anything from Parkson's in June. In fact, on June 29th, he had been staying away, in Wales.

Instantly, Sir Ernest's chin was shooting pugnaciously forward.

"You deny having ordered a black beard from Parkson's on June 29th?"

"I do."

"Ah! In the event of anything happening to your brother, who will inherit Styles Court?"

The brutality of the question called a flush to Lawrence's pale face. The judge gave vent to a faint murmur of disapprobation, and the prisoner in the dock leant forward angrily.

Heavywether cared nothing for his client's anger. "Answer my question, if you please."

"I suppose," said Lawrence quietly, "that I should."

"What do you mean by you 'suppose'? Your brother has no children. You *would* inherit it, wouldn't you?"

"Yes."

"Ah, that's better," said Heavywether, with ferocious geniality. "And you'd inherit a good slice of money too, wouldn't you?"

"Really, Sir Ernest," protested the judge, "these questions are not relevant."

Sir Ernest bowed, and having shot his arrow proceeded.

"On Tuesday, the 17th July, you went, I believe, with another guest, to visit the dispensary at the Red Cross Hospital in Tadminster?"

"Yes."

"Did you — while you happened to be alone for a few seconds — unlock the poison cupboard, and examine some of the bottles?"

"I — I — may have done so."

"I put it to you that you did do so?"

"Yes."

Sir Ernest fairly shot the next question at him.

"Did you examine one bottle in particular?"

"No, I do not think so."

"Be careful, Mr. Cavendish. I am referring to a little bottle of Hydro-chloride of Strychnine."

Lawrence was turning a sickly greenish colour.

"N — o — I am sure I didn't."

"Then how do you account for the fact that you left the unmistakable impress of your finger-prints on it?"

The bullying manner was highly efficacious with a nervous disposition.

"I — I suppose I must have taken up the bottle."

"I suppose so too! Did you abstract any of the contents of the bottle?"

"Certainly not."

"Then why did you take it up?"

"I once studied to be a doctor. Such things naturally interest me."

"Ah! So poisons 'naturally interest' you, do they? Still, you waited to be alone before gratifying that 'interest' of yours?"

"That was pure chance. If the others had been there, I should have done just the same."

"Still, as it happens, the others were not there?"

"No, but—"

"In fact, during the whole afternoon, you were only alone for a couple of minutes, and it happened — I say, it happened — to be during those two minutes that you displayed your 'natural interest' in Hydro-chloride of Strychnine?"

Lawrence stammered pitiably.

"I — I —"

With a satisfied and expressive countenance, Sir Ernest observed:

"I have nothing more to ask you, Mr. Cavendish."

This bit of cross-examination had caused great excitement in court. The heads of the many fashionably attired women present were busily laid together, and their whispers became so loud that the judge angrily threatened to have the court cleared if there was not immediate silence.

There was little more evidence. The hand-writing experts were called upon for their opinion of the signature of "Alfred Inglethorp" in the chemist's poison register. They all declared unanimously that it was certainly not his hand-writing, and gave it as their view that it might be that of the prisoner disguised. Cross-examined, they admitted that it might be the prisoner's hand-writing cleverly counterfeited.

Sir Ernest Heavywether's speech in opening the case for the defence was not a long one, but it was backed by the full force of his emphatic manner. Never, he said, in the course of his long experience, had he known a charge of murder rest on slighter evidence. Not only was it entirely circumstantial, but the greater part of it was practically unproved. Let them take the testimony they had heard and sift it impartially. The strychnine had been found in a drawer in the prisoner's room. That drawer was an unlocked one, as he had pointed out, and he submitted that there was no evidence to prove that it was the prisoner who had concealed the poison there. It was, in fact, a wicked and malicious attempt on the part of some third person to fix the crime on the prisoner. The prosecution had been unable to produce a shred of evidence in support of their contention that it was the prisoner who ordered the black beard from Parkson's. The quarrel which had taken place between prisoner and his stepmother was freely admitted, but both it and his financial embarrassments had been grossly exaggerated.

His learned friend — Sir Ernest nodded carelessly at Mr. Philips — had stated that if the prisoner were an innocent man, he would have come forward at the inquest to explain that it was he, and not Mr. Inglethorp, who had been the participator in the quarrel. He thought the facts had been misrepresented. What had actually occurred was this. The prisoner, returning to the house on Tuesday evening, had been authoritatively told that there had been a violent quarrel between Mr. and Mrs. Inglethorp. No suspicion had entered the prisoner's head that anyone could possibly have mistaken his voice for that of Mr. Inglethorp. He naturally concluded that his stepmother had had two quarrels.

The prosecution averred that on Monday, July 16th, the prisoner had entered the chemist's shop in the village, disguised as Mr. Inglethorp. The prisoner, on the contrary, was at that time at a lonely spot called Marston's Spinney, where he had been summoned by an anonymous note, couched in blackmailing terms, and threatening to reveal certain matters to his wife unless he complied with its demands. The prisoner had, accordingly, gone to the appointed spot, and after waiting there vainly for half an hour had returned home. Unfortunately, he had met with no one on the way there or back who could vouch for the truth of his story, but luckily he had kept the note, and it would be produced as evidence.

As for the statement relating to the destruction of the will, the prisoner had formerly practised at the Bar, and was perfectly well aware that the will made in his favour a year before was automatically revoked by his stepmother's remarriage. He would call evidence to show who did destroy the will, and it was possible that that might open up quite a new view of the case.

Finally, he would point out to the jury that there was evidence against other people besides John Cavendish. He would direct their attention to the fact that the evidence against Mr. Lawrence Cavendish was quite as strong, if not stronger than that against his brother.

He would now call the prisoner.

John acquitted himself well in the witness-box. Under Sir Ernest's skilful handling, he told his tale credibly and well. The anonymous note received by him was produced, and handed to the jury to examine. The readiness with which he admitted his financial difficulties, and the disagreement with his stepmother, lent value to his denials.

At the close of his examination, he paused, and said:

"I should like to make one thing clear. I utterly reject and disapprove of Sir Ernest Heavywether's insinuations against my brother. My brother, I am convinced, had no more to do with the crime than I have."

Sir Ernest merely smiled, and noted with a sharp eye that John's protest had produced a very favourable impression on the jury.

Then the cross-examination began.

"I understand you to say that it never entered your head that the witnesses at the inquest could possibly have mistaken your voice for that of Mr. Inglethorp. Is not that very surprising?"

"No, I don't think so. I was told there had been a quarrel between my mother and Mr. Inglethorp, and it never occurred to me that such was not really the case."

"Not when the servant Dorcas repeated certain fragments of the conversation — fragments which you must have recognized?"

"I did not recognize them."

"Your memory must be unusually short!"

"No, but we were both angry, and, I think, said more than we meant. I paid very little attention to my mother's actual words."

Mr. Philips' incredulous sniff was a triumph of forensic skill. He passed on to the subject of the note.

"You have produced this note very opportunely. Tell me, is there nothing familiar about the hand-writing of it?"

"Not that I know of."

"Do you not think that it bears a marked resemblance to your own hand-writing — carelessly disguised?"

"No, I do not think so."

"I put it to you that it is your own hand-writing!"

"No."

"I put it to you that, anxious to prove an alibi, you conceived the idea of a fictitious and rather incredible appointment, and wrote this note yourself in order to bear out your statement!"

"No."

"Is it not a fact that, at the time you claim to have been waiting about at a solitary and unfrequented spot, you were really in the chemist's shop in Styles St. Mary, where you purchased strychnine in the name of Alfred Inglethorp?"

"No, that is a lie."

"I put it to you that, wearing a suit of Mr. Inglethorp's clothes, with a black beard trimmed to resemble his, you were there — and signed the register in his name!"

"That is absolutely untrue."

"Then I will leave the remarkable similarity of hand-writing between the note, the register, and your own, to the consideration of the jury," said Mr. Philips, and sat down with the air of a man who has done his duty, but who was nevertheless horrified by such deliberate perjury.

After this, as it was growing late, the case was adjourned till Monday.

Poirot, I noticed, was looking profoundly discouraged. He had that little frown between the eyes that I knew so well.

"What is it, Poirot?" I inquired.

"Ah, *mon ami*, things are going badly, badly."

In spite of myself, my heart gave a leap of relief. Evidently there was a likelihood of John Cavendish being acquitted.

When we reached the house, my little friend waved aside Mary's offer of tea.

"No, I thank you, madame. I will mount to my room."

I followed him. Still frowning, he went across to the desk and took out a small pack of patience cards. Then he drew up a chair to the table, and, to my utter amazement, began solemnly to build card houses!

My jaw dropped involuntarily, and he said at once:

"No, *mon ami*, I am not in my second childhood! I steady my nerves, that is all. This employment requires precision of the fingers. With precision of the fingers goes precision of the brain. And never have I needed that more than now!"

"What is the trouble?" I asked.

With a great thump on the table, Poirot demolished his carefully built up edifice.

"It is this, *mon ami!* That I can build card houses seven stories high, but I cannot"—thump—"find"—thump—"that last link of which I spoke to you."

I could not quite tell what to say, so I held my peace, and he began slowly building up the cards again, speaking in jerks as he did so.

"It is done—so! By placing—one card—on another—with mathematical—precision!"

I watched the card house rising under his hands, story by story. He never hesitated or faltered. It was really almost like a conjuring trick.

"What a steady hand you've got," I remarked. "I believe I've only seen your hand shake once."

"On an occasion when I was enraged, without doubt," observed Poirot, with great placidity.

"Yes indeed! You were in a towering rage. Do you remember? It was when you discovered that the lock of the despatch-case in Mrs. Inglethorp's bedroom had been forced. You stood by the mantelpiece, twiddling the things on it in your usual fashion, and your hand shook like a leaf! I must say—"

But I stopped suddenly. For Poirot, uttering a hoarse and inarticulate cry, again annihilated his masterpiece of cards, and putting his hands over his eyes swayed backwards and forwards, apparently suffering the keenest agony.

"Good heavens, Poirot!" I cried. "What is the matter? Are you taken ill?"

"No, no," he gasped. "It is—it is—that I have an idea!"

"Oh!" I exclaimed, much relieved. "One of your 'little ideas'?"

"Ah, *ma foi*, no!" replied Poirot frankly. "This time it is an idea gigantic! Stupendous! And you—*you*, my friend, have given it to me!"

Suddenly clasping me in his arms, he kissed me warmly on both cheeks, and before I had recovered from my surprise ran headlong from the room.

Mary Cavendish entered at that moment.

"What *is* the matter with Monsieur Poirot? He rushed past me crying out: 'A garage! For the love of Heaven, direct me to a garage, madame!' And, before I could answer, he had dashed out into the street."

I hurried to the window. True enough, there he was, tearing down the street, hatless, and gesticulating as he went. I turned to Mary with a gesture of despair.

"He'll be stopped by a policeman in another minute. There he goes, round the corner!"

Our eyes met, and we stared helplessly at one another.

"What can be the matter?"

I shook my head.

"I don't know. He was building card houses, when suddenly he said he had an idea, and rushed off as you saw."

"Well," said Mary, "I expect he will be back before dinner."

But night fell, and Poirot had not returned.

# XII.

## THE LAST LINK.

Poirot's abrupt departure had intrigued us all greatly. Sunday morning wore away, and still he did not reappear. But about three o'clock a ferocious and prolonged hooting outside drove us to the window, to see Poirot alighting from a car, accompanied by Japp and Summerhaye. The little man was transformed. He radiated an absurd complacency. He bowed with exaggerated respect to Mary Cavendish.

"Madame, I have your permission to hold a little *réunion* in the *salon*? It is necessary for everyone to attend."

Mary smiled sadly.

"You know, Monsieur Poirot, that you have *carte blanche* in every way."

"You are too amiable, madame."

Still beaming, Poirot marshalled us all into the drawing-room, bringing forward chairs as he did so.

"Miss Howard — here. Mademoiselle Cynthia. Monsieur Lawrence. The good Dorcas. And Annie. *Bien!* We must delay our proceedings a few minutes until Mr. Inglethorp arrives. I have sent him a note."

Miss Howard rose immediately from her seat.

"If that man comes into the house, I leave it!"

"No, no!" Poirot went up to her and pleaded in a low voice.

Finally Miss Howard consented to return to her chair. A few minutes later Alfred Inglethorp entered the room.

The company once assembled, Poirot rose from his seat with the air of a popular lecturer, and bowed politely to his audience.

"Messieurs, mesdames, as you all know, I was called in by Monsieur John Cavendish to investigate this case. I at once examined the bedroom of the deceased which, by the advice of the doctors, had been kept locked, and was consequently exactly as it had been when the tragedy occurred. I found: first, a fragment of green material; second, a stain on the carpet near the window, still damp; thirdly, an empty box of bromide powders.

"To take the fragment of green material first, I found it caught in the bolt of the communicating door between that room and the adjoining one occupied by Mademoiselle Cynthia. I handed the fragment over to the police who did not consider it of much importance. Nor did they recognize it for what it was — a piece torn from a green land armlet."

There was a little stir of excitement.

"Now there was only one person at Styles who worked on the land — Mrs. Cavendish. Therefore it must have been Mrs. Cavendish who entered the deceased's room through the door communicating with Mademoiselle Cynthia's room."

"But that door was bolted on the inside!" I cried.

"When I examined the room, yes. But in the first place we have only her word for it, since it was she who tried that particular door and reported it fastened. In the ensuing confusion she would have had ample opportunity to shoot the bolt across. I took an early opportunity of verifying my conjectures. To begin with, the fragment corresponds exactly with a tear in Mrs. Cavendish's armlet. Also, at the inquest, Mrs. Cavendish declared that she had heard, from her own room, the fall of the table by the bed. I took an early opportunity of testing that statement by stationing my friend Monsieur Hastings in the left wing of the building, just outside Mrs. Cavendish's door. I myself, in company with the police, went to the deceased's room, and whilst there I, apparently accidentally, knocked over the table in question, but found that, as I had expected, Monsieur Hastings had heard no sound at all. This confirmed my belief that Mrs. Cavendish was not speaking the truth when she declared that she had been dressing in her room at the time of the tragedy. In fact, I was convinced that, far from having been in her own room, Mrs. Cavendish was actually in the deceased's room when the alarm was given."

I shot a quick glance at Mary. She was very pale, but smiling.

"I proceeded to reason on that assumption. Mrs. Cavendish is in her mother-in-law's room. We will say that she is seeking for something and has not yet found it. Suddenly Mrs. Inglethorp awakens and is seized with an alarming paroxysm. She flings out her arm, overturning the bed table, and then pulls desperately at the bell. Mrs. Cavendish, startled, drops her candle, scattering the grease on the carpet. She picks it up, and retreats quickly to Mademoiselle Cynthia's room, closing the door behind her. She hurries out into the passage, for the servants must not find her where she is. But it is too late! Already footsteps are echoing along the gallery which connects the two wings. What can she do? Quick as thought, she hurries back to the young girl's room, and starts shaking her awake. The hastily aroused household come trooping down the passage. They are all busily battering at Mrs. Inglethorp's door. It occurs to nobody that Mrs. Cavendish has not arrived with the rest, but — and this is significant — I can find no one who saw her come from the other wing." He looked at Mary Cavendish. "Am I right, madame?"

She bowed her head.

"Quite right, monsieur. You understand that, if I had thought I would do my husband any good by revealing these facts, I would have done so. But it did not seem to me to bear upon the question of his guilt or innocence."

"In a sense, that is correct, madame. But it cleared my mind of many misconceptions, and left me free to see other facts in their true significance."

"The will!" cried Lawrence. "Then it was you, Mary, who destroyed the will?"

She shook her head, and Poirot shook his also.

"No," he said quietly. "There is only one person who could possibly have destroyed that will — Mrs. Inglethorp herself!"

"Impossible!" I exclaimed. "She had only made it out that very afternoon!"

"Nevertheless, *mon ami*, it was Mrs. Inglethorp. Because, in no other way can you account for the fact that, on one of the hottest days of the year, Mrs. Inglethorp ordered a fire to be lighted in her room."

I gave a gasp. What idiots we had been never to think of that fire as being incongruous! Poirot was continuing:

"The temperature on that day, messieurs, was 80 degrees in the shade. Yet Mrs. Inglethorp ordered a fire! Why? Because she wished to destroy something, and could think of no other way. You will remember that, in consequence of the War economics practiced at Styles, no waste paper was thrown away. There was therefore no means of destroying a thick document such as a will. The moment I heard of a fire being lighted in Mrs. Inglethorp's room, I leaped to the conclusion that it was to destroy some important document — possibly a will. So the discovery of the charred fragment in the grate was no surprise to me. I did not, of course, know at the time that the will in question had only been made this afternoon, and I will admit that, when I learnt that fact, I fell into a grievous error. I came to the conclusion that Mrs. Inglethorp's determination to destroy her will arose as a direct consequence of the quarrel she had that afternoon, and that therefore the quarrel took place after, and not before the making of the will.

"Here, as we know, I was wrong, and I was forced to abandon that idea. I faced the problem from a new standpoint. Now, at four o'clock, Dorcas overheard her mistress saying angrily: 'You need not think that any fear of publicity, or scandal between husband and wife will deter me." I conjectured, and conjectured rightly, that these words were addressed, not to her husband, but to Mr. John Cavendish. At five o'clock, an hour later, she uses almost the same words, but the standpoint is different. She admits to Dorcas, 'I don't know what to do; scandal between husband and wife is a dreadful thing.' At four o'clock she has been angry, but completely mistress of herself. At five o'clock she is in violent distress, and speaks of having had a great shock.

"Looking at the matter psychologically, I drew one deduction which I was convinced was correct. The second 'scandal' she spoke of was not the same as the first — and it concerned herself!

"Let us reconstruct. At four o'clock, Mrs. Inglethorp quarrels with her son, and threatens to denounce him to his wife — who, by the way, overheard the greater part of the conversation. At four-thirty, Mrs. Inglethorp, in consequence of a conversation on the validity of wills, makes a will in favour of her husband, which the two gardeners witness. At five o'clock, Dorcas finds her mistress in a state of considerable agitation, with a slip of paper — 'a letter,' Dorcas thinks — in her hand, and it is then that she orders the fire in her room to be lighted. Presumably, then, between four-thirty and five o'clock, something has occurred to occasion a complete revolution of feeling, since she is now as anxious to destroy the will, as she was before to make it. What was that something?

"As far as we know, she was quite alone during that half-hour. Nobody entered or left that boudoir. What then occasioned this sudden change of sentiment?

"One can only guess, but I believe my guess to be correct. Mrs. Inglethorp had no stamps in her desk. We know this, because later she asked Dorcas to bring her some. Now in the opposite corner of the room stood her husband's desk — locked. She was anxious to find some stamps, and, according to my theory, she tried her own keys in the desk. That one of them fitted I know. She therefore opened the desk, and in searching for the stamps she came across something else — that slip of paper which Dorcas saw in her hand, and which assuredly was never meant for Mrs. Inglethorp's eyes. On the other hand, Mrs. Cavendish believed that the slip of paper to which her mother-in-law clung so tenaciously was a written proof of her own husband's infidelity. She demanded it from Mrs. Inglethorp who assured her, quite truly, that it had nothing to do with that matter. Mrs. Cavendish did not believe her. She thought that Mrs. Inglethorp was shielding her stepson. Now Mrs. Cavendish is a very resolute woman, and, behind her mask of reserve, she was madly jealous of her husband. She determined to get hold of that paper at all costs, and in this resolution chance came to her aid. She happened to pick up the key of Mrs. Inglethorp's despatch-case, which had been lost that morning. She knew that her mother-in-law invariably kept all important papers in this particular case.

"Mrs. Cavendish, therefore, made her plans as only a woman driven desperate through jealousy could have done. Some time in the evening she unbolted the door leading into Mademoiselle Cynthia's room. Possibly she applied oil to the hinges, for I found that it opened quite noiselessly when I tried it. She put off her project until the early hours of the morning as being safer, since the servants were accustomed to hearing her move about her room at that time. She dressed completely in her land kit, and made her way quietly through Mademoiselle Cynthia's room into that of Mrs. Inglethorp."

He paused a moment, and Cynthia interrupted:

"But I should have woken up if anyone had come through my room?"

"Not if you were drugged, mademoiselle."

"Drugged?"

*"Mais, oui!*—You remember"—he addressed us collectively again—"that through all the tumult and noise next door Mademoiselle Cynthia slept. That admitted of two possibilities. Either her sleep was feigned—which I did not believe—or her unconsciousness was indeed by artificial means.

"With this latter idea in my mind, I examined all the coffee-cups most carefully, remembering that it was Mrs. Cavendish who had brought Mademoiselle Cynthia her coffee the night before. I took a sample from each cup, and had them analysed—with no result. I had counted the cups carefully, in the event of one having been removed. Six persons had taken coffee, and six cups were duly found. I had to confess myself mistaken.

"Then I discovered that I had been guilty of a very grave oversight. Coffee had been brought in for seven persons, not six, for Dr. Bauerstein had been there that evening. This changed the face of the whole affair, for there was now one cup missing. The servants noticed nothing, since Annie, the housemaid, who took in the coffee, brought in seven cups, not knowing that Mr. Inglethorp never drank it, whereas Dorcas, who cleared them away the following morning, found six as usual — or strictly speaking she found five, the sixth being the one found broken in Mrs. Inglethorp's room.

"I was confident that the missing cup was that of Mademoiselle Cynthia. I had an additional reason for that belief in the fact that all the cups found contained sugar, which Mademoiselle Cynthia never took in her coffee. My attention was attracted by the story of Annie about some 'salt' on the tray of cocoa which she took every night to Mrs. Inglethorp's room. I accordingly secured a sample of that cocoa, and sent it to be analysed."

"But that had already been done by Dr. Bauerstein," said Lawrence quickly.

"Not exactly. The analyst was asked by him to report whether strychnine was, or was not, present. He did not have it tested, as I did, for a narcotic."

"For a narcotic?"

"Yes. Here is the analyst's report. Mrs. Cavendish administered a safe, but effectual, narcotic to both Mrs. Inglethorp and Mademoiselle Cynthia. And it is possible that she had a mauvais quart d'heure in consequence! Imagine her feelings when her mother-in-law is suddenly taken ill and dies, and immediately after she hears the word 'Poison'! She has believed that the sleeping draught she administered was perfectly harmless, but there is no doubt that for one terrible moment she must have feared that Mrs. Inglethorp's death lay at her door. She is seized with panic, and under its influence she hurries downstairs, and quickly drops the coffee-cup and saucer used by Mademoiselle Cynthia into a large brass vase, where it is discovered later by Monsieur Lawrence. The remains of the cocoa she dare not touch. Too many eyes are upon her. Guess at her relief when strychnine is mentioned, and she discovers that after all the tragedy is not her doing.

"We are now able to account for the symptoms of strychnine poisoning being so long in making their appearance. A narcotic taken with strychnine will delay the action of the poison for some hours."

Poirot paused. Mary looked up at him, the colour slowly rising in her face.

"All you have said is quite true, Monsieur Poirot. It was the most awful hour of my life. I shall never forget it. But you are wonderful. I understand now —"

"What I meant when I told you that you could safely confess to Papa Poirot, eh? But you would not trust me."

"I see everything now," said Lawrence. "The drugged cocoa, taken on top of the poisoned coffee, amply accounts for the delay."

"Exactly. But was the coffee poisoned, or was it not? We come to a little difficulty here, since Mrs. Inglethorp never drank it."

"What?" The cry of surprise was universal.

"No. You will remember my speaking of a stain on the carpet in Mrs. Inglethorp's room? There were some peculiar points about that stain. It was still damp, it exhaled a strong odour of coffee, and imbedded in the nap of the carpet I found some little splinters of china. What had happened was plain to me, for not two minutes before I had placed my little case on the table near the window, and the table, tilting up, had deposited it upon the floor on precisely the identical spot. In exactly the same way, Mrs. Inglethorp had laid down her cup of coffee on reaching her room the night before, and the treacherous table had played her the same trick.

"What happened next is mere guess work on my part, but I should say that Mrs. Inglethorp picked up the broken cup and placed it on the table by the bed. Feeling in need of a stimulant of some kind, she heated up her cocoa, and drank it off then and there. Now we are faced with a new problem. We know the cocoa contained no strychnine. The coffee was never drunk. Yet the strychnine must have been administered between seven and nine o'clock that evening. What third medium was there — a medium so suitable for disguising the taste of strychnine that it is extraordinary no one has thought of it?" Poirot looked round the room, and then answered himself impressively. "Her medicine!"

"Do you mean that the murderer introduced the strychnine into her tonic?" I cried.

"There was no need to introduce it. It was already there — in the mixture. The strychnine that killed Mrs. Inglethorp was the identical strychnine prescribed by Dr. Wilkins. To make that clear to you, I will read you an extract from a book on dispensing which I found in the Dispensary of the Red Cross Hospital at Tadminster:

> *"The following prescription has become famous in text books:*
>
> *Strychninae Sulph: 1 gr.*
> *Potass Bromide: 3vi*
> *Aqua ad: 3viii*
> *Fiat Mistura*
>
> *"This solution deposits in a few hours the greater part of the strychnine salt as an insoluble bromide in transparent crystals. A lady in England lost her life by taking a similar mixture: the precipitated strychnine collected at the bottom, and in taking the last dose she swallowed nearly all of it!*

"Now there was, of course, no bromide in Dr. Wilkins' prescription, but you will remember that I mentioned an empty box of bromide powders. One or two of those powders introduced into the full bottle of medicine would effectually precipitate the strychnine, as the book describes, and cause it to be taken in the last dose. You will learn later that the person who usually poured out Mrs. Inglethorp's medicine was always extremely careful not to shake the bottle, but to leave the sediment at the bottom of it undisturbed.

"Throughout the case, there have been evidences that the tragedy was intended to take place on Monday evening. On that day, Mrs. Inglethorp's bell wire was neatly cut, and on Monday evening Mademoiselle Cynthia was spending the night with friends, so that Mrs. Inglethorp would have been quite alone in the right wing, completely shut off from help of any kind, and would have died, in all probability, before medical aid could have been summoned. But in her hurry to be in time for the village entertainment Mrs. Inglethorp forgot to take her medicine, and the next day she lunched away from home, so that the last — and fatal — dose was actually taken twenty-four hours later than had been anticipated by the murderer; and it is owing to that delay that the final proof — the last link of the chain — is now in my hands."

Amid breathless excitement, he held out three thin strips of paper.

"A letter in the murderer's own hand-writing, *mes amis!* Had it been a little clearer in its terms, it is possible that Mrs. Inglethorp, warned in time, would have escaped. As it was, she realized her danger, but not the manner of it."

In the deathly silence, Poirot pieced together the slips of paper and, clearing his throat, read:

*"Dearest Evelyn:*

*"You will be anxious at hearing nothing. It is all right — only it will be to-night instead of last night. You understand. There's a good time coming once the old woman is dead and out of the way. No one can possibly bring home the crime to me. That idea of yours about the bromides was a stroke of genius! But we must be very circumspect. A false step —*

"Here, my friends, the letter breaks off. Doubtless the writer was interrupted; but there can be no question as to his identity. We all know this hand-writing and —"

A howl that was almost a scream broke the silence.

"You devil! How did you get it?"

A chair was overturned. Poirot skipped nimbly aside. A quick movement on his part, and his assailant fell with a crash.

"*Messieurs, mesdames,*" said Poirot, with a flourish, "let me introduce you to the murderer, Mr. Alfred Inglethorp!"

# XIII.

## POIROT EXPLAINS.

"Poirot, you old villain," I said, "I've half a mind to strangle you! What do you mean by deceiving me as you have done?"

We were sitting in the library. Several hectic days lay behind us. In the room below, John and Mary were together once more, while Alfred Inglethorp and Miss Howard were in custody. Now at last, I had Poirot to myself, and could relieve my still burning curiosity.

Poirot did not answer me for a moment, but at last he said:

"I did not deceive you, *mon ami*. At most, I permitted you to deceive yourself."

"Yes, but why?"

"Well, it is difficult to explain. You see, my friend, you have a nature so honest, and a countenance so transparent, that — *enfin*, to conceal your feelings is impossible! If I had told you my ideas, the very first time you saw Mr. Alfred Inglethorp that astute gentleman would have — in your so expressive idiom — 'smelt a rat'! And then, *bonjour* to our chances of catching him!"

"I think that I have more diplomacy than you give me credit for."

"My friend," besought Poirot, "I implore you, do not enrage yourself! Your help has been of the most invaluable. It is but the extremely beautiful nature that you have, which made me pause."

"Well," I grumbled, a little mollified, "I still think you might have given me a hint."

"But I did, my friend. Several hints. You would not take them. Think now, did I ever say to you that I believed John Cavendish guilty? Did I not, on the contrary, tell you that he would almost certainly be acquitted?"

"Yes, but—"

"And did I not immediately afterwards speak of the difficulty of bringing the murderer to justice? Was it not plain to you that I was speaking of two entirely different persons?"

"No," I said, "it was not plain to me!"

"Then again," continued Poirot, "at the beginning, did I not repeat to you several times that I didn't want Mr. Inglethorp arrested *now*? That should have conveyed something to you."

"Do you mean to say you suspected him as long ago as that?"

"Yes. To begin with, whoever else might benefit by Mrs. Inglethorp's death, her husband would benefit the most. There was no getting away from that. When I went up to Styles with you that first day, I had no idea as to how the crime had been committed, but from what I knew of Mr. Inglethorp I fancied that it would be very hard to find anything to connect him with it. When I arrived at the château, I realized at once that it was Mrs. Inglethorp who had burnt the will; and there, by the way, you cannot complain, my friend, for I tried my best to force on you the significance of that bedroom fire in midsummer."

"Yes, yes," I said impatiently. "Go on."

"Well, my friend, as I say, my views as to Mr. Inglethorp's guilt were very much shaken. There was, in fact, so much evidence against him that I was inclined to believe that he had not done it."

"When did you change your mind?"

"When I found that the more efforts I made to clear him, the more efforts he made to get himself arrested. Then, when I discovered that Inglethorp had nothing to do with Mrs. Raikes and that in fact it was John Cavendish who was interested in that quarter, I was quite sure."

"But why?"

"Simply this. If it had been Inglethorp who was carrying on an intrigue with Mrs. Raikes, his silence was perfectly comprehensible. But, when I discovered that it was known all over the village that it was John who was attracted by the farmer's pretty wife, his silence bore quite a different interpretation. It was nonsense to pretend that he was afraid of the scandal, as no possible scandal could attach to him. This attitude of his gave me furiously to think, and I was slowly forced to the conclusion that Alfred Inglethorp wanted to be arrested. *Eh bien!* from that moment, I was equally determined that he should not be arrested."

"Wait a minute. I don't see why he wished to be arrested?"

"Because, *mon ami*, it is the law of your country that a man once acquitted can never be tried again for the same offence. Aha! but it was clever — his idea! Assuredly, he is a man of method. See here, he knew that in his position he was bound to be suspected, so he conceived the exceedingly clever idea of preparing a lot of manufactured evidence against himself. He wished to be arrested. He would then produce his irreproachable alibi — and, hey presto, he was safe for life!"

"But I still don't see how he managed to prove his alibi, and yet go to the chemist's shop?"

Poirot stared at me in surprise.

"Is it possible? My poor friend! You have not yet realized that it was Miss Howard who went to the chemist's shop?"

"Miss Howard?"

"But, certainly. Who else? It was most easy for her. She is of a good height, her voice is deep and manly; moreover, remember, she and Inglethorp are cousins, and there is a distinct resemblance between them, especially in their gait and bearing. It was simplicity itself. They are a clever pair!"

"I am still a little fogged as to how exactly the bromide business was done," I remarked.

"*Bon!* I will reconstruct for you as far as possible. I am inclined to think that Miss Howard was the master mind in that affair. You remember her once mentioning that her father was a doctor? Possibly she dispensed his medicines for him, or she may have taken the idea from one of the many books lying about when Mademoiselle Cynthia was studying for her exam. Anyway, she was familiar with the fact that the addition of a bromide to a mixture containing strychnine would cause the precipitation of the latter. Probably the idea came to her quite suddenly. Mrs. Inglethorp had a box of bromide powders, which she occasionally took at night. What could be easier than quietly to dissolve one or more of those powders in Mrs. Inglethorp's large sized bottle of medicine when it came from Coot's? The risk is practically nil. The tragedy will not take place until nearly a fortnight later. If anyone has seen either of them touching the medicine, they will have forgotten it by that time. Miss Howard will have engineered her quarrel, and departed from the house. The lapse of time, and her absence, will defeat all suspicion. Yes, it was a clever idea! If they had left it alone, it is possible the crime might never have been brought home to them. But they were not satisfied. They tried to be too clever — and that was their undoing."

Poirot puffed at his tiny cigarette, his eyes fixed on the ceiling.

"They arranged a plan to throw

suspicion on John Cavendish, by buying strychnine at the village chemist's, and signing the register in his hand-writing.

"On Monday Mrs. Inglethorp will take the last dose of her medicine. On Monday, therefore, at six o'clock, Alfred Inglethorp arranges to be seen by a number of people at a spot far removed from the village. Miss Howard has previously made up a cock and bull story about him and Mrs. Raikes to account for his holding his tongue afterwards. At six o'clock, Miss Howard, disguised as Alfred Inglethorp, enters the chemist's shop, with her story about a dog, obtains the strychnine, and writes the name of Alfred Inglethorp in John's handwriting, which she had previously studied carefully.

"But, as it will never do if John, too, can prove an alibi, she writes him an anonymous note — still copying his hand-writing — which takes him to a remote spot where it is exceedingly unlikely that anyone will see him.

"So far, all goes well. Miss Howard goes back to Middlingham. Alfred Inglethorp returns to Styles. There is nothing that can compromise him in any way, since it is Miss Howard who has the strychnine, which, after all, is only wanted as a blind to throw suspicion on John Cavendish.

"But now a hitch occurs. Mrs. Inglethorp does not take her medicine that night. The broken bell, Cynthia's absence — arranged by Inglethorp through his wife — all these are wasted. And then — he makes his slip.

"Mrs. Inglethorp is out, and he sits down to write to his accomplice, who, he fears, may be in a panic at the non-success of their plan. It is probable that Mrs. Inglethorp returned earlier than he expected. Caught in the act, and somewhat flurried he hastily shuts and locks his desk. He fears that if he remains in the room he may have to open it again, and that Mrs. Inglethorp might catch sight of the letter before he could snatch it up. So he goes out and walks in the woods, little dreaming that Mrs. Inglethorp will open his desk, and discover the incriminating document.

"But this, as we know, is what happened. Mrs. Inglethorp reads it, and becomes aware of the perfidy of her husband and Evelyn Howard, though, unfortunately, the sentence about the bromides conveys no warning to her mind. She knows that she is in danger — but is ignorant of where the danger lies. She decides to say nothing to her husband, but sits down and writes to her solicitor, asking him to come on the morrow, and she also determines to destroy immediately the will which she has just made. She keeps the fatal letter."

"It was to discover that letter, then, that her husband forced the lock of the despatch-case?"

"Yes, and from the enormous risk he ran we can see how fully he realized its importance. That letter excepted, there was absolutely nothing to connect him with the crime."

"There's only one thing I can't make out, why didn't he destroy it at once when he got hold of it?"

"Because he did not dare take the biggest risk of all — that of keeping it on his own person."

"I don't understand."

"Look at it from his point of view. I have discovered that there were only five short minutes in which he could have taken it — the five minutes immediately before our own arrival on the scene, for before that time Annie was brushing the stairs, and would have seen anyone who passed going to the right wing. Figure to yourself the scene! He enters the room, unlocking the door by means of one of the other door-keys — they were all much alike. He hurries to the despatch-case — it is locked, and the keys are nowhere to be seen. That is a terrible blow to him, for it means that his presence in the room cannot be concealed as he had hoped. But he sees clearly that everything must be risked for the sake of that damning piece of evidence. Quickly, he forces the lock with a penknife, and turns over the papers until he finds what he is looking for.

"But now a fresh dilemma arises: he dare not keep that piece of paper on him. He may be seen leaving the room — he may be searched. If the paper is found on him, it is certain doom. Probably, at this minute, too, he hears the sounds below of Mr. Wells and John leaving the boudoir. He must act quickly. Where can he hide this terrible slip of paper? The contents of the waste-paper-basket are kept and in any case, are sure to be examined. There are no means of destroying it; and he dare not keep it. He looks round, and he sees — what do you think, *mon ami?*"

I shook my head.

"In a moment, he has torn the letter into long thin strips, and rolling them up into spills he thrusts them hurriedly in amongst the other spills in the vase on the mantle-piece."

I uttered an exclamation.

"No one would think of looking there," Poirot continued. "And he will be able, at his leisure, to come back and destroy this solitary piece of evidence against him."

"Then, all the time, it was in the spill vase in Mrs. Inglethorp's bedroom, under our very noses?" I cried.

Poirot nodded.

"Yes, my friend. That is where I discovered my 'last link,' and I owe that very fortunate discovery to you."

"To me?"

"Yes. Do you remember telling me that my hand shook as I was straightening the ornaments on the mantelpiece?"

"Yes, but I don't see —"

"No, but I saw. Do you know,

my friend, I remembered that earlier in the morning, when we had been there together, I had straightened all the objects on the mantelpiece. And, if they were already straightened, there would be no need to straighten them again, unless, in the meantime, someone else had touched them."

"Dear me," I murmured, "so that is the explanation of your extraordinary behaviour. You rushed down to Styles, and found it still there?"

"Yes, and it was a race for time."

"But I still can't understand why Inglethorp was such a fool as to leave it there when he had plenty of opportunity to destroy it."

"Ah, but he had no opportunity. *I* saw to that."

"You?"

"Yes. Do you remember reproving me for taking the household into my confidence on the subject?"

"Yes."

"Well, my friend, I saw there was just one chance. I was not sure then if Inglethorp was the criminal or not, but if he was I reasoned that he would not have the paper on him, but would have hidden it somewhere, and by enlisting the sympathy of the household I could effectually prevent his destroying it. He was already under suspicion, and by making the matter public I secured the services of about ten amateur detectives, who would be watching him unceasingly, and being himself aware of their watchfulness he would not dare seek further to destroy the document. He was therefore forced to depart from the house, leaving it in the spill vase."

"But surely Miss Howard had ample opportunities of aiding him."

"Yes, but Miss Howard did not know of the paper's existence. In accordance with their prearranged plan, she never spoke to Alfred Inglethorp. They were supposed to be deadly enemies, and until John Cavendish was safely convicted they neither of them dared risk a meeting. Of course I had a watch kept on Mr. Inglethorp, hoping that sooner or later he would lead me to the hiding-place. But he was too clever to take any chances. The paper was safe where it was; since no one had thought of looking there in the first week, it was not likely they would do so afterwards. But for your lucky remark, we might never have been able to bring him to justice."

"I understand that now; but when did you first begin to suspect Miss Howard?"

"When I discovered that she had told a lie at the inquest about the letter she had received from Mrs. Inglethorp."

"Why, what was there to lie about?"

"You saw that letter? Do you recall its general appearance?"

"Yes — more or less."

"You will recollect, then, that Mrs. Inglethorp wrote a very distinctive hand, and left large clear spaces between her words. But if you look at the date at the top of the letter you will notice that 'July 17th' is quite different in this respect. Do you see what I mean?"

"No," I confessed, "I don't."

"You do not see that that letter was not written on the 17th, but on the 7th — the day after Miss Howard's departure? The '1' was written in before the '7' to turn it into the '17th.'"

"But why?"

"That is exactly what I asked myself. Why does Miss Howard suppress the letter written on the 17th, and produce this faked one instead? Because she did not wish to show the letter of the 17th. Why, again? And at once a suspicion dawned in my mind. You will remember my saying that it was wise to beware of people who were not telling you the truth."

"And yet," I cried indignantly, "after that, you gave me two reasons why Miss Howard could not have committed the crime!"

"And very good reasons too," replied Poirot. "For a long time they were a stumbling-block to me until I remembered a very significant fact: that she and Alfred Inglethorp were cousins. She could not have committed the crime single-handed, but the reasons against that did not debar her from being an accomplice. And, then, there was that rather over-vehement hatred of hers! It concealed a very opposite emotion. There was, undoubtedly, a tie of passion between them long before he came to Styles. They had already arranged their infamous plot — that he should marry this rich, but rather foolish old lady, induce her to make a will leaving her money to him, and then gain their ends by a very cleverly conceived crime. If all had gone as they planned, they would probably have left England, and lived together on their poor victim's money.

"They are a very astute and unscrupulous pair. While suspicion was to be directed against him, she would be making quiet preparations for a very different *dénouement*. She arrives from Middlingham with all the compromising items in her possession. No suspicion attaches to her. No notice is paid to her coming and going in the house. She hides the strychnine and glasses in John's room. She puts the beard in the attic. She will see to it that sooner or later they are duly discovered."

"I don't quite see why they tried to fix the blame on John," I remarked. "It would have been much easier for them to bring the crime home to Lawrence."

"Yes, but that was mere chance. All the evidence against him arose out of pure accident. It must, in fact, have been distinctly annoying to the pair of schemers."

"His manner was unfortunate," I observed thoughtfully.

"Yes. You realize, of course, what was at the back of that?"

"No."

"You did not understand that

he believed Mademoiselle Cynthia guilty of the crime?"

"No," I exclaimed, astonished. "Impossible!"

"Not at all. I myself nearly had the same idea. It was in my mind when I asked Mr. Wells that first question about the will. Then there were the bromide powders which she had made up, and her clever male impersonations, as Dorcas recounted them to us. There was really more evidence against her than anyone else."

"You are joking, Poirot!"

"No. Shall I tell you what made Monsieur Lawrence turn so pale when he first entered his mother's room on the fatal night? It was because, whilst his mother lay there, obviously poisoned, he saw, over your shoulder, that the door into Mademoiselle Cynthia's room was unbolted."

"But he declared that he saw it bolted!" I cried.

"Exactly," said Poirot dryly. "And that was just what confirmed my suspicion that it was not. He was shielding Mademoiselle Cynthia."

"But why should he shield her?"

"Because he is in love with her."

I laughed.

"There, Poirot, you are quite wrong! I happen to know for a fact that, far from being in love with her, he positively dislikes her."

"Who told you that, *mon ami?*"

"Cynthia herself."

"*La pauvre petite!* And she was concerned?"

"She said that she did not mind at all."

"Then she certainly did mind very much," remarked Poirot. "They are like that — *les femmes!*"

"What you say about Lawrence is a great surprise to me," I said.

"But why? It was most obvious. Did not Monsieur Lawrence make the sour face every time Mademoiselle Cynthia spoke and laughed with his brother? He had taken it into his long head that Mademoiselle Cynthia was in love with Monsieur John. When he entered his mother's room, and saw her obviously poisoned, he jumped to the conclusion that Mademoiselle Cynthia knew something about the matter. He was nearly driven desperate. First he crushed the coffee-cup to powder under his feet, remembering that *she* had gone up with his mother the night before, and he determined that there should be no chance of testing its contents. Thenceforward, he strenuously, and quite uselessly, upheld the theory of 'Death from natural causes.'"

"And what about the 'extra coffee-cup'?"

"I was fairly certain that it was Mrs. Cavendish who had hidden it, but I had to make sure. Monsieur Lawrence did not know at all what I meant; but, on reflection, he came to the conclusion that if he could find an extra coffee-cup anywhere his lady love would be cleared of suspicion. And he was perfectly right."

"One thing more. What did Mrs. Inglethorp mean by her dying words?"

"They were, of course, an accusation against her husband."

"Dear me, Poirot," I said with a sigh, "I think you have explained everything. I am glad it has all ended so happily. Even John and his wife are reconciled."

"Thanks to me."

"How do you mean — thanks to you?"

"My dear friend, do you not realize that it was simply and solely the trial which has brought them together again? That John Cavendish still loved his wife, I was convinced. Also, that she was equally in love with him. But they had drifted very far apart. It all arose from a misunderstanding. She married him without love. He knew it. He is a sensitive man in his way, he would not force himself upon her if she did not want him. And, as he withdrew, her love awoke. But they are both unusually proud, and their pride held them inexorably apart. He drifted into an entanglement with Mrs. Raikes, and she deliberately cultivated the friendship of Dr. Bauerstein. Do you remember the day of John Cavendish's arrest, when you found me deliberating over a big decision?"

"Yes, I quite understood your distress."

"Pardon me, *mon ami*, but you did not understand it in the least. I was trying to decide whether or not I would clear John Cavendish at once. I could have cleared him — though it might have meant a failure to convict the real criminals. They were entirely in the dark as to my real attitude up to the very last moment — which partly accounts for my success."

"Do you mean that you could have saved John Cavendish from being brought to trial?"

"Yes, my friend. But I eventually decided in favour of 'a woman's happiness.' Nothing but the great danger through which they have passed could have brought these two proud souls together again."

I looked at Poirot in silent amazement. The colossal cheek of the little man! Who on earth but Poirot would have thought of a trial for murder as a restorer of conjugal happiness!

"I perceive your thoughts, *mon ami*," said Poirot, smiling at me. "No one but Hercule Poirot would have attempted such a thing! And you are wrong in condemning it. The happiness of one man and one woman is the greatest thing in all the world."

His words took me back to earlier events. I remembered Mary as she lay white and exhausted on the sofa, listening, listening. There had come the sound of the bell below. She had started up. Poirot had opened the door, and meeting her agonized eyes had nodded gently. "Yes, madame," he said. "I have brought him back to you." He had stood aside, and as I went out I had seen the look in Mary's eyes, as John Cavendish had caught his wife in his arms.

"Perhaps you are right, Poirot," I said gently. "Yes, it is the greatest thing in the world."

Suddenly, there was a tap at the door, and Cynthia peeped in.

"I — I only —"

"Come in," I said, springing up.

She came in, but did not sit down.

"I — only wanted to tell you something —"

"Yes?"

Cynthia fidgeted with a little tassel for some moments, then, suddenly exclaiming: "You dears!" kissed first me and then Poirot, and rushed out of the room again.

"What on earth does this mean?" I asked, surprised.

It was very nice to be kissed by Cynthia, but the publicity of the salute rather impaired the pleasure.

"It means that she has discovered Monsieur Lawrence does not dislike her as much as she thought," replied Poirot philosophically.

"But —"

"Here he is."

Lawrence at that moment passed the door.

"Eh! Monsieur Lawrence," called Poirot. "We must congratulate you, is it not so?"

Lawrence blushed, and then smiled awkwardly. A man in love is a sorry spectacle. Now Cynthia had looked charming.

I sighed.

"What is it, *mon ami?*"

"Nothing," I said sadly. "They are two delightful women!"

"And neither of them is for you?" finished Poirot. "Never mind. Console yourself, my friend. We may hunt together again, who knows? And then —"

# THE MURDER ON THE LINKS

*Agatha Christie's Second Hercule Poirot Novel*
*Published in 1923*

# I.

## A FELLOW-TRAVELLER.

I believe that a well-known anecdote exists to the effect that a young writer, determined to make the commencement of his story forcible and original enough to catch and rivet the attention of the most blasé of editors, penned the following sentence:

"'Hell!' said the Duchess."

Strangely enough, this tale of mine opens in much the same fashion. Only the lady who gave utterance to the exclamation was not a duchess.

It was a day in early June. I had been transacting some business in Paris and was returning by the morning service to London, where I was still sharing rooms with my old friend, the Belgian ex-detective, Hercule Poirot.

The Calais express was singularly empty — in fact, my own compartment held only one other traveller. I had made a somewhat hurried departure from the hotel and was busy assuring myself that I had duly collected all my traps, when the train started. Up till then I had hardly noticed my companion, but I was now violently recalled to the fact of her existence. Jumping up from her seat, she let down the window and stuck her head out, withdrawing it a moment later with the brief and forcible ejaculation "Hell!"

Now I am old-fashioned. A woman, I consider, should be

womanly. I have no patience with the modern neurotic girl who jazzes from morning to night, smokes like a chimney, and uses language which would make a Billingsgate fish-woman blush!

I looked up, frowning slightly, into a pretty, impudent face, surmounted by a rakish little red hat. A thick cluster of black curls hid each ear. I judged that she was little more than seventeen, but her face was covered with powder, and her lips were quite impossibly scarlet.

Nothing abashed, she returned my glance, and executed an expressive grimace.

"Dear me, we've shocked the kind gentleman!" she observed to an imaginary audience. "I apologize for my language! Most unladylike, and all that, but, oh, Lord, there's reason enough for it! Do you know I've lost my only sister?"

"Really?" I said politely. "How unfortunate."

"He disapproves!" remarked the lady. "He disapproves utterly — of me, and my sister — which last is unfair, because he hasn't seen her!"

I opened my mouth, but she forestalled me. "Say no more! Nobody loves me! I shall go into the garden and eat worms! Boohoo. I am crushed!"

She buried herself behind a large comic French paper. In a minute or two I saw her eyes stealthily peeping at me over the top. In spite of myself I could not help smiling, and in a minute she had tossed the paper aside, and had burst into a merry peal of laughter.

"I knew you weren't such a mutt as you looked," she cried.

Her laughter was so infectious that I could not help joining in, though I hardly cared for the word "mutt".

"There! Now we're friends!" declared the minx. "Say you're sorry about my sister —"

"I am desolated!"

"That's a good boy!"

"Let me finish. I was going to add that, although I am desolated, I can manage to put up with her absence very well." I made a little bow.

But this most unaccountable of damsels frowned and shook her head.

"Cut it out. I prefer the 'dignified disapproval' stunt. Oh, your face! 'Not one of us,' it said. And you were right there — though, mind you, it's pretty hard to tell nowadays. It's not everyone who can distinguish between a demi and a duchess. There now, I believe I've shocked you again! You've been dug out of the backwoods, you have. Not that I mind that. We could do with a few more of your sort. I just hate a fellow who gets fresh. It makes me mad."

She shook her head vigorously.

"What are you like when you're mad?" I inquired with a smile.

"A regular little devil! Don't care

what I say, or what I do, either! I nearly did a chap in once. Yes, really. He'd have deserved it too."

"Well," I begged, "don't get mad with me."

"I shan't. I like you — did the first moment I set eyes on you. But you looked so disapproving that I never thought we should make friends."

"Well, we have. Tell me something about yourself."

"I'm an actress. No — not the kind you're thinking of. I've been on the boards since I was a kid of six — tumbling."

"I beg your pardon," I said, puzzled.

"Haven't you ever seen child acrobats?"

"Oh, I understand!"

"I'm American born, but I've spent most of my life in England. We've got a new show now —"

"We?"

"My sister and I. Sort of song and dance, and a bit of patter, and a dash of the old business thrown in. It's quite a new idea, and it hits them every time. There's going to be money in it —"

My new acquaintance leaned forward, and discoursed volubly, a great many of her terms being quite unintelligible to me. Yet I found myself evincing an increasing interest in her. She seemed such a curious mixture of child and woman. Though perfectly worldly-wise, and able, as she expressed it, to take care of herself, there was yet something curiously ingenuous in her single-minded attitude towards life, and her wholehearted determination to "make good."

We passed through Amiens. The name awakened many memories. My companion seemed to have an intuitive knowledge of what was in my mind.

"Thinking of the War?"

I nodded.

"You were through it, I suppose?"

"Pretty well. I was wounded once, and after the Somme they invalided me out altogether. I'm a sort of private secretary now to an MP."

"My! That's brainy!"

"No, it isn't. There's really awfully little to do. Usually a couple of hours every day sees me through. It's dull work too. In fact, I don't know what I should do if I hadn't got something to fall back upon."

"Don't say you collect bugs!"

"No. I share rooms with a very interesting man. He's a Belgian — an ex-detective. He's set up as a private detective in London, and he's doing extraordinarily well. He's really a very marvellous little man. Time and again he has proved to be right where the official police have failed."

My companion listened with widening eyes.

"Isn't that interesting now? I just adore crime. I go to all the mysteries on the movies. And when there's a murder on I just devour the papers."

"Do you remember the Styles Case?" I asked.

"Let me see, was that the old lady who was poisoned? Somewhere down in Essex?"

I nodded.

"That was Poirot's first big case. Undoubtedly, but for him, the murderer would have escaped scot-free. It was a most wonderful bit of detective work."

Warming to my subject, I ran over the heads of the affair, working up to the triumphant and unexpected *dénouement.*

The girl listened spellbound. In fact, we were so absorbed that the train drew into Calais station before we realized it.

I secured a couple of porters, and we alighted on the platform. My companion held out her hand.

"Goodbye, and I'll mind my language better in future."

"Oh, but surely you'll let me look after you on the boat?"

"Mayn't be on the boat. I've got to see whether that sister of mine got aboard after all anywhere. But thanks, all the same."

"Oh, but we're going to meet again, surely? Aren't you even going to tell me your name?" I cried, as she turned away.

She looked over her shoulder. "Cinderella," she said, and laughed.

But little did I think when and how I should see Cinderella again.

# II.

## AN APPEAL FOR HELP.

It was five minutes past nine when I entered our joint sitting-room for breakfast on the following morning. My friend Poirot, exact to the minute as usual, was just tapping the shell of his second egg.

He beamed upon me as I entered.

"You have slept well, yes? You have recovered from the crossing so terrible? It is a marvel, almost you are exact this morning. *Pardon*, but your tie is not symmetrical. Permit that I rearrange him."

Elsewhere, I have described Hercule Poirot. An extraordinary little man! Height, five feet four inches; egg-shaped head carried a little to one side; eyes that shone green when he was excited; stiff military moustache; air of dignity immense! He was neat and dandified in appearance. For neatness of any kind he had an absolute passion. To see an ornament set crookedly, or a speck of dust, or a slight disarray in one's attire, was torture to the little man until he could ease his feelings by remedying the matter. "Order" and "Method" were his gods. He had a certain disdain for tangible evidence, such as footprints and cigarette ash, and would maintain that, taken by themselves, they would never enable a detective to solve a problem. Then he would tap his egg-shaped head with absurd complacency, and remark with great satisfaction: "The true work, it is done from within. The little grey cells — remember always the little grey cells, *mon ami.*"

I slipped into my seat, and remarked idly, in answer to Poirot's greeting, that an hour's sea passage from Calais to Dover could hardly be dignified by the epithet "terrible."

"Anything interesting come by the post?" I asked.

Poirot shook his head with a dissatisfied air. "I have not yet examined my letters, but nothing of interest arrives nowadays. The great criminals, the criminals of method, they do not exist."

He shook his head despondently, and I roared with laughter.

"Cheer up, Poirot, the luck will change. Open your letters. For all you know, there may be a great case looming on the horizon."

Poirot smiled, and taking up the neat little letter opener with which he opened his correspondence he slit the tops of the several envelopes that lay by his plate.

"A bill. Another bill. It is that I grow extravagant in my old age. Aha! a note from Japp."

"Yes?" I pricked up my ears. The Scotland Yard Inspector had more than once introduced us to an interesting case.

"He merely thanks me (in his fashion) for a little point in the Aberystwyth Case on which I was able to set him right. I am delighted to have been of service to him."

Poirot continued to read his correspondence placidly.

"A suggestion that I should give a lecture to our local Boy Scouts. The Countess of Forfanock will be obliged if I will call and see her. Another lap-dog without doubt! And now for the last. Ah —"

I looked up, quick to notice the change of tone. Poirot was reading attentively. In a minute he tossed the sheet over to me.

"This is out of the ordinary, *mon ami.* Read for yourself."

The letter was written on a foreign type of paper, in a bold characteristic hand:

*Villa Geneviève,*
*Merlinville-sur-Mer,*
*France.*

*Dear Sir, — I am in need of the services of a detective and, for reasons which I will give you later, do not wish to call in the official police. I have heard of you from several quarters, and all reports go to show that you are not only a man of decided ability, but one who also knows how to be discreet. I do not wish to trust details to the post, but, on account of a secret I possess, I go in daily fear of my life. I am convinced that the danger is imminent, and therefore I beg that you will lose no time in crossing to France; I will send a car to meet you at Calais, if you will wire me when you are arriving. I shall be obliged if you will drop all cases you have on hand, and devote yourself solely to my interests. I am prepared to pay any compensation necessary. I shall probably need your services for a considerable period of time, as it may be necessary for you to go out to Santiago, where I spent several years of my life. I shall be content for you to name your own fee.*

*Assuring you once more that the matter is urgent.*

*Yours faithfully,*
*P. T. RENAULD.*

Below the signature was a hastily scrawled line, almost illegible:

"For God's sake, come!"

I handed the letter back with quickened pulse.

"At last!" I said. "Here is something distinctly out of the ordinary."

"Yes, indeed," said Poirot meditatively.

"You will go of course," I continued.

Poirot nodded. He was thinking deeply. Finally he seemed to make up his mind, and glanced up at the clock. His face was very grave.

"See you, my friend, there is no time to lose. The Continental express leaves Victoria at 11 o'clock. Do not agitate yourself. There is plenty of time. We can allow ten minutes for discussion. You accompany me, *n'est-ce pas?*"

"Well —"

"You told me yourself that your employer needed you not for the next few weeks."

"Oh, that's all right. But this Mr. Renauld hints strongly that his business is private."

"*Ta-ta-ta!* I will manage Monsieur Renauld. By the way, I seem to know the name?"

"There's a well-known South American millionaire fellow. His name's Renauld. I don't know whether it could be the same."

"But without doubt. That explains the mention of Santiago. Santiago is in Chile, and Chile it is in South America! Ah; but we progress finely! You remarked the postscript? How did it strike you?"

I considered.

"Clearly he wrote the letter keeping himself well in hand, but at the end his self-control snapped and, on the impulse of the moment, he scrawled those four desperate words."

But my friend shook his head energetically. "You are in error. See you not that while the ink of the signature is nearly black, that of the postscript is quite pale?"

"Well?" I said, puzzled.

"*Mon Dieu, mon ami*, but use your little grey cells. Is it not obvious? Mr. Renault wrote his letter. Without blotting it, he re-read it carefully. Then, not on impulse, but deliberately, he added those last words, and blotted the sheet."

"But why?"

"*Parbleu!* so that it should produce the effect upon me that it has upon you."

"What?"

"*Mais oui* — to make sure of my coming! He reread the letter and was dissatisfied. It was not strong enough!"

He paused, and then added softly, his eyes shining with that green light that always betokened inward excitement: "And so, *mon ami*, since that postscript was added, not on impulse, but soberly, in cold blood, the urgency is very great, and we must reach him as soon as possible."

"Merlinville," I murmured thoughtfully. "I've heard of it, I think."

Poirot nodded.

"It is a quiet little place — but *chic!* It lies about midway between Boulogne and Calais. Mr. Renauld has a house in England, I suppose?"

"Yes, in Rutland Gate, as far as I remember. Also a big place in the country, somewhere in Hertfordshire. But I really know very little about him, he doesn't do much in a social way. I believe he has large South American interests in the City, and has spent most of his life out in Chile and the Argentine."

"Well, we shall hear all the details from the man himself. Come, let us pack. A small suit-case each, and then a taxi to Victoria."

Eleven o'clock saw our departure from Victoria on our way to Dover. Before starting Poirot had dispatched a telegram to Mr. Renauld giving the time of our arrival at Calais.

"I'm surprised you haven't invested in a few bottles of some sea-sick remedy, Poirot," I observed maliciously, as I recalled our conversation at breakfast.

My friend, who was anxiously scanning the weather, turned a reproachful face upon me.

"Is it that you have forgotten the method most excellent of Laverguier? His system, I practise it always. One balances oneself, if you remember, turning the head from left to right, breathing in and out, counting six between each breath."

"H'm," I demurred. "You'll be rather tired of balancing yourself and counting six by the time you get to Santiago, or Buenos Aires, or wherever it is you land."

"*Quelle idée*! You do not figure to yourself that I shall go to Santiago?"

"Mr. Renauld suggests it in his letter."

"He did not know the methods of Hercule Poirot. I do not run to and fro, making journeys and agitating myself. My work is done from within — *here* —" he tapped his forehead significantly.

As usual, this remark roused my argumentative faculty.

"It's all very well, Poirot, but I think you are falling into the habit of despising certain things too much. A fingerprint has led sometimes to the arrest and conviction of a murderer."

"And has, without doubt, hanged more than one innocent man," remarked Poirot dryly.

"But surely the study of fingerprints and footprints, cigarette ash, different kinds of mud, and other clues that comprise the minute observation of details — all these are of vital importance?"

"But certainly. I have never said otherwise. The trained observer, the expert, without doubt he is useful! But the others, the Hercules Poirots, they are above the experts! To them the experts bring the facts, their business is the method of the crime, its logical deduction, the proper sequence and order of the facts; above all, the true psychology of the case. You have hunted the fox, yes?"

"I have hunted a bit, now and again," I said, rather bewildered by this abrupt change of subject. "Why?"

"*Eh bien*, this hunting of the fox, you need the dogs, no?"

"Hounds," I corrected gently. "Yes, of course."

"But yet," Poirot wagged his finger at me. "You did not descend from your horse and run along the ground smelling with your nose and uttering loud Ow Ows?"

In spite of myself I laughed immoderately. Poirot nodded in a satisfied manner.

"So. You leave the work of the d — hounds to the hounds. Yet you demand that I, Hercule Poirot, should make myself ridiculous by lying down (possibly on damp grass) to study hypothetical footprints, and should scoop up cigarette ash when I do not know one kind from the other. Remember the Plymouth Express mystery. The good Japp departed to make a survey of the railway line. When he returned, I, without having moved from my apartments, was able to tell him exactly what he had found."

"So you are of the opinion that Japp wasted his time."

"Not at all, since his evidence confirmed my theory. But I should have wasted my time if I had gone. It is the same with so called "experts." Remember the handwriting testimony in the Cavendish Case. One counsel's questioning brings out testimony as to the resemblances, the defence brings evidence to show dissimilarity. All the language is very technical. And the result? What we all knew in the first place. The writing was very like that of John Cavendish. And the psychological mind is faced with the question "Why?" Because it was actually his? Or because someone wished us to think it was his? I answered that question, *mon ami*, and answered it correctly."

And Poirot, having effectually silenced, if not convinced me, leaned back with a satisfied air.

On the boat, I knew better than to disturb my friend's solitude. The weather was gorgeous, and the sea as smooth as the proverbial mill-pond, so I was hardly surprised when a smiling Poirot joined me on disembarking at Calais. A disappointment was in store for us, as no car had been sent to meet us, but Poirot put this down to his telegram having been delayed in transit.

"We will hire a car," he said

cheerfully. And a few minutes later saw us creaking and jolting along, in the most ramshackle of automobiles that ever plied for hire, in the direction of Merlinville.

My spirits were at their highest, but my little friend was observing me gravely.

"You are what the Scotch people call "fey," Hastings. It presages disaster."

"Nonsense. At any rate, you do not share my feelings."

"No, but I am afraid."

"Afraid of what?"

"I do not know. But I have a premonition — a *je ne sais quoi!*"

He spoke so gravely that I was impressed in spite of myself.

"I have a feeling," he said slowly, "that this is going to be a big affair — a long, troublesome problem that will not be easy to work out."

I would have questioned him further, but we were just coming into the little town of Merlinville, and we slowed up to inquire the way to the Villa Geneviève.

"Straight on, monsieur, through the town. The Villa Geneviève is about half a mile the other side. You cannot miss it. A big villa, overlooking the sea."

We thanked our informant, and drove on, leaving the town behind. A fork in the road brought us to a second halt. A peasant was trudging towards us, and we waited for him to come up to us in order to ask the way again. There was a tiny villa standing right by the road, but it was too small and dilapidated to be the one we wanted. As we waited, the gate of it swung open and a girl came out.

The peasant was passing us now, and the driver leaned forward from his seat and asked for direction.

"The Villa Geneviève? Just a few steps up this road to the right, monsieur. You could see it if it were not for the curve."

The chauffeur thanked him, and started the car again. My eyes were fascinated by the girl who still stood, with one hand on the gate, watching us. I am an admirer of beauty, and here was one whom nobody could have passed without remark. Very tall, with the proportions of a young goddess, her uncovered golden head gleaming in the sunlight — I swore to myself that she was one of the most beautiful girls I had ever seen. As we swung up the rough road, I turned my head to look after her.

"By Jove, Poirot," I exclaimed, "did you see that young goddess?"

Poirot raised his eyebrows.

"*Ça commence!*" he murmured. "Already you have seen a goddess!"

"But, hang it all, wasn't she?"

"Possibly, I did not remark the fact."

"Surely you noticed her?"

"*Mon ami*, two people rarely see the same thing. You, for instance, saw a goddess. I —"

He hesitated.

"Yes?"

"I saw only a girl with anxious eyes," said Poirot gravely.

But at that moment we drew up at a big green gate, and, simultaneously, we both uttered an exclamation. Before it stood an imposing *sergent de ville*. He held up his hand to bar our way.

"You cannot pass, messieurs."

"But we wish to see Mr. Renauld," I cried. "We have an appointment. This is his villa, isn't it?"

"Yes, monsieur, but —"

Poirot leaned forward. "But what?"

"Monsieur Renauld was murdered this morning."

# III.

## AT THE VILLA GENEVIÈVE.

In a moment Poirot had leapt from the car, his eyes blazing with excitement.

"What is that you say? Murdered? When? How?"

The *sergent de ville* drew himself up.

"I cannot answer any questions, monsieur."

"True. I comprehend." Poirot reflected for a minute. "The Commissary of Police, he is without doubt within?"

"Yes, monsieur."

Poirot took out a card, and scribbled a few words on it.

"*Voilà*! Will you have the goodness to see that this card is sent in to the commissary at once?"

The man took it and, turning his head over his shoulder, whistled. In a few seconds a comrade joined him, and was handed Poirot's message. There was a wait of some minutes, and then a short, stout man with a huge moustache came bustling down to the gate. The *sergent de ville* saluted and stood aside.

"My dear Monsieur Poirot," cried the newcomer, "I am delighted to see you. Your arrival is most opportune."

Poirot's face had lighted up.

"Monsieur Bex! This is indeed a pleasure." He turned to me. "This is an English friend of mine, Captain Hastings—Monsieur Lucien Bex."

The commissary and I bowed

to each other ceremoniously, and Monsieur Bex turned once more to Poirot.

"*Mon vieux*, I have not seen you since 1909, that time in Ostend. You have information to give which may assist us?"

"Possibly you know it already. You were aware that I had been sent for?"

"No. By whom?"

"The dead man. It seems that he knew an attempt was going to be made on his life. Unfortunately he sent for me too late."

"*Sacré tonnerre!*" ejaculated the Frenchman. "So he foresaw his own murder. That upsets our theories considerably! But come inside."

He held the gate open, and we commenced walking towards the house. Monsieur Bex continued to talk:

"The examining magistrate, Monsieur Hautet, must hear of this at once. He has just finished examining the scene of the crime and is about to begin his interrogations."

"When was the crime committed?" asked Poirot.

"The body was discovered this morning about nine o'clock. Madame Renauld's evidence and that of the doctors goes to show that death must have occurred about 2 a.m. But enter, I pray of you."

We had arrived at the steps which led up to the front door of the villa. In the hall another *sergent de ville* was sitting. He rose at sight of the commissary.

"Where is Monsieur Hautet now?" inquired the latter.

"In the *salon*, monsieur."

Monsieur Bex opened a door to the left of the hall, and we passed in. Monsieur Hautet and his clerk were sitting at a big round table. They looked up as we entered. The commissary introduced us, and explained our presence.

Monsieur Hautet, the *Juge d'Instruction*, was a tall gaunt man, with piercing dark eyes, and a neatly cut grey beard, which he had a habit of caressing as he talked. Standing by the mantelpiece was an elderly man, with slightly stooping shoulders, who was introduced to us as Dr. Durand.

"Most extraordinary," remarked Monsieur Hautet as the commissary finished speaking. "You have the letter here, monsieur?"

Poirot handed it to him, and the magistrate read it.

"H'm! He speaks of a secret. What a pity he was not more explicit. We are much indebted to you, Monsieur Poirot. I hope you will do us the honour of assisting us in our investigations. Or are you obliged to return to London?"

"Monsieur le juge, I propose to remain. I did not arrive in time to prevent my client's death, but I feel myself bound in honour to discover the assassin."

The magistrate bowed.

"These sentiments do you honour. Also, without doubt, Madame Renauld will wish to retain your services. We are expecting Monsieur Giraud from the Súreté in Paris any moment, and I am sure that you and he will be able to give each other mutual assistance in your investigations. In the meantime, I hope that you will do me the honour to be present at my interrogations, and I need hardly say that if there is any assistance you require it is at your disposal."

"I thank you, monsieur. You will comprehend that at present I am completely in the dark. I know nothing whatever."

Monsieur Hautet nodded to the commissary, and the latter took up the tale:

"This morning, the old servant Françoise, on descending to start her work, found the front door ajar. Feeling a momentary alarm as to burglars, she looked into the dining-room, but seeing the silver was safe she thought no more about it, concluding that her master had, without doubt, risen early, and gone for a stroll."

"Pardon, monsieur, for interrupting, but was that a common practice of his?"

"No, it was not, but old Françoise has the common idea as regards the English — that they are mad, and liable to do the most unaccountable things at any moment! Going to call her mistress as usual, a young maid, Léonie, was horrified to discover her gagged and bound, and almost at the same moment news was brought that Monsieur Renauld's body had been discovered, stone dead, stabbed in the back."

"Where?"

"That is one of the most extraordinary features of the case. Monsieur Poirot, the body was lying face downwards, *in an open grave.*"

"What?"

"Yes. The pit was freshly dug — just a few yards outside the boundary of the villa grounds."

"And it had been dead — how long?"

Dr. Durand answered this.

"I examined the body this morning at ten o'clock. Death must have taken place at least seven, and possibly ten hours previously."

"H'm! that fixes it at between midnight and 3 a.m."

"Exactly, and Mrs. Renauld's evidence places it at after 2 a.m., which narrows the field still farther. Death must have been instantaneous, and naturally could not have been self-inflicted."

Poirot nodded, and the commissary resumed:

"Madame Renauld was hastily freed from the cords that bound her by the horrified servants. She was in a terrible condition of weakness, almost unconscious from the pain of her bonds. It appears that two masked men entered the bedroom, gagged and bound her, while forcibly abducting her husband. This we know at second hand from the servants. On hearing the tragic news, she fell at once into an alarming state of agitation. On arrival, Dr. Durand immediately prescribed a sedative, and we have not yet been able to question her. But without doubt she will awake more calm, and be equal to bearing the strain of the interrogation."

The commissary paused.

"And the inmates of the house, monsieur?"

"There is old Françoise, the housekeeper, she lived for many years with the former owners of the Villa Geneviève. Then there are two young girls, sisters, Denise and Léonie Oulard. Their home is in Merlinville, and they come of most respectable parents. Then there is the chauffeur whom Monsieur Renauld brought over from England with him, but he is away on a holiday. Finally there are Madame Renauld and her son, Monsieur Jack Renauld. He, too, is away from home at present."

Poirot bowed his head. Monsieur Hautet spoke: "Marchaud!"

The *sergent de ville* appeared.

"Bring in the woman Françoise."

The man saluted, and disappeared. In a moment or two he returned, escorting the frightened Françoise.

"Your name is Françoise Arrichet?"

"Yes, monsieur."

"You have been a long time in service at the Villa Geneviève?"

"Eleven years with Madame la Vicomtesse. Then when she sold the Villa this spring, I consented to remain on with the English milor.' Never did I imagine —"

The magistrate cut her short.

"Without doubt, without doubt. Now, Françoise, in this matter of the front door, whose business was it to fasten it at night?"

"Mine, monsieur. Always I saw to it myself."

"And last night?"

"I fastened it as usual."

"You are sure of that?"

"I swear it by the blessed saints, monsieur."

"What time would that be?"

"The same time as usual, half past ten, monsieur."

"What about the rest of the household, had they gone up to bed?"

"Madame had retired some time before. Denise and Léonie went up with me. Monsieur was still in his study."

"Then, if anyone unfastened the door afterwards, it must have been Monsieur Renauld himself?"

Françoise shrugged her broad shoulders. "What should he do that for? With robbers and assassins passing every minute! A nice idea! Monsieur was not an *imbecile*. It is not as though he had had to let the lady out —"

The magistrate interrupted sharply: "The lady? What lady do you mean?"

"Why, the lady who came to see him."

"Had a lady been to see him that evening?"

"But yes, monsieur — and many other evenings as well."

"Who was she? Did you know her?"

A rather cunning look spread over the woman's face.

"How should I know who it was?" she grumbled. "I did not let her in last night."

"Aha!" roared the examining magistrate, bringing his hand down with a bang on the table. "You would trifle with the police, would you? I demand that you tell me at once the name of this woman who came to visit Monsieur Renauld in the evenings."

"The police — the police," grumbled Françoise. "Never did I think that I should be mixed up with the police. But I know well enough who she was. It was Madame Daubreuil."

The commissary uttered an exclamation, and leaned forward as though in utter astonishment.

"Madame Daubreuil — from the Villa Marguerite just down the road?"

"That is what I said, monsieur. Oh, she is a pretty one."

The old woman tossed her head scornfully.

"Madame Daubreuil," murmured the commissary. "Impossible."

"*Voilà*," grumbled Françoise. "That is all you get for telling the truth."

"Not at all," said the examining magistrate soothingly. "We were surprised, that is all. Madame Daubreuil then, and Monsieur Renauld, they were — ?" He paused delicately. "Eh? It was that without doubt?"

"How should I know? But what will you? Monsieur, he was *milord anglais* — *très riche* — and Madame Daubreuil, she was poor, that one — and *très chic*, for all that she lives so quietly with her daughter. Not a doubt of it, she has had her history! She is no longer young, but *ma foi!* I who speak to you have seen the men's heads turn after her as she goes down the street. Besides lately, she had had more money to spend — all the town knows it. The little economies, they are at an end." And Françoise shook her head with an air of unalterable certainty.

Monsieur Hautet stroked his beard reflectively.

"And Madame Renauld?" he asked at length. "How did she take this — friendship?"

Françoise shrugged her shoulders.

"She was always most amiable — most polite. One would say that she suspected nothing. But all the same, is it not so, the heart suffers, monsieur? Day by day, I have watched Madame grow paler and thinner. She was not the same woman who arrived here a month ago. Monsieur, too, has changed. He also has had his worries. One could see that he was on the brink of a crisis of the nerves. And who could wonder, with an affair conducted in such a fashion? No reticence, no discretion. *Style anglais*, without doubt!"

I bounded indignantly in my seat, but the examining magistrate was continuing his questions, undistracted by side issues.

"You say that Monsieur Renauld had let Madame Daubreuil out? Had she left, then?"

"Yes, monsieur. I heard them come out of the study and go to the door. Monsieur said goodnight, and shut the door after her."

"What time was that?"

"About twenty-five minutes after ten, monsieur."

"Do you know when Monsieur Renauld went to bed?"

"I heard him come up about ten minutes after we did. The stair creaks so that one hears everyone who goes up and down."

"And that is all? You heard no sound of disturbance during the night?"

"Nothing whatever, monsieur."

"Which of the servants came down the first in the morning?"

"I did, monsieur. At once I saw the door swinging open."

"What about the other downstairs windows, were they all fastened?"

"Every one of them. There was nothing suspicious or out of place anywhere."

"Good. Françoise, you can go."

The old woman shuffled towards the door. On the threshold she looked back.

"I will tell you one thing, monsieur. That Madame Daubreuil she is a bad one! Oh, yes, one woman knows about another. She is a bad one, remember that." And, shaking her head sagely, Françoise left the room.

"Léonie Oulard," called the magistrate.

Léonie appeared dissolved in tears, and inclined to be hysterical. Monsieur Hautet dealt with her adroitly. Her evidence was mainly concerned with the discovery of her mistress gagged and bound, of which she gave rather an exaggerated account. She, like Françoise, had heard nothing during the night.

Her sister, Denise, succeeded her. She agreed that her master had changed greatly of late.

"Every day he became more and more morose. He ate less. He was always depressed." But Denise had her own theory. "Without doubt it was the Mafia he had on his track! Two masked men — who else could it be? A terrible society that!"

"It is, of course, possible," said the magistrate smoothly. "Now, my girl, was it you who admitted Madame Daubreuil to the house last night?"

"Not *last* night, monsieur, the night before."

"But Françoise has just told us that Madame Daubreuil was here last night?"

"No, monsieur. A lady did come to see Monsieur Renauld last night, but it was not Madame Daubreuil."

Surprised, the magistrate insisted, but the girl held firm. She knew Madame Daubreuil perfectly by sight. This lady was dark also, but shorter, and much younger. Nothing could shake her statement.

"Had you ever seen this lady before?"

"Never, monsieur." And then the girl added diffidently: "But I think she was English."

"English?"

"Yes, monsieur. She asked for Monsieur Renauld in quite good French, but the accent — however slight, one can always tell it. Besides, when they came out of the study they were speaking in English."

"Did you hear what they said? Could you understand it, I mean?"

"Me, I speak the English very well," said Denise with pride. "The lady was speaking too fast for me to catch what she said, but I heard Monsieur's last words as he opened the door for her."

She paused, and then repeated carefully and laboriously: "'Yeas — yeas — but for Gaud's saike go nauw!'"

"Yes, yes, but for God's sake go now!" repeated the magistrate.

He dismissed Denise and, after a moment or two for consideration, recalled Françoise. To her he propounded the question as to whether she had not made a mistake in fixing the night of Madame Daubreuil's visit. Françoise, however, proved unexpectedly obstinate. It was last night that Madame Daubreuil had come. Without doubt it was she. Denise wished to make herself interesting, *voilà tout!* So she had cooked up this fine tale about a strange lady. Airing her knowledge of English, too! Probably Monsieur had never spoken that sentence in English at all, and, even if he had, it proved nothing, for Madame Daubreuil spoke English perfectly, and generally used that language when talking to Monsieur and Madame Renauld. "You see, Monsieur Jack, the son of Monsieur, was usually here, and he spoke the French very badly."

The magistrate did not insist. Instead, he inquired about the chauffeur, and learned that only yesterday Monsieur Renauld had declared that he was not likely to use the car, and that Masters might just as well take a holiday.

A perplexed frown was beginning to gather between Poirot's eyes.

"What is it?" I whispered.

He shook his head impatiently, and asked a question:

"Pardon, Monsieur Bex, but without doubt Monsieur Renauld could drive the car himself?"

The commissary looked over at Françoise, and the old woman replied promptly:

"No, Monsieur did not drive himself."

Poirot's frown deepened.

"I wish you would tell me what is worrying you," I said impatiently.

"See you not? In his letter Monsieur Renauld speaks of sending the car for me to Calais."

"Perhaps he meant a hired car," I suggested.

"Doubtless, that is so. But why

hire a car when you have one of your own? Why choose yesterday to send away the chauffeur on a holiday—suddenly, at a moment's notice? Was it that for some reason he wanted him out of the way before we arrived?"

# IV.

## THE LETTER SIGNED "BELLA."

Françoise had left the room. The magistrate was drumming thoughtfully on the table.

"Monsieur Bex," he said at length, "here we have directly conflicting testimony. Which are we to believe, Françoise or Denise?"

"Denise," said the commissary decidedly. "It was she who let the visitor in. Françoise is old and obstinate, and has evidently taken a dislike to Madame Daubreuil. Besides, our own knowledge tends to show that Renauld was entangled with another woman."

"*Tiens!*" cried Monsieur Hautet. "We have forgotten to inform Monsieur Poirot of that." He searched among the papers on the table, and finally handed the one he was in search of to my friend. "This letter, Monsieur Poirot, we found in the pocket of the dead man's overcoat."

Poirot took it and unfolded it. It was somewhat worn and crumpled, and was written in English in a rather unformed hand:

> *My Dearest One, — Why have you not written for so long? You do love me still, don't you? Your letters lately have been so different, cold, and strange, and now this long silence. It makes me afraid. If you were to stop loving me! But that's impossible — what a silly kid I am — always imagining things! But if you did stop loving me, I don't know what I should do — kill myself perhaps!*

*I couldn't live without you. Sometimes I fancy another woman is coming between us. Let her look out, that's all — and you too! I'd as soon kill you as let her have you! I mean it.*

*But there, I'm writing high-flown nonsense. You love me, and I love you — yes, love you, love you, love you!*

*Your own adoring*

*Bella.*

There was no address or date. Poirot handed it back with a grave face.

"And the assumption is — ?"

The examining magistrate shrugged his shoulders.

"Obviously Monsieur Renauld was entangled with this Englishwoman — Bella! He comes over here, meets Madame Daubreuil, and starts an intrigue with her. He cools off to the other, and she instantly suspects something. This letter contains a distinct threat. Monsieur Poirot, at first sight the case seemed simplicity itself. Jealousy! The fact that Monsieur Renauld was stabbed in the back seemed to point distinctly to its being a woman's crime."

Poirot nodded.

"The stab in the back, yes — but not the grave! That was laborious work, hard work — no woman dug that grave, Monsieur. That was a man's doing."

The commissary exclaimed excitedly:

"Yes, yes, you are right. We did not think of that."

"As I said," continued Monsieur Hautet, "at first sight the case seemed simple, but the masked men, and the letter you received from Monsieur Renauld, complicate matters. Here we seem to have an entirely different set of circumstances, with no relationship between the two. As regards the letter written to yourself, do you think it is possible that it referred in any way to this "Bella" and her threats?"

Poirot shook his head.

"Hardly. A man like Monsieur Renauld, who had led an adventurous life in out-of-the-way places, would not be likely to ask for protection against a woman."

The examining magistrate nodded his head emphatically.

"My view exactly. Then we must look for the explanation of the letter —"

"In Santiago," finished the commissary. "I shall cable without delay to the police in that city, requesting full details of the murdered man's life out there, his love affairs, his business transactions, his friendships, and any enmities he may have incurred. It will be strange if, after that, we do not hold a clue to his mysterious murder."

The commissary looked around for approval. "Excellent!" said Poirot appreciatively.

"You have found no other letters from this Bella among Monsieur Renauld's effects?" asked Poirot.

"No. Of course one of our first proceedings was to search through his private papers in the study. We found nothing of interest, however. All seemed square and above-board. The only thing at all out of the ordinary was his will. Here it is."

Poirot ran through the document.

"So. A legacy of a thousand pounds to Mr. Stonor — who is he, by the way?"

"Monsieur Renauld's secretary. He remained in England, but was over here once or twice for a weekend."

"And everything else left unconditionally to his beloved wife, Eloise. Simply drawn up, but perfectly legal. Witnessed by the two servants, Denise and Françoise. Nothing so very unusual about that." He handed it back.

"Perhaps," began Bex, "you did not notice —"

"The date?" twinkled Poirot. "But, yes, I noticed it. A fortnight ago. Possibly it marks his first intimation of danger. Many rich men die intestate through never considering the likelihood of their demise. But it is dangerous to draw conclusions prematurely. It points, however, to his having a real liking and fondness for his wife, in spite of his amorous intrigues."

"Yes," said Monsieur Hautet doubtfully. "But it is possibly a little unfair on his son, since it leaves him entirely dependent on his mother. If she were to marry again, and her second husband obtained an ascendancy over her, this boy might never touch a penny of his father's money."

Poirot shrugged his shoulders.

"Man is a vain animal. Monsieur Renauld figured to himself, without doubt, that his widow would never marry again. As to the son, it may have been a wise precaution to leave the money in his mother's hands. The sons of rich men are proverbially wild."

"It may be as you say. Now, Monsieur Poirot, you would without doubt like to visit the scene of the crime. I am sorry that the body has been removed, but of course photographs have been taken from every conceivable angle, and will be at your disposal as soon as they are available."

"I thank you, monsieur, for all your courtesy."

The commissary rose.

"Come with me, messieurs."

He opened the door, and bowed ceremoniously to Poirot to precede him. Poirot, with equal politeness, drew back and bowed to the commissary.

"Monsieur."

"Monsieur."

At last they got out into the hall.

"That room there, it is the study, *hein?*" asked Poirot suddenly, nodding towards the door opposite.

"Yes. You would like to see it?"

He threw open the door as he spoke, and we entered.

The room which Monsieur Renauld had chosen for his own particular use was small, but furnished with great taste and comfort. A business-like writing-desk, with many pigeonholes, stood in the window. Two large leather-covered armchairs faced the fireplace, and between them was a round table covered with the latest books and magazines.

Poirot stood a moment taking in the room, then he stepped forward, passed his hand lightly over the backs of the leather chairs, picked up a magazine from the table, and drew a finger gingerly over the surface of the oak sideboard. His face expressed complete approval.

"No dust?" I asked, with a smile.

He beamed on me, appreciative of my knowledge of his peculiarities.

"Not a particle, *mon ami!* And for once, perhaps, it is a pity."

His sharp, birdlike eyes darted here and there.

"Ah!" he remarked suddenly, with an intonation of relief. "The hearth-rug is crooked," and he bent down to straighten it.

Suddenly he uttered an exclamation and rose. In his hand he held a small fragment of pink paper.

"In France, as in England," he remarked, "the domestics omit to sweep under the mats?"

Bex took the fragment from him, and I came close to examine it.

"You recognize it — eh, Hastings?"

I shook my head, puzzled — and yet that particular shade of pink paper was very familiar.

The commissary's mental processes were quicker than mine. "A fragment of a cheque," he exclaimed.

The piece of paper was roughly about two inches square. On it was written in ink the word "Duveen."

"*Bien!*" said Bex. "This cheque was payable to, or drawn by, someone named Duveen."

"The former, I fancy," said Poirot. "For, if I am not mistaken, the handwriting is that of Monsieur Renauld."

That was soon established, by comparing it with a memorandum from the desk.

"Dear me," murmured the commissary, with a crestfallen air, "I really cannot imagine how I came to overlook this."

Poirot laughed.

"The moral of that is, always look under the mats! My friend Hastings here will tell you that anything in the least crooked is a torment to me. As soon as I saw that the hearthrug was out of the straight, I said to myself: "*Tiens!* The legs of the chair caught it in being pushed back. Possibly there may be something beneath it which the good Françoise overlooked."'

"Françoise?"

"Or Denise, or Léonie. Whoever did this room. Since there is no dust, the room must have been done this morning. I reconstruct the incident like this. Yesterday, possibly last night, Monsieur Renauld drew a cheque to the order of someone named Duveen. Afterwards it was torn up, and scattered on the floor. This morning —"

But Monsieur Bex was already pulling impatiently at the bell.

Françoise answered it. Yes, there had been a lot of pieces of paper on the floor. What had she done with them? Put them in the kitchen stove of course! What else?

With a gesture of despair, Bex dismissed her. Then, his face lightening, he ran to the desk. In a minute he was hunting through the dead man's cheque book. Then he repeated his former gesture. The last counterfoil was blank.

"*Courage!*" cried Poirot, clapping him on the back. "Without doubt, Madame Renauld will be able to tell us all about this mysterious person named Duveen."

The commissary's face cleared. "That is true. Let us proceed."

As we turned to leave the room, Poirot remarked casually: "It was here that Monsieur Renauld received his guest last night, eh?"

"It was — but how did you know?"

"By this. I found it on the back of the leather chair." And he held up between his finger and thumb a long black hair — a woman's hair!

Monsieur Bex took us out by the back of the house to where there was a small shed leaning against the house. He produced a key from his pocket and unlocked it.

"The body is here. We moved it from the scene of the crime just before you arrived, as the photographers had done with it."

He opened the door and we passed in. The murdered man lay on the ground, with a sheet over him. Monsieur Bex dexterously whipped off the covering.

Renauld was a man of medium height, slender, and lithe in figure. He looked about fifty years of age, and his dark hair was plentifully streaked with grey. He was clean-shaven with a long, thin nose, and eyes set rather close together, and his skin was deeply bronzed, as that of a man who had spent most of his life beneath tropical skies His lips were drawn back from his teeth and an expression of absolute amazement and terror was stamped on the livid features.

"One can see by his face that he was stabbed in the back," remarked Poirot.

Very gently, he turned the dead man over. There, between the shoulder-blades, staining the light fawn overcoat, was a round dark patch. In the middle of it there was a slit in the cloth. Poirot examined it narrowly.

"Have you any idea with what weapon the crime was committed?"

"It was left in the wound." The commissary reached down a large glass jar. In it was a small object that looked to me more like a paper-knife than anything else. It had a black handle and a narrow shining blade.

The whole thing was not more than ten inches long.

Poirot tested the discoloured point gingerly with his fingertip.

"*Ma foi!* but it is sharp! A nice easy little tool for murder!"

"Unfortunately, we could find no trace of fingerprints on it," remarked Bex regretfully. "The murderer must have worn gloves."

"Of course he did," said Poirot contemptuously. "Even in Santiago they know enough for that. The veriest amateur of an English Mees knows it — thanks to the publicity the Bertillon system has been given in the Press. All the same, it interests me very much that there were no fingerprints. It is so amazingly simple to leave the fingerprints of someone else! And then the police are happy." He shook his head. "I very much fear our criminal is not a man of method — either that or he was pressed for time. But we shall see."

He let the body fall back into its original position.

"He wore only underclothes under his overcoat, I see," he remarked.

"Yes, the examining magistrate thinks that is rather a curious point."

At this minute there was a tap on the door which Bex had closed after him. He strode forward and opened it. Françoise was there. She endeavoured to peep in with ghoulish curiosity.

"Well, what is it?" demanded Bex impatiently.

"Madame. She sends a message that she is much recovered and is quite ready to receive the examining magistrate."

"Good," said Monsieur Bex briskly. "Tell Monsieur Hautet and say that we will come at once."

Poirot lingered a moment, looking back towards the body I thought for a moment that he was going to apostrophize it, to declare aloud his determination never to rest till he had discovered the murderer. But when he spoke, it was tamely and awkwardly, and his comment was ludicrously inappropriate to the solemnity of the moment.

"He wore his overcoat very long," he said constrainedly.

# V.

## MRS. RENAULD'S STORY.

We found Monsieur Hautet awaiting us in the hall, and we all proceeded upstairs together, Françoise marching ahead to show us the way. Poirot went up in a zigzag fashion which puzzled me, until he whispered with a grimace:

"No wonder the servants heard Monsieur Renauld the stairs, not a board of them but creaks fit to awake the dead!"

At the head of the staircase, a small passage branched off.

"The servants' quarters," explained Bex.

We continued along a corridor, and Françoise tapped on the last door to the right of it.

A faint voice bade us enter, and we passed into a large, sunny apartment looking out towards the sea, which showed blue and sparkling about a quarter of a mile distant.

On a couch, propped up with cushions, and attended by Dr. Durand, lay a tall, striking-looking woman. She was middle-aged, and her once dark hair was now almost entirely silvered, but the intense vitality and strength of her personality would have made itself felt anywhere. You knew at once that you were in the presence of what the French call *une maîtresse femme.*

She greeted us with a dignified inclination of the head.

"Pray be seated, messieurs."

We took chairs, and the magistrate's clerk established himself at a round table.

"I hope, madame," began Monsieur Hautet, "that it will not distress you unduly to relate to us what occurred last night?"

"Not at all, monsieur. I know the value of time, if these scoundrelly assassins are to be caught and punished."

"Very well, madame. It will fatigue you less, I think, if I ask you questions and you confine yourself to answering them. At what time did you go to bed last night?"

"At half past nine, monsieur. I was tired."

"And your husband?"

"About an hour later, I fancy."

"Did he seem disturbed — upset in any way?"

"No, not more than usual."

"What happened then?"

"We slept. I was awakened by a hand pressed over my mouth. I tried to scream out, but the hand prevented me. There were two men in the room. They were both masked."

"Can you describe them at all, madame?"

"One was very tall, and had a long black beard; the other was short and stout. His beard was reddish. They both wore hats pulled down over their eyes."

"H'm!" said the magistrate thoughtfully. "Too much beard, I fear."

"You mean they were false?"

"Yes, madame. But continue your story."

"It was the short man who was holding me. He forced a gag into my mouth, and then bound me with rope hand and foot. The other man was standing over my husband. He had caught up my little dagger paper-knife from the dressing-table and was holding it with the point just over his heart. When the short man had finished with me, he joined the other, and they forced my husband to get up and accompany them into the dressing-room next door. I was nearly fainting with terror, nevertheless I listened desperately.

"They were speaking in too low a tone for me to hear what they said. But I recognized the language, a bastard Spanish such as is spoken in some parts of South America. They seemed to be demanding something from my husband, and presently they grew angry, and their voices rose a little. I think the tall man was speaking. 'You know what we want?' he said. '*The secret!* Where is it?' I do not know what my husband answered, but the other replied fiercely: 'You lie! We know you have it. Where are your keys?'

"Then I heard sounds of drawers being pulled out. There is a safe on the wall of my husband's dressing-room in which he always keeps a fairly large amount of ready money. Léonie tells me this has been rifled and the money taken, but evidently what they were looking for was not there, for presently I heard the tall man, with an oath, command my husband to dress himself. Soon after that, I think some noise in the house must have disturbed them, for they hustled my husband out into my room only half dressed."

"*Pardon*," interrupted Poirot, "but is there then no other egress from the dressing-room?"

"No, monsieur, there is only the communicating door into my room. They hurried my husband through, the short man in front, and the tall man behind him with the dagger still in his hand. Paul tried to break away to come to me. I saw his agonized eyes. He turned to his captors. "I must speak to her," he said. Then, coming to the side of the bed, "It is all right, Eloise," he said. "Do not be afraid. I shall return before morning." But, although he tried to make his voice confident, I could see the terror in his eyes. Then they hustled him out of the door, the tall man saying: 'One sound—and you are a dead man, remember.'

"After that," continued Mrs. Renauld, "I must have fainted. The next thing I recollect is Léonie rubbing my wrists and giving me brandy."

"Madame Renauld," said the magistrate, "had you any idea what it was for which the assassins were searching?"

"None whatever, monsieur."

"Had you any knowledge that your husband feared something?"

"Yes. I had seen the change in him."

"How long ago was that?"

Mrs. Renauld reflected.

"Ten days, perhaps."

"Not longer?"

"Possibly. I only noticed it then."

"Did you question your husband at all as to the cause?"

"Once. He put me off evasively. Nevertheless, I was convinced that he was suffering some terrible anxiety. However, since he evidently wished to conceal the fact from me, I tried to pretend that I had noticed nothing."

"Were you aware that he had called in the services of a detective?"

"A detective?" exclaimed Mrs. Renauld, very much surprised.

"Yes, this gentleman—Monsieur Hercule Poirot." Poirot bowed. "He arrived today in response to a summons from your husband." And taking the letter written by Monsieur Renauld from his pocket he handed it to the lady.

She read it with apparently genuine astonishment.

"I had no idea of this. Evidently he was fully cognizant of the danger."

"Now, madame, I will beg of you to be frank with me. Is there any incident in your husband's past life in South America which might throw light on his murder?"

Mrs. Renauld reflected deeply, but at last shook her head.

"I can think of none. Certainly my husband had many enemies, people he had got the better of in some way or another, but I can think of no one distinctive case. I do not say there is no such incident — only that I am not aware of it."

The examining magistrate stroked his beard disconsolately.

"And you can fix the time of this outrage?"

"Yes, I distinctly remember hearing the clock on the mantelpiece strike two."

She nodded towards an eight-day travelling clock in a leather case which stood in the centre of the chimney-piece.

Poirot rose from his seat, scrutinized the clock carefully, and nodded, satisfied.

"And here too," exclaimed Monsieur Bex, "is a wristwatch, knocked off the dressing-table by the assassins, without doubt, and smashed to atoms. Little did they know it would testify against them."

Gently he picked away the fragments of broken glass. Suddenly his face changed to one of utter stupefaction.

"*Mon Dieu!*" he ejaculated.

"What is it?"

"The hands of the watch point to seven o'clock!"

"What?" cried the examining magistrate, astonished.

But Poirot, deft as ever, took the broken trinket from the startled commissary, and held it to his ear. Then he smiled.

"The glass is broken, yes, but the watch itself is still going."

The explanation of the mystery was greeted with a relieved smile. But the magistrate bethought him of another point.

"But surely it is not seven o'clock now?"

"No," said Poirot gently, "it is a few minutes after five. Possibly the watch gains, is that so, madame?"

Mrs. Renauld was frowning perplexedly. "It does gain," she admitted. "But I've never known it gain quite so much as that."

With a gesture of impatience the magistrate left the matter of the watch and proceeded with his interrogatory.

"Madame, the front door was found ajar. It seems almost certain that the murderers entered that way, yet it has not been forced at all. Can you suggest any explanation?"

"Possibly my husband went out for a stroll the last thing, and forgot to latch it when he came in."

"Is that a likely thing to happen?"

"Very. My husband was the most absentminded of men."

There was a slight frown on her brow as she spoke, as though this trait in the dead man's character had at times vexed her.

"There is one inference I think we might draw," remarked the commissary suddenly. "Since the men insisted on Monsieur Renauld dressing himself, it looks as though the place they were taking him to, the place where 'the secret' was concealed, lay some distance away."

The magistrate nodded.

"Yes, far, and yet not too far, since he spoke of being back by morning."

"What time does the last train leave the station of Merlinville?" asked Poirot.

"11:50 one way, and 12:17 the other, but it is more probable that they had a motor waiting."

"Of course," agreed Poirot, looking somewhat crestfallen.

"Indeed, that might be one way of tracing them," continued the magistrate, brightening. "A motor containing two foreigners is quite likely to have been noticed. That is an excellent point, Monsieur Bex."

He smiled to himself, and then, becoming grave once more, he said to Mrs.Renauld:

"There is another question. Do you know anyone of the name of "Duveen'?"

"Duveen?" Mrs. Renauld repeated thoughtfully. "No, for the moment, I cannot say I do."

"You have never heard your husband mention anyone of that name."

"Never."

"Do you know anyone whose Christian name is Bella?"

He watched Mrs. Renauld narrowly as he spoke, seeking to surprise any signs of anger or consciousness, but she merely shook her head in quite a natural manner. He continued his questions.

"Are you aware that your husband had a visitor last night?"

Now he saw the red mount slightly in her cheeks, but she replied composedly:

"No, who was that?"

"A lady."

"Indeed?"

But for the moment the magistrate was content to say no more. It seemed unlikely that Madame Daubreuil had any connexion with the crime, and he was anxious not to upset Mrs. Renauld more than necessary.

He made a sign to the commissary, and the latter replied with a nod. Then rising, he went across the room, and returned with the glass jar we had seen in the outhouse in his hand. From this he took the dagger.

"Madame," he said gently, "do you recognize this?"

She gave a little cry.

"Yes, that is my little dagger." Then she saw the stained point, and she drew back, her eyes widening with horror. "Is that—blood?"

"Yes, madame. Your husband was killed with this weapon." He removed it hastily from sight. "You are quite sure about its being the one that was on your dressing-table last night?"

"Oh, yes. It was a present from my son. He was in the Air Force during the War. He gave his age as older than it was." There was a touch of the proud mother in her voice. "This was made from a streamline aeroplane wire, and was given to me by my son as a souvenir of the War."

"I see, madame. That brings us to another matter. Your son, where is he now? It is necessary that he should be telegraphed to without delay."

"Jack? He is on his way to Buenos Aires."

"What?"

"Yes. My husband telegraphed to him yesterday. He had sent him on business to Paris, but yesterday he discovered that it would be necessary for him to proceed without delay to South America. There was a boat leaving Cherbourg for Buenos Aires last night, and he wired him to catch it."

"Have you any knowledge of what the business in Buenos Aires was?"

"No, monsieur, I know nothing of its nature, but Buenos Aires is not my son's final destination. He was going overland from there to Santiago."

And, in unison, the magistrate and the commissary exclaimed:

"Santiago! Again Santiago!"

It was at this moment, when we were all stunned by the mention of that word, that Poirot approached Mrs. Renauld. He had been standing by the window like a man lost in a dream, and I doubt if he had fully taken in what had passed. He paused by the lady's side with a bow.

"*Pardon*, madame, but may I examine your wrists?"

Though slightly surprised at the request, Mrs. Renauld held them out to him. Round each of them was a cruel red mark where the cords had bitten into the flesh. As he examined them, I fancied that a momentary flicker of excitement I had seen in his eyes disappeared.

"They must cause you great pain," he said, and once more he looked puzzled.

But the magistrate was speaking excitedly.

"Young Monsieur Renauld must be communicated with at once by wireless. It is vital that we should know anything he can tell us about this trip to Santiago." He hesitated. "I hoped he might have been near at hand, so that we could have saved you pain, madame." He paused.

"You mean," she said in a low voice, "the identification of my husband's body?"

The magistrate bowed his head.

"I am a strong woman, monsieur. I can bear all that is required of me. I am ready — now."

"Oh, tomorrow will be quite soon enough, I assure you —"

"I prefer to get it over," she said in a low tone, a spasm of pain crossing her face. "If you will be so good as to give me your arm, doctor?"

The doctor hastened forward, a cloak was thrown over Mrs. Renauld's shoulders, and a slow procession went down the stairs. Monsieur Bex hurried on ahead to open the door of the shed. In a minute or two Mrs. Renauld appeared in the doorway. She was very pale, but resolute. She raised her hand to her face.

"A moment, messieurs, while I steel myself."

She took her hand away and looked down at the dead man. Then the marvellous self-control which had upheld her so far deserted her.

"Paul!" she cried. "Husband! Oh, God!" And pitching forward she fell unconscious to the ground.

Instantly Poirot was beside her; he raised the lid of her eye, felt her pulse. When he had satisfied himself that she had really fainted, he drew aside. He caught me by the arm.

"I am an imbecile, my friend! If ever there was love and grief in a woman's voice, I heard it then. My little idea was all wrong. *Eh bien!* I must start again!"

# VI.

## THE SCENE OF THE CRIME.

Between them, the doctor and Monsieur Hautet carried the unconscious woman into the house. The commissary looked after them, shaking his head.

"*Pauvre femme*," he murmured to himself. "The shock was too much for her. Well, well, we can do nothing Now, Monsieur Poirot, shall we visit the place where the crime was committed?"

"If you please, Monsieur Bex."

We passed through the house, and out by the front door. Poirot had looked up at the staircase in passing, and shook his head in a dissatisfied manner.

"It is to me incredible that the servants heard nothing. The creaking of that staircase, with three people descending it, would awaken the dead!"

"It was the middle of the night, remember. They were sound asleep by then."

But Poirot continued to shake his head as though not fully accepting the explanation. On the sweep of the drive he paused, looking up at the house.

"What moved them in the first place to try if the front door were open? It was a most unlikely thing that it should be. It was far more probable that they should at once try to force a window."

"But all the windows on the ground floor are barred with iron shutters," objected the commissary.

Poirot pointed to a window on the first floor.

"That is the window of the bedroom we have just come from, is it not? And see — there is a tree by which it would be the easiest thing in the world to mount."

"Possibly," admitted the other. "But they couldn't have done so without leaving footprints in the flowerbed."

I saw the justice of his words. There were two large oval flower-beds planted with scarlet geraniums, one each side of the steps leading up to the front door. The tree in question had its roots actually at the back of the bed itself, and it would have been impossible to reach it without stepping on the bed.

"You see," continued the commissary, "owing to the dry weather no prints would show on the drive or paths; but, on the soft mould of the flower-bed, it would have been a very different affair."

Poirot went close to the bed and studied it attentively. As Bex had said, the mould was perfectly smooth. There was not an indentation on it anywhere.

Poirot nodded, as though convinced, and we turned away, but he suddenly darted off and began examining the other flower-bed.

"Monsieur Bex!" he called. "See here. Here are plenty of traces for you."

The commissary joined him — and smiled.

"My dear Monsieur Poirot, those are without doubt the footprints of the gardener's large hobnailed boots. In any case, it would have no importance, since this side we have no tree, and consequently no means of gaining access to the upper storey."

"True," said Poirot, evidently crestfallen. "So you think these footprints are of no importance?"

"Not the least in the world."

Then, to my utter astonishment, Poirot pronounced these words:

"I do not agree with you. I have a little idea that these footprints are the most important things we have seen yet."

Monsieur Bex said nothing, merely shrugged his shoulders. He was far too courteous to utter his real opinion.

"Shall we proceed?" he asked, instead.

"Certainly. I can investigate this matter of the footprints later," said Poirot cheerfully.

Instead of following the drive down to the gate, Monsieur Bex turned up a path that branched off at right angles. It led, up a slight incline, round to the right of the house, and was bordered on either side by a kind of shrubbery. Suddenly it emerged into a little clearing from which one obtained a view of the sea. A seat had been placed here, and not far from it was a ramshackle shed. A few steps farther on, a neat line of small bushes marked the boundary of the Villa grounds. Monsieur Bex pushed his way through these, and we found ourselves on a wide stretch of open downs. I looked round, and saw something that filled me with astonishment.

"Why, this is a golf course," I cried.

Bex nodded.

"The links are not completed yet," he explained. "It is hoped to be able to open them sometime next month. It was some of the men working on them who discovered the body early this morning."

I gave a gasp. A little to my left, where for the moment I had overlooked it, was a long narrow pit and by it, face downwards, was the body of a man! For a moment my heart gave a terrible leap, and I had a wild fancy that the tragedy had been duplicated. But the commissary dispelled my illusion by moving forward with a sharp exclamation of annoyance:

"What have my police been about? They had strict orders to allow no one near the place without proper credentials!"

The man on the ground turned his head over his shoulder.

"But I have proper credentials," he remarked, and rose slowly to his feet.

"My dear Monsieur Giraud," cried the commissary. "I had no idea that you had arrived, even. The examining magistrate has been awaiting you with the utmost impatience."

As he spoke, I was scanning the newcomer with the keenest curiosity. The famous detective from the Paris Sûreté was familiar to me by name, and I was extremely interested to see him in the flesh. He was very tall, perhaps about thirty years of age, with auburn hair and moustache, and a military carriage. There was a trace of arrogance in his manner which showed that he was fully alive to his own importance. Bex introduced us, presenting Poirot as a colleague. A flicker of interest came into the detective's eye.

"I know you by name, Monsieur Poirot," he said. "You cut quite a figure in the old days, didn't you? But methods are very different now."

"Crimes, though, are very much the same," remarked Poirot gently.

I saw at once that Giraud was prepared to be hostile. He resented the other being associated with him, and I felt that if he came across any clue of importance he would be more than likely to keep it to himself.

"The examining magistrate —" began Bex again.

But Giraud interrupted rudely:

"A fig for the examining magistrate! The light is the important thing. For all practical purposes it will be gone in another half hour or so. I know all about the case, and the people at the house will do very well until tomorrow; but, if we're going to find a clue to the murderers, here is the spot we shall find it. Is it your police who have been trampling all over the place? I thought they knew better nowadays."

"Assuredly they do. The marks

you complain of were made by the workmen who discovered the body."

The other grunted disgustedly.

"I can see the tracks where the three of them came through the hedge — but they were cunning. You can just recognize the centre footmarks as those of Monsieur Renauld, but those on either side have been carefully obliterated. Not that there would really be much to see anyway on this hard ground, but they weren't taking any chances."

"The external sign," said Poirot. "That is what you seek, eh?"

The other detective stared. "Of course."

A very faint smile came to Poirot's lips. He seemed about to speak, but checked himself. He bent down to where a spade was lying.

"That's what the grave was dug with, right enough," said Giraud. "But you'll get nothing from it. It was Renauld's own spade, and the man who used it wore gloves. Here they are."

He gesticulated with his foot to where two soil-stained gloves were lying. "And they're Renauld's too — or at least his gardener's. I tell you, the men who carried out this crime were taking no chances. The man was stabbed with his own dagger, and would have been buried with his own spade. They counted on leaving no traces! But I'll beat them. There's always something! And I mean to find it."

But Poirot was now apparently interested in something else, a short, discoloured piece of lead-piping which lay beside the spade. He touched it delicately with his finger.

"And does this, too, belong to the murdered man?" he asked, and I thought I detected a subtle flavour of irony in the question.

Giraud shrugged his shoulders to indicate that he neither knew nor cared.

"May have been lying around here for weeks. Anyway, it doesn't interest me."

"I, on the contrary, find it very interesting," said Poirot sweetly.

I guessed that he was merely bent on annoying the Paris detective and, if so, he succeeded. The other turned away rudely, remarking that he had no time to waste, and bending down he resumed his minute search of the ground.

Meanwhile, Poirot, as though struck by a sudden idea, stepped back over the boundary, and tried the door of the little shed.

"That's locked," said Giraud over his shoulder. "But it's only a place where the gardener keeps his rubbish. The spade didn't come from there, but from the toolshed up by the house."

"Marvellous," murmured Monsieur Bex ecstatically to me. "He has been here but half an hour, and he already knows everything! What a man! Undoubtedly Giraud is the greatest detective alive today."

Although I disliked the detective heartily, I nevertheless was secretly impressed. Efficiency seemed to radiate from the man. I could not help feeling that, so far, Poirot had not greatly distinguished himself, and it vexed me. He seemed to be directing his attention to all sorts of silly puerile points that had nothing to do with the case. Indeed, at this juncture, he suddenly asked:

"Monsieur Bex, tell me, I pray you, the meaning of this whitewashed line that extends all round the grave. Is it a device of the police?"

"No, Monsieur Poirot, it is an affair of the golf course. It shows that there is here to be a 'bunkair,' as you call it."

"A bunkair?" Poirot turned to me. "That is the irregular hole filled with sand and a bank at one side, is it not?"

I concurred.

"Monsieur Renauld, without doubt he played the golf?"

"Yes, he was a keen golfer. It's mainly owing to him, and to his large subscriptions, that this work is being carried forward. He even had a say in the designing of it."

Poirot nodded thoughtfully. Then he remarked: "It was not a very good choice they made — of a spot to bury the body? When the men began to dig up the ground, all would have been discovered."

"Exactly," cried Giraud triumphantly. "And that proves that they were strangers to the place. It's an excellent piece of indirect evidence."

"Yes," said Poirot doubtfully. "No one who knew would bury a body there — unless they wanted it to be discovered. And that is clearly absurd, is it not?"

Giraud did not even trouble to reply.

"Yes," said Poirot, in a somewhat dissatisfied voice. "Yes — undoubtedly — absurd!"

# VII.

## THE MYSTERIOUS MADAME DAUBREUIL.

As we retraced our steps to the house, Monsieur Bex excused himself for leaving us, explaining that he must immediately acquaint the examining magistrate with the fact of Giraud's arrival. Giraud himself had been obviously delighted when Poirot declared that he had seen all he wanted. The last thing we observed, as we left the spot, was Giraud, crawling about on all fours, with a thoroughness in his search that I could not but admire. Poirot guessed my thoughts, for as soon as we were alone he remarked ironically:

"At last you have seen the detective you admire — the human foxhound! Is it not so, my friend?"

"At any rate, he's doing something," I said, with asperity. "If there's anything to find he'll find it. Now you —"

"*Eh bien!* I also have found something! A piece of lead-piping."

"Nonsense, Poirot. You know very well that's got nothing to do with it. I meant little things — traces that may lead us infallibly to the murderers."

"*Mon ami*, a clue of two feet long is every bit as valuable as one measuring two millimetres! But it is the romantic idea that all important clues must be infinitesimal. As to the piece of lead-piping having nothing to do with the crime, you say that because Giraud told you so. No"— as

I was about to interpose a question—"we will say no more. Leave Giraud to his search, and me to my ideas. The case seems straightforward enough—and yet—and yet, *mon ami*, I am not satisfied! And do you know why? Because of the wristwatch that is two hours fast. And then there are several curious little points that do not seem to fit in. For instance, if the object of the murderers was revenge, why did they not stab Renauld in his sleep and have done with it?"

"They wanted the 'secret,'" I reminded him.

Poirot brushed a speck of dust from his sleeve with a dissatisfied air.

"Well, where is this 'secret'? Presumably some distance away, since they wish him to dress himself. Yet he is found murdered close at hand, almost within ear-shot of the house. Then again, it is pure chance that a weapon such as the dagger should be lying about casually, ready to hand."

He paused, frowning, and then went on: "Why did the servants hear nothing? Were they drugged? Was there an accomplice, and did that accomplice see to it that the front door should remain open? I wonder if—"

He stopped abruptly. We had reached the drive in front of the house. Suddenly he turned to me.

"My friend, I am about to surprise you—to please you! I have taken your reproaches to heart! We will examine some footprints!"

"Where?"

"In that right-hand bed, yonder. Monsieur Bex says that they are the footmarks of the gardener. Let us see if this is so. See, he approaches with his wheelbarrow."

Indeed an elderly man was just crossing the drive with a barrowful of seedlings. Poirot called to him, and he set down the barrow and came hobbling towards us.

"You are going to ask him for one of his boots to compare with the footmarks?" I asked breathlessly. My faith in Poirot revived a little. Since he said the footprints in this right-hand bed were important, presumably they were.

"Exactly," said Poirot.

"But won't he think it very odd?"

"He will not think about it at all."

We could say no more, for the old man had joined us.

"You want me for something, monsieur?"

"Yes. You have been gardener here a long time, haven't you?"

"Twenty-four years, monsieur."

"And your name is—?"

"Auguste, monsieur."

"I was admiring these magnificent geraniums They are truly superb. They have been planted long?"

"Some time, monsieur. But of course, to keep the beds looking smart, one must keep bedding out a few new plants, and remove those that are over, besides keeping the old blooms well picked off."

"You put in some new plants

yesterday, didn't you? Those in the middle there, and in the other bed also."

"Monsieur has a sharp eye. It takes always a day or so for them to 'pick up.' Yes, I put ten new plants in each bed last night. As monsieur doubtless knows, one should not put in plants when the sun is hot."

Auguste was charmed with Poirot's interest, and was quite inclined to be garrulous.

"That is a splendid specimen there," said Poirot, pointing. "Might I perhaps have a cutting of it?"

"But certainly, monsieur."

The old fellow stepped into the bed, and carefully took a slip from the plant Poirot had admired.

Poirot was profuse in his thanks, and Auguste departed to his barrow.

"You see?" said Poirot with a smile, as he bent over the bed to examine the indentation of the gardener's hobnailed boot. "It is quite simple."

"I did not realize —"

"That the foot would be inside the boot? You do not use your excellent mental capacities sufficiently. Well, what of the footmark?"

I examined the bed carefully.

"All the footmarks in the bed were made by the same boot," I said at length after a careful study.

"You think so? *Eh bien!* I agree with you," said Poirot.

He seemed quite uninterested, and as though he were thinking of something else.

"At any rate," I remarked, "you will have one bee less in your bonnet now."

"*Mon Dieu!* But what an idiom! What does it mean?"

"What I meant was that now you will give up your interest in these footmarks."

But to my surprise Poirot shook his head. "No, no, *mon ami.* At last I am on the right track. I am still in the dark, but, as I hinted just now to Monsieur Bex these footmarks are the most important and interesting things in the case! That poor Giraud — I should not be surprised if he took no notice of them whatever."

At that moment the front door opened, and Monsieur Hautet and the commissary came down the steps.

"Ah, Monsieur Poirot, we were coming to look for you," said the magistrate. "It is getting late, but I wish to pay a visit to Madame Daubreuil. Without doubt she will be very much upset by Monsieur Renauld's death, and we may be fortunate enough to get a clue from her. The secret that he did not confide to his wife, it is possible that he may have told it to the woman whose love held him enslaved. We know where our Samsons are weak, don't we?"

We said no more, but fell into line. Poirot walked with the examining magistrate, and the commissary and I followed a few paces behind.

"There is no doubt that Françoise's story is substantially correct," he remarked to me in a confidential tone. "I have been telephoning headquarters. It seems that three times in the last six weeks — that is to say, since the arrival of Monsieur Renauld at Merlinville — Madame Daubreuil has paid a large sum in notes into her banking account. Altogether the sum totals two hundred thousand francs!"

"Dear me," I said, considering, "that must be something like four thousand pounds!"

"Precisely. Yes, there can be no doubt that he was absolutely infatuated. But it remains to be seen whether he confided his secret to her. The examining magistrate is hopeful, but I hardly share his views."

During this conversation we were walking down the lane towards the fork in the road where our car had halted earlier in the afternoon, and in another moment I realized that the Villa Marguerite, the home of the mysterious Madame Daubreuil, was the small house from which the beautiful girl had emerged.

"She has lived here for many years," said the commissary nodding his head towards the house. "Very quietly, very unobtrusively. She seems to have no friends or relations other than the acquaintances she has made in Merlinville. She never refers to the past, nor to her husband. One does not even know if he is alive or dead. There is a mystery about her, you comprehend."

I nodded, my interest growing. "And — the daughter?" I ventured.

"A truly beautiful young girl — modest, devout, all that she should be. One pities her, for, though she may know nothing of the past, a man who wants to ask her hand in marriage must necessarily inform himself, and then —" The commissary shrugged his shoulders cynically.

"But it would not be her fault!" I cried, with rising indignation.

"No. But what will you? A man is particular about his wife's antecedents."

I was prevented from further argument by our arrival at the door. Monsieur Hautet rang the bell. A few minutes elapsed, and then we heard a footfall within, and the door was opened. On the threshold stood my young goddess of that afternoon. When she saw us, the colour left her cheeks, leaving her deathly white, and her eyes widened with apprehension. There was no doubt about it, she was afraid!

"Mademoiselle Daubreuil," said Monsieur Hautet, sweeping off his hat, "we regret infinitely to disturb you, but the exigencies of the Law, you comprehend? My compliments to madame your mother, and will she have the goodness to grant me a few moments' interview?"

For a moment the girl stood motionless. Her left hand was pressed to her side, as though to still the sudden unconquerable agitation of her heart. But she mastered herself, and said in a low voice:

"I will go and see. Please come inside."

She entered a room on the left of the hall, and we heard the low murmur of her voice. And then another voice, much the same in timbre, but with a slightly harder inflection behind its mellow roundness, said:

"But certainly. Ask them to enter."

In another minute we were face to face with the mysterious Madame Daubreuil.

She was not nearly so tall as her daughter, and the rounded curves of her figure had all the grace of full maturity. Her hair, again unlike her daughter's, was dark, and parted in the middle in the Madonna style. Her eyes, half hidden by the drooping lids, were blue. Though very well preserved, she was certainly no longer young, but her charm was of the quality which is independent of age.

"You wished to see me, monsieur?" she asked.

"Yes, madame." Monsieur Hautet cleared his throat. "I am investigating the death of Monsieur Renauld. You have heard of it, no doubt?"

She bowed her head without speaking. Her expression did not change.

"We came to ask you whether you can — er — throw any light upon the circumstances surrounding it?"

"I?" The surprise of her tone was excellent.

"Yes, madame. We have reason to believe that you were in the habit of visiting the dead man at his villa in the evenings. Is that so?"

The colour rose in the lady's pale cheeks, but she replied quietly:

"I deny your right to ask me such a question!"

"Madame, we are investigating a murder."

"Well, what of it? I had nothing to do with the murder."

"Madame, we do not say that for a moment. But you knew the dead man well. Did he ever confide in you as to any danger that threatened him?"

"Never."

"Did he ever mention his life in Santiago, and any enemies he may have made there?"

"No."

"Then you can give us no help at all?"

"I fear not. I really do not see why you should come to me. Cannot his wife tell you what you want to know?" Her voice held a slender inflection of irony.

"Mrs. Renauld has told us all she can."

"Ah!" said Madame Daubreuil. "I wonder —"

"You wonder what, madame?"

"Nothing."

The examining magistrate looked at her. He was aware that he was fighting a duel, and that he had no mean antagonist.

"You persist in your statement that Monsieur Renauld confided nothing to you?"

"Why should you think it likely that he should confide in me?"

"Because, madame," said

Monsieur Hautet, with calculated brutality, "a man tells to his mistress what he does not always tell to his wife."

"Ah!" She sprang forward. Her eyes flashed fire. "Monsieur, you insult me! And before my daughter! I can tell you nothing. Have the goodness to leave my house!"

The honours undoubtedly rested with the lady. We left the Villa Marguerite like a shamefaced pack of schoolboys. The magistrate muttered angry ejaculations to himself. Poirot seemed lost in thought. Suddenly he came out of his reverie with a start, and inquired of Monsieur Hautet if there was a good hotel near at hand.

"There is a small place, the Hotel des Bains, on this side of the town. A few hundred yards down the road. It will be handy for your investigations. We shall see you in the morning, then, I presume?"

"Yes, I thank you, Monsieur Hautet."

With mutual civilities we parted company, Poirot and I going towards Merlinville, and the others returning to the Villa Geneviève.

"The French police system is very marvellous," said Poirot, looking after them. "The information they possess about everyone's life, down to the most commonplace detail, is extraordinary. Though he has only been here a little over six weeks, they are perfectly well acquainted with Monsieur Renauld's tastes and pursuits, and at a moment's notice they can produce information as to Madame Daubreuil's banking account, and the sums that have lately been paid in! Undoubtedly the dossier is a great institution. But what is that?" He turned sharply.

A figure was running hatless down the road after us. It was Marthe Daubreuil.

"I beg your pardon," she cried breathlessly, as she reached us. "I—I should not do this, I know. You must not tell my mother. But is it true, what the people say, that Monsieur Renauld called in a detective before he died, and—and that you are he?"

"Yes, mademoiselle," said Poirot gently. "It is quite true. But how did you learn it?"

"Françoise told our Amélie," explained Marthe with a blush.

Poirot made a grimace.

"The secrecy, it is impossible in an affair of this kind! Not that it matters. Well, mademoiselle, what is it you want to know?"

The girl hesitated. She seemed longing, yet fearing, to speak. At last, almost in a whisper, she asked:

"Is—anyone suspected?"

Poirot eyed her keenly. Then he replied evasively:

"Suspicion is in the air at present, mademoiselle."

"Yes, I know—but—anyone in particular?"

"Why do you want to know?"

The girl seemed frightened by the question. All at once Poirot's words about her earlier in the day occurred to me. The "girl with the anxious eyes."

"Monsieur Renauld was always very kind to me," she replied at last. "It is natural that I should be interested."

"I see," said Poirot. "Well, mademoiselle, suspicion at present is hovering round two persons."

"Two?"

I could have sworn there was a note of surprise and relief in her voice.

"Their names are unknown, but they are presumed to be Chileans from Santiago. And now, mademoiselle, you see what comes of being young and beautiful! I have betrayed professional secrets for you!"

The girl laughed merrily, and then, rather shyly, she thanked him.

"I must run back now. Maman will miss me."

And she turned and ran back up the road, looking like a modern Atalanta. I stared after her.

"*Mon ami*," said Poirot, in his gentle ironical voice, "is it that we are to remain planted here all night—just because you have seen a beautiful young woman, and your head is in a whirl?"

I laughed and apologized.

"But she is beautiful, Poirot. Anyone might be excused for being bowled over by her."

But to my surprise Poirot shook his head very earnestly.

"Ah, *mon ami*, do not set your heart on Marthe Daubreuil. She is not for you, that one! Take it from Papa Poirot!"

"Why," I cried, "the commissary assured me that she was as good as she is beautiful! A perfect angel!"

"Some of the greatest criminals I have known had the faces of angels," remarked Poirot cheerfully. "A malformation of the grey cells may coincide quite easily with the face of a Madonna."

"Poirot," I cried, horrified, "you cannot mean that you suspect an innocent child like this!"

"*Ta-ta-ta!* Do not excite yourself! I have not said that I suspected her. But you must admit that her anxiety to know about the case is somewhat unusual."

"For once I see farther than you do," I said. "Her anxiety is not for herself—but for her mother."

"My friend," said Poirot, "as usual, you see nothing at all. Madame Daubreuil is very well able to look after herself without her daughter worrying about her. I admit I was teasing you just now, but all the same I repeat what I said before. Do not set your heart on that girl. She is not for you! I, Hercule Poirot, know it. *Sacre!* if only I could remember where I had seen that face?"

"What face?" I asked, surprised. "The daughter's?"

"No. The mother's."

Noting my surprise, he nodded emphatically.

"But yes—it is as I tell you. It was a long time ago, when I was still with the police in Belgium. I have never actually seen the woman before, but I have seen her picture — and in connexion with some case. I rather fancy —"

"Yes?"

"I may be mistaken, but I rather fancy that it was a murder case!"

# VIII.

## AN UNEXPECTED MEETING.

We were up at the villa betimes next morning. The man on guard at the gate did not bar our way this time. Instead, he respectfully saluted us, and we passed on to the house. The maid Léonie was just coming down the stairs, and seemed not averse to the prospect of a little conversation.

Poirot inquired after the health of Mrs. Renauld. Léonie shook her head.

"She is terribly upset, the poor lady! She will eat nothing—but nothing! And she is as pale as a ghost. It is heartrending to see her. Ah, it is not I who would grieve like that for a man who had deceived me with another woman!"

Poirot nodded sympathetically.

"What you say is very just, but what will you? The heart of a woman who loves will forgive many blows. Still undoubtedly there must have been many scenes of recrimination between them in the last few months?"

Again Léonie shook her head.

"Never, monsieur. Never have I heard madame utter a word of protest—of reproach, even! She had the temper and disposition of an angel—quite different to monsieur."

"Monsieur Renauld had not the temper of an angel?"

"Far from it. When he enraged himself, the whole house knew of it. The day that he quarrelled with Monsieur Jack—*ma foi*, they might have been heard in the marketplace, they shouted so loud!"

"Indeed," said Poirot. "And when did this quarrel take place?"

"Oh, it was just before Monsieur Jack went to Paris. Almost he missed his train. He came out of the library, and caught up his bag which he had left in the hall. The automobile, it was being repaired, and he had to run for the station. I was dusting the salon, and I saw him pass, and his face was white — white — with two burning spots of red. Ah, but he was angry!"

Léonie was enjoying her narrative thoroughly.

"And the dispute, what was it about?"

"Ah, that I do not know," confessed Léonie. "It is true that they shouted, but their voices were so loud and high, and they spoke so fast, that only one well acquainted with English could have comprehended. But monsieur, he was like a thundercloud all day! Impossible to please him!"

The sound of a door shutting upstairs cut short Léonie's loquacity.

"And Françoise who awaits me!" she exclaimed, awakening to a tardy remembrance of her duties. "That old one, she always scolds."

"One moment, mademoiselle. The examining magistrate, where is he?"

"They have gone out to look at the automobile in the garage. Monsieur the commissary had some idea that it might have been used on the night of the murder."

"*Quelle idée*," murmured Poirot, as the girl disappeared.

"You will go out and join them?"

"No, I shall await their return in the salon. It is cool there on this hot morning."

This placid way of taking things did not quite commend itself to me.

"If you don't mind —" I said, and hesitated.

"Not in the least. You wish to investigate on your own account, eh?"

"Well, I'd rather like to have a look at Giraud, if he's anywhere about, and see what he's up to."

"The human foxhound," murmured Poirot, as he leaned back in a comfortable chair, and closed his eyes. "By all means, my friend. *Au revoir*."

I strolled out of the front door. It was certainly hot. I turned up the path we had taken the day before. I had a mind to study the scene of the crime myself. I did not go directly to the spot, however, but turned aside into the bushes, so as to come out on the links some hundred yards or so farther to the right. The shrubbery here was much denser, and I had quite a struggle to force my way through. When I emerged at last on the course, it was quite unexpectedly and with such vigour that I cannoned heavily into a young lady who had been standing with her back to the plantation.

She not unnaturally gave a suppressed shriek, but I, too, uttered an exclamation of surprise. For it was my friend of the train, Cinderella!

The surprise was mutual.

"You!" we both exclaimed simultaneously. The young lady recovered herself first. "My only aunt!" she exclaimed. "What are you doing here?"

"For the matter of that, what are you?" I retorted.

"When last I saw you, the day before yesterday, you were trotting home to England like a good little boy."

"When last I saw you," I said, "you were trotting home with your sister, like a good little girl. By the way, how is your sister?"

A flash of white teeth rewarded me.

"How kind of you to ask! My sister is well, I thank you."

"She is here with you?"

"She remained in town," said the minx with dignity.

"I don't believe you've got a sister," I laughed. "If you have, her name is Harris!"

"Do you remember mine?" she asked with a smile.

"Cinderella. But you're going to tell me the real one now aren't you?"

She shook her head with a wicked look. "Not even why you're here?"

"Oh, that! I suppose you've heard of members of my profession 'resting.'"

"At expensive French watering-places?"

"Dirt cheap if you know where to go."

I eyed her keenly.

"Still, you'd no intention of coming here when I met you two days ago?"

"We all have our disappointments," said Miss Cinderella sententiously. "There now, I've told you quite as much as is good for you. Little boys should not be inquisitive. You've not yet told me what you're doing here?"

"You remember my telling you that my great friend was a detective?"

"Yes?"

"And perhaps you've heard about this crime — at the Villa Geneviève — ?"

She stared at me. Her breast heaved, and her eyes grew wide and round.

"You don't mean — that you're in on that?"

I nodded.

There was no doubt that I had scored heavily. Her emotion, as she regarded me, was only too evident. For some few seconds she remained silent, staring at me.

Then she nodded her head emphatically. "Well, if that doesn't beat the band! Tote me round. I want to see all the horrors."

"What do you mean?"

"What I say. Bless the boy, didn't I tell you I doted on crimes? I've been nosing round for hours. It's a real piece of luck happening on you this way. Come on, show me all the sights."

"But look here — wait a

minute — I can't. Nobody's allowed in. They're awfully strict."

"Aren't you and your friends the big bugs?"

I was loath to relinquish my position of importance.

"Why are you so keen?" I asked weakly. "And what is it you want to see?"

"Oh, everything! The place where it happened, and the weapon, and the body, and any fingerprints or interesting things like that. I've never had a chance before of being right in on a murder like this. It'll last me all my life."

I turned away, sickened. What were women coming to nowadays? The girl's ghoulish excitement nauseated me.

"Come off your high horse," said the lady suddenly. "And don't give yourself airs. When you got called to this job, did you put your nose in the air and say it was a nasty business, and you wouldn't be mixed up in it?"

"No, but —"

"If you'd been here on a holiday, wouldn't you be nosing round just the same as I am? Of course you would."

"I'm a man. You're a woman."

"Your idea of a woman is someone who gets on a chair and shrieks if she sees a mouse. That's all prehistoric. But you will show me round, won't you? You see, it might make a big difference to me."

"In what way?"

"They're keeping all the reporters out. I might make a big scoop with one of the papers. You don't know how much they pay for a bit of inside stuff."

I hesitated. She slipped a small soft hand into mine.

"*Please* — there's a dear."

I capitulated. Secretly, I knew that I should rather enjoy the part of showman.

We repaired first to the spot where the body had been discovered. A man was on guard there, who saluted respectfully, knowing me by sight, and raised no questions as to my companion. Presumably he regarded her as vouched for by me. I explained to Cinderella just how the discovery had been made, and she listened attentively, sometimes putting an intelligent question. Then we turned our steps in the direction of the villa. I proceeded rather cautiously, for, truth to tell, I was not at all anxious to meet anyone. I took the girl through the shrubbery round to the back of the house where the small shed was. I recollected that yesterday evening, after relocking the door, Monsieur Bex had left the key with the *sergent de ville*, Marchaud, "in case Monsieur Giraud should require it while we are upstairs." I thought it quite likely that the Sûreté detective, after using it, had returned it to Marchaud again. Leaving the girl out of sight in the shrubbery, I entered the house. Marchaud was on duty outside the door of the salon. From within came the murmur of voices.

"Monsieur desires Monsieur

Hautet? He is within. He is again interrogating Françoise."

"No," I said hastily, "I don't want him. But I should very much like the key of the shed outside if it is not against regulations."

"But certainly, monsieur." He produced it. "Here it is. Monsieur Hautet gave orders that all facilities were to be placed at your disposal. You will return it to me when you have finished out there, that is all."

"Of course."

I felt a thrill of satisfaction as I realized that in Marchaud's eyes, at least, I ranked equally in importance with Poirot.

The girl was waiting for me. She gave an exclamation of delight as she saw the key in my hand.

"You've got it then?"

"Of course," I said coolly. "All the same, you know, what I'm doing is highly irregular."

"You've been a perfect duck, and I shan't forget it. Come along. They can't see us from the house, can they?"

"Wait a minute." I arrested her eager advance. "I won't stop you if you really wish to go in. But do you? You've seen the grave, and the grounds, and you've heard all the details of the affair. Isn't that enough for you? This is going to be gruesome, you know, and—unpleasant."

She looked at me for a moment with an expression that I could not quite fathom. Then she laughed.

"Me for the horrors," she said. "Come along."

In silence we arrived at the door of the shed. I opened it and we passed in. I walked over to the body, and gently pulled down the sheet as Bex had done the preceding afternoon. A little gasping sound escaped from the girl's lips, and I turned and looked at her. There was horror on her face now, and those debonair high spirits of hers were quenched utterly. She had not chosen to listen to my advice, and she was punished now for her disregard of it. I felt singularly merciless towards her. She should go through with it now. I turned the corpse over gently.

"You see," I said. "He was stabbed in the back."

Her voice was almost soundless. "With what?"

I nodded towards the glass jar. "That dagger."

Suddenly the girl reeled, and then sank down in a heap. I sprang to her assistance.

"You are faint. Come out of here. It has been too much for you."

"Water," she murmured. "Quick. Water."

I left her, and rushed into the house. Fortunately none of the servants were about, and I was able to secure a glass of water unobserved and add a few drops of brandy from a pocket flask. In a few minutes I was back again. The girl was lying as I had left her, but a few sips of the brandy and water revived her in a marvellous manner.

"Take me out of here—oh, quickly, quickly!" she cried, shuddering.

Supporting her with my arm, I led her out into the air, and she pulled the door to behind her. Then she drew a deep breath.

"That's better. Oh, it was horrible! Why did you ever let me go in?"

I felt this to be so feminine that I could not forbear a smile. Secretly, I was not dissatisfied with her collapse. It proved that she was not quite so callous as I had thought her. After all she was little more than a child, and her curiosity had probably been of the unthinking order.

"I did my best to stop you, you know," I said gently.

"I suppose you did. Well, goodbye."

"Look here, you can't start off like that—all alone. You're not fit for it. I insist on accompanying you back to Merlinville."

"Nonsense. I'm quite all right now.

"Supposing you felt faint again? No, I shall come with you."

But this she combated with a good deal of energy. In the end, however, I prevailed so far as to be allowed to accompany her to the outskirts of the town. We retraced our steps over our former route, passing the grave again, and making a detour on to the road. Where the first straggling line of shops began, she stopped and held out her hand.

"Goodbye, and thank you ever so much for coming with me."

"Are you sure you're all right now?"

"Quite, thanks. I hope you don't get into any trouble over showing me things."

I disclaimed the idea lightly.

"Well, goodbye."

"*Au revoir*," I corrected. "If you're staying here, we shall meet again."

She flashed a smile at me.

"That's so. *Au revoir*, then."

"Wait a second, you haven't told me your address."

"Oh, I'm staying at the Hotel du Phare. It's a little place, but quite good. Come and look me up tomorrow."

"I will," I said, with perhaps rather unnecessary *empressement*.

I watched her out of sight, then turned and retraced my steps to the villa. I remembered that I had not relocked the door of the shed. Fortunately no one had noticed the oversight, and turning the key I removed it and returned it to the *sergent de ville*. As I did so, it came upon me suddenly that though Cinderella had given me her address I still did not know her name.

# IX.

## MONSIEUR GIRAUD FINDS SOME CLUES.

In the salon I found the examining magistrate busily interrogating the old gardener, Auguste. Poirot and the commissary, who were both present, greeted me respectively with a smile and a polite bow. I slipped quietly into a seat.

Monsieur Hautet was painstaking and meticulous in the extreme, but did not succeed in eliciting anything of importance.

The gardening gloves Auguste admitted to be his. He wore them when handling a certain species of primula plant which was poisonous to some people. He could not say when he had worn them last. Certainly he had not missed them. Where were they kept? Sometimes in one place, sometimes in another. The spade was usually to be found in the small tool-shed. Was it locked? Of course it was locked. Where was the key kept? *Parbleu*, it was in the door of course. There was nothing of value to steal. Who would have expected a party of bandits, or assassins? Such things did not happen in Madame la Vicomtesse's time.

Monsieur Hautet signifying that he had finished with him, the old man withdrew, grumbling to the last. Remembering Poirot's unaccountable insistence on the footprints in the flower-beds, I scrutinized him narrowly as he gave his evidence. Either he had nothing to do with the crime or he was a consummate actor. Suddenly, just as he was going out of the door, an idea struck me.

"*Pardon*, Monsieur Hautet," I cried, "but will you permit me to ask him one question?"

"But certainly, monsieur."

Thus encouraged, I turned to Auguste. "Where do you keep your boots?"

"On my feet," growled the old man. "Where else?"

"But when you go to bed at night?"

"Under my bed."

"But who cleans them?"

"Nobody. Why should they be cleaned? Is it that I promenade myself on the front like a young man? On Sunday I wear the Sunday boots, but otherwise —" He shrugged his shoulders.

I shook my head, discouraged.

"Well, well," said the magistrate, "we do not advance very much. Undoubtedly we are held up until we get the return cable from Santiago. Has anyone seen Giraud? In verity that one lacks politeness! I have a very good mind to send for him and —"

"You will not have to send far."

The quiet voice startled us. Giraud was standing outside looking in through the open window.

He leapt lightly into the room and advanced to the table.

"Here I am, at your service. Accept my excuses for not presenting myself sooner."

"Not at all — not at all!" said the magistrate, rather confused.

"Of course I am only a detective," continued the other. "I know nothing of interrogatories. Were I conducting one, I should be inclined to do so without an open window. Anyone standing outside can so easily hear all that passes. But no matter."

Monsieur Hautet flushed angrily. There was evidently going to be no love lost between the examining magistrate and the detective in charge of the case. They had fallen foul of each other at the start. Perhaps in any event it would have been much the same. To Giraud, all examining magistrates were fools, and to Monsieur Hautet, who took himself seriously, the casual manner of the Paris detective could not fail to give offence.

"*Eh bien*, Monsieur Giraud," said the magistrate rather sharply. "Without doubt you have been employing your time to a marvel! You have the names of the assassins for us, have you not? And also the precise spot where they find themselves now?"

Unmoved by this irony, Monsieur Giraud replied:

"I know at least where they have come from."

Giraud took two small objects from his pocket and laid them down on the table. We crowded round. The objects were very simple ones: the stub of a cigarette and an unlighted match. The detective wheeled round on Poirot.

"What do you see there?" he asked.

There was something almost brutal in his tone. It made my cheeks flush. But Poirot remained unmoved. He shrugged his shoulders.

"A cigarette end and a match."

"And what does that tell you?"

Poirot spread out his hands.

"It tells me — nothing."

"Ah!" said Giraud, in a satisfied voice. "You haven't made a study of these things. That's not an ordinary match — not in this country at least. It's common enough in South America. Luckily it's unlighted. I mightn't have recognized it otherwise. Evidently one of the men threw away his cigarette and lit another, spilling one match out of the box as he did so."

"And the other match?" asked Poirot.

"Which match?"

"The one he *did* light his cigarette with. You have found that also?"

"No."

"Perhaps you didn't search very thoroughly."

"Not search thoroughly —" For a moment it seemed as though the detective was going to break out angrily, but with an effort he controlled himself. "I see you love a joke, Monsieur Poirot. But in any case, match or no match, the cigarette end would be sufficient. It is a South American cigarette with liquorice pectoral paper."

Poirot bowed. The commissary spoke: "The cigarette end and match might have belonged to Monsieur Renauld. Remember, it is only two years since he returned from South America."

"No," replied the other confidently. "I have already searched among the effects of Monsieur Renauld. The cigarettes he smoked and the matches he used are quite different."

"You do not think it odd," asked Poirot, "that these strangers should come unprovided with a weapon, with gloves, with a spade, and that they should so conveniently find all these things?"

Giraud smiled in a rather superior manner.

"Undoubtedly it is strange. Indeed, without the theory that I hold, it would be inexplicable."

"Aha!" said Monsieur Hautet. "An accomplice within the house!"

"Or outside it," said Giraud, with a peculiar smile.

"But someone must have admitted them. We cannot allow that, by an unparalleled piece of good fortune, they found the door ajar for them to walk in?"

"The door was opened for them; but it could just as easily be opened from outside by someone who possessed a key."

"But who did possess a key?"

Giraud shrugged his shoulders.

"As for that, no one who possesses one is going to admit the fact if he can help it. But several people *might* have had one. Monsieur Jack Renauld, the son, for instance.

It is true that he is on his way to South America, but he might have lost the key or had it stolen from him. Then there is the gardener—he has been here many years. One of the younger servants may have a lover. It is easy to take an impression of a key and have one cut. There are many possibilities. Then there is another person who, I should judge, is exceedingly likely to have such a thing."

"Who is that?"

"Madame Daubreuil," said the detective.

"Eh, eh!" said the magistrate. "So you have heard about that, have you?"

"I hear everything," said Giraud imperturbably.

"There is one thing I could swear you have not heard," said Monsieur Hautet, delighted to be able to show superior knowledge, and without more ado he retailed the story of the mysterious visitor the night before. He also touched on the cheque made out to "Duveen," and finally handed Giraud the letter signed "Bella."

"All very interesting. But my theory remains unaffected."

"And your theory is?"

"For the moment I prefer not to say. Remember, I am only just beginning my investigations."

"Tell me one thing, Monsieur Giraud," said Poirot suddenly. "Your theory allows for the door being opened. It does not explain why it was left open. When they departed, would it not have been natural for them to close it behind them? If a *sergent de ville* had chanced to come up to the house, as is sometimes done to see that all is well, they might have been discovered and overtaken almost at once."

"Bah! They forgot it. A mistake, I grant you."

Then, to my surprise, Poirot uttered almost same words as he had uttered to Bex the previous evening:

"I do not agree with you. The door being left open was the result of either design or necessity, and any theory that does not admit that fact is bound to prove vain."

We all regarded the little man with a good deal of astonishment. The confession of ignorance drawn from him over the match end had, I thought, been bound to humiliate him, but here he was self-satisfied as ever, laying down the law to Giraud without a tremor.

The detective twisted his moustache, eyeing my friend in a somewhat bantering fashion.

"You don't agree with me, eh? Well, what strikes you particularly about the case? Let's hear your views."

"One thing presents itself to me as being significant. Tell me, Monsieur Giraud, does nothing strike you as familiar about this case? Is there nothing it reminds you of?"

"Familiar? Reminds me of? I can't say off-hand. I don't think so, though."

"You are wrong," said Poirot

quietly. "A crime almost precisely similar has been committed before."

"When? And where?"

"Ah, that, unfortunately, I cannot for the moment remember, but I shall do so. I had hoped you might be able to assist me."

Giraud snorted incredulously.

"There have been many affairs of masked men. I cannot remember the details of them all. The crimes all resemble each other more or less."

"There is such a thing as the individual touch." Poirot suddenly assumed his lecturing manner, and addressed us collectively. "I am speaking to you now of the psychology of crime. Monsieur Giraud knows quite well that each criminal has his particular method, and that the police, when called in to investigate, say, a case of burglary, can often make a shrewd guess at the offender, simply by the peculiar methods he has employed. (Japp would tell you the same, Hastings.) Man is an unoriginal animal. Unoriginal within the law in his daily respectable life, equally unoriginal outside the law. If a man commits a crime, any other crime he commits will resemble it closely. The English murderer who disposed of his wives in succession by drowning them in their baths was a case in point. Had he varied his methods, he might have escaped detection to this day. But he obeyed the common dictates of human nature, arguing that what had once succeeded would succeed again, and he paid the penalty of his lack of originality."

"And the point of all this?" sneered Giraud.

"That, when you have two crimes precisely similar in design and execution, you find the same brain behind them both. I am looking for that brain, Monsieur Giraud, and I shall find it. Here we have a true clue—a psychological clue. You may know all about cigarettes and match ends, Monsieur Giraud, but I, Hercule Poirot, know the mind of man."

Giraud remained singularly unimpressed.

"For your guidance," continued Poirot, "I will also advise you of one fact which might fail to be brought to your notice. The wristwatch of Madame Renauld, on the day following the tragedy, had gained two hours."

Giraud stared.

"Perhaps it was in the habit of gaining?"

"As a matter of fact, I am told it did."

"Very well, then."

"All the same, two hours is a good deal," said Poirot softly. "Then there is the matter of the footprints in the flower-bed."

He nodded his head towards the open window. Giraud took two eager strides, and looked out.

"But I see no footprints?"

"No," said Poirot, straightening a little pile of books on a table. "There are none."

For a moment an almost murderous rage obscured Giraud's face. He took two strides towards his tormentor, but at that moment the salon door was opened, and Marchaud announced:

"Monsieur Stonor, the secretary, has just arrived from England. May he enter?"

# X.

## GABRIEL STONOR.

The man who now entered the room was a striking figure. Very tall with a well-knit, athletic frame, and a deeply bronzed face and neck, he dominated the assembly. Even Giraud seemed anaemic beside him.

When I knew him better I realized that Gabriel was quite an unusual personality. English by birth, he had knocked about all over the world. He had shot big game in Africa, travelled in Korea, ranched in California, and traded in the South Sea islands.

His unerring eye picked out Monsieur Hautet.

"The examining magistrate in charge of the case? Pleased to meet you, sir. This is a terrible business. How's Mrs. Renauld? Is she bearing up fairly well? It must have been an awful shock to her."

"Terrible, terrible," said Monsieur Hautet. "Permit me to introduce Monsieur Bex, our commissary of police, Monsieur Giraud of the Sûreté. This gentleman is Monsieur Hercule Poirot. Mr. Renauld sent for him, but he arrived too late to do anything to avert the tragedy. A friend of Monsieur Poirot's, Captain Hastings."

Stonor looked at Poirot with some interest. "Sent for you, did he?"

"You did not know, then, that Monsieur Renauld contemplated

calling a detective?" interposed Monsieur Bex.

"No, I didn't. But it doesn't surprise me a bit."

"Why?"

"Because the old man was rattled. I don't know what it was all about. He didn't confide in me. We weren't on those terms. But rattled he was — and badly."

"H'm!" said Monsieur Hautet. "But you have no notion of the cause?"

"That's what I said, sir."

"You will pardon me, Monsieur Stonor, but we must begin with a few formalities. Your name?"

"Gabriel Stonor."

"How long ago was it that you became secretary to Monsieur Renauld?"

"About two years ago, when he first arrived from South America. I met him through a mutual friend, and he offered me the post. A thundering good boss he was too."

"Did he talk to you much about his life in South America?"

"Yes, a good bit."

"Do you know if he was ever in Santiago?"

"Several times, I believe."

"He never mentioned any special incident occurred there — anything that might have provoked some vendetta against him?"

"Never."

"Did he speak of any secret that he had while sojourning there?"

"Not that I can remember. But, for all that, there was a mystery about him. I've never heard him speak of his boyhood, for instance, of any incident prior to his arrival in South America. He was a French-Canadian by birth, I believe, but I've never heard him speak of his life in Canada. He could shut up like a clam if he liked."

"So, as far as you know, he had no enemies, and you can give us no clue as to any secret to obtain possession of which he might have been murdered?"

"That's so."

"Monsieur Stonor, have you ever heard the name of Duveen in connexion with Monsieur Renauld?"

"Duveen. Duveen." He tried the name over thoughtfully. "I don't think I have. And yet it seems familiar."

"Do you know a lady, a friend of Monsieur Renauld's, whose Christian name is Bella?"

Again Mr. Stonor shook his head.

"Bella Duveen? Is that the full name? It's curious. I'm sure I know it. But for the moment I can't remember in what connexion."

The magistrate coughed.

"You understand, Monsieur Stonor — the case is like this. *There must be no reservations.* You might, perhaps, through a feeling of consideration for Madame Renauld — for whom, I gather, you have a great esteem and affection — you might — in fact!" said Monsieur Hautet, getting rather tied up in his sentence, "there must absolutely be no reservations."

Stonor stared at him, a dawning light of comprehension in his eyes.

"I don't quite get you," he said gently. "Where does Mrs. Renauld come in? I've an immense respect and affection for that lady; she's a very wonderful and unusual type, but I don't quite see how my reservations, or otherwise, could affect her."

"Not if this Bella Duveen should prove to have been something more than a friend to her husband?"

"Ah!" said Stonor. "I get you now. But I'll bet my bottom dollar that you're wrong. The old man never so much as looked at a petticoat. He just adored his own wife. They were the most devoted couple I know."

Monsieur Hautet shook his head gently. "Monsieur Stonor, we hold absolute proof—a love-letter written by this Bella to Monsieur Renauld, accusing him of having tired of her. Moreover, we have further proof that, at the time of his death, he was carrying on an intrigue with a Frenchwoman, a Madame Daubreuil, who rents the adjoining villa."

The secretary's eyes narrowed.

"Hold on, sir. You're barking up the wrong tree. I knew Paul Renauld. What you've just been saying is plumb impossible. There's some other explanation."

The magistrate shrugged his shoulders. "What other explanation could there be?"

"What leads you to think it was a love affair?"

"Madame Daubreuil was in the habit of visiting him here in the evenings. Also, since Monsieur Renauld came to the Villa Geneviève, Madame Daubreuil has paid large sums of money into the bank in notes. In all, the amount totals four thousand pounds of your English money."

"I guess that's right," said Stonor quietly. "I transmitted him those sums in notes, at his request. But it wasn't an intrigue."

"What else could it be?"

"Blackmail," said Stonor sharply, bringing down his hand with a slam on the table. "That's what it was."

"Ah!" cried the magistrate, shaken in spite of himself.

"Blackmail," repeated Stonor. "The old man was being bled—and at a good rate too. Four thousand in a couple of months. Whew! I told you just now there was a mystery about Renauld. Evidently this Madame Daubreuil knew enough of it to put the screw on."

"It—is possible," the commissary cried excitedly. "Decidedly it is possible."

"Possible?" roared Stonor. "It's certain. Tell me, have you asked Mrs. Renauld about this love-affair stunt of yours?"

"No, monsieur. We did not wish to occasion her any distress if it could reasonably be avoided."

"Distress? Why, she'd laugh in your face. I tell you, she and Renauld were a couple in a hundred."

"Ah, that reminds me of another point," said Monsieur Hautet. "Did Monsieur Renauld take you into his confidence at all as to the dispositions of his will?"

"I know all about it—took it to the lawyers for him after he'd drawn it out. I can give you the name of his solicitors if you want to see it. They've got it there. Quite simple. Half in trust to his wife for her lifetime, the other half to his son. A few legacies. I rather think he left me a thousand."

"When was this will drawn up?"

"Oh, about a year and a half ago."

"Would it surprise you very much, Monsieur Stonor, to hear that Monsieur Renauld had made another will, less than a fortnight ago?"

Stonor was obviously very much surprised.

"I'd no idea of it. What's it like?"

"The whole of his vast fortune is left unreservedly to his wife. There is no mention of his son."

Mr. Stonor gave vent to a prolonged whistle.

"I call that rather rough on the lad. His mother adores him of course, but to the world at large it looks rather like a want of confidence on his father's part. It will be rather galling to his pride. Still, it all goes to prove what I told you, that Renauld and his wife were on first-rate terms."

"Quite so, quite so," said Monsieur Hautet. "It is possible we shall have to revise our ideas on several points. We have, of course, cabled to Santiago, and are expecting a reply from there any minute. In all probability, everything will then be perfectly clear and straightforward. On the other hand, if your suggestion of blackmail is true, Madame Daubreuil ought to be able to give us valuable information."

Poirot interjected a remark:

"Monsieur Stonor, the English chauffeur, Masters, had he been long with Monsieur Renauld?"

"Over a year."

"Have you any idea whether he has ever been in South America?"

"I'm quite sure he hasn't. Before coming to Monsieur Renauld he had been for many years with some people in Gloucestershire whom I know well."

"In fact, you can answer for him as being above suspicion?"

"Absolutely."

Poirot seemed somewhat crestfallen. Meanwhile the magistrate had summoned Marchaud.

"My compliments to Madame Renauld, and I should be glad to speak to her for a few minutes. Beg her not to disturb herself. I will wait upon her upstairs."

Marchaud saluted and disappeared.

We waited some minutes, and then, to our surprise, the door opened, and Mrs. Renauld, deathly pale in her heavy mourning, entered the room.

Monsieur Hautet brought

forward a chair, uttering vigorous protestations, and she thanked him with a smile. Stonor was holding one hand of hers in his with an eloquent sympathy. Words evidently failed him. Mrs. Renauld turned to Monsieur Hautet.

"You wish to ask me something?"

"With your permission, madame. I understand your husband was a French-Canadian by birth. Can you tell me anything of his youth or upbringing?"

She shook her head.

"My husband was always very reticent about himself, monsieur. He came from the Northwest, I know, but I fancy that he had an unhappy childhood, for he never cared to speak of that time. Our life was lived entirely in the present and the future."

"Was there any mystery in his past life?"

Mrs. Renauld smiled a little and shook her head.

"Nothing so romantic, I am sure, monsieur."

Monsieur Hautet also smiled.

"True, we must not permit ourselves to get melodramatic. There is one thing more —" He hesitated.

Stonor broke in impetuously:

"They've got an extraordinary idea into their heads, Mrs. Renauld. They actually fancy that Mr. Renauld was carrying on an intrigue with a Madame Daubreuil who, it seems, lives next door."

The scarlet colour flamed into Mrs. Renauld's cheeks. She flung her head up, then bit her lip, her face quivering. Stonor stood looking at her in astonishment, but Monsieur Bex leaned forward and said gently:

"We regret to cause you pain, madame, but have you any reason to believe that Madame Daubreuil was your husband's mistress?"

With a sob of anguish, Mrs. Renauld buried her face in her hands. Her shoulders heaved convulsively. At last she lifted her head and said brokenly:

"She may have been."

Never, in all my life, have I seen anything to equal the blank amazement on Stonor's face. He was thoroughly taken aback.

# XI.

## JACK RENAULD.

What the next development of the conversation would have been I cannot say, for at that moment the door was thrown open violently and a tall young man strode into the room.

Just for a moment I had the uncanny sensation that the dead man had come to life again. Then I realized that this dark head was untouched with grey, and that, in point of fact, it was a mere boy who now burst in among us with so little ceremony. He went straight to Mrs. Renauld with an impetuosity that took no heed of the presence of others.

"Mother!"

"Jack!" With a cry she folded him in her arms. "My dearest! But what brings you here? You were to sail on the *Anzora* from Cherbourg two days ago?" Then, suddenly recalling to herself the presence of others, she turned with a certain dignity: "My son, messieurs."

"Aha!" said Monsieur Hautet, acknowledging the young man's bow. "So you did not sail on the *Anzora?*"

"No, monsieur. As I was about to explain, the *Anzora* was detained twenty-four hours through engine trouble. I should have sailed last night instead of the night before, but, happening to buy an evening paper, I saw in it an account of the — the awful tragedy that had befallen us —" His voice broke and the tears came into his eyes. "My poor father — my poor, poor father."

Staring at him like one in a dream, Mrs. Renauld repeated:

"So you did not sail?" And then, with a gesture of infinite weariness, she murmured as though to herself: "After all, it does not matter — now."

"Sit down, Monsieur Renauld, I beg of you," said Monsieur Hautet, indicating a chair. "My sympathy for you is profound. It must have been a terrible shock to you to learn the news as you did. However, it is most fortunate that you were prevented from sailing. I am in hopes that you may be able to give us just the information we need to clear up this mystery."

"I am at your disposal, monsieur. Ask me any questions you please."

"To begin with, I understand that this journey was being undertaken at your father's request?"

"Quite so, monsieur. I received a telegram bidding me to proceed without delay to Buenos Aires, and from thence via the Andes to Valparaiso, and on to Santiago."

"Ah! And the object of this journey?"

"I have no idea."

"What?"

"No. See, here in the telegram."

The magistrate took it and read it aloud:

" 'Proceed immediately Cherbourg embark *Anzora* sailing tonight Buenos Aires. Ultimate destination Santiago. Further instructions will await you Buenos Aires. Do not fail. Matter is of utmost importance. — RENAULD.' And there had been no previous correspondence on the matter?"

Jack Renauld shook his head.

"That is the only intimation of any kind. I knew, of course, that my father, having lived so long out there, had necessarily many interests in South America. But he had never mooted any suggestion of sending me out."

"You have, of course, been a good deal in South America, Monsieur Renauld?"

"I was there as a child. But I was educated in England, and spent most of my holidays in that country, so I really know far less of South America than might be supposed. You see, the War broke out when I was seventeen."

"You served in the English Flying Corps, did you not?"

"Yes, monsieur."

Monsieur Hautet nodded his head and proceeded with his inquiries along the, by now, well-known lines. In response, Jack Renauld declared definitely that he knew nothing of any enmity his father might have incurred in the city of Santiago or elsewhere in the South American continent, that he had noticed no change in his father's manner of late, and that he had never heard him refer to a secret. He had regarded the mission to South America as connected with business interests.

As Monsieur Hautet paused for a minute, the quiet voice of Giraud broke in:

"I should like to put a few questions of my own, Monsieur le juge."

"By all means, Monsieur Giraud, if you wish," said the magistrate coldly.

Giraud edged his chair a little nearer to the table.

"Were you on good terms with your father, Monsieur Renauld?"

"Certainly I was," returned the lad haughtily.

"You assert that positively?"

"Yes."

"No little disputes, eh?"

Jack shrugged his shoulders. "Everyone may have a difference of opinion now and then."

"Quite so, quite so. But, if anyone were to assert that you had a violent quarrel with your father on the eve of your departure for Paris, that person, without doubt, would be lying?"

I could not but admire the ingenuity of Giraud. His boast, "I know everything," had been no idle one. Jack Renauld was clearly disconcerted by the question.

"We—we did have an argument," he admitted.

"Ah, an argument! In the course of that argument, did you use this phrase: "When you are dead I can do as I please'?"

"I may have done," muttered the other. "I don't know."

"In response to that, did your father say: 'But I am not dead yet!' To which you responded: 'I wish you were!'?"

The boy made no answer. His hands fiddled nervously with the things on the table in front of him.

"I must request an answer, please, Monsieur Renauld," said Giraud sharply.

With an angry exclamation, the boy swept a heavy paper-knife to the floor.

"What does it matter? You might as well know. Yes, I did quarrel with my father. I dare say I said all those things—I was so angry I cannot even remember what I said! I was furious—I could almost have killed him at that moment—there, make the most of that!" He leant back in his chair, flushed and defiant.

Giraud smiled, then, moving his chair back a little, said:

"That is all. You would, without doubt, prefer to continue the interrogatory, Monsieur Hautet."

"Ah, yes, exactly," said Monsieur Hautet. "And what was the subject of your quarrel?"

"That I decline to state."

Monsieur Hautet sat up in his chair.

"Monsieur Renauld, it is not permitted to trifle with the law!" he thundered. "What was the subject of the quarrel?"

Young Renauld remained silent, his boyish face sullen and overcast. But another voice spoke, imperturbable and calm, the voice of Hercule Poirot:

"I will inform you, if you like, monsieur."

"You know?"

"Certainly I know. The subject of the quarrel was Mademoiselle Marthe Daubreuil."

Renauld sprang round, startled. The magistrate leaned forward.

"Is that so, monsieur?"

Jack Renauld bowed his head.

"Yes," he admitted. "I love Mademoiselle Daubreuil, and I wish to marry her. When I informed my father of the fact he flew at once into a violent rage. Naturally, I could not stand hearing the girl I loved insulted, and I, too, lost my temper."

Monsieur Hautet looked across at Mrs. Renauld. "You were aware of this — attachment, madame?"

"I feared it," she replied simply.

"Mother," cried the boy. "You too! Marthe is as good as she is beautiful. What can you have against her?"

"I have nothing against Mademoiselle Daubreuil in any way. But I should prefer you to marry an Englishwoman, or if a Frenchwoman, not one who has a mother of doubtful antecedents!"

Her rancour against the older woman showed plainly in her voice, and I could well understand that it must have been a bitter blow to her when her only son showed signs of falling in love with the daughter of her rival.

Mrs. Renauld continued, addressing the magistrate:

"I ought, perhaps, to have spoken, to, my husband on the subject, but I hoped that it was only a boy and girl flirtation which would blow over all the quicker if no notice was taken of it. I blame myself now for my silence, but my husband, as I told you, had seemed so anxious and careworn, different altogether from his normal self, that I was chiefly concerned not to give him any additional worry."

Monsieur Hautet nodded.

"When you informed your father of your intentions towards Mademoiselle Daubreuil," he resumed, "he was surprised?"

"He seemed completely taken aback. Then he ordered me peremptorily to dismiss any such idea from my mind. He would never give his consent to such a marriage. Nettled, I demanded what he had against Mademoiselle Daubreuil. To that he could give no satisfactory reply, but spoke in slighting terms of the mystery surrounding the lives of the mother and daughter. I answered that I was marrying Marthe and not her antecedents, but he shouted me down with a peremptory refusal to discuss the matter in any way. The whole thing must be given up. The injustice and high-handedness of it all maddened me — especially since he himself always seemed to go out of his way to be attentive to the Daubreuils and was always suggesting that they should be asked to the house. I lost my head, and we quarrelled in earnest. My father reminded me that I was entirely dependent on him, and it must have been in answer to that that I made the remark about doing as I pleased after his death —"

Poirot interrupted with a quick question:

"You were aware, then, of the terms of your father's will?"

"I knew that he had left half his fortune to me, the other half in trust for my mother, to come to me at her death," replied the lad.

"Proceed with your story," said the magistrate.

"After that we shouted at each other in sheer rage, until I suddenly realized that I was in danger of missing my train to Paris. I had to run for the station, still in a white heat of fury. However, once well away, I calmed down. I wrote to Marthe, telling her what had happened, and her reply soothed me still further. She pointed out to me that we had only to be steadfast, and any opposition was bound to give way at last. Our affection for each other must be tried and proved, and when my parents realized that it was no light infatuation on my part they would doubtless relent towards us. Of course, to her, I had not dwelt on my father's principal objection to the match. I soon saw that I should do my cause no good by violence."

"To pass to another matter, are you acquainted with the name of Duveen, Monsieur Renauld?"

"Duveen?" said Jack. "Duveen?" He leant forward and slowly picked up the paper-knife he had swept from the table. As he lifted his head his eyes met the watching ones of Giraud. "Duveen? No, I can't say I do."

"Will you read this letter, Monsieur Renauld? And tell me if you have any idea as to who the person was who addressed it to your father."

Jack Renauld took the letter and read it through, the colour mounting in his face as he did so.

"Addressed to my father?" The emotion and indignation in his tones were evident.

"Yes. We found it in the pocket of his coat."

"Does —" He hesitated, throwing the merest fraction of a glance towards his mother.

The magistrate understood.

"As yet — no. Can you give us any clue as to the writer?"

"I have no idea whatsoever."

Monsieur Hautet sighed.

"A most mysterious case. Ah, well, I suppose we can now rule out the letter altogether. Let me see, where were we? Oh, the weapon. I fear this may give you pain, Monsieur Renauld. I understand it was a present from you to your mother. Very sad — very distressing —"

Jack Renauld leaned forward. His face, which had flushed during the perusal of the letter, was now deadly white.

"Do you mean that it was with an aeroplane-wire paper-cutter that my father was — was killed? But it's impossible! A little thing like that!"

"Alas, Monsieur Renauld, it is only too true! An ideal little tool, I fear. Sharp and easy to handle."

"Where is it? Can I see it? Is it still in the — the body?"

"Oh no, it has been removed. You

would like to see it? To make sure? It would be as well, perhaps, though madame has already identified it. Still — Monsieur Bex, might I trouble you?"

"Certainly. I will fetch it immediately."

"Would it not be better to take Monsieur Renauld to the shed?" suggested Giraud smoothly. "Without doubt he would wish to see his father's body."

The boy made a shivering gesture of negation, and the magistrate, always disposed to cross Giraud whenever possible, replied:

"But no — not at present. Monsieur Bex will be so kind as to bring it to us here."

The commissary left the room. Stonor crossed to Jack and wrung him by the hand. Poirot had risen, and was adjusting a pair of candlesticks that struck his trained eye as being a shade askew. The magistrate was reading the mysterious love-letter through a last time, clinging desperately to his first theory of jealousy and a stab in the back.

Suddenly the door burst open and the commissary rushed in.

"Monsieur le juge! Monsieur le juge!"

"But yes. What is it?"

"The dagger! It is gone!"

"What — gone?"

"Vanished. Disappeared. The glass jar that contained it is empty!"

"What?" I cried. "Impossible. Why, only this morning I saw —" The words died on my tongue.

But the attention of the entire room was diverted to me.

"What is that you say?" cried the commissary. "This morning?"

"I saw it there this morning," I said slowly. "About an hour and a half ago, to be accurate."

"You went to the shed, then? How did you get the key?"

"I asked the sergent de ville for it."

"And you went there? Why?"

I hesitated, but in the end I decided that the only thing to do was to make a clean breast of it.

"Monsieur Hautet," I said, "I have committed a grave fault, for which I must crave your indulgence."

"Proceed, monsieur."

"The fact of the matter is," I said, wishing myself anywhere else but where I was, "that I met a young lady, an acquaintance of mine. She displayed a great desire to see everything that was to be seen, and I — well, in short, I took the key to show her the body."

"Ah!" cried the magistrate indignantly. "But it is a grave fault you have committed there, Captain Hastings. It is altogether most irregular. You should not have permitted yourself this folly."

"I know," I said meekly. "Nothing that you can say could be too severe, monsieur."

"You did not invite this lady to come here?"

"Certainly not. I met her quite by accident. She is an English lady who happens to be staying in Merlinville, though I was not aware of that until my unexpected meeting with her."

"Well, well," said the magistrate, softening. "It was most irregular, but the lady is without doubt young and beautiful. What it is to be young!" And he sighed sentimentally.

But the commissary, less romantic and more practical, took up the tale:

"But did you not reclose and lock the door when you departed?"

"That's just it," I said slowly. "That's what I blame myself for so terribly. My friend was upset at the sight. She nearly fainted. I got her some brandy and water, and afterwards insisted on accompanying her back to the town. In the excitement I forgot to relock the door. I only did so when I got back to the villa."

"Then for twenty minutes at least —" said the commissary slowly. He stopped.

"Exactly," I said.

"Twenty minutes," mused the commissary.

"It is deplorable," said Monsieur Hautet, his sternness of manner returning. "Without precedent."

Suddenly another voice spoke.

"You find it deplorable?" asked Giraud.

"Certainly I do."

"I find it admirable!" said the other imperturbably.

This unexpected ally quite bewildered me. "Admirable, Monsieur Giraud?" asked the magistrate, studying him cautiously out of the corner of his eye.

"Precisely."

"And why?"

"Because we know now that the assassin, or an accomplice of the assassin, has been near the villa only an hour ago. It will be strange if, with that knowledge, we do not shortly lay hands upon him."

There was a note of menace in his voice. He continued: "He risked a good deal to gain possession of that dagger. Perhaps he feared that fingerprints might be discovered on it."

Poirot turned to Bex.

"You said there were none?"

Giraud shrugged his shoulders.

"Perhaps he could not be sure."

Poirot looked at him.

"You are wrong, Monsieur Giraud. The assassin wore gloves. So he must have been sure."

"I do not say it was the assassin himself. It may have been an accomplice who was not aware of that fact."

The magistrate's clerk was gathering up the papers on the table. Monsieur Hautet addressed us: "Our work here finished. Perhaps, Monsieur Renauld, you will listen while your evidence is read over to you. I have purposely kept all the proceedings as informal as possible. I have been called original in my methods, but I maintain that there is much to be said for originality. The case is now in the clever hands of the renowned Monsieur Giraud.

He will without doubt distinguish himself. Indeed, I wonder that he has not already laid his hands upon the murderers! Madame, again let me assure you of my heartfelt sympathy. Messieurs, I wish you all good day."

And, accompanied by his clerk and the commissary, he took his departure.

Poirot tugged out that large turnip of a watch of his and observed the time.

"Let us return to the hotel for lunch, my friend," he said. "And you shall recount to me in full the indiscretions of this morning. No one is observing us. We need make no *adieux*."

We went quietly out of the room. The examining magistrate had just driven off in his car. I was going down the steps when Poirot's voice arrested me:

"One little moment, my friend." Dexterously he whipped out his yard measure and proceeded, quite solemnly, to measure an overcoat hanging in the hall, from the collar to the hem. I had not seen it hanging there before, and guessed that it belonged to either Mr. Stonor or Jack Renauld.

Then, with a little satisfied grunt, Poirot returned the measure to his pocket and followed me out into the open air.

# XII.

## POIROT ELUCIDATES CERTAIN POINTS.

"Why did you measure that overcoat?" I asked, with some curiosity, as we walked down the hot white road at a leisurely pace.

"*Parbleu!* to see how long it was," replied my friend imperturbably.

I was vexed. Poirot's incurable habit of making a mystery out of nothing never failed to irritate me. I relapsed into silence, and followed a train of thought of my own.

Although I had not noticed them specially at the time, certain words Mrs. Renauld had addressed to her son now recurred to me, fraught with a new significance. "So you did not sail?" she had said, and then had added: "*After all, it does not matter — now.*"

What had she meant by that? The words were enigmatical — significant. Was it possible that she knew more than we supposed? She had denied all knowledge of the mysterious mission with which her husband was to have entrusted his son. But was she really less ignorant than she pretended? Could she enlighten us if she chose, and was her silence part of a carefully thought out and preconceived plan?

The more I thought about it, the more I was convinced that I was right. Mrs. Renauld knew more than she chose to tell. In her surprise at seeing her son, she had momentarily betrayed herself. I felt convinced that she knew, if not the assassins, at least the motive for the assassination. But some very powerful considerations must keep her silent.

"You think profoundly, my friend," remarked Poirot, breaking in upon my reflections. "What is it that intrigues you so?"

I told him, sure of my ground, though feeling expectant that he would ridicule my suspicions. But to my surprise he nodded thoughtfully.

"You are quite right, Hastings. From the beginning I have been sure that she was keeping something back. At first I suspected her, if not of inspiring, at least of conniving at the crime."

"You suspected her?" I cried.

"But certainly. She benefits enormously—in fact, by this new will, she is the only person to benefit. So, from the start, she was singled out for attention. You may have noticed that I took an early opportunity of examining her wrists. I wished to see whether there was any possibility that she had gagged and bound herself. *Eh bien*, I saw at once that there was no fake, the cords had actually been drawn so tight as to cut into the flesh. That ruled out the possibility of her having committed the crime single-handed. But it was still possible for her to have connived at it, or to have been the instigator with an accomplice. Moreover, the story, as she told it, was singularly familiar to me—the masked men that she could not recognize, the mention of "the secret"—I had heard, or read, all these things before. Another little detail confirmed my belief that she was not speaking the truth. The wristwatch, Hastings, the wristwatch!"

Again that wristwatch! Poirot was eyeing me curiously.

"You see, *mon ami?* You comprehend?"

"No," I replied with some ill humour. "I neither see nor comprehend. You make all these confounded mysteries, and it's useless asking you to explain. You always like keeping something up your sleeve to the last minute."

"Do not enrage yourself, my friend," said Poirot, with a smile. "I will explain if you wish. But not a word to Giraud, *c'est entendu?* He treats me as an old one of no importance! We shall see! In common fairness I gave him a hint. If he does not choose to act upon it, that is his own lookout."

I assured Poirot that he could rely upon my discretion.

"*C'est bien!* Let us then employ our little grey cells. Tell me, my friend, at what time, according to you, did the tragedy take place?"

"Why, at two o'clock or thereabouts," I said, astonished. "You remember, Mrs. Renauld told us that she heard the clock strike while the men were in the room."

"Exactly, and on the strength of that, you, the examining magistrate,

Bex, and everyone else, accept the time without further question. But I, Hercule Poirot, say that Madame Renauld lied. The crime took place at least two hours earlier."

"But the doctors —"

"They declared, after examination of the body, that death had taken place between ten and seven hours previously. *Mon ami*, for some reason it was imperative that the crime should seem to have taken place later than it actually did. You have read of a smashed watch or clock recording the exact hour of a crime? So that the time should not rest on Madame Renauld's testimony alone, someone moved on the hands of that wristwatch to two o'clock, and then dashed it violently to the ground. But, as is often the case, they defeated their own object. The glass was smashed, but the mechanism of the watch was uninjured. It was a most disastrous manoeuvre on their part, for it at once drew my attention to two points — first, that Madame Renauld was lying; secondly, that there must be some vital reason for the postponement of the time."

"But what reason could there be?"

"Ah, that is the question! There we have the whole mystery. As yet, I cannot explain it. There is only one idea that presents itself to me as having a possible connexion."

"And that is?"

"The last train left Merlinville at seventeen minutes past twelve."

I followed it out slowly.

"So that, the crime apparently taking place some two hours later, anyone leaving by that train would have an unimpeachable alibi!"

"Perfect, Hastings! You have it!"

I sprang up.

"But we must inquire at the station! Surely they cannot have failed to notice two foreigners who left by that train! We must go there at once!"

"You think so, Hastings?"

"Of course. Let us go there now."

Poirot restrained my ardour with a light touch upon the arm.

"Go by all means if you wish, *mon ami* — but if you go, I should not ask for particulars of two foreigners."

I stared and he said rather impatiently:

"*Là, là, là,* you do not believe all that rigmarole, do you? The masked men and all the rest of *cette histoire-la!*"

His words took me so much aback, that I hardly knew how to respond. He went on serenely:

"You heard me say to Giraud, did you not, that all the details of this crime were familiar to me? *Eh bien*, that presupposes one of two things, either the brain that planned the first crime also planned this one, or else an account read of a *cause célèbre* unconsciously remained in our assassin's memory and prompted the details. I shall be able to pronounce definitely on that after —"

He broke off.

I was revolving sundry matters in my mind. "But Mr. Renauld's letter? It distinctly mentions a secret and Santiago!"

"Undoubtedly there was a secret in Monsieur Renauld's life — there can be no doubt of that. On the other hand, the word Santiago, to my mind, is a red herring, dragged continually across the track to put us off the scent. It is possible that it was used in the same way on Monsieur Renauld, to keep from directing his suspicions to a quarter at hand. Oh, be assured, Hastings, the danger that threatened him was not in Santiago, it was near at hand, in France."

He spoke so gravely, and with such assurance, that I could not fail to be convinced. But I essayed one final objection: "And the match and cigarette end found near the body? What of them?"

A light of pure enjoyment lit up Poirot's face.

"Planted! Deliberately planted there for Giraud or one of his tribe to find! Ah, he is smart, Giraud, he can do his tricks! So can a good retriever dog. He comes in so pleased with himself. For hours he has crawled on his stomach. "See what I have found," he says. And then again to me: "What do you see here?" Me, I answer, with profound and deep truth, "Nothing." And Giraud, the great Giraud, he laughs, he thinks to himself, 'Oh, he is *imbecile*, this old one.' *But we shall see . . .* "

But my mind had reverted to the main facts.

"Then all this story of the masked men — ?"

"Is false."

"What really happened?"

Poirot shrugged his shoulders.

"One person could tell us — Madame Renauld. But she will not speak. Threats and entreaties would not move her. A remarkable woman that, Hastings. I recognized as soon as I saw her that I had to deal with a woman of unusual character. At first, as I told you, I was inclined to suspect her of being concerned in the crime. Afterwards I altered my opinion."

"What made you do that?"

"Her spontaneous and genuine grief at the sight of her husband's body. I could swear that the agony in that cry of hers was genuine."

"Yes," I said thoughtfully, "one cannot mistake these things."

"I beg your pardon, my friend — one can always be mistaken. Regard a great actress, does not her acting of grief carry you away and impress you with its reality? No, however strong my own impression and belief, I needed other evidence before I allowed myself to be satisfied. The great criminal can be a great actor. I base my certainty in this case not upon my own impression, but upon the undeniable fact that Madame Renauld actually fainted. I turned up her eyelids and felt her pulse. There was no deception — the swoon was genuine.

Therefore I was satisfied that her anguish was real and not assumed. Besides, a small additional point without interest, it was unnecessary for Madame Renauld to exhibit unrestrained grief. She had had one paroxysm on learning of her husband's death, and there would be no need for her to simulate another such a violent one on beholding his body. No, Madame Renauld was not her husband's murderess. But why has she lied? She lied about the wristwatch, she lied about the masked men — she lied about a third thing. Tell me, Hastings, what is your explanation of the open door?"

"Well," I said, rather embarrassed, "I suppose it was an oversight. They forgot to shut it."

Poirot shook his head, and sighed.

"That is the explanation of Giraud. It does not satisfy me. There is a meaning behind that open door which for the moment I cannot fathom. One thing I am fairly sure of — they did not leave through the door. They left by the window."

"What?"

"Precisely."

"But there were no footmarks in the flower-bed underneath."

"No — and there ought to have been. Listen, Hastings. The gardener, Auguste, as you heard him say, planted both those beds the preceding afternoon. In the one there are plentiful impressions of his big hobnailed boots — in the other, none! You see? Someone had passed that way, someone who, to obliterate their footprints, smoothed over the surface of the bed with a rake."

"Where did they get a rake?"

"Where they got the spade and the gardening gloves," said Poirot impatiently. "There is no difficulty about that."

"What makes you think that they left that way, though? Surely it is more probable that they entered by the window, and left by the door?"

"That is possible, of course. Yet I have a strong idea that they left by the window."

"I think you are wrong."

"Perhaps, *mon ami.*"

I mused, thinking over the new field of conjecture that Poirot's deductions had opened up to me. I recalled my wonder at his cryptic allusion to the flower-bed and the wristwatch. His remarks had seemed so meaningless at the moment, and now, for the first time, I realized how remarkably, from a few slight inci dents, he had unravelled much of the mystery that surrounded the case. I paid a belated homage to my friend.

"In the meantime," I said, considering, "although we know a great deal more than we did, we are no nearer to solving the mystery of who killed Mr. Renauld."

"No," said Poirot cheerfully. "In fact we are a great deal farther off."

The fact seemed to afford him such peculiar satisfaction that I gazed at him in wonder. He met my eye and smiled.

Suddenly a light burst upon me.

"Poirot! Mrs. Renauld! I see it now. She must be shielding somebody."

From the quietness with which Poirot received my remark, I could see that the idea had already occurred to him.

"Yes," he said thoughtfully. "Shielding someone — or screening someone. One of the two."

Then, as we entered our hotel, he enjoined silence on me with a gesture.

# XIII.

## THE GIRL WITH THE ANXIOUS EYES.

We lunched with an excellent appetite. For a while we ate in silence, and then Poirot observed maliciously: "*Eh bien*! And your indiscretions! You recount them not?"

I felt myself blushing.

"Oh, you mean this morning?" I endeavoured to adopt a tone of absolute nonchalance.

But I was no match for Poirot. In a very few minutes he had extracted the whole story from me, his eyes twinkling as he did so.

"*Tiens!* A story of the most romantic. What is her name, this charming young lady?"

I had to confess that I did not know.

"Still more romantic! The first *rencontre* in the train from Paris, the second here. Journeys end in lovers' meetings, is not that the saying?"

"Don't be an ass, Poirot."

"Yesterday it was Mademoiselle Daubreuil, today it is Mademoiselle — Cinderella! Decidedly you have the heart of a Turk, Hastings! You should establish a harem!"

"It's all very well to rag me. Mademoiselle Daubreuil is a very beautiful girl, and I do admire her immensely — I don't mind admitting it. The other's nothing — I don't suppose I shall ever see her again."

"You do not propose to see the lady again?"

His last words were almost a question, and I was aware of the sharpness with which he darted a glance at me. And before my eyes, writ large in letters of fire, I saw the words "Hotel du Phare," and I heard again her voice saying, "Come and look me up," and my own answering with *empressement,* "I will."

I answered Poirot lightly enough:

"She asked me to look her up, but, of course, I shan't."

"Why 'of course'?"

"Well, I don't want to."

"Mademoiselle Cinderella is staying at the Hôtel d'Angleterre you told me, did you not?"

"No. Hotel du Phare."

"True, I forgot."

A moment's misgiving shot across my mind. Surely I had never mentioned any hotel to Poirot. I looked across at him and felt reassured. He was cutting his bread into neat little squares, completely absorbed in his task. He must have fancied I had told him where the girl was staying.

We had coffee outside facing the sea. Poirot smoked one of his tiny cigarettes, and then drew his watch from his pocket.

"The train to Paris leaves at 2.25," he observed. "I should be starting."

"Paris?" I cried.

"That is what I said, *mon ami.*"

"You are going to Paris? But why?"

He replied very seriously:

"To look for the murderer of Monsieur Renauld."

"You think he is in Paris?"

"I am quite certain that he is not. Nevertheless, it is there that I must look for him. You do not understand, but I will explain it all to you in good time. Believe me, this journey to Paris is necessary. I shall not be away long. In all probability I shall return tomorrow. I do not propose that you should accompany me. Remain here and keep an eye on Giraud. Also cultivate the society of Monsieur Renauld *fils.*"

"That reminds me," I said. "I meant to ask you how you knew about those two?"

"*Mon ami* — I know human nature. Throw together a boy like young Renauld and a beautiful girl like Mademoiselle Marthe and the result is almost inevitable. Then, the quarrel! It was money, or a woman, and, remembering Léonie's description of the lad's anger, I decided on the latter. So I made my guess — and I was right."

"You already suspected that she loved young Renauld?"

Poirot smiled.

"At any rate, I saw that she had anxious eyes. That is how I always think of Mademoiselle Daubreuil — as *the girl with the anxious eyes.*"

His voice was so grave that it impressed me uncomfortably.

"What do you mean by that, Poirot?"

"I fancy, my friend, that we shall see before very long. But I must start."

"I will come and see you off," I said, rising.

"You will do nothing of the sort. I forbid it."

He was so peremptory that I stared at him in surprise. He nodded emphatically.

"I mean it, *mon ami. Au revoir.*"

I felt rather at a loose end after Poirot had left me. I strolled down to the beach and watched the bathers, without feeling energetic enough to join them. I rather fancied that Cinderella might be disporting herself among them in some wonderful costume; but I saw no signs of her. I strolled aimlessly along the sands towards the farther end of the town. It occurred to me that, after all, it would only be decent feeling on my part to inquire after the girl. And it would save trouble in the end. The matter would then be finished with. There would be no need for me to trouble about her any further. But if I did not go at all, she might quite possibly come and look me up at the villa.

Accordingly, I left the beach, and walked inland. I soon found the Hôtel du Phare, a very unpretentious building. It was annoying in the extreme not to know the lady's name and, to save my dignity, I decided to stroll inside and look around. Probably I should find her in the lounge. I went in, but there was no sign of her. I waited for some time, till my impatience got the better of me. I took the concierge aside and slipped five francs into his hand.

"I wish to see a lady who is staying here. A young English lady, small and dark. I am not sure of her name."

The man shook his head and seemed to be suppressing a grin.

"There is no such lady as you describe staying here."

"But the lady told me she was staying here."

"Monsieur must have made a mistake—or it is more likely the lady did, since there has been another gentleman here inquiring for her."

"What is that you say?" I cried, surprised.

"But yes, monsieur. A gentleman who described her just as you have done."

"What was he like?"

"He was a small gentleman, well dressed, very neat, very spotless, the moustache very stiff, the head of a peculiar shape, and the eyes green."

Poirot! So that was why he refused to let me accompany him to the station. The impertinence of it! I would thank him not to meddle in my concerns. Did he fancy I needed a nurse to look after me?

Thanking the man, I departed, somewhat at a loss, and still much incensed with my meddlesome friend.

But where was the lady? I set aside my wrath and tried to puzzle it out. Evidently, through inadvertence, she had named the wrong hotel.

Then another thought struck me. Was it inadvertence? Or had she deliberately withheld her name and given me the wrong address?

The more I thought about it, the more I felt convinced that this last surmise of mine was right. For some reason or other she did not wish to let the acquaintance ripen into friendship. And, though half an hour earlier this had been precisely my own view, I did not enjoy having the tables turned upon me. The whole affair was profoundly unsatisfactory, and I went up to the Villa Geneviève in a condition of distinct ill humour. I did not go to the house, but went up the path to the little bench by the shed, and sat there moodily enough.

I was distracted from my thoughts by the sound of voices close at hand. In a second or two I realized that they came, not from the garden I was in, but from the adjoining garden of the Villa Marguerite, and that they were approaching rapidly. A girl's voice was speaking, a voice that I recognized as that of the beautiful Marthe.

*"Cheri,"* she was saying, "is it really true? Are all our troubles over?"

"You know it, Marthe," Jack Renauld replied. "Nothing can part us now, beloved. The last obstacle to our union is removed. Nothing can take you from me."

"Nothing?" the girl murmured. "Oh Jack, Jack — I am afraid."

I had moved to depart, realizing that I was quite unintentionally eavesdropping. As I rose to my feet, I caught sight of them through a gap in the hedge. They stood together facing me, the man's arm round the girl, his eyes looking into hers. They were a splendid-looking couple, the dark, well-knit boy and the fair young goddess. They seemed made for each other as they stood there, happy in spite of the terrible tragedy that overshadowed their young lives.

But the girl's face was troubled, and Jack Renauld seemed to recognize it, as he held her closer to him and asked:

"But what are you afraid of, darling? What is there to fear — now?"

And then I saw the look in her eyes, the look Poirot had spoken of, as she murmured, so that I almost guessed at the words:

"I am afraid — for you."

I did not hear young Renauld's answer, for my attention was distracted by an unusual appearance a little farther down the hedge. There appeared to be a brown bush there, which seemed odd, to say the least of it, so early in the summer. I stepped along to investigate, but, at my advance, the brown bush withdrew itself precipitately, and faced me with a finger to its lips. It was Giraud.

Enjoining caution, he led the way round the shed until we were out of ear-shot.

"What were you doing there?" I asked.

"Exactly what you were doing, listening."

"But I was not there on purpose!"

"Ah!" said Giraud. "I was."

As always, I admired the man while disliking him. He looked me up and down with a sort of contemptuous disfavour.

"You didn't help matters by butting in. I might have heard something useful in a minute. What have you done with your old fossil?"

"Monsieur Poirot has gone to Paris," I replied coldly.

Giraud snapped his fingers disdainfully. "So he has gone to Paris, has he? Well, a good thing. The longer he stays there the better. But what does he think he will find there?"

I thought I read in the question a tinge of uneasiness. I drew myself up.

"That I am not at liberty to say," I said quietly.

Giraud subjected me to a piercing stare.

"He has probably enough sense not to tell you," he remarked rudely. "Good afternoon. I'm busy." And with that he turned on his heel, and left me without ceremony.

Matters seemed at a standstill at the Villa Geneviève. Giraud evidently did not desire my company and, from what I had seen, it seemed fairly certain that Jack Renauld did not either.

I went back to the town, had an enjoyable bathe, and returned to the hotel. I turned in early, wondering whether the following day would bring forth anything of interest.

I was wholly unprepared for what it did bring forth. I was eating my *petit dejeuner* in the dining-room when the waiter, who had been talking to someone outside, came back in obvious excitement. He hesitated for a minute, fidgeting with his napkin, and then burst out:

"Monsieur will pardon me, but he is connected, is he not, with the affair at the Villa Geneviève?"

"Yes," I said eagerly. "Why?"

"Monsieur has not heard the news, though?"

"What news?"

"That there has been another murder there last night!"

"*What?*"

Leaving my breakfast, I caught up my hat and ran as fast as I could. Another murder — and Poirot away! What fatality. But who had been murdered?

I dashed in at the gate. A group of servants were in the drive, talking and gesticulating. I caught hold of Françoise.

"What has happened?"

"Oh, monsieur! monsieur! Another death! It is terrible. There is a curse upon the house. But yes, I say it, a curse! They should send for Monsieur le Cure to bring some holy water. Never will I sleep another night under that roof. It might be my turn, who knows?"

She crossed herself.

"Yes," I cried, "but who has been killed?"

"Do I know — me? A man — a stranger. They found him up there — in the shed — not a hundred yards from where they found poor

Monsieur. And that is not all—he is stabbed—stabbed to the heart with the same dagger!"

# XIV.

## THE SECOND BODY.

Waiting for no more, I turned and ran up the path to the shed. The two men on guard there stood aside to let me pass and, filled with excitement, I entered.

The light was dim, the place was a mere rough wooden erection to keep old pots and tools in. I had entered impetuously, but on the threshold I checked myself, fascinated by the spectacle before me.

Giraud was on his hands and knees, a pocket torch in his hand with which he was examining every inch of the ground. He looked up with a frown at my entrance, then his face relaxed a little in a sort of good-humoured contempt.

"There he is," said Giraud, flashing his torch to the far corner.

I stepped across.

The dead man lay straight upon his back. He was of medium height, swarthy of complexion, and possibly about fifty years of age. He was neatly dressed in a dark blue suit, well cut, and probably made by an expensive tailor, but not new. His face was terribly convulsed, and on his left side, just over the heart, the hilt of a dagger stood up, black and shining. I recognized it. It was the same dagger I had seen reposing in the glass jar the preceding morning!

"I'm expecting the doctor any minute," explained Giraud. "Although we hardly need him. There's no doubt what the man died of. He was stabbed to the heart, and death must have been pretty well instantaneous."

"When was it done? Last night?"

Giraud shook his head.

"Hardly. I don't lay down the law on medical evidence, but the man's been dead over twelve hours. When do you say you last saw that dagger?"

"About ten o'clock yesterday morning."

"Then I should be inclined to fix the crime as being done not long after that."

"But people were passing and repassing this shed continually."

Giraud laughed disagreeably.

"You progress to a marvel! Who told you he was killed in this shed?"

"Well —" I felt flustered. "I — I assumed it."

"Oh, what a fine detective! Look at him. Does a man stabbed to the heart fall like that — neatly with his feet together, and his arms to his sides? No. Again, does a man lie down on his back and permit himself to be stabbed without raising a hand to defend himself? It is absurd, is it not? But see here — and here —" He flashed the torch along the ground. I saw curious irregular marks in the soft dirt. "He was dragged here after he was dead. Half dragged, half carried by two people. Their tracks do not show on the hard ground outside, and here they have been careful to obliterate them; but one of the two was a woman, my young friend."

"A woman?"

"Yes."

"But if the tracks are obliterated, how do you know?"

"Because, blurred as they are, the prints of the woman's shoe are unmistakable. Also, by this." And, leaning forward, he drew something from the handle of the dagger and held it up for me to see. It was a woman's long black hair, similar to the one Poirot had taken from the armchair in the library.

With a slightly ironic smile he wound it round the dagger again.

"We will leave things as they are as much as possible," he explained. "It pleases the examining magistrate. Well, do you notice anything else?"

I was forced to shake my head.

"Look at his hands."

I did. The nails were broken and discoloured and the skin was hard. It hardly enlightened me as much as I should have liked it to have done. I looked up at Giraud.

"They are not the hands of a gentleman," he said, answering my look. "On the contrary, his clothes are those of a well-to-do man. That is curious, is it not?"

"Very curious," I agreed.

"And none of his clothing is marked. What do we learn from that? This man was trying to pass himself off as other than he was. He was masquerading. Why? Did he fear something? Was he trying to escape by disguising himself? As yet we do not know, but one thing we do know — he was as anxious to conceal his identity as we are to discover it."

He looked down at the body again.

"As before, there are no fingerprints on the handle of the dagger. The murderer again wore gloves."

"You think, then, that the murderer was the same in both cases?" I asked eagerly.

Giraud became inscrutable.

"Never mind what I think. We shall see. Marchaud!"

The *sergent de ville* appeared at the door.

"Monsieur?"

"Why is Madame Renauld not here? I sent for her a quarter of an hour ago."

"She is coming up the path now, monsieur, and her son with her."

"Good. I only want one at a time, though."

Marchaud saluted and disappeared again. A moment later he reappeared with Mrs. Renauld.

"Here is Madame."

Giraud came forward with a curt bow. "This way, madame." He led her across, and then, standing suddenly aside, "Here is the man. Do you know him?"

And as he spoke, his eyes, gimlet-like, bored into her face, seeking to read her mind, noting every indication of her manner.

But Mrs. Renauld remained perfectly calm — too calm, I felt. She looked down at the corpse almost without interest, certainly without any sign of agitation or recognition.

"No," she said. "I have never seen him in my life. He is quite a stranger to me."

"You are sure?"

"Quite sure."

"You do not recognize in him one of your assailants, for instance?"

"No." She seemed to hesitate, as though struck by the idea. "No, I do not think so. Of course they wore beards — false ones, the examining magistrate thought — but still, no." Now she seemed to make her mind up definitely. "I am sure neither of the two was this man."

"Very well, madame. That is all, then."

She stepped out with head erect, the sun flashing on the silver threads in her hair.

Jack Renauld succeeded her. He, too, failed to identify the man in a completely natural manner.

Giraud merely grunted. Whether he was pleased or chagrined I could not tell. He called to Marchaud.

"You have got the other there?"

"Yes, monsieur."

"Bring her in, then."

The "other" was Madame Daubreuil. She came indignantly, protesting with vehemence. "I object, monsieur! This is an outrage! What have I to do with all this?"

"Madame," said Giraud brutally, "I am investigating not one murder, but two murders! For all I know you may have committed them both."

"How dare you?" she cried. "How dare you insult me by such a wild accusation! It is infamous!"

"Infamous, is it? What about this?"

Stooping, he again detached the hair, and held it up. "Do you see this, madame?" He advanced towards her. "You permit that I see whether it matches?"

With a cry she started backwards, white to the lips.

"It is false, I swear it. I know nothing of the crime — of either crime. Anyone who says I do lies! Ah, *mon Dieu*, what shall I do?"

"Calm yourself, madame," said Giraud coldly. "No one has accused you as yet. But you will do well to answer my questions without more ado."

"Anything you wish, monsieur."

"Look at the dead man. Have you ever seen him before?"

Drawing nearer, a little of the colour creeping back to her face, Madame Daubreuil looked down at the victim with a certain amount of interest and curiosity. Then she shook her head.

"I do not know him."

It seemed impossible to doubt her, the words came so naturally. Giraud dismissed her with a nod of the head.

"You are letting her go?" I asked in a low voice. "Is that wise? Surely that black hair is from her head."

"I do not need teaching my business," said Giraud dryly. "She is under surveillance. I have no wish to arrest her as yet."

Then, frowning, he gazed down at the body.

"Should you say that was a Spanish type at all?" he asked suddenly.

I considered the face carefully.

"No," I said at last. "I should put him down as a Frenchman most decidedly."

Giraud gave a grunt of dissatisfaction.

"Same here."

He stood there for a moment, then with an imperative gesture he waved me aside, and once more, on hands and knees, he continued his search of the floor of the shed. He was marvellous. Nothing escaped him. Inch by inch he went over the floor, turning over pots, examining old sacks. He pounced on a bundle by the door, but it proved to be only a ragged coat and trousers, and he flung it down again with a snarl. Two pairs of old gloves interested him, but in the end he shook his head and laid them aside. Then he went back to the pots, methodically turning them over one by one. In the end he rose to his feet, and shook his head thoughtfully. He seemed baffled and perplexed. I think he had forgotten my presence.

But at that moment a stir and bustle was heard outside, and our old friend, the examining magistrate, accompanied by his clerk and Monsieur Bex, with the doctor behind them, came bustling in.

"But this is extraordinary, Monsieur Giraud," cried Monsieur Hautet. "Another crime! Ah, we have not got to the bottom of this case.

There is some deep mystery here. But who is the victim this time?"

"That is just what nobody can tell us, monsieur. He has not been identified."

"Where is the body?" asked the doctor. Giraud moved aside a little.

"There in the corner. He has been stabbed to the heart, as you see. And with the dagger that was stolen yesterday morning. I fancy that the murder followed hard upon the theft—but that is for you to say. You can handle the dagger freely—there are no fingerprints on it."

The doctor knelt down by the dead man, and Giraud turned to the examining magistrate.

"A pretty little problem, is it not? But I shall solve it."

"And so no one can identify him," mused the magistrate. "Could it possibly be one of the assassins? They may have fallen out among themselves."

Giraud shook his head.

"The man is a Frenchman—I would take my oath on that—"

But at that moment they were interrupted by the doctor, who was sitting back on his heels with a perplexed expression.

"You say he was killed yesterday morning?"

"I fix it by the theft of the dagger," explained Giraud. "He may, of course, have been killed later in the day."

"Later in the day? Fiddlesticks! This man been dead at least forty-eight hours, and probably longer."

We stared at each other in blank amazement.

# XV.

## A PHOTOGRAPH.

The doctor's words were so surprising that we were all momentarily taken aback. Here was a man stabbed with a dagger which we knew to have been stolen only twenty-four hours previously, and yet Dr. Durand asserted positively that he had been dead at least forty-eight hours. The whole thing was fantastic to the last extreme.

We were still recovering from the surprise of the doctor's announcement, when a telegram was brought to me. It had been sent up from the hotel to the villa. I tore it open. It was from Poirot, and announced his return by the train arriving at Merlinville at 12:28.

I looked at my watch and saw that I had just time to get comfortably to the station and meet him there. I felt that it was of the utmost importance that he should know at once of the new and startling developments in the case.

Evidently, I reflected, Poirot had had no difficulty in finding what he wanted in Paris. The quickness of his return proved that. Very few hours had sufficed. I wondered how he would take the exciting news I had to impart.

The train was some minutes late, and I strolled aimlessly up and down the platform, until it occurred to me that I might pass the time by asking a few questions as to who had left Merlinville by the last train on the evening of the tragedy.

I approached the chief porter, an intelligent looking man, and had little difficulty in persuading him to enter upon the subject. It was a disgrace to the police, he hotly affirmed, that such brigands or assassins should be allowed to go about unpunished. I hinted that there was some possibility they might have left by the midnight train, but he negatived the idea decidedly. He would have noticed two foreigners — he was sure of it. Only about twenty people had left by the train, and he could not have failed to observe them.

I do not know what put the idea into my head — possibly it was the deep anxiety underlying Marthe Daubreuil's tones — but I asked suddenly:

"Young Monsieur Renauld — he did not leave by that train, did he?"

"Ah, no, monsieur. To arrive and start off again within half an hour, it would not be amusing, that!"

I stared at the man, the significance of his words almost escaping me. Then I saw.

"You mean," I said, my heart beating a little, "that Monsieur Jack Renauld arrived at Merlinville that evening?"

"But yes, monsieur. By the last train arriving the other way, the 11:40."

My brain whirled. That, then, was the reason of Marthe's poignant anxiety. Jack Renauld had been in Merlinville on the night of the crime. But why had he not said so? Why, on the contrary, had he led us to believe that he had remained in Cherbourg? Remembering his frank boyish countenance, I could hardly bring myself to believe that he had any connexion with the crime. Yet why this silence on his part about so vital a matter? One thing was certain, Marthe had known all along. Hence her anxiety, and her eager questioning of Poirot as to whether anyone was suspected.

My cogitations were interrupted by the arrival of the train, and in another moment I was greeting Poirot. The little man was radiant. He beamed and vociferated and, forgetting my English reluctance, embraced me warmly on the platform.

"*Mon cher ami*, I have succeeded — but succeeded to a marvel!"

"Indeed? I'm delighted to hear it. Have you heard the latest here?"

"How would you that I should hear anything? There have been some developments, eh? The brave Giraud, he has made an arrest? Or even arrests, perhaps? Ah, but I will make him look foolish, that one! But where are you taking me, my friend? Do we not go to the hotel? It is necessary that I attend to my moustaches — they are deplorably limp from the heat of travelling. Also, without doubt, there is dust on my coat. And my tie, that I must rearrange."

I cut short his remonstrances.

"My dear Poirot — never mind

all that. We must go to the villa at once. *There has been another murder!*"

Never have I seen a man so flabbergasted. His jaw dropped. All the jauntiness went out of his bearing. He stared at me open-mouthed.

"What is that you say? Another murder? Ah, then, but I am all wrong, I have failed. Giraud may mock himself at me — he will have reason!"

"You did not expect it, then?"

"I? Not the least in the world. It demolishes my theory — it ruins everything — ah — no!" He stopped dead, thumping himself on the chest. "It is impossible. I *cannot* be wrong! The facts, taken methodically, and in their proper order, admit of only one explanation. I must be right! I *am* right!"

"But then —'

He interrupted me.

"Wait, my friend. I must be right, therefore this new murder is impossible unless — unless — Oh, wait, I implore you. Say no word."

He was silent for a moment or two, then resuming his normal manner, he said in a quiet assured voice:

"The victim is a man of middle age. His body was found in the locked shed near the scene of the crime and had been dead at least forty-eight hours. And it is most probable that he was stabbed in a similar manner to Mr. Renauld, though not necessarily in the back."

It was my turn to gape — and gape I did. In all my knowledge of Poirot he had never done anything so amazing as this. And, almost inevitably, a doubt crossed my mind.

"Poirot," I cried, "you're pulling my leg. You've heard all about it already."

He turned his earnest gaze upon me reproachfully.

"Would I do such a thing? I assure you that I have heard nothing whatsoever. Did you not observe the shock your news was to me?"

"But how on earth could you know all that?"

"I was right, then? But I knew it. The little grey cells, my friend, the little grey cells! They told me. Thus, and in no other way, could there have been a second death. Now tell me all. If we go round to the left here, we can take a short cut across the golf links which will bring us to the back of the Villa Geneviève much more quickly."

As we walked, taking the way he had indicated, I recounted all I knew. Poirot listened attentively.

"The dagger was in the wound, you say? That is curious. You are sure it was the same one?"

"Absolutely certain. That's what makes it so impossible."

"Nothing is impossible. There may have been two daggers."

I raised my eyebrows.

"Surely that is in the highest degree unlikely? It would be a most extraordinary coincidence."

"You speak, as usual, without reflection, Hastings. In some cases two identical weapons would be highly improbable. But not here. This particular weapon was a war souvenir which was made to Jack Renauld's orders. It is really highly unlikely, when you come to think of it, that he should have had only one made. Very probably he would have another for his own use."

"But nobody has mentioned such a thing," I objected.

A hint of the lecturer crept into Poirot's tone.

"My friend, in working upon a case, one does not take into account only the things that are 'mentioned.' There is no reason to mention many things which may be important. Equally, there is often an excellent reason for not mentioning them. You can take your choice of the two motives."

I was silent, impressed in spite of myself.

Another few minutes brought us to the famous shed. We found all our friends there, and after an interchange of polite amenities, Poirot began his task.

Having watched Giraud at work, I was keenly interested. Poirot bestowed but a cursory glance on the surroundings. The only thing he examined was the ragged coat and trousers by the door. A disdainful smile rose to Giraud's lips, and, as though noting it, Poirot flung the bundle down again.

"Old clothes of the gardener's?" he queried.

"Exactly," said Giraud.

Poirot knelt down by the body. His fingers were rapid but methodical. He examined the texture of the clothes, and satisfied himself that there were no marks on them. The boots he subjected to special care, also the dirty and broken fingernails. While examining the latter he threw a quick question at Giraud.

"You saw them?"

"Yes, I saw them," replied the other. His face remained inscrutable.

Suddenly Poirot stiffened.

"Dr. Durand!"

"Yes?" The doctor came forward.

"There is foam on the lips. You observed it?"

"I didn't notice it, I must admit."

"But you observe it now?"

"Oh, certainly."

Poirot again shot a question at Giraud. "You noticed it without doubt?"

The other did not reply.

Poirot proceeded. The dagger had been withdrawn from the wound. It reposed in a glass jar by the side of the body. Poirot examined it, then he studied the wound closely. When he looked up, his eyes were excited and shone with the green light I knew so well.

"It is a strange wound, this! It has not bled. There is no stain on the clothes. The blade of the dagger is slightly discoloured, that is all. What do you think, *monsieur le docteur?*"

"I can only say that it is most abnormal."

"It is not abnormal at all. It is most simple. The man was stabbed after he was dead."

And, stilling the clamour of voices that arose with a wave of his hand, Poirot turned to Giraud and added: "Monsieur Giraud agrees with me, do you not, monsieur?"

Whatever Giraud's real belief, he accepted the position without moving a muscle. Calmly and almost scornfully he replied:

"Certainly I agree."

The murmur of surprise and interest broke out again.

"But what an idea!" cried Monsieur Hautet. "To stab a man after he is dead! Barbaric! Unheard-of! Some unappeasable hate perhaps."

"No," said Poirot. "I should fancy it was done quite cold-bloodedly — to create an impression."

"What impression?"

"The impression it nearly did create," returned Poirot oracularly.

Monsieur Bex had been thinking. "How, then, was the man killed?"

"He was not killed. He died. He died, if I am not much mistaken, of an epileptic fit!"

This statement of Poirot's again aroused considerable excitement. Dr. Durand knelt down again, and made a searching examination. At last he rose to his feet.

"Monsieur Poirot, I am inclined to believe that you are correct in your assertion. I was misled to begin with. The incontrovertible fact that the man had been stabbed distracted my attention from any other indications."

Poirot was the hero of the hour. The examining magistrate was profuse in compliments. Poirot responded gracefully, and then excused himself on the pretext that neither he nor I had yet lunched, and that he wished to repair the ravages of the journey. As we were about to leave the shed, Giraud approached us.

"One other thing, Monsieur Poirot," he said, in his suave mocking voice. "We found this coiled round the handle of the dagger — a woman's hair."

"Ah!" said Poirot. "A woman's hair? What woman's, I wonder?"

"I wonder also," said Giraud. Then, with a bow, he left us.

"He was insistent, the good Giraud," said Poirot thoughtfully, as we walked towards the hotel. "I wonder in what direction he hopes to mislead me? A woman's hair — h'm!"

We lunched heartily, but I found Poirot somewhat distrait and inattentive. Afterwards we went up to our sitting-room, and there I begged him to tell me something of his mysterious journey to Paris.

"Willingly, my friend. I went to Paris to find this."

He took from his pocket a small faded newspaper cutting. It was the reproduction of a woman's photograph. He handed it to me. I uttered an exclamation.

"You recognize it, my friend?"

I nodded. Although the photo obviously dated from very many years back, and the hair was dressed in a different style, the likeness was unmistakable.

"Madame Daubreuil!" I exclaimed.

Poirot shook his head with a smile.

"Not quite correct, my friend. She did not call herself by that name in those days. That is a picture of the notorious Madame Beroldy!"

Madame Beroldy! In a flash the whole thing came back to me. The murder trial that had evoked such world-wide interest.

The Beroldy Case.

# XVI.

## THE BEROLDY CASE.

Some twenty years or so before the opening of the present story, Monsieur Arnold Beroldy, a native of Lyons, arrived in Paris accompanied by his pretty wife and their little daughter, a mere babe. Monsieur Beroldy was a junior partner in a firm of wine merchants, a stout middle-aged man, fond of the good things of life, devoted to his charming wife, and altogether unremarkable in every way. The firm in which Monsieur Beroldy was a partner was a small one and, although doing well, it did not yield a large income to the junior partner. The Beroldys had a small apartment and lived in a very modest fashion to begin with.

But, unremarkable though Monsieur Beroldy might be, his wife was plentifully gilded with the brush of Romance. Young and good-looking, and gifted withal with a singular charm of manner, Madame Beroldy at once created a stir in the quarter, especially when it began to be whispered that some interesting mystery surrounded her birth. It was rumoured that she was the illegitimate daughter of a Russian Grand Duke. Others asserted that it was an Austrian Arch-duke, and that the union was legal, though morganatic. But all stories agreed upon one point, that Jeanne Beroldy was the centre of an interesting mystery.

Among the friends and acquaintances of the Beroldys was a young lawyer, Georges Conneau. It was soon evident that the fascinating Jeanne had completely enslaved his heart. Madame Beroldy encouraged the young man in a discreet fashion, but always being careful to affirm her complete devotion to her middle-aged husband. Nevertheless, many spiteful persons did not hesitate to declare that young Conneau was her lover — and not the only one!

When the Beroldys had been in Paris about three months, another personage came upon the scene. This was Mr. Hiram P. Trapp, a native of the United States, and extremely wealthy. Introduced to the charming and mysterious Madame Beroldy, he fell a prompt victim to her fascinations. His admiration was obvious, though strictly respectful.

About this time, Madame Beroldy became more outspoken in her confidences. To several friends, she declared herself greatly worried on her husband's behalf. She explained that he had been drawn into several schemes of a political nature, and also referred to some important papers that had been entrusted to him for safe-keeping and which concerned a "secret" of far-reaching European importance. They had been entrusted to his custody to throw pursuers off the track, but Madame Beroldy was nervous, having recognized several important members of the Revolutionary Circle in Paris.

On the 28th day of November the blow fell. The woman who came daily to clean and cook for the Beroldys was surprised to find the door of the apartment standing wide open. Hearing faint moans issuing from the bedroom, she went in. A terrible sight met her eyes. Madame Beroldy lay on the floor bound hand and foot, uttering feeble moans, having managed to free her mouth from a gag. On the bed was Monsieur Beroldy, lying in a pool of blood, with a knife driven through his heart.

Madame Beroldy's story was clear enough. Suddenly awakened from sleep, she had discerned two masked men bending over her. Stifling her cries, they had bound and gagged her. They had then demanded of Monsieur Beroldy the famous "secret."

But the intrepid wine merchant refused point-blank to accede to their request. Angered by his refusal, one of the men incontinently stabbed him through the heart. With the dead man's keys, they had opened the safe in the corner, and had carried away with them a mass of papers. Both men were heavily bearded, and had worn masks, but Madame Beroldy declared positively that they were Russians.

The affair created an immense sensation. Time went on, and the mysterious bearded men were never traced. And then, just as public interest was beginning to die down, a startling development occurred: Madame Beroldy was arrested and charged with the murder of her husband.

The trial, when it came on, aroused widespread interest. The youth and beauty of the accused, and her mysterious history, were sufficient to make of it a *cause célèbre*.

It was proved beyond doubt that Jeanne Beroldy's parents were a highly respectable and prosaic couple, fruit merchants, who lived on the outskirts of Lyons. The Russian Grand Duke, the court intrigues, and the political schemes — all the stories current were traced back to the lady herself! Remorselessly, the whole story of her life was laid bare. The motive for the murder was found in Mr. Hiram P. Trapp. Mr. Trapp did his best, but, relentlessly and agilely cross-questioned, he was forced to admit that he loved the lady, and that, had she been free, he would have asked her to be his wife. The fact that the relations between them were admittedly platonic strengthened the case against the accused. Debarred from becoming his mistress by the simple honourable nature of the man, Jeanne Beroldy had conceived the monstrous project of ridding herself of her elderly, undistinguished husband and becoming the wife of the rich American.

Throughout, Madame Beroldy confronted her accusers with complete *sang-froid* and self-possession. Her story never varied. She continued to declare strenuously that she was of royal birth and that she had been substituted for the daughter of the fruit-seller at an early age. Absurd and completely unsubstantiated as these statements were, a great number of people believed implicitly in their truth.

But the prosecution was implacable. It denounced the masked "Russians" as a myth, and asserted that the crime had been committed by Madame Beroldy and her lover, Georges Conneau. A warrant was issued for the arrest of the latter, but he had wisely disappeared. Evidence showed that the bonds which secured Madame Beroldy were so loose that she could easily have freed herself.

And then, towards the close of the trial, a letter, posted in Paris, was sent to the Public Prosecutor. It was from Georges Conneau and, without revealing his whereabouts, it contained a full confession of the crime. He declared that he had indeed struck the fatal blow at Madame Beroldy's instigation. The crime had been planned between them. Believing that her husband ill-treated her, and maddened by his own passion for her, a passion which he believed her to return, he had planned the crime and struck the fatal blow that should free the woman he loved from a hateful bondage. Now, for the first time, he learnt of Mr. Hiram P. Trapp, and realized that the woman he loved had betrayed him! Not for his sake did she wish to be free, but in order to marry the wealthy American. She had used him as a cat's paw, and now, in his jealous rage, he turned and denounced her, declaring that throughout he had acted at her instigation.

And then Madame Beroldy proved herself the remarkable woman she undoubtedly was. Without hesitation, she dropped her previous defence, and admitted that the "Russians" were a pure invention on her part. The real murderer was Georges Conneau. Maddened by passion, he had committed the crime, vowing that if she did not keep silence he would exact a terrible vengeance. Terrified by his threats, she had consented — also fearing it likely that if she told the truth she might be accused of conniving at the crime. But she had steadfastly refused to have anything more to do with her husband's murderer, and it was in revenge for this attitude on her part that he had written this letter accusing her. She swore solemnly that she had had nothing to do with the planning of the crime, that she had awakened on that memorable night to find Georges Conneau standing over her, the blood-stained knife in his hand.

It was a touch-and-go affair. Madame Beroldy's story was hardly credible. But her address to the jury was a masterpiece. The tears streaming down her face, she spoke of her child, of her woman's honour — of her desire to keep her reputation untarnished for the child's sake. She admitted that, Georges Conneau having been her lover, she might perhaps be held morally responsible for the crime — but, before God, nothing more! She knew that she had committed a grave fault in not denouncing Conneau to the law, but she declared in a broken voice that that was a thing no woman could have done. She had loved him! Could she let her hand be the one to send him to the guillotine? She had been guilty of much, but she was innocent of the terrible crime imputed to her.

However that may have been, her eloquence and personality won the day. Madame Beroldy, amidst a scene of unparalleled excitement, was acquitted.

Despite the utmost endeavours of the police, Georges Conneau was never traced. As for Madame Beroldy, nothing more was heard of her. Taking the child with her, she left Paris to begin a new life.

# XVII.

## WE MAKE FURTHER INVESTIGATIONS.

I have set down the Beroldy case in full. Of course all the details did not present themselves to my memory as I have recounted them here. Nevertheless, I recalled the case fairly accurately. It had attracted a great deal of interest at the time, and had been fully reported by the English papers, so that it did not need much effort of memory on my part to recollect the salient details.

Just for the moment, in my excitement, it seemed to clear up the whole matter. I admit that I am impulsive, and Poirot deplores my custom of jumping to conclusions, but I think I had some excuse in this instance. The remarkable way in which this discovery justified Poirot's point of view struck me at once.

"Poirot," I said, "I congratulate you. I see everything now."

Poirot lit one of his little cigarettes with his usual precision. Then he looked up.

"And since you see everything now, *mon ami*, what exactly is it that you see?"

"Why, that it was Madame Daubreuil — Beroldy — who murdered Mr. Renauld. The similarity of the two cases proves that beyond a doubt."

"Then you consider that Madame Beroldy was wrongly acquitted? That in actual fact she was guilty of connivance in her husband's murder?"

I opened my eyes wide. "Of course! Don't you?"

Poirot walked to the end of the room, absentmindedly straightened a chair, and then said thoughtfully:

"Yes, that is my opinion. But there is no 'of course' about it, my friend. Technically speaking, Madame Beroldy is innocent."

"Of that crime, perhaps. But not of this."

Poirot sat down again, and regarded me, his thoughtful air more marked than ever. "So it is definitely your opinion, Hastings, that Madame Daubreuil murdered Monsieur Renauld?"

"Yes."

"Why?"

He shot the question at me with such suddenness that I was taken aback.

"Why?" I stammered. "Why? Oh, because —" I came to a stop.

Poirot nodded his head at me.

"You see, you come to a stumbling-block at once. Why should Madame Daubreuil (I shall call her that for clearness' sake) murder Monsieur Renauld? We can find no shadow of a motive. She does not benefit by his death; considered as either mistress or blackmailer she stands to lose. You cannot have a murder without motive. The first crime was different — there we had a rich lover waiting to step into her husband's shoes."

"Money is not the only motive for murder," I objected.

"True," agreed Poirot placidly. "There are two others, the *crime passionnel* is one. And there is the third rare motive, murder for an idea, which implies some form of mental derangement on the part of the murderer. Homicidal mania and religious fanaticism belong to that class. We can rule it out here."

"But what about the *crime passionnel?* Can you rule that out? If Madame Daubreuil was Renauld's mistress, if she found that his affection was cooling, or if her jealousy was aroused in any way, might she not have struck him down in a moment of anger?"

Poirot shook his head.

"If — I say if, you note — Madame Daubreuil was Renauld's mistress, he had not had time to tire of her. And in any case you mistake her character. She is a woman who can simulate great emotional stress. She is a magnificent actress. But, looked at dispassionately, her life disproves her appearance. Throughout, if we examine it, she has been cold-blooded and calculating in her motives and actions. It was not to link her life with that of her young lover that she connived at her husband's murder. The rich American, for whom she probably did not care a button, was her objective. If she committed a crime, she would always do so for gain. Here there was no gain. Besides, how do you account for the digging of the grave? That was a man's work."

"She might have had an

accomplice," I suggested, unwilling to relinquish my belief.

"I pass to another objection. You have spoken of the similarity between the two crimes. Wherein does that lie, my friend?"

I stared at him in astonishment.

"Why, Poirot, it was you who remarked on that! The story of the masked men, the 'secret,' the papers!"

Poirot smiled a little.

"Do not be so indignant, I beg of you. I repudiate nothing. The similarity of the two stories links the two cases together inevitably. But reflect now on something very curious. It is not Madame Daubreuil who tells us this tale — if it were, all would indeed be plain sailing — it is Madame Renauld. Is she then league with the other?"

"I can't believe that," I said slowly. "If she is, she must be the most consummate actress the world has ever known."

"*Ta-ta-ta!*" said Poirot impatiently. "Again you have the sentiment and not the logic! If it is necessary for a criminal to be a consummate actress, then by all means assume her to be one. But is it necessary? I do not believe Mrs. Renauld to be in league with Madame Daubreuil for several reasons, some of which I have already enumerated to you. The others are self-evident. Therefore, that possibility eliminated, we draw very near to the truth, which is, as always, very curious and interesting."

"Poirot," I cried, "what more do you know?"

"*Mon ami*, you must make your own deductions. You have 'access to the facts.' Concentrate your grey cells. Reason — not like Giraud — but like Hercule Poirot!"

"But are you sure?"

"My friend, in many ways I have been an imbecile. But at last I see clearly."

"You know everything?"

"I have discovered what Monsieur Renauld sent for me to discover."

"And you know the murderer?"

"I know one murderer."

"What do you mean?"

"We talk a little at cross-purposes. There are here not one crime, but two. The first I have solved, the second — *eh bien*, I will confess, I am not sure!"

"But, Poirot, I thought you said the man in the shed had died a natural death?"

"*Ta-ta-ta!*" Poirot made his favourite ejaculation of impatience. "Still you do not understand. One may have a crime without a murderer, but for two crimes it is essential to have two bodies."

His remark struck me as so peculiarly lacking in lucidity that I looked at him in some anxiety. But he appeared perfectly normal. Suddenly, he rose and strolled to the window.

"Here he is," he observed.

"Who?"

"Monsieur Jack Renauld. I sent

a note up to the Villa to ask him to come here."

That changed the course of my ideas, and I asked Poirot if he knew that Jack Renauld had been in Merlinville on the night of the crime. I had hoped to catch my astute little friend napping, but as usual he was omniscient. He, too, had inquired at the station.

"And without doubt we are not original in the idea, Hastings. The excellent Giraud, he also has probably made his inquiries."

"You don't think —" I said, and then, "Ah, no, it would be too horrible!"

Poirot looked inquiringly at me, but I said no more. It had just occurred to me that though there were seven women directly and indirectly connected with the case — Mrs. Renauld, Madame Daubreuil and her daughter, the mysterious visitor, and the three servants — there was, with the exception of old Auguste, who could hardly count, only one man — Jack Renauld. *And a man must have dug the grave.*

I had no time to develop farther the appalling idea that had occurred to me, for Jack Renauld was ushered into the room.

Poirot greeted him in business-like manner. "Take a seat, monsieur. I regret infinitely to derange you, but you will perhaps understand that the atmosphere of the villa is not too congenial to me. Monsieur Giraud and I do not see eye to eye about everything. His politeness to me has not been striking, and you will comprehend that I do not intend any little discoveries I may make to benefit him in any way."

"Exactly, Monsieur Poirot," said the lad. "That fellow Giraud is an ill-conditioned brute, and I'd be delighted to see someone score at his expense."

"Then I may ask a little favour of you?"

"Certainly."

"I will ask you to go to the railway station and take a train to the next station along the line, Abbalac. Ask at the cloakroom whether two foreigners deposited a valise there on the night of the murder. It is a small station, and they are almost certain to remember. Will you do this?"

"Of course I will," said the boy, mystified, though ready for the task.

"I and my friend, you comprehend, have business elsewhere," explained Poirot. "There is a train in a quarter of an hour, and I will ask you not to return to the villa, as I have no wish for Giraud to get an inkling of your errand."

"Very well, I will go straight to the station."

He rose to his feet. Poirot's voice stopped him:

"One moment, Monsieur Renauld, there is one little matter that puzzles me. Why did you not mention to Monsieur Hautet this morning that you were in Merlinville on the night of the crime?"

Jack Renauld's face went crimson. With an effort he controlled himself.

"You have made a mistake. I was in Cherbourg as I told the examining magistrate this morning."

Poirot looked at him, his eyes narrowed, cat-like, until they only showed a gleam of green.

"Then it is a singular mistake that I have made there — for it is shared by the station staff. They say you arrived by the 11:40 train."

For a moment Jack Renauld hesitated, then he made up his mind.

"And if I did? I suppose you do not mean to accuse me of participating in my father's murder?" He asked the question haughtily, his head thrown back.

"I should like an explanation of the reason that brought you here."

"That is simple enough. I came to see my fiancée, Mademoiselle Daubreuil. I was on the eve of a long voyage, uncertain as to when I should return. I wished to see her before I went, to assure her of my unchanging devotion."

"And did you see her?" Poirot's eyes never left the other's face.

There was an appreciable pause before Renauld replied. Then he said:

"Yes."

And afterwards?"

"I found I had missed the last train. I walked to St. Beauvais, where I knocked up a garage and got a car to take me back to Cherbourg."

"St. Beauvais? That is fifteen kilometres. A long walk, Monsieur Renauld."

"I — I felt like walking."

Poirot bowed his head as a sign that he accepted the explanation. Jack Renauld took up his hat and cane and departed. In a trice Poirot jumped to his feet.

"Quick, Hastings. We will go after him."

Keeping a discreet distance behind our quarry, we followed him through the streets of Merlinville. But when Poirot saw that he took the turning to the station he checked himself.

"All is well. He has taken the bait. He will go to Abbalac, and will inquire for the mythical valise left by the mythical foreigners. Yes, *mon ami*, all that was a little invention of my own."

"You wanted him out of the way!" I exclaimed.

"Your penetration is amazing, Hastings! Now, if you please, we will go up to the Villa Geneviève."

# XVIII.

## GIRAUD ACTS.

Arrived at the villa, Poirot led the way up to the shed where the second body had been discovered. He did not, however, go in, but paused by the bench which I have mentioned before as being set some few yards away from it. After contemplating it for a moment or two, he paced carefully from it to the hedge which marked the boundary between the Villa Geneviève and the Villa Marguerite. Then he paced back again, nodding his head as he did so. Returning again to the hedge, he parted the bushes with his hands.

"With good fortune," he remarked to me over his shoulder, "Mademoiselle Marthe may find herself in the garden. I desire to speak to her and would prefer not to call formally at the Villa Marguerite. Ah, all is well, there she is. Pst, Mademoiselle! Pst! *Un moment, s'il vous plait.*"

I joined him at the moment that Marthe Daubreuil, looking slightly startled, came running up to the hedge at his call.

"A little word with you, mademoiselle, if it is permitted?"

"Certainly, Monsieur Poirot."

Despite her acquiescence, her eyes looked troubled and afraid.

"Mademoiselle, do you remember running after me on the road the day that I came to your house with the examining magistrate? You asked me if anyone were suspected of the crime."

"And you told me two Chileans." Her voice sounded rather breathless, and her left hand stole to her breast.

"Will you ask me the same question again, mademoiselle?"

"What do you mean?"

"This. If you were to ask me that question again, I should give you a different answer. Someone is suspected — but not a Chilean."

"Who?" The word came faintly between her parted lips.

"Monsieur Jack Renauld."

"What?" It was a cry. "Jack? Impossible. Who dares to suspect him?"

"Giraud."

"Giraud!" The girl's face was ashy. "I am afraid of that man. He is cruel. He will — he will —" She broke off. There was courage gathering in her face, and determination. I realized in that moment that she was a fighter. Poirot, too, watched her.

"You know, of course, that he was here on the night of the murder?" he asked.

"Yes," she replied mechanically. "He told me."

"It was unwise to have tried to conceal the fact," ventured Poirot.

"Yes, yes," she replied impatiently. "But we cannot waste time on regrets. We must find something to save him. He is innocent, of course; but that will not help him with a man like Giraud, who has his reputation to think of. He must arrest someone, and that someone will be Jack."

"The facts will tell against him," said Poirot. "You realize that?"

She faced him squarely.

"I am not a child, monsieur. I can be brave and look facts in the face. He is innocent, and we must save him."

She spoke with a kind of desperate energy, then was silent, frowning as she thought.

"Mademoiselle," said Poirot, observing her keenly, "is there not something that you are keeping back that you could tell us?"

She nodded perplexedly.

"Yes, there is something, but I hardly know whether you will believe it — it seems so absurd."

"At any rate, tell us, mademoiselle."

"It is this. Monsieur Giraud sent for me, as an afterthought, to see if I could identify the man in there." She signed with her head towards the shed. "I could not. At least I could not at the moment. But since I have been thinking —"

"Well?"

"It seems so queer, and yet I am almost sure. I will tell you. On the morning of the day Monsieur Renauld was murdered, I was walking in the garden here, when I heard a sound of men's voices quarrelling. I pushed aside the bushes and looked through. One of the men was Monsieur Renauld and the other was a tramp, a dreadful-looking creature in filthy rags. He was alternately whining and threatening. I gathered he was asking for money, but at that moment *Maman* called me from the house, and I had to go. That is all, only — I am almost sure that the tramp and the dead man in the shed are one and the same."

Poirot uttered an exclamation.

"But why did you not say at the time, mademoiselle?"

"Because at first it only struck me that the face was vaguely familiar in some way. The man was differently dressed, and apparently belonged to a superior station in life."

A voice called from the house.

"*Maman*," whispered Marthe. "I must go." She slipped away through the trees.

"Come," said Poirot and, taking my arm, turned in the direction of the villa.

"What do you really think?" I asked in some curiosity. "Was that story true, or did the girl make it up in order to divert suspicion from her lover?"

"It is a curious tale," said Poirot, "but I believe it to be the absolute truth. Unwittingly, Mademoiselle Marthe told us the truth on another point — and incidentally gave Jack Renauld the lie. Did you notice his hesitation when I asked him if he saw Marthe Daubreuil on the night of the crime? He paused and then said "Yes." I suspected that he was lying. It was necessary for me to see Mademoiselle Marthe before he could put her on her guard. Three little words gave me the information I wanted. When I asked her if she knew that Jack Renauld was here that night, she answered, "He told me." Now, Hastings, what was Jack Renauld doing here on that eventful evening, and if he did not see Mademoiselle Marthe whom did he see?"

"Surely, Poirot," I cried, aghast, "you cannot believe that a boy like that would murder his own father!"

"*Mon ami*," said Poirot. "You continue to be of a sentimentality unbelievable! I have seen mothers who murdered their little children for the sake of the insurance money! After that, one can believe anything."

"And the motive?"

"Money of course. Remember that Jack Renauld thought that he would come into half his father's fortune at the latter's death."

"But the tramp. Where does he come in?" Poirot shrugged his shoulders.

"Giraud would say that he was an accomplice — an apache who helped young Renauld to commit the crime, and who was conveniently put out of the way afterwards."

"But the hair round the dagger? The woman's hair?"

"Ah!" said Poirot, smiling broadly. "That is the cream of Giraud's little jest. According to him, it is not a woman's hair at all. Remember that the youths of today wear their hair brushed straight back from the forehead with pomade or hair wash to make it lie flat.

Consequently some of the hairs are of considerable length."

"And you believe that too?"

"No," said Poirot, with a curious smile. "For I know it to be the hair of a woman — and more, which woman!"

"Madame Daubreuil," I announced positively.

"Perhaps," said Poirot, regarding me quizzically. But I refused to allow myself to get annoyed.

"What are we going to do now?" I asked, as we entered the hall of the Villa Geneviève.

"I wish to make a search among the effects of Monsieur Jack Renauld. That is why I had to get him out of the way for a few hours."

Neatly and methodically, Poirot opened each drawer in turn, examined the contents, and returned them exactly to their places. It was a singularly dull and uninteresting proceeding. Poirot waded on through collars, pyjamas, and socks. A purring noise outside drew me to the window. Instantly I became galvanized into life.

"Poirot!" I cried. "A car has just driven up. Giraud is in it, and Jack Renauld, and two gendarmes."

"*Sacré tonnerre!*" growled Poirot. "That animal of a Giraud, could he not wait? I shall not be able to replace the things in this last drawer with the proper method. Let us be quick."

Unceremoniously he tumbled out the things on the floor, mostly ties and handkerchiefs. Suddenly with a cry of triumph Poirot pounced on something, a small square of cardboard, evidently a photograph. Thrusting it into his pocket, he returned the things pell-mell to the drawer, and seizing me by the arm dragged me out of the room and down the stairs. In the hall stood Giraud, contemplating his prisoner.

"Good afternoon, Monsieur Giraud," said Poirot. "What have we here?"

Giraud nodded his head towards Jack.

"He was trying to make a getaway, but I was too sharp for him. He's under arrest for the murder of his father, Monsieur Paul Renauld."

Poirot wheeled round to confront the boy, who was leaning limply against the door, his face ashy pale.

"What do you say to that, *jeune homme*?"

Jack Renauld stared at him stonily.

"Nothing," he said.

# XIX.

## I USE MY GREY CELLS.

I was dumbfounded. Up to the last, I had not been able to bring myself to believe Jack Renauld guilty. I had expected a ringing proclamation of his innocence when Poirot challenged him. But now, watching him as he stood, white and limp against the wall, and hearing the damning admission fall from his lips, I doubted no longer.

But Poirot had turned to Giraud.

"What are your grounds for arresting him?"

"Do you expect me to give them to you?"

"As a matter of courtesy, yes."

Giraud looked at him doubtfully. He was torn between a desire to refuse rudely and the pleasure of triumphing over his adversary.

"You think I have made a mistake, I suppose?" he sneered.

"It would not surprise me," replied Poirot, with a *soupçon* of malice.

Giraud's face took on a deeper tinge of red.

"*Eh bien*, come in here. You shall judge for yourself."

He flung open the door of the salon, and we passed in, leaving Jack Renauld in the care of the two other men.

"Now, Monsieur Poirot," said Giraud, laying his hat on the table and speaking with the utmost sarcasm, "I will treat you to a little lecture on detective work. I will show how we moderns work."

"*Bien!*" said Poirot, composing himself to listen. "I will show you how admirably the Old Guard can listen." And he leaned back and closed his eyes, opening them for a moment to remark: "Do not fear that I shall sleep. I will attend most carefully."

"Of course," began Giraud, "I soon saw through all that Chilean tomfoolery. Two men were in it — but they were not mysterious foreigners! All that was a blind."

"Very creditable so far, my dear Giraud," murmured Poirot. "Especially after that clever trick of theirs with the match and cigarette end."

Giraud glared, but continued.

"A man must have been connected with the case, in order to dig the grave. There is no man who actually benefits by the crime, but there was a man who *thought* he would benefit. I heard of Jack Renauld's quarrel with his father, and of the threats that he had used. The motive was established. Now as to means. Jack Renauld was in Merlinville that night. He concealed the fact — which turned suspicion into certainty. Then we found a second victim — *stabbed with the same dagger*. We know when that dagger was stolen. Captain Hastings here can fix the time. Jack Renauld, arriving from Cherbourg, was the only person who could have taken it. I have accounted for all the other members of the household."

Poirot interrupted.

"You are wrong. There is one other person who could have taken the dagger."

"You refer to Monsieur Stonor? He arrived at the front door, in an automobile which had brought him straight from Calais. Ah! believe me, I have looked into everything. Monsieur Jack Renauld arrived by train. An hour elapsed between his arrival and the moment when he presented himself at the house. Without doubt, he saw Captain Hastings and his companion leave the shed, slipped in himself and took the dagger, stabbed his accomplice in the shed —"

"Who was already dead!"

Giraud shrugged his shoulders.

"Possibly he did not observe that. He may have judged him to be sleeping. Without doubt they had a rendezvous. In any case he knew this apparent second murder would greatly complicate the case. It did."

"But it could not deceive Giraud," murmured Poirot.

"You mock at me! But I will give you one last irrefutable proof. Madame Renauld's story was false — a fabrication from beginning to end. We believe Madame Renauld to have loved her husband — *yet she lied to shield his murderer*. For whom will a woman lie? Sometimes for herself, usually for the man she loves, *always* for her children. That is the last — the irrefutable proof. You cannot get round it."

Giraud paused, flushed and triumphant.

Poirot regarded him steadily.

"That is my case," said Giraud. "What have you to say to it?"

"Only that there is one thing you have failed to take into account."

"What is that?"

"Jack Renauld was presumably acquainted with the planning out of the golf course. He knew that the body would be discovered almost at once, when they started to dig the bunker."

Giraud laughed out loud.

"But it is idiotic what you say there! He wanted the body to be found! Until it was found, he could not presume death, and would have been unable to enter into his inheritance."

I saw a quick flash of green in Poirot's eyes as he rose to his feet.

"Then why bury it?" he asked very softly. "Reflect, Giraud. Since it was to Jack Renauld's advantage that the body should be found without delay, why dig a grave at all?"

Giraud did not reply. The question found him unprepared. He shrugged his shoulders as though to intimate that it was of no importance.

Poirot moved towards the door. I followed him.

"There is one more thing that you have failed to take into account," he said over his shoulder.

"What is that?"

"The piece of lead piping," said Poirot, and left the room.

Jack Renauld still stood in the hall, with a white dumb face, but as we came out of the salon he looked up sharply. At the same moment there was the sound of a footfall on the staircase. Mrs. Renauld was descending it. At the sight of her son, standing between the myrmidons of the law, she stopped as though petrified.

"Jack," she faltered. "Jack, what is this?"

He looked up at her, his face set. "They have arrested me, mother."

"What?"

She uttered a piercing cry, and before anyone could get to her, swayed, and fell heavily. We both ran to her and lifted her up. In a minute Poirot stood up again.

"She has cut her head badly, on the corner of the stairs. I fancy there is slight concussion also. If Giraud wants a statement from her, he will have to wait. She will probably be unconscious for at least a week."

Denise and Françoise had run to their mistress, and leaving her in their charge Poirot left the house. He walked with his head down, frowning thoughtfully. For some time I did not speak, but at last I ventured to put a question to him:

"Do you believe then, in spite of all appearances to the contrary, that Jack Renauld may not be guilty?"

Poirot did not answer at once, but after a long wait he said gravely:

"I do not know, Hastings. There is just a chance of it. Of course Giraud is all wrong—wrong from beginning to end. If Jack Renauld is guilty, it is in spite of Giraud's arguments, not because of them. And the gravest indictment against him is known only to me."

"What is that?" I asked, impressed.

"If you would use your grey cells, and see the whole case clearly as I do, you too would perceive it, my friend."

This was what I called one of Poirot's irritating answers. He went on, without waiting for me to speak:

"Let us walk this way to the sea. We will sit on that little mound there, overlooking the beach, and review the case. You shall know all that I know, but I would prefer that you should come at the truth by your own efforts — not by my leading you by the hand."

We established ourselves on the grassy knoll as Poirot had suggested, looking out to sea.

"Think, my friend," said Poirot's voice encouragingly. "Arrange your ideas. Be methodical. Be orderly. There is the secret of success."

I endeavoured to obey him, casting my mind back over all the details of the case. And suddenly I started as an idea of bewildering luminosity shot into my brain. Tremblingly I built up my hypothesis.

"You have a little idea, I see, *mon ami*. Capital. We progress."

I sat up, and lit my pipe.

"Poirot," I said, "it seems to me we have been strangely remiss. I say *we* — although I dare say *I* would be nearer the mark. But you must pay the penalty of your determined secrecy. So I say again we have been remiss. There is someone we have forgotten."

"And who is that?" inquired Poirot, with twinkling eyes.

"Georges Conneau!"

# XX.

## AN AMAZING STATEMENT.

The next moment Poirot embraced me warmly on the cheek.

"*Enfin!* You have arrived! And all by yourself. It is superb! Continue your reasoning. You are right. Decidedly we have done wrong to forget Georges Conneau."

I was so flattered by the little man's approval that I could hardly continue. But at last I collected my thoughts and went on.

"Georges Conneau disappeared twenty years ago, but we have no reason to believe that he is dead."

"*Aucunement*," agreed Poirot. "Proceed."

"Therefore we will assume that he is alive."

"Exactly."

"Or that he was alive until recently."

"*De mieux en mieux!*"

"We will presume," I continued, my enthusiasm rising, "that he has fallen on evil days. He has become a criminal, an apache, a tramp—a what-you-will. He chances to come to Merlinville. There he finds the woman he has never ceased to love."

"Eh eh! The sentimentality," warned Poirot.

"Where one hates one also loves," I quoted, or misquoted. "At any rate he finds her there, living under an assumed name. But she has a new lover, the Englishman, Renauld. Georges Conneau, the memory of old wrongs rising in him, quarrels with this Renauld. He lies in wait for him as he comes to visit his mistress, and stabs him in the back. Then, terrified at what he has done, he starts to dig a grave. I imagine it likely that Madame Daubreuil comes out to look for her lover. She and Conneau have a terrible scene. He drags her into the shed, and there suddenly falls down in an epileptic fit.

"Now supposing Jack Renauld to appear. Madame Daubreuil tells him all, points out to him the dreadful consequences to her daughter if this scandal of the past is revived. His father's murderer is dead — let them do their best to hush it up. Jack Renauld consents — goes to the house and has an interview with his mother, winning her over to his point of view. Primed with the story that Madame Daubreuil has suggested to him, she permits herself to be gagged and bound.

"There, Poirot, what do you think of that?"

I leaned back, flushed with the pride of successful reconstruction.

Poirot looked at me thoughtfully.

"I think that you should write for the Kinema, *mon ami*," he remarked at last.

"You mean —"

"It would mean a good film, the story that you have recounted to me there — but it bears no sort of resemblance to everyday life."

"I admit that I haven't gone into all the details, but —"

"You have gone farther — you have ignored them magnificently. What about the way the two men were dressed? Do you suggest that after stabbing his victim, Conneau removed his suit of clothes, donned it himself, and replaced the dagger?"

"I don't see that that matters," I objected rather huffily. "He may have obtained clothes and money from Madame Daubreuil by threats earlier in the day."

"By threats, eh? You seriously advance that supposition?"

"Certainly. He could have threatened to reveal her identity to the Renaulds, which would probably have put an end to all hopes of her daughter's marriage."

"You are wrong, Hastings. He could not blackmail her, for she had the whip-hand. Georges Conneau, remember, is still wanted for murder. A word from her and he is in danger of the guillotine."

I was forced, rather reluctantly, to admit the truth of this.

"Your theory," I remarked acidly, "is doubtless correct as to all the details?"

"My theory is the truth," said Poirot quietly. "And the truth is necessarily correct. In your theory you made a fundamental error. You permitted your imagination to lead you astray with midnight assignations and passionate love scenes. But in investigating crime we must take our stand upon the commonplace. Shall I demonstrate my methods to you?"

"Oh, by all means let us have a demonstration!"

Poirot sat very upright and began, wagging his forefinger emphatically to emphasize his points:

"I will start as you started from the basic fact of Georges Conneau. Now the story told by Madame Beroldy in court as to the 'Russians' was admittedly a fabrication. If she was innocent of connivance in the crime, it was concocted by her, and by her only as she stated. If, on the other hand, she was not innocent, it might have been invented by either her or Georges Conneau.

"Now, in this case we are investigating, we meet the same tale. As I pointed out to you, the facts render it very unlikely that Madame Daubreuil inspired it. So we turn to the hypothesis that the story had its origin in the brain of Georges Conneau. Very good. Georges Conneau, therefore, planned the crime, with Mrs. Renauld as his accomplice. She is in the limelight, and behind her is a shadowy figure whose present alias is unknown to us.

"Now let us go carefully over the Renauld Case from the beginning, setting down each significant point in its chronological order. You have a notebook and pencil? Good. Now what is the earliest point to note down?"

"The letter to you?"

"That was the first we knew of it, but it is not the proper beginning of the case. The first point of any significance, I should say, is the change that came over Monsieur Renauld shortly after arriving in Merlinville, and which is attested to by several witnesses. We have also to consider his friendship with Madame Daubreuil, and the large sums of money paid over to her. From thence we can come directly to the 23rd May."

Poirot paused, cleared his throat, and signed to me to write:

"*23rd May.* Monsieur Renauld quarrels with his son over latter's wish to marry Marthe Daubreuil. Son leaves for Paris.

"*24th May.* Monsieur Renauld alters his will, leaving entire control of his fortune in his wife's hands.

"*7th June.* Quarrel with tramp in garden, witnessed by Marthe Daubreuil.

"Letter written to Monsieur Hercule Poirot, imploring assistance.

"Telegram sent to Monsieur Jack Renauld, bidding him proceed by the *Anzora* to Buenos Aires.

"Chauffeur, Masters, sent off on a holiday.

"Visit of a lady that evening. As he is seeing her out, his words are 'Yes, yes — but for God's sake go now ....'"

Poirot paused.

"There, Hastings, take each of those facts one by one, consider them carefully by themselves and in relation to the whole, and see if you do not get new light on the matter."

I endeavoured conscientiously to do as he had said. After a moment or two, I said rather doubtfully:

"As to the first points, the question seems to be whether we adopt the theory of blackmail, or of an infatuation for this woman."

"Blackmail, decidedly. You heard what Stonor said as to his character and habits."

"Mrs. Renauld did not confirm his view," I argued.

"We have already seen that Madame Renauld's testimony cannot be relied upon in any way. We must trust to Stonor on that point."

"Still, if Renauld had an affair with a woman called Bella, there seems no inherent improbability in his having another with Madame Daubreuil."

"None whatever, I grant you, Hastings. But did he?"

"The letter, Poirot. You forget the letter."

"No, I do not forget. But what makes you think that letter was written to Monsieur Renauld?"

"Why, it was found in his pocket, and — and —"

"And that is all!" cut in Poirot. "There was no mention of any name to show to whom the letter was addressed. We assumed it was to the dead man because it was in the pocket of his overcoat. Now, *mon ami*, something about that overcoat struck me as unusual. I measured it, and made the remark that he wore his overcoat very long. That remark should have given you to think."

"I thought you were just saying it for the sake of saying something," I confessed.

"Ah, *quelle idée*! Later you observed me measuring the overcoat of Monsieur Jack Renauld. *Eh bien*, Monsieur Jack Renauld wears his overcoat very short. Put those two facts together with a third, namely, that Monsieur Jack Renauld flung out of the house in a hurry on his departure for Paris, and tell me what you make of it!"

"I see," I said slowly, as the meaning of Poirot's remarks bore in upon me. "That letter was written to Jack Renauld — not to his father. He caught up the wrong overcoat in his haste and agitation."

Poirot nodded.

"*Précisément*! We can return to this point later. For the moment let us content ourselves with accepting the letter as having nothing to do with Monsieur Renauld *père*, and pass to the next chronological event."

"'23rd May,'" I read: "'Monsieur Renauld quarrels with his son over latter's wish to marry Marthe Daubreuil. Son leaves for Paris.' I don't see anything much to remark upon there, and the altering of the will the following day seems straightforward enough. It was the direct result of the quarrel."

"We agree, *mon ami* — at least as to the cause. But what exact motive underlay this procedure of Monsieur Renauld's?"

I opened my eyes in surprise.

"Anger against his son of course."

"Yet he wrote him affectionate letters to Paris?"

"So Jack Renauld says, but he cannot produce them."

"Well, let us pass from that."

"Now we come to the day of the tragedy. You have placed the events of the morning in a certain order. Have you any justification for that?"

"I have ascertained that the letter to me was posted at the same time as the telegram was dispatched. Masters was informed he could take a holiday shortly afterwards. In my opinion the quarrel with the tramp took place anterior to these happenings."

"I do not see that you can fix that definitely unless you question Madame Daubreuil again."

"There is no need. I am sure of it. And if you do not see that, you see nothing, Hastings!"

I looked at him for a moment.

"Of course! I am an idiot. If the tramp was Georges Conneau, it was after the stormy interview with him that Mr. Renauld apprehended danger. He sent away the chauffeur, Masters, whom he suspected of being in the other's pay, he wired to his son, and sent for you."

A faint smile crossed Poirot's lips.

"You do not think it strange that he should use exactly the same expressions in his letter as Madame Renauld used, later in her story? If the mention of Santiago was a blind, why should Renauld speak of it, and—what is more—send his son there?"

"It is puzzling, I admit, but perhaps we shall find some explanation later. We come now to the evening, and the visit of the mysterious lady. I confess that that fairly baffles me, unless it was indeed Madame Daubreuil, as Françoise all along maintained."

Poirot shook his head.

"My friend, my friend, where are your wits wandering? Remember the fragment of cheque, and the fact that the name Bella Duveen was faintly familiar to Stonor, and I think we may take it for granted that Bella Duveen is the full name of Jack's unknown correspondent, and that it was she who came to the Villa Geneviève that night. Whether she intended to see Jack, or whether she meant all along to appeal to his father, we cannot be certain, but I think we may assume that this is what occurred. She produced her claim upon Jack, probably showed letters that he had written her, and the older man tried to buy her off by writing a cheque. This she indignantly tore up. The terms of her letter are those of a woman genuinely in love, and she would probably deeply resent being offered money. In the end he got rid of her, and here the words that he used are significant."

"'Yes, yes, but for God's sake go now,'" I repeated. "They seem to me a little vehement, perhaps, that is all."

"That is enough. He was desperately anxious for the girl to go. Why? Not because the interview was unpleasant. No, it was the time that was slipping by, and for some reason time was precious."

"Why should it be?" I asked, bewildered.

"That is what we ask ourselves. Why should it be? But later we have the incident of the wristwatch — which again shows us that time plays a very important part in the crime. We are now fast approaching the actual drama. It is half past ten when Bella Duveen leaves, and by the evidence of the wristwatch we know that the crime was committed, or at any rate that it was staged, before twelve o'clock. We have reviewed all the events anterior to the murder, there remains only one unplaced. By the doctor's evidence, the tramp, when found, had been dead at least forty-eight hours — with a possible margin of twenty-four hours more. Now, with no other facts to help me than those we have discussed, I place the death as having occurred on the morning of 7th June."

I stared at him, stupefied.

"But how? Why? How can you possibly know?"

"Because only in that way can the sequence of events be logically explained. *Mon ami*, I have taken you step by step along the way. Do you not now see what is so glaringly plain?"

"My dear Poirot, I can't see anything glaring about it. I did think I was beginning to see my way before, but I'm now hopelessly fogged. For goodness' sake, get on, and tell me who killed Mr. Renauld."

"That is just what I am not sure of as yet."

"But you said it was glaringly clear!"

"We talk at cross-purposes, my friend. Remember, it is two crimes we are investigating — for which, as I pointed out to you, we have the necessary two bodies. There, there, *ne vous impatientez pas!* I explain all. To begin with, we apply our psychology. We find three points at which Monsieur Renauld displays a distinct change of view and action — three psychological points therefore. The first occurs immediately after arriving in Merlinville, the second after quarrelling with his son on a certain subject, the third on the morning of 7th June. Now for the three causes. We can attribute No. 1 to meeting Madame Daubreuil. No. 2 is indirectly connected with her, since it concerns a marriage between Monsieur Renauld's son and her daughter. But the cause of No 3 is hidden from us. We had to deduce it. Now, *mon ami*, let me ask you a question: whom do we believe to have planned this crime?"

"Georges Conneau," I said doubtfully, eyeing Poirot warily.

"Exactly. Now Giraud laid it down as an axiom that a woman lies to save herself, the man she loves, and her child. Since we are satisfied that it was Georges Conneau who dictated the lie to her, and as Georges Conneau is not Jack Renauld, it follows that the third case is put out of court. And, still attributing the crime to Georges Conneau, the first is equally so. So we are forced to the second — that Madame Renauld lied for the sake of the man she loved — or in other words, for the sake of Georges Conneau. You agree to that?"

"Yes," I admitted. "It seems logical enough."

"*Bien!* Madame Renauld loves Georges Conneau. Who, then, is Georges Conneau?"

"The tramp."

"Have we any evidence to show that Madame Renauld loved the tramp?"

"No, but —"

"Very well then. Do not cling to theories where facts no longer support them. Ask yourself instead whom Madame Renauld *did* love."

I shook my head, perplexed.

"*Mais oui*, you know perfectly. Whom did Madame Renauld love so dearly that when she saw his dead body she fell down in a swoon?"

I stared dumbfounded.

"Her husband?" I gasped.

Poirot nodded.

"Her husband — or Georges Conneau, whichever you like to call him."

I rallied myself.

"But it's impossible."

"How 'impossible'? Did we not agree just now that Madame Daubreuil was in a position to blackmail Georges Conneau?"

"Yes, but —"

"And did she not very effectively blackmail Monsieur Renauld?"

"That may be true enough, but —"

"And is it not a fact that we know nothing of Monsieur Renauld's youth and upbringing? That he springs suddenly into existence as a French-Canadian exactly twenty-two years ago?"

"All that is so," I said more firmly, "but you seem to me to be overlooking one salient point."

"What is that, my friend?"

"Why, we have admitted that Georges planned the crime. That brings us to the ridiculous statement that he planned his own murder!"

"*Eh bien, mon ami*," said Poirot placidly, "that is just what he *did* do!"

# XXI.

## HERCULE POIROT ON THE CASE.

In a measured voice Poirot began his exposition.

"It seems strange to you, *mon ami*, that a man should plan his own death? So strange, that you prefer to reject the truth as fantastic, and to revert to a story that is in reality ten times more impossible. Yes, Monsieur Renauld planned his own death, but there is one detail that perhaps escapes you — he did not intend to die."

I shook my head, bewildered.

"But no, it is all most simple really," said Poirot kindly. "For the crime that Monsieur Renauld proposed a murderer was not necessary, as I told you, but a body was. Let us reconstruct, seeing events this time from a different angle.

"Georges Conneau flies from justice — to Canada. There, under an assumed name, he marries, and finally acquires a vast fortune in South America. But there is a nostalgia upon him for his own country. Twenty years have elapsed, he is considerably changed in appearance, besides being a man of such eminence that no one is likely to connect him with a fugitive from justice many years ago. He deems it quite safe to return. He takes up his headquarters in England, but intends to spend the summers in France. And ill fortune, or that obscure justice which shapes men's ends and will not allow them to evade the consequences of their acts, takes him to Merlinville. There, in the whole of France, is the one person who is capable of recognizing him. It is, of course, a gold mine to Madame Daubreuil, and a gold mine of which she is not slow to take advantage. He is helpless, absolutely in her power. And she bleeds him heavily.

"And then the inevitable happens. Jack Renauld falls in love with the beautiful girl he sees almost daily, and wishes to marry her. That rouses his father. At all costs, he will prevent his son marrying the daughter of this evil woman. Jack Renauld knows nothing of his father's past, but Madame Renauld knows everything. She is a woman of great force of character and passionately devoted to her husband. They take counsel together. Renauld sees only one way of escape — death. He must appear to die, in reality escaping to another country where he will start again under an assumed name and where Madame Renauld, having played the widow's part for a while, can join him. It is essential that she should have control of the money, so he alters his will. How they meant to manage the body business originally, I do not know — possibly an art student's skeleton and a fire — or something of the kind, but long before their plans have matured an event occurs which plays into their hands. A rough tramp, violent and abusive, finds his way into the garden. There is a struggle, Renauld seeks to eject him, and suddenly the tramp, an epileptic, falls down in a fit. He is dead. Renauld calls his wife. Together they drag him into the shed — as we know the event had occurred just outside — and they realize the marvellous opportunity that has been vouchsafed them. The man bears no resemblance to Renauld, but he is middle-aged, of a usual French type. That is sufficient.

"I rather fancy that they sat on the bench up there, out of earshot from the house; discussing matters. Their plan was quickly made. The identification must rest solely on Madame Renauld's evidence. Jack Renauld and the chauffeur (who had been with his master two years) must be got out of the way. It was unlikely that the French women servants would go near the body, and in any case Renauld intended to take measures to deceive anyone not likely to appreciate details. Masters was sent off, a telegram dispatched to Jack, Buenos Aires being selected to give credence to the story that Renauld had decided upon. Having heard of me as a rather obscure elderly detective, he wrote his appeal for help, knowing that when I arrived, the production of the letter would have a profound effect upon the examining magistrate — which, of course, it did.

"They dressed the body of the tramp in a suit of Renauld's and left his ragged coat and trousers by the door of the shed, not daring to take them into the house. And then, to give credence to the tale Madame Renauld was to tell, they drove the aeroplane dagger through his heart. That night Renauld will first bind and gag his wife, and then, taking a spade, will dig a grave in that particular plot of ground where he knows a — how do you call it? — bunkair? is to be made. It is essential that the body should be found — Madame Daubreuil must have no suspicions. On the other hand, if a little time elapses, any dangers as to identity will be greatly lessened. Then, Renauld will don the tramp's rags, and shuffle off to the station, where he will leave, unnoticed, by the 12:10 train. Since the crime will be supposed to have taken place two hours later, no suspicion can possibly attach to him.

"You see now his annoyance at the inopportune visit of the girl, Bella. Every moment of delay is fatal to his plans. He gets rid of her as soon as he can, however. Then, to work! He leaves the front door slightly ajar to create the impression that assassins left that way. He binds and gags Madame Renauld, correcting his mistake of twenty-two years ago, when the looseness of the bonds caused suspicion to fall upon his accomplice, but leaving her primed with essentially the same story as he had invented before, proving the unconscious recoil of the mind against originality. The night is chilly, and he slips on an overcoat over his under-clothing, intending to cast it into the grave with the dead man. He goes out by the window, smoothing over the flower-bed carefully, and thereby furnishing the most positive evidence against himself. He goes out on to the lonely golf links, and he digs — And then —"

"Yes?"

"And then," said Poirot gravely, "the justice that he has so long eluded overtakes him. An unknown hand stabs him in the back .... Now, Hastings, you understand what I mean when I talk of *two* crimes. The first crime, the crime that Monsieur Renauld, in his arrogance, asked us to investigate, is solved. But behind it lies a deeper riddle. And to solve that will be difficult — since the criminal, in his wisdom, has been content to avail himself of the devices prepared by Renauld. It has been a particularly perplexing and baffling mystery to solve."

"You're marvellous, Poirot," I said, with admiration. "Absolutely marvellous. No one on earth but you would have done it!"

I think my praise pleased him. For once in his life he looked almost embarrassed.

"That poor Giraud," said Poirot, trying unsuccessfully to look modest. "Without doubt it is not all stupidity. He has had *la mauvaise chance* once or twice. That dark hair coiled round the dagger, for instance. To say the least, it was misleading."

"To tell you the truth, Poirot," I said slowly, "even now I don't quite see — whose hair was it?"

"Madame Renauld's, of course. That is where *la mauvaise chance* came in. Her hair, dark originally, is almost completely silvered. It might just as easily have been a grey hair — and then, by no conceivable effort could Giraud have persuaded himself it came from the head of Jack Renauld! But it is all of a piece. Always the facts must be twisted to fit the theory!

"Without doubt, when Madame Renauld recovers, she will speak. The possibility of her son being accused of the murder never occurred to her. How should it, when she believed him safely at sea on board the *Anzora?* Ah! *voilà une femme*, Hastings! What force, what self-command! She only made one slip. On his unexpected return: "It does not matter — now." And no one noticed — no one realized the significance of those words. What a terrible part she has had to play, poor woman. Imagine the shock when she goes to identify the body and, instead of what she expects, sees the actual lifeless form of the husband she has believed miles away by now. No wonder she fainted! But since then, despite her grief and her despair, how resolutely she has played her part and how the anguish of it must wring her. She cannot say a word to set us on the track of the real murderers. For her son's sake, no one must know that Paul Renauld was Georges Conneau, the criminal. Final and most bitter blow, she has admitted publicly that Madame Daubreuil was her husband's mistress — for a hint of blackmail might be fatal to her secret. How cleverly she dealt with the examining magistrate when he asked her if there was any mystery in her husband's past life. "Nothing so romantic, I am sure, monsieur." It was perfect, the indulgent tone, the *soupçon* of sad mockery. At once Monsieur Hautet felt himself foolish and melodramatic. Yes, she is a great woman! If she loved a criminal, she loved him royally!"

Poirot lost himself in contemplation.

"One thing more, Poirot, what about the piece of lead-piping?"

"You do not see? To disfigure the victim's face so that it would be unrecognizable. It was that which first set me on the right track. And that imbecile of a Giraud, swarming all over it to look for match ends! Did I not tell you that a clue of two foot long was quite as good as a clue of two inches? You see, Hastings, we must now start again. Who killed Monsieur Renauld? Someone who was near the villa just before twelve o'clock that night, someone who would benefit by his death — the description fits Jack Renauld only too well. The crime need not have been premeditated. And then the dagger!"

I started. I had not realized that point.

"Of course," I said, "Mrs. Renauld's dagger was the second one we found in the tramp. There were two, then?"

"Certainly, and since they were

duplicates, it stands to reason that Jack Renauld was the owner. But that would not trouble me so much. In fact, I had a little idea as to that. No, the worst indictment against him is again psychological — heredity, *mon ami*, heredity! Like father, like son — Jack Renauld, when all is said or done, is the son of Georges Conneau."

His tone was grave and earnest, and I was impressed in spite of myself.

"What is your little idea that you mentioned just now?" I asked.

For answer, Poirot consulted his turnip faced watch, and then asked:

"What time is the afternoon boat from Calais?"

"About five, I believe."

"That will do very well. We shall just have time."

"You are going to England?"

"Yes, my friend."

"Why?"

"To find a possible — witness."

"Who?"

With a rather peculiar smile upon his face, Poirot replied:

"Miss Bella Duveen."

"But how will you find her — what do you know about her?"

"I know nothing about her — but I can guess a good deal. We may take it for granted that her name *is* Bella Duveen, and since that name was faintly familiar to Monsieur Stonor, though evidently not in connexion with the Renauld family, it is probable that she is on the stage. Jack Renauld was a young man with plenty of money, and twenty years of age. The stage is sure to have been the home of his first love. It tallies, too, with Monsieur Renauld's attempt to placate her with a cheque. I think I shall find her all right — especially with the help of this."

And he brought out the photograph I had seen him take from Jack Renauld's drawer. "With love from Bella" was scrawled across the corner, but it was not that which held my eyes fascinated. The likeness was not first rate — but for all that it was unmistakable to me. I felt a cold sinking, as though some unutterable calamity had befallen me.

It was the face of Cinderella.

# XXII.

## I FIND LOVE.

For a moment or two I sat as though frozen, the photograph still in my hand. Then summoning all my courage to appear unmoved, I handed it back. At the same time I stole a quick glance at Poirot. Had he noticed anything? But to my relief he did not seem to be observing me. Anything unusual in my manner had certainly escaped him.

He rose briskly to his feet.

"We have no time to lose. We must make our departure with all dispatch. All is well — the sea, it will be calm!"

In the bustle of departure, I had no time for thinking, but once on board the boat, secure from Poirot's observation, I pulled myself together, and attacked the facts dispassionately. How much did Poirot know, and why was he bent on finding this girl? Did he suspect her of having seen Jack Renauld commit the crime? Or did he suspect — But that was impossible! The girl had no grudge against the elder Renauld, no possible motive for wishing his death. What had brought her back to the scene of the murder? I went over the facts carefully. She must have left the train at Calais where I parted from her that day. No wonder I had been unable to find her on the boat. If she had dined in Calais, and then taken a train out to Merlinville, she would have arrived at the Villa

Geneviève just about the time that Françoise said. What had she done when she left the house just after ten? Presumably either gone to a hotel, or returned to Calais. And then? The crime had been committed on Tuesday night. On Thursday morning she was once more in Merlinville — had she ever left France at all? I doubted it very much. What kept her there — the hope of seeing Jack Renauld? I had told her (as at the time we believed) that he was on the high seas en route to Buenos Aires. Possibly she was aware that the Anzora had not sailed. But to know that she must have seen Jack. Was that what Poirot was after? Had Jack Renauld, returning to see Marthe Daubreuil, come face to face instead with Bella Duveen, the girl he had heartlessly thrown over?

I began to see daylight. If that were indeed the case, it might furnish Jack with the alibi he needed. Yet under those circumstances his silence seemed difficult to explain. Why could he not have spoken out boldly? Did he fear for this former entanglement of his to come to the ears of Marthe Daubreuil? I shook my head, dissatisfied. The thing had been harmless enough, a foolish boy-and-girl affair, and I reflected cynically that the son of a millionaire was not likely to be thrown over by a penniless French girl, who moreover loved him devotedly, without a much graver cause.

Poirot reappeared brisk and smiling at Dover, and our journey to London was uneventful. It was past nine o'clock when we arrived, and I supposed that we should return straight away to our rooms and do nothing till the morning.

But Poirot had other plans.

"We must lose no time, *mon ami*. The news of the arrest will not be in the English papers until the day after tomorrow, but still we must lose no time."

I did not quite follow his reasoning, but I merely asked how he proposed to find the girl.

"You remember Joseph Aarons, the theatrical agent? No? I assisted him in a little matter of a Japanese wrestler. A pretty little problem, I must recount it to you one day. He, without doubt, will be able to put us in the way of finding out what we want to know."

It took us some time to run Mr. Aarons to earth, and it was after midnight when we finally managed it. He greeted Poirot with every evidence of warmth, and professed himself ready to be of service to us in any way.

"There's not much about the profession I don't know," he said, beaming genially.

"*Eh bien*, Monsieur Aarons, I desire to find a young girl called Bella Duveen."

"Bella Duveen. I know the name, but for a moment I can't place it. What's her line?"

"That I do not know — but here is her photograph."

Mr. Aarons studied it for a moment, then his face lighted.

"Got it!" He slapped his thigh. "The Dulcibella Kids, by the Lord!"

"The Dulcibella Kids?"

"That's it. They're sisters. Acrobats, dancers, and singers. Give quite a good little turn. They're in the provinces, somewhere, I believe — if they're not resting. They've been on in Paris for the last two or three weeks."

"Can you find out for me exactly where they are?"

"Easy as a bird. You go home, and I'll send you round the dope in the morning."

With this promise we took leave of him.

He was as good as his word. About eleven o'clock the following day, a scribbled note reached us:

"The Dulcibella Sisters are on at the Palace in Coventry. Good luck to you."

Without more ado, we started for Coventry. Poirot made no inquiries at the theatre, but contented himself with booking stalls for the variety performance that evening.

The show was wearisome beyond words — or perhaps it was only my mood that made it seem so. Japanese families balanced themselves precariously, would-be fashionable men, in greenish evening dress and exquisitely slicked hair, reeled off society patter and danced marvellously. Stout prima donnas sang at the top of the human register; a comic comedian endeavoured to be Mr. George Robey and failed signally.

At last the number went up which announced the Dulcibella Kids. My heart beat sickeningly. There she was — there they both were, the pair of them, one flaxen haired, one dark, matching as to size, with short fluffy skirts and immense "Buster Brown" bows. They looked a pair of extremely piquant children. They began to sing. Their voices were fresh and true, rather thin and music-hally, but attractive.

It was quite a pretty little turn. They danced neatly, and did some clever little acrobatic feats. The words of their songs were crisp and catchy. When the curtain fell, there was a full meed of applause. Evidently the Dulcibella Kids were a success.

Suddenly I felt that I could remain no longer. I must get out into the air. I suggested leaving to Poirot.

"Go by all means, *mon ami*. I amuse myself, and will stay to the end. I will rejoin you later."

It was only a few steps from the theatre to the hotel. I went up to the sitting-room, ordered a whisky and soda, and sat drinking it, staring meditatively into the empty grate. I heard the door open, and turned my head, thinking it was Poirot. Then I jumped to my feet. It was Cinderella who stood in the doorway.

She spoke haltingly, her breath coming in little gasps.

"I saw you in front. You and your friend. When you got up to go, I was waiting outside and followed you. Why are you here — in Coventry? What were you doing there tonight? Is the man who was with you the — the detective?"

She stood there, the cloak she had wrapped round her stage dress slipping from her shoulders. I saw the whiteness of her cheeks under the rouge, and heard the terror in her voice. And in that moment I understood everything — understood why Poirot was seeking her, and what she feared, and understood at last my own heart.

"Yes," I said gently.

"Is he looking for — me?" she half whispered.

Then, as I did not answer for a moment, she slipped down by the big chair, and burst into violent bitter weeping.

I knelt down by her, holding her in my arms, and smoothing the hair back from her face.

"Don't cry, child, don't cry, for God's sake. You're safe here. I'll take care of you. Don't cry, darling. Don't cry. I know — I know everything."

"Oh, but you don't!"

"I think I do." And after a moment, as her sobs grew quieter, I asked: "It was you who took the dagger, wasn't it?"

"Yes."

"That was why you wanted me to show you round? And why you pretended to faint?"

Again she nodded.

"Why did you take the dagger?" I asked presently.

She replied as simply as a child:

"I was afraid there might be finger-marks on it."

"But didn't you remember that you had worn gloves?"

She shook her head as though bewildered, and then said slowly:

"Are you going to give me up to — to the police?"

"Good God! no."

Her eyes sought mine long and earnestly, and then she asked in a little quiet voice that sounded afraid of itself:

"Why not?"

It seemed a strange place and a strange time for a declaration of love — and God knows, in all my imagining, I had never pictured love coming to me in such a guise. But I answered simply and naturally enough:

"Because I love you, Cinderella."

She bent her head down, as though ashamed, and muttered in a broken voice:

"You can't — you can't — not if you knew —" And then, as though rallying herself, she faced me squarely, and asked, "What do you know, then?"

"I know that you came to see Mr. Renauld that night. He offered you a cheque and you tore it up indignantly. Then you left the house —" I paused.

"Go on — what next?"

"I don't know whether you knew Jack Renauld would be coming that night, or whether you just waited about on the chance of seeing him, but you did wait about. Perhaps you were just miserable and walked aimlessly — but at any rate just before twelve you were still near there, and you saw a man on the golf links —"

Again I paused. I had leapt to the truth in a flash as she entered the room, but now the picture rose before me even more convincingly. I saw vividly the peculiar pattern of the overcoat on the dead body of Mr. Renauld, and I remembered the amazing likeness that had startled me into believing for one instant that the dead man had risen from the dead when his son burst into our conclave in the salon.

"Go on," repeated the girl steadily.

"I fancy his back was to you — but you recognized him, or thought you recognized him. The gait and the carriage were familiar to you, and the pattern of his overcoat." I paused. "You used a threat in one of your letters to Jack Renauld. When you saw him there, your anger and jealousy drove you mad — and you struck! I don't believe for a minute that you meant to kill him. But you did kill him, Cinderella."

She had flung up her hands to cover her face, and in a choked voice she said:

"You're right ... you're right ... I can see it all as you tell it." Then she turned on me almost savagely. "And you love me? Knowing what you do, how can you love me?"

"I don't know," I said a little wearily. "I think love is like that — a thing one cannot help. I have tried, I know — ever since the first day I met you. And love has been too strong for me."

And then suddenly, when I least expected it, she broke down again, casting herself down on the floor and sobbing wildly.

"Oh, I can't!" she cried. "I don't know what to do. I don't know which way to turn. Oh, pity me, pity me, someone, and tell me what to do!"

Again I knelt by her, soothing her as best I could.

"Don't be afraid of me, Bella. For God's sake don't be afraid of me. I love you, that's true — but I don't want anything in return. Only let me help you. Love him still if you have to, but let me help you, as he can't."

It was as though she had been turned to stone by my words. She raised her head from her hands and stared at me.

"You think that?" she whispered. "You think that I love Jack Renauld?"

Then, half laughing, half crying, she flung her arms passionately round my neck, and pressed her sweet wet face to mine.

"Not as I love you," she whispered. "Never as I love you!"

Her lips brushed my cheek, and then, seeking my mouth, kissed me again and again with a sweetness and fire beyond belief. The wildness of it — and the wonder, I shall not forget — no, not as long as I live!

It was a sound in the doorway that made us look up. Poirot was standing there looking at us.

I did not hesitate. With a bound I reached him and pinioned his arms to his sides.

"Quick," I said to the girl. "Get out of here. As fast as you can. I'll hold him."

With one look at me, she fled out of the room past us. I held Poirot in a grip of iron.

"*Mon ami*," observed the latter mildly, "you do this sort of thing very well. The strong man holds me in his grasp and I am helpless as a child. But all this is uncomfortable and slightly ridiculous. Let us sit down and be calm."

"You won't pursue her?"

"*Mon Dieu!* no. Am I Giraud? Release me, my friend."

Keeping a suspicious eye upon him, for I paid Poirot the compliment of knowing that I was no match for him in astuteness, I relaxed my grip, and he sank into an armchair, feeling his arms tenderly.

"It is that you have the strength of a bull when you are roused, Hastings! *Eh bien*, and do you think you have behaved well to your old friend? I show you the girl's photograph and you recognize it, but you never say a word."

"There was no need if you knew that I recognized it," I said rather bitterly. So Poirot had known all along! I had not deceived him for an instant.

"*Ta-ta!* You did not know that I knew that. And tonight you help the girl to escape when we have found her with so much trouble. *Eh bien!* it comes to this — are you going to work with me or against me, Hastings?"

For a moment or two I did not answer. To break with my old friend gave me great pain. Yet I must definitely range myself against him. Would he ever forgive me, I wondered? He had been strangely calm so far, but I knew him to possess marvellous self-command.

"Poirot," I said, 'I'm sorry. I admit I've behaved badly to you over this. But sometimes one has no choice. And in future I must take my own line."

Poirot nodded his head several times.

"I understand," he said. The mocking light had quite died out of his eyes, and he spoke with a sincerity and kindness that surprised me. "It is that, my friend, is it not? It is love that has come — not as you imagined it, all cock-a-hoop with fine feathers, but sadly, with bleeding feet. Well, well — I warned you. When I realized that this girl must have taken the dagger, I warned you. Perhaps you remember. But already it was too late. But, tell me, how much do you know?"

I met his eyes squarely.

"Nothing that you could tell me would be any surprise to me, Poirot. Understand that. But in case you think of resuming your search for Miss Duveen, I should like you to know one thing clearly. If you have any idea that she was concerned in the crime, or was the mysterious lady who called upon Mr. Renauld that night, you are wrong. I travelled home from France with her that day, and parted from her at Victoria that evening, so that it is clearly impossible for her to have been in Merlinville."

"Ah!" Poirot looked at me thoughtfully. "And you would swear to that in a court of law?"

"Most certainly I would."

Poirot rose and bowed.

"*Mon ami! Vive l'amour!* It can perform miracles. It is decidedly ingenious what you have thought of there. It defeats even Hercule Poirot!"

# XXIII.

## DIFFICULTIES AHEAD.

After a moment of stress, such as I have just described, reaction is bound to set in. I retired to rest that night on a note of triumph, but I awoke to realize that I was by no means out of the wood. True, I could see no flaw in the alibi I had so suddenly conceived. I had but to stick to my story, and I failed to see how Bella could be convicted in face of it.

But I felt the need of treading warily. Poirot would not take defeat lying down. Somehow or other, he would endeavour to turn the tables on me, and that in the way, and at the moment, when I least expected it.

We met at breakfast the following morning as though nothing had happened. Poirot's good temper was imperturbable, yet I thought I detected a film of reserve in his manner which was new. After breakfast, I announced my intention of going out for a stroll. A malicious gleam shot through Poirot's eyes.

"If it is information you seek, you need not be at the pains of deranging yourself. I can tell you all you wish to know. The Dulcibella Sisters have cancelled their contract, and have left Coventry for an unknown destination."

"Is that really so, Poirot?"

"You can take it from me, Hastings. I made inquiries the first thing this morning. After all, what else did you expect?"

True enough, nothing else could be expected under the circumstances. Cinderella had profited by the slight start I had been able to secure her, and would certainly not lose a moment in removing herself from the reach of the pursuer. It was what I had intended and planned. Nevertheless, I was aware of being plunged into a network of fresh difficulties.

I had absolutely no means of communicating with the girl, and it was vital that she should know the line of defence that had occurred to me, and which I was prepared to carry out. Of course it was possible that she might try to send word to me in some way or another, but I hardly thought it likely. She would know the risk she ran of a message being intercepted by Poirot, thus setting him on her track once more. Clearly her only course was to disappear utterly for the time being.

But, in the meantime, what was Poirot doing? I studied him attentively. He was wearing his most innocent air, and staring meditatively into the far distance. He looked altogether too placid and supine to give me reassurance. I had learned, with Poirot, that the less dangerous he looked, the more dangerous he was. His quiescence alarmed me. Observing a troubled quality in my glance, he smiled benignantly.

"You are puzzled, Hastings? You ask yourself why I do not launch myself in pursuit?"

"Well — something of the kind."

"It is what you would do, were you in my place. I understand that. But I am not of those who enjoy rushing up and down a country seeking a needle in a haystack, as you English say. No — let Mademoiselle Bella Duveen go. Without doubt, I shall be able to find her when the time comes. Until then, I am content to wait."

I stared at him doubtfully. Was he seeking to mislead me? I had an irritating feeling that, even now, he was master of the situation. My sense of superiority was gradually waning. I had contrived the girl's escape, and evolved a brilliant scheme for saving her from the consequences of her rash act — but I could not rest easy in my mind. Poirot's perfect calm awakened a thousand apprehensions.

"I suppose, Poirot," I said rather diffidently, "I mustn't ask what your plans are? I've forfeited the right."

"But not at all. There is no secret about them. We return to France without delay."

"*We?*"

"Precisely — "*we*"! You know very well that you cannot afford to let Papa Poirot out of your sight. Eh? is it not so, my friend? But remain in England by all means if you wish —"

I shook my head. He had hit the nail on the head. I could not afford to let him out of my sight. Although

I could not expect his confidence after what had happened, I could still check his actions. The only danger to Bella lay with him. Giraud and the French police were indifferent to her existence. At all costs I must keep near Poirot.

Poirot observed me attentively as these reflections passed through my mind, and gave me a nod of satisfaction.

"I am right, am I not? And as you are quite capable of trying to follow me, disguised with some absurdity such as a false beard which everyone would perceive, *bien entendu*— I much prefer that we should voyage together. It would annoy me greatly that anyone should mock themselves at you."

"Very well, then. But it's only fair to warn you—"

"I know—I know all. You are my enemy! Be my enemy, then. It does not worry me at all."

"So long as it's all fair and aboveboard, I don't mind."

"You have to the full the English passion for "fair play'! Now your scruples are satisfied, let us depart immediately. There is no time to be lost. Our stay in England has been short but sufficient. I know—what I wanted to know."

The tone was light, but I read a veiled menace into the words.

"Still—" I began, and stopped.

"Still—as you say! Without doubt you are satisfied with the part you are playing. Me, I preoccupy myself with Jack Renauld."

Jack Renauld! The words gave me a start. I had completely forgotten that aspect of the case. Jack Renauld, in prison, with the shadow of the guillotine looming over him. I saw the part I was playing in a more sinister light. I could save Bella—yes, but in doing so I ran the risk of sending an innocent man to his death.

I pushed the thought from me with horror. It could not be. He would be acquitted. Certainly he would be acquitted. But the cold fear came back. Suppose he were not? What then? Could I have it on my conscience—horrible thought! Would it come to that in the end? A decision. Bella or Jack Renauld?

The promptings of my heart were to save the girl I loved at any cost to myself. But, if the cost were to another, the problem was altered.

What would the girl herself say? I remembered that no word of Jack Renauld's arrest had passed my lips. As yet she was in total ignorance of the fact that her former lover was in prison charged with a hideous crime which he had not committed. When she knew, how would she act? Would she permit her life to be saved at the expense of his? Certainly she must do nothing rash. Jack Renauld might, and probably would, be acquitted without any intervention on her part. If so, good. But if he was not! That was the terrible, the unanswerable problem. I fancied she ran no risk of the extreme penalty. The circumstances of the crime were quite different in her case. She could plead jealousy and extreme provocation, and her youth and beauty would go for much. The fact that by a tragic mistake it was Mr. Renauld, and not his son, who paid the penalty would not alter the motive of the crime. But in any case, however lenient the sentence of the Court, it must mean a long term of imprisonment.

No, Bella must be protected. And, at the same time, Jack Renauld must be saved. How this was to be accomplished I did not see clearly. But I pinned my faith to Poirot. He knew. Come what might, he would manage to save an innocent man. He must find some pretext other than the real one. It might be difficult, but he would manage it somehow. And with Bella unsuspected, and Jack Renauld acquitted, all would end satisfactorily.

So I told myself repeatedly, but at the bottom of my heart there still remained a cold fear.

# XXIV.

## "SAVE HIM!"

We crossed from England by the evening boat, and the following morning saw us in St. Omer, whither Jack Renauld had been taken. Poirot lost no time in visiting Monsieur Hautet. As he did not seem disposed to make any objections to my accompanying him, I bore him company.

After various formalities and preliminaries, we were conducted to the examining magistrate's room. He greeted us cordially.

"I was told that you had returned to England, Monsieur Poirot. I am glad that such is not the case."

"It is true I went there, monsieur, but it was only for a flying visit. A side issue, but one that I fancied might repay investigation."

"And it did — eh?"

Poirot shrugged his shoulders. Monsieur Hautet nodded, sighing.

"We must resign ourselves, I fear. That animal Giraud, his manners are abominable, but he is undoubtedly clever! Not much chance of that one making a mistake."

"You think not?"

It was the examining magistrate's turn to shrug his shoulders.

"Oh, well, speaking frankly — in confidence, of course — can you come to any other conclusion?"

"Frankly, there seem to me to be many points that are obscure."

"Such as — ?"

But Poirot was not to be drawn.

"I have not yet tabulated them,"

he remarked. "It was a general reflection that I was making. I liked the young man, and should be sorry to believe him guilty of such a hideous crime. By the way, what has he to say for himself on the matter?"

The magistrate frowned.

"I cannot understand him. He seems incapable of putting up any sort of defence. It has been most difficult to get him to answer questions. He contents himself with a general denial, and beyond that takes refuge in a most obstinate silence. I am interrogating him again tomorrow, perhaps you would like to be present?"

We accepted the invitation with *empressement*.

"A distressing case," said the magistrate with a sigh. "My sympathy for Madame Renauld is profound."

"How is Madame Renauld?"

"She has not yet recovered consciousness. It is merciful in a way, poor woman; she is being spared much. The doctors say that there is no danger, but that when she comes to herself she must be kept as quiet as possible. It was, I understand, quite as much the shock as the fall which caused her present state. It would be terrible if her brain became unhinged; but I should not wonder at all — no, really, not at all."

Monsieur Hautet leaned back, shaking his head, with a sort of mournful enjoyment, as he envisaged the gloomy prospect.

He roused himself at length, and observed with a start:

"That reminds me. I have here a letter for you, Monsieur Poirot. Let me see, where did I put it?"

He proceeded to rummage among his papers. At last he found the missive, and handed it to Poirot.

"It was sent under cover to me in order that I might forward it to you," he explained. "But as you left no address I could not do so."

Poirot studied the letter curiously. It was addressed in a long, sloping, foreign hand, and the writing was decidedly a woman's. Poirot did not open it. Instead he put it in his pocket and rose to his feet.

"Till tomorrow then. Many thanks for your courtesy and amiability."

"But not at all. I am always at your service."

We were just leaving the building when we came face to face with Giraud, looking more dandified than ever, and thoroughly pleased with himself.

"Aha! Monsieur Poirot," he cried airily. "You have returned from England then?"

"As you see," said Poirot.

"The end of the case is not far off now, I fancy."

"I agree with you, Monsieur Giraud."

Poirot spoke in a subdued tone. His crestfallen manner seemed to delight the other.

"Of all the milk-and-water criminals! Not an idea of defending himself. It is extraordinary!"

"So extraordinary that it gives one to think, does it not?" suggested Poirot mildly.

But Giraud was not even listening. He twirled his cane amicably.

"Well, good day, Monsieur Poirot. I am glad you're satisfied of young Renauld's guilt at last."

"*Pardon!* But I am not in the least satisfied. Jack Renauld is innocent."

Giraud stared for a moment—then burst out laughing, tapping his head significantly with the brief remark: "*Toqué!*"

Poirot drew himself up. A dangerous light showed in his eyes.

"Monsieur Giraud, throughout the case your manner to me has been deliberately insulting. You need teaching a lesson. I am prepared to wager you five hundred francs that I find the murderer of Monsieur Renauld before you do. Is it agreed?"

Giraud stared helplessly at him, and murmured again: "*Toqué!*"

"Come now," urged Poirot; "is it agreed?"

"I have no wish to take your money from you."

"Make your mind easy—you will not!"

"Oh, well then, I agree! You speak of my manner to you being insulting. Well, once or twice, *your* manner has annoyed *me*."

"I am enchanted to hear it," said Poirot. "Good morning, Monsieur Giraud. Come, Hastings."

I said no word as we walked along the street. My heart was heavy. Poirot had displayed his intentions only too plainly. I doubted more than ever my powers of saving Bella from the consequences of her act. This unlucky encounter with Giraud had roused Poirot and put him on his mettle.

Suddenly I felt a hand laid on my shoulder, and turned to face Gabriel Stonor. We stopped and greeted him, and he proposed strolling with us back to our hotel.

"And what are you doing here, Monsieur Stonor?" inquired Poirot.

"One must stand by one's friends," replied the other dryly. "Especially when they are unjustly accused."

"Then you do not believe that Jack Renauld committed the crime?" I asked eagerly.

"Certainly I don't. I know the lad. I admit that there have been one or two things in this business that have staggered me completely, but none the less, in spite of his fool way of taking it, I'll never believe that Jack Renauld is a murderer."

My heart warmed to the secretary. His words seemed to lift a secret weight from my heart.

"I have no doubt that many people feel as you do," I exclaimed. "There is really absurdly little evidence against him. I should say that there was no doubt of his acquittal—no doubt whatever."

But Stonor hardly responded as I could have wished.

"I'd give a lot to think as you do," he said gravely. He turned to Poirot. "What's your opinion, monsieur?"

"I think that things look very black against him," said Poirot quietly.

"You believe him guilty?" said Stonor sharply.

"No. But I think he will find it hard to prove his innocence."

"He's behaving so damned queerly," muttered Stonor. "Of course, I realize that there's a lot more in this affair than meets the eye. Giraud's not wise to that because he's an outsider, but the whole thing has been damned odd. As to that, least said soonest mended. If Mrs. Renauld wants to hush anything up, I'll take my cue from her. It's her show, and I've too much respect for her judgement to shove my oar in, but I can't get behind this attitude of Jack's. Anyone would think he wanted to be thought guilty."

"But it's absurd," I cried, bursting in. "For one thing, the dagger —" I paused, uncertain as to how much Poirot would wish me to reveal. I continued, choosing my words carefully, "We know that the dagger could not have been in Jack Renauld's possession that evening. Mrs. Renauld knows that."

"True," said Stonor. "When she recovers, she will doubtless say all this and more. Well, I must be leaving you."

"One moment." Poirot's hand arrested his departure. "Can you arrange for word to be sent to me at once should Mrs. Renauld recover consciousness?"

"Certainly. That's easily done."

"That point about the dagger is good, Poirot," I urged as we went upstairs. "I couldn't speak very plainly before Stonor."

"That was quite right of you. We might as well keep the knowledge to ourselves as long as we can. As to the dagger, your point hardly helps Jack Renauld. You remember that I was absent for an hour this morning, before we started from London?"

"Yes?"

"Well, I was employed in trying to find the firm Jack Renauld employed to convert his souvenirs. It was not very difficult. *Eh bien*, Hastings, they made to his order not two paper knives, but three."

"So that —"

"So that, after giving one to his mother and one to Bella Duveen, there was a third which he doubtless retained for his own use. No, Hastings, I fear the dagger question will not help us to save him from the guillotine."

"It won't come to that," I cried, stung. Poirot shook his head uncertainly. "You will save him," I cried positively. Poirot glanced at me dryly.

"Have you not rendered it impossible, *mon ami?*"

"Some other way," I muttered.

"Ah! *Sapristi!* But it is miracles

you ask from me. No — say no more. Let us instead see what is in this letter."

And he drew out the envelope from his breast pocket.

His face contracted as he read, then he handed the one flimsy sheet to me.

"There are other women in the world who suffer, Hastings."

The writing was blurred and the note had evidently been written in great agitation.

> *Dear Monsieur Poirot — If you get this, I beg of you to come to my aid. I have no one to turn to, and at all costs Jack must be saved. I implore of you on my knees to help us.*
>
> *—Marthe Daubreuil*

I handed it back, moved.

"You will go?"

"At once. We will command an auto."

Half an hour later saw us at the Villa Marguerite. Marthe was at the door to meet us, and let Poirot in, clinging with both hands to one of his.

"Ah, you have come — it is good of you. I have been in despair, not knowing what to do. They will not let me go to see him in prison even. I suffer horribly. I am nearly mad! Is it true what they say, that he does not deny the crime? But that is madness! It is impossible that he should have done it! Never for one minute will I believe it."

"Neither do I believe it, mademoiselle," said Poirot gently.

"But then why does he not speak? I do not understand."

"Perhaps because he is screening someone," suggested Poirot, watching her.

Marthe frowned.

"Screening someone? Do you mean his mother? Ah, from the beginning I have suspected her. Who inherits all that vast fortune? She does. It is easy to wear widow's weeds and play the hypocrite. And they say that when he was arrested she fell down like that!" She made a dramatic gesture. "And without doubt, Monsieur Stonor, the secretary, he helped her. They are thick as thieves, those two. It is true she is older than he — but what do men care — if a woman is rich!"

There was a hint of bitterness in her tone.

"Stonor was in England," I put in.

"He says so — but who knows?"

"Mademoiselle," said Poirot quietly, "if we are to work together, you and I, we must have things clear. First, I will ask you a question."

"Yes, monsieur?"

"Are you aware of your mother's real name?"

Marthe looked at him for a minute, then, letting her head fall forward on her arms, she burst into tears.

"There, there," said Poirot, patting her on the shoulder. "Calm yourself, *petite*, I see that you know. Now a second question — did you know who Monsieur Renauld was?"

"Monsieur Renauld." She raised her head from her hands and gazed at him wonderingly.

"Ah, I see you do not know that. Now listen to me carefully."

Step by step, he went over the case, much as he had done to me on the day of our departure for England. Marthe listened spellbound. When he had finished she drew a long breath.

"But you are wonderful — magnificent! You are the greatest detective in the world."

With a swift gesture she slipped off her chair and knelt before him with an abandonment that was wholly French.

"Save him, monsieur," she cried. "I love him so. Oh, save him, save him — save him!"

# XXV.

## AN UNEXPECTED DÉNOUEMENT.

We were present the following morning at the examination of Jack Renauld. Short as the time had been, I was shocked at the change that had taken place in the young prisoner. His cheeks had fallen in, there were deep black circles round his eyes, and he looked haggard and distraught, as one who had wooed sleep in vain for several nights. He betrayed no emotion at seeing us.

"Renauld," began the magistrate, "do you deny that you were in Merlinville on the night of the crime?"

Jack did not reply at once, then he said with a hesitancy of manner which was piteous:

"I — I — told you that I was in Cherbourg."

The magistrate turned sharply.

"Send in the station witnesses."

In a moment or two the door opened to admit a man whom I recognized as being a porter at Merlinville station.

"You were on duty on the night of 7th June?"

"Yes, monsieur."

"You witnessed the arrival of the 11:40 train?"

"Yes, monsieur."

"Look at the prisoner. Do you recognize him as having been one of the passengers to alight?"

"Yes, monsieur."

"There is no possibility of your being mistaken?"

"No, monsieur. I know Monsieur Jack Renauld well."

"Nor of your being mistaken as to the date?"

"No, monsieur. Because it was the following morning, 8th June, that we heard of the murder."

Another railway official was brought in, and confirmed the first one's evidence. The magistrate looked at Jack Renauld.

"These men have identified you positively. What have you to say?"

Jack shrugged his shoulders. "Nothing."

"Renauld," continued the magistrate, "do you recognize this?"

He took something from the table by his side and held it out to the prisoner. I shuddered as I recognized the aeroplane dagger.

"Pardon," cried Jack's counsel, Maître Grosier. "I demand to speak to my client before he answers the question."

But Jack Renauld had no consideration for the feelings of the wretched Grosier. He waved him aside, and replied quietly:

"Certainly I recognize it. It was a present given by me to my mother, as a souvenir of the War."

"Is there, as far as you know, any duplicate of that dagger in existence?"

Again Maître Grosier burst out, and again Jack overrode him.

"Not that I know of. The setting was my own design."

Even the magistrate almost gasped at the boldness of the reply. It did, in very truth, seem as though Jack was rushing on his fate. I realized, of course, the vital necessity he was under of concealing, for Bella's sake, the fact that there was a duplicate dagger in the case. So long as there was supposed to be only one weapon, no suspicion was likely to attach to the girl who had had the second paper-knife in her possession. He was valiantly shielding the woman he had once loved — but at what cost to himself! I began to realize the magnitude of the task I had so lightly set Poirot. It would not be easy to secure the acquittal of Jack Renauld by anything short of the truth.

Monsieur Hautet spoke again, with a peculiarly biting inflection:

"Madame Renauld told us that this dagger was on her dressing-table on the night of the crime. But Madame Renauld is a mother! It will doubtless astonish you, Renauld, but I consider it highly likely that Madame Renauld was mistaken, and that, by inadvertence perhaps, you had taken it with you to Paris. Doubtless you will contradict me."

I saw the lad's handcuffed hands clench themselves. The perspiration stood out in beads upon his brow, as with a supreme effort he interrupted Monsieur Hautet in a hoarse voice:

"I shall not contradict you. It is possible."

It was a stupefying moment. Maître Grosier rose to his feet, protesting:

"My client has undergone a

considerable nervous strain. I should wish it put on the record that I do not consider him answerable for what he says."

The magistrate quelled him angrily. For a moment a doubt seemed to arise in his own mind. Jack Renauld had almost overdone his part. He leaned forward, and gazed at the prisoner searchingly.

"Do you fully understand, Renauld, that on the answers you have given me I shall have no alternative but to commit you for trial?"

Jack's pale face flushed. He looked steadily back.

"Monsieur Hautet, I swear that I did not kill my father."

But the magistrate's brief moment of doubt was over. He laughed a short unpleasant laugh.

"Without doubt, without doubt—they are always innocent, our prisoners! By your own mouth you are condemned. You can offer no defence, no alibi—only a mere assertion which would not deceive a babe!—That you are not guilty. You killed your father, Renauld—a cruel and cowardly murder—for the sake of the money which you believed would come to you at his death. Your mother was an accessory after the fact. Doubtless, in view of the fact that she acted as a mother, the courts will extend an indulgence to her that they will not accord to you. And rightly so! Your crime was a horrible one—to be held in abhorrence by gods and men!"

Monsieur Hautet was interrupted—to his intense annoyance. The door was pushed open.

"Monsieur le juge, Monsieur le juge," stammered the attendant, "there is a lady who says—who says—"

"Who says what?" cried the justly incensed magistrate. "This is highly irregular. I forbid it—I absolutely forbid it."

But a slender figure pushed the stammering gendarme aside. Dressed all in black, with a long veil that hid her face, she advanced into the room.

My heart gave a sickening throb. She had come then! All my efforts were in vain. Yet I could not but admire the courage that had led her to take this step so unfalteringly.

She raised her veil—and I gasped. For, though as like her as two peas, this girl was not Cinderella! On the other hand, now that I saw her without the fair wig she had worn on the stage, I recognized her as the girl of the photograph in Jack Renauld's room.

"You are the Juge d'Instruction, Monsieur Hautet?" she queried.

"Yes, but I forbid—"

"My name is Bella Duveen. I wish to give myself up for the murder of Mr. Renauld."

# XVI.

## I RECEIVE A LETTER.

*My friend,—*

*You will know all when you get this. Nothing that I can say will move Bella. She has gone out to give herself up. I am tired out with struggling.*

*You will know now that I deceived you, that where you gave me trust I repaid you with lies. It will seem, perhaps, indefensible to you, but I should like, before I go out of your life for ever, to show you just how it all came about. If I knew that you forgave me, it would make life easier for me. It wasn't for myself I did it—that's the only thing I can put forward to say for myself.*

*I'll begin from the day I met you in the boat train from Paris. I was uneasy then about Bella. She was just desperate about Jack Renauld, she'd have lain down on the ground for him to walk on, and when he began to change, and to stop writing so often, she began getting in a state. She got it into her head that he was keen on another girl—and of course, as it turned out afterwards, she was quite right there. She'd made up her mind to go to their villa at Merlinville, and try and see Jack. She knew I was against it, and tried to give me the slip. I found she was not on the train at Calais, and determined I would not go on to England without her. I'd an uneasy feeling that something awful was going to happen if I couldn't prevent it.*

*I met the next train from Paris. She was on it, and set upon going out then and there to Merlinville. I argued with her for all I was worth, but it wasn't any good — she was all strung up and set upon having her own way. Well, I washed my hands of it. I'd done all I could. It was getting late. I went to a hotel, and Bella started for Merlinville. I still couldn't shake off my feeling of what the books call 'impending disaster.'*

*The next day came — but no Bella. She'd made a date with me to meet at the hotel, but she didn't keep it. No sign of her all day. I got more and more anxious. Then came the evening paper with the news.*

*It was awful! I couldn't be sure, of course — but I was terribly afraid. I figured it out that Bella had met Papa Renauld and told him about her and Jack, and that he'd insulted her or something like that. We've both got terribly quick tempers.*

*Then all the masked foreigner business came out, and I began to feel more at ease. But it still worried me that Bella hadn't kept her date with me.*

*By the next morning I was so rattled that I'd just got to go and see what I could. First thing, I ran up against you. You know all that.... When I saw the dead man, looking so like Jack, and wearing Jack's fancy overcoat, I knew! And there was the identical paper-knife — wicked little thing! — that Jack had given Bella! Ten to one it had her fingermarks on it. I can't hope to explain to you the sort of helpless horror of that moment. I only saw one thing clearly — I must get hold of that dagger, and get right away with it before they found out it was gone. I pretended to faint, and while you were away getting water I took the thing and hid it away in my dress.*

*I told you that I was staying at the Hotel du Phare, but of course really I made a bee-line back to Calais, and then on to England by the first boat. When we were in mid-Channel I dropped that little devil of a dagger into the sea. Then I felt I could breathe again.*

*Bella was in our digs in London. She looked like nothing on God's earth. I told her what I'd done, and that she was pretty safe for the time being. She stared at me, and then began laughing ... laughing ... laughing ... it was horrible to hear her! I felt that the best thing to do was to keep busy. She'd go mad if she had time to brood on what she'd done. Luckily we got an engagement at once.*

*And then, I saw you and your friend watching us that night... I was frantic. You must suspect, or you wouldn't have tracked us down. I had to know the worst, so I followed you. I was desperate. And then, before I'd had time to say anything, I tumbled to it that it was me you suspected, not Bella! Or at least that you thought I was Bella, since I'd stolen the dagger.*

*I wish, honey, that you could see back into my mind at that moment... you'd forgive me, perhaps... I was so frightened, and muddled, and desperate ... All I could get clearly was that you would try and save me — I didn't know whether you'd be willing to save her... I thought very likely not — it wasn't the same thing! And I couldn't risk it! Bella's my twin — I'd got to do the best for her. So I went on lying. I felt mean — I feel mean still . . . That's all — enough, too, you'll say, I expect. I ought to have trusted you . . . If I had —*

*As soon as the news was in the paper that Jack Renauld had been arrested, it was all up. Bella wouldn't even wait to see how things went . . . .*

*I'm very tired. I can't write any more.*

She had begun to sign herself Cinderella, but had crossed that out and written instead "Dulcie Duveen."

It was an ill — written, blurred epistle — but I have kept it to this day.

Poirot was with me when I read it. The sheets fell from my hand, and I looked across at him. "Did you know all the time that it was — the other?"

"Yes, my friend."

"Why did you not tell me?'

"To begin with, I could hardly believe it conceivable that you could make such a mistake. You had seen the photograph. The sisters are very alike, but by no means incapable of distinguishment."

"But the fair hair?'

"A wig, worn for the sake of a piquant contrast on the stage. Is it conceivable that with twins one should be fair and one dark?"

"Why didn't you tell me that night at the hotel in Coventry?"

"You were rather high-handed in your methods, *mon ami*," said Poirot dryly. "You did not give me a chance."

"But afterwards?'

"Ah, afterwards! Well, to begin with, I was hurt at your want of faith in me. And then, I wanted to see whether your — feelings would stand the test of time. In fact, whether it was love, or a flash in the pan, with you. I should not have left you long in your error."

I nodded. His tone was too affectionate for me to bear resentment. I looked down on the sheets of the letter. Suddenly I picked them up from the floor, and pushed them across to him.

"Read that," I said. "I'd like you to."

He read it through in silence, then he looked up at me.

"What is it that worries you, Hastings?'

This was quite a new mood in Poirot. His mocking manner seemed laid quite aside. I was able to say what I wanted without too much difficulty.

"She doesn't say — she doesn't say — well, not whether she cares for me or not?"

Poirot turned back the pages.

"I think you are mistaken, Hastings."

"Where?" I cried, leaning forward eagerly.

Poirot smiled. "She tells you that in every line of the letter, *mon ami*."

"But where am I to find her? There's no address on the letter. There's a French stamp, that's all."

"Excite yourself not! Leave it to Papa Poirot. I can find her for you as soon as soon as I have five little minutes!"

# XXVII.

## JACK RENAULD'S STORY.

"Congratulations, Monsieur Jack," said Poirot, wringing the lad warmly by the hand.

Young Renauld had come to us as soon as he was liberated — before starting for Merlinville to rejoin Marthe and his mother. Stonor accompanied him. His heartiness was in strong contrast to the lad's wan looks. It was plain that the boy was on the verge of a nervous breakdown. He smiled mournfully at Poirot, and said in a low voice:

"I went through it to protect her, and now it's all no use."

"You could hardly expect the girl to accept the price of your life," remarked Stonor dryly. "She was bound to come forward when she saw you heading straight for the guillotine."

"Eh, *ma foi!* and you were heading for it too!" added Poirot, with a slight twinkle. "You would have had Maître Grosier's death from rage on your conscience if you had gone on."

"He was a well-meaning ass, I suppose," said Jack. "But he worried me horribly. You see, I couldn't very well take him into my confidence. But, my God! what's going to happen about Bella?'

"If I were you," said Poirot frankly, "I should not distress myself unduly. The French Courts are very lenient to youth and beauty, and the *crime passionnel!* A clever lawyer will make out a great case of extenuating circumstances. It will not be pleasant for you —"

"I don't care about that. You see, Monsieur Poirot, in a way I do feel guilty of my father's murder. But for me, and my entanglement with this girl, he would be alive and well today. And then my cursed carelessness in taking away the wrong overcoat. I can't help feeling responsible for his death. It will haunt me forever!"

"No, no," I said soothingly.

"Of course it's horrible to me to think that Bella killed my father," resumed Jack. "But I'd treated her shamefully. After I met Marthe, and realized I'd made a mistake, I ought to have written and told her so honestly. But I was so terrified of a row, and of its coming to Marthe's ears, and her thinking there was more in it than there ever had been — well, I was a coward, and went on hoping the thing would die down of itself. I just drifted, in fact — not realizing that I was driving the poor kid desperate. If she'd really knifed me, as she meant to, I should have got no more than my deserts. And the way she's come forward now is downright plucky. I'd have stood the racket, you know — up to the end."

He was silent for a moment or two, and then burst out on another tack:

"What gets me is why the Governor should be wandering about in underclothes and my overcoat at that time of night. I suppose he'd just given the foreign johnnies the slip, and my mother must have made a mistake about its being two o'clock when they came. Or — or, it wasn't all a frame-up, was it? I mean, my mother didn't think — couldn't think — that — that it was me?"

Poirot reassured him quickly.

"No, no, Monsieur Jack. Have no fears on that score. As for the rest, I will explain it to you one of these days. It is rather curious. But will you recount to us exactly what did occur on that terrible evening?'

"There's very little to tell. I came from Cherbourg, as I told you, in order to see Marthe before going to the other end of the world. The train was late, and I decided to take the short cut across the golf links. I could easily get into the grounds of the Villa Marguerite from there. I had nearly reached the place when —"

He paused and swallowed.

"Yes?'

"I heard a terrible cry. It wasn't loud — a sort of choke and gasp — but it frightened me. For a moment I stood rooted to the spot. Then I came round the corner of a bush. There was moonlight. I saw the grave, and a figure lying face downwards with a dagger sticking in the back. And then — and then — I looked up and saw her. She was looking at me as though she saw a ghost — it's what she must have thought me at first — all expression seemed frozen out of her face by horror. And then she gave a cry, and turned and ran."

He stopped, trying to master his emotion.

"And afterwards?" asked Poirot.

"I really don't know. I stayed there for a time, dazed. And then I realized I'd better get away as fast as I could. It didn't occur to me that they would suspect me, but I was afraid of being called upon to give evidence against her. I walked to St. Beauvais as I told you, and got a car from there back to Cherbourg."

A knock came at the door, and a page entered with a telegram which he delivered to Stonor. He tore it open. Then he got up from his seat.

"Mrs. Renauld has regained consciousness," he said.

"Ah!" Poirot sprang to his feet. "Let us all go to Merlinville at once!"

A hurried departure was made forthwith. Stonor, at Jack's insistence, agreed to stay behind and do all that could be done for Bella Duveen. Poirot, Jack Renauld, and I set off in the Renauld car.

The run took just over forty minutes. As we approached the doorway of the Villa Marguerite Jack Renauld shot a questioning glance at Poirot.

"How would it be if you went on first — to break the news to my mother that I am free —"

"While you break it in person to Mademoiselle Marthe, eh?" finished Poirot, with a twinkle. "But yes, by all means, I was about to propose such an arrangement myself."

Jack Renauld did not wait for more. Stopping the car, he swung himself out, and ran up the path to the front door. We went on in the car to the Villa Geneviève.

"Poirot," I said, "do you remember how we arrived here that first day? And were met by the news of Mr. Renauld's murder?"

"Ah, yes, truly. Not so long ago either. But what a lot of things have happened since then — especially for you, *mon ami!*"

"Yes, indeed," I sighed.

"You are regarding it from the sentimental standpoint, Hastings. That was not my meaning. We will hope that Mademoiselle Bella will be dealt with leniently, and after all Jack Renauld cannot marry both the girls! I spoke from a professional standpoint. This is not a crime well-ordered and regular, such as a detective delights in. The *mise en scène* designed by Georges Conneau, that indeed is perfect, but the *dénouement* — ah, no! A man killed by accident in a girl's fit of anger — ah, indeed, what order or method is there in that?"

And in the midst of a fit of laughter on my part at Poirot's peculiarities, the door was opened by Françoise.

Poirot explained that he must see Mrs. Renauld at once, and the old woman conducted him upstairs. I remained in the salon.

It was some time before Poirot reappeared. He was looking unusually grave. "*Vous voilà,* Hastings! *Sacré tonnerre!* But there are squalls ahead!"

"What do you mean?" I cried.

"I would hardly have credited it," said Poirot thoughtfully, "but women are very unexpected."

"Here are Jack and Marthe Daubreuil," I exclaimed, looking out of the window.

Poirot bounded out of the room, and met the young couple on the steps outside.

"Do not enter. It is better not. Your mother is very upset."

"I know, I know," said Jack Renauld. "I must go up to her at once."

"But no, I tell you. It is better not."

"But Marthe and I —"

"In any case, do not take Mademoiselle with you. Mount, if you must, but you would be wise to be guided by me."

A voice on the stairs behind made us all start.

"I thank you for your good offices, Monsieur Poirot, but I will make my own wishes clear."

We stared in astonishment. Descending the stairs, leaning on Léonie's arm, was Mrs. Renauld, her head still bandaged. The French girl was weeping, and imploring her mistress to return to bed.

"Madame will kill herself. It is contrary to all the doctor's orders!"

But Mrs. Renauld came on.

"Mother," cried Jack, starting forward. But with a gesture she drove him back.

"I am no mother of yours! You are no son of mine! From this day and hour I renounce you."

"Mother!" cried the lad, stupefied.

For a moment she seemed to waver, to falter before the anguish in his voice. Poirot made a mediating gesture. But instantly she regained command of herself.

"Your father's blood is on your head. You are morally guilty of his death. You thwarted and defied him over this girl, and by your heartless treatment of another girl, you brought about his death. Go out from my house. Tomorrow I intend to take such steps as shall make it certain that you shall never touch a penny of his money. Make your way in the world as best you can with the help of the girl who is the daughter of your father's bitterest enemy!"

And slowly, painfully, she retraced her way upstairs.

We were all dumbfounded — totally unprepared for such a demonstration. Jack Renauld, worn out with all he had already gone through, swayed and nearly fell. Poirot and I went quickly to his assistance.

"He is overdone," murmured Poirot to Marthe. "Where can we take him?"

"But home! To the Villa Marguerite. We will nurse him, my mother and I. My poor Jack!"

We got the lad to the villa, where he dropped limply on to a chair in a semi-dazed condition. Poirot felt his head and hands.

"He has fever. The long strain

begins to tell. And now this shock on top of it. Get him to bed, and Hastings and I will summon a doctor."

A doctor was soon procured. After examining the patient, he gave it as his opinion that it was simply a case of nerve strain. With perfect rest and quiet, the lad might be almost restored by the next day, but, if excited, there was a chance of brain fever. It would be advisable for someone to sit up all night with him.

Finally, having done all we could, we left him in the charge of Marthe and her mother, and set out for the town. It was past our usual hour of dining, and we were both famished. The first restaurant we came to assuaged the pangs of hunger with an excellent omelette, and an equally excellent entrecôte to follow.

"And now for quarters for the night," said Poirot, when at length *café noir* had completed the meal. "Shall we try our old friend, the Hotel de Bains?"

We traced our steps there without more ado. Yes, Messieurs could be accommodated with two good rooms overlooking the sea. Then Poirot asked a question which surprised me:

"Has an English lady, Miss Robinson, arrived?"

"Yes, Monsieur. She is in the little salon."

"Ah!"

"Poirot," I cried, keeping pace with him, as he walked along the corridor, "who on earth is Miss Robinson?"

Poirot beamed kindly on me.

"It is that I have arranged you a marriage, Hastings."

"But I say —"

"Bah!" said Poirot, giving me a friendly push over the threshold of the door. "Do you think I wish to trumpet aloud in Merlinville the name of Duveen?"

It was indeed Cinderella who rose to greet us. I took her hand in both of mine. My eyes said the rest.

Poirot cleared his throat.

"Mes enfants," he said, "for the little moment we have no time for sentiment. There is work ahead of us. Mademoiselle, were you able to do what I asked you?"

In response, Cinderella took from her bag an object wrapped up in paper, and handed it silently to Poirot. The latter unwrapped it. It gave me a start — for it was the aeroplane dagger which I understood she had cast into the sea. Strange, how reluctant women always are to destroy the most compromising of objects and documents!

"*Très bien, mon enfant*," said Poirot. "I am pleased with you. Go now and rest yourself. Hastings here and I have work to do. You shall see him tomorrow."

"Where are you going?" asked the girl, her eyes widening.

"You shall hear all about it tomorrow."

"Because wherever you're going, I'm coming too."

"But, mademoiselle —"

"I'm coming too, I tell you."

Poirot realized that it was futile to argue. He gave in.

"Come then, mademoiselle. But it will not be amusing. In all probability nothing will happen."

The girl made no reply.

Twenty minutes later we set forth. It was quite dark now, a close oppressive evening. Poirot led the way out of the town in the direction of the Villa Geneviève. But when he reached the Villa Marguerite he paused.

"I should like to assure myself that all goes well with Jack Renauld. Come with me, Hastings. Mademoiselle will perhaps remain outside. Madame Daubreuil might say something which would wound her."

We unlatched the gate, and walked up the path. As we went round to the side of the house, I drew Poirot's attention to a window on the first floor. Thrown sharply on the blind was the profile of Marthe Daubreuil.

"Ah!" said Poirot. "I figure to myself that that is the room where we shall find Jack Renauld."

Madame Daubreuil opened the door to us. She explained that Jack was much the same, but perhaps we would like to see for ourselves. She led us upstairs and into the bedroom. Marthe Daubreuil was sitting by a table with a lamp on it, working. She put her finger to her lips as we entered.

Jack Renauld was sleeping an uneasy, fitful sleep, his head turning from side to side, and his face still unduly flushed.

"Is the doctor coming again?" asked Poirot in a whisper.

"Not unless we send. He is sleeping — that is the great thing. *Maman* made him a *tisane.*"

She sat down again with her embroidery as we left the room. Madame Daubreuil accompanied us down the stairs. Since I had learned of her past history, I viewed this woman with increased interest. She stood there with her eyes cast down, the same faint enigmatical smile that I remembered on her lips. And suddenly I felt afraid of her, as one might feel afraid of a beautiful poisonous snake.

"I hope we have not deranged you, madame," said Poirot politely, as she opened the door for us to pass out.

"Not at all, monsieur."

"By the way," said Poirot, as though struck by an afterthought, "Monsieur Stonor has not been in Merlinville today, has he?"

I could not at all fathom the point of this question, which I well knew to be meaningless as far as Poirot was concerned.

Madame Daubreuil replied quite composedly.

"Not that I know of."

"He has not had an interview with Madame Renauld?'

"How should I know that, monsieur?"

"True," said Poirot. "I thought you might have seen him coming or going, that is all. Goodnight, madame."

"Why —" I began.

"No whys, Hastings. There will be time for that later."

We rejoined Cinderella and made our way rapidly in the direction of the Villa Geneviève. Poirot looked over his shoulder once at the lighted window and the profile of Marthe as she bent over her work.

"He is being guarded at all events," he muttered.

Arrived at the Villa Geneviève, Poirot took up his stand behind some bushes to the left of the drive, where, while enjoying a good view ourselves, we were completely hidden from sight. The villa itself was in total darkness; everybody was without doubt in bed and asleep. We were almost immediately under the window of Mrs. Renauld's bedroom, which window, I noticed, was open. It seemed to me that it was upon this spot that Poirot's eyes were fixed.

"What are we going to do?" I whispered.

"Watch."

"But —"

"I do not expect anything to happen for at least an hour, probably two hours, but the —"

His words were interrupted by a long, thin drawn cry:

"Help!"

A light flashed up in the first bedroom on the right-hand side of the front door. The cry came from there. And even as we watched there came a shadow on the blind as of two people struggling.

"*Mille tonnerres!*" cried Poirot. "She must have changed her room."

Dashing forward, he battered wildly on the front door. Then rushing to the tree in the flower-bed, he swarmed up it with the agility of a cat. I followed him, as with a bound he sprang in through the open window. Looking over my shoulder, I saw Dulcie reaching the branch behind me.

"Take care," I exclaimed.

"Take care of your grandmother!" retorted the girl. "This is child's play to me."

Poirot had rushed through the empty room and was pounding on the door.

"Locked and bolted on the outside," he growled. "And it will take time to burst it open."

The cries for help were getting noticeably fainter. I saw despair in Poirot's eyes. He and I together put our shoulders to the door.

Cinderella's voice, calm and dispassionate, came from the window:

"You'll be too late. I guess I'm the only one who can do anything."

Before I could move a hand to stop her, she appeared to leap from the window into space. I rushed and looked out. To my horror, I saw her hanging by her hands from the roof, propelling herself along by jerks in the direction of the lighted window.

"Good heavens! She'll be killed," I cried.

"You forget. She's a professional acrobat, Hastings. It was the providence of the good God that made her insist on coming with us tonight. I only pray that she may be in time. Ah!"

A cry of absolute terror floated out on to the night, as the girl disappeared through the window, and then in Cinderella's clear tones came the words:

"No, you don't! I've got you — and my wrists are just like steel."

At the same moment the door of our prison was opened cautiously by Françoise. Poirot brushed her aside unceremoniously and rushed down the passage to where the other maids were grouped round the farther door.

"It's locked on the inside, monsieur."

There was the sound of a heavy fall within. After a moment or two the key turned and the door swung slowly open. Cinderella, very pale, beckoned us in.

"She is safe?' demanded Poirot.

"Yes, I was just in time. She was exhausted."

Mrs. Renauld was half sitting, half lying on the bed. She was gasping for breath.

"Nearly strangled me," she murmured painfully.

The girl picked up something from the floor and handed it to Poirot. It was a rolled-up ladder of silk rope, very fine, but quite strong.

"A getaway," said Poirot. "By the window, while we were battering at the door. Where is — the other?"

The girl stood aside a little and pointed. On the ground lay a figure wrapped in some dark material, a fold of which hid the face.

"Dead?"

She nodded.

"I think so. Head must have struck the marble fender."

"But who is it?" I cried.

"The murderer of Renauld, Hastings. And the would-be murderer of Madame Renauld."

Puzzled and uncomprehending, I knelt down, and lifting the fold of cloth, looked into the dead beautiful face of Marthe Daubreuil!

# XXVIII.

## JOURNEY'S END.

I have confused memories of the further events of that night. Poirot seemed deaf to my repeated questions. He was engaged in overwhelming Françoise with reproaches for not having told him of Mrs. Renauld's change of sleeping quarters.

I caught him by the shoulder, determined to attract his attention, and make myself heard.

"But you must have known," I expostulated. "You were taken up to see her this afternoon."

Poirot deigned to attend to me for a moment.

"She had been wheeled on a sofa to the middle room — her boudoir," he explained.

"But, monsieur," cried Françoise, "Madame changed her room almost immediately after the crimes. The associations — they were too distressing!"

"Then why was I not told?" vociferated Poirot, striking the table, and working himself into a first-class passion. "I demand of you — why — was — I — not — told? You are an old woman completely *imbecile!* And Léonie and Denise are no better. All of you are triple idiots! Your stupidity has nearly caused the death of your mistress. But for this courageous child —"

He broke off, and, darting across the room to where the girl was bending over ministering to Mrs.

Renauld, he embraced her with Gallic fervour — slightly to my annoyance.

I was aroused from my condition of mental fog by a sharp command from Poirot to fetch the doctor immediately on Mrs. Renauld's behalf. After that, I might summon the police. And he added, to complete my dudgeon:

"It will hardly be worth your while to return here. I shall be too busy to attend to you, and of Mademoiselle here I make a *garde-malade*."

I retired with what dignity I could command. Having done my errands, I returned to the hotel. I understood next to nothing of what had occurred. The events of the night seemed fantastic and impossible. Nobody would answer my questions. Nobody had seemed to hear them. Angrily, I flung myself into bed, and slept the sleep of the bewildered and utterly exhausted.

I awoke to find the sun pouring in through the open windows and Poirot, neat and smiling, sitting beside the bed.

"*Enfin*, you wake! But it is that you are a famous sleeper, Hastings! Do you know that it is nearly eleven o'clock?"

I groaned and put a hand to my head.

"I must have been dreaming," I said. "Do you know, I actually dreamt that we found Marthe Daubreuil's body in Mrs. Renauld's room, and that you declared her to have murdered Mr. Renauld?"

"You were not dreaming. All that is quite true."

"But Bella Duveen killed Mr. Renauld?"

"Oh no, Hastings, she did not! She said she did — yes — but that was to save the man she loved from the guillotine."

"What?"

"Remember Jack Renauld's story? They both arrived on the scene on the same instant, and each took the other to be the perpetrator of the crime. The girl stares at him in horror, and then with a cry rushes away. But, when she hears that the crime has been brought home to him, she cannot bear it, and comes forward to accuse herself and save him from certain death."

Poirot leaned back in his chair, and brought the tips of his fingers together in familiar style.

"The case was not quite satisfactory to me," he observed judicially. "All along I was strongly under the impression that we were dealing with a cold-blooded and premeditated crime committed by someone who had contented themselves (very cleverly) with using Monsieur Renauld's own plans for throwing the police off the track. The great criminal (as you may remember my remarking to you once) is always supremely simple."

I nodded.

"Now, to support this theory, the criminal must have been fully cognizant of Monsieur Renauld's plans. That leads us to Mrs. Renauld. But facts fail to support any theory of her guilt. Is there anyone else who might have known of them? Yes. From Marthe Daubreuil's own lips we have the admission that she overheard Mr. Renauld's quarrel with the tramp. If she could overhear that, there is no reason why she should not have heard everything else, especially if Mr. and Madame Renauld were imprudent enough to discuss their plans sitting on the bench. Remember how easily you overheard Marthe's conversation with Jack Renauld from that spot."

"But what possible motive could Marthe have for murdering Mr. Renauld?" I argued.

"What motive! Money! Renauld was a millionaire several times over, and at his death (or so she and Jack believed) half that vast fortune would pass to his son. Let us reconstruct the scene from the standpoint of Marthe Daubreuil.

"Marthe Daubreuil overhears what passes between Renauld and his wife. So far he has been a nice little source of income to the Daubreuil mother and daughter, but now he proposes to escape from their toils. At first, possibly, her idea is to prevent that escape. But a bolder idea takes its place, and one that fails to horrify the daughter of Jeanne Beroldy! At present Renauld stands inexorably in the way of her marriage with Jack. If the latter defies his father, he will be a pauper — which is not at all to the mind of Mademoiselle Marthe. In fact, I doubt if she has ever cared a straw for Jack Renauld. She can simulate emotion but in reality she is of the same cold, calculating type as her mother. I doubt, too, whether she was really very sure of her hold over the boy's affections. She had dazzled and captivated him, but separated from her, as his father could so easily manage to separate him, she might lose him. But, with Renauld dead, and Jack the heir to half his millions, the marriage can take place at once, and at a stroke she will attain wealth — not the beggarly thousands that have been extracted from him so far. And her clever brain takes in the simplicity of the thing. It is all so easy. Renauld is planning all the circumstances of his death — she has only to step in at the right moment and turn the farce into a grim reality. And here comes in the second point which led me infallibly to Marthe Daubreuil — the dagger! Jack Renauld had three souvenirs made. One he gave to his mother, one to Bella Duveen — was it not highly probable that he had given the third one to Marthe Daubreuil?

"So, then, to sum up, there were four points of note against Marthe Daubreuil:

"1. Marthe Daubreuil could have overheard Renauld's plans.

"2. Marthe Daubreuil had a direct interest in causing Renauld's death.

"3. Marthe Daubreuil was the daughter of the notorious Madame Beroldy who in my opinion was morally and virtually the murderess of her husband, although it may have been Georges Conneau's hand which struck the actual blow.

"4. Marthe Daubreuil was the only person, besides Jack Renauld, likely to have the third dagger in her possession."

Poirot paused and cleared his throat.

"Of course, when I learned of the existence of the other girl, Bella Duveen, I realized that it was quite possible that she might have killed Renauld. The solution did not commend itself to me, because, as I pointed out to you, Hastings, an expert, such as I am, likes to meet a foeman worthy of his steel. Still, one must take crimes as one finds them, not as one would like them to be. It did not seem very likely that Bella Duveen would be wandering about carrying a souvenir paper-knife in her hand, but of course she might have had some idea all the time of revenging herself on Jack Renauld. When she actually came forward and confessed to the murder, it seemed that all was over. And yet, I was not satisfied, *mon ami*. I was not satisfied ....

"I went over the case again minutely, and I came to the same conclusion as before: If it was not Bella Duveen, the only other person who could have committed the crime was Marthe Daubreuil. But I had not one single proof against her!

"And then you showed me that letter from Mademoiselle Dulcie, and I saw a chance of settling the matter once for all. The original dagger was stolen by Dulcie Duveen and thrown into the sea — since, as she thought, it belonged to her sister. But if, by any chance, it was not her sister's, but the one given by Jack to Marthe Daubreuil? Why then, Bella Duveen's dagger would be still intact! I said no word to you, Hastings (it was no time for romance), but I sought out Mademoiselle Dulcie, told her as much as I deemed needful, and set her to search among the effects of her sister. Imagine my elation, when she sought me out (according to my instructions) as Miss Robinson, with the precious souvenir in her possession!

"In the meantime I had taken steps to force Mademoiselle Marthe into the open. By my orders, Madame Renauld repulsed her son, and declared her intention of making a will on the morrow which should cut him off from ever enjoying even a portion of his father's fortune. It was a desperate step, but a necessary one, and Madame Renauld was fully prepared to take the risk — though unfortunately she also never thought of mentioning her change of room. I suppose she took it for granted that I knew. All happened as I thought. Marthe Daubreuil made a last bold bid for the Renauld millions — and failed!"

"What absolutely bewilders

me," I said, "is how she ever got into the house without our seeing her. It seems an absolute miracle. We left her behind at the Villa Marguerite, we go straight to the Villa Geneviève — and yet she is there before us!"

"Ah, but we did not leave her behind. She was out of the Villa Marguerite by the back way while we were talking to her mother in the hall. That is where, as the Americans say, she 'put it over' on Hercule Poirot!"

"But the shadow on the blind? We saw it from the road."

"*Eh bien*, when we looked up, Madame Daubreuil had just had time to run upstairs and take her place."

"Madame Daubreuil?"

"Yes. One is old, and one is young, one dark, and one fair, but, for the purpose of a silhouette on a blind, their profiles are singularly alike. Even I did not suspect — triple imbecile that I was! I thought I had plenty of time before me — that she would not try to gain admission to the villa until much later. She had brains, that beautiful Mademoiselle Marthe."

"And her object was to murder Mrs. Renauld?"

"Yes. The whole fortune would then pass to her son. But it would have been suicide, *mon ami*! On the floor by Marthe Daubreuil's body, I found a pad and a little bottle of chloroform and a hypodermic syringe containing a fatal dose of morphine. You understand? The chloroform first then when the victim is unconscious the prick of the needle. By the morning the smell of the chloroform has quite disappeared, and the syringe lies where it has fallen from Madame Renauld's hand. What would he say, the excellent Monsieur Hautet? 'Poor woman! What did I tell you? The shock of joy, it was too much on top of the rest! Did I not say that I should not be surprised if her brain became unhinged? Altogether a most tragic case, the Renauld Case!'"

"However, Hastings, things did not go quite as Mademoiselle Marthe had planned. To begin with, Madame Renauld was awake and waiting for her. There is a struggle. But Madame Renauld is terribly weak still. There is a last chance for Marthe Daubreuil. The idea of suicide is at an end, but if she can silence Madame Renauld with her strong hands, make a getaway with her little silk ladder while we are still battering on the inside of the farther door, and be back at the Villa Marguerite before we return there, it will be hard to prove anything against her. But she was checkmated, not by Hercule Poirot, but by la petite acrobate with her wrists of steel."

I mused over the whole story.

"When did you first begin to suspect Marthe Daubreuil, Poirot? When she told us she had overheard the quarrel in the garden?"

Poirot smiled.

"My friend, do you remember when we drove into Merlinville that first day? And the beautiful girl we saw standing at the gate? You asked me if I had noticed a young goddess, and I replied to you that I had seen only a girl with anxious eyes. That is how I have thought of Marthe Daubreuil from the beginning. The girl with the anxious eyes! Why was she anxious? Not on Jack Renauld's behalf, for she did not know then that he had been in Merlinville the previous evening."

"By the way," I exclaimed, "how is Jack Renauld?"

"Much better. He is still at the Villa Marguerite. But Madame Daubreuil has disappeared. The police are looking for her."

"Was she in with her daughter, do you think?"

"We shall never know. Madame is a lady who can keep her secrets. And I doubt very much if the police will ever find her."

"Has Jack Renauld been — told?"

"Not yet."

"It will be a terrible shock to him."

"Naturally. And yet, do you know, Hastings, I doubt if his heart was ever seriously engaged? So far we have looked upon Bella Duveen as a siren, and Marthe Daubreuil as the girl he really loved. But I think that if we reversed the terms we should come nearer to the truth. Marthe Daubreuil was very beautiful. She set herself to fascinate Jack, and she succeeded, but remember his curious reluctance to break with the other girl. And see how he was willing to go to the guillotine rather than implicate her. I have a little idea that when he learns the truth, he will be horrified — revolted, and his false love will wither away."

"What about Giraud?"

"He has a *crise* of the nerves, that one! He has been obliged to return to Paris."

We both smiled.

Poirot proved a fairly true prophet. When at length the doctor pronounced Jack Renauld strong enough to hear the truth, it was Poirot who broke it to him. The shock was indeed terrific. Yet Jack rallied better than I could have supposed possible. His mother's devotion helped him to live through those difficult days. The mother and son were inseparable now.

There was a further revelation to come. Poirot had acquainted Mrs. Renauld with the fact that he knew her secret, and had represented to her that Jack should not be left in ignorance of his father's past.

"To hide the truth, never does it avail, madame! Be brave and tell him everything."

With a heavy heart Mrs. Renauld consented, and her son learned that the father he had loved had been in actual fact a fugitive from justice. A halting question was promptly answered by Poirot.

"Reassure yourself, Monsieur

Jack. The world knows nothing. As far as I can see, there is no obligation for me to take the police into my confidence. Throughout the case I have acted, not for them, but for your father. Justice overtook him at last, but no one need ever know that he and Georges Conneau were one and the same."

There were, of course, various points in the case that remained puzzling to the police, but Poirot explained things in so plausible a fashion that all query about them was gradually stilled.

Shortly after we got back to London, I noticed a magnificent model of a foxhound adorning Poirot's mantelpiece. In answer to my inquiring glance, Poirot nodded.

"*Mais oui!* I got my five hundred francs. Is he not a splendid fellow? I call him Giraud!"

A few days later Jack Renauld came to see us with a resolute expression on his face.

"Monsieur Poirot, I've come to say goodbye. I'm sailing for South America almost immediately. My father had large interests over the continent, and I mean to start a new life out there."

"You go alone, Monsieur Jack?"

"My mother comes with me—and shall keep Stonor on as my secretary. He likes out-of-the-way parts of the world."

"No one else goes with you?"

Jack flushed.

"You mean—?"

"A girl who loves you very dearly—who has been willing to lay down her life for you?"

"How could I ask her?" muttered the boy. "After all that has happened, could I go to her and—Oh, what sort of a lame story could I tell?"

"Les femmes—they have a wonderful genius for manufacturing crutches for stories like that."

"Yes, but—I've been such a damned fool."

"So have all of us, one time and another," observed Poirot philosophically.

But Jack's face had hardened.

"There's something else. I'm my father's son. Would anyone marry me, knowing that?"

"You are your father's son, you say. Hastings here will tell you that I believe in heredity —"

"Well, then —"

"Wait. I know a woman, a woman of courage and endurance, capable of great love, of supreme self-sacrifice —"

The boy looked up. His eyes softened. "My mother!"

"Yes. You are your mother's son as well as your father's. Then go to Mademoiselle Bella. Tell her everything. Keep nothing back—and see what she will say!"

Jack looked irresolute.

"Go to her as a boy no longer, but a man—a man bowed by the fate of the Past, and the fate of Today, but looking forward to a new and wonderful life. Ask her to share it with you. You may not realize it, but your love for each other has been tested in the fire and not found wanting. You have both been willing to lay down your lives for each other."

And what of Captain Arthur Hastings, humble chronicler of these pages?

There is some talk of his joining the Renaulds on a ranch across the seas, but for the end of this story I prefer to go back to a morning in the garden of the Villa Geneviève.

"I can't call you Bella," I said, "since it isn't your name. And Dulcie seems so unfamiliar. So it's got to be Cinderella. Cinderella married the Prince, you remember. I'm not a prince, but —"

She interrupted me.

"Cinderella warned him, I'm sure. You see, she couldn't promise to turn into a princess. She was only a little scullion after all —"

"It's the Prince's turn to interrupt," I interpolated. "Do you know what he said?"

"No?"

"'Hell!' said the Prince — and kissed her!"

And I suited the action to the word.

# "TALES WITH A STING."

*The first series of twelve short stories published in*
**The Sketch: A Journal of Art and Actuality**
*from March to May 1923.*

# THE AFFAIR AT THE VICTORY BALL.

"The Affair at the Victory Ball" was first published in *The Sketch* on March 7, 1923.

Formerly Chief of the Belgian Force, my friend Hercule Poirot came to England as a refugee in the early days of the war. Pure chance led him to be connected with the case which I have already chronicled elsewhere under the title of "The Mysterious Affair at Styles." His success brought him notoriety, and he decided to remain in this country and devote himself to the solving of problems in crime.

Having been wounded on the Somme and invalided out of the Army, I finally took up my quarters with him in London. Since I have a firsthand knowledge of most of his cases, it has been suggested to me that I select some of the most interesting and place them on record. In doing so, I feel that I cannot do better than begin with that strange tangle which aroused such widespread public interest at the time. I refer to the affair at the Victory Ball.

Although perhaps it is not so fully demonstrative of Poirot's peculiar methods as some of the more obscure cases, its sensational features, the well-known people involved, and the tremendous publicity given it by the press, make it stand out as a *cause célèbre* and I have long felt that it is only fitting that Poirot's connection with the solution should be given to the world.

It was a fine morning in spring, and we were sitting in Poirot's rooms. My little friend, neat and dapper as ever, his egg-shaped head tilted on one side, was delicately applying a new pomade to his moustaches. A certain harmless vanity was a characteristic of Poirot's and fell into line with his general love of order and method.

"Of what are you thinking so deeply, *mon ami*?"

"To tell you the truth," I replied, "I was puzzling over this unaccountable affair at the Victory Ball."

I tapped the newspaper with my finger as I spoke.

"Yes?"

"The more one reads of it, the more shrouded in mystery the whole thing becomes!" I warmed to my subject. "Who killed Lord Cronshaw? Was Coco Courtenay's death on the same night a mere coincidence? Was it an accident? Or did she deliberately take an overdose of cocaine?" I stopped, and then added dramatically: "These are the questions I ask myself."

Poirot, somewhat to my annoyance, did not play up. He was peering into the glass, and merely murmured: "Decidedly, this new pomade, it is a marvel for the moustaches!" Catching my eye, however, he added hastily: "Quite so — and how do you reply to your questions?"

"Well —" I hesitated.

"The little grey cells, Hastings. Employ the little grey cells of brain. They alone can solve a problem."

But before I could answer, the door opened, and our landlady announced Inspector Japp.

The Scotland Yard man was an old friend of ours, and we greeted him warmly.

"Ah, my good Japp," cried Poirot, "and what brings you to see us?"

"Well, Moosior Poirot," said Japp, seating himself and nodding to me, "I'm on a case that strikes me as being very much in your line, and I came along to know whether you'd care to have a finger in the pie?"

Poirot had a good opinion of Japp's abilities (though deploring his lamentable lack of method), but I, for my part, considered that the detective's highest talent lay in the gentle art of seeking favours under the guise of conferring them.

"It's the Victory Ball, Moosior," said Japp persuasively. "Come, now, you'd like to have a hand in that."

Poirot smiled at me.

"My friend Hastings would, at all events. He was just holding forth on the subject, *n'est-ce pas, mon ami?*"

"Well, Sir," said Japp condescendingly, "you shall be in it too. I can tell you, it's something of a feather in your cap to have inside knowledge of a case like this. Well, here's to business. You know the main facts of the case, I suppose, Moosior Poirot?"

"From the papers only — and

the imagination of the journalist is sometimes misleading. Recount the whole story to me."

Japp crossed his legs comfortably and began.

"As all the world and his wife knows, on Tuesday last a grand Victory Ball was held. Every twopenny-halfpenny hop calls itself that nowadays, but this was the real thing, held at the Colossus Hall, and all London at it—including your Lord Cronshaw and his party."

"His *dossier*?" interrupted Poirot. "I should say his bioscope—no, how do you call it?—Biograph?"

"Viscount Cronshaw was fifth viscount, twenty-five years of age, rich, unmarried, and very fond of the theatrical world. There were rumours of his being engaged to Miss Courtenay of the Albany Theatre, who was known to her friends as 'Coco' and who was, by all accounts, a very fascinating young lady."

"Good. *Continuez*!"

"Lord Cronshaw's party consisted of six people—he himself; his uncle, the Honourable Eustace Beltane; a pretty American widow, Mrs. Mallaby; a young actor, Chris Davidson; his wife; and last but not least, Miss Coco Courtenay. It was a fancy dress ball, as you know, and the Cronshaw party represented the old Italian Comedy—whatever that may be."

"The *Commedia dell' Arte*," murmured Poirot. "I know."

"Anyway, the costumes were copied from a set of china figures forming part of Eustace Beltane's collection. Lord Cronshaw was Harlequin; Beltane was Punchinello; Mrs. Mallaby matched him as Pulcinella; the Davidsons were Pierrot and Pierette; and Miss Courtenay, of course, was Columbine.

"Now, quite early in the evening it was apparent that there was something wrong. Lord Cronshaw was moody and strange in his manner. When the party met together for supper in a small private room engaged by the host, everyone noticed that he and Miss Courtenay were no longer on speaking terms. She had obviously been crying, and seemed on the verge of hysterics. The meal was an uncomfortable one, and as they all left the supper-room, she turned to Chris Davidson and requested him audibly to take her home, as she was 'sick of the ball.' The young actor hesitated, glancing at Lord Cronshaw, and finally drew them both back to the supper-room.

"But all his efforts to secure a reconciliation were unavailing, and he accordingly got a taxi and escorted the now weeping Miss Courtenay back to her flat. Although obviously very much upset, she did not confide in him, merely reiterating again and again that she would 'make old Cronch sorry for this!' That is the only hint we have that her death might not have been accidental, and it's precious little to go upon. By the time Davidson had quieted her down somewhat, it was too late to return to the Colossus Hall, and Davidson accordingly went straight home to his flat in Chelsea, where his wife arrived shortly afterwards, bearing the news of the terrible tragedy that had occurred after his departure.

"Lord Cronshaw, it seems, became more and more moody as the ball went on. He kept away from his party, and they hardly saw him during the rest of the evening. It was about 1:30 a.m., just before the Grand Cotillion when everyone was to unmask, that Captain Digby, a brother-officer who knew his disguise, noticed him standing in a box gazing down on the scene.

"'Hullo, Cronch!' he called. 'Come down and be sociable! What are you moping about up there for like a boiled owl? Come along; there's a good old rag coming on now.'

"'Right!' responded Cronshaw. 'Wait for me, or I'll never find you in the crowd.'

"He turned and left the box as he spoke. Captain Digby, who had Mrs. Davidson with him, waited. The minutes passed, but Lord Cronshaw did not appear. Finally Digby grew impatient.

"'Does the fellow think we're going to wait all night for him?' he exclaimed.

"At that moment Mrs. Mallaby joined them, and they explained the situation. "'Say, now,' cried the pretty widow vivaciously, 'he's like a bear with a sore head to-night. Let's go right away and rout him out.'

"The search commenced, but met with no success until it occurred to Mrs. Mallaby that he might possibly be found in the room where they had supped an hour earlier. They made their way there. What a sight met their eyes! There was Harlequin, sure enough, but stretched on the ground with a table-knife in his heart!"

Japp stopped, and Poirot nodded, and said with the relish of the specialist—

"*Une belle affaire*! And there was no clue as to the perpetrator of the deed? But how should there be?"

"Well," continued the Inspector, "you know the rest. The tragedy was a double one. Next day there were headlines in all the papers, and a brief statement to the effect that Miss Courtenay, the popular actress, had been discovered dead in her bed, and that her death was due to an overdose of cocaine. Now, was it accident or suicide? Her maid, who was called upon to give evidence, admitted that Miss Courtenay was a confirmed taker of the drug, and a verdict of accidental death was returned. Nevertheless we can't leave the possibility of suicide out of account. Her death is particularly unfortunate, since it leaves us no clue now to the cause of the quarrel the preceding night. By the way, a small enamel box was found on the dead man. It had 'Coco' written across it in diamonds, and was half-full of cocaine. It was identified by

Miss Courtenay's maid as belonging to her mistress, who nearly always carried it about with her, since it contained her supply of the drug, to which she was fast becoming a slave."

"Was Lord Cronshaw himself addicted to the drug?"

"Very far from it. He held unusually strong views on the subject of dope."

Poirot nodded thoughtfully.

"But since the box was in his possession, he knew that Miss Courtenay took it. Suggestive, that, is it not, my good Japp?"

"Ah!" said Japp rather vaguely.

I smiled.

"Well," said Japp, "that's the case. What do you think of it, Moosior?"

"You found no clue of any kind that has not been reported?"

"Yes, there was this." Japp took a small object from his pocket and handed it over to Poirot. It was a small pompon of emerald green silk, with some ragged threads hanging from it, as though it had been wrenched violently away.

"We found it in the dead man's hand, which was tightly clenched over it," explained the inspector.

Poirot handed it back without any comment and asked: "Had Lord Cronshaw any enemies?"

"None that anyone knows of. He seemed a popular young fellow."

"Who benefits by his death?"

"His uncle, the Hon. Eustace Beltane, comes into the title and estates. There are one or two suspicious facts against him. Several people declare that they heard a violent altercation going on in the little supper-room, and that Eustace Beltane was one of the disputants. You see, the table-knife being snatched up off the table would fit in with the murder being done in the heat of a quarrel."

"What does Mr. Beltane say about the matter?"

"Declares one of the waiters was the worse for liquor, and that he was giving him a dressing-down. Also that it was nearer to one than half past. You see, Captain Digby's evidence fixes the time pretty accurately. Only about ten minutes elapsed between his speaking to Cronshaw and the finding of the body."

"And in any case I suppose Mr. Beltane, as Punchinello, was wearing a hump and a ruffle?"

"I don't know the exact details of the costumes," said Japp, looking curiously at Poirot. "And anyway, I don't quite see what that has got to do with it?"

"No?" There was a hint of mockery in Poirot's smile. He continued quietly, his eyes shining with the green light I had learnt to recognize so well: "There was a curtain in this little supper room, was there not?"

"Yes, but —"

"With a space behind it sufficient to conceal a man?"

"Yes; in fact, there's a small

recess, but how you knew about it — you haven't been to the place, have you, Monsieur Poirot?"

"No, my good Japp, I supplied the curtain from my brain. Without it, the drama is not reasonable. And always one must be reasonable. But tell me, did they not send for a doctor?"

"At once, of course. But there was nothing to be done. Death must have been instantaneous."

Poirot nodded rather impatiently.

"Yes, yes, I understand. This doctor, now, he gave evidence at the inquest?"

"Yes."

"Did he say nothing of any unusual symptom — was there nothing about the appearance of the body which struck him as being abnormal?"

Japp stared hard at the little man.

"Yes, Moosior Poirot. I don't know what you're getting at, but he did mention that there was a tension and stiffness about the limbs which he was quite at a loss to account for."

"Aha!" said Poirot. "Aha! *Mon Dieu!* Japp, that gives one to think, does it not?"

I saw that it had certainly not given Japp to think.

"If you're thinking of poison, Moosior, who on earth would poison a man first and then stick a knife into him?"

"In truth that would be ridiculous," agreed Poirot placidly.

"Now is there anything you want to see, Moosior? If you'd like to examine the room where the body was found —"

Poirot waved his hand.

"*Inutile!* There is not the slightest necessity."

"Do you want to question Miss Courtenay's maid?"

"Not in the least. You have told me the only thing that interests me — Lord Cronshaw's views on the subject of drug taking."

"Then there's nothing you want to see?"

"Just one thing."

"What is that?"

"The set of china figures from which the costumes were copied."

Japp stared.

"Well, you're a funny one!"

"You can manage that for me?"

"Come round to Berkeley Square now if you like. Mr. Beltane — or His Lordship, as I should say now — won't object."

We set off at once in a taxi. The new Lord Cronshaw was not at home, but at Japp's request we were shown into the "China Room," where the gems of the collection were kept. Japp looked round him rather helplessly.

"I don't see how you'll ever find the ones you want, Moosior."

But Poirot had already drawn a chair in front of the mantelpiece and was hopping up upon it like a nimble robin. Above the mirror, on a small shelf to themselves, stood six china figures. Poirot examined them minutely, making a few comments to us as he did so.

"*Les voilà!* The old Italian Comedy. Three pairs. Harlequin and Columbine, Pierrot and Pierrette — very dainty in white and green — and Punchinello and Pulcinella in mauve and yellow. Very elaborate, the costume of Punchinello — ruffles and frills, a hump, a high hat. Yes, as I thought, very elaborate."

He replaced the figures carefully, and jumped down.

"I am satisfied, *mon ami* Japp."

Japp looked unsatisfied, but as Poirot had clearly no intention of explaining anything, the detective put the best face he could upon the matter.

As we were preparing to leave, the master of the house came in, and Japp performed the necessary introductions.

The sixth Viscount Cronshaw was a man of about fifty, suave in manner, with a handsome, dissolute face. Evidently an elderly roué, with the languid manner of a poseur. I took an instant dislike to him. He greeted us graciously enough, declaring he had heard great accounts of Poirot's skill, and placing himself at our disposal in every way.

"The police are doing all they can, I know," he said. "But I much fear the mystery of my nephew's death will never be cleared up. The whole thing seems utterly mysterious."

Poirot was watching him keenly.

"Your nephew had no enemies that you know of?"

"None whatever. I am sure of that." He paused, and then went on: "If there are any questions you would like to ask —"

"Only one." Poirot's voice was serious. "The costumes — they were reproduced *exactly* from your *Commedia*?"

"To the smallest detail."

"Thank you, Milor'. That is all I wanted to be sure of. I wish you good-day."

"And what next?" inquired Japp as we hurried down the street. "I've got to report at the Yard, you know."

"*Bien!* I will not detain you. I have one other little matter to attend to, and then —"

"Yes?"

"The case will be complete."

"What? You don't mean it! You know who killed Lord Cronshaw?"

"*Parfaitement.*"

"Who was it? Eustace Beltane?"

"Ah, *mon ami*, you know my little weakness! Always I have a desire to keep the threads in my own hands up to the last minute. But have no fear. I will reveal all when the time comes. I want no credit — the affair shall be yours, on the condition that you permit me to play the *dénouement* my own way."

"That's fair enough," said Japp. "That is, if the *dénouement* ever comes! But I say, you *are* an oyster, aren't you?" Poirot smiled. "Well, so long. I'm off to the Yard."

He strode off down the street, and Poirot hailed a passing taxi.

"Where are we going now?" I asked in lively curiosity.

"To Chelsea to see the Davidsons."

He gave the address to the driver.

"What do you think of the new Lord Cronshaw?" I asked.

"What says my good friend Hastings?"

"I distrust him instinctively."

"You think he is the 'wicked uncle' of the storybooks, eh?"

"Don't you?"

"Me, I think he was most amiable towards us," said Poirot noncommittally.

"Because he had his reasons!"

Poirot looked at me, shook his head sadly, and murmured something that sounded like: "No method."

The Davidsons lived on the third floor of a block of "mansion" flats. Mr. Davidson was out, we were told, but Mrs. Davidson was at home. We were ushered into a long, low room with garish Oriental hangings. The air felt close and oppressive, and there was an overpowering fragrance of joss sticks.

Mrs. Davidson came to us almost immediately, a small, fair creature whose fragility would have seemed pathetic and appealing had it not been for the rather shrewd and calculating gleam in her light-blue eyes.

Poirot explained our connection with the case, and she shook her head sadly. "Poor Cronch — and poor Coco too! We were both so fond of her, and her death has been a terrible grief to us. What is it you want to ask me? Must I really go over all that dreadful evening again?"

"Oh, Madame, believe me, I would not harass your feelings unnecessarily. Indeed, Inspector Japp has told me all that is needful. I only wish to see the costume you wore at the ball that night."

The lady looked somewhat surprised, and Poirot continued smoothly: "You comprehend, Madame, that I work on the system of my country. There we always 'reconstruct' the crime. It is possible that I may have an actual *représentation*, and if so, you understand, the costumes would be important."

Mrs. Davidson still looked a bit doubtful.

"I've heard of reconstructing a crime, of course," she said. "But I didn't know you were so particular about details. But I'll fetch the dress now."

She left the room and returned almost immediately with a dainty wisp of white satin and green. Poirot took it from her and examined it, handing it back with a bow.

"*Merci,* Madame! I see you have had the misfortune to lose one of your green pompons — the one on the shoulder here."

"Yes, it got torn off at the ball. I picked it up and gave it to poor Lord Cronshaw to keep for me."

"That was after supper?"

"Yes."

"Not long before the tragedy, perhaps?"

A faint look of alarm came into Mrs. Davidson's pale eyes, and she replied quickly: "Oh no! — long before that. Quite soon after supper, in fact."

"I see. Well, that is all. I will not *dérange* you further. *Bonjour,* Madame."

"Well," I said as we emerged from the building. "That explains the mystery of the green pompon."

"I wonder."

"Why, what do you mean?"

"You saw me examine the dress, Hastings?"

"Yes?"

"*Eh bien*, the pompon that was missing had not been wrenched off, as the lady said. On the contrary, it had been *cut* off, my friend, cut off with scissors. The threads were all quite even."

"Dear me!" I exclaimed. "This becomes more and more involved."

"On the contrary," replied Poirot placidly, "it becomes more and more simple."

"Poirot," I cried, "one day I shall murder you! Your habit of finding everything perfectly simple is aggravating to the last degree!"

"But when I explain, *mon ami*, is it not always perfectly simple?"

"Yes; that is the annoying part of it! I feel then that I could have done it myself."

"And so you could, Hastings, so you could, if you would but take the trouble of arranging your ideas! Without method —"

"Yes, yes," I said hastily, for I knew Poirot's eloquence when started on his favourite theme only too well. "Tell me, what do we do next? Visit Mrs. Mallaby?"

"No, she can wait, that one. She will be at my little *répresentation*."

"Are you really going to reconstruct the crime?"

"Hardly that. Shall we say that the drama is over — but that I propose to add — a Harlequinade?"

The following Tuesday was fixed upon by Poirot as the day for this mysterious performance. The preparations greatly intrigued me. A white screen was erected at one side of the room, flanked by heavy curtains at either side. A man with some lighting apparatus arrived next, and finally a group of members of the theatrical profession, who disappeared into Poirot's bed-room, which had been rigged up as a temporary dressing-room.

Shortly before eight, Japp arrived, in no very cheerful mood. I gathered that the official detective hardly approved of Poirot's plan.

"Bit melodramatic, like all his ideas. But there, it can do no harm, and as he says, it might save us a good bit of trouble. He's been very smart over the case. I was on the same scent myself, of course" — I felt instinctively that Japp was straining the truth here — "but there, I promised to let him play the thing out his own way. Ah! Here are the crowd."

His Lordship arrived first, escorting Mrs. Mallaby, whom I had not as yet seen. She was a pretty, dark-haired woman, and appeared perceptibly nervous. The Davidsons followed. Chris Davidson also I saw for the first time. He was handsome enough in a rather obvious style, tall and dark, with the easy grace of the actor.

Poirot had arranged seats for the party facing the screen. This was illuminated by a bright light. Poirot switched out the other lights so that the room was in darkness except for the screen. Poirot's voice rose out of the gloom.

"*Messieurs, mesdames,* a word of explanation. Six figures in turn will pass across the screen. They are familiar to you. Pierrot and his Pierrette; Punchinello the buffoon, and elegant Pulcinella; beautiful Columbine, lightly dancing, Harlequin, the sprite, invisible to man!"

With these words of introduction, the show began. In turn each figure that Poirot had mentioned bounded before the screen, stayed there a moment poised, and then vanished. The lights went up, and a sigh of relief went round. Everyone had been nervous, fearing they knew not what. It seemed to me that the proceedings had gone singularly flat. If the criminal was among us, and Poirot expected him to break down at the mere sight of a familiar figure, the device had failed signally — as it was almost bound to do. Perhaps dealing with the impressionable Latin race, it might be different; but certainly in this case the thing was a fiasco. Poirot, however, appeared not a whit discomposed. He stepped forward, beaming.

"Now, *messieurs et mesdames,* will you be so good as to tell me, one at a time, what it is that we have just seen? Will you begin, Milor'?"

The gentleman looked rather puzzled. "I'm afraid I don't quite understand."

"Just tell me what we have been seeing."

"I — er — well, I should say we have seen six figures passing in front of a screen and dressed to represent the personages in the old Italian Comedy, or — er — ourselves the other night —"

"Never mind the other night, Milor'," broke in Poirot. "The first part of your speech was what I wanted. Madame, you agree with Milor' Cronshaw?"

He had turned as he spoke to Mrs. Mallaby.

"I — er — yes, of course."

"You agree that you have seen

six figures representing the Italian Comedy?"

"Why, certainly."

"Monsieur Davidson? You too?"

"Yes."

"Madame?"

"Yes."

"Hastings? Japp? Yes? You are all in accord?"

He looked around upon us; his face grew rather pale, and his eyes were green as any cat's.

"And yet—*you are all wrong!* Your eyes have lied to you—as they lied to you on the night of the Victory Ball. To 'see things with your eyes,' as they say, is not always to see the truth. One must see with the eyes of the mind; one must employ the little cells of grey! Know, then, that tonight and on the night of the Victory Ball, you saw not *six* figures but *five!* See!"

The lights went out again. A figure bounded in front of the screen—Pierrot!

"Who is that?" demanded Poirot. "Is it Pierrot?"

"Yes," we all cried.

"Look again!"

With a swift movement the man divested himself of his loose Pierrot garb. There in the limelight stood glittering Harlequin!

At the same moment there was a cry and an overturned chair.

"Curse you," snarled Davidson's voice. "Curse you! How did you guess?"

Then came the clink of handcuffs and Japp's calm official voice. "I arrest you, Christopher Davidson—charge of murdering Viscount Cronshaw—anything you say—used in evidence against you."

It was a quarter of an hour later. A *recherché* little supper had appeared; and Poirot, beaming all over his face, was dispensing hospitality and answering our eager questions.

"It was all very simple. The circumstances in which the green pompon was found suggested at once that it had been torn from the costume of the murderer. I dismissed Pierrette from my mind (since it takes considerable strength to drive a table-knife home) and fixed upon Pierrot as the criminal. But Pierrot left the ball nearly two hours before the murder was committed. So he must either have returned to the ball later to kill Lord Cronshaw, or—*eh bien*, he must have killed him before he left! Was that impossible? Who had seen Lord Cronshaw after supper that evening? Only Mrs. Davidson, whose statement, I suspected, was a deliberate fabrication uttered with the object of accounting for the missing pompon, which, of course, she cut from her own dress to replace the one missing on her husband's costume. But then the Harlequin who was seen in the box at 1:30, must have been an impersonation.

"For a moment, earlier, I had considered the possibility of Mr. Beltane being the guilty party. But with his elaborate costume, it was clearly impossible that he could have doubled the roles of Punchinello and Harlequin. On the other hand, to Davidson, a young man of about the same height as the murdered man and an actor by profession, the thing was simplicity itself.

"But one thing worried me. Surely a doctor could not fail to perceive the difference between a man who had been dead two hours and one who had been dead ten minutes! *Eh bien!* the doctor *did* perceive it! But he was not taken to the body and asked, 'How long has this man been dead?' On the contrary, he was informed that the man had been seen alive ten minutes ago, and so he merely commented at the inquest on the abnormal stiffening of the limbs for which he was quite unable to account!

"All was now marching famously for my theory. Davidson had killed Lord Cronshaw immediately after supper, when, as you remember, he was seen to draw him back into the supper room. Then he departed with Miss Courtenay, left her at the door of her flat (instead of going in and trying to pacify her as he affirmed) and returned posthaste to the Colossus — but as Harlequin, not Pierrot — a simple transformation effected by removing his outer costume."

The uncle of the dead man leaned forward, his eyes perplexed.

"But if so, he must have come to the ball prepared to kill his victim. What earthly motive could he have had? The motive, that's what I can't get."

"Ah! There we come to the second tragedy — that of Miss Courtenay. There was one simple point which everyone overlooked. Miss Courtenay died of cocaine poisoning — but her supply of the drug was in the enamel box which was found on Lord Cronshaw's body. Where, then, did she obtain the dose which killed her? Only one person could have supplied her with it — Davidson. And that explains everything. It accounts for her friendship with the Davidsons and her demand that Davidson should escort her home. Lord Cronshaw, who was almost fanatically opposed to drug taking, discovered that she was addicted to cocaine, and suspected that Davidson supplied her with it. Davidson doubtless denied this, but Lord Cronshaw determined to get the truth from Miss Courtenay at the ball. He could forgive the wretched girl, but he would certainly have no mercy on the man who made a living by trafficking in drugs. Exposure and ruin confronted Davidson. He went to the ball determined that Cronshaw's silence must be obtained at any cost."

"Was Coco's death an accident, then ?"

"I suspect that it was an accident cleverly engineered by Davidson. She was furiously angry with Cronshaw, first for his reproaches, and secondly for taking her cocaine from her. Davidson supplied her with more, and probably suggested her augmenting the dose as a defiance to 'old Cronch!'"

"One other thing," I said. "The recess and the curtain? How did you know about them?"

"Why, *mon ami*, that was the most simple of all. Waiters had been in and out of that little room, so, obviously, the body could not have been lying where it was found on the floor. There must be some place in the room where it could be hidden. I deduced a curtain and a recess behind it. Davidson dragged the body there, and later, after drawing attention to himself in the box, he dragged it out again before finally leaving the Hall. It was one of his best moves. He is a clever fellow!"

But in Poirot's green eyes I read unmistakably the unspoken remark—

"But not quite so clever as Hercule Poirot!"

# THE CURIOUS DISAPPEARANCE OF THE OPALSEN PEARLS.

"The Curious Disappearance of the Opalsen Pearls" was first published in *The Sketch* on March 14, 1923.

"Poirot," I said, "a change of air would do you good."

"You think so, *mon ami?*"

"I am sure of it."

"Eh — eh?" said my friend, smiling. "It is all arranged, then?"

"You will come?"

"Where do you propose to take me?"

"Brighton. As a matter of fact, a friend of mine in the City put me on to a very good thing, and — well, I have money to burn, as the saying goes. I think a week-end at the Grand Metropolitan would do us all the good in the world."

"Thank you, I accept most gratefully. You have the good heart to think of an old man. And the good heart, it is in the end worth all the little grey cells. Yes — yes, I who speak to you am in danger of forgetting that sometimes."

I did not quite relish the implication. I fancy that Poirot is sometimes a little inclined to under-estimate my mental capacities. But his pleasure was so evident that I put my slight annoyance aside.

"Then that's all right," I said hastily.

Saturday evening saw us dining at the Grand Metropolitan in the midst of a gay throng. All the world and his wife seemed to be at Brighton. The dresses were marvellous, and the jewels — worn sometimes with more love of display than good taste — were something magnificent.

"*Hein*, it is a good sight, this!" murmured Poirot. "This is the home of the Profiteer, is it not so, Hastings?"

"Supposed to be," I replied. "But we'll hope they aren't all tarred with the Profiteering brush."

Poirot gazed round him placidly.

"The sight of so many jewels makes me wish I had turned my brains to crime, instead of to its detection. What a magnificent opportunity for some thief of distinction! Regard, Hastings, that stout woman by the pillar. She is, as you would say, plastered with gems."

I followed his eyes.

"Why," I exclaimed, "it's Mrs. Opalsen."

"You know her?"

"Slightly. Her husband is a rich stockbroker who made a fortune in the recent oil boom."

After dinner we ran across the Opalsens in the lounge, and I introduced Poirot to them. We chatted for a few minutes, and ended by having our coffee together.

Poirot said a few words in praise of some of the costlier gems displayed on the lady's ample bosom, and she brightened up at once.

"It's a perfect hobby of mine, Mr. Poirot. I just *love* jewellery. Ed knows my weakness, and every time things go well he brings me something new. You are interested in precious stones?"

"I have had a good deal to do with them one time and another, Madame. My profession has brought me into contact with some of the most famous jewels in the world."

He went on to narrate, with discreet pseudonyms, the story of the historic jewels of a reigning house, and Mrs. Opalsen listened with bated breath.

"There now," she exclaimed, as he ended. "If it isn't just like a play! You know, I've got some pearls of my own that have a history attached to them. I believe it's supposed to be one of the finest necklaces in the world — the pearls are so beautifully matched and so perfect in colour. I declare I really must run up and get it!"

"Oh, Madame," protested Poirot, "you are too amiable. Pray do not *dérange* yourself!"

"Oh, but I'd like to show it to you."

The buxom dame waddled across to the lift briskly enough. Her husband, who had been talking to me, looked at Poirot inquiringly.

"Madame your wife is so amiable as to insist on showing me her pearl necklace," explained the latter.

"Oh, the pearls!" Opalsen smiled in a satisfied fashion. "Well, they *are* worth seeing. Cost a pretty penny too! Still, the money's there all right; I could get what I paid for them any day — perhaps more. May have to, too, if things go on as they are now. Money's confoundedly tight in the City. All this infernal E.P.D." He rambled on, launching into technicalities where I could not follow him.

He was interrupted by a small page-boy who approached him and murmured something in his ear.

"Eh — what? I'll come at once. Not taken ill, is she? Excuse me, gentlemen." He left us abruptly.

Poirot leaned back and lit one of his tiny Russian cigarettes. Then, carefully and meticulously, he arranged the empty coffee-cups in a neat row, and beamed happily on the result.

The minutes passed. The Opalsens did not return.

"Curious," I remarked, at length. "I wonder when they will come back."

Poirot watched the ascending spirals of smoke, and then said thoughtfully: "They will not come back."

"Why?"

"Because, my friend, something has happened."

"What sort of thing? How do you know?" I asked curiously.

Poirot smiled.

"A few minutes ago the manager came hurriedly out of his office and ran upstairs. He was much agitated. The lift boy is deep in talk with one of the pages. The lift-bell has rung three times, but he heeds it not. Thirdly, even the waiters are *distraits*; and to make a waiter *distrait* —" Poirot shook his head with an air of finality. "The affair must indeed be of the first magnitude. Ah, it is as I thought! Here come the police."

Two men had just entered the hotel — one in uniform, the other in plain clothes. They spoke to a page, and were immediately ushered upstairs. A few minutes later, the same boy descended and came up to where we were sitting.

"Mr. Opalsen's compliments, and would you step upstairs?"

Poirot sprang nimbly to his feet. One would have said that he had awaited the summons. I followed with no less alacrity.

The Opalsens' apartments were situated on the first floor. After knocking on the door, the page boy retired, and we answered the summons: "Come in!"

A strange scene met our eyes. The room was Mrs. Opalsen's bed-room, and in the centre of it, lying back in an armchair, was the lady herself, weeping violently. She presented an extraordinary spectacle, with the tears making great furrows in the powder with which her complexion was liberally coated. Mr. Opalsen was striding up and down angrily. The two police officials stood in the middle of the room, one with a notebook in hand. A hotel chambermaid, looking frightened to death, stood by the fireplace; and on the other side of the room a

Frenchwoman, obviously Mrs. Opalsen's maid, was weeping and wringing her hands, with an intensity of grief that rivalled that of her mistress.

Into this pandemonium stepped Poirot, neat and smiling. Immediately, with an energy surprising in one of her bulk, Mrs. Opalsen sprang from her chair towards him.

"There now; Ed may say what he likes, but I believe in luck, I do. It was fated I should meet you the way I did this evening, and I've a feeling that if you can't get my pearls back for me nobody can."

"Calm yourself, I pray of you, Madame." Poirot patted her hand soothingly. "Reassure yourself. All will be well. Hercule Poirot will aid you!"

Mr. Opalsen turned to the police inspector.

"There will be no objection to my — er — calling in this gentleman, I suppose?"

"None at all, Sir," replied the man civilly, but with complete indifference. "Perhaps now your lady's feeling better she'll just let us have the facts?"

Mrs. Opalsen looked helplessly at Poirot. He led her back to her chair.

"Seat yourself, Madame, and recount to us the whole history without agitating yourself."

Thus abjured, Mrs. Opalsen dried her eyes gingerly, and began.

"I came upstairs after dinner to fetch my pearls for Mr. Poirot here to see. The chambermaid and Célestine were both in the room as usual —"

"Excuse me, Madame, but what do you mean by 'as usual?'"

Mr. Opalsen explained.

"I make it a rule that no one is to come into this room unless Célestine, the maid, is there also. The chambermaid does the room in the morning while Célestine is present, and comes in after dinner to turn down the beds under the same conditions; otherwise she never enters the room."

"Well, as I was saying," continued Mrs. Opalsen, "I came up. I went to the drawer here"— she indicated the bottom right-hand drawer of the kneehole dressing table — "took out my jewel case and unlocked it. It seemed quite as usual — but, the pearls were not there!"

The inspector had been busy with his notebook. "When had you last seen them?" he asked.

"They were there when I went down to dinner."

"You are sure?"

"Quite sure. I was uncertain whether to wear them or not, but in the end I decided on the emeralds, and put them back in the jewel-case."

"Who locked up the jewel-case?"

"I did. I wear the key on a chain round my neck." She held it up as she spoke.

The inspector examined it, and shrugged his shoulders.

"The thief must have had a duplicate key. No difficult matter. The lock is quite a simple one. What did you do after you'd locked the jewel case?"

"I put it back in the bottom drawer where I always keep it."

"You didn't lock the drawer?"

"No, I never do. My maid remains in the room till I come up, so there's no need."

The inspector's face grew greyer.

"Am I to understand that the jewels were there when you went down to dinner, and that since then *the maid has not left the room?*"

Suddenly, as though the horror of her own situation for the first time burst upon her, Célestine uttered a piercing shriek, and, flinging herself upon Poirot, poured out a torrent of incoherent French.

The suggestion was infamous! That she, Célestine, should be suspected of robbing Madame! The police were well known to be of a *stupidité incredible!* But Monsieur, who was a Frenchman—

"A Belgian," interjected Poirot, but Célestine paid no attention to the correction. Monsieur would not stand by and see her falsely accused, while that infamous chambermaid was allowed to go scot-free. She, Célestine, had never liked her—a bold, red-faced thing—a born thief. She had said from the first that she was not honest. And had kept a sharp watch over her, too, when she was doing Madame's room! Let those idiots of policemen search her, and if they did not find Madame's pearls on her it would be very surprising!

Although this harangue was uttered in rapid and virulent French, Célestine had interlarded it with a wealth of gesture, and the chambermaid realized at least a part of her meaning. She reddened angrily.

"If that foreign woman's saying I took the pearls, it's a lie!" she declared heatedly. "I never so much as saw them."

"Search her!" screamed the other. "You will find it is as I say."

"You're a liar—do you hear?" said the chambermaid, advancing upon her. "Stole 'em yourself, and want to put it on me. Why, I was only in the room about three minutes before the lady came up, and then you were sitting here the whole time, as you always do, like a cat watching a mouse."

The inspector looked across inquiringly at Celestine. "Is that true? Didn't you leave the room at all?"

"I did not actually leave her alone," admitted Celestine reluctantly, "but I went into my own room through the door here twice—once to fetch a reel of cotton, and once for my scissors. She must have done it then."

"You wasn't gone a minute," retorted the chambermaid angrily. "Just popped out and in again. I'd be glad if the police *would* search me. *I've* nothing to be afraid of."

At this moment there was a tap

at the door. The inspector went to it. His face brightened when he saw who it was.

"Ah!" he said. "That's rather fortunate. I sent for one of our female searchers, and she's just arrived. Perhaps if you wouldn't mind going into the room next door"—he looked at the chambermaid, who stepped across the threshold with a toss of her head, the searcher following her closely.

The French girl had sunk sobbing into a chair. Poirot was looking round the room, the main features of which I have made clear by a sketch:

*(See bottom of this page)*

"Where does that door lead?" he inquired, nodding his head towards the one by the window.

"Into the next apartment, I believe," said the inspector. "It's bolted, anyway, on this side."

Poirot walked across to it, tried it, then drew back the bolt and tried it again. "And on the other side as well," he remarked. "Well, that seems to rule out that."

He walked over to the windows, examining each of them in turn. "And again—nothing. Not even a balcony outside."

"Even if there were," said the inspector impatiently, "I don't see how that would help us, if the maid never left the room."

"*Évidemment*," said Poirot, not disconcerted. "As Mademoiselle is positive she did not leave the room—"

He was interrupted by the reappearance of the chambermaid and the police searcher.

"Nothing," said the latter laconically.

"I should hope not, indeed," said the chambermaid virtuously. "And that French hussy ought to be ashamed of herself taking away an honest girl's character!"

"There, there, my girl; that's all

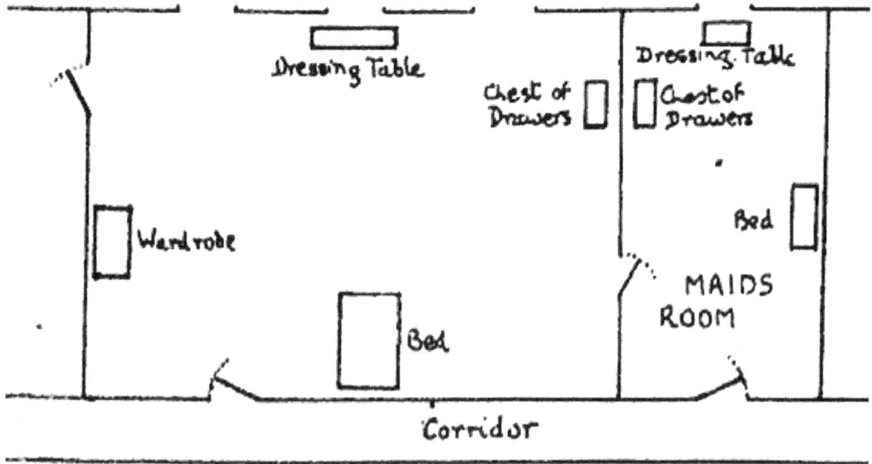

right," said the inspector, opening the door. "Nobody suspects you. You go along and get on with your work."

The chambermaid went unwillingly.

"Going to search *her?*" she demanded, pointing at Célestine.

"Yes, yes!" He shut the door on her and turned the key.

Célestine accompanied the searcher into the small room in her turn. A few minutes later she also returned. Nothing had been found on her.

The inspector's face grew graver.

"I'm afraid I'll have to ask you to come along with me all the same, Miss." He turned to Mrs. Opalsen. "I'm sorry, madam, but all the evidence points that way. If she's not got them on her, they're hidden somewhere about the room."

Célestine uttered a piercing shriek, and clung to Poirot's arm. The latter bent and whispered something in the girl's ear. She looked up at him doubtfully.

"*Si, si, mon enfant*—I assure you it is better not to resist." Then he turned to the inspector. "You permit, Monsieur? A little experiment—purely for my own satisfaction."

"Depends on what it is," replied the police officer noncommittally.

Poirot addressed Célestine once more.

"You have told us that you went into your room to fetch a reel of cotton ... whereabouts was it?"

"On top of the chest of drawers, Monsieur."

"And the scissors?"

"They also."

"Would it be troubling you too much, Mademoiselle, to ask you to repeat those two actions? You were sitting here with your work, you say?"

Célestine sat down, and then, at a sign from Poirot, rose, passed into the adjoining room, took up an object from the chest of drawers, and returned.

Poirot divided his attention between her movements and a large turnip of a watch which he held in the palm of his hand.

"Again, if you please, Mademoiselle."

At the conclusion of the second performance, he made a note in his pocketbook, and returned the watch to his pocket.

"Thank you, Mademoiselle. And you, Monsieur"—he bowed to the inspector—"for your courtesy."

The inspector seemed somewhat entertained by this excessive politeness. Célestine departed in a flood of tears, accompanied by the woman and the plainclothes official.

Then, with a brief apology to Mrs. Opalsen, the inspector set to work to ransack the room. He pulled out drawers, opened cupboards, completely unmade the bed, and tapped the floor. Mr. Opalsen looked on sceptically.

"You really think you will find them?"

"Yes, Sir. It stands to reason. She

hadn't time to take them out of the room. The lady's discovering the robbery so soon upset her plans. No, they're here right enough. One of the two must have hidden them — and it's very unlikely for the chambermaid to have done so."

"More than unlikely — impossible!" said Poirot quietly.

"Eh?" The inspector stared.

Poirot smiled modestly.

"I will demonstrate. Hastings, my good friend, take my watch in your hand — with care. It is a family heirloom! — Just now I timed Mademoiselle's movements — her first absence from the room was of twelve seconds, her second of fifteen. Now observe my actions. Madame will have the kindness to give me the key of the jewel case. I thank you. My friend Hastings will have the kindness to say 'Go!'"

"Go!" I said.

With almost incredible swiftness, Poirot wrenched open the drawer of the dressing table, extracted the jewel-case, fitted the key in the lock, opened the case, selected a piece of jewellery, shut and locked the case, and returned it to the drawer, which he pushed to again. His movements were like lightning.

"Well, *mon ami*?" he demanded of me breathlessly.

"Forty-six seconds," I replied.

"You see?" He looked round. "There would have not been time for the chambermaid even to take the necklace out, far less hide it."

"Then that settles it on the maid," said the inspector with satisfaction, and returned to his search. He passed into the maid's bed-room next door.

Poirot was frowning thoughtfully. Suddenly he shot a question at Mr. Opalsen.

"This necklace — it was, without doubt, insured?"

Mr. Opalsen looked a trifle surprised at the question. "Yes," he said hesitatingly; "that is so."

"But what does that matter?" broke in Mrs. Opalsen tearfully. "It's my necklace I want. It was unique. No money could be the same."

"I comprehend, Madame," said Poirot soothingly. "I comprehend perfectly. To *la femme* sentiment is everything — is it not so? But Monsieur, who has not the so fine susceptibility, will doubtless find some slight consolation in the fact."

"Of course, of course," said Mr. Opalsen rather uncertainly. "Still —"

He was interrupted by a shout of triumph from the inspector. He came in dangling something from his fingers.

With a cry, Mrs. Opalsen heaved herself up from her chair. She was a changed woman.

"Oh, oh, my necklace!"

She clasped it to her breast with both hands. We crowded round.

"Where was it?" demanded Opalsen.

"Maid's bed. In among the springs of the wire mattress. She

must have stolen it and hidden it there before the chambermaid arrived on the scene."

"You permit, Madame?" said Poirot gently. He took the necklace from her and examined it closely; then handed it back with a bow.

"I'm afraid, madam, you'll have to hand it over to us for the time being," said the inspector. "We shall want it for the charge. But it shall be returned to you as soon as possible."

Mr. Opalsen frowned. "Is that necessary?"

"I'm afraid so, Sir. Just a formality."

"Oh, let him take it, Ed!" cried his wife. "I'd feel safer if he did. I shouldn't sleep a wink thinking someone else might try to get hold of it. That wretched girl! And I would never have believed it of her."

"There, there, my dear, don't take on so."

I felt a gentle pressure on my arm. It was Poirot.

"Shall we slip away, my friend? I think our services are no longer needed."

Once outside, however, he hesitated, and then, much to my surprise, he remarked:

"I should rather like to see the room next door."

The door was not locked, and we entered. The room, which was a large double one, was unoccupied. Dust lay about rather noticeably, and my sensitive friend gave a characteristic grimace as he ran his finger round a rectangular mark on a table near the window.

"The *service* leaves to be desired," he observed dryly.

He was staring thoughtfully out of the window, and seemed to have fallen into a brown study.

"Well?" I demanded impatiently. "What did we come in here for?"

He started.

"*Je vous demande pardon, mon ami.* I wished to see if the door was really bolted on this side also."

"Well," I said, glancing at the door which communicated with the room we had just left, "it *is* bolted."

Poirot nodded. He still seemed to be thinking.

"And anyway," I continued, "what does it matter? The case is over. I wish you'd had more chance of distinguishing yourself. But it was the kind of case that even a stiff-backed idiot like that inspector couldn't go wrong over."

Poirot shook his head.

"The case is not over, my friend. It will not be over until we find out who stole the pearls."

"But the maid did!"

"Why do you say that?"

"Why," I stammered, "they were found — actually in her mattress."

"*Ta-ta-ta!*" said Poirot impatiently. "Those were not the pearls."

"What?"

"Imitation, *mon ami*."

The statement took my breath away. Poirot was smiling placidly.

"The good inspector obviously knows nothing of jewels. But presently there will be a fine hullabaloo!"

"Come!" I cried, dragging at his arm.

"Where?"

"We must tell the Opalsens at once."

"I think not."

"But that poor woman —"

"*Eh bien;* that poor woman, as you call her, will have a much better night believing the jewels to be safe."

"But the thief may escape with them!"

"As usual, my friend, you speak without reflection. How do you know that the pearls Mrs. Opalsen locked up so carefully tonight were not the false ones, and that the real robbery did not take place at a much earlier date?"

"Oh!" I said, bewildered.

"Exactly," said Poirot, beaming. "We start again."

He led the way out of the room, paused a moment as though considering, and then walked down to the end of the corridor, stopping outside the small den where the chambermaids and valets of the respective floors congregated. Our particular chambermaid appeared to be holding a small court there, and to be retailing her late experiences to an appreciative audience. She stopped in the middle of a sentence. Poirot bowed with his usual politeness.

"Excuse that I *dérange* you, but I shall be obliged if you will unlock for me the door of Mr. Opalsen's room."

The woman rose willingly, and we accompanied her down the passage again. Mr. Opalsen's room was on the other side of the corridor, its door facing that of his wife's room. The chambermaid unlocked it with her pass-key, and we entered.

As she was about to depart Poirot detained her.

"One moment; have you ever seen among the effects of Mr. Opalsen a card like this?"

He held out a plain white card, rather highly glazed and uncommon in appearance. The maid took it and scrutinized it carefully.

"No, Sir, I can't say I have. But, anyway, the valet has most to do with the gentlemen's rooms."

"I see. Thank you."

Poirot took back the card. The woman departed. Poirot appeared to reflect a little. Then he gave a short, sharp nod of the head.

"Ring the bell, I pray you, Hastings. Three times for the valet."

I obeyed, devoured with curiosity. Meanwhile Poirot had emptied the wastepaper basket on the floor, and was swiftly going through its contents.

In a few moments the valet answered the bell. To him Poirot put the same question, and handed him the card to examine. But the response was the same. The valet had never seen a card of that particular quality among Mr. Opalsen's belongings. Poirot thanked him, and he withdrew, somewhat unwillingly, with an inquisitive glance at the overturned wastepaper basket and the litter on the floor. He could hardly have helped overhearing Poirot's thoughtful remark as he bundled the torn papers back again: "And the necklace was heavily insured ...."

"Porot," I cried, "I see —"

"You see nothing, my friend," he replied quickly. "As usual, nothing at all! It is incredible — but there it is. Let us return to our own apartments."

We did so in silence. Once there, to my intense surprise, Poirot effected a rapid change of clothing.

"I go to London to-night," he explained. "It is imperative."

"What?"

"Absolutely. The real work, that of the brain (ah, those brave little grey cells), it is done. I go to seek the confirmation. I shall find it! Impossible to deceive Hercule Poirot!"

"You'll come a cropper one of these days," I observed, rather disgusted by his vanity.

"Do not be enraged, I beg of you, *mon ami*. I count on you to do me a service — of your friendship."

"Of course," I said eagerly, rather ashamed of my moroseness. "What is it?"

"The sleeve of my coat that I have taken off — will you brush it? See you, a little white powder has clung to it. You without doubt observed me run my finger round the drawer of the dressing table?"

"No — I didn't."

"You should observe my actions, my friend. Thus I obtained the powder on my finger, and, being a little overexcited, I rubbed it on my sleeve — an action without method which I deplore — false to all my principles."

"But what was the powder?" I asked, not particularly interested in Poirot's principles.

"Not the poison of the Borgias," replied Poirot with a twinkle. "I see your imagination mounting. I should say it was French chalk."

"French chalk?"

"Yes, cabinet-makers use it to make drawers run smoothly."

I laughed.

"You old sinner! I thought you were working up to something exciting."

"*Au revoir*, my friend. I save myself. I fly!"

The door shut behind him. With a smile, half of derision, half of affection, I picked up the coat and stretched out my hand for the clothes brush.

The next morning, hearing nothing from Poirot, I went out for a stroll, met some old friends, and lunched with them at their hotel. In the afternoon we went for a spin. A punctured tyre delayed us, and it was past eight when I got back to the Grand Metropolitan.

The first sight that met my eyes

was Poirot, looking even more diminutive than usual, sandwiched between the Opalsens, beaming in a state of placid satisfaction. "*Mon ami* Hastings!" he cried, and sprang to meet me. "Embrace me, my friend; all has marched to a marvel!"

Luckily, the embrace was merely figurative — not a thing one is always sure of with Poirot.

"Do you mean —" I began.

"Just wonderful, I call it!" said Mrs. Opalsen, smiling all over her fat face. "Didn't I tell you, Ed, that if he couldn't get back my pearls nobody would?"

"You did, my dear, you did. And you were right."

I looked helplessly at Poirot, and he answered the glance.

"My friend Hastings is, as you say in England, all at the seaside. Seat yourself, and I will recount to you all the affair that has so happily ended."

"Ended?"

"But yes. They are arrested."

"Who are arrested?"

"The chambermaid and the valet, *parbleu!* You did not suspect? Not with my parting hint about the French chalk?"

"You said cabinet-makers used it."

"Certainly they do — to make drawers slide easily. Somebody wanted the drawer to slide in and out without any noise. Who could that be? Obviously, only the chambermaid. The plan was so ingenious that it did not at once leap to the eye — not even to the eye of Hercule Poirot.

"Listen, this was how it was done. The valet was in the empty room next door, waiting. The French maid leaves the room. Quick as a flash the chambermaid whips open the drawer, takes out the jewel case and, slipping back the bolt, passes it through the door. The valet opens it at his leisure with the duplicate key with which he has provided himself, extracts the necklace, and waits his time. Célestine leaves the room again, and — pst! — in a flash the case is passed back again and replaced in the drawer.

"Madame arrives, the theft is discovered. The chambermaid demands to be searched, with a good deal of righteous indignation, and leaves the room without a stain on her character. The imitation necklace with which they have provided themselves has been concealed in the French girl's bed that morning by the chambermaid — a master stroke, *ça!*"

"But what did you go to London for?"

"You remember the card?"

"Certainly. It puzzled me — and puzzles me still. I thought —"

I hesitated delicately, glancing at Mr. Opalsen.

Poirot laughed heartily.

"*Une blague!* For the benefit of the valet. The card was one with a specially prepared surface — for fingerprints. I went straight to Scotland Yard, asked for our old friend Inspector Japp, and laid the facts before him. As I had suspected, the fingerprints proved to be those of two well-known jewel thieves who have been 'wanted' for some time. Japp came down with me, the thieves were arrested, and the necklace was discovered in the valet's possession. A clever pair, but they failed in *method*. Have I not told you, Hastings, at least thirty-six times, that without method —"

"At least thirty-six thousand times!" I interrupted. "But where did their 'method' break down?"

"*Mon ami,* it is a good plan to take a place as chambermaid or valet — but you must not shirk your work. They left an empty room undusted; and therefore, when the man put down the jewel case on the little table near the communicating door, it left a square mark —"

"I remember," I cried.

"Before, I was undecided. Then — I *knew!*"

There was a moment's silence.

"And I've got my pearls," said Mrs. Opalsen as a sort of Greek chorus.

"Well," I said, "I'd better have some dinner."

Poirot accompanied me.

"This ought to mean kudos for you," I observed.

"*Pas du tout*," replied Poirot tranquilly. "Japp and the local inspector will divide the credit between them. But"— he tapped his pocket — "I have a cheque here, from Mr. Opalsen, and, how you say, my friend? This week-end has not gone according to plan. Shall we return here next week-end — at my expense this time?"

# THE ADVENTURE OF THE KING OF CLUBS.

"The Adventure of the King of Clubs" was first published in *The Sketch* on March 21, 1923.

"Truth," I observed, laying aside the *Daily Newsmonger*, "is stranger than fiction!"

The remark was not, perhaps, an original one. It appeared to incense my friend. Tilting his egg-shaped head on one side, the little man carefully flicked an imaginary fleck of dust from his carefully creased trousers, and observed sarcastically—

"How profound! What a thinker is my friend Hastings!"

Without displaying any annoyance at this quite-uncalled-for gibe, I tapped the sheet I had laid aside.

"You've read this morning's paper?"

"I have. And after reading it, I folded it anew symmetrically. I did not cast it on the floor as you have done, with your so lamentable absence of order and method."

(That is the worst of Poirot. Order and Method are his gods. He goes so far as to attribute all his success to them.)

"Then you saw the account of the murder of Heinrich Rosenblumn, the impresario? It was that which prompted my remark. Not only is truth stranger than fiction — it is more dramatic. Think of that solid middle-class English family, the Oglanders. Father and mother, son and daughter, typical of thousands of families all over this country. The men of the family go to the City every day, the women look after the house. Their lives are perfectly peaceful, and utterly monotonous. Last night they were sitting in their neat suburban drawing room at Daisymead, Streatham, playing bridge. Suddenly, without any warning, the French window bursts open, and a woman staggers into the room. Her grey satin frock is marked with a crimson stain. She utters one word, "Murder!" before she sinks to the ground insensible. It is possible that they recognize her from her pictures as Valérie Saintclair, the famous dancer who has lately taken London by storm!"

"Is this your eloquence, or that of the *Daily Newsmonger?*" inquired Poirot.

"The *Daily Newsmonger* was in a hurry to go to press, and contented itself with bare facts. But the dramatic possibilities of the story struck me at once."

Poirot nodded thoughtfully. "Wherever there is human nature, there is drama. *But* — it is not always just where you think it is. Remember that. Still, I too am interested in the case, since it is likely that I shall be connected with it."

"Indeed?"

"Yes. A gentleman rang me up this morning, and made an appointment with me on behalf of Prince Paul of Maurania."

"But what has that to do with it?"

"You do not read your pretty little English scandal-papers. The ones with the funny stories, and 'a little mouse has heard,' or 'a little bird would like to know.' See here."

I followed his short stubby finger along the paragraph —

"... whether the foreign prince and the famous dancer are *really* affinities! And if the lady likes her new diamond ring!"

"And now to resume your so-dramatic narrative," said Poirot. "Mademoiselle Saintclair had just fainted on the drawing room carpet at Daisymead, you remember."

I shrugged my shoulders. "As a result of Mademoiselle's first murmured words when she came round, the two male Oglanders stepped out, one to fetch a doctor to attend to the lady, who was evidently suffering terribly from shock, and the other to the police station — whence after telling his story, he accompanied the police to Mon Désir, Mr. Rosenblumn's magnificent villa, which is situated at no great distance from Daisymead. There they found the great man, who by the way suffers from a somewhat unsavoury reputation, lying in the library with the back of his head cracked open like an eggshell."

"I have cramped your style," said Poirot kindly. "Forgive me, I pray ...

ah, here is *Monsieur le Prince!*"

Our distinguished visitor was announced under the title of Count Feodor. He was a strange-looking youth, tall, eager, with a weak chin, the famous Mauranberg mouth, and the dark, fiery eyes of a fanatic.

"Monsieur Poirot?"

My friend bowed.

"Monsieur, I am in terrible trouble, greater than I can well express —"

Poirot waved his hand. "I comprehend your anxiety. Mademoiselle Saintclair is a very dear friend, is it not so?"

The prince replied simply: "I hope to make her my wife."

Poirot sat up in his chair, and his eyes opened.

The prince continued: "I should not be the first of my family to make a morganatic marriage. My brother Alexander has also defied the Emperor. We are living now in more enlightened days, free from the old caste-prejudice. Besides, Mademoiselle Saintclair, in actual fact, is quite my equal in rank. You have heard hints as to her history?"

"There are many romantic stories of her origin — not an uncommon thing with famous dancers. I have heard that she is the daughter of an Irish charwoman, also the story which makes her mother a Russian grand duchess."

"The first story is, of course, nonsense." said the young man. "But the second is true. Valérie, though bound to secrecy, has let me guess as much. Besides, she proves it unconsciously in a thousand ways. I believe in heredity, Monsieur Poirot."

"I too believe in heredity," said Poirot thoughtfully. "I have seen some strange things in connection with it — *moi qui vous parle* ... But to business, *Monsieur le Prince*. What do you want of me? What do you fear? I may speak freely, may I not? Is there anything to connect Mademoiselle Saintclair with the crime? She knew Rosenblumn, of course?"

"Yes. He professed to be in love with her. But she would have nothing to say to him."

Poirot looked at him keenly. "Had she any reason to fear him?"

The young man hesitated. "There was an incident. You know Zara, the clairvoyant ?"

"No."

"She is wonderful. You should consult her some time. Valérie and I went to see her last week. She read the cards for us. She spoke to Valérie of trouble, of gathering clouds; then she turned up the last card — the covering card, they call it. It was the king of clubs. She said to Valérie: 'Beware. There is a man who holds you in his power. You fear him — you are in great danger through him. You know whom I mean?' Valerie was white to the lips. She nodded and said: 'Yes, yes, I know.' Shortly afterwards we left. Zara's last words to Valerie were: 'Beware of the king of clubs. Danger threatens you.' I questioned Valerie. She would tell me nothing — assured me that all was well. But now — after last night — I am more sure than ever that in the King of Clubs Valérie saw Rosenblumn, and that he was the man she feared."

The Prince paused abruptly. "Now you understand my agitation when I opened the paper this morning. Supposing Valérie, in a fit of madness — oh, it is impossible!"

Poirot rose from his seat, and patted the young man kindly on the shoulder. "Do not distress yourself, I beg of you. Leave it in my hands."

"You will go to Streatham? I gather she is still there — at Daisymead, prostrated by the shock."

"I will go at once."

"I have arranged matters — through the Embassy. You will be allowed access everywhere."

"Then we will depart — Hastings, you will accompany me? *Au revoir, Monsieur le Prince.*"

Mon Désir was an exceptionally fine villa, thoroughly modern and comfortable, whilst containing a rather heterogeneous collection of works of art. A short carriage-drive led up to it from the road, and beautiful gardens extended behind the house for some acres.

On mentioning Prince Paul's name, the butler who answered the door at once took us to the scene of the tragedy. The library was a magnificent room, running from back to front of the whole building, with a window at either end — one giving on the front carriage-drive, and the other on the garden. It was in the recess of the latter that the body had lain. It had been removed not long before, the police having concluded their examination.

"That is annoying," I murmured to Poirot. "Who knows what clues they may have destroyed?"

My little friend smiled. "Eh — eh? How often must I tell you that clues come from *within?* In the little grey cells of the brain lies the solution of every mystery."

He turned to the butler. "I suppose, except for the removal of the body, the room has not been touched?"

"No, Sir. It's just as it was when the police came up last night."

"These curtains, now. I see they pull right across the window recess. They are the same in the other window. Were they drawn last night?"

"Yes, Sir, I draw them every night."

"Then Mr. Rosenblumn must have drawn them back himself?"

"I suppose so, Sir."

"Did you know your master expected a visitor last night?"

"He did not say so, Sir. But he gave orders he was not to be disturbed after dinner. You see, Sir, there is a door leading out of the library on to the terrace at the side of the house. He could have admitted anyone that way."

"Was he in the habit of doing that?"

The butler coughed discreetly. "I believe so, Sir."

Poirot strode to the door in question. It was unlocked. He stepped through it on to the terrace which joined the drive on the right, whilst on the left it led up to a red brick wall.

"The fruit garden, Sir. There is a door leading into it farther along, but it was always locked at six o'clock."

Poirot nodded, and reëntered the library.

"Did you hear nothing of last night's events?"

"Well, Sir, we heard voices in the library, a little before nine. But that wasn't unusual, especially being a lady's voice. But of course, once we were all in the servants' hall, right the other side, we didn't hear anything at all. And then, about eleven o'clock, the police came."

" How many voices did you hear?"

"I couldn't say, Sir. I only noticed the lady's."

"Ah!"

"I beg pardon, Sir, but Dr. Ryan is still in the house, if you would care to see him."

We jumped at the suggestion, and in a few minutes the doctor, a cheery, middle-aged man, joined us, and gave Poirot all the information he required. Rosenblumn had been lying near the window, his head by the marble window-seat. There were two wounds, one between the eyes, and the other — the fatal one — on the back of the head.

"He was lying on his back?"

"Yes. There is the mark." He pointed to a small dark stain on the floor.

"Could not the blow on the back of the head have been caused by his striking the floor?"

"Impossible. Whatever the weapon was, it penetrated some distance into the skull."

Poirot looked thoughtfully in front of him. In the embrasure of each window was a carved marble seat, the arms being fashioned in the form of a lion's head. A light came into Poirot's eyes. "Supposing he had fallen backwards on this projecting lion's head, and slipped from there to the ground. Would not that cause a wound such as you describe?"

"Yes, it would. But the angle at which he was lying makes that theory impossible. And besides there could not fail to be traces of blood on the marble of the seat."

"Unless they were washed away?"

The doctor shrugged his shoulders. "That is hardly likely. It would be to no one's advantage to give an accident the appearance of murder."

"Quite so," acquiesced Poirot. "Could either of the blows have been struck by a woman, do you think?"

"Oh, quite out of the question, I should say. You are thinking of Mademoiselle Saintclair, I suppose?"

Poirot turned his attention to

the open French window, and the doctor continued —

"It is through here that Mademoiselle Saintclair fled. You can just catch a glimpse of Daisymead between the trees. Of course, there are many houses nearer to the front of the house on the road, but as it happens, Daisymead, though some distance away, is the only house visible this side."

"Come, Hastings, we will follow the footsteps of Mademoiselle. Good day to you, *Monsieur le Docteur*; many thanks for your amiability."

Poirot led the way down through the garden, out through an iron gate, across a short stretch of green and in through the garden gate of Daisymead, which was an unpretentious little house in about half an acre of ground. There was a small flight of steps leading up to a French window. Poirot nodded in their direction.

"That is the way Mademoiselle Saintclair went. For us, who have not her urgency to plead, it will be better to go round to the front door."

A maid admitted us and took us into the drawing-room, whilst she went in search of Mrs. Oglander. The room had evidently not been touched since the night before. The ashes were still in the grate, and the bridge table was still in the centre of the room, with a dummy exposed, and the hands thrown down. The place was somewhat overloaded with gimcrack ornaments, and a good many family portraits of surpassing ugliness adorned the walls.

Poirot gazed at them more leniently than I did, and straightened one or two that were hanging a shade askew. "*La famille* — it is a strong tie, is it not? Sentiment, it takes the place of beauty."

I agreed, my eyes being fixed on a family group comprising a gentleman with whiskers, a lady with a high "front" of hair, a solid, thick-set boy, and two little girls tied up with a good many unnecessary bows of ribbon. I took this to be the Oglander family in earlier days.

The door opened, and a young woman came in. Her dark hair was neatly arranged, and she wore a drab-coloured sports coat and a tweed skirt.

Poirot stepped forward. "Miss Oglander? I regret to *dérange* you — especially after all you have been through. The whole affair must have been most disturbing."

"It has been rather upsetting," admitted the young lady cautiously.

I began to think that the elements of drama were wasted on Miss Oglander, that her lack of imagination rose superior to any tragedy. I was confirmed in this belief as she continued: "I must apologize for the state this room is in. Servants get so foolishly excited."

"It was here that you were sitting last night, *n'est-ce pas?*"

"Yes, we were playing bridge after supper, when —"

"Excuse me — how long had you been playing?"

"Well —" Miss Oglander considered. "I really can't say. I suppose it must have been about ten o'clock. We had had several rubbers, I know."

"And you yourself were sitting — where?"

"Facing the window. I was playing with my mother and had gone one 'No Trump.' Suddenly, without any warning. the window burst open, and Miss Saintclair staggered into the room."

"You recognized her?"

"I had a vague idea her face was familiar."

"She is still here, is she not?"

"Yes, but she refuses to see anyone. She is still quite prostrated."

"I think she will see me. Will you tell her that I am here at the express request of Prince Paul of Maurania?"

I fancied that the mention of a royal prince rather shook Miss Oglander's imperturbable calm. But she left the room on her errand without any further remark, and returned almost immediately to say that Miss Saintclair would see us in her room.

We followed her upstairs, and into a fair-sized light bed-room. On a couch by the window a woman was lying who turned her head as we entered. The contrast between the two women struck me at once, the more so as in actual features and colouring they were not unlike — but, oh! the difference. Not a look, not a gesture of Valérie Saintclair's but expressed drama. She seemed to exhale an atmosphere of romance. A scarlet flannel dressing gown covered her feet — a homely garment in all conscience; but the charm of her personality invested it with an exotic flavour, and it seemed an Eastern robe of glowing colour.

Her large dark eyes fastened themselves on Poirot.

"You come from Paul?" Her voice matched her appearance — it was full and languid.

"Yes, Mademoiselle. I am here to serve him — and you."

"What do you want to know?"

"Everything that happened last night. *But everything!*"

She smiled rather wearily.

"Do you think I should lie? I am not stupid. I see well enough that there can be no concealment. He held a secret of mine, that man who is dead. He threatened me with it. For Paul's sake, I endeavoured to make terms with him. I could not risk losing Paul .... Now that he is dead, I am safe. But for all that, I did not kill him."

Poirot shook his head with a smile. "It is not necessary to tell me that, Mademoiselle. Now recount to me what happened last night."

"I offered him money. He appeared to be willing to treat with me. He appointed last night at nine o'clock. I was to go to Mon Désir. I knew the place; I had been there before. I was to go round to the side door into the library, so that the servants should not see me."

"Excuse me, Mademoiselle, but were you not afraid to trust yourself alone there at night?"

Was it my fancy, or was there a momentary pause before she answered?

"Perhaps I was. But you see, there was no one I could ask to go with me. And I was desperate. Rosenblumn admitted me to the library. Oh, that man! I am glad he is dead! He played with me, as a cat does with a mouse. He taunted me. I begged and implored him on my knees. I offered him every jewel I have. All in vain! Then he named his own terms. Perhaps you can guess what they were. I refused. I told him what I thought of him. I raved at him. He remained calmly smiling. And then — as I fell to silence at last, there was a sound — from behind the curtain in the window .... He heard it too. He strode to the curtains and flung them wide apart. There was a man there, hiding — a dreadful-looking man, a sort of tramp. He struck at Mr. Rosenblumn — then he struck again, and he went down. The tramp clutched at me with his bloodstained hand. I tore myself free, slipped through the window, and ran for my life. Then I perceived the lights in this house, and made for them. The blinds were up, and I saw some people playing bridge. I almost fell into the room. I just managed to gasp out 'Murder!' and then everything went black —"

"Thank you, Mademoiselle. It must have been a great shock to your nervous system. As to this tramp, could you describe him? Do you remember what he was wearing?"

"No — it was all so quick. But I should know the man anywhere. His face is burnt in on my brain."

"Just one more question, Mademoiselle. The curtains of the *other* window, the one giving on the drive, were they drawn?"

For the first time a puzzled expression crept over the dancer's face. She seemed to be trying to remember.

"*Eh bien,* Mademoiselle?"

"I think — I am almost sure — yes, quite sure! They were *not* drawn."

"That is curious, since the other ones were. No matter. It is, I dare say, of no great importance. You are remaining here long, Mademoiselle?"

"The doctor thinks I shall be fit to return to town to-morrow." She looked round the room. Miss Oglander had gone out. "These people, they are very kind — but they are not of my world. I shock them! And to me — well, I am not fond of the *bourgeoisie!*"

A faint note of bitterness underlay her words.

Poirot nodded. "I understand. I hope I have not fatigued you unduly with my questions?"

"Not at all, Monsieur. I am only too anxious Paul should know all as soon as possible."

"Then I will wish you good day, Mademoiselle."

As Poirot was leaving the room, he paused, and pounced on a pair of patent-leather slippers. "Yours, Mademoiselle?"

"Yes, Monsieur. They have just been cleaned and brought up."

"Ah!" said Poirot, as we descended the stairs. "It seems that the domestics are not too excited to clean shoes, though they forget a grate. Well, *mon ami*, at first there appeared to be one or two points of interest, but I fear, I very much fear, that we must regard the case as finished. It all seems straightforward enough."

"And the murderer?"

"Hercule Poirot does not hunt down tramps," replied my friend grandiloquently.

Miss Oglander met us in the hall. "If you will wait in the drawing room a minute, Mamma would like to speak to you."

The room was still untouched, and Poirot idly gathered up the cards, shuffling them with his tiny, fastidiously groomed hands.

"Do you know what I think, my friend?"

"No?" I said eagerly.

"I think that Miss Oglander made a mistake in going one No Trump. She should have gone three Spades."

"Poirot! You are the limit."

"*Mon Dieu*, I cannot always be talking blood and thunder."

Suddenly he stiffened: "Hastings, Hastings — see! The King of Clubs is missing from the pack!"

"Zara!" I cried.

"Eh?" He did not seem to understand my allusion. Mechanically he stacked the cards and put them away in their cases. His face was very grave.

"Hastings," he said at last, "I, Hercule Poirot, have come near to making a big mistake — a very big mistake."

I gazed at him, impressed, but utterly uncomprehending.

"We must begin again, Hastings. Yes, we must begin again. But this time we shall not err."

He was interrupted by the entrance of a handsome middle-aged lady. She carried some household books in her hand. Poirot bowed to her.

"Do I understand, Sir, that you are a friend of — er — Miss Saintclair's?"

"I come from a friend of hers, Madame."

"Oh, I see. I thought perhaps —"

Poirot suddenly waved brusquely at the window. "Your blinds were not pulled down last night?"

"No — I suppose that is why Miss Saintclair saw the light so plainly."

"There was moonlight last night. I wonder that you did not see Mademoiselle Saintclair from your seat here facing the window?"

"I suppose we were engrossed

with our game. Nothing like this has ever happened before to us."

"I can quite believe that, Madame. And I will put your mind at rest. Mademoiselle Saintclair is leaving to-morrow."

"Oh!" The good lady's face cleared.

"And I will wish you good morning, Madame."

A servant was cleaning the steps as we went out of the front door. Poirot addressed her.

"Was it you who cleaned the shoes of the young lady upstairs?"

The maid shook her head. "No, Sir. I don't think they've been cleaned."

"Who cleaned them, then?" I inquired of Poirot, as we walked down the road.

"Nobody. They did not need cleaning."

"I grant that walking on the road or path on a fine night would not soil them. But surely after going through the long grass of the garden, they would have been soiled and stained."

"Yes," said Poirot with a curious smile. "In that case, I agree, they would have been stained."

"But —"

"Have patience a little half hour, my friend. We are going back to Mon Désir."

The butler looked surprised at our reappearance, but offered no objection to our returning to the library.

"Hi, that's the wrong window, Poirot," I cried as he made for the one overlooking the front carriage-drive.

"I think not, my friend. See here."

He pointed to the marble lion's head. On it was a faint discoloured smear. He shifted his finger and pointed to a similar stain on the polished floor.

"Someone struck Rosenblumn a blow with his clenched fist between the eyes. He fell backward on this projecting bit of marble, then slipped to the floor. Afterwards, he was dragged across the floor to the other window, and laid there instead, but not quite at the same angle, as the doctor's evidence told us."

"But why? It seems utterly unnecessary."

"On the contrary, it was essential. Also, it is the key to the murderer's identity — though, by the way, he had no intention of killing Rosenblumn, and so it is hardly permissible to call him a murderer. He must be a very strong man!"

"Because of having dragged the body across the floor?"

"Not altogether. It has been an interesting case. I nearly made an imbecile of myself, though."

"Do you mean to say it is over, that you know everything?"

"Yes."

A remembrance smote me. "No," I cried. "There is one thing you do *not* know!"

"And that?"

"You do not know where the missing king of clubs is!"

"Eh? Oh, that is droll! That is very droll, my friend."

"Why?"

"*Because it is in my pocket!*" He drew it forth with a flourish.

"Oh!" I said, rather crestfallen. "Where did you find it? Here?"

"There was nothing sensational about it. It had simply not been taken out with the other cards. It was in the box."

"H'm! All the same, it gave you an idea, didn't it?"

"Yes, my friend. I present my respects to His Majesty."

"Well, what are we going to do now?"

"We are going to return to town. But I must have a few words with a certain lady at Daisymead first."

The same little maid opened the door to us.

"They're all at lunch now, Sir. Unless it's Miss Saintclair you want to see; and she's resting."

"It will do if I can see Mrs. Oglander for a few minutes. Will you tell her?"

We were led into the drawing room to wait. I had a glimpse of the family in the dining room as we passed, now reinforced by the presence of two heavy, solid-looking men, one with a moustache, the other with a beard.

In a few minutes Mrs. Oglander came into the room, looking inquiringly at Poirot. Poirot bowed.

"Madame, we, in our country, have a great tenderness, a great respect for the mother. The *mère de famille*, she is everything!"

Mrs. Oglander looked rather astonished at this opening.

"It is for that reason that I have come — to allay a mother's anxiety. The murderer of Mr. Rosenblumn will not be discovered. Have no fear. I, Hercule Poirot, tell you so. I am right, am I not? Or is it a wife that I must reassure?"

There was a moment's pause. Mrs. Oglander seemed searching Poirot with her eyes. At last she said quietly: "I don't know how you know — but — yes, you are right."

Poirot nodded gravely. "That is all, Madame. But do not be uneasy. Your English policemen have not the eyes of Hercule Poirot."

He tapped the family portrait on the wall with his fingernail.

"You had another daughter once. She is dead, Madame?"

Again there was a pause, as she searched him with her eyes. Then she answered: "Yes, she is dead —"

"Ah!" said Poirot briskly. "Well, we must return to town. You permit that I return the king of clubs to the pack? It was your only slip. You understand to have played bridge for an hour or so, with only fifty-one cards — well, no one who knows anything of the game would credit it for a minute! *Bonjour!*"

"And now, my friend," said Poirot as we stepped towards the station, "you see it all!"

"I see nothing! Who killed Rosenblumn?"

"John Oglander, Junior. I was not quite sure if it was the father or the son, but I fixed on the son as being the stronger and younger of the two. It had to be one of them, because of the window."

"Why?"

"There were four exits from the library — two doors, two windows; but evidently only one would do. Three exits gave on the front, directly or indirectly. The tragedy had to occur in the back window in order to make it appear that Valérie Saintclair came to Daisymead by chance. Really, of course, she fainted, and John Oglander carried her across over his shoulders. That is why I said he must be a strong man."

"Did they go there together, then?"

"Yes. You remember Valérie's hesitation when I asked her if she was not afraid to go alone? John Oglander went with her — which didn't improve Rosenblumn's temper, I fancy. They quarrelled, and it was probably some insult levelled at Valerie that made Oglander hit him. The rest, you know."

"But why the bridge?"

"Bridge presupposes four players. A simple thing like that carries a lot of conviction. Who would have supposed that there had been only three people in that room all the evening?"

I was still puzzled.

"There's one thing I don't understand. What have the Oglanders to do with the dancer Valérie Saintclair?"

"Ah! That I wonder you did not see. And yet you looked long enough at that picture on the wall — longer than I did. Mrs. Oglander's other daughter may be dead to her family, but the world knows her as Valérie Saintclair!"

"*What?*"

"Did you not see the resemblance the moment you saw the two sisters together?"

"No," I confessed. "I only thought how extraordinarily dissimilar they were."

"That is because your mind is so open to external romantic impressions, my dear Hastings. The features are almost identical. So is the colouring. The interesting thing is that Valérie is ashamed of her family, and her family is ashamed of her! Nevertheless, in a moment of peril, she turned to her brother for help, and when things went wrong, they all hung together in a remarkable way. Family strength is a marvellous thing. They can all act, that family. That is where Valerie gets her histrionic talent from. I, like Prince Paul, believe in heredity! They deceived *me!* But for a lucky accident, and test question to Mrs. Oglander by which I got her to contradict her daughter's account of how they were sitting, the

Oglander family would have put a defeat on Hercule Poirot."

"What shall you tell the Prince?"

"That Valérie could not possibly have committed the crime, and that I doubt if that tramp will ever be found. Also, to convey my compliments to 'Zara.' A curious coincidence, that! I think I shall call this little affair 'The Adventure of the King of Clubs.' What do you think, my friend?"

# THE DISAPPEARANCE OF MR. DAVENHEIM.

"The Disappearance of Mr. Davenheim" was first published in *The Sketch* on March 28, 1923.

Poirot and I were expecting our old friend Inspector Japp of Scotland Yard to tea. We were sitting round the tea table awaiting his arrival. Poirot had just finished carefully straightening the cups and saucers which our landlady was in the habit of throwing, rather than placing, on the table. He had also breathed heavily on the metal teapot, and polished it with a silk handkerchief. The kettle was on the boil, and a small enamel saucepan beside it contained some thick, sweet chocolate which was more to Poirot's palate than what he described as "your English poison."

A sharp "rat-tat" sounded below, and a few minutes afterwards Japp entered briskly.

"Hope I'm not late," he said as he greeted us. "To tell the truth, I was yarning with Miller, the man who's in charge of the Davenheim case."

I pricked up my ears. For the last three days the papers had been full of the strange disappearance of Mr. Davenheim, senior partner of Davenheim and Salmon, the well-known bankers and financiers. On

Saturday last he had walked out of his house, and had never been seen since. I looked forward to extracting some interesting details from Japp.

"I should have thought," I remarked, "that it would be almost impossible for anyone to 'disappear' nowadays."

Poirot brushed a speck of dust from his coat, moved a plate of bread and butter the eighth of an inch, and said sharply: "Be exact, my friend. What do you mean by 'disappear'? To which class of disappearance are you referring?"

"Are disappearances classified and labelled, then?" I laughed. Japp smiled also. Poirot frowned at both of us.

"But certainly they are! They fall into three categories: First, and most common, the voluntary disappearance. Second, the much abused 'loss of memory' case — rare, but occasionally genuine. Third, murder, and a more or less successful disposal of the body. Do you refer to all three as impossible of execution?"

"Very nearly so, I should think. You might lose your own memory, but someone would be sure to recognize you — especially in the case of a well-known man like Davenheim. Then 'bodies' can't be made to vanish into thin air. Sooner or later they turn up, concealed in lonely places, or in trunks. Murder will out. In the same way, the absconding clerk, or the domestic defaulter, is bound to be run down in these days of wireless telegraphy. He can be headed off from foreign countries; ports and railway stations are watched; and as for concealment in this country, his features and appearance will be known to everyone who reads a daily newspaper. He's up against civilization."

"*Mon ami*," said Poirot, "you make one error. You do not allow for the fact that a man who had decided to make away with another man — or with himself in a figurative sense — might be that rare machine, a man of method! He might bring intelligence, talent, a careful calculation of detail to the task; and then —"

"Yes, then?"

"Why, then I do not see why he should not be successful in baffling the police force."

"But not *you*, I suppose?" said Japp good-humouredly, winking at me. "He couldn't baffle *you*, eh, Monsieur Poirot?"

Poirot endeavoured, with a marked lack of success, to look modest. "Me also! Why not? It is true that I approach such problems with an exact science, a mathematical precision, which seems, alas, only too rare in the new generation of detectives!"

Japp grinned more widely. "I don't know," he said. "Miller, the man who's on this case, is a smart chap. You may be very sure he won't overlook a footprint, or a cigar ash, or a crumb even! He's got eyes that see everything."

"So, *mon ami*," said Poirot, "has

the London sparrow. But all the same, I should not ask this little brown bird here to solve the problem of Mr. Davenheim."

"Come now, Moosior. you're not going to run down the value of details as clues?"

"By no means. These things are all good in their way. The danger is they may assume undue importance. Most details are insignificant — one or two are vital! It is the brain — the little grey cells" — he tapped his forehead — "on which one must rely. The senses mislead. One must seek the truth within — not without."

"You don't mean to say, Moosior Poirot, that you would undertake to solve a case without moving from your chair, do you?"

"That is exactly what I do mean — granted the facts were placed before me. I regard myself as a consulting specialist."

Japp slapped his knee. "Hanged if I don't take you at your word. Bet you a fiver that you can't lay your hand — or rather tell me where to lay my hand — on Mr.Davenheim, dead or alive, before a week is out."

Poirot considered. "*Eh bien, mon ami*, I accept. *Le sport*, it is the passion of you English! Now — the facts."

"On Saturday last, as is his usual custom, Mr. Davenheim took the 12:40 train from Victoria to Chingside, where his palatial country seat, The Cedars, is situated. After lunch, he strolled round the grounds, and gave various directions to the gardeners. Everybody agrees that his manner was absolutely normal and as usual. After tea he put his head into his wife's boudoir, saying that he was going to stroll down to the village and post some letters. He added that he was expecting a Mr. Lowenthal on business. If he should come before he himself returned, he was to be shown into the study and asked to wait. Mr. Davenheim then left the house by the front door, passed leisurely down the drive, and out at the gate, and — was never seen again. From that hour, he vanished completely."

"Pretty — very pretty — altogether a charming little problem," murmured Poirot. "Proceed, my good friend."

"About a quarter of an hour later a tall, dark man, with a Jewish cast of features and a thick black moustache, rang the front doorbell, and explained that he had an appointment with Mr. Davenheim. He gave the name of Lowenthal, and, in accordance with the banker's instructions, was shown into the study. Nearly an hour passed. Mr. Davenheim did not return. Finally Mr. Lowenthal rang the bell, and explained that he was unable to wait any longer, as he must catch his train back to town.

"Mrs. Davenheim apologized for her husband's absence, which seemed unaccountable, as she knew him to have been expecting the visitor. Mr. Lowenthal reiterated his regret and took his departure.

"Well, as everyone knows, Mr. Davenheim did *not* return. Early on Sunday morning the police were communicated with, but could make neither head nor tail of the matter. Mr. Davenheim seemed literally to have vanished into thin air. He had not been to the post office; nor had he been seen passing through the village. At the station they were positive he had not departed by any train. His own motor had not left the garage. If he had hired a car to meet him in some lonely spot, it seems almost certain that by this time, in view of the large reward offered for information, the driver of it would have come forward to tell what he knew. True, there was a small race-meeting at Entfield, five miles away, and if he had walked to that station he might have passed unnoticed in the crowd. But since then his photograph and a full description of him have been circulated in every newspaper, and nobody has been able to give any news of him. We have, of course, received many letters from all over England, but each clue, so far, has ended in disappointment.

"On Monday morning a further sensational discovery came to light. Behind a portière in Mr. Davenheim's study stands a safe, and that safe had been broken into and rifled. The windows were fastened securely on the inside, which seems to put an ordinary burglary out of court, unless, of course, an accomplice within the house fastened them again afterwards. On the other hand, Sunday having intervened, and the household being in a state of chaos, it is likely that the burglary was committed on the Saturday, and remained undetected until Monday."

"*Précisément*," said Poirot dryly. "Well, is he arrested, *ce pauvre* Monsieur Lowenthal?"

Japp grinned. "Not yet. But he's under pretty close supervision."

Poirot nodded. "What was taken from the safe? Have you any idea?"

"We've been going into that with the junior partner of the firm and Mrs. Davenheim. Apparently there was a considerable amount in bearer bonds, and a very large sum in notes, owing to some large transaction having been just carried through. There was also a small fortune in jewellery. All Mrs. Davenheim's jewels were kept in the safe. The purchasing of them had become a passion with her husband of late years, and hardly a month passed that he did not make her a present of some rare and costly gem."

"Altogether a good haul," said Poirot thoughtfully. "Now, what about Lowenthal? Is it known what his business was with Davenheim that evening?"

"Well, the two men were apparently not on very good terms. Lowenthal is a speculator in quite a small way. Nevertheless, he has been able once or twice to score a coup off Davenheim in the market, though it seems they seldom, or never, actually met. It was a matter concerning some South American shares which led the banker to make his appointment."

"Had Davenheim interests in South America, then?"

"I believe so. Mrs. Davenheim happened to mention that he spent all last autumn in Buenos Aires."

"Any trouble in his home life? Were the husband and wife on good terms?"

"I should say his domestic life was quite peaceful and uneventful. Mrs. Davenheim is a pleasant, rather unintelligent woman. Quite a nonentity, I think."

"Then we must not look for the solution of the mystery there. Had he any enemies?"

"He had plenty of financial rivals, and no doubt there are many people whom he has got the better of who bear him no particular good-will. But there was no one likely to make away with him — and, if they had, where is the body?"

"Exactly. As Hastings says, bodies have a habit of coming to light with fatal persistency."

"By the way, one of the gardeners says he saw a figure going round to the side of the house towards the rose-garden. The long French window of the study opens on to the rose-garden, and Mr. Davenheim frequently entered and left the house that way. But the man was a good way off, at work on some cucumber frames, and cannot even say whether it was the figure of his master or not. Also, he cannot fix the time with any accuracy. It must have been before six, as the gardeners cease work at that time."

"And Mr. Davenheim left the house?"

"About half past five or thereabouts."

"What lies beyond the rose garden?"

"A lake."

"With a boat-house?"

"Yes, a couple of punts are kept there. I suppose you're thinking of suicide, Moosior Poirot? Well, I don't mind telling you that Miller's going down to-morrow expressly to see that piece of water dragged. That's the kind of man he is!"

Poirot smiled faintly, and turned to me. "Hastings, I pray you, hand me that copy of *Daily Megaphone*. If I remember rightly, there is an unusually clear photograph there of the missing man."

I rose, and found the sheet required. Poirot studied the features attentively.

"H'm!" he murmured. "Wears his hair rather long and wavy, full moustache and pointed beard, bushy eyebrows. Distinctly Jewish cast of countenance. Eyes dark?"

"Yes."

"Hair and beard turning grey?"

The detective nodded. "Well, Moosior Poirot, what have you got to say to it all? Clear as daylight, eh?"

"On the contrary, most obscure."

The Scotland Yard man looked pleased.

"Which gives me great hopes of solving it," finished Poirot placidly.

"Eh?"

"I find it a good sign when a case is obscure. If a thing is clear as daylight — *eh bien*, mistrust it! *Someone has made it so.*"

Japp shook his head almost pityingly. "Well, each to their fancy. But it's not a bad thing to see your way clear ahead."

"I do not see," murmured Poirot. "I shut my eyes — and think."

Japp sighed. "Well, you've got a clear week to think in."

"And you will bring me any fresh developments that arise — the result of the labours of the hard-working and lynx-eyed Inspector Miller, for instance?"

"Certainly. That's in the bargain."

"Seems a shame, doesn't it?" said Japp to me as I accompanied him to the door. "Like robbing a child."

I replied that in this case Poirot had certainly brought his fate upon himself, and that there was no need for Japp to reproach himself.

"That's true. He certainly did ask for it! Past his day, of course, but a shrewd old fellow in many ways. But in a case like this he's out of his depth. Fancies himself, though, doesn't he? Thinks there's nothing on God's earth like Hercule Poirot!"

I could not help agreeing with a smile. I was still smiling as I reëntered the room.

"*Eh bien!*" said Poirot immediately. "You make fun of Papa Poirot, is it not so?" He shook his finger at me. "You do not trust his grey cells? Ah, do not be confused! Let us discuss this little problem — incomplete as yet, I admit, but already showing one or two points of interest."

"The lake!" I said significantly.

"And even more than the lake, the boathouse!"

I looked sidewise at Poirot. He was smiling in his most inscrutable fashion. I felt that, for the moment, it would be quite useless to question him further.

We heard nothing of Japp until the following evening, when he walked in about nine o'clock. I saw at once by his expression that he was bursting with news of some kind.

"*Eh bien*, my friend," remarked Poirot. "All goes well? But do not tell me that you have discovered the body of Mr. Davenheim in your lake, because I shall not believe you."

"We haven't found the body, but I'll tell you what we have found, right enough, his *clothes* — the identical clothes he was wearing that day! What do you say to that?"

"Any other clothes missing from the house?"

"No, his valet was quite positive on that point. The rest of his wardrobe is intact. There's more. We've arrested Lowenthal! One of the maids, whose business it is to fasten the bed-room windows, declares that she saw Lowenthal coming *towards* the study through the rose garden about a quarter past six. That would be about ten minutes before he left the house."

"What does he himself say to that?"

"Denied first of all that he had ever left the study. But the maid was positive, and he pretended afterwards that he had forgotten just stepping out of the window to examine an unusual species of rose. Rather a weak story. And there's fresh evidence against him come to light. Mr. Davenheim always wore a thick gold ring set with a solitaire diamond on the little finger of his right hand. Well, that ring was pawned in London on Saturday night by a man called Billy Kellett. He's already known to the police — did three months last autumn for lifting an old gentleman's watch. It seems he tried to pawn the ring at no fewer than five different places, succeeded at the last one, got gloriously drunk on the proceeds, assaulted a policeman, and was run in in consequence. I went to Bow Street with Miller and saw him. He's sober enough now, and I don't mind admitting we pretty well frightened the life out of him, hinting he might be charged with murder.

"This is his yarn, and a very queer one it is. He was at Entfield races on Saturday, though I daresay scarf-pins was his line of business, rather than betting. Anyway, he had a bad day, and was down on his luck. He was tramping along the road to Chingside, and sat down in a ditch to rest just before he got into the village. A few minutes later he noticed a man coming along the road to the village, 'dark, Jewish-looking gent, with a big moustache, one of them City toffs,' is his description of the man.

"Kellett was half concealed from the road by a heap of stones. Just before he got abreast of him, the man looked quickly up and down the road, and seeing it apparently deserted he took a small object from his pocket and threw it over the hedge. Then he went on towards the station.

"Now, the object he had thrown over the hedge had fallen with a slight 'chink' which aroused the curiosity of the human derelict in the ditch. He investigated and, after a short search, discovered the ring!

"That is Kellett's story. It's only fair to say that Lowenthal denies it utterly, and of course the word of a man like Kellett can't be relied upon in the slightest. It's within the bounds of possibility that he met Davenheim in the lane and robbed and murdered him."

Poirot shook his head.

"Very improbable, *mon ami*. He had no means of disposing of the body. It would have been found by now. Secondly, the open way in which he pawned the ring makes it unlikely that he did murder to get it. Thirdly, your sneak-thief is rarely a murderer. Fourthly, as he has been in prison since Saturday, it would be too much of a coincidence that he is able to give so accurate a description of Lowenthal."

Japp nodded. "I don't say you're not right. But all the same, you won't get a jury to take much note of a gaol-bird's evidence. What seems odd to me is that Lowenthal couldn't find a cleverer way of disposing of the ring."

Poirot shrugged his shoulders. "Well, after all, if it were found in the neighbourhood, it might be argued that Davenheim himself had dropped it."

"But why remove it from the body at all?" I cried.

"There might be a reason for that," said Japp. "Do you know that just beyond the lake, a little gate leads out on to the hill, and not three minutes' walk brings you to — what do you think? — a *lime kiln*."

"Good heavens!" I cried. "You mean that the lime which destroyed the body would be powerless to affect the metal of the ring?"

"Exactly."

"It seems to me," I said, "that that explains everything. What a horrible crime!"

By common consent we both turned and looked at Poirot. He seemed lost in reflection, his brow knitted, as though with some supreme mental effort. I felt at last his keen intellect was asserting itself. What would his first words be?

We were not long left in doubt. With a sigh, the tension of his attitude relaxed and, turning to Japp, he asked —

"Have you any idea, my friend, whether Mr. and Mrs. Davenheim occupied the same bed-room?"

The question seemed so ludicrously inappropriate that for a moment we both stared in silence. Then Japp burst into a laugh. "Good Lord, Monsieur Poirot, I thought you were coming out with something startling. As to your question, I'm sure I don't know."

"You could find out?" asked Poirot with curious persistence.

"Oh, certainly — if you *really* want to know."

"*Merci, mon ami.* I should be obliged if you would make a point of it."

Japp stared at him a few minutes longer, but Poirot seemed to have forgotten us both. The detective shook his head sadly at me, and, murmuring, "Poor old fellow! War's been too much for him!," gently withdrew from the room.

As Poirot seemed sunk in a daydream, I took a sheet of paper, and amused myself by scribbling notes upon it. My friend's voice aroused me. He had come out of his reverie, and was looking brisk and alert.

"*Que faites-vous là, mon ami?*"

"I was jotting down what occurred to me as the main points of interest in this affair."

"You become methodical — at

last!" said Poirot approvingly.

I concealed my pleasure. "Shall I read them to you?"

"By all means."

I cleared my throat.

"'1. All the evidence points to Lowenthal having been the man who forced the safe.

"'2. He had a grudge against Davenheim.

"'3. He lied in his first statement that he had never left the study.

"'4. If you accept Billy Kellett's story as true, Lowenthal is unmistakably implicated.'"

I paused. "Well?" I asked, for I felt that I had put my finger on all the vital facts.

Poirot looked at me pityingly, shaking his head very gently. "*Mon pauvre ami!* But it is that you have not the gift! The important detail, you appreciate him never! Also, your reasoning is false."

"How?"

"Let me take your four points—

"1. Mr. Lowenthal could not possibly know that he would have the chance to open the safe. He came for a business interview. He could not know beforehand that Mr. Davenheim would be absent posting a letter, and that he would consequently be alone in the study!"

"He might have seized the opportunity," I suggested.

"And the tools? City gentlemen do not carry round housebreaker's tools on the off-chance! And one could not cut into that safe with penknife, *bien entendu.*"

"Well, what about No. 2?"

"You say Lowenthal had a grudge against Mr. Davenheim. What you mean is that he had once or twice got the better of him. And presumably those transactions were entered into with the view of benefiting himself. In any case you do not as a rule bear a grudge against a man you have got the better of—it is more likely to be the other way about. Whatever grudge there might have been would have been on Mr. Davenheim's side."

"Well, you can't deny that he lied about never having left the study?"

"No. But he may have been frightened. Remember, the missing man's clothes had just been discovered in the lake. Of course, as usual, he would have done better to speak the truth."

"And the fourth point?"

"I grant you that. If Kellett's story is true, Lowenthal is undeniably implicated. That is what makes the affair so very interesting."

"Then I did appreciate *one* vital fact?"

"Perhaps—but you have entirely overlooked the two most important points, the ones which undoubtedly hold the clue to the whole matter."

"And pray, what are they?"

"One, the passion which has grown upon Mr. Davenheim in the last few years for buying jewellery. Two, his trip to Buenos Aires last autumn."

"Poirot, you are joking?"

"I am serious. Ah, sacred thunder, but I hope Japp will not forget my little commission."

But the detective, entering into the spirit of the joke, had remembered it so well that a telegram was handed to Poirot about eleven o'clock the next day. At his request I opened it and read it out:

"'Husband and wife have occupied separate rooms since last winter.'"

"Aha!" cried Poirot. "And now we are in mid-June! All is solved!"

I stared at him.

"You have no moneys in the bank of Davenheim and Salmon, *mon ami?*"

"No," I said wondering. "Why?"

"Because I should advise you to withdraw it — before it is too late."

"Why, what do you expect?"

"I expect a big smash in a few days — perhaps sooner. Which reminds me, we will return the compliment of a *dépêche* to Japp. A pencil, I pray you, and a form. *Voilà!* 'Advise you to withdraw any money deposited with firm in question.' That will intrigue him, the good Japp! His eyes will open wide — wide! He will not comprehend in the slightest — until to-morrow, or the next day!"

I remained sceptical, but the morrow forced me to render tribute to my friend's remarkable powers. In every paper was a huge headline telling of the sensational failure of the Davenheim bank. The disappearance of the famous financier took on a totally different aspect in the light of the revelation of the financial affairs of the bank.

Before we were halfway through breakfast, the door flew open and Japp rushed in. In his left hand was a paper; in his right was Poirot's telegram, which he banged down on the table in front of my friend.

"How did you know, Moosior Poirot? How the blazes could you know?"

Poirot smiled placidly at him. "Ah, *mon ami*, after your wire, it was a certainty! From the *commencement*, see you, it struck me that the safe burglary was somewhat remarkable. Jewels, ready money, bearer bonds — all so conveniently arranged for — whom? Well, the good Monsieur Davenheim was of those who 'look after Number One,' as your saying goes! It seemed almost certain that it was arranged for — himself! Then his passion of late years for buying jewellery. How simple! The funds he embezzled, he converted into jewels, very likely replacing them in turn with paste replicas; and so he put away in a safe place, under another name, a considerable fortune to be enjoyed all in good time when everyone has been thrown off the track. His arrangements completed, he makes an appointment with Mr. Lowenthal (who has been imprudent enough in the past to cross the great man once or twice), drills a hole in the safe, leaves orders that the guest is to be shown into the study, and walks out of the house — where?"

Poirot stopped, and stretched out his hand for another boiled egg. He frowned. "It is really insupportable," he murmured, "that every hen lays an egg of a different size! What symmetry can there be on the breakfast table? At least they should sort them in dozens at the shop!"

"Never mind the eggs," said Japp impatiently. "Let 'em lay 'em square if they like. Tell us where our customer went to when he left The Cedars — that is, if you know!"

"*Eh bien*, he went to his hiding place. Ah, this Monsieur Davenheim, there may be some malformation in his grey cells, but they are of the first quality!"

"Do you know where he is hiding?"

"Certainly! It is most ingenious."

"For the Lord's sake, tell us, then!"

Poirot gently collected every fragment of shell from his plate, placed them in the egg-cup, and reversed the empty eggshell on top of them. This little operation concluded, he smiled on the neat effect, and then beamed affectionately on us both. "Come, my friends, you are men of intelligence. Ask yourself the question I asked myself: 'If *I* were this man, where should *I* hide?' Hastings, what do you say?"

"Well," I said, "I'm rather inclined to think I'd not do a bolt at all. I'd stay in London — in the heart of things, travel by tubes and 'buses; ten to one I'd never be recognized. There's safety in a crowd."

Poirot turned inquiringly to Japp.

"I don't agree. Get clear away at once — that's the only chance. I would have had plenty of time to prepare things beforehand. I'd have a yacht waiting, with steam up, and I'd be off to one of the most out-of-the-way corners of the world before the hue and cry began!"

We both looked at Poirot. "What do you say, Moosior?"

For a moment he remained silent. Then a very curious smile flitted across his face.

"My friends, if *I* were hiding from the police, do you know *where* I should hide? *In a prison!*"

"*What?*"

"You are seeking Monsieur Davenheim in order to put him in prison, so you never dream of looking to see if he may not be already there!"

"What do you mean?"

"You tell me Madame Davenheim is not a very intelligent woman. Nevertheless I think if you took her up to Bow Street and confronted her with the man Billy Kellett, she would recognize him! In spite of the fact that he has shaved his beard and moustache and those bushy eyebrows, and has cropped his hair close. A woman nearly always knows her husband, though the rest of the world may be deceived."

"Billy Kellett? But he's known to the police!"

"Did I not tell you Davenheim was a clever man? He prepared his alibi long beforehand. He was not in Buenos Aires last autumn — he was creating the character of Billy Kellett, 'doing three months,' so that the police should have no suspicions when the time came. He was playing, remember, for a large fortune, as well as liberty. It was worth while doing the thing thoroughly. Only —"

"Yes?"

"*Eh bien*, afterwards he had to wear a false beard and wig, et cetera — he had to *make up as himself again*; and to sleep with a false beard is not easy — it invites detection! He cannot risk continuing to share the chamber of Madame his wife. You found out for me that for the last six months, or ever since his supposed return from Buenos Aires, he and Mrs. Davenheim occupied separate rooms. Then I was sure! Everything fitted in. The gardener who fancied he saw his master going round to the side of the house was quite right. He went to the boathouse, donned his 'tramp' clothes, which you may be sure had been safely hidden from the eyes of his valet, dropped the others in the lake, and proceeded to carry out his plan by pawning the ring in an obvious manner, and then assaulting a policeman, getting himself safely into the haven of Bow Street, where nobody would ever dream of looking for him!"

"It's impossible," murmured Japp.

"Ask Madame," said my friend, smiling.

The next day a registered letter lay beside Poirot's plate. He opened it and a five-pound note fluttered out. My friend's brow puckered.

"*Ah, sacré!* But what shall I do with it? I have much remorse! *Ce pauvre* Japp! Ah, an idea! We will have a little dinner, we three! That consoles me. It was really too easy. I am ashamed. I, who would not rob a child — *mille tonnerres, mon ami!* What have you, that you laugh so heartily?"

# THE MYSTERY OF THE PLYMOUTH EXPRESS.

"The Mystery of the Plymouth Express" was first published in *The Sketch* on April 4, 1923.

## I.

Lieutenant Alec Simpson, R.N., stepped from the platform at Newton Abbot into a first-class compartment of the Plymouth Express. A porter followed him with a heavy suit-case. He was about to swing it up to the rack, but the young sailor stopped him.

"No—leave it on the seat. I'll put it up later. Here you are."

"Thank you, Sir." The porter, generously tipped, withdrew.

Doors banged; a stentorian voice shouted: "Plymouth only. Change for Torquay. Plymouth next stop." Then a whistle blew, and, with a long, reluctant jerk, the train drew slowly out of the station.

Lieutenant Simpson had the carriage to himself. The December air was chilly, and he pulled up the window. Then he sniffed vaguely, and frowned. What a smell there was. Reminded him of that time in hospital, and the operation on his leg. Yes, chloroform—that was it!

He let the window down again, changing his seat to one with its back to the engine. He pulled a pipe out of his pocket and lit it. For a little time he sat inactive, looking out into the night and smoking.

At last he roused himself, and opening the suitcase, took out some papers and magazines, then closed the suitcase again and endeavoured to shove it under the opposite seat — without success. Some obstacle resisted it. He shoved harder with rising impatience, but it still stuck out halfway into the carriage.

"Why the devil won't it go in?" he muttered, and, hauling it out completely, he stooped down and peered under the seat....

A moment later a cry rang out into the night, and the great train came to an unwilling halt in obedience to the imperative jerking of the communication cord.

## II.

"M*on ami*," said Poirot, "you have, I know, been deeply interested in this mystery of the Plymouth Express. Read this."

I picked up the note he flicked across the table to me. It was brief and to the point.

> *Dear Sir,—*
>
> *I shall be obliged if you will call upon me at your earliest convenience.—Yours faithfully,*
>
> *Ebenezer Halliday.*

The connection was not clear to my mind, and I looked inquiringly at Poirot.

For answer he took up the newspaper and read aloud: "'A sensational discovery was made last night. A young naval officer returning to Plymouth found under the seat of his compartment the body of a woman, stabbed through the heart. The officer at once pulled the communication cord, and the train was brought to a standstill. The woman, who was about thirty years of age, and richly dressed, has not yet been identified.'

"And later we have this: 'The woman found dead in the Plymouth Express has been identified as the Hon. Mrs. Rupert Carstairs.' You see now, my friend? Or if you do not I will add this — Mrs. Rupert Carrington was, before her marriage, Flossie Halliday, daughter of old man Halliday, the steel king of America."

"And he has sent for you? Splendid!"

"I did him a little service in the past — an affair of bearer bonds. And once, when I was in Paris for a royal visit, I had Mademoiselle Flossie pointed out to me. *La jolie petite pensionnaire.* She had the *joli dot* too! It caused trouble. She nearly made a bad affair."

"How was that?"

"A certain Count de la Rochefour. *Un bien mauvais sujet!* A bad hat, as you would say. An adventurer pure and simple, who knew how to appeal to a romantic young girl. Luckily her father got wind of it in time. He took her back to America in haste. I heard of her marriage some years later, but I know nothing of her husband."

"H'm," I said. "The Hon. Rupert Carstairs is no beauty, by all accounts. He'd pretty well run through his own money on the turf, and I should imagine old man Halliday's dollars came along in the nick of time. I should say that for a good-looking, well-mannered, utterly unscrupulous young scoundrel, it would be hard to find his match!"

"Ah, the poor little lady! *Elle n'est pas bien tombée!*"

"I fancy he made it pretty obvious at once that it was her money, and not she, that had attracted him. I believe they drifted apart almost at once. I have heard rumours lately that there was to be a definite legal separation."

"Old man Halliday is no fool. He would tie up her money pretty tight."

"I dare say. Anyway, I know as a fact that the Honourable Rupert is said to be extremely hard up."

"Aha! I wonder —"

"You wonder what?"

"My good friend, do not jump down my throat like that. You are interested, I see. Suppose you accompany me to see Mr. Halliday. There is a taxi stand at the corner."

### III.

A very few minutes sufficed to whirl us to the superb house in Park Lane rented by the American magnate. We were shown into the library, and almost immediately we were joined by a large stout man, with piercing eyes and an aggressive chin.

"Monsieur Poirot?" said Mr. Halliday. "I guess I don't need to tell you what I want you for. You've read the papers, and I'm never one to let the grass grow under my feet. I happened to hear you were in London, and I remembered the good work you did over those bombs. Never forget a name. I've the pick of Scotland Yard, but I'll have my own man as well. Money no object. All the dollars were made for my little girl — and now she's gone, I'll spend my last cent to catch the damned scoundrel that did it! See? So it's up to you to deliver the goods."

Poirot bowed.

"I accept, Monsieur, all the more willingly that I saw your daughter in Paris several times. And now I will ask you to tell me the circumstances of her journey to Plymouth and any other details that seem to you to bear upon the case."

"Well, to begin with, she wasn't going to Plymouth. She was going to join a house party at Avonmead Court, the Duchess of Swansea's place. She left London by the 12:14 from Paddington, arriving at Bristol (where she had to change) at 2:50. The principal Plymouth expresses, of course, run via Westbury, and do not go near Bristol at all. The 12:14 does a non-stop run to Bristol, afterwards stopping at Weston, Taunton,

Exeter and Newton Abbot. My daughter travelled alone in her carriage, which was reserved as far as Bristol, her maid being in a third-class carriage in the next coach."

Poirot nodded, and Mr. Halliday went on: "The party at Avonmead Court was to be a very gay one, with several balls, and in consequence my daughter had with her nearly all her jewels — amounting in value, perhaps, to about £20,000."

"*Un moment*," interrupted Poirot. "Who had charge of the jewels? Your daughter, or the maid?"

"My daughter always took charge of them herself, carrying them in a small blue morocco case."

"Continue, Monsieur."

"At Bristol the maid, Jane Mason, collected her mistress's dressing-bag and wraps, which were with her, and came to the door of Flossie's compartment. To her intense surprise, my daughter told her that she was not getting out at Bristol, but was going on farther. She directed Mason to get out the luggage and put it in the cloak-room. She could have tea in the refreshment room, but she was to wait at the station for her mistress, who would return to Bristol by an up-train in the course of the afternoon. The maid, although very much astonished, did as she was told. She put the luggage in the cloakroom and had some tea. But up-train after up-train came in, and her mistress did not appear. After the arrival of the last train, she left the luggage where it was, and went to a hotel near the station for the night. This morning she read of the tragedy, and returned to town by the first available train."

"Is there nothing to account for your daughter's sudden change of plan?"

"Well there is this: According to Jane Mason, at Bristol, Flossie was no longer alone in her carriage. There was a man in it who stood looking out of the farther window so that she could not see his face."

"The train was a corridor one, of course?"

"Yes."

"Which side was the corridor?"

"On the platform side. My daughter was standing in the corridor as she talked to Mason."

"And there is no doubt in your mind — excuse me!" He got up, and carefully straightened the inkstand which was a little askew. "*Je vous demande pardon*," he continued, re-seating himself; "it affects my nerves to see anything crooked. Strange, is it not? I was saying, Monsieur, that there is no doubt in your mind as to this probably unexpected meeting being the cause of your daughter's sudden change of plan?"

"It seems the only reasonable supposition."

"You have no idea as to who the gentleman in question might be?"

The millionaire hesitated for a moment, and then replied: "No — I do not know at all."

"Now — as to the discovery of the body?"

"It was discovered by a young naval officer who at once gave the alarm. There was a doctor on the train. He examined the body. She had been first chloroformed, and then stabbed. He gave it as his opinion that she had been dead about four hours, so it must have been done not long after leaving Bristol. Probably between there and Weston, possibly between Weston and Taunton."

"And the jewel-case?"

"The jewel-case, Monsieur Poirot, was missing."

"One thing more, Monsieur. Your daughter's fortune — to whom does it pass at her death?"

"Flossie made a will soon after her marriage, leaving everything to her husband." He hesitated for a minute, and then went on: "I may as well tell you, Monsieur Poirot, that I regard my son-in-law as an unprincipled scoundrel, and that, by my advice, my daughter was on the eve of freeing herself from him by legal means — no difficult matter. I settled her money upon her in such a way that he could not touch it during her lifetime, but although they have lived entirely apart for some years, she had frequently acceded to his demands for money, rather than face an open scandal. However, I was determined to put an end to this. At last Flossie agreed, and my lawyers were instructed to take proceedings."

"And where is Monsieur Carstairs?"

"In town. I believe he was away in the country yesterday, but he returned last night."

Poirot considered a little while. Then he said: "I think that is all, Monsieur."

"You would like to see the maid, Jane Mason?"

"If you please."

Halliday rang the bell, and gave a short order to the footman. A few minutes later Jane Mason entered the room — a respectable, hard-featured woman, as emotionless in the face of tragedy as only a good servant can be.

"You will permit me to put a few questions? Your mistress, she was quite as usual before starting yesterday morning? Not excited or flurried?"

"Oh no, Sir."

"But at Bristol she was quite different?"

"Yes, Sir; regular upset. So nervous she didn't seem to know what she was saying."

"What did she say exactly?"

"Well, Sir, as near as I can remember, she said: 'Mason, I've got to alter my plans. Something has happened — I mean, I'm not getting out here after all. I must go on. Get out the luggage and put it in the cloakroom; then have some tea, and wait for me in the station.'

"'Wait for you here, M'm?' I asked.

"'Yes, yes. Don't leave the station.

I shall return by a later train. I don't know when. It mayn't be until quite late.'

"'Very well, M'm,' I says. It wasn't my place to ask questions, but I thought it very strange."

"It was unlike your mistress, eh?"

"Very unlike her, Sir."

"What do you think?"

"Well, Sir, I thought it was to do with the gentleman in the carriage. She didn't speak to him, but she turned round once or twice as though to ask him if she was doing right."

"But you didn't see the gentleman's face?"

"No, Sir; he stood with his back to me all the time."

"Can you describe him at all?"

"He had on a light fawn overcoat, and a travelling-cap. He was tall and slender-like, and the back of his head was dark."

"You didn't know him?"

"Oh no, I don't think so, Sir."

"It was not your master, Mr. Carstairs, by any chance?"

Mason looked rather startled.

"Oh—I don't think so, Sir!"

"But you are not *sure?*"

"It was about the master's build, Sir—but I never thought of it being him. We so seldom saw him .... I couldn't say it *wasn't* him!"

Poirot picked up a pin from the carpet, and frowned at it severely; then he continued: "Would it be possible for the man to have entered the train at Bristol before you reached the carriage?"

Mason considered.

"Yes, Sir, I think it would. My compartment was very crowded, and it was some minutes before I could get out—and then there was a very large crowd on the platform, and that delayed me too. But he'd only have had a minute or two to speak to the mistress, that way. I took it for granted that he'd come along the corridor."

"That is more probable, certainly."

He paused, still frowning.

"You know how the mistress was dressed, Sir?"

"The papers give a few details, but I would like you to confirm them."

"She was wearing a white fox fur toque, Sir, with a white spotted veil, and a blue frieze coat and skirt—the shade of blue they call electric."

"H'm, rather striking."

"Yes," remarked Mr. Halliday. "Inspector Japp is in hopes that that may help us to fix the spot where the crime took place. Anyone who saw her would remember her."

"*Precisément!*—Thank you, Mademoiselle."

The maid left the room.

"Well"—Poirot got up briskly—"That is all I can do here—except, Monsieur, that I would ask you to tell me everything, but *everything!*"

"I have done so."

"You are sure?"

"Absolutely."

"Then there is nothing more to be said. I must decline the case."

"Why?"

"Because you have not been frank with me."

"I assure you —"

"No, you are keeping something back."

There was a moment's pause, and then Halliday drew a paper from his pocket and handed it to my friend.

"I guess that's what you're after, Monsieur Poirot. Though how you know about it fairly gets my goat."

Poirot smiled, and unfolded the paper. It was a letter written in thin sloping handwriting. Poirot read it aloud.

> *Chère Madame,—*
>
> *It is with infinite pleasure that I look forward to the felicity of meeting you again. After your so amiable reply to my letter, I can hardly restrain my impatience. I have never forgotten those days in Paris. It is most cruel that you should be leaving London to-morrow. However, before very long, and perhaps sooner than you think, I shall have the joy of beholding once more the lady whose image has ever reigned supreme in my heart.*
>
> *Believe, chère Madame, all the assurances of my most devoted and unaltered sentiments—*
>
> *Armand de la Rochefour.*

Poirot handed the letter back to Halliday with a bow.

"I fancy, Monsieur, that you did not know that your daughter intended renewing her acquaintance with the Count de la Rochefour?"

"It came as a thunderbolt to me. I found this letter in my daughter's handbag. As you probably know, Monsieur Poirot, this so-called Count is an adventurer of the worst type."

Poirot nodded.

"But I want to know how you knew of the existence of this letter?"

My friend smiled. "Monsieur, I did not. But to track footmarks and recognize cigarette ash is not sufficient for a detective. He must also be a good psychologist! I knew that you disliked and mistrusted your son-in-law. He benefits by your daughter's death; the maid's description of the mysterious man bears a sufficient resemblance to him. Yet you are not keen on his track! Why? Surely because your suspicions lie in another direction. Therefore you were keeping something back."

"You're right, Monsieur Poirot. I was sure of Rupert's guilt until I found this letter. It unsettled me horribly."

"Yes. The Count says, 'Before very long, and perhaps sooner than you think.' Obviously he would not want to wait until you should get wind of his reappearance. Was it he who travelled down from London by the 12:14, and came along the corridor to your daughter's compartment? The Count de la Rochefour is also, if I remember rightly, tall and dark?"

The millionaire nodded.

"Well, Monsieur, I will wish you good day. Scotland Yard has, I presume, a list of the jewels?"

"Yes, I believe Inspector Japp is here now if you would like to see him."

Japp was an old friend of ours, and greeted Poirot with a sort of affectionate contempt.

"And how are you, Moosior? No bad feeling between us, though we *have* got our different ways of looking at things. How are the 'little grey cells,' eh? Going strong?"

Poirot beamed upon him. "They function, my good Japp; assuredly they function!"

"Then that's all right. Think it was the Hon. Rupert, or a crook? We're keeping an eye on all the regular places, of course. We shall know if the shiners are disposed of, and of course whoever did it isn't going to keep them to admire their sparkle. Not likely! I'm trying to find out where Rupert Carstairs was yesterday. Seems a bit of a mystery about it. I've got a man watching him."

"A great precaution, but perhaps a day late," suggested Poirot gently.

"You always will have your joke, Mr. Poirot. Well, I'm off to Paddington. Bristol, Weston, Taunton — that's my beat. So long."

"You will come round and see me this evening, and tell me the result?"

"Sure thing, if I'm back."

"The good inspector believes in matter in motion," murmured Poirot as our friend departed. "He travels; he measures footprints; he collects mud and cigarette ash! He is extremely busy! He is zealous beyond words! And if I mentioned psychology to him, do you know what he would do, my friend? He would smile! He would say to himself: 'Poor old Poirot! He ages! He grows senile!' Japp is the 'younger generation knocking on the door,' and *ma foi!* They are so busy knocking that they do not notice that the door is open!"

"And what are you going to do?"

"As we have *carte blanche*, I shall expend threepence in ringing up the Ritz — where you may have noticed our Count is staying. After that, as my feet are a little damp, and I have sneezed twice, I shall return to my rooms and make myself a *tisane* over the spirit-lamp."

## IV.

I did not see Poirot again until the following morning. I found him placidly finishing his breakfast.

"Well?" I inquired eagerly. "What has happened?"

"Nothing."

"But Japp?"

"I have not seen him."

"The Count?"

"He left the Ritz the day before yesterday."

"The day of the murder?"

"Yes."

"Then that settles it! Rupert Carstairs is cleared."

"Because the Count de la Rochefour has left the Ritz? You go too fast, my friend."

"Anyway, he must be followed — arrested! But what could be his motive?"

"Twenty thousand pounds' worth of jewellery is a very good motive for anyone. No, the question to my mind is: why kill her? Why not simply steal the jewels? She would not prosecute."

"Why not?"

"Because she is a woman, *mon ami*. She once loved this man — therefore she would suffer her loss in silence. And the Count, who is an extremely good psychologist where women are concerned — hence his successes — would know that perfectly well! On the other hand, if Rupert Carrington killed her, why take the jewels which would incriminate him fatally?"

"As a blind."

"Perhaps you are right, my friend. Ah, here is Japp; I recognize his knock."

The inspector was beaming good-humouredly.

"Morning, Moosior. Only just got back. I've done some good work. And you?"

"Me, I have arranged my ideas," replied Poirot placidly.

Japp laughed heartily.

"Old chap's getting on in years," he observed beneath his breath to me. "That won't do for us young folk," he said aloud.

"*Quel dommage!*"

"Well, do you want to hear what I've done?"

"You permit me to make a guess? You have found the knife with which the crime was committed, by the side of the line between Weston and Taunton, and you have interviewed the paperboy who spoke to Mrs. Carstairs at Weston!"

Japp's jaw fell. "How on earth did you know? Don't tell me it was those almighty 'little grey cells' of yours!"

"I am glad you admit for once that they are *almighty!* Tell me, did she give the paperboy a shilling for himself?"

"No, it was half a crown!" Japp had recovered his temper, and grinned. "Pretty extravagant, these rich Americans!"

"And in consequence the boy did not forget her?"

"Not he. Half-crowns don't come his way every day. She hailed him and bought two magazines. One had a picture of a girl in blue on the cover. 'That'll match me,' she said. Oh, he remembered her perfectly. Well, that was enough for me. By the doctor's evidence, the crime *must* have been committed before Taunton. I guessed they'd throw the knife away at once, and I walked down the line looking for it; and sure enough, there it was. I made inquiries at Taunton about our man, but of course it's a big station, and it wasn't likely they'd notice him. He probably got back to London by a later train."

Poirot nodded. "Very likely."

"But I found another bit of news when I got back. They're passing the jewels, all right! That large emerald was pawned last night — by one of the regular lot. Who do you think it was?"

"I don't know — except that he was a short man."

Japp stared. "Well, you're right there. He's short enough. It was Red Narky."

"Who is Red Narky?" I asked.

"A particularly sharp jewel thief, Sir. And not one to stick at murder. Usually works with a woman — Gracie Kidd; but she doesn't seem to be in it this time — unless she's got off to Holland with the rest of the swag."

"You've arrested Narky?"

"Sure thing. But mind you, it's the other man we want — the man who went down with Mrs. Carstairs in the train. He was the one who planned the job, right enough. But Narky won't squeal on a pal."

I noticed Poirot's eyes had become very green.

"I think," he said gently, "that I can find Narky's pal for you, all right."

"One of your little ideas, eh?" Japp eyed Poirot sharply. "Wonderful how you manage to deliver the goods sometimes, at your age and all. Devil's own luck, of course."

"Perhaps, perhaps," murmured my friend. "Hastings, my hat. And the brush. So! My galoshes, if it still rains! We must not undo the good work of that *tisane. Au revoir*, Japp!"

"Good luck to you, Moosior."

Poirot hailed the first taxi we met, and directed the driver to Park Lane.

When we drew up before Halliday's house, he skipped out nimbly, paid the driver and rang the bell. To the footman who opened the door he made a request in a low voice, and we were immediately taken upstairs. We went up to the top of the house, and were shown into a small neat bed-room.

Poirot's eyes roved round the room and fastened themselves on a small black trunk. He knelt in front of it, scrutinized the labels on it, and took a small twist of wire from his pocket.

"Ask Mr. Halliday if he will be so kind as to mount to me here," he said over his shoulder to the footman.

The man departed, and Poirot gently coaxed the lock of the trunk with a practised hand. In a few minutes the lock gave, and he raised the lid of the trunk. Swiftly he began rummaging among the clothes it contained, flinging them out on the floor.

There was a heavy step on the stairs, and Halliday entered the room. "What in hell are you doing here?" he demanded, staring.

"I was looking, Monsieur, for *this*." Poirot withdrew from the trunk a coat and skirt of bright-blue frieze, and a small toque of white fox fur.

"What are you doing with my trunk?" I turned to see that the maid, Jane Mason, had entered the room.

"If you will just shut the door, Hastings. Thank you. Yes, and stand with your back against it. Now, Mr. Halliday, let me introduce you to Gracie Kidd, otherwise Jane Mason, who will shortly rejoin her accomplice, Red Narky, under the kind escort of Japp."

## V.

"It was of the most simple." Poirot waved a deprecating hand, then helped himself to more caviar. It is not every day that one lunches with a millionaire.

"It was the maid's insistence on the clothes that her mistress was wearing that first struck me. Why was she so anxious that our attention should be directed to them? I reflected that we had only the maid's word for the mysterious man in the carriage at Bristol. As far as the doctor's evidence went, Mrs. Carstairs might easily have been murdered *before* reaching Bristol. But if so, then the maid must be an accomplice. And if she were an accomplice, she would not wish this point to rest on her evidence alone. The clothes Mrs. Carstairs was wearing were of a striking nature. A maid usually has a good deal of choice as to what her mistress shall wear. Now if, after Bristol, anyone saw a lady in a bright blue coat and skirt, and a fur toque, he will be quite ready to swear he had seen Mrs. Carstairs.

"I began to reconstruct. The maid would provide herself with duplicate clothes. She and her accomplice chloroform and stab Mrs. Carrington between London and Bristol, probably taking advantage of a tunnel. Her body is rolled under the seat; and the maid takes her place. At Weston she must make herself noticed. How? In all probability, a newspaper boy will be selected. She will insure his remembering her by giving him a large tip. She also drew his attention to the colour of her dress by a remark about one of the magazines. After leaving Weston, she throws the knife out of the window to mark the place where the crime presumeably occurred, and changes her clothes, or buttons a long mackintosh over them. At Taunton she leaves the train and returns to Bristol as soon as possible, where her accomplice has duly left the luggage in the cloakroom. He hands over the ticket and himself returns to London. She waits on the platform, carrying out her rôle, goes to a hotel for the night and returns to town in the morning, exactly as she said.

"When Japp returned from his expedition, he confirmed all my deductions. He also told me that a well-known crook was passing the jewels. I knew that whoever it was would be the exact opposite of the man Jane Mason described. When I heard that it was Red Narky, who always worked with Gracie Kidd—well, I knew just where to find her."

"And the Count?"

"The more I thought of it, the more I was convinced that he had nothing to do with it. That gentleman is much too careful of his own skin to risk murder. It would be out of keeping with his character."

"Well, Monsieur Poirot," said Halliday, "I owe you a big debt. And the cheque I write after lunch won't go near to settling it. You're the goods all right!"

Poirot smiled modestly, and murmured to me: "The good Japp, he shall get the official credit, all right; but though he has got his 'Kidd,' *ma foi,* I think that I, as the Americans say, have 'got his goat!'"

# THE ADVENTURE OF "THE WESTERN STAR."

"The Adventure of 'The Western Star'" was first published in *The Sketch* on April 11, 1923.

I was standing at the window of Poirot's rooms looking out idly on the street below.

"That's queer," I ejaculated suddenly beneath my breath.

"What is, *mon ami?*" asked Poirot placidly, from the depths of his comfortable chair.

"Deduce, Poirot, from the following facts! Here is a young lady, richly dressed — fashionable hat, magnificent furs. She is coming along slowly, looking up at the houses as she goes. Unknown to her, she is being shadowed by three men and a middle-aged woman. They have just been joined by an errand boy who points after the girl, gesticulating as he does so. What drama is this being played? Is the girl a crook, and are the shadows detectives preparing to arrest her? Or are they the scoundrels, and are they plotting to attack an innocent victim? What does the great detective say?"

"The great detective, *mon ami*, chooses, as ever, the simplest course. He rises to see for himself." And my friend joined me at the window.

In a minute he gave vent to an amused chuckle.

"As usual, your facts are tinged with your incurable romanticism. This is Miss Mary Marvell, the film star. She is being followed by a bevy of admirers who have recognized her. And, *en passant*, my dear Hastings, she is quite aware of the fact!"

I laughed.

"So all is explained! But you get no marks for that, Poirot. It was a mere matter of recognition."

"*En verite!* And how many times have you seen Mary Marvell on the screen, *mon cher?*"

I thought.

"About a dozen times perhaps."

"And I—once! Yet *I* recognize her, and *you* do not."

"She looks so different," I replied rather feebly.

"Ah, *sacré!*" cried Poirot. "Is it that you expect her to promenade herself in the streets of London in a cowboy hat, or with bare feet and a bunch of curls, as an Irish colleen? Always with you it is the nonessentials! Remember the case of the dancer, Valerie Saintclair."

I shrugged my shoulders, slightly annoyed.

"But console yourself, *mon ami*," said Poirot, calming down. "All cannot be as Hercule Poirot! I know it well."

"You really have the best opinion of yourself of anyone I ever knew!" I cried, divided between amusement and annoyance.

"What will you? When one is unique, one knows it! And others share that opinion—even, if I mistake it not, Miss Mary Marvell."

"What?"

"Without doubt. She is coming here."

"How do you make that out?"

"Very simply. This street, it is not aristocratic, *mon ami!* In it there is no fashionable doctor, no fashionable dentist—still less is there a fashionable milliner! But there *is* a fashionable detective. *Si*, my friend, it is true—I am become the mode, the *dernier cri!* One says to another: '*Comment?* You have lost your gold pencil case? You must go to the little Belgian. He is too marvellous! Everyone goes! *Courez!*' And they arrive! In flocks, *mon ami!* With problems of the most foolish!"

A bell rang below.

"What did I tell you? That is Miss Marvell."

As usual, Poirot was right. After a short interval, the American film star was ushered in, and we rose to our feet.

Mary Marvell was undoubtedly one of the most popular actresses on the screen. She had only lately arrived in England in company with her husband, Gregory B. Rolf, also a film actor. Their marriage had taken place about a year ago in the States, and this was their first visit to England. They had been given a great reception. Everyone was prepared to go mad over Mary Marvell, her wonderful clothes, her furs, her jewels—above all one jewel, the great diamond which had been nicknamed, to match its owner, "The Western Star." Much, true and untrue, had been written about this famous stone, which was reported to be insured for the enormous sum of fifty thousand pounds.

All these details passed rapidly through my mind as I joined with Poirot in greeting our fair client.

Miss Marvell was small and slender, very fair and girlish looking, with the wide innocent blue eyes of a child.

Poirot drew forward a chair for her, and she commenced talking at once.

"You will probably think me very foolish, Monsieur Poirot, but Lord Cronshaw was telling me last night how wonderfully you cleared up the mystery of his nephew's death, and I felt that I just must have your advice. I dare say it's only a silly hoax — Gregory says so — but it's just worrying me to death."

She paused for breath. Poirot beamed encouragement. "Proceed, Madame. You comprehend, I am still in the dark."

"It's these letters." Miss Marvell unclasped her handbag, and drew out three envelopes which she handed to Poirot.

The latter scrutinized them closely.

"Cheap paper — the name and address carefully printed. Let us see the inside."

He drew out the enclosure. I had joined him, and was leaning over his shoulder. The writing consisted of a single sentence, carefully printed like the envelope. It ran as follows —

> *The great diamond which is the left eye of the god must return whence it came.*

The second letter was couched in precisely the same terms; but the third was more explicit:

> *You have been warned. You have not obeyed. Now the diamond will be taken from you. At the full of the moon, the two diamonds which are the left and right eye of the god shall return. So it is written.*

"The first letter I treated as a joke," explained Miss Marvell. "When I got the second, I began to wonder. The third one came yesterday, and it seemed to me that, after all, the matter might be more serious than I had imagined."

"I see they did not come by post, these letters."

"No; they were left by hand — by a *Chinaman*. That is what frightens me."

"Why?"

"Because it was from a Chink in San Francisco that Gregory bought the stone three years ago."

"I see, Madame, that you believe the diamond referred to to be —"

" 'The Western Star,' " finished Miss Marvell. "That's so. At the time, Gregory remembers that there was some story attached to the stone, but the Chink wasn't handing out any information. Gregory says he seemed just scared to death, and in a mortal hurry to get rid of the thing. He only asked about a tenth of its value. It was Greg's wedding present to me."

Poirot nodded thoughtfully.

"The story seems of an almost unbelievable romanticism. And yet — who knows? I pray of you, Hastings, hand me my little almanack."

I complied.

"*Voyons,*" said Poirot, turning the leaves. "When is the date of the full moon? Ah, Friday next. That is, in three days' time. *Eh bien*, Madame, you seek my advice — I give it to you. This *belle histoire* may be a hoax — but it may not! Therefore I counsel you to place the diamond in my keeping until after Friday next. Then we can take what steps we please."

A slight cloud passed over the actress's face, and she replied constrainedly: "I'm afraid that's impossible."

"You have it with you — *hein?*" Poirot was watching her narrowly.

The girl hesitated a moment, then slipped her hand into the bosom of her gown, drawing out a long thin chain. She leaned forward, unclosing her hand. In the palm, a stone of white fire, exquisitely set in platinum, lay and winked at us solemnly.

Poirot drew in his breath with a long hiss.

"*Épatant!*" he murmured. "You permit, Madame?" He took the jewel in his own hand and scrutinized it keenly, then restored it to her with a little bow. "A magnificent stone — without a flaw. Ah, *cent tonnerres!* And you carry it about with you, *comme ça!*"

"No — no, I'm very careful really, Monsieur Poirot. As a rule it's locked up in my jewel-case, and left in the hotel safe deposit. We're staying at the Magnificent, you know. I just brought it along to-day for you to see."

"And you will leave it with me, *n'est-ce pas?* You will be advised by Papa Poirot?"

"Well, you see, it's this way, Monsieur Poirot. On Friday we're going down to Yardly Chase to spend a few days with Lord and Lady Yardly."

Her words awoke a vague echo of remembrance in my mind. Some gossip — what was it now? A few years ago Lord and Lady Yardly had paid a visit to the States; rumour had it that his lordship had rather gone the pace out there with the assistance of some lady friends — but surely there was something more, more gossip which coupled Lady Yardly's name with that of a "movie" star in California — why! it came to me in a flash — of course it was none other than Gregory B. Rolf.

"I'll let you into a little secret, Monsieur Poirot," Miss Marvell was continuing. "We've got a deal on with Lord Yardly. There's some chance of our arranging to film a play down there in his ancestral pile."

"At Yardly Chase?" I cried,

interested. "Why, it's one of the show places of England."

Miss Marvell nodded.

"I guess it's the real old feudal stuff all right. But he wants a pretty stiff price, and of course I don't know yet whether the deal will go through, but Greg and I always like to combine business with pleasure."

"But — I demand pardon if I am dense, Madame — surely it is possible to visit Yardly Chase without taking the diamond with you?"

A shrewd, hard look came into Miss Marvell's eyes which belied their child-like appearance. She looked suddenly a good deal older.

"I want to wear it down there."

"Surely," I said suddenly, "there are some very famous jewels in the Yardly collection, a large diamond amongst them?"

"That's so," said Miss Marvell briefly.

I heard Poirot murmur beneath his breath: "Ah, *c'est comme ça!*" Then he said aloud, with his usual uncanny luck in hitting the bull's-eye (he dignifies it by the name of psychology): "Then you are without doubt already acquainted with Lady Yardly, or perhaps your husband is?"

"Gregory knew her when she was out West three years ago," said Miss Marvell. She hesitated a moment, and then added abruptly: "Do either of you ever see *Society Gossip?*"

We both pleaded guilty rather shamefacedly.

"I ask because in this week's number there is an article on famous jewels, and it's really very curious —" She broke off.

I rose, went to the table at the other side of the room and returned with the paper in question in my hand. She took it from me, found the article, and began to read aloud:

*Amongst other famous stones may be included The Star of the East, a diamond in the possession of the Yardly family. An ancestor of the present Lord Yardly brought it back with him from China, and a romantic story is said to attach to it. According to this, the stone was once the right eye of a temple god. Another diamond, exactly similar in form and size, formed the left eye, and the story goes that this jewel, too, would in course of time be stolen. 'One eye shall go West, the other East, till they shall meet once more. Then, in triumph shall they return to the god.' It is a curious coincidence that there is at the present time a stone corresponding closely in description with this one, and known as 'The Star of the West,' or 'The Western Star.' It is the property of the celebrated film star, Miss Mary Marvell. A comparison of the two stones would be interesting.*

She stopped.

"*Épatant!*" murmured Poirot. "Without doubt a romance of the first water." He turned to Mary Marvell. "And you are not afraid, Madame? You have no superstitious terrors? You do not fear to introduce these two Siamese twins to each other lest a Chinaman should appear and, hey presto! whisk them both back to China?"

His tone was mocking, but I fancied that an undercurrent of seriousness lay beneath it.

"I don't believe that Lady Yardly's diamond is anything like as good as mine," said Miss Marvell. "Anyway, I'm going to see."

What more Poirot would have said I do not know, for at that moment the door flew open, and a splendid-looking man strode into the room. From his crisply curling black head, to the tips of his patent leather boots, he was a hero fit for romance.

"I said I'd call round for you, Mary," said Gregory Rolf, "and here I am. Well, what does Monsieur Poirot say to our little problem? Just one big hoax — same as I do?"

Poirot smiled up at the big actor. They made a ridiculous contrast.

"Hoax or no hoax, Mr. Rolf," he said dryly, "I have advised Madame your wife not to take the jewel with her to Yardly Chase on Friday."

"I' m with you there, Sir. I've already said so to Mary. But there! She's a woman through and through, and I guess she can't bear to think of another woman outshining her in the jewel line."

"What nonsense, Gregory!" said Mary Marvell sharply. But she flushed angrily.

Poirot shrugged his shoulders.

"Madame, I have advised. I can do no more. *C'est fini.*"

He bowed them both to the door.

"Ah! *Là, là*," he observed, returning. "*Histoire des femmes!* The good husband, he hit the nail — *tout de même*, but he was not tactful! Assuredly not."

I imparted to him my vague remembrances, and he nodded vigorously.

"So I thought. All the same, there is something curious underneath all this. With your permission, *mon ami*, I will take the air. Await my return, I beg of you, I shall not be long."

I was half-asleep in my chair when the landlady tapped on the door, and put her head in.

"It's another lady to see Mr. Poirot, Sir. I've told her he was out, but she says as how she'll wait, seeing as she's come up from the country."

"Oh, show her in here, Mrs. Murchinson. Perhaps I can do something for her."

In another moment the lady had been ushered in. My heart gave a leap as I recognized her. Lady Yardly's portrait had figured too often in the Society papers to allow her to remain unknown.

"Do sit down, Lady Yardly," I said, drawing forward a chair. "My friend, Poirot, is out, but I know for a fact that he'll be back very shortly."

She thanked me and sat down. A very different type, this, from Miss

Mary Marvell. Tall, dark, with flashing eyes, and a pale proud face — yet something wistful in the curves of the mouth.

I felt a desire to rise to the occasion. Why not? In Poirot's presence I have frequently felt a difficulty — I do not appear at my best. And yet there is no doubt that I, too, possess the deductive sense in a marked degree. I leant forward on a sudden impulse.

"Lady Yardly," I said, "I know why you have come here. You have received blackmailing letters about the diamond."

There was no doubt as to my bolt having shot home. She stared at me open-mouthed, all colour banished from her cheeks.

"You know?" she gasped. "How?"

I smiled. "By a perfectly logical process. If Miss Marvell has had warning letters —"

"Miss Marvell? She has been here?"

"She has just left. As I was saying, if she, as the holder of one of the twin diamonds, has received a mysterious series of warnings, you, as the holder of the other stone, must necessarily have done the same. You see how simple it is? I am right, then — you have received these strange communications also?"

For a moment she hesitated, as though in doubt whether to trust me or not; then she bowed her head in assent with a little smile.

"That is so," she acknowledged.

"Were yours, too, left by hand — by a Chinaman?"

"No, they came by post. But tell me, has Miss Marvell undergone the same experience, then?"

I recounted to her the events of the morning. She listened attentively.

"It all fits in. My letters are the duplicate of hers. It is true that they came by post, but there is a curious perfume impregnating them — something in the nature of joss-stick — that at once suggested the East to me. What does it all mean?"

I shook my head.

"That is what we must find out. You have the letters with you? We might learn something from the postmarks."

"Unfortunately I destroyed them. You understand, at the time I regarded it as some foolish joke. Can it be true that some Chinese gang are really trying to recover the diamonds? It seems too incredible."

We went over the facts again and again, but could get no further towards the elucidation of the mystery. At last Lady Yardly rose.

"I really don't think I need wait for Monsieur Poirot. You can tell him all this, can't you? Thank you so much Mr. —"

She hesitated, her hand outstretched.

"Captain Hastings."

"Of course! How stupid of me. You're a friend of the Cavendishes, aren't you? It was Mary Cavendish who sent me to Monsieur Poirot."

When my friend returned, I enjoyed telling him the tale of what had occurred during his absence. He cross-questioned me rather sharply over the details of our conversation and I could read between the lines that he was not best pleased to have been absent. I also fancied that the dear old fellow was just the least inclined to be jealous. It had become rather a pose with him to consistently belittle my abilities, and I think he was chagrined at finding no loophole for criticism. I was secretly rather pleased with myself, though I tried to conceal the fact for fear of irritating him. In spite of his idiosyncrasies, I was deeply attached to my quaint little friend.

"*Bien!*" he said at length, with a curious look on his face. "The plot develops. Pass me, I pray you, that *Peerage* on the top shelf there."

He turned the leaves. "Ah, here we are. Yardly ... tenth Viscount—born ... educated ... *tout ça n'a pas d'importance* ... married 1907 the Hon. Maude Stopperton, fourth daughter of third Baron Cotteril ... um, um, um, has iss. two daughters, born 1908, 1910; served South African war, et cetera ... clubs ... residences ...' *Voilà*, that does not tell us much. But to-morrow morning we see this milor'!"

"What?"

"Yes. I telegraphed him."

"I thought you had washed your hands of the case?"

"I am not acting for Miss Marvell since she refuses to be guided by my advice. What I do now is for my own satisfaction — the satisfaction of Hercule Poirot! Decidedly, I must have a finger in this pie."

"And you calmly wire Lord Yardly to dash up to town just to suit your convenience? He won't be pleased."

"*Au contraire*, if I preserve for him his family diamond, he ought to be very grateful."

"Then you really think there is any chance of it being stolen?" I asked eagerly.

"Almost a certainty," replied Poirot placidly. "Everything points that way."

"But how —"

Poirot stopped my eager questions with an airy gesture of the hand.

"Not now, I pray you. Let us not confuse the mind. And observe that *Peerage* — how you have replaced him. See you not that the tallest books go in the top shelf, the next tallest in the row beneath, and so on. Thus we have order — *method* — which, as I have often told you, Hastings —"

"Exactly," I said hastily, and put the offending volume in its proper place.

Lord Yardly turned out to be a cheery, loud-voiced sportsman with a rather red face, but with a good-humoured bonhomie about him that was distinctly attractive and made up for any lack of mentality.

"Extraordinary business this, Monsieur Poirot. Can't make head or tail of it. Seems my wife's been getting odd kind of letters, and that Miss Marvell's had 'em too. What does it all mean?"

Poirot handed him the copy of *Society Gossip*.

"First, Milor', I would ask you if these facts are substantially correct?"

The peer took it. His face darkened with anger as he read.

"Damned nonsense!" he spluttered. "There's never been any romantic story attaching to the diamond. It came from India originally, I believe. I never heard of all this Chinese god stuff."

"Still, the stone is known as 'The Star of the East,' Milor'?"

"Well, what if it is?" demanded the gentleman wrathfully.

Poirot smiled a little, but made no direct reply.

"What I would ask you to do, Milor', is to place yourself in my hands. If you do so unreservedly, I have great hopes of averting the catastrophe."

"Then you think there's actually something in these wild-cat tales?"

"Will you do as I ask you?"

"Of course I will, but —"

"*Bien!* Then permit that I ask you a few questions. This affair of Yardly Chase, is it, as you say, all fixed up between you and Mr. Rolf?"

"Oh, he told you about it, did he? No, there's nothing settled." He hesitated, the brick-red colour of his face deepening. "Might as well get the thing straight. I've made rather an ass of myself in many ways, Monsieur Poirot — and I'm head over ears in debt — but I want to pull up. I'm fond of the kids, and I want to straighten things up, and be able to live on at the old place. Gregory Rolf is offering me big money — enough to set me on my feet again. I don't want to do it — I hate the thought of all that crowd play-acting round the Chase — but I may have to, unless —"

He broke off.

Poirot eyed him keenly. "You have, then, another string to your bow? Permit that I make a guess? It is to sell The Star of the East?"

Lord Yardly nodded. "That's it. It's been in the family for some generations, but it's not entailed. Still, it's not the easiest thing in the world to find a purchaser. Hoffberg, the Hatton Garden man, is on the lookout for a likely customer, but he'll have to find one soon, or it's a washout."

"One more question, *permettez*. Milady your wife, which plan does she approve?"

"Oh, she's bitterly opposed to my selling the jewel. You know what women are. She's all for this film stunt."

"I comprehend," said Poirot. He remained a moment or so in thought, then rose briskly to his feet. "You return to Yardly Chase at once? *Bien!* Say no word to anyone — to *anyone*, mind — but expect us there this evening. We will arrive shortly after five."

"All right, but I don't see —"

"*Ça n'a pas d'importance*," said Poirot kindly. "You will that I preserve for you your diamond, *n'est-ce pas?*"

"Yes, but —"

"Then do as I say."

A sadly bewildered nobleman left the room.

It was half past five when we arrived at Yardly Chase, and followed the dignified butler to the old panelled hall with its fire of blazing logs. A pretty picture met our eyes: Lady Yardly and her two children, the mother's proud dark head bent down over the two fair ones. Lord Yardly stood nearby, smiling down on them.

"Monsieur Poirot and Captain Hastings," announced the butler.

Lady Yardly looked up with a start; her husband came forward uncertainly, his eyes seeking instruction from Poirot.

The little man was equal to the occasion.

"All my excuses! It is that I investigate still this affair of Miss Marvell's. She comes to you on Friday, does she not? I make a little tour first to make sure that all is secure. Also I wanted to ask of Milady if she recollected at all the postmarks on the letters she received."

Lady Yardly shook her head regretfully. "I'm afraid I don't. It's stupid of me. But, you see, I never dreamt of taking them seriously."

"You'll stay the night?" said Lord Yardly.

"Oh, Milor', I fear to incommode you. We have left our bags at the inn."

"That's all right." Lord Yardly had his cue. "We'll send down for them. No, no — no trouble, I assure you."

Poirot permitted himself to be persuaded, and sitting down by Lady Yardly, began to make friends with the children. In a short time they were all romping together, and had dragged me into the game.

"*Vous êtes bonne mère*, Milady," said Poirot, with a gallant little bow, as the children were removed reluctantly by a stern nurse.

Lady Yardly smoothed her ruffled hair.

"I adore them," she said with a little catch in her voice.

"And they you — with reason!" Poirot bowed again.

A dressing-gong sounded, and we rose to go up to our rooms. At that moment the butler emerged with a telegram on a salver which he handed to Lord Yardly. The latter tore it open with a brief word of apology. As he read it he stiffened visibly.

With an ejaculation he handed it to his wife. Then he glanced at my friend. "Just a minute. Monsieur Poirot, I feel you ought to know about this. It's from Hoffberg. He thinks he's found a customer for the diamond — an American, sailing for the States to-morrow. They're sending down a chap tonight to vet the stone. By Jove, though, if this goes through —" Words failed him.

Lady Yardly had turned away. She still held the telegram in her hand.

"I wish you wouldn't sell it, George," she said, in a low voice. "It's been in the family so long." She waited, as though for a reply, but when none came her face hardened. She shrugged her shoulders. "I must go and dress. I suppose I had better display 'the goods.'" She turned to Poirot with a slight grimace. "It's one of the most hideous necklaces that was ever designed! George has always promised to have the stones reset for me, but it's never been done."

She left the room.

Half an hour later, we three were assembled in the great drawing room awaiting the lady. It was already a few minutes past the dinner-hour.

Suddenly there was a low rustle, and Lady Yardly appeared framed in the doorway, a radiant figure in a long white shimmering dress. Round the column of her neck was a rivulet of fire. She stood there with one hand just touching the necklace.

"Behold the sacrifice," she said gaily. Her ill-humour seemed to have vanished. "Wait while I turn the big light on and you shall feast your eyes on the ugliest necklace in England."

The switches were just outside the door. As she stretched out her hand to them, the incredible thing happened. Suddenly, without any warning, every light was extinguished, the door banged, and from the other side of it came a long-drawn piercing woman's scream.

"My God!" cried Lord Yardly. "That was Maude's voice! What has happened?"

We rushed blindly for the door, cannoning into each other in the darkness. It was some minutes before we could find it. What a sight met our eyes! Lady Yardly lay senseless on the marble floor, a crimson mark on her white throat where the necklace had been wrenched from her neck.

As we bent over her, uncertain for the moment whether she was dead or alive, her eyelids opened.

"The Chinaman," she whispered painfully. "The Chinaman — the side door."

Lord Yardly sprang up with an oath. I accompanied him, my heart beating wildly. The Chinaman again! The side door in question was a small one in the angle of the wall, not more than a dozen yards from the scene of the tragedy. As we reached it, I gave a cry. There, just short of the threshold, lay the glittering necklace, evidently dropped by the thief in the panic of his flight.

I swooped joyously down on it. Then I uttered another cry which Lord Yardly echoed. For in the middle of the necklace was a great gap. The Star of the East was missing!

"That settles it," I breathed. "These were no ordinary thieves. This one stone was all they wanted."

"But how did the fellow get in?"

"Through this door."

"But it's always locked."

I shook my head. "It's not locked now. See!" I pulled it open as I spoke.

As I did so something fluttered to the ground. I picked it up. It was a piece of silk, and the embroidery was unmistakable. It had been torn from a Chinaman's robe.

"In his haste it caught in the door," I explained. "Come, hurry. He cannot have gone far as yet."

But in vain we hunted and searched. In the pitch darkness of the night, the thief had found it easy to make his getaway. We returned reluctantly, and Lord Yardly sent off one of the footmen post-haste to fetch the police.

Lady Yardly, aptly ministered to by Poirot, who is as good as a woman in these matters, was soon sufficiently recovered to be able to tell her story.

"I was just going to turn on the other light," she said, "when a man sprang on me from behind. He tore my necklace from my neck with such force that I fell headlong to the floor. As I fell I saw him disappearing through the side door. Then I realized by the pigtail and the embroidered robe that he was a Chinaman." She stopped with a shudder.

The butler reappeared. He spoke in a low voice to Lord Yardly.

"A gentleman from Mr. Hoffberg's, m'lord. He says you expect him."

"Good heavens!" cried the distracted nobleman. "I must see him, I suppose. No, not here, Mullings, in the library."

I drew Poirot aside.

"Look here, my dear fellow, hadn't we better get back to London?"

"You think so, Hastings? Why?"

"Well"— I coughed delicately — "things haven't gone very well, have they? I mean, you tell Lord Yardly to place himself in your hands and all will be well — and then, hey, presto! — the diamond vanishes from under your very nose!"

"True," said Poirot, rather crestfallen. "It was not one of my most striking triumphs."

This way of describing events almost caused me to smile, but I stuck to my guns.

"So, having — pardon the expression — rather made a mess of things, don't you think it would be more graceful to leave immediately?"

"And the dinner — the without-doubt-excellent dinner — that the *chef* of Lord Yardly has prepared?"

"Oh, what's dinner?" I said impatiently.

Poirot held up his hands in horror.

"*Mon Dieu!* It is that in this country you treat the affairs gastronomic with a criminal indifference."

"There's another reason why we should get back to London as soon as possible," I continued.

"What is that, my friend?"

"The other diamond," I said, lowering my voice. "Miss Marvell's."

"*Eh bien*, what of it?"

"Don't you see?" His unusual obtuseness annoyed me. What had happened to his usually keen wits? "They've got one, now they'll go for the other."

"*Tiens!*" cried Poirot, stepping back a pace and regarding me with admiration. "But your brain marches to a marvel, my friend! Figure to yourself that for the moment I had not thought of that! But there is plenty of time. The full of the moon, it is not until Friday."

I shook my head dubiously. The full of the moon theory left me entirely cold.

I had my way with Poirot, however, and we departed immediately, leaving behind us a note of explanation and apology for Lord Yardly.

My idea was to go at once to the Magnificent, and relate to Miss Marvell what had occurred, but Poirot vetoed the plan, and insisted that the morning would be time enough. I gave in rather grudgingly.

In the morning Poirot seemed strangely disinclined to stir out. I began to suspect that, having made a mistake to start with, he was singularly loath to proceed with the case. In answer to my persuasions, he pointed out, with admirable common sense, that as the details of the affair at Yardly Chase were already in the morning papers the Rolfs would know quite as much as we could tell them. I gave way unwillingly.

Events proved my forebodings to be justified. About two o'clock, the telephone rang. Poirot answered it. He listened for some moments, then with a brief "*Bien, j'y serai,*" he rang off, and turned to me.

"What do you think, *mon ami?*" He looked half ashamed, half excited. "The diamond of Miss Marvell, it has been stolen."

"What?" I cried, springing up. "And what about the 'full of the moon' now?"—Poirot hung his head—"When did this happen?"

"This morning, I understand."

I shook my head sadly. "If only you had listened to me. You see I was right."

"It appears so, *mon ami,*" said Poirot cautiously. "Appearances are deceptive, they say—but it certainly appears so."

As we hurried in a taxi to the Magnificent, I puzzled out the true inwardness of the scheme.

"That 'full of the moon' idea was clever. The whole point of it was to get us to concentrate on the Friday, and so be off our guard beforehand. It is a pity you did not realize that."

"*Ma foi!*" said Poirot airily, his nonchalance quite restored after its brief eclipse. "One cannot think of everything."

I felt sorry for him. He did so hate failure of any kind. "Cheer up," I said consolingly. "Better luck next time."

At the Magnificent, we were ushered at once into the manager's office. Gregory Rolf was there with two men from Scotland Yard. A pale-faced clerk sat opposite them.

Rolf nodded to us as we entered.

"We're getting to the bottom of it," he said. "But it's almost unbelievable. How the guy had the nerve I can't think."

A very few minutes sufficed to give us the facts. Mr. Rolf had gone out of the hotel at 11:15. At 11:30, a gentleman, so like him in appearance as to pass muster, entered the hotel and demanded the jewel case from the safe deposit. He duly signed the receipt, remarking carelessly as he did so: "Looks a bit different from my ordinary one, but I hurt my hand getting out of the taxi." The clerk merely smiled and remarked that he saw very little difference. "Rolf" laughed and said: "Well, don't run me in as a crook this time, anyway. I've been getting threatening letters from a Chinaman, and the worst of it is I look rather like a Chink myself— it's something about the eyes."

"I looked at him," said the clerk who was telling us this, "and I saw at once what he meant. The eyes slanted up at the corners like an Oriental's. I'd never noticed it before."

"Darn it all, man," roared Gregory Rolf, leaning forward. "do you notice it now?"

The man looked up at him and started.

"No, Sir," he said. "I can't say I do." And indeed there was nothing even remotely Oriental about the frank brown eyes that looked into ours.

The Scotland Yard man grunted. "Bold customer. Thought the eyes might be noticed, and took the bull by the horns to disarm suspicion. He must have watched you out of the hotel, Sir, and nipped in as soon as you were well away."

"What about the jewel-case?" I asked.

"It was found in the corridor of the hotel. Only one thing had been taken — 'The Western Star.'"

We stared at each other — the whole thing was so bizarre, so unreal.

Poirot hopped briskly to his feet. "I have not been of much use, I fear," he said regretfully. "Is it permitted to see Madame?"

"I guess she's prostrated with the shock," exclaimed Rolf.

"Then perhaps I might have a few words alone with you, Monsieur?"

"Certainly."

In about five minutes Poirot reappeared.

"Now, my friend," he said gaily—"to a post office. I have to send a telegram."

"To whom?"

"Lord Yardly." He discounted further inquiries by slipping his arm through mine. "Come, come, *mon ami*. I know all that you feel about this terrible business. I have not distinguished myself! You, in my place, might have distinguished yourself. *Bien!* All is admitted. Let us forget it and have lunch."

It was about four o'clock when we entered Poirot's rooms. A figure rose from a chair by the window. It was Lord Yardly. He looked haggard and distraught.

"I got your wire and came up at once. Look here, I've been round to Hoffberg, and they know nothing about that man of theirs last night, or the wire either. Do you think that —"

Poirot held up his hand.

"My excuses! I sent that wire, and hired the gentleman in question."

"*You?* But why? What?" the nobleman spluttered impotently.

"My little idea was to bring things to a head," explained Poirot placidly.

"Bring things to a head! Oh, my God!" cried Lord Yardly.

"And the ruse succeeded," said Poirot cheerfully. "Therefore, Milor', I have much pleasure in returning you—this!" With a dramatic gesture he produced a glittering object. It was a great diamond.

"The Star of the East," gasped Lord Yardly. "But I don't understand —"

"No?" said Poirot. "It makes no matter. Believe me, it was necessary for the diamond to be stolen. I promised you that it would be preserved to you, and I have kept my word. You must permit me to keep my little secret. Convey, I beg of you, the assurance of my deepest respect to Lady Yardly, and tell her how pleased I am to be able to restore her jewel to her. What *beau temps*, is it not? Good day, Milor'."

And smiling and talking, the amazing little man conducted the bewildered nobleman to the door. He returned gently rubbing his hands.

"Poirot," I said. "Am I quite demented?"

"No, *mon ami*, but you are, as always, in a mental fog."

"How did you get the diamond?"

"From Mr. Rolf."

"Rolf?"

"*Mais oui!* The warning letters, the Chinaman, the article in *Society Gossip*, all sprang from the ingenious brain of Mr. Rolf! The two diamonds, supposed to be so miraculously alike—bah! they did not exist. There was only *one* diamond, my friend! Originally in the Yardly collection, for three years it has been in the possession of Mr. Rolf. He stole it this morning with the assistance of a touch of grease paint at the corner of each eye! Ah, I must see him on the film. He is indeed an artist, *celui-lá!*"

"But why should he steal his own diamond?" I asked, puzzled.

"For many reasons. To begin with, Lady Yardly was getting restive."

"Lady Yardly?"

"You comprehend she was left much alone in California. Her husband was amusing himself elsewhere. Mr. Rolf was handsome, he had an air about him of romance. But *au fond*, he is very businesslike, *ce monsieur*! He made love to Lady Yardly, and then he blackmailed her. I taxed the lady with the truth the other night, and she admitted it. She swore that she had only been indiscreet, and I believe her. But, undoubtedly, Rolf had letters of hers that could be twisted to bear a different interpretation. Terrified by the threat of a divorce, and the prospect of being separated from her children, she agreed to all he wished. She had no money of her own, and she was forced to permit him to substitute a paste replica for the real stone. The coincidence of the date of the appearance of 'The Western Star' struck me at once.

All goes well. Lord Yardly prepares to range himself — to settle down. And then comes the menace of the possible sale of the diamond. The substitution will be discovered. Without doubt she writes off frantically to Gregory Rolf who has just arrived in England. He soothes her by promising to arrange all — and prepares for a double robbery. In this way he will quiet the lady, who might conceivably tell all to her husband (an affair which would not suit our blackmailer at all), he will have £50,000 insurance money — aha, you had forgotten that! — and he will still have the diamond! At this point I put my fingers in the pie. The arrival of a diamond expert is announced — Lady Yardly, as I felt sure she would, immediately arranges a robbery — and does it very well too!

"But Hercule Poirot, he sees nothing but facts. What happens in actuality? The lady switches off the light, bangs the door, throws the necklace down the passage, and screams. She has already wrenched out the diamond with pliers upstairs —"

"But we saw the necklace round her neck!" I objected.

"I demand pardon, my friend. Her hand concealed the part of it where the gap would have shown. To place a piece of silk in the door beforehand is child's play! Of course, as soon as Rolf read of the robbery, he arranged his own little comedy. And very well he played it!"

"What did you say to him?" I asked with lively curiosity.

"I said to him that Lady Yardly had told her husband all, that I was empowered to recover the jewel, and that if it were not immediately handed over proceedings would be taken. Also a few more little lies which occurred to me. He was as wax in my hands!"

I pondered the matter.

"It seems a little unfair on Mary Marvell. She has lost her diamond through no fault of her own."

"Bah!" said Poirot brutally. "She has a magnificent advertisement. That is all she cares for, that one! Now the other, she is different. *Bonne mere — trés femme!*"

"Yes," I said doubtfully, hardly sharing Poirot's views on femininity. "I suppose it was Rolf who sent her the duplicate letters."

"*Pas du tout*," said Poirot briskly. "She came by the advice of Mary Cavendish to seek my aid in her dilemma. Then she heard that Mary Marvell, whom she knew to be her enemy, had been here, and she changed her mind jumping at a pretext that you, my friend, offered her. A very few questions sufficed to show me that you told her of the letters, not she you! She jumped at the chance your words offered."

"I don't believe it," I cried, stung.

"*Si, si, mon ami*, it is a pity that you study not the psychology. She told you that the letters were destroyed? Oh, *là, là*, never does a woman destroy a letter if she can avoid it! Not even if it would be more prudent to do so!"

"It's all very well," I said, my anger rising, "but you've made a perfect fool of me! From beginning to end! No, it's all very well to try and explain it away afterwards. There really is a limit!"

"But you were so enjoying yourself, my friend, I had not the heart to shatter your illusions."

# THE TRAGEDY AT MARSDON MANOR.

"The Tragedy at Marsdon Manor" was first published in *The Sketch* on April 18, 1923.

I had been called away from town for a few days, and on my return found Poirot in the act of strapping up his small valise.

"*A la bonheur*, Hastings. I feared you would not have returned in time to accompany me."

"You are called away on a case, then?"

"Yes, though I am bound to admit that, on the face of it, the affair does not seem promising. The Northern Union Insurance Company have asked me to investigate the death of a Mr. Maltravers, who a few weeks ago insured his life with them for the large sum of fifty thousand pounds."

"Yes?" I said, much interested.

"There was, of course, the usual suicide clause in the policy. In the event of his committing suicide within a year the premiums would be forfeited. Mr. Maltravers was duly examined by the Company's own doctor, and although he was a man slightly past the prime of life was passed as being in quite sound health. However, on Wednesday last — the day before yesterday — the body of Mr. Maltravers was found in the grounds of his house in Essex,

Marsdon Manor, and the cause of his death is described as some kind of internal haemorrhage. That in itself would be nothing remarkable; but sinister rumours as to Mr. Maltravers' financial position have been in the air of late, and the Northern Union have ascertained beyond any possible doubt that the deceased gentleman stood upon the verge of bankruptcy. Now that alters matters considerably. Maltravers had a beautiful young wife, and it is suggested that he got together all the ready money he could for the purpose of paying the premiums on a life insurance for his wife's benefit, and then committed suicide. Such a thing is not uncommon. In any case, my friend Alfred Wright, who is a director of the Northern Union, has asked me to investigate the facts of the case; but, as I told him, I am not very hopeful of success. If the cause of the death had been heart failure, I should have been more sanguine. Heart failure may always be translated as the inability of the local 'G.P.' to discover what his patient really did die of; but a haemorrhage seems fairly definite. Still, we can but make some necessary inquiries. Five minutes to pack your bag, Hastings, and we will take a taxi to Liverpool Street."

About an hour later, we alighted from a Great Eastern train at the little station of Marsdon Leigh. Inquiries at the station yielded the information that Marsdon Manor was about a mile distant. Poirot decided to walk, and we betook ourselves along the main street.

"What is our plan of campaign?" I asked.

"First I will call upon the doctor. I have ascertained that there is only one doctor in Marsdon Leigh, Dr. Ralph Bernard. Ah, here we are at his house."

The house in question was a kind of superior cottage, standing back a little from the road. A brass plate on the gate bore the doctor's name and, passing up the path, we rang the bell.

We proved to be fortunate in our call. It was the doctor's consulting hour, and for the moment there were no patients waiting for him. Dr. Bernard was an elderly man, high-shouldered and stooping, with a pleasant vagueness of manner.

Poirot introduced himself and explained the purpose of our visit, adding that insurance companies were bound to investigate fully in a case of this kind.

"Of course, of course," said Dr. Bernard vaguely. "I suppose, as he was such a rich man, his life was insured for a big sum?"

"You consider him a rich man, doctor?"

The doctor looked rather surprised.

"Was he not? He kept two cars, you know, and Marsdon Manor is a pretty big place to keep up, although I believe he bought it very cheap."

"I understand that he had had considerable losses of late," said Poirot, watching the doctor narrowly.

The latter, however, merely shook his head sadly.

"Is that so? Indeed. It is fortunate for his wife, then, that there is this life insurance. A very beautiful and charming young creature, but terribly unstrung by this sad catastrophe. A mass of nerves, poor thing. I have tried to spare her all I can, but of course the shock was bound to be considerable."

"You had been attending Mr. Maltravers recently?"

"My dear Sir, I never attended him."

"What?"

"I understand Mr. Maltravers was a Christian Scientist — or something of that kind."

"But you examined the body?"

"Certainly. I was fetched by one of the under-gardeners."

"And the cause of death was clear?"

"Absolutely. There was blood on the lips, but most of the bleeding must have been internal."

"Was he still lying where he had been found?"

"Yes, the body had not been touched. He was lying at the edge of a small plantation. He had evidently been out shooting rooks; a small rook-rifle lay beside him. The haemorrhage must have occurred quite suddenly. Gastric ulcer, without a doubt."

"No question of his having been shot, eh?"

"My dear Sir!"

"I demand pardon," said Poirot humbly. "But, if my memory is not at fault, in the case of a recent murder, the doctor first gave a verdict of heart failure, altering it when the local constable pointed out that there was a bullet wound through the head."

"You will not find any bullet wounds on the body of Mr. Maltravers," said Dr. Bernard dryly. "Now gentlemen, if there is nothing further —"

We took the hint.

"Good morning, and many thanks to you, Doctor, for so kindly answering our questions. By the way, you saw no need for an autopsy?"

"Certainly not." The doctor became quite apoplectic. "The cause of death was clear, and in my profession we see no need to distress unduly the relatives of a dead patient."

And, turning, the doctor slammed the door sharply in our faces.

"And what do you think of Dr. Bernard, Hastings?" inquired Poirot, as we proceeded on our way to the Manor.

"Rather an old ass."

"Exactly. Your judgements of character are always profound, my friend."

I glanced at him uneasily, but he seemed perfectly serious. A twinkle, however, came into his eye, and he added slyly—

"That is to say, where there is no question of a beautiful woman!"

I looked at him coldly.

On our arrival at the manor house, the door was opened to us by a middle-aged parlourmaid. Poirot handed her his card, and a letter from the Insurance Company for Mrs. Maltravers. She showed us into a small morning room, and retired to tell her mistress. About ten minutes elapsed, and then the door opened, and a slender figure in widow's weeds stood upon the threshold.

"Monsieur Poirot?" she faltered.

"Madame!" Poirot sprang gallantly to his feet and hastened towards her. "I cannot tell you how I regret to *dérange* you in this way. But what will you? *Les affaires*—they know no mercy."

Mrs. Maltravers permitted him to lead her to a chair. Her eyes were red with weeping, but the temporary disfigurement could not conceal her extraordinary beauty. She was about twenty-seven or twenty-eight, and very fair, with large blue eyes and a pretty, pouting mouth.

"It is something about my husband's insurance, is it? But must I be bothered *now*—so soon?"

"Courage, my dear Madame. Courage! You see, your late husband insured his life for rather a large sum, and in such a case the company always has to satisfy itself as to a few details. They have empowered me to act for them. You can rest assured that I will do all in my power to render the matter not too unpleasant for you. Will you recount to me briefly the sad events of Wednesday?"

"I was changing for tea when my maid came up—one of the gardeners had just run to the house. He had found —"

Her voice trailed away. Poirot pressed her hand sympathetically.

"I comprehend. Enough! You had seen your husband earlier in the afternoon?"

"Not since lunch. I had walked down to the village for some stamps, and I believe he was out pottering round the grounds."

"Shooting rooks, eh?"

"Yes, he usually took his little rook-rifle with him, and I heard one or two shots in the distance."

"Where is this little rook-rifle now?"

"In the hall, I think."

She led the way out of the room and found and handed the little weapon to Poirot, who examined it cursorily.

"Two shots fired, I see," he observed, as he handed it back. "And now, Madame, if I might see —"

He paused delicately.

"The servants shall take you," she murmured, averting her head.

The parlourmaid, summoned, led Poirot upstairs. I remained with the lovely and unfortunate woman. It was hard to know whether to speak or remain silent. I essayed one or two general reflections, to which she responded absently, and in a very few minutes Poirot rejoined us.

"I thank you for all your courtesy, Madame. I do not think you need be troubled any further with this matter. By the way, do you know anything of your husband's financial position?"

She shook her head.

"Nothing whatever. I am very stupid over business things."

"I see. Then you can give us no clue as to why he suddenly decided to insure his life? He had not done so previously, I understand."

"Well, we had only been married a little over a year. But, as to why he insured his life, it was because he had absolutely made up his mind that he would not live long. He had a strong premonition of his own death. I gather that he had had one haemorrhage already, and that he knew that another one would prove fatal. I tried to dispel these gloomy fears of his, but without avail. Alas! he was only too right."

Tears in her eyes, she bade us a dignified farewell. Poirot made a characteristic gesture as we walked down the drive together.

"*Eh bien*, that is that! Back to London, my friend, there appears to be no mouse in this mouse-hole. And yet —"

"Yet what?"

"A slight discrepancy, that is all! You noticed it? You did not? Still, life is full of discrepancies, and assuredly the man cannot have taken his life — there is no poison that would fill his mouth with blood. No, no, I must resign myself to the fact that all here is clear and aboveboard — but who is this?"

A tall young man was striding up the drive towards us. He passed us without making any sign, but I noted that he had a lean, deeply bronzed face that spoke of life in a tropic clime. A gardener who was sweeping up leaves had paused for a minute in his task, and Poirot ran quickly up to him.

"Tell me, I pray you, who is that gentleman? Do you know him?"

"I don't remember his name, Sir, though I did hear it. He was staying down here last week for a night. Tuesday, it was."

"Quick, *mon ami*, let us follow him."

We hastened up the drive after the retreating figure. A glimpse of a black-robed figure on the terrace at the side of the house, and our quarry swerved and we after him, so that we were witnesses of the meeting.

Mrs. Maltravers staggered slightly, and her hand crept to her side.

"You," she gasped. "I thought you were on the sea — on your way to East Africa?"

"I got some news from my lawyers that detained me," explained the young man. "My old uncle in Scotland died unexpectedly and left me some money. Under the circumstances I thought it better to cancel my passage. Then I saw this bad news in the paper and I came down to see if there was anything I could do. You'll want someone to look after things for you a bit, perhaps?"

At that moment they became aware of our presence. Poirot stepped forward, and with many apologies explained that he had left his stick in the hall. Rather reluctantly, it seemed to me, Mrs. Maltravers made the necessary introduction.

"Monsieur Poirot, Captain Black."

A few minutes' chat ensued, in the course of which Poirot elicited the fact that Captain Black was putting up at the Anchor Inn. The missing stick not having been discovered (which was not surprising), Poirot uttered more apologies and we withdrew.

We returned to the village at a great pace, and Poirot made a bee-line for the Anchor Inn.

"Here we establish ourselves until our friend the Captain returns," he explained. "You noticed that I emphasized the point that we were returning to London by the first train? Possibly you thought I meant it. You observed Mrs. Maltravers' face when she caught sight of this young Black? She was clearly taken aback, and he — *eh bien*, he was very devoted, did you not think so? And he was here on Tuesday night — the day before Mr. Maltravers died. We must investigate the doings of Captain Black, Hastings."

In about half an hour we espied our quarry approaching the inn. Poirot went out and accosted him and presently brought him up to the room we had engaged.

"I have been telling Captain Black of the mission which brings us here," he explained. "You can understand, *Monsieur le Capitaine*, that I am anxious to arrive at Mr. Maltravers' state of mind immediately before his death, and that at the same time I do not wish to distress Mrs. Maltravers unduly by asking her painful questions. Now, you were here just before the occurrence, and can give us equally valuable information."

"I'll do anything I can to help you, I'm sure," replied the young soldier; "but I'm afraid I didn't notice anything out of the ordinary. You see, although Maltravers was an old friend of my people's, I didn't know him very well myself."

"You came down — when?"

"Tuesday afternoon. I went up to town early Wednesday morning, as my boat sailed from Tilbury about twelve o'clock. But some news I got made me alter my plans, as I dare say you heard me explain to Mrs. Maltravers."

"You were returning to East Africa, I understand?"

"Yes. I've been out there ever since the War — a great country."

"Exactly. Now what was the talk about at dinner on Tuesday night?"

"Oh, I don't know. The usual odd topics. Maltravers asked after my people, and then we discussed the question of German reparations, and then Mrs. Maltravers asked a lot of questions about East Africa, and I told them one or two yarns — that's about all, I think."

"Thank you."

Poirot was silent for a moment, then he said gently: "With your permission, I should like to try a little experiment. You have told us all that your conscious self knows, I want now to question your sub-conscious self."

"Psychoanalysis, what?" said Black, with visible alarm.

"Oh, no," said Poirot reassuringly. "You see, it is like this, I give you a word, you answer with another, and so on. Any word, the first one you think of. Shall we begin?"

"All right," said Black slowly, but he looked uneasy.

"Note down the words, please, Hastings," said Poirot. Then he took from his pocket his big turnip-faced watch and laid it on the table beside him. "We will commence. Day."

There was a moment's pause, and then Black replied:

"Night."

As Poirot proceeded, his answers came quicker. "Name," said Poirot.

"*Place.*"

"Bernard."

"*Shaw.*"

"Tuesday."

"*Dinner.*"

"Journey."

"*Ship.*"

"Country."

"*Uganda.*"

"Story."

"*Lions.*"

"Rook Rifle."

"*Farm.*"

"Shot."

"*Suicide.*"

"Elephant."

"*Tusks.*"

"Money."

"*Lawyers.*"

"Thank you, Captain Black. Perhaps you could spare me a few minutes in about half an hour's time."

"Certainly." The young soldier looked at him curiously and wiped his brow as he got up.

"And now, Hastings," said Poirot, smiling at me as the door closed behind him. "You see it all, do you not?"

"I don't know what you mean."

"Does that list of words tell you nothing?"

I scrutinized it, but was forced to shake my head.

"I will assist you. To begin with, Black answered well within the normal time limit, with no pauses, so we can take it that he himself has no guilty knowledge to conceal. 'Day' to 'Night' and 'Place' to 'Name' are normal associations. I began work with 'Bernard,' which might have suggested the local doctor had he come across him at all. Evidently he had not. After our recent conversation, he gave 'Dinner' to my 'Tuesday,' but 'Journey' and 'Country' were answered by 'Ship' and 'Uganda,' showing clearly that it was his journey abroad that was important to him and not the one which brought him down here. 'Story' recalls to him one of the 'Lion' stories he told at dinner. I proceeded to 'Rook Rifle' and he answered with the totally unexpected word 'Farm.' When I say 'Shot,' he answers at once 'Suicide.' The association seems clear. A man he knows committed suicide with a rook-rifle on a farm somewhere. Remember, too, that his mind is still on the stories he told at dinner, and I think you will agree that I shall not be far from the truth if I recall Captain Black and ask him to repeat the particular suicide story which he told at the dinner table on Tuesday evening."

Black was straightforward enough over the matter.

"Yes, I did tell them that story now that I come to think of it. Chap shot himself on a farm out there. Did it with a rook-rifle through the roof of the mouth, bullet lodged in the brain. Doctors were no end puzzled over it — there was nothing to show except a little blood on the lips. But what — ?"

"What has it got to do with Mr. Maltravers? You did not know, I see, that he was found with a rook-rifle by his side."

"You mean my story suggested to him — oh, but that is awful!"

"Do not distress yourself — it would have been one way or another. Well, I must get on the telephone to London."

Poirot had a lengthy conversation over the wire, and came back thoughtful.

He went off by himself in the afternoon, and it was not till seven o'clock that he announced that he could put it off no longer, but must break the news to the young widow. My sympathy had already gone out to her unreservedly. To be left penniless, and with the knowledge that her husband had killed himself to assure her future, was a hard burden for any woman to bear. I cherished a secret hope, however, that young Black might prove capable of consoling her after her first grief had passed. He evidently admired her enormously.

Our interview with the lady was painful. She refused vehemently to believe the facts that Poirot advanced, and, when she was at last convinced, broke down into bitter weeping.

An examination of the body turned our suspicions into certainty. Poirot was very sorry for the poor lady, but, after all, he was employed by the Insurance Company, and what could he do? As he was preparing to leave he said gently to Mrs. Maltravers:

"Madame, you of all people should know that there are no dead!"

"What do you mean?" she faltered, her eyes growing wide.

"Have you never taken part in any spiritualistic seances? You are mediumistic, you know."

"I have been told so. But you do not believe in Spiritualism, surely?"

"Madame — I have seen some strange things. You know that they say in the village that this house is haunted?"

She nodded, and at that moment

the parlourmaid announced that dinner was ready.

"Won't you just stay and have something to eat?"

We accepted gracefully, and I felt that our presence could not but help distract her a little from her own griefs.

Suddenly there was a scream outside the door, and the sound of breaking crockery. We jumped up. The parlourmaid appeared, her hand to her heart.

"It was a man standing in the passage."

Poirot rushed out, returning quickly.

"There is no one there."

"Isn't there, Sir?" said the parlourmaid weakly. "Oh it did give me a start!"

"But why?"

She dropped her voice to a whisper.

"I thought — I thought it was the master — it looked like 'im."

I saw Mrs. Maltravers give a terrified start, and my mind flew to the old superstition that a suicide cannot rest. She thought of it too, I am sure, for a minute later, she caught Poirot's arm with a scream.

"Didn't you hear that? Those three taps on the window? That's how *he* always used to tap when he passed round the house."

"The ivy," I cried, "it was the ivy against the pane."

But a sort of terror was gaining on us all. The parlourmaid was obviously unstrung, and when the meal was over Mrs. Maltravers besought Poirot not to go at once. She was clearly terrified to be left alone. We sat in the little morning room. The wind was getting up, and moaning round the house in an eerie fashion. Twice the door of the room came unlatched and the door slowly opened, and each time she clung to me with a terrified gasp.

"Ah, but this door, it is bewitched!" cried Poirot angrily at last. He got up and shut it once more, then turned the key in the lock. "I shall lock it — so!"

"Don't do that," she gasped. "If it should come open now —"

Even as she spoke, the impossible happened. The locked door slowly swung open. I could not see into the passage from where I sat, but she and Poirot were facing it. She gave one long shriek as she turned to him.

"You saw him, there in the passage?" she cried.

He was staring down at her with a puzzled face, then shook his head.

"I *saw* him — my husband — you must have seen him too?"

"Madame — I saw nothing. You are not well — unstrung —"

"I am perfectly well, I — Oh God!"

Suddenly, without warning, the lights quivered and went out. Out of the darkness came three loud raps. I could hear Mrs. Maltravers moaning.

And then — I saw!

The man I had seen on the bed

upstairs stood there facing us, gleaming with a faint ghostly light. There was blood on his lips, and he held his right hand out pointing. Suddenly a brilliant light seemed to proceed from it. It passed over Poirot and me, and fell on Mrs. Maltravers. I saw her white terrified face, and something else!

"My God, Poirot!" I cried, "look at her hand, her right hand! It's all red!"

Her own eyes fell on it, and she collapsed in a heap on the floor.

"Blood!" she cried hysterically. "Yes, it's blood. I killed him. I did it. He was showing me, and then I put my hand on the trigger and pressed. Save me from him — save me! He's come back!"

Her voice died away in a gurgle.

"Lights," said Poirot briskly.

The lights went on as if by magic.

"That's it," he continued. "You heard, Hastings? And you, Everett? Oh, by the way, this is Mr. Everett, rather a fine member of the theatrical profession. I phoned to him this afternoon. His makeup is good, isn't it? Quite like the dead man, and with a pocket torch and the necessary phosphorescence he made the proper impression. I shouldn't touch her right hand if I were you, Hastings. Red paint marks so. When the lights went out I clasped her hand, you see. By the way, we mustn't miss our train. Inspector Japp is outside the window. A bad night — but he has been able to while away the time by tapping on the window every now and then."

"You see," continued Poirot, as we walked briskly through the wind and rain, "there was a little discrepancy. The doctor seemed to think the deceased was a Christian Scientist; and who could have given him that impression but Mrs. Maltravers? But to us she represented him as being in a great state of apprehension about his own health. Again, why was she so taken aback by the reappearance of young Black? And lastly, although I know that convention decrees that a woman must make a decent pretence of mourning for her husband, I do not care for such heavily rouged eyelids. You did not observe them, Hastings? No! As I always tell you, you see nothing!

"Well, there it was. There were the two possibilities. Did Black's story suggest an ingenious method of committing suicide to Mr. Maltravers, or did his other listener, the wife, see an equally ingenious method of committing murder? It was a slender chance, and one had to revise all one's ideas of the case. It is now not the husband who seeks refuge in oblivion, whilst leaving his wife provided for, but a shrewd and scheming woman who, knowing her husband's financial débâcle, and tired of the elderly mate she has married only for his money, induces him to insure his life for a large sum, and then seeks for the means to accomplish her purpose. An accident gives her that — the young soldier's strange story.

The next afternoon, when *Monsieur le Capitaine*, as she thinks, is on the high seas, she and her husband are strolling round the grounds. 'What a curious story that was last night,' she observes. 'Could a man shoot himself in such a way? Do show me if it is possible!' The poor fool, he shows her. 'Like that?' she says, and then laughs. 'Supposing I pull the trigger?' she says saucily.

"And then she pulls it."

# THE KIDNAPPED PRIME MINISTER.

"The Kidnapped Prime Minister" was first published in *The Sketch* on April 25, 1923.

I.

Now that war and the problems of war are things of the past, I think I may safely venture to reveal to the world the part which my friend Poirot played in a moment of national crisis. The secret has been well guarded. Not a whisper of it reached the press. But, now that the need for secrecy has gone by, I feel it is only just that England should know the debt it owes to my quaint little friend, whose marvellous brain so ably averted a great catastrophe.

One evening after dinner — I will not particularize the date; it suffices to say that it was at the time when "Peace by negotiation" was the parrot-cry of England's enemies — my friend and I were sitting in his rooms. After being invalided out of the Army I had been given a recruiting job, and it had become my custom to drop in on Poirot in the evenings after dinner and talk with him of any cases of interest that he might have had on hand.

I was attempting to discuss with him the sensational news of the day — no less than an attempted assassination of Mr. David

MacAdam, England's Prime Minister. The account in the papers had evidently been carefully censored. No details were given, save that the Prime Minister had had a marvellous escape, the bullet just grazing his cheek.

I considered that our police must have been shamefully careless for such an outrage to be possible. I could well understand that the German agents in England would be willing to risk much for such an achievement. "Fighting Mac," as his own party had nicknamed him, had strenuously and unequivocally combated the Pacifist influence which was becoming so prevalent.

He was more than England's Prime Minister — he *was* England; and to have removed him from his sphere of influence would have been a crushing and paralysing blow to Britain.

Poirot was busy mopping a grey suit with a minute sponge. Never was there a dandy such as Hercule Poirot. Neatness and order were his passion. Now, with the odour of benzine filling the air, he was quite unable to give me his full attention.

"In a little minute I am with you, my friend. I have all but finished. The spot of grease — he is not good — I remove him — so!" He waved his sponge.

I smiled as I lit another cigarette.

"Anything interesting on?" I inquired, after a minute or two.

"I assist a — how do you call it? — 'charlady' to find her husband. A difficult affair, needing the tact. For I have a little idea that when he is found he will not be pleased. What would you? For my part, I sympathize with him. He was a man of discrimination to lose himself."

I laughed.

"At last! The spot of grease, he is gone! I am at your disposal."

"I was asking you what you thought of this attempt to assassinate MacAdam?"

"*Enfantillage!*" replied Poirot promptly. "One can hardly take it seriously. To fire with the rifle — never does it succeed. It is a device of the past."

"It was very near succeeding this time," I reminded him.

Poirot shook his head impatiently. He was about to reply when the landlady thrust her head round the door and informed him that there were two gentlemen below who wanted to see him.

"They won't give their names, Sir, but they says as it's very important."

"Let them mount," said Poirot, carefully folding his grey trousers.

In a few minutes the two visitors were ushered in, and my heart gave a leap as in the foremost I recognized no less a personage than Lord Estair, Leader of the House of Commons; whilst his companion, Mr. Bernard Dodge, was also a member of the War Cabinet, and, as I knew, a close personal friend of the Prime Minister.

"Monsieur Poirot?" said Lord

Estair interrogatively. My friend bowed. The great man looked at me and hesitated. "My business is private."

"You may speak freely before Captain Hastings," said my friend, nodding to me to remain. "He has not all the gifts, no! But I answer for his discretion."

Lord Estair still hesitated, but Mr. Dodge broke in abruptly:

"Oh, come on — don't let's beat about the bush! As far as I can see, the whole of England will know the hole we're in soon enough. Time's everything."

"Pray be seated, messieurs," said Poirot politely. "Will you take the big chair, Milor'?"

Lord Estair started slightly. "You know me?"

Poirot smiled. "Certainly. I read the little papers with the pictures. How should I not know you?"

"Monsieur Poirot, I have come to consult you upon a matter of the most vital urgency. I must ask for absolute secrecy."

"You have the word of Hercule Poirot — I can say no more!" said my friend grandiloquently.

"It concerns the Prime Minister. We are in grave trouble."

"We're up a tree!" interposed Mr. Dodge.

"The injury is serious then?" I asked.

"What injury?"

"The bullet wound."

"Oh, that!" cried Mr. Dodge contemptuously. "That's old history."

"As my colleague says," continued Lord Estair, "that affair is over and done with. Luckily, it failed. I wish I could say as much for the second attempt."

"There has been a second attempt, then?"

"Yes, though not of the same nature. Monsieur Poirot, the Prime Minister has disappeared."

"What?"

"He has been kidnapped!"

"Impossible!" I cried, stupefied.

Poirot threw a withering glance at me, which I knew enjoined me to keep my mouth shut.

"Unfortunately, impossible as it seems, it is only too true," continued his lordship.

Poirot looked at Mr. Dodge. "You said just now, Monsieur, that time was everything. What did you mean by that?"

The two men exchanged glances, and then Lord Estair said:

"You have heard, Monsieur Poirot, of the approaching Allied Conference?"

My friend nodded.

"For obvious reasons, no details have been given of when and where it is to take place. But, although it has been kept out of the newspapers, the date is, of course, widely known in diplomatic circles. The Conference is to be held to-morrow — Thursday — evening at Versailles. Now you perceive the terrible gravity of the situation. I will not conceal from you that the Prime Minister's presence at the Conference is a vital necessity. The Pacifist propaganda, started and maintained by the German agents in our midst, has been very active. It is the universal opinion that the turning point of the Conference will be the strong personality of the Prime Minister. His absence may have the most serious results — possibly a premature and disastrous peace. And we have no one who can be sent in his place. He alone can represent England."

Poirot's face had grown very grave. "Then you regard the kidnapping of the Prime Minister as a direct attempt to prevent his being present at the Conference?"

"Most certainly I do. He was actually on his way to France at the time."

"And the Conference is to be held?"

"At nine o'clock to-morrow night."

Poirot drew an enormous watch from his pocket. "It is now a quarter to nine."

"Twenty-four hours," said Mr. Dodge thoughtfully.

"And a quarter," amended Poirot. "Do not forget the quarter, Monsieur — it may come in useful. Now for the details — the abduction, did it take place in England or in France?"

"In France. Mr. MacAdam crossed to France this morning. He was to stay tonight as the guest of the Commander-in-Chief, proceeding to-morrow to Paris. He was conveyed across the Channel by destroyer. At Boulogne he was met by a car from General Headquarters and one of the Commander-in-Chief's A.D.C.s."

"*Eh bien?*"

"Well, they started from Boulogne — but they never arrived."

"What?"

"Monsieur Poirot, it was a bogus car and a bogus A.D.C. The real car was found in a side road, with the chauffeur and the A.D.C. neatly gagged and bound."

"And the bogus car?"

"Is still at large."

Poirot made a gesture of impatience. "Incredible! Surely it cannot escape attention for long?"

"So we thought. It seemed merely a question of searching thoroughly. That part of France is under Military Law. We were convinced that the car could not go long unnoticed. The French police and our own Scotland Yard men and the military are straining every nerve. It is, as you say, incredible — but nothing has been discovered!"

At that moment a tap came at the door, and a young officer entered with a heavily sealed envelope which he handed to Lord Estair.

"Just through from France, Sir. I brought it on here, as you directed."

The Minister tore it open eagerly, and uttered an exclamation. The officer Withdrew.

"Here is news at last! This telegram has just been decoded. They have found the second car, also the secretary, Daniels, chloroformed, gagged, and bound, in an abandoned farm near C—. He remembers nothing, except something being pressed against his mouth and nose from behind, and struggling to free himself. The police are satisfied as to the genuineness of his statement."

"And they have found nothing else?"

"No."

"Not the Prime Minister's dead body? Then, there is hope. But it is strange. Why, after trying to shoot him this morning, are they now taking so much trouble to keep him alive?"

Dodge shook his head. "One thing's quite certain. They're determined at all costs to prevent his attending the Conference."

"If it is humanly possible, the Prime Minister shall be there. God grant it is not too late. Now, messieurs, recount to me everything — from the beginning. I must know about this shooting affair as well."

"Last night, the Prime Minister, accompanied by — one of his secretaries, Captain Daniels —"

"The same who accompanied him to France?"

"Yes. As I was saying, they motored down to Windsor, where the Prime Minister was granted an Audience. Early this morning he returned to town, and it was on the way that the attempted assassination took place."

"One moment, if you please. Who is this Captain Daniels? You have his dossier?"

Lord Estair smiled. "I thought you would ask me that. We do not know very much of him. He is of no particular family. He has served in the English Army, and is an extremely able secretary, being an exceptionally fine linguist. I believe he speaks seven languages. It is for that reason that the Prime Minister chose him to accompany him to France."

"Has he any relatives in England?"

"Two aunts. A Mrs. Everard, who lives at Hampstead, and a Miss Daniels, who lives near Ascot."

"Ascot? That is near to Windsor, is it not?"

"That point has not been overlooked. But it has led to nothing."

"You regard the *Capitaine* Daniels, then, as above suspicion?"

A shade of bitterness crept into Lord Estair's voice, as he replied:

"No, Monsieur Poirot. In these days, I should hesitate before I pronounced anyone above suspicion."

"*Très bien*. Now I understand, Milor', that the Prime Minister would, as a matter of course, be under vigilant police protection, which ought to render any assault upon him an impossibility?"

Lord Estair bowed his head. "That is so. The Prime Minister's car was closely followed by another car containing detectives in plain clothes. Mr. MacAdam knew nothing of these precautions. He is personally a most fearless man, and would be inclined to sweep them away arbitrarily. But, naturally, the police make their own arrangements. In fact, the Premier's chauffeur, O'Murphy, is a CID man."

"O'Murphy? That is a name of Ireland, is it not so?"

"Yes, he is an Irishman."

"From what part of Ireland?"

"County Clare, I believe."

"*Tiens!* But proceed, Milor'."

"The Premier started for London. The car was a closed one. He and Captain Daniels sat inside. The second car followed as usual. But, unluckily, for some unknown reason, the Prime Minister's car deviated from the main road —"

"At a point where the road curves?" interrupted Poirot.

"Yes — but how did you know?"

"Oh, *c'est evident!* Continue!"

"For some unknown reason," continued Lord Estair, "the Premier's car left the main road. The police car, unaware of the deviation, continued to keep to the high road. At a short distance down the unfrequented lane, the Prime Minister's car was suddenly held up by a band of masked men. The chauffeur —"

"That brave O'Murphy!" murmured Poirot thoughtfully.

"The chauffeur, momentarily taken aback, jammed on the brakes. The Prime Minister put his head out of the window. Instantly a shot rang out — then another. The first one grazed his cheek, the second, fortunately, went wide. The chauffeur, now realizing the danger, instantly forged straight ahead, scattering the band of men."

"A near escape," I ejaculated, with a shiver.

"Mr. MacAdam refused to make any fuss over the slight wound he had received. He declared it was only a scratch. He stopped at a local cottage hospital, where it was dressed and bound up — he did not, of course, reveal his identity. He then drove, as per schedule, straight to Charing Cross, where a special train for Dover was awaiting him, and, after a brief account of what had happened had been given to the anxious police by Captain Daniels, he duly departed for France. At Dover, he went on board the waiting destroyer. At Boulogne, as you know, the bogus car was waiting for him, carrying the Union Jack, and correct in every detail."

"That is all you have to tell me?"

"Yes."

"There is no other circumstance that you have omitted, Milor'?"

"Well, there is one rather peculiar thing."

"Yes?"

"The Prime Minister's car did not return home after leaving the Prime Minister at Charing Cross. The police were anxious to interview O'Murphy, so a search was instituted at once. The car was discovered standing outside a certain unsavoury little restaurant in Soho, which is well known as a meeting place of German agents."

"And the chauffeur?"

"The chauffeur was nowhere to be found. He, too, had disappeared."

"So," said Poirot thoughtfully, "there are two disappearances: the Prime Minister in France, and O'Murphy in London."

He looked keenly at Lord Estair, who made a gesture of despair.

"I can only tell you, Monsieur Poirot, that, if anyone had suggested to me yesterday that O'Murphy was a traitor, I should have laughed in his face."

"And to-day?"

"To-day I do not know what to think."

Poirot nodded gravely. He looked at his turnip of a watch again.

"I understand that I have *carte blanche*, messieurs — in every way, I mean? I must be able to go where I choose, and how I choose."

"Perfectly. There is a special train leaving for Dover in an hour's time, with a further contingent from Scotland Yard. You shall be accompanied by a Military officer and a CID man, who will hold themselves at your disposal in every way. Is that satisfactory?"

"Quite. One more question before you leave, messieurs. What made you come to me? I am unknown, obscure in this great London of yours."

"We sought you out on the express recommendation and wish of a very great man of your own country."

"*Comment?* My old friend the Prefet — ?"

Lord Estair shook his head.

"One higher than the Prefet. One whose word was once law in Belgium — and shall be again! That England has sworn!"

Poirot's hand flew swiftly to a dramatic salute. "Amen to that! Ah, but my Master does not forget .... Messieurs, I, Hercule Poirot, will serve you faithfully. Heaven only send that it will be in time. But this is dark — dark ... I cannot see."

## II.

"Well, Poirot," I cried impatiently, as the door closed behind the Ministers, "what do you think?"

My friend was busy packing a minute suitcase, with quick, deft movements.

He shook his head thoughtfully.

"I don't know what to think. My brains desert me."

"Why, as you said, kidnap him, when a knock on the head would do as well?" I mused.

"Pardon me, *mon ami*, but I did not quite say that. It is undoubtedly far more their affair to kidnap him."

"But why?"

"Because uncertainty creates panic. That is one reason. Were the

Prime Minister dead, it would be a terrible calamity, but the situation would have to be faced. But now you have paralysis. Will the Prime Minister reappear, or will he not? Is he dead or alive? Nobody knows, and until they know nothing definite can be done. And, as I tell you, uncertainty breeds panic, which is what *les Boches* are playing for.

"Then, again, if the kidnappers are holding him secretly somewhere, they have the advantage of being able to make terms with both sides. The German Government is not a liberal paymaster, as a rule, but no doubt they can be made to disgorge substantial remittances in such a case as this.

"Thirdly, they run no risk of the hangman's rope. Oh, decidedly, kidnapping is their affair."

"Then, if that is so, why should they first try to shoot him?"

Poirot made a gesture of anger. "Ah, that is just what I do not understand! It is inexplicable — stupid! They have all their arrangements made (and very good arrangements too!) for the abduction, and yet they imperil the whole affair by a melodramatic attack, worthy of a cinema, and quite as unreal. It is almost impossible to believe in it, with its band of masked men, not twenty miles from London!"

"Perhaps they were two quite separate attempts which happened irrespective of each other," I suggested.

"Ah, no, that would be too much of a coincidence! Then, further — who is the traitor? There must have been a traitor — in the first affair, anyway. But who was it — Daniels or O'Murphy? It must have been one of the two, or why did the car leave the main road? We cannot suppose that the Prime Minister connived at his own assassination! Did O'Murphy take that turning of his own accord, or was it Daniels who told him to do so?"

"Surely it must have been O'Murphy's doing."

"Yes, because if it was Daniels' the Prime Minister would have heard the order, and would have asked the reason. But there are altogether too many 'whys' in this affair, and they contradict each other. If O'Murphy is an honest man, why did he leave the main road? But if he was a dishonest man, why did he start the car again when only two shots had been fired — thereby, in all probability, saving the Prime Minister's life? And, again, if he was honest, why did he, immediately on leaving Charing Cross, drive to a well-known rendezvous of German spies?"

"It looks bad," I said.

"Let us look at the case with method. What have we for and against these two men? Take O'Murphy first. Against: that his conduct in leaving the main road was suspicious; that he is an Irishman from County Clare; that he has disappeared in a highly suggestive manner. For: that his promptness in restarting the car saved the Premier's life; that he is a Scotland Yard man, and, obviously, from the post allotted to him, a trusted detective. Now for Daniels. There is not much against him, except the fact that nothing is known of his antecedents, and that he speaks too many languages for a good Englishman! (Pardon me, *mon ami*, but, as linguists, you are deplorable!) Now *for* him, we have the fact that he was found gagged, bound, and chloroformed—which does not look as though he had anything to do with the matter."

"He might have gagged and bound himself, to divert suspicion."

Poirot shook his head. "The French police would make no mistake of that kind. Besides, once he had attained his object, and the Prime Minister was safely abducted, there would not be much point in his remaining behind. His accomplices could have gagged and chloroformed him, of course, but I fail to see what object they hoped to accomplish by it. He can be of little use to them now, for, until the circumstances concerning the Prime Minister have been cleared up, he is bound to be closely watched."

"Perhaps he hoped to start the police on a false scent?"

"Then why did he not do so? He merely says that something was pressed over his nose and mouth, and that he remembers nothing more. There is no false scent there. It sounds remarkably like the truth."

"Well," I said, glancing at the clock, "I suppose we'd better start for the station. You may find more clues in France."

"Possibly, *mon ami*, but I doubt it. It is still incredible to me that the Prime Minister has not been discovered in that limited area, where the difficulty of concealing him must be tremendous. If the military and the police of two countries have not found him, how shall I?"

At Charing Cross we were met by Mr. Dodge.

"This is Detective Barnes, of Scotland Yard, and Major Norman. They will hold themselves entirely at your disposal. Good luck to you. It's a bad business, but I've not given up hope. Must be off now." And the Minister strode rapidly away.

We chatted in a desultory fashion with Major Norman. In the centre of the little group of men on the platform I recognized a little ferret-faced fellow talking to a tall, fair man. He was an old acquaintance of Poirot's—Detective-Inspector Japp, supposed to be one of the smartest of Scotland Yard's officers. He came over and greeted my friend cheerfully.

"I heard you were on this job too. Smart bit of work. So far they've got away with the goods all right. But I can't believe they can keep him hidden long. Our people are going through France with a toothcomb. So are the French. I can't help feeling it's only a matter of hours now."

"That is, if he's still alive,"

remarked the tall detective gloomily.

Japp's face fell. "Yes ... but somehow I've got the feeling he's still alive all right."

Poirot nodded. "Yes, yes; he's alive. But can he be found in time? I, like you, did not believe he could be hidden so long."

The whistle blew, and we all trooped up into the Pullman car. Then, with a slow, unwilling jerk, the train drew out of the station.

It was a curious journey. The Scotland Yard men crowded together. Maps of Northern France were spread out, and eager forefingers traced the lines of roads and villages. Each man had his own pet theory. Poirot showed none of his usual loquacity, but sat staring in front of him, with an expression on his face that reminded me of a puzzled child. I talked to Norman, whom I found quite an amusing fellow.

On arriving at Dover Poirot's behaviour moved me to intense amusement. The little man, as he went on board the boat, clutched desperately at my arm. The wind was blowing lustily.

"*Mon Dieu!* " he murmured. "This is terrible!"

"Have courage, Poirot," I cried. "You will succeed. You will find him. I am sure of it."

"Ah, *mon ami*, you mistake my emotion. It is this villainous sea that troubles me! The *mal de mer*—it is horrible suffering!"

"Oh!" I said, rather taken aback.

The first throb of the engines was felt, and Poirot groaned and closed his eyes.

"Major Norman has a map of Northern France if you would like to study it?"

Poirot shook his head impatiently.

"But no, but no! Leave me, my friend. See you, to think, the stomach and the brain must be in harmony. Laverguier has a method most excellent for averting the *mal de mer*. You breathe in—and out—slowly, so—turning the head from left to right and counting six between each breath."

I left him to his gymnastic endeavours, and went on deck.

As we came slowly into Boulogne Harbour Poirot appeared, neat and smiling, and announced to me in a whisper that Laverguier's system had succeeded "to a marvel!"

Japp's forefinger was still tracing imaginary routes on his map. "Nonsense! The car started from Boulogne—here they branched off. Now, my idea is that they transferred the Prime Minister to another car. See?"

"Well," said the tall detective, "I shall make for the seaports. Ten to one, they've smuggled him on board a ship."

Japp shook his head. "Too obvious. The order went out at once to close all the ports."

The day was just breaking as we

landed. Major Norman touched Poirot on the arm. "There's a military car here waiting for you, Sir."

"Thank you, Monsieur. But, for the moment, I do not propose to leave Boulogne."

"What?"

"No, we will enter this hotel here, by the quay."

He suited the action to the word, demanded and was accorded a private room.

We three followed him, puzzled and uncomprehending.

He shot a quick glance at us. "It is not so that the good detective should act, eh? I perceive your thought. He must be full of energy. He must rush to and fro. He should prostrate himself on the dusty road and seek the marks of tyres through a little glass. He must gather up the cigarette end, the fallen match? That is your idea, is it not?"

His eyes challenged us. "But I — Hercule Poirot — tell you that it is not so! The true clues are within — here!" He tapped his forehead. "See you, I need not have left London. It would have been sufficient for me to sit quietly in my rooms there. All that matters is the little grey cells within. Secretly and silently they do their part, until suddenly I call for a map, and I lay my finger on a spot — so — and I say: the Prime Minister is there! And it is so! With method and logic one can accomplish anything! This frantic rushing to France was a mistake — it is playing a child's game of hide-and-seek. But now; though it may be too late, I will set to work the right way, from within. Silence, my friends, I beg of you."

And for five long hours the little man sat motionless, blinking his eyelids like a cat, his green eyes flickering and becoming steadily greener and greener. The Scotland Yard man was obviously contemptuous, Major Norman was bored and impatient, and I myself found the time passed with wearisome slowness.

Finally, I got up, and strolled as noiselessly as I could to the window. The matter was becoming a farce. I was secretly concerned for my friend. If he failed, I would have preferred him to fail in a less ridiculous manner. Out of the window I idly watched the daily leave boat, belching forth columns of smoke, as she lay alongside the quay.

Suddenly I was aroused by Poirot's voice close to my elbow.

"*Mes amis*, let us start!"

I turned. An extraordinary transformation had come over my friend. His eyes were flickering with excitement, his chest was swelled to the uttermost.

"I have been an imbecile, my friends! But I see daylight at last."

Major Norman moved hastily to the door. "I'll order the car."

"There is no need. I shall not use it. Thank Heaven the wind has fallen."

"Do you mean you are going to walk, Sir?"

"No, my young friend. I am no

St. Peter. I prefer to cross the sea by boat."

"To cross the sea?"

"Yes. To work with method, one must begin from the beginning. And the beginning of this affair was in England. Therefore, we return to England."

### III.

At three o'clock, we stood once more upon Charing Cross platform. To all our expostulations, Poirot turned a deaf ear, and reiterated again and again that to start at the beginning was not a waste of time, but the only way. On the way over, he had conferred with Norman in a low voice, and the latter had despatched a sheaf of telegrams from Dover.

Owing to the special passes held by Norman, we got through everywhere in record time. In London, a large police car was waiting for us, with some plain-clothesmen, one of whom handed a typewritten sheet of paper to my friend. He answered my inquiring glance.

"A list of the cottage hospitals within a certain radius west of London. I wired for it from Dover."

We were whirled rapidly through the London streets. We were on the Bath Road. On we went, through Hammersmith, Chiswick and Brentford. I began to see our objective. Through Windsor and so on to Ascot. My heart gave a leap. Ascot was where Daniels had an aunt living. We were after him, then, not O'Murphy.

We duly stopped at the gate of a trim villa. Poirot jumped out and rang the bell. I saw a perplexed frown dimming the radiance of his face. Plainly, he was not satisfied.

The bell was answered. He was ushered inside. In a few moments he reappeared, and climbed into the car with a short, sharp shake of his head. My hopes began to die down. It was past four now. Even if he found certain evidence incriminating Daniels, what would be the good of it, unless he could wring from someone the exact spot in France where they were holding the Prime Minister?

Our return progress towards London was an interrupted one. We deviated from the main road more than once, and occasionally stopped at a small building, which I had no difficulty in recognizing as a cottage hospital. Poirot only spent a few minutes at each, but at every halt his radiant assurance was more and more restored.

He whispered something to Norman, to which the latter replied:

"Yes, if you turn off to the left, you will find them waiting by the bridge."

We turned up a side road, and in the failing light I discerned a second car, waiting by the side of the road. It contained two men in plain clothes. Poirot got down and spoke to them, and then we started off in a northerly direction, the other car following close behind.

We drove for some time, our objective being obviously one of the northern suburbs of London. Finally, we drove up to the front door of a tall house, standing a little back from the road in its own grounds.

Norman and I were left in the car. Poirot and one of the detectives went up to the door and rang. A neat parlourmaid opened it. The detective spoke.

"I am a police officer, and I have a warrant to search this house."

The girl gave a little scream, and a tall, handsome woman of middle age appeared behind her in the hall.

"Shut the door, Edith. They are burglars, I expect."

But Poirot swiftly inserted his foot in the door, and at the same moment blew a whistle. Instantly the other detectives ran up, and poured into the house, shutting the door behind them.

Norman and I spent about five minutes cursing our forced inactivity. Finally the door reopened, and the men emerged, escorting three prisoners — a woman and two men. The woman, and one of the men, were taken to the second car. The other man was placed in our car by Poirot himself.

"I must go with the others, my friend. But have great care of this gentleman. You do not know him, no? *Eh bien*, let me present to you, Monsieur O'Murphy!"

O'Murphy! I gaped at him open-mouthed as we started again. He was not handcuffed, but I did not fancy he would try to escape. He sat there staring in front of him as though dazed. Anyway, Norman and I would be more than a match for him.

To my surprise, we still kept a northerly route. We were not returning to London, then! I was much puzzled.

Suddenly, as the car slowed down, I recognized that we were close to Hendon Aerodrome. Immediately I grasped Poirot's idea. He proposed to reach France by aeroplane.

It was a sporting idea, but, on the face of it, impracticable. A telegram would be far quicker. Time was everything. He must leave the personal glory of rescuing the Prime Minister to others.

As we drew up, Major Norman jumped out, and a plainclothesman took his place. He conferred with Poirot for a few minutes, and then went off briskly.

I, too, jumped out, and caught Poirot by the arm.

"I congratulate you, old fellow! They have told you the hiding place? But, look here, you must wire to France at once. You'll be too late if you go yourself."

Poirot looked at me curiously for a minute or two.

"Unfortunately, my friend, there are some things that cannot be sent by telegram."

At that moment Major Norman returned, accompanied by a young officer in the uniform of the Flying Corps.

"This is Captain Lyall, who will fly you over to France. He can start at once."

"Wrap up warmly, Sir," said the young pilot. "I can lend you a coat, if you like."

Poirot was consulting his enormous watch. He murmured to himself: "Yes, there is time — just time." Then he looked up and bowed politely to the young officer. "I thank you, Monsieur. But it is not I who am your passenger. It is this gentleman here."

He moved a little aside as he spoke, and a figure came forward out of the darkness. It was the second male prisoner who had gone in the other car, and as the light fell on his face, I gave a start of surprise.

It was the Prime Minister!

## IV.

"For Heaven's sake, tell me all about it," I cried impatiently, as Poirot, Norman and I motored back to London. "How in the world did they manage to smuggle him back to England?"

"There was no need to smuggle him back," replied Poirot dryly. "The Prime Minister has never left England. He was kidnapped on his way from Windsor to London."

"What?"

"I will make all clear. The Prime Minister was in his car, his secretary beside him. Suddenly a pad of chloroform is clapped on his face —"

"But by whom?"

"By the clever linguistic Captain Daniels. As soon as the Prime Minister is unconscious, Daniels picks up the speaking tube, and directs O'Murphy to turn to the right, which the chauffeur, quite unsuspicious, does. A few yards down that unfrequented road a large car is standing, apparently broken down. Its driver signals to O'Murphy to stop. O'Murphy slows up. The stranger approaches. Daniels leans out of the window, and, probably with the aid of an instantaneous anaesthetic, such as ethylchloride, the chloroform trick is repeated. In a few seconds, the two helpless men are dragged out and transferred to the other car, and a pair of substitutes take their places."

"Impossible!"

"*Pas du tout!* Have you not seen music hall turns imitating celebrities with marvellous accuracy? Nothing is easier than to personate a public character. The Prime Minister of England is far easier to understudy than Mr. John Smith of Clapham, say. As for O'Murphy's 'double,' no one was going to take much notice of him until after the departure of the Prime Minister, and by then he would have made himself scarce. He drives straight from Charing Cross to the meeting place of his friends. He goes in as O'Murphy, he emerges as someone quite different. O'Murphy has disappeared, leaving a conveniently suspicious trail behind him."

"But the man who personated the Prime Minister was seen by everyone!"

"He was not seen by anyone who knew him privately or intimately. And Daniels shielded him from contact with anyone as much as possible. Moreover, his face was bandaged up, and anything unusual in his manner would be put down to the fact that he was suffering from shock as a result of the attempt upon his life. Mr. MacAdam has a weak throat, and always spares his voice as much as possible before any great speech. The deception was perfectly easy to keep up as far as France. There it would be impracticable and impossible — so the Prime Minister disappears. The police of this country hurry across the Channel, and no one bothers to go into the details of the first attack. To sustain the illusion that the abduction has taken place in France, Daniels is gagged and chloroformed in a convincing manner."

"And the man who has enacted the part of the Prime Minister?"

"Rids himself of his disguise. He and the bogus chauffeur may be arrested as suspicious characters, but no one will dream of suspecting their real part in the drama, and they will eventually be released for lack of evidence."

"And the real Prime Minister?"

"He and O'Murphy were driven straight to the house of 'Mrs. Everard,' at Hampstead, Daniels' so-called 'aunt.' In reality, she is Frau Bertha Ebenthal, and the police have been looking for her for some time. It is a valuable little present that I have made them — to say nothing of Daniels! Ah, it was a clever plan, but he did not reckon on the cleverness of Hercule Poirot!"

I think my friend might well be excused his moment of vanity. "When did you first begin to suspect the truth of the matter?"

"When I began to work the right way — from within! I could not make that shooting affair fit in — but when I saw that the net result of it was that the Prime Minister went to France with his face bound up I began to comprehend! And when I visited all the cottage hospitals between Windsor and London, and found that no one answering to my description had had his face bound up and dressed that morning, I was sure! After that, it was child's play for a mind like mine!"

## V.

The following morning, Poirot showed me a telegram he had just received. It had no place of origin, and was unsigned.

It ran: "In time."

Later in the day the evening papers published an account of the Allied Conference. They laid particular stress on the magnificent ovation accorded to Mr. David MacAdam, whose inspiring speech had produced a deep and lasting impression.

# THE MILLION-DOLLAR BOND ROBBERY.

"The Million-Dollar Bond Robbery" was first published in *The Sketch* on May 2, 1923.

"What a number of bond robberies there have been lately!" I observed one morning, laying aside the newspaper. "Poirot, let us forsake the science of detection, and take to crime instead!"

"You are on the—how do you say it?—get-rich-quick tack, eh, *mon ami?*"

"Well, look at this last coup, the million dollars' worth of Liberty Bonds which the London and Scottish Bank were sending to New York, and which disappeared in such a remarkable manner on board the *Olympia*."

"If it were not for *mal de mer*, and the difficulty of practising the so-excellent method of Laverguier for a longer time than the few hours of crossing the Channel, I should delight to voyage myself on one of these big liners," murmured Poirot dreamily.

"Yes, indeed," I said enthusiastically. "Some of them must be perfect palaces; the swimming baths, the lounges, the restaurant, the palm courts—really, it must be hard to believe that one is on the sea."

"Me, I always know when I am on the sea," said Poirot sadly. "And all those bagatelles that you enumerate, they say nothing to me; but, my friend, consider for a moment the genuises that travel, as it were, incognito! On board these floating palaces, as you so justly call them, one would meet the *élite*, the *haute noblesse* of the criminal world!"

I laughed.

"So that's the way your enthusiasm runs! You would have liked to cross sword with the man who sneaked the Liberty Bonds?"

The landlady interrupted us.

"A young lady as wants to see you, Mr. Poirot. Here's her card."

The card bore the inscription: "Miss Esmé Farquhar"; and Poirot, after diving under the table to retrieve a stray crumb, and putting it carefully in the wastepaper basket, nodded to the landlady to admit her.

In another minute one of the most charming girls I have ever seen was ushered into the room. She was perhaps about five-and-twenty, with big brown eyes and a perfect figure. She was well-dressed and perfectly composed in manner.

"Sit down, I beg of you, Mademoiselle. This is my friend, Captain Hastings, who aids me in my little problems."

"I am afraid it is a big problem I have brought you to-day, Monsieur Poirot," said the girl, giving me a pleasant bow as she seated herself. "I dare say you have read about it in the papers. I am referring to the theft of Liberty Bonds on the *Olympia*." Some astonishment must have shown itself on Poirot's face, for she continued quickly: "You are doubtless asking yourself what I have to do with a grave institution like the London and Scottish Bank. In one sense nothing, in another sense everything. You see, Monsieur Poirot, I am engaged to Mr. Philip Ridgeway."

"Aha! and Mr. Philip Ridgeway —"

"Was in charge of the bonds when they were stolen. Of course no actual blame can attach to him; it was not his fault in any way. Nevertheless, he is half distraught over the matter, and his uncle, I know, insists that he must carelessly have mentioned having them in his possession. It is a terrible setback to his career."

"Who is his uncle?"

"Mr. Vavasour, joint general manager of the London and Scottish Bank."

"Suppose, Miss Farquhar, that you recount to me the whole story?"

"Very well. As you know, the Bank wished to extend their credits in America, and for this purpose decided to send over a million dollars in Liberty Bonds. Mr. Vavasour selected his nephew, who had occupied a position of trust in the Bank for many years and who was conversant with all the details of the Bank's dealings in New York, to make the trip. The *Olympia* sailed from Liverpool on the 23rd, and the bonds were handed over to Philip on the morning of that day by Mr. Vavasour and Mr. Shaw, the two joint general managers of the London and Scottish Bank. They were counted, enclosed in a package, and sealed in his presence, and he then locked the package at once in his portmanteau."

"A portmanteau with an ordinary lock?"

"No, Mr. Shaw insisted on a special lock being fitted to it by Hubbs. Philip, as I say, placed the package at the bottom of the trunk. It was stolen just a few hours before reaching New York. A rigorous search of the whole ship was made, but without result. The bonds seemed literally to have vanished into thin air."

Poirot made a grimace.

"But they did not vanish absolutely, since I gather that they were sold in small parcels within half an hour of the docking of the *Olympia!* Well, undoubtedly the next thing is for me to see Mr. Ridgeway."

"I was about to suggest that you should lunch with me at the Cheshire Cheese. Philip will be there. He is meeting me, but does not yet know that I have been consulting you on his behalf."

Philip Ridgeway was a pleasant-faced man of thirty-odd, with just a touch of greying hair at his temples. His face looked drawn and haggard. The theft of the bonds which had been placed in his charge had almost demoralised him, and he reproached himself vainly for not having exercised greater care. Over the excellent steak-and-kidney pudding of the establishment he confirmed his fiancée's story in every particular. Poirot then proceeded to question him.

"What led you to discover that the bonds had been stolen, Mr. Ridgeway?"

The man laughed rather bitterly.

"The thing stared me in the face, Monsieur Poirot. I couldn't have missed it. My cabin trunk was half out from under the bunk and all scratched and cut about where they'd tried to force the lock."

"But I understood that it had been opened with a key?"

"That's so. They tried to force it, but couldn't. And in the end, they must have got it unlocked somehow or other."

"Curious," said Poirot, his eyes beginning to flicker with the green light I knew so well. "Very curious! They waste much, much time trying to prise it open, and then — *sapristi!* they find they have the key all the time — for each of Messieurs Hubbs's locks is unique!"

"They couldn't have had the key. It never left me day or night."

"You are sure of that?"

"I can swear to it, and besides, if they had had the key or a duplicate, why should they waste time trying to force an obviously unforceable lock?"

"Ah, there is exactly the question

we are asking ourselves! You will see, the solution, if we ever find it, will hinge on that curious fact. I beg of you not to assault me if I ask you one more question: Are you perfectly certain that you did not leave the trunk unlocked?"

Philip Ridgeway merely looked at him, and Poirot gesticulated apologetically. "Ah, but these things can happen, I assure you! Very well, the bonds were stolen from the trunk. What did the thief do with them? How did he manage to get ashore with them?"

"Ah!" cried Ridgeway. "That's just it. How? Word was passed to the Customs authorities, and every soul that left the ship was gone over with a tooth-comb!"

"And the bonds, I gather, made a bulky package?"

"Certainly they did. They could hardly have been hidden on board — and any way we know they weren't, because they were offered for sale within half an hour of the Olympia's arrival, long before I got the cables going and the numbers sent out. One broker swears he bought some of them even before the Olympia got in! But you can't send bonds by wireless!"

"Not by wireless; but did any tug come alongside?"

"Only the official ones, and that was after the alarm was given when everyone was on the lookout. I was watching out myself for their being passed over to someone that way. My God, Monsieur Poirot, this thing will drive me mad! People are beginning to say I stole them myself."

"But you also were searched on landing, weren't you?" asked Poirot gently.

"Yes."

The young man stared at him in a puzzled manner.

"You do not catch my meaning, I see," said Poirot, smiling enigmatically. "Now I should like to make a few inquiries at the Bank."

Ridgeway produced a card and scribbled a few words on it.

"Send this in and my uncle will see you at once."

Poirot thanked him, bade farewell to Miss Farquhar, and together we started out for Threadneedle Street and the head office of the London and Scottish Bank.

On production of Ridgeway's card, we were led through the labyrinth of counters and desks, skirting paying-in clerks and paying-out clerks, and up to a small office on the first floor where the joint general managers received us. They were two grave gentlemen, who had grown grey in the service of the Bank. Mr. Vavasour had a short white beard, Mr. Shaw was clean-shaven.

"I understand you are strictly a private inquiry agent?" said Mr. Vavasour. "Quite so, quite so. We have, of course, placed ourselves in the hands of Scotland Yard. Inspector

McNeil has charge of the case. A very able officer, I believe."

"I am sure of it," said Poirot politely. "You will permit a few questions, on your nephew's behalf? About this lock, who ordered it from Messieurs Hubbs's?"

"I ordered it myself," said Mr. Shaw. "I would not trust to any clerk in the matter. As to the keys, Mr. Ridgeway had one, and the other two are held by my colleague and myself."

"And no clerk has had access to them?"

Mr. Shaw turned inquiringly to Mr. Vavasour.

"I think I am correct in saying that they have remained in the safe where we placed them on the twenty-third," said Mr. Vavasour. "My colleague was unfortunately taken ill a fortnight ago — in fact on the very day that Philip left us. He has only just recovered."

"Severe bronchitis is no joke to a man of my age," said Mr. Shaw ruefully. "But I'm afraid Mr. Vavasour has suffered from the hard work entailed by my absence, especially with this unexpected worry coming on top of everything."

Poirot asked a few more questions. I judged that he was endeavouring to gauge the exact amount of intimacy between uncle and nephew. Mr. Vavasour's answers were brief and punctilious. His nephew was a trusted official of the Bank, and had no debts or money difficulties that he knew of. He had been entrusted with similar missions in the past. Finally we were politely bowed out.

"I am disappointed," said Poirot, as we emerged into the street.

"You hoped to discover more? They are such stodgy old men."

"It is not their stodginess which disappoints me, *mon ami*. I do not expect to find in a Bank manager, a 'keen financier with an eagle glance,' as your favourite works of fiction put it. No, I am disappointed in the case — it is too easy!"

"*Easy?*"

"Yes, do you not find it almost childishly simple?"

"You know who stole the bonds?"

"I do."

"But then — we must — why —"

"Do not confuse and fluster yourself, Hastings. We are not going to do anything at present."

"But why? What are you waiting for?"

"For the *Olympia*. She is due on her return trip from New York on Tuesday."

"But if you know who stole the bonds, why wait? He may escape."

"To a South Sea island where there is no extradition? No, *mon ami*, he would find life very uncongenial there. As to why I wait — *eh bien*, to the intelligence of Hercule Poirot the case is perfectly clear, but for the benefit of others, not so greatly gifted by the good God — the Inspector, McNeil, for instance — it would be as well to make a few inquiries to establish the facts. One must have consideration for those less gifted than oneself."

"Good Lord, Poirot! Do you know, I'd give a considerable sum of money to see you make a thorough ass of yourself—just for once. You're so confoundedly conceited!"

"Do not enrage yourself, Hastings. In verity, I observe that there are times when you almost detest me! Alas, I suffer the penalties of greatness!"

The little man puffed out his chest, and sighed so comically that I was forced to laugh.

Tuesday saw us speeding to Liverpool in a first-class carriage of the L. and N.W.R. Poirot had obstinately refused to enlighten me as to his suspicions—or certainties. He contented himself with expressing surprise that I, too, was not equally *au fait* with the situation. I disdained to argue, and entrenched my curiosity behind a rampart of pretended indifference.

Once arrived at the quay alongside which lay the big transatlantic liner, Poirot became brisk and alert. Our proceedings consisted in interviewing four successive stewards and inquiring after a friend of Poirot's who had crossed to New York on the twenty-third.

"An elderly gentleman, wearing glasses. A great invalid, hardly moved out of his cabin."

The description appeared to tally with one Mr. Ventnor, who had occupied the cabin C24, which was next to that of Philip Ridgeway. Although unable to see how Poirot had deduced Mr. Ventnor's existence and personal appearance, I was keenly excited.

"Tell me," I cried, "was this gentleman one of the first to land when you got to New York?"

The steward shook his head.

"No, indeed, Sir, he was one of the last off the boat."

I retired crestfallen, and observed Poirot grinning at me. He thanked the steward, a note changed hands, and we took our departure.

"It's all very well," I remarked heatedly, "but that last answer must have damned your precious theory, grin as you please!"

"As usual, you see nothing, Hastings. That last answer is, on the contrary, the coping-stone of my theory."

I flung up my hands in despair.

"I give it up."

Once more we were in the train—speeding towards London this time. Poirot wrote busily for few minutes, then sealed up the result in an envelope.

"This is for the good Inspector McNeil. We will leave it at Scotland Yard in passing, and then to the Rendez-Vous Restaurant, where I have asked Miss Esmé Farquhar to do us the honour of dining with us."

"What about Ridgeway?"

"What about him?" asked Poirot with a twinkle.

"Why, you surely don't think—you can't—"

"The habit of incoherence is growing upon you, Hastings. As a matter of fact I *did* think. If Ridgeway had been the thief — which was perfectly possible — the case would have been charming — a piece of neat, methodical work."

"But not so charming for Miss Farquhar."

"Possibly you are right. Therefore all is for the best. Now, Hastings, let us review the case. The sealed package is removed from the trunk and vanishes, as Miss Farquhar puts it, into thin air. We will dismiss the thin air theory, which is not practicable at the present stage of science, and consider what is likely to have become of it. Everyone asserts the incredibility of it being smuggled ashore —"

"Yes, but we know —"

"*You* may know, Hastings, I do not. I take the view that, since it seemed incredible, it *was* incredible. Two possibilities remain. It was hidden on board — also rather difficult; or — it was thrown overboard."

"With a cork on it, do you mean?"

"Without a cork."

I stared.

"But if the bonds were thrown overboard, they could not have been sold in New York."

"I admire your logical mind, Hastings. The bonds were sold in New York, therefore they were not thrown overboard. You see where that leads us?"

"Where we were when we started."

"*Jamais de la vie!* If the package was thrown overboard and the bonds were sold in New York, the package could not have contained the bonds. Is there any evidence that the package did contain the bonds? Remember, Mr. Ridgeway never opened it from the time it was placed in his hands in London."

"Yes, but then —"

Poirot waved an impatient hand.

"Permit me to continue. The last moment that the bonds are seen as bonds is in the office of the London and Scottish Bank on the morning of the twenty-third. They reappear in New York half an hour after the *Olympia* gets in, and according to one man, whom nobody listens to, actually *before* she gets in. Supposing then, that they have never been on the *Olympia* at all? Is there any other way they could get to New York? Yes. The *Gigantic* leaves Southampton on the same day as the *Olympia*, and she holds the record for the Atlantic. Mailed by the *Gigantic*, the bonds would be in New York the day before the *Olympia* arrived. All is clear, the case begins to explain itself. The sealed packet is only a dummy, and the moment of its substitution must be in the office in the bank. It would be an easy matter for any of the three men present to have prepared a duplicate package which could be substituted for the genuine one. *Très bien*, the bonds are mailed to a confederate in

New York, with instructions to sell as soon as the *Olympia* is in; but someone must travel on the *Olympia* to engineer the supposed moment of robbery."

"But why?"

"Because, if Ridgeway merely opens the packet and finds it a dummy, suspicion flies at once to London. No; the man on board in the cabin next door does his work, pretends to force the lock in an obvious manner so as to draw immediate attention to the theft, really unlocks the trunk with a duplicate key, throws the package overboard and waits until the last to leave the boat. Naturally he wears glasses to conceal his eyes, and is an invalid since he does not want to run the risk of meeting Ridgeway. He steps ashore in New York and returns by the first boat available."

"But who — which was he?"

"The man who had a duplicate key, the man who ordered the lock, the man who has not been severely ill with bronchitis at his home in the country — *enfin*, the stodgy old man, Mr. Shaw! There are criminals in high places sometimes, my friend. Ah, here we are, Mademoiselle, I have succeeded! You permit?"

And, beaming, Poirot kissed the astonished girl lightly on either cheek!

# THE ADVENTURE OF THE CHEAP FLAT.

"The Adventure of the Cheap Flat" was first published in *The Sketch* on May 9, 1923.

So far, in the cases which I have recorded, Poirot's investigations have started from the central fact, whether murder or robbery, and have proceeded from thence by a process of logical deduction to the final triumphant unravelling. In the events I am now about to chronicle a remarkable chain of circumstances led from the apparently trivial incidents which first attracted Poirot's attention to the sinister happenings which completed a most unusual case.

I had been spending the evening with an old friend of mine, Gerald Parker. There had been, perhaps, about half a dozen people there besides my host and myself, and the talk fell, as it was bound to do sooner or later wherever Parker found himself, on the subject of house-hunting in London. Houses and flats were Parker's special hobby. Since the end of the War, he had occupied at least half a dozen different flats and maisonettes. No sooner was he settled anywhere than he would light unexpectedly upon a new find, and would forthwith depart bag and baggage. His moves were nearly always accomplished at a slight pecuniary gain, for he had a shrewd business head; but it was sheer love of the sport that actuated him, and not a desire to make money at it.

We listened to Parker for some time with the respect of the novice for the expert. Then it was our turn, and a perfect babel of tongues was let loose. Finally the floor was left to Mrs. Robinson, a charming little bride who was there with her husband. I had never met them before, as Robinson was only a recent acquaintance of Parker's.

"Talking of flats," she said, "have you heard of our piece of luck, Mr. Parker? We've got a flat — at last! In Montagu Mansions."

"Well," said Parker, "I've always said there are plenty of flats — at a price."

"Yes, but this isn't at a price. It's dirt cheap — £80 a year!"

"But — but Montagu Mansions is just off Knightsbridge, isn't it? Big handsome building. Or are you talking of a poor relation of the same name stuck in the slums somewhere?"

"No, it's the Knightsbridge one. That's what makes it so wonderful."

"Wonderful is the word! It's a blinking miracle! But there must be a catch somewhere. Big premium, I suppose?"

"No premium!"

"No prem — Oh, hold my head, somebody!" groaned Parker.

"But we've got to buy the furniture," continued Mrs. Robinson.

"Ah!" Parker brisked up. "I knew there was a catch!"

"For £50. And it's beautifully furnished!"

"I give it up," said Parker. "The present occupants must be lunatics with a taste for philanthropy."

Mrs. Robinson was looking a little troubled. A little pucker appeared between her dainty brows.

"It *is* queer, isn't it? You don't think that — that — the place is *haunted?*"

"Never heard of a haunted flat," declared Parker decisively.

"No —" Mrs. Robinson appeared far from convinced. "But there were several things about it all that struck me as — well, queer."

"For instance —" I suggested.

"Ah," said Parker, "our criminal expert's attention is aroused! Unburden yourself to him, Mrs. Robinson. Hastings is a great unraveller of mysteries."

I laughed, embarrassed, but not wholly displeased with the rôle thrust upon me.

"Oh, not really queer, Captain Hastings, but when we went to the agents, Stosser and Paul — we hadn't tried them before because they only have the expensive Mayfair flats, but we thought at any rate it would do no harm — well, we went there, and everything they offered us was four and five hundred a year, or else huge premiums; and then, just as we were going, they mentioned that they had a flat at eighty, but that they doubted if it would be any good our going there, because it had been on their books some time and they had sent so many people to see it that it was almost sure to be taken — 'snapped up' as the clerk put it — only people were *so* tiresome in not letting them know, and then they went on sending, and people got annoyed at being sent to a place that had perhaps been let some time."

Mrs. Robinson paused for some much-needed breath, and then continued:

"We thanked him, and said that we quite understood it would probably be no good, but that we should like an order all the same — just in case. And we went there straight away in a taxi, for, after all, you never know. No. 4 was on the second floor, and just as we were waiting for the lift, Elsie Ferguson — she's a friend of mine, Captain Hastings, and they are looking for a flat too — came hurrying down the stairs. 'Ahead of you for once, my dear,' she said. 'But it's no good. It's already let.' Well, that seemed to finish it, but — well, as John said, the place was very cheap — we could afford to give more, and perhaps if we offered a premium — a horrid thing to do, of course, and I feel quite ashamed of telling you, but you know what flat-hunting is —"

I assured her that I was well aware that in the struggle for houseroom the baser side of human nature frequently triumphed over the higher, and that the well-known rule of diamond cut diamond always applied.

"So we went up and, would you believe it, the flat wasn't let at all. We were shown over it by the maid, and then we saw the mistress, and the thing was settled then and there. Immediate possession and £50 for the furniture. We signed the agreement next day, and we are to move in to-morrow!"

Mrs. Robinson paused triumphantly.

"And what about Mrs. Ferguson?" asked Parker. "Let's have your deductions, Hastings."

"'Obvious, my dear Watson,'" I quoted lightly; "she went to the wrong flat."

"Oh, Captain Hastings, how clever of you!" cried Mrs. Robinson admiringly.

I rather wished Poirot had been there. Sometimes I have the feeling that he rather underestimates my capabilities.

The whole thing was rather amusing, and I propounded the thing as a mock problem to Poirot on the following morning. He seemed interested, and questioned me rather narrowly as to the rents of flats in various localities.

"A curious story," he said thoughtfully. "Excuse me, Hastings, I must take a short stroll."

When he returned, about an hour later, his eyes were gleaming with a peculiar excitement. He laid his stick on the table, and brushed the nap of his hat with his usual tender care before he spoke.

"It is as well, *mon ami*, that we have no affairs of moment on hand. We can devote ourselves wholly to the present investigation."

"What investigation are you talking about?"

"The remarkable cheapness of your friend, Mrs. Robinson's, new flat."

"Poirot, you are not serious!"

"I am most serious. Figure to yourself, my friend, that the real rent of those flats is £350. I have just ascertained that from the landlord's agents. And yet this particular flat is being sublet at £80! Why?"

"There must be something wrong with it. Perhaps it is haunted, as Mrs. Robinson suggested."

Poirot shook his head in a dissatisfied manner.

"Then again how curious it is that her friend tells her the flat is let, and when she goes up—behold, it is not so at all!"

"But surely you agree with me that the other woman must have gone to the wrong flat. That is the only possible solution."

"You may or may not be right on that point, Hastings. The fact still remains that numerous other applicants were sent to see it, and yet, in spite of its remarkable cheapness, it was still in the market when Mrs. Robinson arrived."

"That shows that there must be something wrong about it."

"Mrs. Robinson did not seem to notice anything amiss. Very curious, is it not? Did she impress you as being a truthful woman, Hastings?"

"She was a delightful creature!"

"*Évidemment,* since she renders you incapable of replying to my question. Describe her to me, then."

"Well, she's tall and fair—her hair's really a beautiful shade of auburn —"

"Always you have had a *penchant* for auburn hair!" murmured Poirot. "But continue —"

"Blue eyes and a very nice complexion and—well, that's all, I think," I concluded lamely.

"And her husband?"

"Oh! he's quite a nice fellow—nothing startling."

"Dark or fair?"

"I don't know—betwixt and between, and just an ordinary sort of face."

Poirot nodded.

"Yes, there are hundreds of these average men—and anyway, you bring more sympathy and appreciation to your description of women. Do you know anything about these people? Does Parker know them well?"

"They are just recent acquaintances, I believe. But surely, Poirot, you don't think for an instant —"

Poirot raised his hand.

"*Tout doucement, mon ami.* Have I said that I think anything? All I say is—it is a curious story. And there is nothing to throw light upon it—except perhaps the lady's name, eh, Hastings?"

"Her name is Stella," I said stiffly; "but I don't see —"

Poirot interrupted me with a tremendous chuckle. Something seemed to be amusing him vastly.

"And Stella means a star, does it not? Famous!"

"What on earth —"

"And stars give light! *Voilà!* Calm yourself, Hastings. Do not put on that air of injured dignity. Come, we will go to Montagu Mansions and make a few inquiries."

I accompanied him, nothing loath.

The Mansions were a handsome block of buildings in excellent repair, situated near Brompton Road. A uniformed porter was sunning himself on the threshold, and it was to him that Poirot addressed himself.

"Pardon, but would you tell me if a Mr. and Mrs. Robinson reside here?"

The porter was a man of few words, and apparently of a sour or suspicious disposition. He hardly looked at us and grunted out: "Number four. Second floor."

"I thank you. Can you tell me how long they have been here?"

"Six months."

I started forward in amazement, conscious as I did so of Poirot's malicious grin.

"Impossible," I cried. "You must be making a mistake."

"Six months."

"Are you sure? The lady I mean is tall and fair, with reddish gold hair and —"

"That's 'er," said the porter. "Come in the Michaelmas quarter, they did. Just six months ago."

He appeared to lose interest in us and retreated slowly up the hall. I followed Poirot outside.

"*Eh bien*, Hastings?" my friend demanded slyly. "Are you so sure now that delightful women always speak the truth?"

I did not reply.

Poirot had steered his way into Brampton Road before I asked him what he was going to do and where we were going.

"To the house agents, Hastings. I have a great desire to have a flat in Montagu Mansions. If I am not mistaken, several interesting things will take place there before long."

We were fortunate in our quest. No. 8, on the fourth floor, was to be let furnished at ten guineas a week. Poirot promptly took it for a month. Outside in the street again, he silenced my protests:

"But I make money nowadays! Why should I not indulge a whim? By the way, Hastings, have you a revolver?"

"Yes — somewhere," I answered, slightly thrilled. "Do you think —"

"That you will need it? It is quite possible. The idea pleases you, I see. Always the spectacular and romantic appeals to you."

The following day saw us installed in our temporary home. The flat was pleasantly furnished. It was in the same block of the buildings as that of the Robinsons, but was two floors higher.

The day after our installation was a Sunday. In the afternoon, Poirot left the front door ajar, and summoned me hastily as a bang reverberated from somewhere below.

"Look over the banisters. Are those your friends? Do not let them see you."

I craned my neck over the staircase. "That's them," I declared in an ungrammatical whisper.

"Good. Wait awhile."

About half an hour later, a young woman emerged in brilliant and varied clothing. With a sigh of satisfaction, Poirot tiptoed back into the flat.

"*C'est ça.* After the master and mistress, the maid. The flat should now be empty."

"What are we going to do?" I asked uneasily.

Poirot had trotted briskly into the scullery and was hauling at the rope of the coal-lift.

"We are about to descend after the method of the dustbins," he explained cheerfully. "No one will observe us. The Sunday concert, the Sunday 'afternoon out,' and finally the Sunday nap after the Sunday dinner of England — *le rosbif* — all these will distract attention from the doings of Hercule Poirot. Come, my friend."

He stepped into the rough wooden contrivance and I followed him gingerly. "Are we going to break into the flat?" I asked dubiously.

Poirot's answer was not too reassuring:

"Not precisely to-day," he replied.

Pulling on the rope, we descended slowly till we reached the second floor. Poirot uttered an exclamation of satisfaction as he perceived that the wooden door into the scullery was open.

"You observe? Never do they bolt these doors in the day time. And yet anyone could mount or descend as we have done. At night, yes — though not always then — and it is against that that we are going to make provision."

He had drawn some tools from his pocket as he spoke, and at once set deftly to work, his object being to arrange the bolt so that it could be pulled back from the lift. The operation only occupied about three minutes. Then Poirot returned the tools to his pocket, and we reascended once more to our own domain.

On Monday Poirot was out all day, but when he returned in the evening he flung himself into his chair with a sigh of satisfaction.

"Hastings, shall I recount to you a little history? A story after your own heart and which will remind you of your favourite cinema?"

"Go ahead," I laughed. "I presume that it is a true story — not one of your efforts of fancy."

"It is true enough. Inspector

Japp of Scotland Yard will vouch for its accuracy, since it was through his kind offices that it came to my ears. Listen, Hastings. A little over six months ago some important Naval plans were stolen from an American Government department. They showed the position of some of the most important Harbour defences, and were worth a considerable sum to any foreign Government — that of Japan, for example. Suspicion fell upon a young man named Luigi Valdarno, an Italian by birth, who was employed in a minor capacity in the Department and who was missing at the same time as the papers. Whether Luigi Valdarno was the thief or not, he was found two days later on the East Side in New York, shot dead. The papers were not on him.

"Now for some time past Luigi Valdarno had been going about with a Miss Elsa Hardt, a young concert singer who had recently appeared, and who lived with a brother in an apartment in Washington. Nothing was known of the antecedents of Miss Elsa Hardt, and she disappeared suddenly about the time of Valdarno's death. There are reasons for believing that she was in reality an accomplished international spy who has done much nefarious work under various aliases. The American Secret Service, while doing their best to trace her, also kept an eye upon certain insignificant Japanese gentlemen living in Washington. They felt pretty certain that, when Elsa Hardt had covered her tracks sufficiently, she would approach the gentlemen in question. One of them left suddenly for England a fortnight ago. On the face of it, therefore, it would seem that Elsa Hardt is in England."

Poirot paused, and then added softly: "The official description of Elsa Hardt is — Height five feet seven; eyes, blue; hair, auburn; fair complexion; nose straight; no special distinguishing marks."

"Mrs. Robinson!" I gasped.

"Well, there is a chance of it, anyhow," amended Poirot. "Also I learn that a swarthy man, a foreigner of some kind, was inquiring about the occupants of No. 4 only this morning. Therefore, *mon ami*, I fear that you must forego your beauty sleep to-night, and join me in my all-night vigil in the flat below, armed with that excellent revolver of yours, *bien entendu!*"

"Rather," I cried with enthusiasm. "When shall we start?"

"The hour of midnight is both solemn and suitable, I fancy. Nothing is likely to occur before then."

At twelve o'clock precisely, we crept cautiously into the coal lift and lowered ourselves to the second floor. Under Poirot's manipulation, the wooden door quickly swung inwards, and we climbed into the flat. From the scullery we passed into the kitchen where we established ourselves comfortably in two chairs with the door into the hall ajar.

"Now we have but to wait," said Poirot contentedly, closing his eyes.

To me, the waiting appeared endless. I was terrified of going to sleep. Just when it seemed to me that I had been there about eight hours (and had, as I found out afterwards, in reality been exactly one hour and twenty minutes) a faint scratching sound came to my ears. Poirot's hand touched mine. I rose, and together we moved carefully in the direction of the hall. The noise came from there. Poirot placed his lips to my ear.

"Outside the front door. He is cutting out the lock. When I give the word, not before, fall upon him from behind and hold him fast. Be careful, he will have a knife."

Presently there was a rending sound, and a little circle of light appeared through the door. It was extinguished immediately and then the door was slowly opened. Poirot and I flattened ourselves against the wall. I heard a man's breathing as he passed us. Then he flashed on his torch, and as he did so, Poirot hissed in my ear: "*Allez!*"

We sprang together; Poirot with a quick movement enveloped the intruder's head with a light woollen scarf, whilst I pinioned his arms. The whole affair was quick and noiseless. I twisted a dagger from his hand, and as Poirot brought down the scarf from his eyes, whilst keeping it wound tightly round his mouth, I jerked up my revolver where he could see it and understand that resistance was useless. As he ceased to struggle Poirot put his mouth close to his ear and began to whisper rapidly. After a minute the man nodded. Then enjoining silence with a movement of the hand, Poirot led the way out of the flat and down the stairs. Our captive followed, and I brought up the rear with the revolver.

When we were out in the street, Poirot turned to me.

"There is a taxi waiting just round the corner. Give me the revolver. We shall not need it now."

"But if this fellow tries to escape?"

Poirot smiled.

"He will not."

I returned in a minute with the waiting taxi. The scarf had been unwound from the stranger's face, and I gave a start of surprise.

"He's not a Jap," I ejaculated in a whisper to Poirot.

"Observation was always your strong point, Hastings! Nothing escapes you. No, the man is not a Jap. He is an Italian."

We got into the taxi, and Poirot gave the driver an address in St. John's Wood. I was by now completely fogged. I did not like to ask Poirot where we were going in front of our captive, and strove in vain to obtain some light upon the proceedings.

We alighted at the door of a small house standing back from the road. A returning wayfarer, slightly drunk, was lurching along the pavement and almost collided with Poirot, who said something sharply to him which I did not catch. All three of us went up the steps of the house. Poirot rang the bell and motioned us to stand a little aside. There was no answer and he rang again and then seized the knocker, which he plied for some minutes vigorously.

A light appeared suddenly above the fanlight, and the door opened cautiously a little way.

"What the devil do you want?" a man's voice demanded harshly.

"I want the doctor. My wife is taken ill."

"There's no doctor here."

The man prepared to shut the door, but Poirot thrust his foot in adroitly. He became suddenly a perfect caricature of an infuriated Frenchman.

"What you say, there is no doctor? I will have the law of you. You must come! I will stay here and ring and knock all night."

"My dear Sir —" The door was opened again; the man, clad in a dressing-gown and slippers, stepped forward to pacify Poirot with an uneasy glance round.

"I will call the police —"

Poirot prepared to descend the steps.

"No, don't do that, for Heaven's sake," the man cried as he dashed after him.

With a neat push Poirot sent him staggering down the steps. In another minute all three of us were inside the door and it was pushed to and bolted.

"Quick — in here." Poirot led the way into the nearest room, switching on the light as he did so. "And you — behind the curtain."

"*Si, Signor*," said the Italian and slid rapidly behind the full folds of rose-coloured velvet which draped the embrasure of the window.

Not a minute too soon. Just as he disappeared from view a woman rushed into the room. She was tall with reddish hair and held a scarlet kimono round her slender form.

"Where is my husband?" she cried, with a quick frightened glance. "Who are you?"

Poirot stepped forward with a bow.

"It is to be hoped your husband will not suffer from a chill. I observed that he had slippers on his feet, and that his dressing-gown was a warm one."

"Who are you? What are you doing in my house?"

"It is true that none of us have the pleasure of your acquaintance, Madame. It is especially to be regretted as one of our number has come specially from New York in order to meet you."

The curtains parted and the Italian stepped out. To my horror I observed that he was brandishing my revolver, which Poirot must doubtless have put down through inadvertence in the cab.

The woman gave a piercing scream and turned to fly, but Poirot was standing in front of the closed door.

"Let me by!" she shrieked. "He will murder me!"

"Who was it dat croaked Luigi Valdarno?" asked the Italian hoarsely, brandishing the weapon, and sweeping each one of us with it. We dared not move.

"My God, Poirot, this is awful. What shall we do?" I cried.

"You will oblige me by refraining from talking so much, Hastings. I can assure you that our friend will not shoot until I give the word."

"Youse sure o' dat, eh?" said the Italian, leering unpleasantly.

It was more than I was, but the woman turned to Poirot like a flash.

"What is it you want?"

Poirot bowed.

"I do not think it is necessary to insult Miss Elsa Hardt's intelligence by telling her."

With a swift movement, the woman snatched up a big black velvet cat which served as a cover for the telephone.

"They are stitched in the lining of that."

"Clever," murmured Poirot appreciatively. He stood aside from the door.

"Good evening, Madame. I will detain your friend from New York whilst you make your getaway."

"Whatta fool!" roared the big Italian, and raising the revolver he fired pointblank at the woman's retreating figure just as I flung myself upon him.

But the weapon merely clicked harmlessly and Poirot's voice rose in mild reproof.

"Never will you trust your old friend, Hastings. I do not care for my friends to carry loaded pistols about with them and never would I permit a mere acquaintance to do so."

The Italian was swearing hoarsely. Poirot continued to address him in a tone of mild reproof: "See now, what I have done for you. I have saved you from being hanged. And do not think that our beautiful lady will escape. No, no, the house is watched, back and front. Straight into the arms of the police she will go. Is not that a beautiful and consoling thought? Yes, you may leave the room now. But be careful — be very careful. I — ah, he is gone! And my friend Hastings looks at me with eyes of reproach. But it was all so simple! It was clear, from the first, that out of several hundred (probable) applicants for No. 4, Montagu Mansions, only the Robinsons were considered suitable. Why? What was there that singled them out from the rest — at practically a glance? The appearance? Possibly, but it was not so unusual. Their name, then!"

"But there's nothing unusual about the name of Robinson," I cried.

"It's quite a common name."

"Ah, *sapristi*, but exactly! That was the point. Elsa Hardt and her husband, or brother, or whatever he really is, come from New York, and take a flat in the name of Mr. and Mrs. Robinson. Suddenly they learn that one of these secret societies, the Mafia, or the Camorra, to which doubtless Luigi Valdarno belonged, is on the track. What do they do? They hit on a scheme of transparent simplicity. Evident they knew that their pursuers were not personally acquainted with either of them. What, then, can be simpler? They offer the flat at an absurdly low rental. Of the thousands of young couples in London looking for flats, there cannot fail to be several Robinsons. It is only a matter of waiting. If you will look at the name Robinson in the telephone directory, you will realize that a fair-haired Mrs. Robinson was pretty sure to come along sooner or later. Then what will happen? The avenger arrives. He knows the name, he knows the address. He strikes! All is over, vengeance is satisfied, and Miss Elsa Hardt has escaped by the skin of her teeth once more. By the way, Hastings, you must present me to the real Mrs. Robinson — that delightful and truthful creature! What will they think when they find their flat has been broken into! We must hurry back. Ah, that sounds like Japp and his friend arriving!"

A mighty tattoo sounded on the knocker.

"How do you know this address?" I asked as I followed Poirot out into the hall. "Oh, of course, you had the first Mrs. Robinson followed when she left the other flat."

"*À la bonheur*, Hastings! You use your grey cells at last. Now for a little surprise for Japp."

Softly unbolting the door, he stuck the cat's head round the edge and ejaculated a piercing "Miaow."

The Scotland Yard inspector, who was standing outside with another man, jumped in spite of himself.

"Oh, it's only Moosior Poirot at one of his little jokes!" he exclaimed, as Poirot's head followed that of the cat. "Let us in, Moosior."

"You have our friends safe and sound?"

"Yes, we've got the birds all right. But they hadn't got the goods with them."

"I see. So you come to search. Well, I am about to depart with Hastings, but I should like to give you a little lecture upon the history and habits of the domestic cat."

"For the Lord's sake, have you gone completely balmy?"

"The cat," declaimed Poirot, "was worshipped by the ancient Egyptians. It is still regarded as a symbol of good luck if a black cat crosses your path. This cat crossed your path tonight, Japp. To speak of the interior of any animal or any person is not. I know, considered polite in England. But the interior of this cat is perfectly delicate. I refer to the lining."

With a sudden grunt, the second man seized the cat from Poirot's hand.

"Oh, I forgot to introduce you," said Japp. "Mr. Poirot, this is Mr. Burt of the United States Secret Service."

The American's trained fingers had felt what he was looking for. He held out his hand, and for a moment speech failed him. Then he rose to the occasion.

"Pleased to meet you," said Mr. Burt.

# THE MYSTERY OF HUNTER'S LODGE.

"The Mystery of Hunter's Lodge" was first published in *The Sketch* on May 16, 1923.

"After all," murmured Poirot, "it is possible that I shall not die this time."

Coming from a convalescent influenza patient, I hailed the remark as showing a beneficial optimism. I myself had been the first sufferer from the disease. Poirot in his turn had gone down. He was now sitting up in bed, propped up with pillows, his head muffled in a woollen shawl, and was slowly sipping a particularly noxious *tisane* which I had prepared according to his directions. His eye rested with pleasure upon a neatly graduated row of medicine bottles which adorned the mantelpiece.

"Yes, yes," my little friend continued. "Once more shall I be myself again, the great Hercule Poirot, the terror of evildoers! Figure to yourself, *mon ami*, that I have a little paragraph to myself in *Society Gossip*. But yes! Here it is: 'Go it—criminals—all out! Hercule Poirot (and believe me, girls, he's some Hercules!), our own pet society detective can't get a grip on you. 'Cause why? 'Cause he's got *la grippe* himself!'"

I laughed.

"Good for you, Poirot. You are becoming quite a public character.

And fortunately you haven't missed anything of particular interest during this time."

"That is true. The few cases I have had to decline did not fill me with any regret."

Our landlady stuck her head in at the door.

"There's a gentleman downstairs. Says he must see Monsieur Poirot or you, Captain. Seeing as he was in a great to-do — and with all that quite the gentleman — I brought up 'is card."

She handed me a bit of pasteboard. "Mr. Roger Havering," I read.

Poirot motioned with his head towards the bookcase, and I obediently pulled forth *Who's Who.* Poirot took it from me and scanned the pages rapidly.

"Second son of fifth Baron Windsor. Married 1913 Zoe, fourth daughter of William Crabb."

"H'm!" I said. "I rather fancy that's the girl who used to act at the Frivolity — only she called herself Zoe Carrisbrook. I remember she married some young man-about-town just before the War."

"Would it interest you, Hastings, to go down and hear what our visitor's particular little trouble is? Make him all my excuses."

Roger Havering was a man of about forty, well set up and of smart appearance. His face, however, was haggard, and he was evidently labouring under great agitation.

"Captain Hastings? You are Monsieur Poirot's partner, I understand. It is imperative that he should come with me to Derbyshire to-day."

"I'm afraid that's impossible," I replied. "Poirot is ill in bed — influenza."

His face fell.

"Dear me, that is a great blow to me."

"The matter on which you want to consult him is serious?"

"My God, yes! My uncle, the best friend I have in the world, was foully murdered last night."

"Here in London?"

"No, in Derbyshire. I was in town and received a telegram from my wife this morning. Immediately upon its receipt I determined to come round and beg Monsieur Poirot to undertake the case."

"If you will excuse me a minute," I said, struck by a sudden idea.

I rushed upstairs, and in a few brief words acquainted Poirot with the situation. He took any further words out of my mouth.

"I see. I see. You want to go yourself, is it not so? Well, why not? You should know my methods by now. All I ask is that you should report to me fully every day, and follow implicitly any instructions I may wire you."

To this I willingly agreed, and an hour later I was sitting opposite Mr. Havering in a first-class carriage on the Midland Railway, speeding rapidly away from London.

"To begin with, Captain Hastings, you must understand that Hunter's Lodge, where we are going, and where the tragedy took place, is only small shooting box in the heart of the Derbyshire moors. Our real home is near Newmarket, and we usually rent a flat in town for the season. Hunter's Lodge is looked after by a housekeeper who is quite capable of doing all we need when we run down for an occasional week-end. Of course, during the shooting season, we take down some of our own servants from Newmarket. My uncle, Mr. Harrington Pace (as you may know, my mother was a Miss Pace of New York), has, for the last three years, made his home with us. He never got on well with my father, or my elder brother, and I suspect that my being somewhat of a prodigal son myself rather increased than diminished his affection towards me. Of course I am a poor man, and my uncle was a rich one — in other words, he paid the piper! But, though exacting in many ways, he was not really hard to get on with, and we all three lived very harmoniously together.

"Two days ago, my uncle, rather wearied with some recent gaieties of ours in town, suggested that we should run down to Derbyshire for a day or two. My wife telegraphed to Mrs. Middleton, the housekeeper, and we went down that same afternoon. Yesterday evening I was forced to return to town, but my wife and my uncle remained on. This morning I received this telegram."

He handed it over to me:

> *Come at once uncle Harrington murdered last night bring good detective if you can but do come — Zoe.*

"Then, as yet you know no details?"

"No, I suppose it will be in the evening papers. Without doubt the police are in charge."

It was about three o'clock when we arrived at the little station of Elmer's Dale. From there a five-mile drive brought us to a small grey stone building in the midst of the rugged moors.

"A lonely place," I observed with a shiver.

Havering nodded.

"I shall try and get rid of it. I could never live here again."

We unlatched the gate and were walking up the narrow path to the oak door when a familiar figure emerged and came to meet us.

"Japp!" I ejaculated.

The Scotland Yard inspector grinned at me in a friendly fashion before addressing my companion.

"Mr. Havering, I think? I've been sent down from London to take charge of this case, and I'd like a word with you, if I may, Sir."

"My wife —"

"I've seen your good lady, Sir — and the housekeeper. I won't keep you a moment, but I am anxious to get back to the village now that I've seen all there is to see here."

"I know nothing as yet as to what —"

"Ex-actly," said Japp soothingly. "But there are just one or two little points I'd like your opinion about all the same. Captain Hastings here, he knows me, and he'll go on up to the house and tell them you're coming. What have you done with the little man, by the way, Captain Hastings?"

"He's ill in bed with influenza."

"Is he now? I'm sorry to hear that. Rather the case of the cart without the horse, you being here without him, isn't it?"

And on this rather ill-timed jest I went on to the house. I rang the bell, as Japp had closed the door behind him. After some moments it was opened to me by a middle-aged woman in black.

"Mr. Havering will be here in a moment," I explained. "He has been detained by the inspector. I have come down with him from London to look into the case. Perhaps you can tell me briefly what occurred last night."

"Come inside, Sir." She closed the door behind me, and we stood in the dimly-lighted hall. "It was after dinner last night, Sir, that the man came. He asked to see Mr. Pace, Sir, and, seeing that he spoke the same way, I thought it was an American gentleman friend of Mr. Pace's and I showed him into the gun-room, and then went to tell Mr. Pace. He wouldn't give no name, which, of course, was a bit odd, now I come to think of it. I told Mr. Pace, and he seemed puzzled-like, but he said to the mistress: 'Excuse me, Zoe, while I see what this fellow wants.' He went off to the gun-room, and I went back to the kitchen; but after a while I heard loud voices, as if they were quarrelling, and I came out into the hall. At the same time, the mistress she comes out too, and just then there was a shot and then a dreadful silence. We both ran to the gun room door, but it was locked and we had to go round to the window. It was open, and there inside was Mr. Pace, all shot and bleeding."

"What became of the man?"

"He must have got away through the window, Sir, before we got to it."

"And then?"

"Mrs. Havering sent me to fetch the police. Five miles to walk it was. They came back with me, and the constable he stayed all night, and this morning the police gentleman from London arrived."

"What was this man like who called to see Mr. Pace?"

The housekeeper reflected.

"He had a black beard, Sir, and was about middle-aged, and had on a light overcoat. Beyond the fact that he spoke like an American I didn't notice much about him."

"I see. Now I wonder if I can see Mrs. Havering?"

"She's upstairs, Sir. Shall I tell her?"

"If you please. Tell her that Mr. Havering is outside with Inspector Japp, and that the gentleman he has brought back with him from London is anxious to speak to her as soon as possible."

"Very good, Sir."

I was in a fever of impatience to get all the facts. Japp had two or three hours' start on me, and his anxiety to be gone made me keen to be close at his heels.

Mrs. Havering did not keep me waiting long. In a few minutes I heard a light step descending the stairs, and looked up to see a very handsome young woman coming towards me. She wore a flame-coloured jumper, that set off the slender boyishness of her figure. On her dark head was a little hat of flame-coloured leather. Even the present tragedy could not dim the vitality of her personality.

I introduced myself, and she nodded in quick comprehension.

"Of course I have often heard of you and your colleague, Monsieur Poirot. You have done some wonderful things together, haven't you? It was very clever of my husband to get you so promptly. Now will you ask me questions? That is the easiest way, isn't it, of getting to know all you want to about this dreadful affair?"

"Thank you, Mrs. Havering. Now what time was it that this man arrived?"

"It must have been just before nine o'clock. We had finished dinner, and were sitting over our coffee and cigarettes."

"Your husband had already left for London?"

"Yes, he went up by the 6:15."

"Did he go by car to the station, or did he walk?"

"Our own car isn't down here. One came out from the garage in Elmer's Dale to fetch him in time for the train."

"Was Mr. Pace quite his usual self?"

"Absolutely. Quite normal in every way."

"Now, can you describe this visitor at all?"

"I'm afraid not. I didn't see him. Mrs. Middleton showed him straight into the gun room and then came to tell my uncle."

"What did your uncle say?"

"He seemed rather annoyed, but went off at once. It was about five minutes later that I heard the sound of raised voices. I ran out into the hall and almost collided with Mrs. Middleton. Then we heard the shot. The gun room door was locked on the inside, and we had to go right round the house to the window. Of course that took some time, and the murderer had been able to get well away. My poor uncle"—her voice faltered—"had been shot through the head. I saw at once that he was dead. I sent Mrs. Middleton for the police, I was careful to touch nothing in the room, but to leave it exactly as I found it."

I nodded approval.

"Now, as to the weapon?"

"Well, I can make a guess at it, Captain Hastings. A pair of revolvers of my husband's were mounted upon the wall. One of them is missing. I pointed this out to the police, and they took the other one away with them. When they have extracted the bullet, I suppose they will know for certain."

"May I go to the gun-room?"

"Certainly. The police have finished with it. But the body has been removed."

She accompanied me to the scene of the crime. At that moment Havering entered the hall, and with a quick apology his wife ran to him. I was left to undertake my investigations alone.

I may as well confess at once that they were rather disappointing. In detective novels clues abound, but here I could find nothing that struck me as out of the ordinary except a large bloodstain on the carpet where I judged the dead man had fallen. I examined everything with painstaking care, and took a couple of pictures of the room with my little camera, which I had brought with me. I also examined the ground outside the window, but it appeared to have been so heavily trampled underfoot that I judged it was useless to waste time over it. No, I had seen all that Hunter's Lodge had to show me. I must go back to Elmer's Dale and get into touch with Japp. Accordingly I took leave of the Haverings, and was driven off in the car that had brought us from the station.

I found Japp at the Matlock Arms and he took me forthwith to see the body. Harrington Pace was a small, spare, clean-shaven man, typically American in appearance. He had been shot through the back of the head, and the revolver had been discharged at close quarters.

"Turned away for a moment," remarked Japp, "and the other fellow snatched up a revolver and shot him. The one Mrs. Havering handed over to us was fully loaded, and I suppose the other one was also. Curious what darn fool things people do. Fancy keeping two loaded revolvers hanging up on your wall."

"What do you think of the case?" I asked, as we left the gruesome chamber behind us.

"Well, I'd got my eye on Havering to begin with. Oh, yes," noting my exclamation of astonishment; "Havering has one or two shady incidents in his past. When he was a boy at Oxford there was some funny business about the signature on one of his father's cheques. All hushed up, of course. Then, he's pretty heavily in debt now, and they're the kind of debts he wouldn't like to go to his uncle about, whereas you may be sure the uncle's will would be in his favour. Yes, I'd got my eye on him, and that's why I wanted to speak to him before he saw his wife; but their statements dovetail all right, and I've been to the station and there's no doubt whatever that he left by the 6:15. That gets up to London about 10:30. He went straight to his club, he says, and if that's confirmed all right—why, he couldn't have been shooting his uncle here at nine o'clock in a black beard!"

"Ah, yes, I was going to ask you what you thought about that beard?"

Japp winked.

"I think it grew pretty fast—grew in the five miles from Elmer's Dale to Hunter's Lodge. Americans that I've met are mostly clean-shaven. Yes, it's amongst Mr. Pace's American associates that we'll have to look for the murderer. I questioned the housekeeper first, and then her mistress, and their stories agree all right, but I'm sorry Mrs. Havering didn't get a look at the fellow. She's a smart woman, and she might have noticed something that would set us on the track."

I sat down and wrote a minute and lengthy account to Poirot. I was able to add various further items of information before I posted the letter.

The bullet had been extracted and was proved to have been fired from a revolver identical with the one held by the police. Furthermore, Mr. Havering's movements on the night in question had been checked and verified, and it was proved beyond doubt that he had actually arrived in London by the train in question. And, thirdly, a sensational development had occurred. A city gentleman, living at Ealing, on crossing Haven Green to get to the District Railway Station that morning, had observed a brown-paper parcel stuck between the railings. Opening it, he found that it contained a revolver. He handed the parcel over to the local police station, and before night it was proved to be the one we were in search of, the fellow to that given us by Mrs. Havering. One bullet had been fired from it.

All this I added to my report.

A wire from Poirot arrived whilst I was at breakfast the following morning:

*OF COURSE BLACK-BEARDED MAN WAS NOT HAVERING ONLY YOU OR JAPP WOULD HAVE SUCH AN IDEA WIRE ME DESCRIPTION OF HOUSEKEEPER AND WHAT CLOTHES SHE WORE THIS MORNING SAME OF MRS. HAVERING DO NOT WASTE TIME TAKING PHOTOGRAPHS OF INTERIORS THEY ARE UNDER-EXPOSED AND NOT IN THE LEAST ARTISTIC.*

It seemed to me that Poirot's style was unnecessarily facetious. I also fancied he was a shade jealous of my position on the spot with full facilities for handling the case.

His request for a description of the clothes worn by the two women appeared to me to be simply ridiculous, but I complied as well as I, a mere man, was able to.

At eleven a reply wire came from Poirot:

*ADVISE JAPP ARREST HOUSEKEEPER BEFORE IT IS TOO LATE.*

Dumbfounded, I took the wire to Japp. He swore softly under his breath.

"He's the goods, Monsieur Poirot: if he says so, there's something in it. And I hardly noticed the woman. I don't know that I can go so far as arresting her, but I'll have her watched. We'll go up right away, and take another look at her."

But it was too late. Mrs. Middleton, that quiet middle-aged woman, who had appeared so normal and respectable, had vanished into thin air. Her box had been left behind. It contained only ordinary wearing apparel. There was no clue to her identity, or as to her whereabouts.

From Mrs. Havering we elicited all the facts we could:

"I engaged her about three weeks ago when Mrs. Emery, our former house-keeper, left. She came to me from Mrs. Selbourne's Agency in Fount Street—a very well-known place. I get all my servants from there. They sent several women to see me, but this Mrs. Middleton seemed much the nicest, and had splendid references. I engaged her on the spot, and notified the Agency of the fact. I can't believe that there was anything wrong with her. She was such a nice quiet woman."

The thing was certainly a mystery. Whilst it was clear that the woman herself could not have committed the crime, since at the moment the shot was fired Mrs. Havering was with her in the hall, nevertheless she must have some connection with the murder, or why should she suddenly take to her heels and bolt?

I wired the latest development to Poirot and suggested returning to London and making inquiries at Selbourne's Agency.

Poirot's reply was prompt—

*USELESS TO INQUIRE AT AGENCY THEY WILL NEVER HAVE HEARD OF HER FIND OUT WHAT VEHICLE TOOK HER UP TO HUNTERS LODGE WHEN SHE FIRST ARRIVED THERE.*

Though mystified, I was obedient. The means of transport in Elmer's Dale were limited. The local garage had two battered Ford cars, and there were two station flies. None of these had been requisitioned on the date in question. Questioned, Mrs. Havering explained that she had given the woman the money for her fare down to Derbyshire and sufficient to hire a car or fly to take her up to Hunter's Lodge. There was usually one of the Fords at the station on the chance of its being required. Taking into consideration the further fact that nobody at the station had noticed the arrival of a stranger, black-bearded or otherwise, on the fatal evening, everything seemed to point to the conclusion that the murderer had come to the spot in a car, which had been waiting near at hand to aid his escape, and that the same car had brought the mysterious housekeeper to her new post. I may mention that inquiries at the Agency in London bore out Poirot's prognostication. No such woman as "Mrs. Middleton" had ever been on their books. They had received the Hon. Mrs. Havering's application for a housekeeper, and had sent her various applicants for the post. When she sent them the engagement fee, she omitted to mention which woman she had selected.

Somewhat crestfallen, I returned to London. I found Poirot established in an armchair by the fire in a garish, silk dressing gown. He greeted me with much affection.

"*Mon ami* Hastings! But how glad I am to see you. Veritably I have for you a great affection! And you have enjoyed yourself? You have run to and fro with the good Japp? You have interrogated and investigated to your heart's content?"

"Poirot," I cried, "the thing's a dark mystery! It will never be solved."

"It is true that we are not likely to cover ourselves with glory over it."

"No, indeed. It's a hard nut to crack."

"Oh, as far as that goes — me, I am very good at cracking the nuts! A veritable squirrel! It is not that which embarrasses me. I know well enough who killed Mr. Harrington Pace."

"You know? How did you find out?"

"Your illuminating answers to my wires supplied me with the truth. See here, Hastings, let us examine the facts methodically and in order. Mr. Harrington Pace is a man with a considerable fortune which at his death will doubtless pass to his nephew: point number one. His nephew is known to be desperately hard up: point number two. His nephew is also known to be — shall we say a man of rather loose moral fibre? Point number three."

"But Roger Havering is proved to have journeyed straight up to London."

"*Précisément*; therefore, as Mr. Havering left Elmer's Dale at 6:15, and since Mr. Pace cannot have been killed before he left (or the doctor would have spotted the time of the crime as being given wrongly when he examined the body), we conclude quite rightly, that Mr. Havering did *not* shoot his uncle. But there is a Mrs. Havering, Hastings."

"Impossible! The housekeeper was with her when the shot was fired."

"Ah, yes; the housekeeper. But she has disappeared."

"She will be found."

"I think not. There is something

peculiarly elusive about that housekeeper — don't you think so, Hastings? It struck me at once."

"She played her part, I suppose, and then got out in the nick of time."

"And what was her part?"

"Well — presumably, to admit her confederate, the black-bearded man."

"Oh, no, that was not her part! Her part was what you have just mentioned — to provide an alibi for Mrs. Havering at the moment the shot was fired. And no one will ever find her, *mon ami*, because she does not exist! 'There's no sich a person,' as your so great Shakespeare says."

"It was Dickens," I murmured, unable to suppress a smile. "But what do you mean, Poirot?"

"I mean that Zoe Havering was an actress before her marriage, that you and Japp only saw the housekeeper in a dark hall — a dim middle-aged figure in black with a faint subdued voice; and finally that neither you nor Japp, nor the local police whom the housekeeper fetched, ever saw Mrs. Middleton and her mistress at one and the same time. It was child's play for that clever and daring woman. On the pretext of summoning her mistress, she runs upstairs, slips on a bright jumper and a hat with black curls attached which she jams down over the grey transformation. A few deft touches, and the make-up is removed, a slight dusting of rouge, and the brilliant Zoe Havering comes down with her clear-ringing voice. Nobody looks particularly at the housekeeper. Why should they? There is nothing to connect her with the crime. She, too, has an alibi."

"But the revolver that was found at Ealing? Mrs. Havering could not have placed it there?"

"No; that was Roger Havering's job — but it was a mistake on their part. It put me on the right track. A man who has committed murder with a revolver which he found on the spot would fling it away at once — he would not carry it up to London with him. No; the motive was clear — the criminals wished to focus the interest of the police on a spot far removed from Derbyshire; they were anxious to get the police away as soon as possible from the vicinity of Hunter's Lodge. Of course the revolver found at Ealing was not the one with which Mr. Pace was shot. Roger Havering discharged one shot from it, brought it up to London, went straight to his club to establish his alibi, then went quickly out to Ealing by the District — a matter of about twenty minutes only — placed the parcel where it was found and so back to town. That charming creature, his wife, quietly shoots Mr. Pace after dinner (you remember he was shot from behind? Another significant point, that!) — reloads the revolver and puts it back in its place, and then starts off with her desperate little comedy."

"It's incredible," I muttered, fascinated, "and yet —"

"And yet it is true. *Bien sûr*, my friend, it is true. But to bring that precious pair to justice, that is another matter. Well, Japp must do what he can (I have written him fully). But I very much fear, Hastings, that we shall be obliged to leave them to Fate, or *le bon Dieu*, whichever you prefer."

"The wicked flourish like a green bay-tree," I reminded him.

"But at a price, Hastings, always at a price, *croyez-moi*."

Poirot's forebodings were confirmed, Japp, though convinced of the truth of his theory, was unable to get together the necessary evidence to ensure a conviction.

Mr. Pace's huge fortune passed into the hands of his murderers. Nevertheless, Nemesis did overtake them, and when I read in the paper that the Hon. Roger and Mrs. Havering were amongst those killed in the crashing of the Air Mail to Paris I knew that Justice was satisfied.

# THE CLUE OF THE CHOCOLATE BOX.

"The Clue of the Chocolate Box" was first published in *The Sketch* on May 23, 1923.

It was a wild night. Outside, the wind howled malevolently, and the rain beat against the windows in great gusts.

Poirot and I sat facing the hearth, our legs stretched out to the cheerful blaze. Between us was a small table. On my side of it stood some carefully brewed hot toddy; on Poirot's was a cup of thick, rich chocolate which I would not have drunk for hundreds of pounds. My pipe was ready to my hand. I filled it with loving care and lit it. Leaning back in my chair, and watching the smoke rise through half-closed lids, I breathed a sigh of utter content. Poirot sipped the thick brown mess in the pink china cup, and he too sighed the sigh of those who are at peace with the world.

"*Quelle belle vie!*" he murmured.

"Yes, it's a good old world," I agreed. "Here am I with a job, and a good job too! And here are you, famous —"

"Oh, *mon ami,*" protested Poirot modestly.

"But you are. And rightly so! When I think back on your long line of successes, I am positively amazed. I don't believe you know what failure is."

"He would be a droll kind of

original who could say that."

"No; but, seriously, *have* you ever failed?"

"Innumerable times, my friend. What would you? *La bonne chance* cannot always be on your side. I have been called in too late. Very often another, working towards the same goal, has arrived there first. Twice have I been stricken down with illness just as I was on the point of success. One must take the downs with the ups, my friend."

"I didn't quite mean that," I said. "I meant, had you ever been completely down and out over a case through your own fault?"

"Ah, I comprehend! You ask if I have ever made the complete prize ass of myself, as you say over here? Once, my friend"—a slow, reflective smile hovered over his face—"yes, once I made a fool of myself."

He sat up suddenly in his chair.

"See here, my friend, you have, I know, kept a record of my little successes. You shall add one more story to the collection, the story of a failure."

He leaned forward and placed a log on the fire. Then, after carefully wiping his hands on a little duster that hung on a nail by the fireplace, he leaned back and commenced his story.

"That of which I tell you took place in Belgium many years ago. It was at the time of the terrible struggle in France between church and state. Monsieur Paul Déroulard was a French deputy of note. It was an open secret that the portfolio of a Minister awaited him. He was among the bitterest of the anti-Catholic party, and it was certain that on his accession to power, he would have to face violent enmity. He was in many ways a peculiar man. Though he neither drank nor smoked, he was nevertheless not so scrupulous in other ways. You comprehend, Hastings, *c'était des femmes—toujours des femmes!*

"He had married some years earlier a young lady from Brussels who had brought him a substantial *dot*. Undoubtedly the money was useful to him in his career, as his family was not rich—though on the other hand he was entitled to call himself *Monsieur le Baron* if he chose. There were no children of the marriage, and his wife died after two years—the result of a fall downstairs. Amongst the property which his wife bequeathed to him was a house in the Avenue Louise in Brussels. This he did not sell, and he always spent a part of the year in the Belgian capitol.

"It was in this house that his sudden death took place, the event coinciding with the resignation of the Minister whose portfolio he was to inherit. All the papers printed long notices of his career. His death, which had taken place quite suddenly in the evening after dinner, was attributed to heart failure.

"At that time, *mon ami*, I was, as you know, a member of the Belgian detective force. The death of Monsieur Paul Déroulard was not particularly interesting to me. I am, as you also know, *bon catholique*, and his demise seemed to me both fortunate and providential, so far as I thought about it at all.

"It was some three days afterwards that I received a visitor at my own apartments. My vacation had just begun, and I was thinking of a little trip to Spa. I was reading an account of the various sources and the maladies that were benefited thereby when I was informed that a young lady was demanding me. Thinking that it was, perhaps, my little sister Yvonne, I prayed my landlady to make her mount. To my astonishment, the lady who entered the room was a total stranger to me. She was heavily veiled, but evidently quite young, and I perceived at once that she was a *jeune fille tout à fait comme il faut*.

"'You are Monsieur Hercule Poirot?' she asked in a low sweet voice.

"I bowed.

"'Of the detective service?'

"Again I bowed. 'Be seated, I pray of you, Mademoiselle,' I said.

"She accepted a chair and drew aside her veil. Her face was charming, though marred with tears, and haunted as though with some poignant anxiety.

"'Monsieur,' she said, 'I understand that you are now taking a vacation. Therefore you will be free to take up a private case. You understand that I do not wish to call in the police.'

"I shook my head. 'I fear what you ask is impossible, Mademoiselle. Even though on vacation, I am still of the police.'

"She leaned forward. '*Ecoutez, Monsieur.* All that I ask of you is to investigate. The result of your investigations you are at perfect liberty to report to the police. If what I believe to be true is true, we shall need all the machinery of the law.'

"That placed a somewhat different complexion on the matter, and I placed myself at her service without more ado.

"A slight colour rose in her cheeks. 'I thank you, Monsieur. It is the death of Monsieur Paul Déroulard that I ask you to investigate.'

"'*Comment?*' I exclaimed, surprised.

"'Monsieur, I have nothing to go upon — nothing but my woman's instinct; but I am convinced — *convinced*, I tell you — that Monsieur Déroulard did not die a natural death.'

"'But surely the doctors —'

"'Doctors may be mistaken. He was so robust, so strong — ah, Monsieur Poirot, I beseech you to help me!'

"The poor child was almost beside herself. She would have knelt to me. I soothed her as best I could.

"'I will help you, Mademoiselle. I feel almost sure that your fears are unfounded, but we will see. First, I will ask you to describe to me the inmates of the house.'

"'There are the domestics, of course, Jeannette, Félicie, and Denise the cook. She has been there many years; the others are simple country girls. Also there is François, but he too is an old servant. Then there is Monsieur Déroulard's mother ,who lived with him, and myself. My name is Virginie Mesnard. I am a poor cousin of the late Madame Déroulard, Monsieur Paul's wife, and I have been a member of their *ménage* for over three years. I have now described to you the household. There were also two guests staying in the house.'

"'And they were?'

"'Monsieur de Saint Alard, a neighbour of Monsieur Déroulard's in France. Also an English friend, Mr. John Wilson.'

"'Are they still with you?'

"'Mr. Wilson, yes, but Monsieur de Saint Alard departed yesterday.'

"'And what is your plan, Mademoiselle Mesnard?'

"'If you will present yourself at the house in half an hour's time, I will have arranged some story to account for your presence. I had better represent you to be connected with journalism in some way. I shall say you have come from Paris, and that you have brought a card of introduction from Monsieur de Saint Alard. Madame Déroulard is very feeble in health, and will pay little attention to details.'

"On Mademoiselle's ingenious pretext I was admitted to the house, and after a brief interview with the dead deputy's mother—who was a wonderfully imposing and aristocratic figure though obviously in failing health—I was made free of the premises."

Poirot paused in his narrative, drank off the remainder of his fast-cooling chocolate at a draught, and wiped his lips delicately.

"I wonder, my friend, whether you can possibly figure to yourself the difficulties of my task? Here was a man whose death had taken place three days previously. If there *had* been foul play, only one possibility was admittable—*poison.* And I had no chance of seeing the body, and there was no possibility of examining, or analysing, any medium in which the poison could have been administered. There were no clues, false or otherwise, to consider. Had the man been poisoned? Had he died a natural death? I, Hercule Poirot, with nothing to help me, had to decide.

"First, I interviewed the domestics, and with their aid I recapitulated the evening. I paid especial notice to the food at dinner, and the method of serving it. The soup had been served by Monsieur Déroulard himself from a tureen. Next a dish of cutlets. Then a chicken. Finally, a compote of fruits. And all placed on the table and served by Monsieur himself. The coffee was brought in a big pot to the dinner-table. Nothing there, *mon ami* — impossible to poison one without poisoning all!

"After dinner Madame Déroulard had retired to her own apartments and Mademoiselle Virginie had accompanied her. The three men had adjourned to Monsieur Déroulard's study. Here they had chatted amicably for some time, when suddenly, without any warning, the deputy had fallen heavily to the ground. Monsieur de Saint Alard had rushed out and told François to fetch the doctor immediately. 'He said it was without doubt an apoplexy,' explained the man. But when the doctor arrived, the patient was past help.

"Mr. John Wilson, to whom I was presented by Mademoiselle Virginie, was what was known in those days as a regular 'John Bull Englishman,' middle-aged and burly. His account, delivered in very British French, was substantially the same.

" 'Déroulard went very red in the face, and down he fell. A fit of some kind, I thought.'

"There was nothing further to be found out there. Next I went to the scene of the tragedy — the study — and was left alone there at my own request. So far there was nothing to support Mademoiselle Mesnard's theory. I could not but believe that it was a delusion on her part. Evidently she had entertained a romantic passion for the dead man which had not permitted her to take a normal view of the case. Nevertheless, I searched the study with meticulous care. It was just possible that a hypodermic needle might have been introduced into the dead man's chair in such a way as to allow of a fatal injection. The minute puncture it would cause was likely to remain unnoticed. But I could discover no sign to support the theory. I flung myself down in the chair with a gesture of despair.

" '*Enfin*, I abandon it!' I said aloud. 'There is not a clue anywhere! Everything is perfectly normal.'

"As I said the words, my eyes fell on a large box of chocolates standing on a table nearby, and my heart gave a leap. It might not be a clue to Monsieur Déroulard's death, but here at least was something that was *not* normal. I lifted the lid. The box was full, untouched; not a chocolate was missing — but that only made the peculiarity that had caught my eye more striking. For, see you, Hastings, while the box itself was *pink*, the lid was *blue*. Now, one often sees a blue ribbon on a pink box, and vice-versa; but a box of one colour, and a lid of another — no, decidedly — *ça ne se voit jamais!*

"I did not as yet see that this little incident was of any use to me, yet I determined to investigate it as being out of the ordinary. I rang the bell for François, and asked him if his late master had been fond of sweets. A faint, melancholy smile came to his lips.

" 'Passionately fond of them, Monsieur. He would always have a box of chocolates in the house. He did not drink wine of any kind, you see.'

"'Yet this box has not been touched?' I lifted the lid to show him.

"'*Pardon*, Monsieur, but that was a new box purchased on the day of his death, the other being nearly finished.'

"'Then the other box was finished on the day of his death?' I said slowly.

"'Yes, Monsieur, I found it empty in the morning and threw it away.'

"'Did Monsieur Déroulard eat sweets at all hours of the day?'

"'Usually after dinner, Monsieur.'

"I began to see light.

"'François,' I said, 'you can be discreet?'

"'If there is need, Monsieur.'

"'*Bon*. Know, then, that I am of the police. Can you find me that other box?'

"'Without doubt, Monsieur. It will be in the dustbin.'

"He departed, and returned in a few minutes with a dust-covered object. It was the duplicate of the box I held, save for the fact that this time the box was *blue* and the lid was *pink*. I thanked François, recommended him once more to be discreet, and left the house in the Avenue Louise without more ado.

"Next I called upon the doctor who had attended Monsieur Déroulard. With him I had a difficult task. He entrenched himself prettily behind a wall of learned phraseology, but I fancied that he was not quite as sure about the case as he would like to be.

"'There have been many curious occurrences of the kind,' he observed, when I had managed to disarm him somewhat. 'A sudden fit of anger, a violent emotion — after a heavy dinner, *c'est entendu* — then, with an access of rage, the blood flies to the head, and — pst! — there you are!'

"'But Monsieur Déroulard had had no violent emotion.'

"'No? I made sure that he had been having a stormy altercation with Monsieur de Saint Alard.'

"'Why should he?'

"'*C'est evident!*' The doctor shrugged his shoulders. 'Was not Monsieur de Saint Alard a Catholic of the most fanatical? Their friendship was being ruined by this question of Church and State. Not a day passed without discussions. To Monsieur de Saint Alard, Déroulard appeared almost as Antichrist.'

"This was unexpected, and gave me food for thought.

"'One more question, Doctor: would it be possible to introduce a fatal dose of poison into a chocolate?'

"'It would be *possible*, I suppose,' said the doctor slowly. 'Pure prussic acid would meet the case if there were no chance of evaporation, and a tiny globule of anything might be swallowed unnoticed — but it does not seem a very likely supposition. A chocolate full of morphine or strychnine —' He made a wry face. 'You comprehend, Monsieur

Poirot — one bite would be enough! The unwary one would not stand upon ceremony.'

"'Thank you, *Monsieur le Docteur.*'

"I withdrew. Next I made inquiries of the chemists, especially those in the neighbourhood of the Avenue Louise. It is good to be of the police. I got the information I wanted without any trouble. Only in one case could I hear of any poison having been supplied to the house in question. This was some eye drops of atropine sulphate for Madame Déroulard. Atropine is a potent poison, and for the moment I was elated, but the symptoms of atropine poisoning are closely allied to those of ptomaine, and bear no resemblance to those I was studying. Besides, the prescription was an old one. Madame Déroulard had suffered from cataracts in both eyes for many years.

"I was turning away discouraged when the chemist's voice called me back.

"'*Un moment*, Monsieur Poirot. I remember, the girl who brought that prescription, she said something about having to go on to the *English* chemist. You might try there.'

"I did. Once more enforcing my official status, I got the information I wanted. On the day before Monsieur Déroulard's death they had made up a prescription for Mr. John Wilson. Not that there was any making up about it. They were simply little tablets of trinitrin. I asked if I might see some. He showed me them, and my heart beat faster — for the tiny tablets were of *chocolate*.

"'Is it a poison?' I asked.

"'No, Monsieur.'

"'Can you describe to me its effect?'

"'It lowers the blood pressure. It is given for some forms of heart trouble — angina pectoris for instance. It relieves the arterial tension. In arterio-sclerosis —'

"I interrupted him. '*Ma foi!* This rigmarole says nothing to me. Does it cause the face to flush?'

"'Certainly it does.'

"'And supposing I ate ten — twenty — of your little tablets, what then?'

"'I should not advise you to attempt it,' he replied drily.

"'And yet you say it is not poison?'

"'There are many things not called poison which can kill a man,' he replied as before.

"I left the shop elated. At last, things had begun to march!"

"But the whole thing was solved," I cried. "You knew then that it was John Wilson who had committed the crime."

"As usual, Hastings, you speak without reflection. I knew that John Wilson had the means for the crime — but what about the motive? He had come to Belgium on business, and had asked Monsieur

Déroulard, whom he knew slightly, to put him up. There was apparently no way in which Déroulard's death could benefit him. Moreover, I discovered by inquiries in England that he had suffered for some years from that painful form of heart disease known as angina. Therefore he had a genuine right to have those tablets in his possession. Nevertheless, I was convinced that someone had gone to the chocolate box, opening the full one first by mistake, and had abstracted the contents of the last chocolate, cramming in instead as many little trinitrin tablets as it would hold. The chocolates were large ones. Between twenty and thirty tablets, I felt sure, could have been inserted. But who had done this?

"There were two guests in the house. John Wilson had the means. Saint Alard had the motive. Remember, he was a fanatic, and there is no fanatic like a religious fanatic. Could he, by any means, have got hold of John Wilson's trinitrin?

"Another little idea came to me. Ah, you smile at my 'little ideas!' Why had Wilson run out of trinitrin? Surely he would bring an adequate supply from England. I called once more at the house in the Avenue Louise. Wilson was out, but saw the girl who did his room, Félicie. I demanded of her immediately whether it was not true that Monsieur Wilson had lost a bottle from his wash-stand some little time ago. The girl responded eagerly. It was quite true. She, Félicie, had been blamed for it. The English gentleman had evidently thought that she had broken it, and did not like to say so. Whereas she had never even touched it. Without doubt it was Jeannette — always nosing round where she had no business to be —

"I calmed the flow of words, and took my leave. I knew now all that I wanted to know. It remained for me to prove my case. That, I felt, would not be easy. *I* might be sure that Saint Alard had removed the bottle of trinitrin from John Wilson's washstand; but to convince others, I would have to produce evidence. And I had none to produce!

"Never mind. I *knew* — that was the great thing. You remember our difficulty in the Styles case, Hastings? There again, I *knew* — but it took me a long time to find the last link which made my chain of evidence against the murderer complete.

"I asked for an interview with Mademoiselle Mesnard. She came at once. I demanded of her the address of Monsieur de Saint Alard. A look of trouble came over her face.

" 'Why do you want it, Monsieur?'

" 'Mademoiselle, it is necessary.'

"She seemed doubtful — troubled.

" 'He can tell you nothing. He is a man whose thoughts are not in this world. He hardly notices what goes on around him.'

"'Possibly, Mademoiselle. Nevertheless, he was an old friend of Monsieur Deroulard's. There may be things he can tell me — things of the past — old grudges — old love-affairs.'

"The girl flushed and bit her lip. 'As you please — but — but I feel sure now that I have been mistaken. It was good of you to accede to my demand, but I was upset — almost distraught at the time. I see now that there is no mystery to solve. Leave it, I beg of you, Monsieur.'

"I eyed her closely.

"'Mademoiselle,' I said, 'it is sometimes difficult for a dog to find a scent, but once he *has* found it, nothing on earth will make him leave it! Not if he is a good dog. And I, Mademoiselle, I, Hercule Poirot, am a very good dog.'

"Without a word she turned away. A few minutes later she returned with the address written on a sheet of paper. I left the house. François was waiting for me outside. He looked at me anxiously.

"'There is no news, Monsieur?'

"'None as yet, my friend.'

"'Ah! Pauvre Monsieur Déroulard!' he sighed. 'I too was of his way of thinking. I do not care for priests. Not that I would say so in the house. The women are all devout — a good thing perhaps. *Madame est très pieuse — et Mademoiselle Virginie aussi.*'

"Mademoiselle Virginie? Was she '*très pieuse?*' Thinking of the tear-stained passionate face I had seen that first day, I wondered.

"Having obtained the address of Monsieur de Saint Alard, I wasted no time. I arrived in the neighbourhood of his chateau in the Ardennes, but it was some days before I could find a pretext for gaining admission to the house. In the end I did — how do you think? — as a plumber, *mon ami!* It was the affair of a moment to arrange a neat little gas-leak in his bed-room. I departed for my tools, and took care to return with them at an hour when I knew I should have the field pretty well to myself. What I was searching for, I hardly knew. The one thing needful, I could not believe there was any chance of finding. He would never have run the risk of keeping it.

"Still when I found the little cupboard above the washstand locked, I could not resist the temptation of seeing what was inside it. The lock was quite a simple one to pick. The door swung open. It was full of old bottles. I took them up one by one with a trembling hand. Suddenly, I uttered a cry. Figure to yourself, my friend, I held in my hand a little phial with an English chemist's label. On it were the words: 'Trinitrin Tablets. One to be taken when required. Mr. John Wilson.'"

Poirot paused dramatically.

"Well?" I cried interestedly. "What happened next?"

"*Ma foi!* I controlled my emotion, closed the cupboard, slipped the bottle into my pocket, and continued to repair the gas leak. One must be methodical. Then I left the château, and took train for my own country as soon as possible. I arrived in Brussels late that night. I was writing out a report for the *préfet* in the morning, when a note was brought to me. It was from old Madame Déroulard, and it summoned me to the house in the Avenue Louise without delay.

"François opened the door to me.

"'Madame la Baronne is awaiting you.'

"He conducted me to her apartments. She sat in state in a large armchair. There was no sign of Mademoiselle Virginie.

"'Monsieur Poirot,' said the old lady, 'I have just learned that you are not what you pretend to be. You are a police officer.'

"'That is so, Madame.'

"'You came here to inquire into the circumstances of my son's death?'

"Again I replied: 'That is so, Madame.'

"'I should be glad if you would tell me what progress you have made.'

"I hesitated.

"'First I would like to know how you have learned all this, Madame.'

"'From one who is no longer of this world.'

"Her words, and the brooding way she uttered them, sent a chill to my heart. I was incapable of speech.

"'Therefore, Monsieur, I would beg of you most urgently to tell me exactly what progress you have made in your investigation.'

"'Madame, my investigation is finished.'

"'My son?'

"'Was killed deliberately.'

"'You know by whom?'

"'Yes, Madame.'

"'Who, then?'

"'Monsieur de Saint Alard.'

"'You are wrong. Monsieur de Saint Alard is incapable of such a crime.'

"'The proofs are in my hands.'

"'I beg of you once more to tell me all.'

"This time I obeyed, going over each step that had led me to the discovery of the truth. She listened attentively. At the end she nodded her head.

"'Yes, yes, it is all as you say, all but one thing. It was not Monsieur de Saint Alard who killed my son. It was I, his mother.'

"I stared at her. She continued to nod her head gently.

"'It is well that I sent for you. It is the providence of the good God that Virginie told me before she departed for the convent, what she had done. Listen, Monsieur Poirot! My son was an evil man. He persecuted the church. He led a life of mortal sin. He dragged down the other souls beside his own. But there was worse than that. As I came out of my room in this house one morning, I saw my daughter-in-law standing at the head of the stairs. She was reading a letter. I saw my son steal up behind her. One swift push, and she fell, striking her head on the marble steps. When they picked her up she was dead. My son was a murderer, and only I, his mother, knew it.'

"She closed her eyes for a moment. 'You cannot conceive, Monsieur, of my agony, my despair. What was I to do? Denounce him to the police? I could not bring myself to do it. It was my duty, but my flesh was weak. Besides, would they believe me? My eyesight had been failing for some time — they would say I was mistaken. I kept silence. But my conscience gave me no peace. By keeping silence I too was a murderer.

"'My son inherited his wife's money. He flourished as the green bay tree. And now he was to have a Minister's portfolio. His persecution of the church would be redoubled. And there was Virginie. She, poor child, beautiful, naturally pious, was fascinated by him. He had a strange and terrible power over women. I saw it coming. I was powerless to prevent it. He had no intention of marrying her. The time came when she was ready to yield everything to him.

"'Then I saw my path clear. He was my son. I had given him life. I was responsible for him. He had killed one woman's body, now he would kill another's soul! I went to Mr. Wilson's room, and took the bottle of tablets. He had once said laughingly that there were enough in it to kill a man! I went into the study and opened the big box of chocolates that always stood on the table. I opened a new box by mistake. The other was on the table also. There was just one chocolate left in it. That simplified things. No one ate chocolates except my son and Virginie. I would keep her with me that night. All went as I had planned —'

"She paused, closing her eyes a minute then opened them again.

"'Monsieur Poirot, I am in your hands. They tell me I have not many days to live. I am willing to answer for my action before the good God. Must I answer for it on earth also?'

"I hesitated. 'But the empty bottle, Madame,' I said, to gain time. 'How came that into Monsieur de Saint Alard's possession?'

"'When he came to say goodbye to me, Monsieur, I slipped it into his pocket. I did not know how to get rid of it. I am so infirm that I cannot move about much without help, and finding it empty in my rooms might have caused suspicion. You understand, Monsieur —' she drew herself up to her full height — 'it was with no idea of casting suspicion on Monsieur de Saint Alard! I never dreamed of such a thing. I thought his valet would find an empty bottle and throw it away without question.'

"I bowed my head. 'I comprehend, Madame,' I said.

"'And your decision, Monsieur?'

"Her voice was firm and unfaltering, her head held as high as ever.

"I rose to my feet.

"'Madame,' I said, 'I have the honour to wish you good day. I have made my investigations — and failed! The matter is closed.'

Poirot was silent for a moment, then said quietly: "She died just a week later. Mademoiselle Virginie passed through her novitiate, and duly took the veil. That, my friend, is the story. I must admit that I do not make a fine figure in it."

"But that was hardly a failure," I expostulated. "What else could you have thought under the circumstances?"

"Ah, *sacré, mon ami*!" cried Poirot, becoming suddenly animated. "Is it that you do not see? But I was thirty-six times an idiot! My grey cells, they functioned not at all. The whole time I had the clue in my hands."

"What clue?"

"*The chocolate box!* Do you not see? Would anyone in possession of their full eyesight make such a mistake? I knew Madame Déroulard had cataracts — the atropine drops told me that. There was only one person in the household whose eyesight was such that she could not see which lid to replace. It was the chocolate box that started me on the track, and yet up to the end I failed consistently to perceive its real significance!

"Also my psychology was at fault. Had Monsieur de Saint Alard been the criminal, he would never have kept an incriminating bottle. Finding it was a proof of his innocence. I had learned already from Mademoiselle Virginie that he was absent-minded. Altogether it was a miserable affair that I have recounted to you there! Only to you have I told the story. You comprehend, I do not figure well in it! An old lady commits a crime in such a simple and clever fashion that I, Hercule Poirot, am completely deceived! *Sapristi,* it does not bear thinking of! Forget it. Or no — remember it, and if you think at any time that I am growing conceited — it is not likely, but it might arise" — I concealed a smile — "*eh bien*, my friend, you shall say to me, 'Chocolate box.' Is it agreed?"

"It's a bargain!"

"After all," said Poirot reflectively, "it was an experience! I, who have undoubtedly the finest brain in Europe at present, can afford to be magnanimous!"

"Chocolate box," I murmured gently.

"Pardon, *mon ami*?"

I looked at Poirot's innocent face, as he bent forward inquiringly, and my heart smote me. I had suffered often at his hands, but I, too, though not possessing the finest brain in Europe, could afford to be magnanimous!

"Nothing," I lied, and lit another pipe, smiling to myself.

# THE GREY CELLS OF MONSIEUR POIROT.

*The second series of short stories published in* ***The Sketch: A Journal of Art and Actuality*** *from September to December 1923.*

# THE ADVENTURE OF THE EGYPTIAN TOMB.

"The Adventure of the Egyptian Tomb" was first published in *The Sketch* on September 26, 1923.

I have always considered that one of the most thrilling and dramatic of the many adventures I have shared with Poirot was that of our investigation into the strange series of deaths which followed upon the discovery and opening of the Tomb of King Men-her-Ra.

Hard upon the discovery of the Tomb of Tutankhamen by Lord Carnarvon, Sir John Willard and Mr. Bleibner of New York, pursuing their excavations not far from Cairo, in the vicinity of the Pyramids of Gizeh, came unexpectedly on a series of funeral chambers. The greatest interest was aroused by their discovery. The tomb appeared to be that of King Men-her-Ra, one of those shadowy kings of the Eighth Dynasty, when the Old Kingdom was falling to decay. Little was known about this period, and the discoveries were fully reported in the newspapers.

An event soon occurred which took a profound hold on the public mind. Sir John Willard died quite suddenly of heart failure.

The more sensational newspapers immediately took the opportunity of reviving all the old superstitious stories connected with the ill luck of certain Egyptian treasures. The unlucky Mummy at the British Museum, that hoary old chestnut, was dragged out with fresh zest, was quietly denied by the Museum, but nevertheless enjoyed all its usual vogue.

A fortnight later Mr. Bleibner died of acute blood poisoning, and a few days afterwards a nephew of his shot himself in New York. The "Curse of Men-her-Ra" was the talk of the day, and the magic power of dead-and-gone Egypt was exalted to a feverish point.

It was then that Poirot received a brief note from Lady Willard, widow of the dead archaeologist, asking him to go and see her at her house in Kensington Square. I accompanied him.

Lady Willard was a tall, thin woman, dressed in deep mourning. Her haggard face bore eloquent testimony to her recent grief.

"It is kind of you to have come so promptly, Monsieur Poirot."

"I am at your service, Lady Willard. You wished to consult me?"

"You are, I am aware, a detective, but it is not only as a detective that I wish to consult you. You are a man of original views, I know, you have experience of the world; tell me, Monsieur Poirot, what are your views on the supernatural?"

Poirot hesitated for a moment before he replied. He seemed to be considering. Finally he said:

"Let us not misunderstand each other, Lady Willard. It is not a general question that you are asking me there. It has a personal application, has it not? You are referring obliquely to the death of your late husband?"

"That is so," she admitted.

"You want me to investigate the circumstances of his death?"

"I want you to ascertain for me exactly how much is newspaper chatter, and, how much may be said to be founded on fact. Three deaths, Monsieur Poirot — each one explicable taken by itself, but taken together surely an almost unbelievable coincidence, and all within a month of the opening of the tomb! It may be mere superstition, it may be some potent curse from the past that operates in ways undreamed of by modern science. The fact remains — three deaths! And I am afraid, Monsieur Poirot, horribly afraid. It may not yet be the end."

"For whom do you fear?"

"For my son. When the news of my husband's death came I was ill. My son, who has just come down from Oxford, went out there. He brought the — the body home; but now he has gone out again — in spite of my prayers and entreaties. He is so fascinated by the work that he intends to take his father's place and carry on the system of excavations. You may think me a foolish, credulous woman, but, Monsieur Poirot, I am afraid. Supposing that the spirit of the dead king is not yet appeased?

Perhaps to you I seem to be talking nonsense —"

"No, indeed, Lady Willard," said Poirot quickly. "I, too, believe in the force of superstition, one of the greatest forces the world has ever known."

I looked at him in surprise. I should never have credited Poirot with being superstitious. But the little man was obviously in earnest.

"What you really demand, Milady, is that I shall protect your son? I will do my utmost to keep him from harm."

"Yes, in the ordinary way, but against an occult influence?"

"In volumes of the Middle Ages, Lady Willard, you will find many ways of counteracting black magic. Perhaps they knew more than we moderns with all our boasted science. Now let us come to facts, that I may have guidance. Your husband had always been a devoted Egyptologist, hadn't he?"

"Yes, from his youth upwards. He was one of the greatest living authorities upon the subject."

"But Mr. Bleibner, I understand, was more or less of an amateur?"

"Oh, quite. He was a very wealthy man who dabbled freely in any subject that happened to take his fancy. My husband managed to interest him in Egyptology, and it was his money that was so useful in financing the expedition."

"And the nephew? What do you know of his tastes? Was he with the party at all?"

"I do not think so. In fact I never knew of his existence till I read of his death in the paper. I do not think he and Mr. Bleibner can have been at all intimate. He never spoke of having any relations."

"Who are the other members of the party?"

"Well, there is Dr. Tosswill, a minor official connected with the British Museum; Mr. Schneider, of the Metropolitan Museum in New York; a young American secretary; Dr. Ames, who accompanies the expedition in his professional capacity; and Hassan, my husband's devoted native servant."

"Do you remember the name of the American secretary?"

"Harper, I think, but I cannot be sure. He had not been with Mr. Bleibner very long, I know. He was a very pleasant young fellow."

"Thank you, Lady Willard."

"If there is anything else —"

"For the moment, nothing. Leave it now in my hands, and be assured that I will do all that is humanly possible to protect your son."

They were not exactly reassuring words, and I observed Lady Willard wince as he uttered them. Yet, at the same time, the fact that he had not pooh-poohed her fears seemed in itself to be a relief to her.

For my part I had never before suspected that Poirot had so deep a vein of superstition in his nature. I tackled him on the subject as we went homewards. His manner was grave and earnest.

"But yes, Hastings. I believe in these things. You must not underrate the force of superstition."

"What are we going to do about it?"

"*Toujours pratique*, the good Hastings! *Eh bien*, to begin with we are going to cable to New York for fuller details of young Mr. Bleibner's death."

He duly sent off his cable. The reply was full and precise. Young Rupert Bleibner had been in low water for several years. He had been a beachcomber and a remittance man in several South Sea islands, but had returned to New York two years ago, where he had rapidly sunk lower and lower. The most significant thing, to my mind, was that he had recently managed to borrow enough money to take him to Egypt. "I've a good friend there I can borrow from," he had declared. Here, however, his plans had gone awry. He had returned to New York cursing his skinflint of an uncle who cared more for the bones of dead-and-gone kings than his own flesh and blood. It was during his sojourn in Egypt that the death of Sir John Willard had occurred. Rupert had plunged once more into his life of dissipation in New York, and then, without warning, he had committed suicide, leaving behind him a letter which contained some curious phrases. It seemed written in a sudden fit of remorse. He referred to himself as a leper and an outcast, and the letter ended by declaring that such as he were better dead.

A shadowy theory leapt into my brain. I had never really believed in the vengeance of a long-dead Egyptian king. I saw here a more modern crime. Supposing this young man had decided to do away with his uncle—preferably by poison. By mistake, Sir John Willard receives the fatal dose. The young man returns to New York, haunted by his crime. The news of his uncle's death reaches him. He realizes how unnecessary his crime has been, and stricken with remorse, takes his own life.

I outlined my solution to Poirot. He was interested.

"It is ingenious what you have thought of there—decidedly it is ingenious. It may even be true. But you leave out of count the fatal influence of the Tomb."

I shrugged my shoulders.

"You still think that has something to do with it?"

"So much so, *mon ami*, that we start for Egypt to-morrow."

"What?" I cried, astonished.

"I have said it." An expression of conscious heroism spread over Poirot's face. Then he groaned. "But oh," he lamented, "the sea! The hateful sea!"

It was a week later. Beneath our feet was the golden sand of the desert. The hot sun poured down overhead. Poirot, the picture of misery, wilted by my side. The little man was not a good traveller.

Our four days' voyage from Marseilles had been one long agony to him. He had landed at Alexandria the wraith of his former self; even his usual neatness had deserted him. We had arrived in Cairo and had driven out at once to the Mena House Hotel, right in the shadow of the Pyramids.

The charm of Egypt had laid hold of me. Not so Poirot. Dressed precisely the same as in London, he carried a small clothes brush in his pocket, and waged an unceasing war on the dust which accumulated on his dark apparel.

"And my boots," he wailed. "Regard them, Hastings. My boots, of the neat patent leather, usually so smart and shining. See, the sand is *inside* them, which is painful, and *outside* them, which outrages the eyesight! Also the heat, it causes my moustaches to become limp — but limp!"

"Look at the Sphinx," I urged. "Even I can feel the mystery and the charm it exhales."

Poirot looked at it discontentedly.

"It has not the air happy," he declared. "How could it, half-buried in sand in that untidy fashion. Ah, this cursed sand!"

"Come, now, there's a lot of sand in Belgium," I reminded him, mindful of a holiday spent at Knocke-sur-mer in the midst of "*les dunes impeccables*," as the guidebook had phrased it.

"Not in Brussels," declared Poirot. He gazed at the Pyramids thoughtfully. "It is true that they, at least, are of a shape solid and geometrical, but their surface is of an unevenness most unpleasing. And the palm-trees, I like them not. Not even do they plant them in rows!"

I cut short his lamentations, by suggesting that we should start for the camp. We were to ride there on camels, and the beasts were patiently kneeling, waiting for us to mount, in charge of several picturesque boys headed by a voluble dragoman.

I pass over the spectacle of Poirot on a camel. He started by groans and lamentations and ended by shrieks, gesticulations and invocations to the Virgin Mary and every Saint in the calendar. In the end, he descended ignominiously and finished the journey on a diminutive donkey. I must admit that a trotting camel is no joke for the amateur. I was stiff for several days.

At least we neared the scene of the excavations. A sunburnt man with a grey beard, in white clothes and wearing a helmet, came to meet us.

"Monsieur Poirot and Captain Hastings? We received your cable. I'm sorry that there was no one to meet you in Cairo. An unforeseen event occurred which completed disorganized our plans."

Poirot paled. His hand, which had stolen to his clothes brush, stayed its course.

"Not another death?" he breathed.

"Yes."

"Sir Guy Willard?" I cried.

"No, Captain Hastings. My American colleague, Mr. Schneider."

"And the cause?" demanded Poirot.

"Tetanus."

I blanched. All around me I seemed to feel an atmosphere of evil, subtle and menacing. A horrible thought flashed across me. Supposing I were the next?

Two other men joined us — the American doctor, Dr. Ames, and a good-looking, impetuous young fellow of twenty-one whom I recognized from his likeness to Lady Willard, and also from the fact that he was less sunburnt than the rest. Our first friend proved to be Dr. Tosswill, the British expert.

Poirot made a bee-line for the medical man, who took us into his tent. We let down the flap, and Poirot asked question after question. Dr. Ames gave his replies clearly and precisely. He looked a thoroughly efficient man of the most modern type.

"When did this death take place?"

"Three days ago."

"Did you not inject antiserum?"

"Certainly we did, but it was of no avail."

"Had you it with you, or did you procure it from Cairo?"

"We procured it from Cairo."

"Have there been any other cases of tetanus?"

"This was the only one."

"Are you certain that the death of Mr. Bleibner was not due to tetanus in any form?"

"Absolutely certain. He had a scratch on his thumb which became poisoned. The symptoms were entirely different."

"There have been four deaths, all entirely different — one heart failure, one blood-poisoning, one suicide and one tetanus. Tell me, *Monsieur le Docteur*, is there nothing to link the four? No — disrespect, shall we say? — offered to the dead Men-Her-Ra?"

"Why, Monsieur Poirot, don't tell me you believe all that nonsense?"

"Do not you?"

"No, Sir; I am a scientific man," said the doctor warmly.

"Was there no science then in Ancient Egypt?"

Dr. Ames seemed rather at a loss for a reply. Poirot pursued his advantage.

"What do the native workmen think of all this?"

"I guess that where white folk lose their heads, native aren't going to be far behind. I'll admit that they're getting what you might call scared, but they've no cause to be. The thing's pure coincidence."

"I do not agree with you," said Poirot in his haughtiest manner.

"What do you believe?"

For answer Poirot produced a little book from his pocket, an ancient tattered volume. As he held it out I saw its title, *The Magic of the Egyptians and Chaldeans*. Then, wheeling round, he strode out of the tent. The doctor stared at me.

"What is his little idea?"

The phrase, so familiar on Poirot's lips, made me smile as it came from another.

"I don't know exactly," I confessed. "He's got some plan of exorcising the evil spirits, I believe."

I went in search of Poirot, and found him talking to a pleasant, lean-faced young man. This was Mr. Harper, the late Mr. Bleibner's secretary.

"No," he was saying; "I've only been six months with the expedition. Yes, I knew Mr. Bleibner's affairs pretty well."

"Can you recount to me anything concerning his nephew?"

"He turned up here one day, not a bad-looking fellow. I'd never met him before, but some of the others had—Ames, I think, and Schneider. The old man wasn't at all pleased to see him. They were at it in no time, hammer and tongs. 'Not a cent,' the old man shouted. 'Not one cent now or when I'm dead. I intend to leave my money to the furtherance of my life's work. I've been talking it over with Mr. Schneider to-day.' And a bit more of the same. Young Bleibner lit out for Cairo right away."

"Was he in perfectly good health at the time?"

"The old man?"

"No, the young one."

"I believe he did mention there was something wrong with him. But it couldn't have been anything serious, or I should have remembered."

"One thing more, has Mr. Bleibner left a will?"

"So far as we know, he has not."

"Are you remaining with the expedition, Mr. Harper?"

"No, Sir, I am not. I'm for New York as soon as I can square up things here. You may laugh if you like, but I'm not going to be this blasted old Men-her-Ra's next victim. He'll get me if I stop here."

The young man wiped the perspiration from his brow.

Poirot turned away. Over his shoulder he said with a peculiar smile—

"Remember, he got one of his victims in New York."

"Oh, hell!" said Mr. Harper forcibly.

"That young man is nervous," said Poirot thoughtfully. "He is on the edge, but absolutely on the edge."

I glanced at Poirot curiously, but his enigmatical smile told me nothing.

In company with Sir Guy Willard and Dr. Tosswill we were taken round the excavations. The principal finds had been removed to Cairo, but some of the tomb furniture was extremely interesting. The enthusiasm of the young baronet was obvious, but I fancied that I detected a shade of nervousness in his manner as though he could not quite escape from the feeling of menace in the air. As we entered the tent which had been assigned to us, for a wash before joining the evening meal, a tall dark figure in white robes stood aside to let us pass, with a graceful gesture and a murmured greeting in Arabic. Poirot stopped.

"You are Hassan, the late Sir John Willard's servant?"

"I served my lord Sir John; now I serve his son." He took a step nearer to us and lowered his voice. "You are a wise one, they say, learned in dealing with evil spirits. Let the young master depart from here. There is evil in the air around us."

And with an abrupt gesture, not waiting for a reply, he strode away.

"Evil in the air," muttered Poirot. "Yes, I feel it."

Our meal was hardly a cheerful one. The floor was left to Dr. Tosswill, who discoursed at length upon Egyptian antiquities.

Just as we were preparing to retire to rest, Sir Guy caught Poirot by the arm and pointed. A shadowy figure was moving amidst the tents. It was no human one: I recognized distinctly the dog-headed figure I had seen carved on the walls of the tomb.

My blood literally froze at the sight.

"*Mon Dieu*," murmured Poirot, crossing himself vigorously. "Anubis, the jackal-headed, the god of departing souls!"

"Someone is hoaxing us," cried Dr. Tosswill, rising indignantly to his feet.

"It went into your tent, Harper," muttered Sir Guy, his face dreadfully pale.

"No," said Poirot, shaking his head, "into that of Dr. Ames."

The doctor stared at him incredulously; then, repeating Dr. Tosswill's words: "Someone is hoaxing us," he cried: "come, we'll soon catch the fellow."

He dashed energetically in pursuit of the shadowy apparition. I followed him; but, search as we would, we could find no trace of any living soul having passed that way. We returned, somewhat disturbed in mind, to find Poirot taking energetic measures in his own way to ensure his personal safety. He was busily surrounding our tent with various diagrams and inscriptions which he was drawing in the sand. I recognized the five-pointed star, or pentagon, many times repeated. As was his wont, Poirot was at the same time delivering an impromptu lecture on witchcraft and magic in general; white magic as opposed to black; with various references to the Ka and the Book of the Dead thrown in.

It appeared to excite the liveliest contempt in Dr. Tosswill, who drew me aside literally snorting with rage.

"Balderdash, Sir," he exclaimed angrily. "Pure balderdash. The man's an impostor! He doesn't know the difference between the superstitions of the Middle Ages and the beliefs of Ancient Egypt. Never have I heard such a hotch-potch of ignorance and credulity."

I calmed the excited expert, and joined Poirot in the tent. My little friend was beaming cheerfully.

"We can now sleep in peace," he declared happily. "And I can do with some sleep. My head, it aches abominably. Ah, for a good *tisane!*"

As though in answer to prayer, the flap of the tent was lifted and Hassan appeared, bearing a steaming cup which he offered to Poirot. It proved to be camomile tea, a beverage of which he is inordinately fond. Having thanked Hassan and refused his offer of another cup for myself, we were left alone once more. I stood at the door of the tent some time after undressing, looking out over the desert.

"A wonderful place," I said aloud, "and a wonderful work. I can feel the fascination. This desert life, this probing into the heart of a vanished civilization. Surely, Poirot, you, too, must feel the charm?"

I got no answer, and I turned, a little annoyed. My annoyance was quickly changed to concern. Poirot was lying back across the rude couch, his face horribly convulsed. Beside him was the empty cup. I rushed to his side, then dashed out and across the camp to Dr. Ames's tent.

"Dr. Ames!" I cried—"come at once!"

"What's the matter?" said the doctor, appearing in pyjamas.

"My friend. He's ill. Dying. The camomile tea. Don't let Hassan leave the camp."

Like a flash the doctor ran to our tent. Poirot was lying as I left him.

"Extraordinary," cried Ames. "Looks like a seizure—or—what did you say about something he drank?" He picked up the empty cup.

"Only I did not drink it!" said a placid voice.

We turned in amazement. Poirot was sitting up on the bed. He was smiling.

"No," he said gently. "I did not drink it. While my good friend Hastings was apostrophising the night, I took the opportunity of pouring it, not down my throat, but into a little bottle. That little bottle will go to the analytical chemist. No"—as the doctor made a sudden movement—"as a sensible man, you will understand that violence will be of no avail. During Hastings' brief absence to fetch you, I have had time to put the bottle in safe keeping. Ah, quick, Hastings, hold him!"

I misunderstood Poirot's anxiety. Eager to save my friend, I flung myself in front of him. But the doctor's swift movement had another meaning. His hand went to his mouth, a smell of bitter almonds filled the air, and he swayed forward and fell.

"Another victim," said Poirot gravely, "but the last. Perhaps it is the best way. He has three deaths on his head."

"Dr. Ames?" I cried, stupefied. "But I thought you believed in some occult influence?"

"You misunderstood me, Hastings. What I meant was that I believe in the terrific force of superstition. Once get it firmly established that a series of deaths are supernatural, and you might almost stab a man in broad daylight, and it would still be put down to the curse, so strongly is the instinct of the supernatural implanted in the human race! I suspected from the first that a man was taking advantage of that instinct. The idea came to him, I imagine, with the death of Sir John Willard. A fury of superstition arose at once. As far as I could see, nobody could derive any particular profit from Sir John's death. Mr. Bleibner was a different case. He was a man of great wealth. The information I received from New York contained several suggestive points. To begin with, young Bleibner was reported to have said he had a good friend in Egypt from whom he could borrow. It was tacitly understood that he meant his uncle; but it seemed to me that in that case he would have said so outright. The words suggest some boon companion of his own. Another thing, he scraped up enough money to take him to Egypt, his uncle refused outright to advance him a penny, yet he was able to pay the return passage to New York. Someone must have lent him the money."

"All that was very thin," I objected.

"But there was more. Hastings, there occur often enough words spoken metaphorically which are taken literally. The opposite can happen too. In this case, words which were meant literally were taken metaphorically. Young Bleibner wrote plainly enough, 'I am a leper'; but nobody realized that he shot himself because he believed that he had contracted the dread disease of leprosy."

"What?" I ejaculated.

"It was the clever invention of a diabolical mind. Young Bleibner was suffering from some minor skin trouble; he had lived in the South Sea Islands, where the disease is common enough. Ames was a former friend of his, and a well-known medical man; he would never dream of doubting his word. When I arrived here, my suspicions were divided between Harper and Dr. Ames, but I soon realized that only the doctor could have perpetrated and concealed the crimes, and I learn from Harper that he was previously acquainted with young Bleibner. Doubtless the latter at some time or another had made a will or had insured his life in favour of the doctor. The latter saw his chance of acquiring wealth. It was easy for him to inoculate Mr. Bleibner with the deadly germs. Then the nephew, overcome with despair at the dread news his friend had conveyed to him, shot himself. Mr. Bleibner, whatever his intentions, had made no will. His fortune would pass to his nephew and from him to the doctor."

"And Mr. Schneider?"

"We cannot be sure. He knew young Bleibner too, remember, and may have suspected something, or, again, the doctor may have thought that a further death, motiveless and purposeless, would enmesh the matter more deeply than ever in the coils of superstition. Furthermore, I will tell you an interesting psychological fact, Hastings. A murderer has always a strong desire to repeat his successful crime — the performance of it grows upon him. Hence my fears for young Willard. The figure of Anubis you saw tonight was Hassan dressed up by my orders. I wanted to see if I could frighten the doctor. But it would take more than the supernatural to frighten *him*. I could see that he was not entirely taken in by my pretences of belief in the occult. The little comedy I played for him did not deceive him. I suspected that he would endeavour to make me the next victim. Ah, but in spite of *la mer maudite*, the heat abominable, and the annoyances of the sand, the little grey cells still functioned!"

Poirot proved to be perfectly right in his premises. Young Bleibner, some years ago, in a fit of drunken merriment, had made a jocular will, leaving "my cigarette case you admire so much and everything else of which I die possessed (which will be principally debts) to my good friend Robert Ames, who once saved my life from drowning."

The case was hushed up as far as possible, and, to this day, people talk of the remarkable series of deaths in connection with the Tomb of Men-her-Ra as a triumphal proof of the vengeance of a bygone king upon the desecrators of his tomb — a belief which, as Poirot pointed out to me, is contrary to all Egyptian belief and thought.

# THE CASE OF THE VEILED LADY.

"The Case of the Veiled Lady" was first published in *The Sketch* on October 3, 1923.

I had noticed that for some time Poirot had been growing increasingly dissatisfied and restless. We had had no interesting cases of late, nothing on which my little friend could exercise his keen wits and remarkable powers of deduction.

This morning he flung down the newspaper with an impatient "Tchah!"— a favourite exclamation of his which sounded exactly like a cat sneezing.

"They fear me, Hastings; the criminals of your England they fear me! When the cat is there, the little mice, they come no more to the cheese!"

"I don't suppose the greater part of them even know of your existence," I said, laughing.

Poirot looked at me reproachfully. He always imagines that the whole world is thinking and talking of Hercule Poirot. He had certainly made a name for himself in London, but I could hardly believe that his existence struck terror into the criminal world.

"What about that daylight robbery of jewels in Bond Street the other day?" I asked.

"A neat coup," said Poirot approvingly, "though not in my line. *Pas de finesse, seulement de l'audace!* A man with a loaded cane smashes the plate-glass window of a jeweller's shop and grabs a number of precious stones. Worthy citizens immediately seize him; a policeman arrives. He is caught red-handed with the jewels on him. He is marched off to the police, and then it is discovered that the stones are paste replicas. He has passed the real ones to a confederate — one of the afore-mentioned worthy citizens. He will go to prison, true — but when he comes out, there will be a little fortune awaiting him. Yes, not badly imagined. But I could do better than that. Sometimes, Hastings, I regret that I am of such a moral disposition. To work against the law, it would be pleasing for a change."

"Cheer up, Poirot; you know you are unique in your own line."

"*Ça se peut* — but what is there on hand in my own line? Nothing!"

I picked up the paper.

"Here's an Englishman mysteriously done to death in Holland," I said persuasively.

"They always say that — and later they find that he ate the tinned fish and that his death is perfectly natural."

"Well, if you're determined to grouse!"

"*Tiens!*" said Poirot, who had strolled across to the window. "Here in the street is what they call in novels a 'heavily veiled lady.' She mounts the steps; she rings the bell — she comes to consult us. Here is a possibility of something interesting. When one is as young and pretty as that one, one does not veil the face except for a big affair."

A minute later our visitor was ushered in. As Poirot had said, she was indeed heavily veiled. It was impossible to distinguish her features until she raised her veil of black Spanish lace. Then I saw that Poirot's intuition had been right; the lady was extremely pretty, with fair hair and large blue eyes. From the costly simplicity of her attire I deduced at once that she belonged to the upper strata of society.

"Monsieur Poirot," said the lady in a soft, musical voice, "I am in great trouble. I can hardly believe that you can help me, but I have heard such wonderful things of you that I come literally as the last hope to beg you to do the impossible."

"The impossible, it pleases me always," said Poirot. "Continue, I beg of you, Mademoiselle."

Our fair guest hesitated.

"But you must be frank," added Poirot. "You must not leave me in the dark on any point."

"I will trust you," said the girl suddenly. "You have heard of Lady Millicent Castle Vaughan?"

I looked up with keen interest. The announcement of Lady Millicent's engagement to the young Duke of Southshire had appeared a few days previously. She was, I knew, the fifth daughter of an impecunious Irish peer, and the Duke of Southshire was one of the best matches in England.

"I am Lady Millicent," continued the girl. "You may have read of my engagement. I should be one of the happiest girls alive; but oh! Monsieur Poirot, I am in terrible trouble. There is a man, a horrible man — his name is Lavington; and he — I hardly know how to tell you. There was a letter I wrote — I was only sixteen at the time; and he — he —"

"A letter that you wrote to this Mr. Lavington?"

"Oh! *no* — not to him. To a young soldier — I was very fond of him — he was killed in the war."

"I understand," said Poirot kindly.

"It was a foolish letter, an indiscreet letter, but indeed, Monsieur Poirot, nothing more. But there are phrases in it which — which might bear a different interpretation."

"I see," said Poirot. "And this letter has come into the possession of Mr. Lavington?"

"Yes, and he threatens, unless I pay him an enormous sum of money, a sum that is quite impossible for me to raise, to send it to the Duke."

"The dirty swine!" I ejaculated. "I beg your pardon, Lady Millicent."

"Would it not be wiser to confess all to your future husband?"

"I dare not, Monsieur Poirot. The Duke is a rather peculiar character, jealous and suspicious and prone to believe the worst. I might as well break off my engagement at once."

"Dear, dear," said Poirot with an expressive grimace. "And what do you want me to do, Milady?"

"I thought perhaps that I might ask Mr. Lavington to call upon you. I would tell him that you were empowered by me to discuss the matter. Perhaps you could reduce his demands."

"What sum does he mention?"

"£20,000 — an impossibility. I doubt if I could raise a thousand, even."

"You might perhaps borrow the money on the prospect of your approaching marriage — but I doubt if you could get hold of half that sum. Besides — *eh bien*, it is repugnant to me that you should pay. No; the ingenuity of Hercule Poirot shall defeat your enemies! Send me this Mr. Lavington. Is he likely to bring the letter with him?"

The girl shook her head.

"I do not think so. He is very cautious."

"I suppose there is no doubt that he really has it?"

"He showed it to me when I went to his house."

"You went to his house? That was very imprudent, Milady."

"Was it? I was so desperate. I hoped my entreaties might move him."

"Oh, *là, là!* The Lavingtons of this world are not moved by entreaties! He would welcome them as showing how much importance you attached to the document. Where does he live, this fine gentleman?"

"At Buona Vista, Wimbledon. I went there after dark." Poirot groaned. "I declared that I would inform the police in the end, but he only laughed in a horrid, sneering manner. 'By all means, my dear Lady Millicent, do so if you wish,' he said."

"Yes, it is hardly an affair for the police," murmured Poirot.

"'But I think you will be wiser than that,' he continued. 'See, here is your letter — in this little Japanese puzzle box!' He held it so that I could see. I tried to snatch at it, but he was too quick for me. With a horrid smile he folded it up and replaced it in the little wooden box. 'It will be quite safe here, I assure you,' he said, 'and the box itself lives in such a clever place that you would never find it.' My eyes turned to the small wall safe, and he shook his head and laughed. 'I have a better safe than that,' he said. Oh, he was odious! Monsieur Poirot, do you think that you can help me?"

"Have faith in Papa Poirot. I will find a way."

These reassurances were all very well, I thought, as Poirot gallantly ushered his fair client down the stairs. It seemed to me that we had a tough nut to crack. I said as much to Poirot when he returned. He nodded ruefully.

"Yes — the solution does not leap to the eye. He has the whip hand, this Monsieur Lavington. For the moment I do not see how we are to circumvent him."

Mr. Lavington duly called upon us that afternoon. Lady Millicent had spoken truly when she described him as an odious man. I felt a positive tingling in the end of my boot, so keen was I to kick him down the stairs. He was blustering and overbearing in manner, laughed Poirot's gentle suggestions to scorn, and generally showed himself as master of the situation. I could not help feeling that Poirot was hardly appearing at his best. He looked discouraged and crestfallen.

"Well, gentlemen," said Lavington, as he took up his hat, "we don't seem to be getting much further. The case stands like this: I'll let the Lady Millicent off cheap, as she is such a charming young lady." He leered odiously. "We'll say eighteen thousand. I'm off to Paris to-day — a little piece of business to attend to over there. I shall be back on Tuesday. Unless the money is paid by Tuesday evening, the letter goes to the Duke. Don't tell me Lady Millicent can't raise the money. Some of her gentlemen friends would be only too willing to oblige such a pretty woman with a loan — if she goes the right way about it."

My face flushed, and I took a step forward, but Lavington had wheeled out of the room as he finished his sentence.

"My God!" I cried. "Something has got to be done. You seem to be taking this lying down, Poirot."

"You have an excellent heart, my friend—but your grey cells are in deplorable condition. I have no wish to impress Mr. Lavington with my capabilities. The more pusillanimous he thinks me, the better."

"Why?"

"It is curious," murmured Poirot reminiscently, "that I should have uttered a wish to work against the law just before Lady Millicent arrived!"

"You are going to burgle his house while he is away?" I gasped.

"Sometimes, Hastings, your mental processes are amazingly quick."

"Suppose he takes the letter with him?"

Poirot shook his head.

"That is very unlikely. He has evidently a hiding place in his house that he fancies to be pretty impregnable."

"When do we—er—do the deed?"

"To-morrow night. We will start from here about eleven o'clock."

At the time appointed I was ready to set off. I had donned a dark suit, and a soft dark hat. Poirot beamed kindly on me.

"You have dressed the part, I see," he observed. "Come let us take the underground to Wimbledon."

"Aren't we going to take anything with us? Tools to break in with?"

"My dear Hastings, Hercule Poirot does not adopt such crude methods."

I retired, snubbed, but my curiosity was alert.

It was just on midnight that we entered the small suburban garden of Buona Vista. The house was dark and silent. Poirot went straight to a window at the back of the house, raised the sash noiselessly and bade me enter.

"How did you know this window would be open?" I whispered, for really it seemed uncanny.

"Because I sawed through the catch this morning."

"What?"

"But yes, it was most simple. I called, presented a fictitious card and one of Inspector Japp's official ones. I said I had been sent, recommended by Scotland Yard, to attend to some burglar-proof fastenings that Mr. Lavington wanted fixed whilst he was away. The housekeeper welcomed me with enthusiasm. It seems they have had two attempted burglaries here lately—evidently our little idea has occurred to other clients of Mr. Lavington's—with nothing of value taken. I examined all the windows, made my little arrangement, forbade the servants to touch the windows until to-morrow, as they were electrically connected up, and withdrew gracefully."

"Really, Poirot, you are wonderful."

"*Mon ami*, it was of the simplest. Now, to work! The servants sleep at the top of the house, so we will run little risk of disturbing them."

"I presume the safe is built into the wall somewhere?"

"Safe? Fiddlesticks! There is no safe. Mr. Lavington is an intelligent man. You will see, he will have devised a hiding place much more intelligent than a safe. A safe is the first thing everyone looks for, and by going round the principal firms who make such things, you can find out exactly where it was placed. No, my friend, it is not for a safe that I shall look."

I was silent. I did not agree with him altogether. Still, it was possible that a recess in the panelling would answer the purpose better. The hall and study were panelled, and I tapped the walls gently, and ran my fingers over the surface seeking a concealed spring.

Poirot did not seem much interested in my efforts.

"Too obvious, *mon ami*," he said. "The bed-room, that is a more likely place."

He vanished upstairs, to return about half an hour later, crestfallen and irritable.

"Nothing, Hastings. I have searched all the rooms on that floor. Let us try the other rooms here."

The time was going on rapidly. We had been here over two hours. We had ransacked the house and our search had been unavailing. I saw symptoms of anger gathering on Poirot's face.

"Ah, *sapristi!* Is Hercule Poirot to be beaten? Never. Let us be calm. Let us reflect. Let us reason. Let us — *enfin!* — employ our little grey cells. Me, I have been nosing about like a retriever dog. *Voilà tout!*"

He paused for a moment, bending his brows in concentration; then the green light I knew so well stole into his eyes.

"I have been an imbecile! The kitchen!"

"The kitchen," I cried. "But that's impossible. The servants!"

"Exactly. Just what ninety-nine people out of a hundred would say! And for that very reason the kitchen is the ideal place to choose. It is full of various homely objects. *En avant*, to the kitchen!"

I followed him, completely sceptical, and watched whilst he dived into bread-bins, tapped saucepans, and put his head into the gas-oven. In the end, tired of watching him, I strolled back to the study. I was convinced that there, and there only, would we find the *cache*. I made a further minute search, noted that it was now a quarter past four and that therefore it would soon be growing light, and then went back to the kitchen regions.

To my utter amazement, Poirot was now standing right inside the coal bin, to the utter ruin of his neat light suit. He made a grimace.

"But yes, my friend, it is against

all my instincts so to ruin my appearance, but what will you?"

"But Lavington can't have buried it under the coal?"

"If you would use your eyes, you would see that it is not the coal that I examine."

I then saw on a shelf behind the coal bunker some logs of wood were piled. Poirot was dexterously taking them down one by one. Suddenly he uttered a low exclamation.

"Your knife, Hastings!"

I handed it to him. He appeared to inset it in the wood, and suddenly the log split in two. It had been neatly sawn in half and a cavity hollowed out in the centre. From this cavity Poirot took a little wooden box of Japanese make.

"Well done!" I cried, carried out of myself.

"Gently, Hastings, do not raise your voice too much. Come, let us be off, before the daylight is upon us."

Slipping the box into his pocket, he leaped lightly out of the coal-bunker, brushed himself down as well as he could, and leaving the house by the same way as we had come, we walked rapidly in the direction of London.

"But what an extraordinary place!" I expostulated. "Anyone might have used the log."

"In July, Hastings? And it was at the bottom of the pile — a very ingenious hiding place. Ah, here is a taxi! Now for home, a wash, and a refreshing sleep."

After the excitement of the night, I slept late. When I finally strolled into our sitting room just before one o'clock, I was surprised to see Poirot, leaning back in an armchair, the Japanese box open beside him, calmly reading the letter he had taken from it.

He smiled at me affectionately, and tapped the sheet he held.

"She was right, the Lady Millicent. Never would the Duke have pardoned this letter. It contains some of the most extravagant terms of affection I have ever come across."

"Really, Poirot," I said, rather disgustedly, "I don't think you should have read the letter. That's the sort of thing that isn't done."

"It is done by Hercule Poirot," replied my friend imperturbably.

"And another thing," I said. "I don't think using Japp's official card yesterday was quite playing the game."

"But I was not playing a game, Hastings. I was conducting a case."

I shrugged my shoulders. One can't argue with a point of view.

"A step on the stairs," said Poirot. "That will be Lady Millicent."

Our fair client came in with an anxious expression on her face which changed to one of delight on seeing the letter and box which Poirot held up.

"Oh, Monsieur Poirot. How wonderful of you! How did you do it?"

"By rather reprehensible

methods, Milady. But Mr. Lavington will not prosecute. This is your letter, is it not?"

She glanced through it.

"Yes. Oh, how can I ever thank you! You are a wonderful, wonderful man. Where was it hidden?"

Poirot told her.

"How very clever of you!" She fingered the small box on the table. "I shall keep this as a souvenir."

"I had hoped, Milady, that you would permit me to keep it — also as a souvenir."

"I hope to send you a better souvenir than that — on my wedding day. You shall not find me ungrateful, Monsieur Poirot."

"The pleasure of doing you a service will be more to me than a cheque. So you permit that I retain the box?"

"Oh no, Monsieur Poirot, I simply must have that!" she cried laughingly.

She stretched out her hand, but Poirot was before her. His hand closed over it.

"I think not." His voice had changed.

"What do you mean?"

Her voice, too, seemed to have grown sharper.

"At any rate, permit me to abstract its further contents. You observed that the original cavity has been reduced by half. In the top half, the compromising letter; in the bottom —"

He made a nimble gesture, then held out his hand. On the palm were four large glittering stones, and two big milky-white pearls.

"The jewels stolen in Bond Street the other day, I rather fancy," murmured Poirot. "Japp will tell us."

To my utter amazement, Japp himself stepped out from Poirot's bed-room.

"An old friend of yours, I believe," said Poirot politely to Lady Millicent.

"Nabbed, by the Lord!" said Lady Millicent, with a complete change of manner. "You nippy old devil!" She looked at Poirot with almost affectionate awe.

"Well, Gertie, my dear," said Japp, "the game's up this time, I fancy. Fancy seeing you again so soon! We've got your pal, too, the gentleman who called here the other day calling himself Lavington. As for Lavington himself, *alias* Croker, *alias* Reed, I wonder which of the gang it was who stuck a knife into him the other day in Holland? Thought he'd got the goods with him, didn't you? And he hadn't. He double-crossed you properly — hid 'em in his own house. You had two shots at looking for them, and then you tackled Monsieur Poirot here, and by a piece of amazing luck he found them."

"You do like talking, don't you?" said the late Lady Millicent. "Easy there, now. I'll go quietly. You can't say that I'm not the perfect lady. Ta-ta, all!"

"The shoes were wrong," said Poirot dreamily, while I was still too stupefied to speak. "I have made my little observations of your English nation, and a lady, a born lady, is always particular about her shoes. She may have shabby clothes, but she will be well shod. Now, this Lady Millicent had smart, expensive clothes, and cheap shoes. It was not likely that either you or I should have seen the real Lady Millicent; she has been very little in London, and this girl had a certain superficial resemblance which would pass well enough. As I say, the shoes first awakened my suspicions, and then her story—and her veil—were a little melodramatic, eh? The Japanese box with a bogus compromising letter in the top must have been known to all the gang; but the log of wood was the late Mr. Lavington's idea. *Eh, par example*, Hastings, I hope you will not again wound my feelings as you did yesterday by saying that I am unknown to the criminal classes. *Ma foi*, they even employ me when they themselves fail!"

# THE KIDNAPPING OF JOHNNIE WAVERLY.

"The Kidnapping of Johnnie Waverly" was first published in *The Sketch* on October 10, 1923.

"You can understand the feelings of a mother," said Mrs. Waverly for, perhaps, the sixth time.

She looked appealingly at Poirot. My little friend, always sympathetic to motherhood in distress, gesticulated reassuringly.

"But yes, but yes, I comprehend perfectly. Have faith in Papa Poirot."

"The police —" began Mr. Waverly.

His wife waved the interruption aside.

"I won't have anything more to do with the police. We trusted to them and look what happened! But I'd heard so much of Monsieur Poirot and the wonderful things he'd done, that I felt he might possibly be able to help us. A mother's feelings —"

Poirot hastily stemmed the reiteration with an eloquent gesture. Mrs. Waverly's emotion was obviously genuine, but it assorted strangely with her shrewd, rather hard type of countenance. When I heard later that she was the daughter of a prominent steel manufacturer of Sheffield who had worked his way up in the world from an office-boy to his present eminence, I realized that she had inherited many of the paternal qualities.

Mr. Waverly was a big, florid, jovial-looking man. He stood with his legs straddled wide apart and looked the type of the country squire.

"I suppose you know all about this business, Monsieur Poirot?"

The question was almost superfluous. For some days past the papers had been full of the sensational kidnapping of little Johnnie Waverly, the three-year-old son and heir of Marcus Waverly, Esq., of Waverly Court, Surrey, one of the oldest families in England.

"The main facts I know, of course; but recount to me the whole story, Monsieur, I beg of you. And in detail if you please."

"Well, I suppose the beginning of the whole thing was about ten days ago when I got an anonymous letter — beastly things, anyway — that I couldn't make head or tail of. The writer had the impudence to demand that I should pay him £25,000 — twenty-five thousand pounds, Monsieur Poirot! Failing my agreement, he threatened to kidnap Johnnie. Of course I threw the thing into the wastepaper basket without more ado. Thought it was some silly joke. Five days later I got another letter. 'Unless you pay, your son will be kidnapped on the twenty-ninth.' That was on the twenty-seventh. Ada was worried, but I couldn't bring myself to treat the matter seriously. Damn it all, we're in *England!* Nobody goes about kidnapping children and holding them up to ransom."

"It is not a common practice, certainly," said Poirot. "Proceed, Monsieur."

"Well, Ada gave me no peace, so — feeling a bit of a fool — I laid the matter before Scotland Yard. They didn't seem to take the thing very seriously — inclined to my view that it was some silly joke. On the twenty-eighth I got a third letter. 'You have not paid. Your son will be taken from you at twelve o'clock noon to-morrow, the twenty-ninth. It will cost you £50,000 to recover him.' Up I tooled to Scotland Yard again. This time they were more impressed. They inclined to the view that the letters were written by a lunatic, and that in all probability an attempt of some kind would be made at the hour stated. They assured me that they would take all due precautions. Inspector McNeil and a sufficient force would come down to Waverly on the morrow and take charge.

"I went home much relieved in mind. Yet we already had the feeling of being in a state of siege. I gave orders that no stranger was to be admitted, and that no one was to leave the house. The evening passed off without any untoward incident, but on the following morning my wife was seriously unwell. Alarmed by her condition, I sent for Dr. Dakers. Her symptoms appeared to puzzle him. While hesitating to suggest that she had been poisoned,

I could see that that was what was in his mind. There was no danger, he assured me, but it would be a day or two before she would be able to get about again. Returning to my own room, I was startled and amazed to find a note pinned to my pillow. It was in the same handwriting as the others and contained just three words: 'At twelve o'clock.'

"I admit, Monsieur Poirot, that then I saw red! Someone in the house was in this — one of the servants. I had them all up, blackguarded them right and left. They never split on each other; it was Miss Collins, my wife's companion, who informed me that she had seen Johnnie's nurse slip down the drive early that morning. I taxed her with it, and she broke down. She had left the child with the nursery maid and stolen out to meet a friend of hers — a man! Pretty goings-on! She denied having pinned the note to my pillow — she may have been speaking the truth, I don't know. I felt I couldn't take the risk of the child's own nurse being in the plot. One of the servants was implicated — of that I was sure. Finally I lost my temper and sacked the whole bunch, nurse and all. I gave them an hour to pack their boxes and get out of the house."

Mr. Waverly's face was quite two shades redder as he remembered his just wrath.

"Was not that a little injudicious, Monsieur?" suggested Poirot. "For all you know, you might have been playing into the enemy's hands."

Mr. Waverly stared at him. "I don't see that. Send the whole damned lot packing, that was my idea. I wired to London for a fresh lot to be sent down that evening. In the meantime, there'd be only people I could trust in the house — my wife's secretary, Miss Collins, and Tredwell, the butler, who has been with me since I was a boy."

"And this Miss Collins, how long has she been with you?"

"Just a year," said Mrs. Waverly. "She has been invaluable to me as a secretary-companion, and is also a very efficient housekeeper."

"The nurse?"

"She has been with me six months. She came to me with excellent references. All the same, I never really liked her, although Johnnie was quite devoted to her."

"Still, I gather she had already left when the catastrophe occurred. Perhaps, Monsieur Waverly, you will be so kind as to continue."

Mr. Waverly resumed his narrative.

"Inspector McNeil arrived about 10:30. The servants had all left by then. He declared himself quite satisfied with the internal arrangements. He had various men posted in the park outside, guarding all the approaches to the house, and he assured me that if the whole thing were not a hoax, we should undoubtedly catch my mysterious correspondent.

"I had Johnnie with me, and he and I and the inspector went

together into the room we call the council chamber. The inspector locked the door. There is a big grandfather clock there, and as the hands drew near to twelve I don't mind confessing that I was as nervous as a cat. There was a whirring sound, and the clock began to strike. I clutched at Johnnie. I had a feeling a man might drop from the skies. The last stroke sounded, and as it did so, there was a great commotion outside — shouting and running. The inspector flung up the window, and a constable came running up.

"'We've got him Sir!' he panted. 'He was sneaking up through the bushes. He's got a whole dope outfit on him.'

"We hurried out on the terrace where two constables were holding a ruffianly-looking fellow in shabby clothes, who was twisting and turning in a vain endeavour to escape. One of the policemen held out an unrolled parcel which they had wrested from their captive. It contained a pad of cotton wool and a bottle of chloroform. It made my blood boil to see it. There was a note, too, addressed to me. I tore it open. It bore the following words: 'You should have paid up. To ransom your son will now cost you £50,000. In spite of all your precautions he has been abducted at twelve o'clock on the twenty-ninth, as I said.'

"I gave a great laugh, the laugh of relief, but as I did so I heard the hum of a motor and a shout. I turned my head. Racing down the drive towards the south lodge at a furious speed was a low, long grey car. It was the man who drove it who shouted, but that was not what gave me a shock of horror. It was the sight of Johnnie's flaxen curls. The child was in the car beside him.

"The inspector ripped out an oath. 'The child was here not a minute ago,' he cried. His eyes swept over us. We were all there: myself, Tredwell, Miss Collins. 'When did you last see him, Mr. Waverly?'

"I cast my mind back, trying to remember. When the constable had called us I had run out with the inspector, forgetting all about Johnnie.

"And then there came a sound that startled us, the chiming of a church clock from the village. With an exclamation the inspector pulled out his watch. It was exactly twelve o'clock. With one common accord we ran to the council chamber; the clock there marked the hour as ten minutes past. Someone must have deliberately tampered with it, for I have never known it gain or lose before. It is a perfect timekeeper."

Mr. Waverly paused. Poirot smiled to himself and straightened a little mat which the anxious father had pushed askew.

"A pleasing little problem, obscure and charming," murmured Poirot. "I will investigate it for you with pleasure. Truly it was planned *à merveille*."

Mrs. Waverly looked at him

reproachfully. "But my boy," she wailed.

Poirot hastily composed his face and looked the picture of earnest sympathy again. "He is safe, Madame, he is unharmed. Rest assured, these miscreants will take the greatest care of him. Is he not to them the turkey — no, the goose — that lays the golden eggs?"

"Monsieur Poirot, I'm sure there's only one thing to be done — pay up. I was all against it at first — but now! A mother's feelings —"

"But we have interrupted Monsieur in his history," cried Poirot hastily.

"I expect you know the rest pretty well from the papers," said Mr. Waverly. "Of course, Inspector McNeil got on to the telephone immediately. A description of the car and the man was circulated all round, and it looked at first as though everything was going to turn out all right. A car, answering to the description, with a man and a small boy, had passed through various villages, apparently making for London. At one place they had stopped, and it was noticed that the child was crying and obviously afraid of his companion. When Inspector McNeil announced that the car had been stopped and the man and boy detained, I was almost ill with relief. You know the sequel. The boy was not Johnnie, and the man was an ardent motorist, fond of children, who had picked up a small child playing in the streets of Edenswell, a village about fifteen miles from us, and was kindly giving him a ride. Thanks to the cocksure blundering of the police, all traces have disappeared. Had they not persistently followed the wrong car, they might by now have found the boy."

"Calm yourself, Monsieur. The police are a brave and intelligent force of men. Their mistake was a very natural one. And altogether it was a clever scheme. As to the man they caught in the grounds, I understand that his defence has consisted all along of a persistent denial. He declared that the note and parcel were given to him to deliver at Waverly Court. The man who gave them to him handed him a ten-shilling note and promised him another if it were delivered at exactly ten minutes to twelve. He was to approach the house through the grounds and knock at the side door."

"I don't believe a word of it," declared Mrs. Waverly hotly. "It's all a parcel of lies."

"*En verité*, it is a thin story," said Poirot reflectively. "But so far they have not shaken it. I understand, also, that he made a certain accusation?"

His glance interrogated Mr. Waverly. The latter got rather red again.

"The fellow had the impertinence to pretend that he recognized in Tredwell the man who gave him the parcel. 'Only the bloke has shaved off his moustache.' Tredwell, who was born on the estate!"

Poirot smiled a little at the country gentleman's indignation. "Yet you yourself suspect an inmate of the house to have been accessory to the abduction."

"Yes, but not Tredwell."

"And you, Madame?" asked Poirot, suddenly turning to her.

"It could not have been Tredwell who gave this tramp the letter and parcel — if anybody ever did, which I don't believe. It was given him at ten o'clock, he says. At ten o'clock Tredwell was with my husband in the smoking room."

"Were you able to see the face of the man in the car, Monsieur? Did it resemble that of Tredwell in any way?"

"It was too far away for me to see his face."

"Has Tredwell a brother, do you know?"

"He had several, but they are all dead. The last one was killed in the war."

"I am not yet clear as to the grounds of Waverly Court. The car was heading for the south lodge. Is there another entrance?"

"Yes, what we call the east lodge. It can be seen from the other side of the house."

"It seems to me strange that nobody saw the car entering the grounds."

"There is a right of way through, and access to a small chapel. A good many cars pass through. The man must have stopped the car in a convenient place and run up to the house just as the alarm was given and attention attracted elsewhere."

"Unless he was already inside the house," mused Poirot. "Is there any place where he could have hidden?"

"Well, we certainly didn't make a thorough search of the house beforehand. There seemed no need. I suppose he might have hidden himself somewhere, but who would have let him in?"

"We shall come to that later. One thing at a time — let us be methodical. There is no special hiding place in the house? Waverly Court is an old place, and there are sometimes 'priests' holes,' as they call them."

"By gad, there *is* a priest's hole. It opens from one of the panels in the hall."

"Near the Council Chamber?"

"Just outside the door."

*"Voilà!"*

"But nobody knows of its existence except my wife and myself."

"Tredwell?"

"Well — he might have heard of it."

"Miss Collins?"

"I have never mentioned it to her."

Poirot reflected for a minute.

"Well, Monsieur, the next thing is for me to come down to Waverly Court. If I arrive this afternoon, will it suit you?"

"Oh, as soon as possible, please, Monsieur Poirot!" cried Mrs. Waverly. "Read this once more."

She thrust into his hands the last

missive from the enemy which had reached the Waverlys that morning and which had sent her post-haste to Poirot. It gave clever and explicit directions for the paying over of the money, and ended with a threat that the boy's life would pay for any treachery. It was clear that a love of money warred with the essential mother love of Mrs. Waverly, and that the latter was at last gaining the day.

Poirot detained her for a minute behind her husband.

"Madame, the truth, if you please — do you share your husband's faith in the butler, Tredwell?"

"I have nothing against him, Monsieur Poirot, I cannot see how he can have been concerned in this, but — well, I have never liked him — never!"

"One other thing, Madame — can you give me the address of the child's nurse?"

"149, Netherall Road, Hammersmith. You don't imagine —"

"Never do I imagine. Only — I employ the little grey cells. And sometimes, just sometimes, I have a little idea."

Poirot came back to me as the door closed.

"So Madame has never liked the butler. It is interesting, that, eh, Hastings?"

I refused to be drawn. Poirot has deceived me so often that I now go warily. There is always a catch somewhere.

After completing an elaborate outdoor toilet, we set off for Netherall Road. We were fortunate enough to find Miss Jessie Withers at home. She was a pleasant-faced woman of thirty-five, capable and superior. I could not believe that she could be mixed up in the affair. She was bitterly resentful of the way she had been dismissed, but admitted that she had been in the wrong. She was engaged to be married to a painter and decorator who happened to be in the neighbourhood, and she had run out to meet him. The thing seemed natural enough.

I could not quite understand Poirot. All his questions seemed to me quite irrelevant. They were concerned mainly with the daily routine of her life at Waverly Court. I was frankly bored and glad when Poirot took his departure.

"Kidnapping is an easy job, *mon ami*," he observed, as he hailed a taxi in the Hammersmith Road and ordered it to drive to Waterloo. "That child could have been abducted with the greatest ease any day for the last three years."

"I don't see that that advances us much," I remarked coldly.

"*Au contraire*, it advances us enormously, but enormously! — If you must wear a tie pin, Hastings, at least let it be in the exact centre of your tie. At present it is at least a sixteenth of an inch too much to the right."

Waverly Court was a fine old place and had recently been restored with taste and care. Mr. Waverly showed us the Council Chamber, the terrace, and all the various spots connected with the case. Finally, at Poirot's request, he pressed a spring in the wall, a panel slid aside, and a short passage led us into the "Priest's Hole."

"You see," said Waverly. "There is nothing here."

The tiny room was bare enough, there was not even the mark of a footstep on the floor. I joined Poirot where he was bending attentively over a mark in the corner.

"What do you make of this, my friend?"

There were four imprints close together.

"A dog," I cried.

"A very small dog, Hastings."

"A Pom."

"Smaller than a Pom."

"A griffon?" I suggested doubtfully.

"Smaller even than a griffon. A species unknown to the Kennel Club."

I looked at him. His face was alight with excitement and satisfaction.

"I was right," he murmured. "I knew I was right. Come, Hastings."

As we stepped out into the hall and the panel closed behind us, a young lady came out of a door farther down the passage. Mr. Waverly presented her to us.

"Miss Collins."

Miss Collins was about thirty years of age, brisk and alert in manner. She had fair, rather dull hair, and wore pince-nez.

At Poirot's request, we passed into a small morning room, and he questioned her closely as to the servants and particularly as to Tredwell. She admitted that she did not like the butler.

"He gives himself airs," she explained.

They then went into the question of the food eaten by Mrs. Waverly on the night of the 28th. Miss Collins declared that she had partaken of the same dishes upstairs in her sitting room and had felt no ill effects. As she was departing I nudged Poirot.

"The dog," I whispered.

"Ah, yes, the dog!" He smiled broadly. "Is there a dog kept here by any chance, Mademoiselle?"

"There are two retrievers in the kennels outside."

"No, I mean a small dog, a toy dog."

"No — nothing of the kind."

Poirot permitted her to depart. Then, pressing the bell, he remarked to me, "She lies, that Mademoiselle Collins. Possibly I should, also, in her place. Now for the butler."

Tredwell was a dignified individual. He told his story with perfect aplomb, and it was essentially the same as that of Mr. Waverly. He admitted that he knew the secret of the priest's hole.

When he finally withdrew, pontifical to the last, I met Poirot's quizzical eyes.

"What do you make of it all, Hastings?"

"What do you?" I parried.

"How cautious you become! Never, never will the grey cells function unless you stimulate them. Ah, but I will not tease you! Let us make our deductions together. What points strike us specially as being difficult?"

"There is one thing that strikes me," I said. "Why did the man who kidnapped the child go out by the south lodge instead of by the east lodge where no one would see him?"

"That is a very good point, Hastings, an excellent one. I will match it with another. Why warn the Waverlys beforehand? Why not simply kidnap the child and hold him to ransom?"

"Because they hoped to get the money without being forced to action."

"Surely it was very unlikely that the money would be paid on a mere threat?"

"Also they wanted to focus attention on twelve o'clock, so that when the tramp man was seized, the other could emerge from his hiding place and get away with the child unnoticed."

"That does not alter the fact that they were making a thing difficult that was perfectly easy. If they do not specify a time or date, nothing would be easier than to wait their chance, and carry off the child in a motor one day when he is out with his nurse."

"Ye-es," I admitted doubtfully.

"In fact, there is a deliberate playing of the farce! Now let us approach the question from another side. Everything goes to show that there was an accomplice inside the house. Point number one, the mysterious poisoning of Mrs. Waverly; point number two, the letter pinned to the pillow; point number three, the putting on of the clock ten minutes — all inside jobs. And an additional fact that you may not have noticed. There was no dust in the priest's hole. It had been swept out with a broom.

"Now then, we have four people in the house. (We can exclude the nurse, since she could not have swept out the priest's hole, though she could have attended to the other three points.) Four people! Mr. and Mrs. Waverly, Tredwell, the butler, and Miss Collins. We will take Miss Collins first. We have nothing much against her, except that we know very little about her, that she is obviously an intelligent young woman, and that she has only been here a year."

"She lied about the dog, you said," I reminded him.

"Ah, yes, the dog." Poirot gave a peculiar smile. "Now let us pass to Tredwell. There are several suspicious facts against him. For one thing, the tramp declares that it was Tredwell who gave him the parcel in the village."

"But Tredwell can prove an alibi on that point."

"Even then, he could have poisoned Mrs. Waverly, pinned the note to the pillow, put on the clock, and swept out the Priest's Hole. On the other hand, he has been born and bred in the service of the Waverlys. It seems unlikely in the last degree that he should connive at the abduction of the son of the house. It is not in the picture!"

"Well, then?"

"We must proceed logically — however absurd it may seem. We will briefly consider Mrs. Waverly. But she is rich, the money is hers. It is her money which has restored this impoverished estate. There would be no reason for her to kidnap her son and pay over her money to herself. Her husband, now, is in a different position. He has a rich wife. It is not the same thing as being rich himself — in fact I have a little idea that the lady is not very fond of parting with her money, except on a very good pretext. But Mr. Waverly, you can see at once, he is a *bon viveur*."

"Impossible!" I spluttered.

"Not at all. Who sends away the servants? Mr. Waverly. He can write the notes, drug his wife, put on the hands of the clock, and establish an excellent alibi for his faithful retainer Tredwell. Tredwell has never liked Mrs. Waverly. He is devoted to his master and is willing to obey his orders implicitly. There were three of them in it. Waverly, Tredwell, and some friend of Waverly. That is the mistake the police made, they made no further inquiries about the man who drove the grey car with the wrong child in it. He was the third man. He picks up a child in a village near by, a boy with flaxen curls. He drives in through the east lodge and passes out through the south lodge just at the right moment, waving his hand and shouting. They cannot see his face or the number of the car, so obviously they cannot see the child's face, either. Then he lays a false trail to London. In the meantime, Tredwell has done his part in arranging for the parcel and note to be delivered by a rough-looking gentleman. His master can provide an alibi in the unlikely case of the man recognizing him, in spite of the false moustache he wore. As for Mr. Waverly, as soon as the hullabaloo occurs outside, and the inspector rushes out, he quickly hides the child in the Priest's Hole, follows him out. Later in the day, when the inspector is gone and Miss Collins is out of the way, it will be easy enough to drive him off to some safe place in his own car."

"But what about the dog?" I asked. "And Miss Collins lying?"

"That was my little joke. I asked her if there were any toy dogs in the house, and she said no — but doubtless there are some — *in the nursery!* You see, Mr. Waverly placed some toys in the Priest's Hole to keep Johnnie amused and quiet."

"Monsieur Poirot —" Mr.

Waverly entered the room — "have you discovered anything? Have you any clue to where the boy has been taken?"

Poirot handed him a piece of paper.

"Here is the address."

"But this is a blank sheet."

"Because I am waiting for you to write it down for me."

"What the —" Mr. Waverly's face turned purple.

"I know everything, Monsieur. I give you twenty-four hours to return the boy. Your ingenuity will be equal to the task of explaining his reappearance. Otherwise, Mrs. Waverly will be informed of the exact sequence of events."

Mr. Waverly sank down in a chair and buried his face in his hands. "He is with my old nurse, ten miles away. He is happy and well cared for."

"I have no doubt of that. If I did not believe you to be a good father at heart, I should not be willing to give you another chance."

"The scandal —"

"Exactly. Your name is an old and honoured one. Do not jeopardize it again. Good evening, Mr. Waverly. Ah, by the way, one word of advice. Always sweep in the corners!"

# THE MARKET BASING MYSTERY.

"The Market Basing Mystery" was first published in *The Sketch* on October 17, 1923.

"After all, there's nothing like the country, is there?" said Inspector Japp, breathing in heavily through his nose and out through his mouth in the most approved fashion.

Poirot and I applauded the sentiment heartily. It had been the Scotland Yard inspector's idea that we should all go for the week-end to the little country town of Market Basing. When off duty, Japp was an ardent botanist, and discoursed upon minute flowers possessed of unbelievably lengthy Latin names (somewhat strangely pronounced) with an enthusiasm even greater than that he gave to his cases.

"Nobody knows us, and we know nobody," explained Japp. "That's the idea."

This was not to prove quite the case, however, for the local constable happened to have been transferred from a village fifteen miles away where a case of arsenical poisoning had brought him into contact with the Scotland Yard man. However, his delighted recognition of the great man only enhanced Japp's sense of well-being; and as we sat down to breakfast on Sunday morning in the parlour of the village inn, with the sun shining, and tendrils of honeysuckle thrusting themselves in at the window, we were all in the best of spirits. The bacon and eggs were excellent; the coffee not so good, but passable and boiling hot.

"This is the life," said Japp. "When I retire, I shall have a little place in the country. Far from crime, like this!"

"*Le crime, il est partout*," remarked Poirot, helping himself to a neat square of bread, and frowning at a sparrow which had balanced itself impertinently on the windowsill.

I quoted lightly:

*That rabbit has a pleasant face,*
*His private life is a disgrace;*
*I really could not tell to you*
*The awful things that rabbits do.*

"Lord," said Japp, stretching himself backward, "I believe I could manage another egg, and perhaps a rasher or two of bacon. What do you say, Captain?"

"I'm with you," I returned heartily. "What about you, Poirot?"

Poirot shook his head.

"One must not so replenish the stomach that the brain refuses to function," he remarked.

"I'll risk replenishing the stomach a bit more," laughed Japp. "I take a large size in stomachs; and by the way, you're getting stout yourself, Monsieur Poirot. Here, Miss, eggs and bacon twice."

But at that moment, an imposing form blocked the doorway. It was Constable Pollard.

"I hope you'll excuse me troubling the inspector, gentlemen, but I'd be glad of his advice."

"I'm on holiday," said Japp hastily. "No work for me. What is the case?"

"Gentleman up at Leigh Hall. Shot himself. Through the head."

"Well, they will do it," said Japp prosaically. "Debt, or a woman, I suppose. Sorry I can't help you, Pollard."

"The point is," said the constable, "that he can't have shot himself—leastways, that's what Dr. Giles says."

Japp put down his cup.

"*Can't* have shot himself? What do you mean?"

"That's what Dr. Giles says," repeated Pollard. "He says it's plumb impossible. He's puzzled to death, the door being locked on the inside and the windows bolted; but he sticks to it as the man couldn't have committed suicide."

That settled it. The further supply of bacon and eggs was waved aside, and a few minutes later saw us all walking as fast as we could in the direction of Leigh House, Japp eagerly questioning the constable.

The name of the deceased was Walter Protheroe; he was a man of middle age, and something of a recluse. He had come to Market Basing eight years ago and rented Leigh House—a rambling, dilapidated old mansion fast falling into ruin. He lived in a corner of it, his wants attended to by a housekeeper whom he had brought with him. Miss Clegg was her name, and she was a very superior woman and highly thought of in the village. Just lately Mr. Protheroe had had visitors staying with him, a Mr. and Mrs. Parker from London. This morning, unable to get a reply when she went to call her master, and finding the door locked, Miss Clegg became alarmed, and telephoned for the police and the doctor. Constable Pollard and Dr. Giles had arrived at the same moment. Their united efforts had succeeded in breaking down the oak door of his bed-room.

Mr. Protheroe was lying on the floor, shot through the head, and the pistol was clasped in his right hand. It looked a clear case of suicide.

After examining the body, however, Dr. Giles became clearly perplexed, and finally he drew the constable aside, and communicated his perplexities to him; whereupon Pollard had at once thought of Japp. Leaving the doctor in charge, he had hurried down to the inn.

By the time the constable's recital was over, we had arrived at Leigh House, a big, desolate house surrounded by an unkempt, weed-ridden garden. The front door was open, and we passed at once into the hall and from there into a small morning roo, from whence proceeded the sound of voices.

Four people were in the room: a somewhat flashily dressed man with a shifty, unpleasant face to whom I took an immediate dislike; a woman of much the same type, though handsome in a coarse fashion; another woman dressed in neat black who stood apart from the rest, and whom I took to be the housekeeper; and a tall man dressed in sporting tweeds, with a clever, capable face, and who was clearly in command of the situation.

"Dr. Giles," said the constable, " this is Detective-Inspector Japp of Scotland Yard, and his two friends."

The doctor greeted us and made us known to Mr. and Mrs. Parker. Then we accompanied them upstairs. Pollard, in obedience to a sign from Japp, remained below — as it were, on guard over the household. The doctor led us upstairs and along a passage. A door was open at the end; splinters hung from the hinges, and the door itself had crashed to the floor inside the room.

We went in. The body was still lying on the floor. Mr. Protheroe had been a man of middle age, bearded, with hair grey at the temples. Japp went and knelt by the body.

"Why couldn't you leave it as you found it?" he grumbled.

The doctor shrugged his shoulders. "We thought it a clear case of suicide."

"H'm!" said Japp. "Bullet entered the head behind the left ear."

"Exactly," said the doctor. "Clearly impossible for him to have fired it himself. He'd have had to twist his right hand round his head. It couldn't have been done."

"Yet you found the pistol clasped

in his hand? Where is it, by the way?"

The doctor nodded to the table.

"But it wasn't clasped in his hand," he said. "It was inside the hand; but the fingers weren't closed over it."

"Put there afterwards," said Japp; "that's clear enough." He was examining the weapon. "One cartridge fired. We'll test it for fingerprints, but I doubt if we'll find any but yours, Dr. Giles. How long has he been dead?"

"Some time last night. I can't give the time to an hour or so, as those wonderful doctors in detective stories do. Roughly, he's been dead about twelve hours."

So far Poirot had not made a move of any kind. He had remained by my side, watching Japp at work and listening to his questions. Only, from time to time, he had sniffed the air very deliberately and as if puzzled. I too had sniffed, but could detect nothing to arouse interest. The air seemed perfectly fresh and devoid of odour. And yet, from time to time, Poirot continued to sniff it dubiously, as though his keener nose detected something I had missed.

Now, as Japp moved away from the body, Poirot knelt down by it. He took no interest in the wound. I thought at first that he was examining the fingers of the hand that had held the pistol, but in a minute I saw that it was a handkerchief carried in the coat-sleeve that interested him. Mr. Protheroe was dressed in a dark grey lounge-suit.

Finally Poirot got up from his knees, but his eyes still strayed back to the handkerchief as though puzzled.

Japp called to him to come and help to lift the door. Seizing my opportunity, I too knelt down, and, taking the handkerchief from the sleeve, scrutinized it minutely. It was a perfectly plain handkerchief of white cambric; there was no mark or stain on it of any kind. I replaced it, shaking my head and confessing myself baffled.

The others had raised the door. I realized that they were hunting for the key. They looked in vain.

"That settles it," said Japp. "The window's shut and bolted. The murderer left by the door, locking it and taking the key with him. He thought it would be accepted that Protheroe had locked himself in and shot himself, and that the absence of the key would not be noticed. You agree, Moosior Poirot?"

"I agree, yes; but it would have been simpler and better to slip the key back inside the room under the door. Then it would look as though it had fallen from the lock."

"Ah, well, you can't expect everybody to have the bright ideas that you have. You'd have been a holy terror if you'd taken to crime. Any remarks to make, Moosior Poirot?"

Poirot, it seemed to me, was somewhat at a loss. He looked round the room and remarked mildly and almost apologetically—

"He smoked a lot, this monsieur."

True enough, the grate was filled with cigarette stubs, as was an ashtray that stood on a small table near the big armchair.

"He must have got through about twenty cigarettes last night," remarked Japp. Stooping down, he examined the contents of the grate carefully, then transferred his attention to the ash-tray. "They're all the same kind," he announced, "and smoked by the same man. There's nothing there, Monsieur Poirot."

"I did not suggest that there was," murmured my friend.

"Ha," cried Japp, "what's this?" He pounced on something bright and glittering that lay on the floor near the dead man. "A broken cuff-link. I wonder who this belongs to. Dr. Giles, I'd be obliged if you'd go down and send up the housekeeper."

"What about the Parkers? He's very anxious to leave the house—says he's got urgent business in London."

"I dare say. It'll have to get on without him. By the way things are going, it's likely that there'll be some urgent business down here for him to attend to! Send up the housekeeper, and don't let either of the Parkers give you and Pollard the slip. Did any of the household come in here this morning?"

The doctor reflected.

"No, they stood outside in the corridor while Pollard and I came in."

"Sure of that?"

"Absolutely certain."

The doctor departed on his mission.

"Good man, that," said Japp approvingly. "Some of these sporting doctors are first-class fellows. Well, I wonder who shot this chap. It looks like one of the three in the house. I hardly suspect the housekeeper. She's had eight years to shoot him in if she wanted to. I wonder who these Parkers are? They're not a prepossessing-looking couple."

Miss Clegg appeared at this juncture. She was a thin, gaunt woman with neat grey hair parted in the middle, very staid and calm in manner. Nevertheless there was an air of efficiency about her which commanded respect. In answer to Japp's questions, she explained that she had been with the dead man for fourteen years. He had been a generous and considerate master. She had never seen Mr. and Mrs. Parker until three days ago, when they arrived unexpectedly to stay. She was of the opinion that they had asked themselves—the master had certainly not seemed pleased to see them. The cuff-link which Japp showed her had not belonged to Mr. Protheroe—she was sure of that. Questioned about the pistol, she said that she believed her master had a weapon of that kind. He kept it locked up. She had seen it once some years ago, but could not say whether this was the same one. She had heard no shot last night, but that was not surprising, as it was a big, rambling house, and her rooms and those prepared for the Parkers were at the other end of the building. She did not know what time Mr. Protheroe had gone to bed; he was still up when she retired at half-past nine. It was not his habit to go at once to bed when he went to his room. Usually he would sit up half the night, reading and smoking. He was a great smoker.

Then Poirot interposed a question:

"Did your master sleep with his window open or shut, as a rule?"

Miss Clegg considered.

"It was usually open, at any rate at the top."

"Yet now it is closed. Can you explain that?"

"No, unless he felt a draught and shut it."

Japp asked her a few more questions and then dismissed her. Next he interviewed the Parkers separately. Mrs. Parker was inclined to be hysterical and tearful; Mr. Parker was full of bluster and abuse. He denied that the cuff-link was his, but as his wife had previously recognized it, this hardly improved matters for him; and as he had also denied ever having been in Protheroe's room, Japp considered that he had sufficient evidence to apply for a warrant.

Leaving Pollard in charge, Japp bustled back to the village and got into telephonic communication with headquarters. Poirot and I strolled back to the inn.

"You're unusually quiet," I said. "Doesn't the case interest you?"

"*Au contraire*, it interests me enormously. But it puzzles me also."

"The motive is obscure," I said thoughtfully, "but I'm certain that Parker's a bad lot. The case against him seems pretty clear but for the lack of motive, and that may come out later."

"Nothing struck you as being especially significant, although overlooked by Japp?"

I looked at him curiously.

"What have you got up your sleeve, Poirot?"

"What did the dead man have up his sleeve?"

"Oh, that handkerchief!"

"Exactly, that handkerchief."

"A sailor carries his handkerchief in his sleeve," I said thoughtfully.

"An excellent point, Hastings, though not the one I had in mind."

"Anything else?"

"Yes, over and over again I go back to the smell of cigarette smoke."

"I didn't smell any," I cried wonderingly.

"No more did I, *cher ami*."

I looked earnestly at him. It is so difficult to know when Poirot is pulling one's leg, but he seemed thoroughly in earnest and was frowning to himself.

The inquest took place two days later. In the meantime other evidence had come to light. A tramp had admitted that he had climbed over the wall into the Leigh House garden, where he often slept in a shed that was left unlocked. He declared that at twelve o'clock he had heard two men quarrelling loudly in a room on the first floor. One was demanding a sum of money; the other was angrily refusing. Concealed behind a bush, he had seen the two men as they passed and repassed the lighted window. One he knew well as being Mr. Protheroe, the owner of the house; the other he identified positively as Mr. Parker.

It was clear now that the Parkers had come to Leigh House to blackmail Protheroe; and when later it was discovered that the dead man's real name was Wendover, and that he had been a lieutenant in the Navy and had been concerned in the blowing-up of the first-class cruiser *Merrythought* in 1910, the case seemed to be rapidly clearing. It was supposed that Parker, cognizant of the part Wendover had played, had tracked him down and demanded hush money which the other refused to pay. In the course of the quarrel, Wendover drew his revolver, and Parker snatched it from him and shot him, subsequently endeavouring to give it the appearance of suicide.

Parker was committed for trial, reserving his defence. We had attended the police-court proceedings. As we left, Poirot nodded his head.

"It must be so," he murmured to himself. "Yes, it must be so. I will delay no longer."

He went into the post office and wrote off a note, which he despatched by special messenger. I did not see to whom it was addressed.

Then we returned to the inn where we had stayed on that memorable week-end.

Poirot was restless, going to and from the window.

"I await a visitor," he explained. "It cannot be — surely it cannot be — that I am mistaken. No, here she is."

To my utter astonishment, in another minute Miss Clegg walked into the room. She was less calm than usual, and was breathing hard as though she had been running. I saw the fear in her eyes as she looked at Poirot.

"Sit down, Mademoiselle," he said kindly. "I guessed rightly, did I not?"

For answer she burst into tears.

"Why did you do it?" asked Poirot gently. "Why?"

"I loved him so," she answered. "I was nursemaid to him when he was a little boy. Oh, be merciful to me!"

"I will do all I can. But you understand that I cannot permit an innocent man to hang — even though he is an unpleasing scoundrel."

She sat up and said in a low voice: "Perhaps in the end I could not have, either. Do whatever must be done."

Then, rising, she hurried from the room.

"Did *she* shoot him?" I asked, utterly bewildered.

Poirot smiled and shook his head.

"He shot himself. Do you remember that he carried his handkerchief in his *right* sleeve? That showed me that he was left-handed. Fearing exposure, after his stormy interview with Mr. Parker, he shot himself. In the morning Miss Clegg came to call him as usual and found him lying dead. As she has just told us, she had known him from a little boy upward, and was filled with fury against the Parkers, who had driven him to this shameful death. She regarded them as murderers, and then suddenly she saw a chance of making them suffer for the deed they had inspired. She alone knew that he was left-handed. She changed the pistol to his right hand, closed and bolted the window, dropped the bit of cuff-link she had picked up in one of the downstairs rooms, and went out, locking the door and removing the key."

"Poirot," I said, in a burst of enthusiasm, "you are magnificent. All that from the one little clue of the handkerchief."

"And the cigarette smoke. If the window had been closed, and all those cigarettes smoked, the room ought to have been full of stale tobacco. Instead, it was perfectly fresh, so I deduced at once that the window must have been open all night, and only closed in the morning, and that gave me a very interesting line of speculation. I could conceive of no circumstances under which a murderer could want to shut the window. It would be to his advantage to leave it open, and pretend that the murderer had escaped that way, if the theory of suicide did not go down. Of course, the tramp's evidence, when I heard it, confirmed my suspicions. He could never have overheard that conversation unless the window had been open."

"Splendid!" I said heartily. "Now, what about some tea?"

"Spoken like a true Englishman," said Poirot with a sigh. "I suppose it is not likely that I could obtain here a glass of *sirop?*"

# THE ADVENTURE OF THE ITALIAN NOBLEMAN.

"The Adventure of the Italian Nobleman" was first published in *The Sketch* on October 24, 1923.

Poirot and I had many friends and acquaintances of an informal nature. Amongst these was to be numbered Dr. Hawker, a near neighbour of ours, and a member of the medical profession. It was the genial doctor's habit to drop in sometimes of an evening and have a chat with Poirot, of whose genius he was an ardent admirer. The doctor himself, frank and unsuspicious to the last degree, admired the talents so far removed from his own.

On one particular evening in early June, he arrived about half-past eight and settled down to a comfortable discussion on the cheery topic of the prevalence of arsenical poisoning in crimes. It must have been about a quarter of an hour later when the door of our sitting-room flew open, and a distracted female precipitated herself into the room.

"Oh, doctor, you're wanted! Such a terrible voice. It gave me a turn, it did indeed."

I recognized in our new visitor Dr. Hawker's housekeeper, Miss Rider. The doctor was a bachelor, and lived in a gloomy old house a few streets away. The usually placid Miss Rider was now in a state bordering on incoherence.

"What terrible voice? Who is it, and what's the trouble?"

"It was the telephone, doctor. I answered it — and a voice spoke. 'Help,' it said. 'Doctor — help. They've killed me!' Then it sort of tailed away. 'Who's speaking?' I said. 'Who's speaking?' Then I got a reply, just a whisper, it seemed, 'Foscatine' — something like that — 'Regent's Court.'"

The doctor uttered an exclamation.

"Count Foscatini. He has a flat in Regent's Court. I must go at once. What can have happened?"

"A patient of yours?" asked Poirot.

"I attended him for some slight ailment a few weeks ago. An Italian, but he speaks English perfectly. Well, I must wish you good night, Monsieur Poirot, unless —" He hesitated.

"I perceive the thought in your mind," said Poirot, smiling. "I shall be delighted to accompany you. Hastings, run down and get hold of a taxi."

Taxis always make themselves sought for when one is particularly pressed for time, but I captured one at last, and we were soon bowling along in the direction of Regent's Park. Regent's Court was a new block of flats, situated just off St. John's Wood Road. They had only recently been built, and contained the latest service devices.

There was no one in the hall. The doctor pressed the lift bell impatiently, and when the lift arrived questioned the uniformed attendant sharply.

"Flat 11. Count Foscatini. There's been an accident there, I understand."

The man stared at him.

"First I've heard of it. Mr. Graves — that's Count Foscatini's man — went out about half an hour ago, and he said nothing."

"Is the Count alone in the flat?"

"No, Sir, he's got two gentlemen dining with him."

"What are they like?" I asked eagerly.

We were in the lift now, ascending rapidly to the second floor, on which Flat 11 was situated.

"I didn't see them myself, Sir, but I understand that they were foreign gentlemen."

He pulled back the iron door, and we stepped out on the landing. No. 11 was opposite to us. The doctor rang the bell. There was no reply, and we could hear no sound from within. The doctor rang again and again; we could hear the bell trilling within, but no sign of life rewarded us.

"This is getting serious," muttered the doctor. He turned to the lift attendant.

"Is there any pass-key to this door?"

"There is one in the porter's office downstairs."

"Get it, then, and — look here — I think you'd better send for the police."

Poirot approved with a nod of the head.

The man returned shortly; with him came the manager.

"Will you tell me, gentlemen, what is the meaning of all this?"

"Certainly. I received a telephone message from Count Foscatini stating that he had been attacked and was dying. You can understand that we must lose no time — if we are not already too late."

The manager produced the key without more ado, and we all entered the flat.

We passed first into the small square lounge hall. A door on the right of it was half open. The manager indicated it with a nod.

"The dining-room."

Dr. Hawker led the way. We followed close on his heels. As we entered the room I gave a gasp. The round table in the centre bore the remains of a meal; three chairs were pushed back, as though their occupants had just risen. In the corner, to the right of the fireplace, was a big writing table, and sitting at it was a man — or what had been a man. His right hand still grasped the base of the telephone, but he had fallen forward, struck down by a terrific blow on the head from behind. The weapon was not far to seek. A marble statue stood where it had been hurriedly put down, the base of it stained with blood.

The doctor's examination did not take a minute. "Stone dead. Must have been almost instantaneous. I wonder he even managed to telephone. It will be better not to move him until the police arrive."

On the manager's suggestion we searched the flat, but the result was a foregone conclusion. It was not likely that the murderers would be concealed there when all they had to do was to walk out.

We came back to the dining-room. Poirot had not accompanied us in our tour. I found him studying the centre table with close attention. I joined him. It was a well-polished round mahogany table. A bowl of roses decorated the centre, and white lace mats reposed on the gleaming surface. There was a dish of fruit, but the three dessert plates were untouched. There were three coffee-cups with remains of coffee in them — two black, one with milk. All three men had taken port, and the decanter, half full, stood before the centre plate. One of the men had smoked a cigar, the other two cigarettes. A tortoiseshell-and-silver box, holding cigars and cigarettes, stood open upon the table.

I enumerated all these facts to myself, but I was forced to admit that they did not shed any brilliant light on the situation. I wondered what Poirot saw in them to make him so intent. I asked him.

"*Mon ami*," he replied, "you miss the point. I am looking for something that I do *not* see."

"What is that?"

"A mistake — even a little

mistake — on the part of the murderer."

He stepped swiftly to the small adjoining kitchen, looked in, and shook his head.

"Monsieur," he said to the manager, "explain to me, I pray, your system of serving meals here."

The manager stepped to a small hatch in the wall.

"This is the service lift," he explained. "It runs to the kitchens at the top of the building. You order through this telephone, and the dishes are sent down in the lift, one course at a time. The dirty plates and dishes are sent up in the same manner. No domestic worries, you understand, and at the same time you avoid the wearying publicity of always dining in a restaurant."

Poirot nodded.

"Then the plates and dishes that were used tonight are on high in the kitchen. You permit that I mount there?"

"Oh, certainly, if you like! Roberts, the lift man, will take you up and introduce you; but I'm afraid you won't find anything that's of any use. They're handling hundreds of plates and dishes, and they'll be all lumped together."

Poirot remained firm, however, and together we visited the kitchens and questioned the man who had taken the order from Flat 11.

"The order was given from the *à la carte* menu — for three," he explained. "Soup julienne, filet de sole normande, tournedos of beef, and a rice soufflé. What time? Just about eight o'clock, I should say. No, I'm afraid the plates and dishes have been all washed up by now. Unfortunate. You were thinking of fingerprints, I suppose?"

"Not exactly," said Poirot, with an enigmatical smile. "I am more interested in Count Foscatini's appetite. Did he partake of every dish?"

"Yes; but of course I can't say how much of each he ate. The plates were all soiled, and the dishes empty — that is to say, with the exception of the rice soufflé. There was a fair amount of that left."

"Ah!" said Poirot, and seemed satisfied with the fact.

As we descended to the flat again he remarked in a low tone —

"We have decidedly to do with a man of method."

"Do you mean the murderer, or Count Foscatini?"

"The latter was undoubtedly an orderly gentleman. After imploring help and announcing his approaching demise, he carefully hung up the telephone receiver."

I stared at Poirot. His words now and his recent inquiries gave me the glimmering of an idea.

"You suspect poison?" I breathed. "The blow on the head was a blind."

Poirot merely smiled.

We reentered the flat to find the local inspector of police had arrived with two constables. He was inclined to resent our appearance, but Poirot calmed him with the mention of our Scotland Yard friend, Inspector Japp, and we were accorded a grudging permission to remain. It was a lucky thing we were, for we had not been back five minutes before an agitated middle-aged man came rushing into the room with every appearance of grief and agitation.

This was Graves, valet-butler to the late Count Foscatini. The story he had to tell was a sensational one.

On the previous morning, two gentlemen had called to see his master. They were Italians, and the elder of the two, a man of about forty, gave his name as Signor Ascanio. The younger was a well-dressed lad of about twenty-four.

Count Foscatini was evidently prepared for their visit and immediately sent Graves out upon some trivial errand. Here the man paused and hesitated in his story. In the end, however, he admitted that, curious as to the purport of the interview, he had not obeyed immediately, but had lingered about endeavouring to hear something of what was going on.

The conversation was carried on in so low a tone that he was not as successful as he had hoped; but he gathered enough to make it clear that some kind of monetary proposition was being discussed, and that the basis of it was a threat. The discussion was anything but amicable. In the end, Count Foscatini raised his voice slightly, and the listener heard these words clearly:

"I have no time to argue further now, gentlemen. If you will dine with me to-morrow night at eight o'clock, we will resume the discussion."

Afraid of being discovered listening, Graves had then hurried out to do his master's errand.

This evening the two men had arrived punctually at eight. During dinner they had talked of indifferent matters — politics, the weather, and the theatrical world. When Graves had placed the port upon the table and brought in the coffee his master told him that he might have the evening off.

"Was that a usual proceeding of his when he had guests?" asked the Inspector.

"No, Sir; it wasn't. That's what made me think it must be some business of a very unusual kind that he was going to discuss with these gentlemen."

That finished Graves's story. He had gone out about 8:30, and meeting a friend, had accompanied him to the Metropolitan Music Hall in Edgware Road.

Nobody had seen the two men leave, but the time of the murder was fixed clearly enough at 8:47. A small clock on the writing-table had been swept off by Foscatini's arm, and had stopped at that hour, which agreed with Miss Rider's telephone summons.

The police surgeon had made his examination of the body, and it was now lying on the couch. I saw the face for the first time — the olive complexion, the long nose, the luxuriant black moustache, and the full red lips drawn back from the dazzlingly white teeth. Not altogether a pleasant face.

"Well," said the inspector, refastening his notebook, "the case seems clear enough. The only difficulty will be to lay our hands on this Signor Ascanio. I suppose his address is not in the dead man's pocketbook by any chance?"

As Poirot had said, the late Foscatini was an orderly man. Neatly written in small, precise handwriting was the inscription, "Signor Paolo Ascanio, Grosvenor Hotel."

The inspector busied himself with the telephone, then turned to us with a grin.

"Just in time. Our fine gentleman was off to catch the boat train to the Continent. Well, gentlemen, that's about all we can do here. It's a bad business, but straightforward enough. One of these Italian vendetta things, as likely as not."

Thus airily dismissed, we found our way downstairs. Dr. Hawker was full of excitement.

"Like the beginning of a novel, eh? Real exciting stuff. Wouldn't believe it if you read about it."

Poirot did not speak. He was very thoughtful. All the evening he had hardly opened his lips.

"What says the master detective, eh?" asked Hawker, clapping him on the back. "Nothing to work your grey cells over this time."

"You think not?"

"What could there be?"

"Well, for example, there is the window."

"The window? But it was fastened. Nobody could have got out or in that way. I noticed it specially."

"And why were you able to notice it?"

The doctor looked puzzled. Poirot hastened to explain.

"It is to the curtains that I refer. They were not drawn. A little odd, that. And then there was the coffee. It was very black coffee."

"Well, what of it?"

"Very black," repeated Poirot. "In conjunction with that let us remember that very little of the rice soufflé was eaten, and we get — what?"

"Moonshine," laughed the doctor. "You're pulling my leg."

"Never do I pull the leg. Hastings here knows that I am perfectly serious."

"I don't know what you are getting at, all the same," I confessed. "You don't suspect the manservant, do you? He might have been in with the gang, and put some dope in the coffee. I suppose they'll test his alibi?"

"Without doubt, my friend; but it is the alibi of Signor Ascanio that interests me."

"You think he has an alibi?"

"That is just what worries me. I have no doubt that we shall soon be enlightened on that point."

The *Daily Newsmonger* enabled us to become conversant with succeeding events.

Signor Ascanio was arrested and charged with the murder of Count Foscatini. When arrested, he denied knowing the Count, and declared he had never been near Regent's Court either on the evening of the crime or on the previous morning. The younger man had disappeared entirely. Signor Ascanio had arrived alone at the Grosvenor Hotel from the Continent two days before the murder. All efforts to trace the second man failed.

Ascanio, however, was not sent for trial. No less a personage than the Italian Ambassador himself came forward and testified at the police court proceedings that Ascanio had been with him at the Embassy from eight till nine that evening. The prisoner was discharged. Naturally, a lot of people thought that the crime was a political one, and was being deliberately hushed up.

Poirot had taken a keen interest in all these points. Nevertheless, I was somewhat surprised when he suddenly informed me one morning that he was expecting a visitor at eleven o'clock, and that the visitor was none other than Ascanio himself.

"He wishes to consult you?"

"*Du tout*, Hastings, I wish to consult him."

"What about?"

"The Regent's Court murder."

"You are going to prove that he did it?"

"A man cannot be tried twice for murder, Hastings. Endeavour to have the common sense. Ah, that is our friend's ring."

A few minutes later Signor Ascanio was ushered in — a small, thin man with a secretive and furtive glance in his eyes. He remained standing, darting suspicious glances from one to the other of us.

"Monsieur Poirot?"

My little friend tapped himself gently on the chest.

"Be seated, signor. You received my note. I am determined to get to the bottom of this mystery. In some small measure. you can aid me. Let us commence.

"You — in company with a friend — visited the late Count Foscatini on the morning of Tuesday the 9th —"

The Italian made an angry gesture.

"I did nothing of the sort. I have sworn in court —"

"*Précisément* — and I have a little idea that you have sworn falsely."

"You threaten me? Bah! I have nothing to fear from you. I have been acquitted."

"Exactly; and as I am not an imbecile, it is not with the gallows I threaten you — but with publicity. Publicity! I see that you do not like the word. I had an idea that you would not. My little ideas, you know, they are very valuable to me. Come, signor, your only chance is to be frank with me. I do not ask to know whose indiscretions brought you to England. I know this much, you came for the special purpose of seeing Count Foscatini."

"He was not a count," growled the Italian.

"I have already noted the fact that his name does not appear in the *Almanach de Gotha*. Never mind, the title of Count is often useful in the profession of blackmailing."

"I suppose I might as well be frank. You seem to know a good deal."

"I have employed my grey cells to some advantage. Come, Signor Ascanio, you visited the dead man on the Tuesday morning — that is so, is it not?"

"Yes; but I never went there on the following evening. There was no need. I will tell you all. Certain information concerning a man of great position in Italy had come into this scoundrel's possession. He demanded a big sum of money in return for the papers. I came over to England to arrange the matter. I called upon him by appointment that morning. One of the young secretaries of the Embassy was with me. The Count was more reasonable than I had hoped, although even then the sum of money I paid him was a huge one."

"Pardon, how was it paid?"

"In Italian notes of comparatively small denomination. I paid over the money then and there. He handed me the incriminating papers. I never saw him again."

"Why did you not say all this when you were arrested?"

"In my delicate position I was forced to deny any association with the man."

"And how do you account for the events of the evening then?"

"I can only think that someone must have deliberately impersonated me. I understand that no money was found in the flat."

Poirot looked at him and shook his head.

"Strange," he murmured. "We all have the little grey cells. And so few of us know how to use them. Good morning, Signor Ascanio. I believe your story. It is very much as I had imagined. But I had to make sure."

After bowing his guest out, Poirot returned to his armchair and smiled at me. "Let us hear *Monsieur le Capitaine* Hastings on the case."

"Well, I suppose Ascanio is right — somebody impersonated him."

"Never, never will you use the brains the good God has given you. Recall to yourself some words I uttered after leaving the flat that night. I referred to the window-curtains not being drawn. We are in the month of June. It is still light at eight o'clock. The light is failing by half past. *Ça vous dit quelque chose?* I perceive a struggling impression that you will arrive some day. Now let us continue. The coffee was, as I said, very black. Count Foscatini's teeth were magnificently white. Coffee stains the teeth. We reason from that that Count Foscatini did not drink any coffee. Yet there was coffee in all three cups. Why should anyone pretend Count Foscatini had drunk coffee when he had not done so?"

I shook my head, utterly bewildered.

"Come, I will help you. What evidence have we that Ascanio and his friend, or two men posing as them, ever came to the flat that night? Nobody saw them go in; nobody saw them go out. We have the evidence of one man and of a host of inanimate objects."

"You mean?"

"I mean knives and forks and plates and empty dishes. Ah, but it was a clever idea! Graves is a thief and a scoundrel, but what a man of method! He overhears a portion of the conversation in the morning, enough to realize that Ascanio will be in an awkward position to defend himself. The following evening, about eight o'clock, he tells his master he is wanted at the telephone. Foscatini sits down, stretches out his hand to the telephone, and from behind Graves strikes him down with the marble figure. Then quickly to the service telephone — dinner for three! It comes, he lays the table, dirties the plates, knives, and forks, etc. But he has to get rid of the food too. Not only is he a man of brain; he has a resolute and capacious stomach! But after eating three tournedos, the rice soufflé is too much for him! He even smokes a cigar and two cigarettes to carry out the illusion. Ah, but it was magnificently thorough! Then, having moved on the hands of the clock to 8:47, he smashes it and stops it. The one thing he does not do is to draw the curtains. But if there had been a real dinner party the curtains would have been drawn as soon as the light began to fail. Then he hurries out, mentioning the guests to the lift man in passing. He hurries to a telephone box, and as near as possible to 8:47 rings up the doctor with his master's dying cry. So successful is his idea that no one ever inquires if a call was put through from Flat 11 at that time."

"Except Hercule Poirot, I suppose?" I said sarcastically.

"Not even Hercule Poirot," said my friend, with a smile. "I am about to inquire now. I had to prove my point to you first. But you will see, I shall be right; and then Japp, to whom I have already given a hint, will be able to arrest the respectable Graves. I wonder how much of the money he has spent."

Poirot was right. He always is, confound him!

# THE CASE OF THE MISSING WILL.

"The Case of the Missing Will" was first published in *The Sketch* on October 31, 1923.

The problem presented to us by Miss Violet Marsh made rather a pleasant change from our usual routine work. Poirot had received a brisk and businesslike note from the lady asking for an appointment, and had replied asking her to call upon him at eleven o'clock the following day.

She arrived punctually—a tall, handsome young woman, plainly but neatly dressed, with an assured and businesslike manner. Clearly a young woman who meant to get on in the world. I am not a great admirer of the so-called New Woman myself, and, in spite of her good looks, I was not particularly prepossessed in her favour.

"My business is of a somewhat unusual nature, Monsieur Poirot," she began, after she had accepted a chair. "I had better begin at the beginning and tell you the whole story."

"If you please, Mademoiselle."

"I am an orphan. My father was one of two brothers, sons of a small yeoman farmer in Devonshire. The farm was a poor one, and the elder brother, Andrew, emigrated to Australia, where he did very well indeed, and by means of successful speculation in land became a very rich man. The younger brother, Roger (my father), had no leanings towards the agricultural life. He managed to educate himself a little, and obtained a post as clerk with a small firm. He married slightly above him; my mother was the daughter of a poor artist. My father died when I was six years old. When I was fourteen, my mother followed him to the grave. My only living relation then was my uncle Andrew, who had recently returned from Australia and bought a small place, Crabtree Manor, in his native county. He was exceedingly kind to his brother's orphan child, took me to live with him, and treated me in every way as though I was his own daughter.

"Crabtree Manor, in spite of its name, is really only an old farm-house. Farming was in my uncle's blood, and he was intensely interested in various modern farming experiments. Although kindness itself to me, he had certain peculiar and deeply-rooted ideas as to the upbringing of women. Himself a man of little or no education, though possessing remarkable shrewdness, he placed little value on what he called 'book knowledge.' He was especially opposed to the education of women. In his opinion, girls should learn practical housework and dairy work, be useful about the home, and have as little to do with book learning as possible. He proposed to bring me up on these lines, to my bitter disappointment and annoyance. I rebelled frankly. I knew that I possessed a good brain, and had absolutely no talent for domestic duties. My uncle and I had many bitter arguments on the subject, for, though much attached to each other, we were both self-willed. I was lucky enough to win a scholarship, and up to a certain point was successful in getting my own way. The crisis arose when I resolved to go to Girton. I had a little money of my own, left me by my mother, and I was quite determined to make the best use of the gifts God had given me. I had one long, final argument with my uncle. He put the facts plainly before me. He had no other relations, and he had intended me to be his sole heiress. As I have told you, he was a very rich man. If I persisted in these 'new-fangled notions' of mine, however, I need look for nothing from him. I remained polite, but firm. I should always be deeply attached to him, I told him, but I must lead my own life. We parted on that note. 'You fancy your brains, my girl,' were his last words. 'I've no book learning, but, for all that, I'll pit mine against yours any day. We'll see what we shall see.'

"That was nine years ago. I have stayed with him for a week-end occasionally, and our relations were perfectly amicable, though his views remained unaltered. He never referred to my having matriculated, nor to my B.Sc. For the last three years his health had been failing, and a month ago he died.

"I am now coming to the point of my visit. My uncle left a most extraordinary will. By its terms, Crabtree Manor and its contents are to be at my disposal for a year from his death — 'during which time my clever niece may prove her wits,' the actual words run. At the end of that period, 'my wits having been proved better than hers,' the house and all my uncle's large fortune pass to various charitable institutions."

"That is a little hard on you, Mademoiselle, seeing that you were Mr. Marsh's only blood relation."

"I do not look on it in that way. Uncle Andrew warned me fairly, and I chose my own path. Since I would not fall in with his wishes, he was at perfect liberty to leave his money to whom he pleased."

"Was the will drawn up by a lawyer?"

"No; it was written on a printed will form and witnessed by the man and his wife who live at the house and do for my uncle."

"There might be a possibility of upsetting such a will?"

"I would not even attempt to do such a thing."

"You regard it then as a sporting challenge on the part of your uncle?"

"That is exactly how I look upon it."

"It bears that interpretation, certainly," said Poirot thoughtfully. "Somewhere in this rambling old manor house your uncle has concealed either a sum of money in notes or possibly a second will, and has given you a year in which to exercise your ingenuity to find it."

"Exactly, Monsieur Poirot; and I am paying you the compliment of assuming that your ingenuity will be greater than mine."

"Eh, eh! but that is very charming of you. My grey cells are at your disposal. You have made no search yourself?"

"Only a cursory one; but I have too much respect for my uncle's undoubted abilities to fancy that the task will be an easy one."

"Have you the will or a copy of it with you?"

Miss March handed a document across the table. Poirot ran through it, nodding to himself.

"Made three years ago. Dated March 25; and the time is given also — eleven a.m. — that is very suggestive. It narrows the field of search. Assuredly it is another will we have to seek for. A will made even half an hour later would upset this. *Eh bien*, Mademoiselle, it is a problem charming and ingenious that you have presented to me here. I shall have all the pleasure in the world in solving it for you. Granted that your uncle was a man of ability, his grey cells cannot have been of the quality of Hercule Poirot's!"

(Really, Poirot's vanity is blatant!)

"Fortunately, I have nothing of moment on hand at the minute. Hastings and I will go down to

Crabtree Manor tonight. The man and wife who attended on your uncle are still there, I presume?"

"Yes, their name is Baker."

The following morning saw us started on the hunt proper. We had arrived late the night before. Mr. and Mrs. Baker, having received a telegram from Miss Marsh, were expecting us. They were a pleasant couple, the man gnarled and pink-cheeked, like a shrivelled pippin, and his wife a woman of vast proportion and true Devonshire calm.

Tired with our journey and the eight-mile drive from the station, we had retired at once to bed after a supper of roast chicken, apple pie, and Devonshire cream. We had now disposed of an excellent breakfast, and were sitting in a small panelled room which had been the late Mr. Marsh's study and living room. A roll-top desk stuffed with papers, all neatly docketed, stood against the wall, and a big leather armchair showed plainly that it had been its owner's constant resting place. A big chintz-covered settee ran along the opposite wall, and the deep low window seats were covered with the same faded chintz of an old-fashioned pattern.

"*Eh bien, mon ami,*" said Poirot, lighting one of his tiny cigarettes, "we must map out our plan of campaign. Already I have made a rough survey of the house, but I am of the opinion that any clue will be found in this room. We shall have to go through the documents in the desk with meticulous care. Naturally, I do not expect to find the will amongst them; but it is likely that some apparently innocent paper may conceal the clue to its hiding place. But first we must have a little information. Ring the bell, I pray of you."

I did so. While we were waiting for it to be answered, Poirot walked up and down, looking about him approvingly.

"A man of method, this Mr. Marsh. See how neatly the packets of papers are docketed; then the key to each drawer has its ivory label — so has the key of the china cabinet on the wall; and see with what precision the china within is arranged. It rejoices the heart. Nothing here offends the eye —"

He came to an abrupt pause, as his eye was caught by the key of the desk itself, to which a dirty envelope was affixed. Poirot frowned at it and withdrew it from the lock. On it were scrawled the words: "Key of Roll Top Desk," in a crabbed handwriting, quite unlike the neat superscriptions on the other keys.

"An alien note," said Poirot, frowning. "I could swear that here we have no longer the personality of Mr. Marsh. But who else has been in the house? Only Miss Marsh, and she, if I mistake not, is also a young lady of method and order."

Baker came in answer to the bell.

"Will you fetch Madame your wife, and answer a few questions?"

Baker departed, and in a few moments returned with Mrs. Baker, wiping her hands on her apron and beaming all over her face.

In a few clear words Poirot set forth the object of his mission. The Bakers were immediately sympathetic.

"Us don't want to see Miss Violet done out of what's hers," declared the woman. "Cruel hard 'twould be for hospitals to get it all."

Poirot proceeded with his questions. Yes, Mr. and Mrs. Baker remembered perfectly witnessing the will. Baker had previously been sent into the neighbouring town to get two printed will forms.

"Two?" said Poirot sharply .

"Yes, Sir, for safety like, I suppose, in case he should spoil one — and sure enough, so he did do. Us had signed one —"

"What time of day was that?"

Baker scratched his head, but his wife was quicker.

"Why, to be sure, I'd just put the milk on for the cocoa at eleven. Don't 'ee remember? It had all boiled over on the stove when us got back to kitchen ."

"And afterwards?"

"'Twould be about an hour later. Us had to go in again. 'I've made a mistake,' said old master, 'had to tear the whole thing up. I'll trouble you to sign again,' and us did. And afterwards master gave us a tidy sum of money each. 'I've left you nothing in my will,' says he, 'but each year I live you'll have this to be a nest egg when I'm gone'; and sure enough, so he did."

Poirot reflected.

"After you had signed the second time, what did Mr. Marsh do? Do you know?"

"Went out to the village to pay tradesmen's books."

That did not seem very promising. Poirot tried another tack. He held out the key of the desk.

"Is that your master's writing?"

I may have imagined it, but I fancied that a moment or two elapsed before Baker replied: "Yes, Sir, it is."

"He's lying," I thought. "But why?"

"Has your master let the house? — have there been any strangers in it during the last three years?"

"No, Sir."

"No visitors?"

"Only Miss Violet."

"No strangers of any kind been inside this room?"

"No, Sir."

"You forget the workmen, Jim," his wife reminded him.

"Workmen?" Poirot wheeled round on her. "What workmen?"

The woman explained that about two years and a half ago workmen had been in the house to do certain repairs. She was quite vague as to what the repairs were. Her view seemed to be that the whole thing was a fad of her master's and quite unnecessary. Part of the time the workmen had been in the study; but what they had done there she could not say, as her master had not let either of them into the room whilst the work was in progress. Unfortunately, they could not remember the name of the firm employed, beyond the fact that it was a Plymouth one.

"We progress, Hastings," said Poirot, rubbing his hands as the Bakers left the room. "Clearly he made a second will and then had workmen from Plymouth in to make a suitable hiding place. Instead of wasting time taking up the floor and tapping the walls, we will go to Plymouth."

With a little trouble, we were able to get the information we wanted. After one or two essays we found the firm employed by Mr. Marsh.

Their employees had all been with them many years, and it was easy to find the two men who had worked under Mr. Marsh's orders. They remembered the job perfectly. Amongst various other minor jobs, they had taken up one of the bricks of the old-fashioned fireplace, made a cavity beneath, and so cut the brick that it was impossible to see the joint. By pressing on the second brick from the end, the whole thing was raised. It had been quite a complicated piece of work, and the old gentleman had been very fussy about it. Our informant was a man called Coghan, a big, gaunt man with a grizzled moustache. He seemed an intelligent fellow.

We returned to Crabtree Manor in high spirits, and, locking the study door, proceeded to put our newly acquired knowledge into effect. It was impossible to see any sign on the bricks, but when we pressed in the manner indicated, a deep cavity was at once disclosed.

Eagerly Poirot plunged in his hand. Suddenly his face fell from complacent elation to consternation. All he held was a charred fragment of stiff paper. But for it, the cavity was empty.

"*Sacre!*" cried Poirot angrily. "Someone has been before us."

We examined the scrap of paper anxiously. Clearly it was a fragment of what we sought. A portion of Baker's signature remained, but no indication of what the terms of the will had been.

Poirot sat back on his heels. His expression would have been comical if we had not been so overcome. "I understand it not," he growled. "Who destroyed this? And what was their object?"

"The Bakers?" I suggested.

"*Pourquoi?* Neither will makes any provision for them, and they are more likely to be kept on with Miss Marsh than if the place became the property of a hospital. How could it be to anyone's advantage to destroy the will? The hospitals benefit — yes; but one cannot suspect institutions."

"Perhaps the old man changed

his mind and destroyed it himself," I suggested.

Poirot rose to his feet, dusting his knees with his usual care.

"That may be," he admitted. "One of your more sensible observations, Hastings. Well, we can do no more here. We have done all that mortal man can do. We have successfully pitted our wits against the late Andrew Marsh's; but, unfortunately, his niece is not better off for our success."

By driving to the station at once, we were just able to catch a train to London, though not the principal express. Poirot was sad and dissatisfied. For my part, I was tired and dozed in a corner. Suddenly, as we were just moving out of Taunton, Poirot uttered a piercing squeal.

"*Vite*, Hastings! Awake and jump! But jump I say!"

Before I knew where I was we were standing on the platform, bareheaded and minus our valises, whilst the train disappeared into the night. I was furious. But Poirot paid no attention.

"Imbecile that I have been!" he cried. "Triple imbecile! Not again will I vaunt my little grey cells!"

"That's a good job at any rate," I said grumpily. "But what is this all about?"

As usual, when following out his own ideas, Poirot paid absolutely no attention to me.

"The tradesmen's books — I have left them entirely out of account? Yes, but where? Where? Never mind, I cannot be mistaken. We must return at once."

Easier said than done. We managed to get a slow train to Exeter, and there Poirot hired a car. We arrived back at Crabtree Manor in the small hours of the morning.

I pass over the bewilderment of the Bakers when we had at last aroused them. Paying no attention to anybody, Poirot strode at once to the study.

"I have been, not a triple imbecile, but thirty-six times one, my friend," he deigned to remark. "Now, behold!"

Going straight to the desk he drew out the key, and detached the envelope from it. I stared at him stupidly. How could he possibly hope to find a big will form in that tiny envelope? With great care he cut open the envelope, laying it out flat. Then he lighted the fire and held the plain inside surface of the envelope to the flame. In a few minutes faint characters began to appear.

"Look, *mon ami*!" cried Poirot in triumph.

I looked. There were just a few lines of faint writing stating briefly that he left everything to his niece, Violet Marsh. It was dated March 25, 12:30 p.m., and witnessed by Albert Pike, confectioner, and Jessie Pike, married woman.

"But is it legal?" I gasped.

"As far as I know, there is no law

against writing your will in a blend of disappearing and sympathetic ink. The intention of the testator is clear, and the beneficiary is his only living relation. But the cleverness of him! He foresaw every step that a searcher would take — that I, miserable imbecile, took. He gets two will forms, makes the servants sign twice, then sallies out with his will written on the inside of a dirty envelope and a fountain pen containing his little ink mixture. On some excuse he gets the confectioner and his wife to sign their names under his own signature, then he ties it to the key of his desk and chuckles to himself. If his niece sees through his little ruse, she will have justified her choice of life and elaborate education and be thoroughly welcome to his money."

"She didn't see through it, did she?" I said slowly. "It seems rather unfair. The old man really won."

"But no, Hastings. It is *your* wits that go astray. Miss Marsh proved the astuteness of her wits and the value of the higher education for women by at once putting the matter in *my* hands. Always employ the expert. She has amply proved her right to the money."

I wonder — I very much wonder — what old Andrew Marsh would have thought!

# THE SUBMARINE PLANS.

"The Submarine Plans" was first published in *The Sketch* on November 7, 1923.

A note had been brought by special messenger. Poirot read it, and a gleam of excitement and interest came into his eyes as he did so. He dismissed the man with a few curt words and then turned to me.

"Pack a bag with all haste, my friend. We are going down to Sharples."

I started at the mention of the famous country place of Lord Alloway. Head of the newly formed Ministry of Defence, Lord Alloway was a prominent member of the Cabinet. As Sir Ralph Curtis, head of a great engineering firm, he had made his mark in the House of Commons, and he was now freely spoken of as *the* coming man, and the one most likely to be asked to form a ministry should the rumours as to Mr. David MacAdams' health prove well-founded.

A big Rolls-Royce car was waiting for us below, and as we glided off into the darkness I plied Poirot with questions.

"What on earth can they want us for at this time of night?" I demanded.

It was past eleven.

Poirot shook his head. "Something of the most urgent, without doubt."

"I remember," I said, "that some years ago there was some rather ugly scandal about Ralph Curtis, as he then was — some jugglery with shares, I believe. In the end, he was completely exonerated — but perhaps something of the kind has arisen again?"

"It would hardly be necessary for him to send for me in the middle of the night, my friend."

I was forced to agree, and the remainder of the journey was passed in silence. Once out of London, the powerful car fairly forged ahead, and we arrived at Sharples in a little under the hour.

A pontifical butler conducted us at once to a small study where Lord Alloway was awaiting us. He sprang up to greet us — a tall, spare man who seemed actually to radiate power and vitality.

"Monsieur Poirot, I am delighted to see you! It is the second time the government has demanded your services. I remember only too well what you did for us during the war, when the Prime Minister was kidnapped in that astounding fashion. Your masterly deductions — and, may I add, your discretion? — saved the situation."

Poirot's eyes twinkled a little.

"Do I gather, then, Milor', that this is another case for — discretion?"

"Most emphatically. Sir Harry and I — oh, let me introduce you — Admiral Sir Harry Weardale, our First Sea Lord, Monsieur Poirot and — let me see, Captain —?"

"Hastings," I said.

"Exactly. The Doctor Watson, as it were, to our friend's Sherlock Holmes."

I maintained a frozen silence. I thought the comparison hardly a happy one, and it struck me that a man so deficient in tact would not be the most successful of prime ministers.

"I've often heard of you, Monsieur Poirot," said Sir Harry, shaking hands. "This is a most unaccountable business, and if you can solve it we'll be extremely grateful to you."

I liked the First Sea Lord immediately — a square, bluff sailor of the good old-fashioned type.

Poirot looked inquiringly at them both, and Alloway took up the tale.

"Of course, you understand that all this is in confidence, Monsieur Poirot. We have had a most serious loss. The plans of the new 'Z' type of submarine have been stolen."

"When was that?"

"To-night — less than three hours ago. You can appreciate, perhaps, Monsieur Poirot, the magnitude of the disaster. It is essential that the loss should not be made public. I will give you the facts as briefly as possible. My guests over the week-end were the admiral here, his wife and son, and a Mrs. Conrad, a lady well known in London society. The ladies retired to bed early—about 10 o'clock; so did Mr. Leonard Weardale. Sir Harry is down here partly for the purpose of discussing the construction of this new type of submarine with me. Accordingly, I asked Mr. Fitzroy, my secretary, to get out the plans from the safe in the corner there, and to arrange them ready for me, as well as various other documents that bore upon the subject in hand. Whilst he was doing this the Admiral and I strolled up and down the terrace, smoking cigars and enjoying the warm June air.

"We finished our smoke and our chat, and decided to get down to business. Just as we turned at the far end of the terrace I fancied I saw a shadow slip out of the French-window here, cross the terrace, and disappear. I paid very little attention, however. I knew Fitzroy to be in this room, and it never entered my head that anything might be amiss. There, of course, I am to blame. Well, we retraced our steps along the terrace and entered this room by the window just as Fitzroy entered it from the hall.

"'Got everything out we are likely to need, Fitzroy?' I asked.

"'I think so, Lord Alloway. The papers are all on your desk.'

"He then wished us both good-night.

"'Just wait a minute,' I said, going to the desk. 'I may want something I haven't mentioned.'

"I looked quickly through the papers that were lying there.

"'You forgotten the most important of the lot, Fitzroy,' I said—'the actual plans of the submarine!'

"'The plans are right on top, Lord Alloway.'

"'Oh, no, they're not,' I said, turning over the papers.

"'But I put them there not a minute ago.'

"'Well, they're not there now,' I said.

"Fitzroy advanced with a bewildered expression on his face. The thing seemed incredible. We turned over the papers on the desk, we hunted through the safe, but at last we had to make up our minds to it that the papers were gone—and gone within the short space of about three minutes whilst Fitzroy was absent from the room."

"Why did he leave the room?" asked Poirot quickly.

"Just what I asked him," exclaimed Sir Harry.

"It appears," said Lord Alloway, "that just when he had finished arranging the papers on my desk, he was startled by hearing a woman scream. He dashed out into the hall. On the stairs he discovered Mrs. Conrad's French maid. The girl looked very white and upset, and declared that she had seen a ghost—a tall figure dressed all in white that moved without a sound. Fitzroy laughed at her fears and told her, in more or less polite language, not to be a fool. Then he returned to this room just as we entered from the window."

"It all seems very clear," said Poirot thoughtfully. "The only question is, was the maid an accomplice? Did she scream by arrangement with her confederate lurking outside, or was he merely waiting there in the hope of an opportunity presenting itself? It was a man, I suppose—not a woman you saw?"

"I can't tell you, Monsieur Poirot. It was just a—shadow."

The admiral gave such a peculiar snort that it could not fail to attract attention.

"*Monsieur l'Amiral* has something to say, I think," said Poirot quietly, with a slight smile. "You saw this shadow, Sir Harry?"

"No, I didn't," returned the other. "And neither did Alloway. The branch of a tree flapped or something, and then, afterwards, when we discovered the theft, he leapt to the conclusion that he had seen someone pass across the terrace. His imagination played a trick on him, that's all."

"I am not usually credited with having much imagination," said Lord Alloway, with a slight smile.

"Nonsense! We've all got imagination. We can all work ourselves up to believe that we've seen more than we have. I've had a lifetime of experience at sea, and I'll back my eyes against those of any landsman. I was looking right down the terrace, and I'd have seen the same if there was anything to see."

He was quite excited over the matter. Poirot rose and stepped quickly to the window.

"You permit?" he asked. "We must settle this point if possible."

He went out upon the terrace, and we followed him. He had taken a torch from his pocket, and was playing the light along the edge of the grass that bordered the terrace.

"Where did he cross the terrace, Milor'?" he asked.

"About opposite the window, I should say."

Poirot continued to play the torch for some minutes longer, walking the entire length of the terrace and back. Then he shut it off and straightened himself up.

"Sir Harry is right—and you are wrong, Milor'," he said quietly. "It rained heavily earlier this evening. Anyone who passed over that grass could not avoid leaving foot marks. But there are none—none at all."

His eyes went from one man's face to the others. Lord Alloway looked bewildered and unconvinced; the admiral expressed a noisy gratification.

"Knew I couldn't be wrong," he declared. "Trust my eyes anywhere."

He was such a picture of an honest old sea dog that I could not help smiling at him.

"So that brings us to the people in the house," said Poirot smoothly. "Let us come inside again. Now, Milor', whilst Mr. Fitzroy was speaking to the maid on the stairs, could anyone have seized the opportunity to enter the study from the hall?"

Lord Alloway shook his head.

"Quite impossible; they would have had to pass him in order to do so."

"And Mr. Fitzroy himself—you are sure of him, eh?"

Lord Alloway flushed.

"Absolutely, Monsieur Poirot. I will answer confidently for my secretary. It is quite impossible that he should be concerned in the matter in any way."

"Everything seems to be impossible," remarked Poirot rather dryly. "Possibly the plans attached to themselves a little pair of wings and flew away—*comme ça*!" He blew his lips out like a comical cherub.

"The whole thing is impossible," declared Lord Alloway impatiently. "But I beg, Monsieur Poirot, that you will not dream of suspecting Fitzroy. Consider for one moment—had he wished to take the plans, what could have been easier for him then to take a tracing of them without going to the trouble of stealing them?"

"There, Milor'," said Poirot with approval, "you make a remark *bien juste*—I see that you have a mind orderly and methodical. *L'Angleterre* is happy in possessing you."

Lord Alloway looked rather embarrassed by this sudden burst of praise. Poirot returned to the matter in hand.

"The room in which you had been sitting all the evening—"

"The drawing-room? Yes?"

"That also has a window on the terrace, since I remember your saying you went out that way. Would it not be possible for someone to come out by the drawing-room window and in by this one whilst Mr. Fitzroy was out of the room, and return the same way?"

"But we'd have seen them," objected the Admiral.

"Not if you had your backs turned, walking the other way."

"Fitzroy was only out of the room a few minutes—the time it would take us to walk to the end and back."

"No matter; it is a possibility—in fact, the only one as things stand."

"But there was no one in the drawing-room when we went out," said the Admiral.

"They may have come there afterwards."

"You mean," said Lord Alloway slowly, "that when Fitzroy heard the maid scream and went out, someone was already concealed in the drawing-room, that they darted in and out through the windows, and only left the drawing-room when Fitzroy had returned to this room?"

"The methodical mind again," said Poirot, bowing. "You express the matter perfectly."

"One of the servants, perhaps?"

"Or a guest. It was Mrs. Conrad's maid who screamed. What exactly can you tell me of Mrs. Conrad?"

Lord Alloway considered for a minute or two.

"I told you that she is a lady well known in society. That is true in the sense that she gives large parties and goes everywhere. But very little is known as to where she really comes from and what her past life has been. She is a lady who frequents diplomatic and Foreign Office circles as much as possible. The Secret Service is inclined to ask—why?"

"I see," said Poirot. "And she was asked here this week-end—?"

"So that—shall we say?—we might observe her at close quarters."

"*Parfaitement!* It is possible that she has turned the tables on you rather neatly."

Lord Alloway looked discomfited, and Poirot continued—

"Tell me, Milor', was any reference made in her hearing to the subject to you and the admiral were going to discuss together?"

"Yes," admitted the other. "Sir Harry said, 'and now for our submarine! To work!'—or something of that sort. The others had left the room, but she had come back for a book."

"I see," said Poirot thoughtfully. "Milor', it is very late—but this is an urgent affair. I would like to question the members of the house-party at once if it is possible."

"It can be managed, of course," said Lord Alloway. "The awkward thing is, we don't want to let it get about more than can be helped. Of course, Lady Juliet Weardale and young Leonard are all right—but Mrs. Conrad, if she is not guilty, is rather a different proposition. Perhaps you could just state that an important paper is missing, without specifying what it is about, or going into any of the circumstances of the disappearance?"

"Exactly what I was about to propose myself," said Poirot, beaming. "In fact, in all three cases. Monsieur the Admiral will pardon me, but even the best of wives—"

"No offence," said Sir Harry. "All women talk, bless 'em! I wish Juliet would talk a little more and play bridge a little less. But women are like that nowadays—never happy unless they're dancing or gambling. I'll get Juliet and Leonard up—shall I, Alloway?"

"Thank you. I'll knock up the French maid. Monsieur Poirot will want to see her, and she can rouse her mistress. I'll go and attend to it now. In the meantime, I'll send Fitzroy along."

Mr. Fitzroy was a pale, thin young man with pince-nez and a frigid expression. His statement was practically word for word what Lord Alloway had already told us.

"What is your own theory, Mr. Fitzroy?"

Mr. Fitzroy shrugged his shoulders.

"Undoubtedly someone who knew the hang of things was waiting his chance outside. He could see what went on through the window, and he slipped in when I left the room. It's a pity Lord Alloway didn't give chase then and there when he saw the fellow leave."

Poirot did not undeceive him. Instead, he asked —

"Do you believe the story of the French maid — that she had seen a ghost?"

"Well — hardly, Monsieur Poirot!"

"I mean — that she really thought so?"

"Oh, as to that I can't say. She certainly seemed rather upset. She had her hands to her head."

"Aha!" cried Poirot, with the air of one who has made a discovery. "Is that so, indeed — and she was, without doubt, a pretty girl?"

"I didn't notice particularly," said Mr. Fitzroy, in a repressive voice.

"You did not see her mistress, I suppose?"

"As a matter of fact, I did. She was in the gallery at the top of the steps and was calling her — 'Léonie.' Then she saw me — and, of course, retired."

"Upstairs," said Poirot, frowning. He bit his lip, and angrily straightened a match-box and a candlestick that did not quite please his symmetrical eye.

"Of course, I realize that all this is very unpleasant for me — or rather would have been, if Lord Alloway had not chanced to see the man actually leaving. In any case, I should be glad if you would make a point of searching my room — and myself, of course."

"You really wish that?"

"Certainly, I do."

What Poirot would have replied I do not know, but at that moment Lord Alloway reappeared, and informed us that the two ladies and Mr. Leonard Weardale were in the drawing-room.

The women were in becoming négligées. Mrs. Conrad was a beautiful woman of thirty-five with golden hair and a slight tendency to *embonpoint*. Lady Juliet Weardale must have been forty, tall and dark, very thin, still beautiful, with exquisite hands and feet, and a restless, haggard manner. Her son was rather an effeminate-looking young man, as great a contrast to his bluff, hearty father as could well be imagined.

Poirot gave forth the little rigmarole we had agreed upon, and then explained that he was anxious to know if anyone had heard or seen anything that night which might assist us.

Turning to Mrs. Conrad first, he asked her if she would be so kind as to inform him exactly what her movements had been.

"Let me see — I went upstairs. I rang for my maid. Then as she did not put in an appearance, I came out and called her. I could hear her talking on the stairs. After she had brushed my hair, I sent her away — she was in a very curious nervous state. I read a while and then went to bed.

"And you, lady Juliet?"

"I went straight upstairs into bed. I was very tired."

"What about your book, dear?" asked Mrs. Conrad, with a sweet smile.

"My book?" Lady Juliet flushed.

"Yes, you know — when I sent Léonie away, you were coming up the stairs. You had been down to the drawing-room for a book, you said."

"Oh, yes! I did go down — I — I forgot."

Lady Juliet clasped her hands nervously together.

"Did you hear Mrs. Conrad's maid scream, Milady?"

"No — no, I didn't."

"How curious — because you must have been in the drawing-room at the time."

"I heard nothing," said Lady Juliet in a firmer voice.

Poirot turned to young Leonard.

"Monsieur?"

"Nothing doing. I went straight upstairs and turned in."

Poirot stroked his chin.

"Alas! I fear that there is nothing to help me here. Mesdames and Monsieur, I regret — I regret infinitely to have deranged you from your slumbers for so little. Accept my apologies, I pray of you."

Gesticulating and apologizing, he marshalled them out. He returned with the French maid, a pretty, impudent-looking girl. Alloway and Weardale had gone out with the ladies.

"Now, Mademoiselle," said Poirot, in a brisk tone, "let us have the truth. Recount to me no histories. Why did you scream on the stairs?"

"Ah, Monsieur, I saw a tall figure — all in white —"

Poirot arrested her with an energetic shake of his forefinger.

"Did I not say, recount to me no histories? I will make a guess. He kissed you, did he not? Monsieur Leonard Weardale, I mean?"

"*Eh bien*, Monsieur, and after all? What is a kiss?"

"Under the circumstances, it is most natural," replied Poirot gallantly. "I myself — or Hastings here — but tell me just what occurred."

"He came up behind me, and caught me. I was startled and I screamed. If I had known I would not have screamed — but he came upon me like a cat. Then came *Monsieur le Secretaire.* Monsieur Leonard flew up the stairs, and what could I say? Especially to a *jeune homme comme ça — tellement comme il faut? Ma foi,* I invent a ghost."

"And all is explained," cried Poirot geniality. "You then mounted to the chamber of Madame your mistress. Which is her room, by the way?"

"It is at the end, Monsieur. That way."

"Directly over the study, then. *Bien*, Mademoiselle, I will detain you no longer. And, *la prochaine fois*, do not scream."

Handing her out, he came back to me with a smile.

"An interesting case, is it not,

Hastings? I begin to have a few little ideas. *Et vous*?"

"What was Leonard Weardale doing on the stairs? I don't like that young man, Poirot. He's a thorough young rake, I should say."

"I agree with you, *mon ami*."

"Fitzroy seems an honest fellow."

"Lord Alloway is certainly insistent on that point."

"And yet there is something in his manner —"

"That is almost too good to be true? I felt it myself. On the other hand, our friend Mrs. Conrad is certainly not good at all."

"And her room is over the study," I said musingly, and keeping a sharp eye on Poirot.

He shook his head with a slight smile.

"No, *mon ami*; I cannot bring myself seriously to believe that that immaculate lady swarmed down the chimney or let herself down from the balcony."

As he spoke the door opened, and, to my great surprise, lady Juliet Weardale flitted in.

"Monsieur Poirot," she said somewhat breathlessly, "can I speak to you alone?"

"Milady, Captain Hastings is as my other self. You can speak before him as though he were a thing of no account — not there at all. Be seated, I pray you."

She sat down, still keeping her eyes fixed on Poirot.

"What I have to say is — rather difficult. You are in charge of this case. If the — papers were to be returned, would that end the matter? I mean, could it be done without questions being asked?"

Poirot stared hard at her.

"Let me understand you, Madame. They are to be placed in my hands — is that right? And I am to return them to Lord Alloway on the condition that he asks no questions as to where I got them?"

She bowed her head. "That is what I mean. But I must be sure there will be no — publicity."

"I do not think Lord Alloway is particularly anxious for publicity," said Poirot grimly.

"You accept, then?" she cried eagerly.

"A little moment, Milady. It depends on how soon you can place those papers in my hands."

"Almost immediately."

Poirot glanced up at the clock.

"How soon exactly?"

"Say — ten minutes," she whispered.

"I accept, Milady."

She hurried from the room. I pursed my mouth up for a whistle.

"Can you sum up the situation for me, Hastings?"

"Bridge," I replied succinctly.

"Ah, you remember the careless words of Monsieur the Admiral. What a memory! I felicitate you, Hastings."

We said no more, for Lord Alloway came in and looked inquiringly at Poirot.

"Have you any further ideas,

Monsieur Poirot? I am afraid the answers to your questions have been rather disappointing."

"Not at all, Milor'. They have been quite sufficiently illuminating. It will be unnecessary for me to stay here any longer, so, with your permission, I will return at once to London."

Lord Alloway seemed dumbfounded.

"But — but what have you discovered? Do you know who took the plans?"

"Yes, Milor', I do. Tell me, in the case of the papers being returned to you anonymously, you would prosecute no further inquiry?"

Lord Alloway stared at him. "Do you mean on payment of a sum of money?"

"No, Milor'; returned unconditionally."

"Of course, the recovery of the plans is the great thing," said Lord Alloway slowly. He still looked puzzled and uncomprehending.

"Then I should seriously recommend you to adopt that course. Only you, the Admiral, and your secretary know of the loss. Only they need know of the restitution. And you may count on me to support you in every way — lay the mystery on my shoulders. You asked me to restore the papers — I have done so. You know no more."

He rose and held out his hand. "Milor', I am glad to have met you. I have faith in you — and your devotion to England. You will guide her destinies with a strong, sure hand."

"Monsieur Poirot, I swear to you that I will do my best. It may be a fault or it may be a virtue — but I believe in myself."

"So does every great man. Me, I am the same!" said Poirot grandiloquently.

The car came around to the door in a few minutes, and Lord Alloway bade us farewell on the steps with renewed cordiality.

"That is a great man, Hastings," said Poirot, as we drove off. "He has brains, resource, power. He is the strong man that England needs to guide her through these difficult days of reconstruction."

"I'm quite ready to agree with all you say, Poirot — but what about Lady Juliet? Is she to return the paper straight to Alloway? What will she think when she finds you have gone off without a word?"

"Hastings, I will ask you a little question. Why, when she was talking with me, did she not hand me the plans then and there?"

"She hadn't got them with her."

"Perfectly. How long would it take her to fetch them from her room? Or from any hiding place in the house? You need not answer. I will tell you. Probably about two minutes and a half. Yet she asks for ten minutes. Why? Clearly she has to obtain them from some other person, and to reason or argue with that person before they give them up. Now what person could that be? Not Mrs. Conrad clearly, but a member of her own family—her husband or son. Which is it likely to be? Leonard Weardale said he went straight to bed. We know that to be untrue. Supposing his mother went to his room and found it empty, supposing she came downstairs with a nameless dread— he is no beauty, that son of hers! She does not find him, but later she hears him deny that he ever left his room. She leaps to the conclusion that he is the thief. Hence her interview with me.

"But, *mon ami,* we know something that Lady Juliet does not. We know that her son could not have been in the study, because he was on the stairs, making love to the pretty French maid. Although she does not know it, Leonard Weardale has an alibi."

"Well then, who did steal the papers? We seem to have eliminated everybody—Lady Juliet, her son, Mrs. Conrad, the French maid —"

"Exactly. Use your little grey cells, my friend. The solution stares you in the face."

I shook my head blankly.

"But yes! If you would only persevere! See, then, Fitzroy goes out of the study; he leaves the papers on the desk. A few minutes later Lord Alloway enters the room, goes to the desk, and the papers are gone. Only two things are possible: either Fitzroy did *not* leave the papers on the desk, but put them in his pocket (and that is not reasonable, because, as Alloway pointed out, he could have taken a tracing at his own convenience any time), or else the papers were still on the desk when Lord Alloway went to it—in which case they went into *his* pocket...."

"Lord Alloway the thief!" I said, dumbfounded. "But why? Why?"

"Did you not tell me of some scandal in the past? He was exonerated, you said; but suppose, after all, it had been true? In English public life there must be no scandal. If this were raked up and proved against him now—good-bye to his political career. We will suppose that he was being blackmailed and the price asked was the submarine plans."

"But the man's a black traitor!" I cried.

"Oh, no, he is not. He is clever and resourceful. Supposing, my friend, that he copied those plans, making—for he is a clever engineer—a slight alteration in each part which will render them quite impracticable. He hands the fake plans to the enemy's agent—Mrs. Conrad, I fancy; but, in order that no suspicion of their genuineness may arise, the plans must seem to be stolen. He does his best to throw no suspicion on anyone in the house by pretending to see a man leaving the window—but there he ran up against the obstinacy of the Admiral. So his next anxiety is that no suspicion shall fall on Fitzroy."

"This is all guess-work on your part, Poirot," I objected.

"It is psychology, *mon ami.* A

man who had handed over the real plans would not be over-scrupulous as to who was likely to fall under suspicion. And why was he so anxious that no details of the robbery should be given to Mrs. Conrad? Because he had handed over the fake plans earlier in the evening, and did not want her to know that the theft could only have taken place later."

"I wonder if you are right," I said slowly.

"Of course I am right. I spoke to Alloway as one great man to another — and he understood perfectly. You will see."

One thing is quite certain. On the day when Lord Alloway became Prime Minister, a cheque and a signed photograph arrived. On the photograph were the words: "To my discreet friend, Hercule Poirot — from Alloway."

I believe that the "Z" type of submarine is causing great exultation in naval circles. They say it will revolutionize modern naval warfare. I have heard that a certain foreign power essayed to construct something of the same kind and the result was a dismal failure.

But I still consider that Poirot was guessing. He will do it once too often one of these days.

# THE ADVENTURE OF THE CLAPHAM COOK.

"The Adventure of the Clapham Cook" was first published in *The Sketch* on November 14, 1923.

"Absconding Bank Clerk," I read from the pages of the *Daily Newsmonger*, "Disappears with £15,000 Worth of Negotiable Securities"... "Husband Puts His Head in Gas-Oven. Unhappy Home Life" ... "Missing Typist. Pretty Girl of Twenty-One. Where Is Edna Field?"

"There you are, Poirot, plenty to choose from. An absconding bank clerk, a mysterious suicide, a missing typist—which will you have?"

"I am not greatly attracted to any of them, *mon ami*. To-day I feel inclined for the life of ease. It would have to be a very interesting problem to tempt me from my chair. See you, I have affairs of importance of my own to attend to."

"Such as?"

"My wardrobe, Hastings. If I mistake not, there is on my new grey suit the spot of grease—only the unique spot, but it is sufficient to trouble me. Then there is my winter overcoat—I must lay him aside in the powder of Keatings. And I think—yes, I think—the moment is ripe for the trimmings of my moustaches – and afterwards I must apply the pomade."

"Well," I said, strolling to the

window, "I doubt if you'll be able to carry out this delirious programme. That was a ring at the bell."

"Unless the affair is one of national importance, I touch it not," declared Poirot with dignity.

A moment later our privacy was invaded by a stout red-faced lady who panted audibly as a result of her rapid ascent of the stairs.

"You're Monsieur Poirot?" she demanded, as she sank into a chair.

"I am Hercule Poirot, yes, Madame."

"You're not a bit like what I thought you'd be," said the lady, eyeing him with some disfavour. "Did you pay for the bit in the paper saying what a clever detective you were, or did they put it in themselves?"

"Madame!" said Poirot, drawing himself up.

"I'm sorry, I'm sure, but you know what these papers are nowadays. You begin reading a nice article: 'What a bride said to her plain unmarried friend,' and it's all about a simple thing you buy at the chemist's and shampoo your hair with. Nothing but puff. But no offence taken, I hope? I'll tell you what I want you to do for me. I want you to find my cook."

Poirot stared at her; for once his ready tongue failed him. I turned aside to hide the broadening smile I could not control.

"It's all this wicked dole," continued the lady. "Putting ideas into servants' heads, wanting to be typists and what-nots. Stop the dole, that's what I say. I'd like to know what my servants have to complain of — afternoon and evening off a week, alternate Sundays, washing put out, same food as we have — and never a bit of margarine in the house, nothing but the very best butter."

"I fear you are making a mistake, Madame. I am not holding an inquiry into the conditions of domestic service. I am a private detective."

"I know that. Didn't I tell you I wanted you to find my cook for me? Walked out of the house on Wednesday, without so much as a word to me, and never came back."

"I am sorry, Madame, but I do not touch this particular kind of business. I wish you good morning."

Our visitor snorted with indignation.

"That's it, is it, my fine fellow? Too proud, eh? Only deal with Government secrets and countesses' jewels? Let me tell you a servant's every bit as important as a tiara to a woman in my position. We can't all be fine ladies going out in our motors with our diamonds and our pearls. A good cook's a good cook — and when you lose her, it's as much to you as her pearls are to some fine lady."

For a moment or two it appeared to be a toss up between Poirot's dignity and his sense of humour. Finally he laughed and sat down again.

"Madame, you are in the right,

and I am in the wrong. Your remarks are just and intelligent. This case will be a novelty. Never yet have I hunted a missing domestic. Truly here is the problem of national importance that I was demanding of fate just before your arrival. *En avant!* You say this jewel of a cook went out on Wednesday and did not return. That is the day before yesterday."

"Yes, it was her day out."

"But probably, Madame, she has met with some accident. Have you inquired at any of the hospitals? "

"That's exactly what I thought yesterday, but this morning, if you please, she sent for her box. And not so much as a line to me! If I'd been at home, I'd not have let it go — treating me like that! But I'd just stepped out to the butcher."

"What kind of a woman was she?"

"She was middle-aged, stout, black hair turning grey — most respectable. She'd been ten years in her last place. Eliza Dunn, her name was."

"And you had had — no disagreement with her on the Wednesday?"

"None whatsoever. That's what makes it all so queer."

"How many servants do you keep, Madame?"

"Two. The house-parlourmaid, Bessie, is a very nice girl. A bit forgetful and her head full of young men, but a good servant if you keep her up to her work."

"Did she and the cook get on well together?"

"They had their ups and downs, of course — but on the whole, very well."

"And the girl can throw no light on the mystery?"

"She says not — but you know what servants are: they all hang together."

"Well, well, we must look into this. Where did you say you resided, Madame?"

"At Clapham; 88 Prince Albert Road."

"*Bien*, Madame, I will wish you good morning, and you may count upon seeing me at your residence during the course of the day."

Mrs. Todd, for such was our new friend's name, then took her departure. Poirot looked at me somewhat ruefully.

"Well, well, Hastings, this is a novel affair that we have here. The Disappearance of the Clapham Cook! Never, never, must our friend Inspector Japp get to hear of this!"

He then proceeded to heat an iron and carefully removed the grease-spot from his grey suit by means of a piece of blotting paper. His moustaches he regretfully postponed to another day, and we set out for Clapham.

Prince Albert Road proved to be a street of small prim houses, all exactly alike, with neat lace curtains veiling the windows, and well-polished brass knockers on the doors. We rang the bell at No. 88, and the door was opened by a neat maid with a pretty face. Mrs. Todd came out in the hall to greet us.

"Don't go, Bessie," she cried. "This gentleman's a detective and he'll want to ask you some questions."

Bessie's face displayed a struggle between alarm and a pleasurable excitement.

"I thank you, Madame," said Poirot bowing. "I would like to question your maid now — and to see her alone, if I may."

We were shown into a small drawing room, and when Mrs. Todd, with obvious reluctance, had left the room, Poirot commenced his cross-examination.

"*Voyons*, Mademoiselle Bessie, all that you shall tell us will be of the greatest importance. You alone can shed any light on the case. Without your assistance I can do nothing."

The alarm vanished from the girl's face and the pleasurable excitement became more strongly marked. "I'm sure, Sir, I'll tell you anything I can."

"Well, Bessie, what is your own idea? You are a girl of remarkable intelligence; what is your own explanation of Eliza's disappearance?"

"White slavers, Sir, I've said so all along! Cook was always warning *me* against them. 'Don't you sniff no scent, or eat any sweets — no matter how gentlemanly the fellow,' those were her words to me. And now they've got her! I'm sure of it. As likely as not, she's been shipped to Turkey or one of them Eastern places where I've heard they like them fat!"

Poirot preserved an admirable gravity. "But in that case — and it is indeed an idea! — would she have sent for her trunk?"

"Well, I don't know, Sir. She'd want her things — even in those foreign places."

"Who came for the trunk — a man?"

"It was Carter Paterson, Sir."

"Did you pack it?"

"No, Sir, it was already packed and corded."

"That's interesting. That shows that when she left the house on Wednesday, she had already determined not to return. You see that, do you not?"

"Yes, Sir; I hadn't thought of that. But it might still have been white slavers, mightn't it, Sir?" she added wistfully.

"Undoubtedly," said Poirot gravely. "Did you both occupy the same bed-room?"

"No, Sir, we had separate rooms."

"And had Eliza expressed any dissatisfaction with her present post to you at all? Were you both happy here?"

"She'd never mentioned leaving. The place is all right —" The girl hesitated.

"Speak freely," said Poirot kindly. "I shall not tell your mistress."

"Well, of course, Sir, she's a caution, Missus is. But the food's good. Plenty of it, and no stinting. Something hot for supper, good outings, and as much frying-fat as you like. And anyway, if Eliza did want to make a change, she'd never have gone off this way, I'm sure. She'd have stayed her month. Why, Missus could have a month's wages out of her for doing this!"

"And the work, it is not too hard?"

"Well, she's particular — always poking round in corners and looking for dust. And then there's the lodger, or paying guest as he's always called. But that's only breakfast and dinner, same as Master. They're out all day in the City."

"You like your master?"

"He's all right — very quiet and a bit on the stingy side."

"You can't remember, I suppose, the last thing Eliza said before she went out?"

"Yes, I can. 'If there's any stewed peaches over from the dining room,' she says, 'we'll have them for supper, and a bit of bacon and some fried potatoes.' Mad over stewed peaches, she was. I shouldn't wonder if they didn't get her that way."

"Was Wednesday her regular day out?"

"Yes, she had Wednesdays and I had Thursdays."

Poirot asked a few more questions, then declared himself satisfied. Annie departed, and Mrs. Todd hurried in, her face alight with curiosity. Poirot brought the conversation round to her husband and elicited the information that he worked with a firm in the City and would not be home until after six.

"Doubtless he is very disturbed and worried by this unaccountable business, eh? It is not so?"

"He's never worried," declared Mrs. Todd. "'Well, well, get another, my dear.' That's all he said! He's so calm that it drives me to distraction sometimes. 'An ungrateful woman,' he said. 'We are well rid of her.'"

"What about the other inmates of the house, Madame?"

"You mean Mr. Simpson, our paying guest? Well, as long as he gets his breakfast and his evening meal all right, he doesn't worry."

"What is his profession, Madame?"

"He works in a bank." She mentioned its name, and I started slightly, remembering my perusal of the *Daily Newsmonger*.

"A young man?"

"Twenty-eight, I believe. Nice quiet young fellow."

"I should like to have a few words with him, and also with your husband, if I may. I will return for that purpose this evening. I venture to suggest that you should repose yourself a little, Madame; you look fatigued."

"I should just think I am! First the worry about Eliza, and then I was at the sales practically all yesterday, and you know what *that* is, Monsieur Poirot, and what with one thing and another and a lot to do in the house — because, of course, Annie can't do it all; and very likely she'll give notice anyway, being unsettled in this way — well, what with it all, I'm tired out!"

Poirot murmured sympathetically, and we took our leave.

"It's a curious coincidence," I said, "but that absconding clerk, Davis, was from the same bank as Simpson. Can there be any connection, do you think?"

Poirot smiled.

"At the one end, a defaulting clerk, at the other a vanishing cook. It is hard to see any relation between the two, unless possibly Davis visited Simpson, fell in love with the cook, and persuaded her to accompany him on his flight!"

I laughed.

"He might have done worse," said Poirot. "If you are going into exile, a good cook may be of more comfort than a pretty face. It is a curious case, Hastings, full of contradictory features. I am interested — yes, I am distinctly interested."

That evening we returned to 88 Prince Albert Road and interviewed both Todd and Simpson. The former was a melancholy lantern-jawed man of forty-odd; the latter a quiet, inconspicuous young man who displayed little interest in the problem. Neither of them added at all to our sum of knowledge.

On the following morning Poirot received a letter. On reading it he turned purple with indignation, and handed it to me to read.

"Mrs. Todd regrets that after all she will not avail herself of Mr. Poirot's services. After talking the matter over with her husband she sees that it is foolish to call in a detective about a purely domestic affair. Mrs. Todd encloses a guinea for consultation fee."

"Aha!" cried Poirot angrily. "And they think to get rid of Hercule Poirot like that! As a favour — a great favour — I consent to investigate their miserable little twopenny-halfpenny affair — and they dismiss me *comme ça!* That is the hand of Mr. Todd. But I say — No! Thirty-six times no! I will spend my own guineas, thirty-six hundred of them if need be, but I will get to the bottom of this matter. First, we will advertise in the papers: 'If Eliza Dunn will communicate with this address, she will hear of something to her advantage.' Put it in all the papers you can think of, Hastings. Then I will make some little inquiries of my own. Go, go — all must be done as quickly as possible!"

I did not see him again until the evening, when he condescended to tell me what he had been doing.

"I have made inquiries at the firm of Mr. Todd. He was not absent on Wednesday, and he bears a good character — so much for him. Then Simpson, he was not absent on Wednesday either, but on Thursday he was ill and did not come to the bank. He was moderately friendly with Davis. Does that lead us anywhere? It does not. We must place our reliance on the advertisements."

The advertisement duly appeared in all the principal daily papers. By Poirot's orders it was to be continued every day for a week. His eagerness over this uninteresting matter of a defaulting cook was extraordinary, but I realized that he considered it a point of honour to persevere until he finally succeeded. Several extremely interesting cases were brought to him about this time, but he declined them all. Every morning he would rush at his letters, scrutinize them earnestly and then lay them down with a sigh.

But our patience was rewarded at last. On the Wednesday following Mrs. Todd's visit, our landlady informed us that a person of the name of Eliza Dunn had called.

"*Enfin!*" cried Poirot. "But make her mount then! At once! Immediately!"

Thus admonished, our landlady hurried out and returned a moment or two later, ushering in Miss Dunn. Our quarry was much as described — tall, stout, and eminently respectable.

"I came in answer to the advertisement," she explained. "I thought there must be some muddle or other, and that perhaps you didn't know I'd already got my legacy."

Poirot was studying her attentively. He drew forward a chair with a flourish. "The truth of the matter is," he explained, "that your late mistress, Mrs. Todd, was much concerned about you. She feared some accident might have befallen you."

Eliza Dunn seemed very much surprised. "Didn't she get my letter then?"

"She got no word of any kind." He paused, and then said persuasively: "Recount to me the whole story, will you not?"

Eliza Dunn needed no encouragement. She plunged at once into a lengthy narrative.

"I was just coming home on Wednesday night and had nearly got to the house, when a gentleman stopped me. A tall gentleman he was, with a beard and a big hat.

"'Miss Eliza Dunn?' he said.

"'Yes,' I said.

"'I've been inquiring for you at No. 88,' he said. 'They told me I might meet you coming along here. Miss Dunn, I have come from Australia specially to find you. Do you happen to know the maiden name of your maternal grandmother?'

"'Jane Emmott,' I said.

"'Exactly,' he said. 'Now, Miss Dunn, although you may never have heard of the fact, your grandmother had a great friend, Eliza Leech. This friend went to Australia where she married a very wealthy settler. Her two children died in infancy, and she inherited all her husband's property.

She died a few months ago, and by her will you inherit a house in this country and a considerable sum of money.'

"You could have knocked me down with a feather," continued Miss Dunn. "For a minute, I was suspicious, and he must have seen it, for he smiled. 'Quite right to be on your guard, Miss Dunn,' he said. 'Here are my credentials.' He handed me a letter from some lawyers in Melbourne, Hurst and Crotchet, and a card. He was Mr. Crotchet. 'There are one or two conditions,' he said. 'Our client was a little eccentric, you know. The bequest is conditional on your taking possession of the house (it is in Cumberland) before twelve o'clock to-morrow. The other condition is of no importance — it is merely a stipulation that you should not be in domestic service.'

"My face fell. 'Oh, Mr. Crotchet,' I said. 'I'm a cook. Didn't they tell you at the house?'

" 'Dear, dear,' he said. 'I had no idea of such a thing. I thought you might possibly be a companion or governess there. This is very unfortunate — very unfortunate indeed.'

" 'Shall I have to lose all the money?' I said, anxious like.

He thought for a minute or two. 'There are always ways of getting round the law, Miss Dunn,' he said at last. 'We as lawyers know that. The way out here is for you to have left your employment this afternoon.'

" 'But — my month ?' I said.

" 'My dear Miss Dunn,' he said with a smile. 'You can leave an employer any minute by forfeiting a month's wages. Your mistress will understand in view of the circumstances. The difficulty is time! It is imperative that you should catch the 11:05 from King's Cross to the north. I can advance you ten pounds or so for the fare, and you can write a note at the station to your employer. I will take it to her myself and explain the whole circumstances.'

"I agreed, of course, and an hour later I was in the train, so flustered that I didn't know whether I was on my head or heels. Indeed by the time I got to Carlisle, I was half inclined to think the whole thing was one of those confidence tricks you read about. But I went to the address he had given me — solicitors they were, and it was all right. A nice little house, and an income of three hundred a year. These lawyers knew very little, they'd just got a letter from a gentleman in London instructing them to hand over the house to me and £150 for the first six months. Mr. Crotchet sent up my things to me, but there was no word from Missus. I supposed she was angry and grudged me my bit of luck. She kept back my box too, and sent my clothes in paper parcels. But there, of course if she never had my letter, she might think it a bit cool of me."

Poirot had listened attentively to this long history. Now he nodded his head as though completely satisfied.

"Thank you, Mademoiselle. There had been, as you say, a little muddle. Permit me to recompense you for your trouble." He handed her an envelope. "You return to Cumberland immediately? A little word in your ear. Do not forget how to cook. It is always useful to have something to fall back upon in case things go wrong."

"Credulous," he murmured, as our visitor departed, "but perhaps not more than most of her class. Come, Hastings, there is no time to be lost. Get a taxi while I write a note to Japp."

Poirot was waiting on the doorstep when I returned with the taxi. The note was despatched by special messenger, and we sped on to Clapham.

"Though frankly, Hastings, I expect our bird will have flown."

"Who is our bird?"

"The inconspicuous Mr. Simpson, of course. Do not tell me that all is not clear to you now!"

"The cook was got out of the way, I realize that. But why? Why should Simpson wish to get her out of the house? Did she know something about him?"

"Nothing whatever."

"Well, then —"

"But he wanted something that she had."

"Money? The Australian legacy?"

"No, my friend — something quite different. A battered tin trunk."

I looked sideways at him. His statement seemed so fantastic that I suspected him of pulling my leg, but he was perfectly grave and serious.

"Surely he could buy a trunk if he wanted one," I cried.

"He did not want a new trunk. He wanted a trunk of pedigree. A trunk of assured respectability."

"Look here, Poirot," I cried, "this really is a bit thick. You're pulling my leg."

"You lack the brains and the imagination of Mr. Simpson, Hastings. See here: On Wednesday evening, Simpson decoys away the cook. A printed card and a printed sheet of notepaper are simple matters to obtain, and he is willing to pay £150 and a year's house rent to assure the success of his plan. Miss Dunn does not recognize him; the beard and the hat and the slight colonial accent completely deceive her. That is the end of Wednesday — except for the trifling fact that Simpson has helped himself to £15,000 worth of negotiable securities."

"Simpson — but it was Davis —"

"If you will kindly permit me to continue, Hastings! He knows that the theft will be discovered on Thursday afternoon. He does not go to the bank on Thursday, but he lies in wait for Davis when he comes out to lunch. Perhaps he admits the theft and tells Davis he will return the securities to him — anyhow he succeeds in getting Davis to come to Clapham with him. It is the maid's day out, and Mrs. Todd was at the sales, so there is no one in the house.

When the theft is discovered and Davis is missing, the implication will be overwhelming. Davis is the thief! Mr. Simpson will be perfectly safe, and can return to work on the morrow like the honest clerk they think him."

"And Davis?"

Poirot made an expressive gesture, and slowly shook his head.

"It seems too cold-blooded to be believed, and yet what other explanation can there be, *mon ami*? The one difficulty for a murderer is the disposal of the body—and Simpson had planned that out beforehand. I was struck at once by the fact that although Eliza Dunn obviously meant to return that night when she went out (witness her remark about the stewed peaches), yet her trunk was all ready packed when they came for it. It was Simpson who sent word to Carter Paterson to call on Friday, and it was Simpson who corded up the box on Thursday afternoon. What suspicion could possibly arise? A maid leaves and sends for her box, it is labelled and addressed ready in her name, probably to a railway station within easy reach of London. On Saturday afternoon, Simpson, in his Australian disguise, claims it, he affixes a new label and address and redespatches it somewhere else, again 'to be left till called for.' When the authorities get suspicious, for excellent reasons, and open it, all that can be elicited will be that a bearded colonial despatched it from some junction near London. There will be nothing to connect it with 88 Prince Albert Road. Ah! Here we are."

Poirot's prognostications had been correct. Simpson had left days previously. But he was not to escape the consequences of his crime. By the aid of wireless, he was discovered on the *Olympia*, en route to America.

A tin trunk, addressed to Mr. Henry Wintergreen, attracted the attention of railway officials at Glasgow. It was opened and found to contain the body of the unfortunate Davis.

But for Poirot and his amazing powers of reasoning, a particularly cold-blooded murderer would have escaped scot-free.

# THE LOST MINE.

"The Lost Mine" was first published in *The Sketch* on November 21, 1923.

I laid down my bank-book with a sigh.

"It is a curious thing," I observed, "but my overdraft never seems to grow any less."

"And it perturbs you not? Me, if I had an overdraft, never should I close an eye all night," declared Poirot.

"You deal in comfortable balances, I suppose," I retorted.

"Four hundred and forty-four pounds, four and fourpence," said Poirot with some complacency. "A neat figure, is it not?"

"It must be tact on the part of your bank manager. He is evidently acquainted with your passion for symmetrical details. What about investing, say, three hundred of it in the Porcupine Oilfields? Their prospectus, which is advertised in the papers to-day, says that they will pay one hundred per cent. in dividends next year."

"Not for me," said Poirot, shaking his head. "I like not the sensational. For me the safe, the prudent investment — *les Rentes*, the Consols, the — how do you call it? — the Conversion."

"Have you never made a speculative investment?"

"No, *mon ami*," replied Poirot

severely, "I have not. And the only shares I own which have not what you call the gilded edge are fourteen thousand shares in the Burma Mines Ltd."

Poirot paused with an air of waiting to be encouraged to go on.

"Yes?" I prompted.

"And for them I paid no cash — no; they were the reward of the exercise of my little grey cells. You would like to hear the story? Yes?"

"Of course I would."

"These mines are situated in the interior of Burma, about two hundred miles inland from Rangoon. They were discovered by the Chinese in the fifteenth century, and worked down to the time of the Mohammedan Rebellion, being finally abandoned in the year 1868. The Chinese extracted the rich lead-silver ore from the upper part of the ore body, smelting it for the silver alone, and leaving large quantities of rich lead-bearing slag. This, of course, was soon discovered when prospecting work was carried out in Burma, but owing to the fact that the old workings had become full of loose filling and water, all attempts to find the source of the ore proved fruitless. Many parties were sent out by syndicates, and they dug over a large area, but this rich prize still eluded them. A representative of one of the syndicates, however, got on the track of a Chinese family, who were supposed to have still kept a record of the situation of the mine. The present head of the family was one Wu Ling."

"What a fascinating page of commercial romance!" I exclaimed.

"Is it not? Ah, *mon ami*, one can have romance without golden-haired girls of matchless beauty — no, I am wrong; it is auburn hair that so excites you always. You remember —"

"Go on with the story," I said hastily.

"*Eh bien*, my friend, this Wu Ling was approached. He was an estimable merchant, much respected in the province where he lived. He admitted at once that he owned the documents in question, and was perfectly prepared to negotiate for this sale, but he objected to dealing with anyone other than principals. Finally it was arranged that he should journey to England and meet the directors of an important company.

"Wu Ling made the journey to England in the *S.S. Assunta*, and the *Assunta* docked at Southampton on a cold, foggy morning in November. One of the directors, Mr. Pearson, went down to Southampton to meet the boat, but owing to the fog, the train down was very much delayed, and by the time he arrived, Wu Ling had disembarked and left by special train for London. Mr. Pearson returned to town somewhat annoyed, as he had no idea where the Chinaman proposed to stay. Later in the day, however, the offices of the company were rung up on the telephone. Wu Ling was staying at the

Russell Square Hotel. He was feeling somewhat unwell after the voyage, but declared himself perfectly able to attend the board meeting on the following day.

"The meeting of the board took place at eleven o'clock. When half past eleven came, and Wu Ling had not put in an appearance, the secretary rang up the Russell Square Hotel. In answer to his inquiries, he was told that the Chinaman had gone out with a friend about half past ten. It seemed clear that he had started out with the intention of coming to the meeting, but the morning wore away, and he did not appear. It was, of course, possible that he had lost his way, being unacquainted with London, but at a late hour that night he had not returned to the hotel. Thoroughly alarmed now, Mr. Pearson put matters in the hands of the police. On the following day, there was still no trace of the missing man, but towards evening of the day after that again, a body was found in the Thames which proved to be that of the ill-fated Chinaman. Neither on the body, nor in the luggage at the hotel, was there any trace of the papers relating to the mine.

"At this juncture, *mon ami*, I was brought into the affair. Mr. Pearson called upon me. Whilst profoundly shocked by the death of Wu Ling, his chief anxiety was to recover the papers which were the object of the Chinaman's visit to England. The main anxiety of the police, of course, would be to track down the murderer — the recovery of the papers would be a secondary consideration. What he wanted me to do was to cooperate with the police whilst acting in the interests of the company.

"I consented readily enough. It was clear that there were two fields of search open to me. I might look amongst the employees of the company who knew of the Chinaman's coming, on the one hand; and amongst the passengers on the boat who might have been acquainted with his mission on the other. I started with the second, as being a narrower field of search. In this I coincided with Inspector Miller, who was in charge of the case; a man altogether different from our friend Japp — conceited, ill-mannered and altogether insufferable. Together we interviewed the officers of the ship. They had little to tell us. Wu Ling had kept much to himself on the voyage. He had been intimate with but two of the other passengers — one a broken-down European named Dyer, who appeared to bear a somewhat unsavoury reputation; the other a young bank clerk named Charles Lester, who was returning from Hong Kong. We were lucky enough to obtain snapshots of both these men. At the moment there seemed little doubt that if either of the two was implicated, Dyer was the man. He was known to be mixed up with a gang of Chinese crooks, and was altogether a most likely suspect.

"Our next step was to visit the Russell Square Hotel. Shown a snapshot of Wu Ling, they recognized him at once. We then showed them the snapshot of Dyer, but to our disappointment, the hall porter declared positively that that was not the man who had come to the hotel on the fatal morning. Almost as an afterthought, I produced the photograph of Lester, and, to my surprise, the man at once recognized it.

" 'Yes, Sir,' he asserted, 'that's the gentleman who came in at half past ten and asked for Mr. Wu Ling, and afterwards went out with him.'

"The affair was progressing. Our next move was to interview Mr. Charles Lester. He met us with the utmost frankness, was desolated to hear of the Chinaman's untimely death, and put himself at our disposal in every way. His story was as follows: By arrangement with Wu Ling, he called for him at the hotel at 10:30. Wu Ling, however, did not appear. Instead, his servant came, explained that his master had had to go out, and offered to conduct the young man to where his master now was. Suspecting nothing, Lester agreed, and the Chinaman procured a taxi. They drove for some time in the direction of the docks. Suddenly becoming mistrustful, Lester stopped the taxi and got out, disregarding the servant's protests. That, he assured us, was all he knew.

"Apparently satisfied, we thanked him and took our leave. His story was soon proved to be a somewhat inaccurate one. To begin with, Wu Ling had had no servant with him, either on the boat or at the hotel. In the second place, the taxi driver who had driven the two men on that morning came forward. Far from Lester's having left the taxi *en route*, he and the Chinese gentleman had driven to a certain unsavoury dwelling-place in Limehouse, right in the heart of Chinatown. The place in question was more or less well known as an opium-den of the lowest description. The two gentlemen had gone in — about an hour later the English gentleman, whom he identified from the photograph, came out alone. He looked very pale and ill, and directed the taxi man to take him to the nearest underground station.

"Inquiries were made about Charles Lester's standing, and it was found that, though bearing an excellent character, he was heavily in debt, and had a secret passion for gambling. Dyer, of course, was not lost sight of. It seemed just faintly possible that he might have impersonated the other man; but that idea was proved utterly groundless. His alibi for the whole of the day in question was absolutely unimpeachable. Of course, the proprietor of the opium-den denied everything with Oriental stolidity. He had never seen Wu Ling; he had never seen Charles Lester. No two gentlemen had been to the place that morning. In any case, the police were wrong: no opium was ever smoked there.

"His denials, however well meant, did little to help Charles Lester. He was arrested for the murder of Wu Ling. A search of his effects was made, but no papers relating to the mine were discovered. The proprietor of the opium-den was also taken into custody, but a cursory raid of his premises yielded nothing. Not even a stick of opium rewarded the zeal of the police.

"In the meantime, my friend Mr. Pearson was in a great state of agitation. He strode up and down my room, uttering great lamentations.

" 'But you must have some ideas, Monsieur Poirot!' he kept urging. 'Surely you must have some ideas!'

" 'Certainly I have ideas,' I replied cautiously. 'That is the trouble; one has too many — therefore they all lead in different directions.'

" 'For instance?' he suggested.

" 'For instance, the taxi-driver. We have only his word for it that he drove the two men to that house. That is one idea. Then, was it really that house they went to? Supposing that they left the taxi there, passed through the house and out by another entrance and went elsewhere?'

"Mr. Pearson seemed struck by that.

" 'But you do nothing but sit and think? Can't we *do* something?'

"He was of an impatient temperament, you comprehend.

" 'Monsieur,' I said with dignity, 'It is not for Hercule Poirot to run up and down the evil-smelling streets of Limehouse like a little dog of no breeding. Be calm. My agents are at work.'

"On the following day I had news for him. The two men had indeed passed through the house in question, but their real objective was a small eating-house close to the river. They were seen to pass in there, and Lester came out alone.

"And then, figure to yourself, Hastings, an idea of the most unreasonable seized this Mr. Pearson. Nothing would suit him but that we should go ourselves to this eating-house and make investigations. I argued and prayed, but he would not listen. He talked of disguising himself — he even suggested that I — *I* should — I hesitate to say it — should shave off my moustache! Yes, *rien que ça*! I pointed out to him that that was an idea ridiculous and absurd. One destroys not a thing of beauty wantonly. Besides, shall not a Belgian gentleman with a moustache desire to see life and smoke opium just as readily as one without a moustache?

"*Eh bien*, he gave in on that, but he still insisted on his project. He turned up that evening — *Mon dieu*, what a figure! He wore what he called the 'pea jacket'; his chin was dirty and unshaved; he had a scarf of the vilest that offended the nose. And figure to yourself, he was enjoying himself! Truly, the English are mad! He made some changes in my own appearance. I permitted it.

Can one argue with a maniac? We started out — after all, could I let him go alone, a child dressed up to the charades?"

"Of course you couldn't," I replied, stifling a wild desire to laugh long and loudly. The idea of the fastidious Poirot starting out on such a quest was deliciously ludicrous.

"To continue, we arrived. Mr. Pearson talked English of the strangest. He represented himself to be a man of the sea. He talked of 'lubbers' and 'fo'c'sles' and I know not what. It was a low little room with many Chinese in it. We ate of peculiar dishes. Ah, *Dieu, mon estomac*!" Poirot clasped that portion of his anatomy tenderly before continuing. "Then there came to us the proprietor, a Chinaman with a face of evil smiles.

"'You gentlemen no likee food here,' he said. 'You come for what you likee better. Piecee pipe, eh?'

"Mr. Pearson, he gave me the great kick under the table — he had on the boots of the sea too — and he said: 'I don't mind if I do, John. Lead ahead.'

"The Chinaman smiled, and he took us through a door and to a cellar and through a trap-door, and down some steps and up again into a room all full of divans and cushions of the most comfortable. We lay down and a Chinese boy took off our boots. It was the best moment of the evening. Then they brought us the opium pipes and cooked the opium pills, and we pretended to smoke and then to sleep and dream. But when we were alone, Mr. Pearson called softly to me, and immediately he began crawling along the floor. We went into another room where other people were asleep, and so on, until we heard two men talking. We stayed behind a curtain and listened. They were speaking of Wu Ling.

"'What about the papers?' said one.

"'Mr. Lester, he takee those,' answered the other, who was a Chinaman. 'He say, puttee them allee in safee place — where pleeceman no lookee.'

"'Ah, but he's nabbed,' said the first one.

"'He gettee free. Pleeceman not sure he done it.'

"There was more of the same kind of thing, then apparently the two men were coming our way, and we scuttled back to our beds.

"'We'd better get out of here,' said Pearson, after a few minutes had elapsed. 'This place isn't healthy.'

"'You are right, Monsieur,' I agreed. 'We have played the farce long enough.'

"We succeeded in getting away, all right, paying handsomely for our smoke.

"Once clear of Limehouse, Pearson drew a long breath.

"'I'm glad to get out of that,' he said. 'But it's something to be sure.'

"'It is indeed,' I agreed. 'And I fancy that we shall not have much difficulty in finding what we want — after this evening's masquerade.'

"And there was no difficulty whatsoever," finished Poirot suddenly.

This abrupt ending seemed so extraordinary that I stared at him. "But — but where were they?" I asked.

"In his pocket — *tout simplement.*"

"But in whose pocket?"

"Mr. Pearson's, *parbleu!*" Then, observing my look of bewilderment, he continued gently: "You do not yet see it? Mr. Pearson, like Charles Lester, was in debt. Mr. Pearson, like Charles Lester, was fond of gambling. And he conceived the idea of stealing the papers from the Chinaman. He met him all right at Southampton, came up to London with him, and took him straight to Limehouse. It was foggy that day; the Chinaman would not notice where he was going. I fancy Mr. Pearson smoked the opium fairly often down there and had some peculiar friends in consequence. I do not think he meant murder. His idea was that one of the Chinamen should impersonate Wu Ling and receive the money for the sale of the document. So far, so good. But, to the Oriental mind, it was infinitely simpler to kill Wu Ling and throw his body into the river, and Pearson's Chinese accomplices followed their own methods without consulting him. Imagine, then, what you would call the *'funk bleu'* of Monsieur Pearson! Someone may have seen him in the train with Wu Ling — murder is a very different thing from simple abduction.

"His salvation lies with the Chinaman who is personating Wu Ling at the Russell Square Hotel. If only the body is not discovered too soon! Probably Wu Ling had told him of the arrangement between him and Charles Lester whereby the latter was to call for him at the hotel. Pearson sees there an excellent way of diverting suspicion from himself. Charles Lester shall be the last person to be seen in company with Wu Ling. The impersonator has orders to represent himself to Lester as the servant of Wu Ling, and to bring him as speedily as possible to Limehouse. There, very likely, he was offered a drink. The drink would be suitably drugged, and when Lester emerged an hour later he would have a very hazy impression of what had happened. So much was this the case, that as soon as Lester learned of Wu Ling's death, he loses his nerve and denies that he ever reached Limehouse.

"By that, of course, he plays right into Pearson's hands. But is Pearson content? No — my manner disquiets him, and he determines to complete the case against Lester. So he arranges an elaborate masquerade. Me, I am to be gulled completely. Did I not say just now that he was as a child acting the charades? *Eh bien*, I play my part. He goes home rejoicing. But in the morning, Inspector Miller arrives on his doorstep. The papers are found on him. The game is up. Bitterly he regrets permitting himself to play the farce with Hercule Poirot! There was only one real difficulty in the affair."

"What was that?" I demanded curiously.

"Convincing Inspector Miller! What an animal, that! Both obstinate and imbecile. And in the end he took all the credit!"

"Too bad," I cried.

"Ah, well, I had my compensations. The other directors of the Burma Mines, Ltd., awarded me fourteen thousand shares as a small recompense for my services. Not so bad, eh? But when investing money, keep, I beg of you, Hastings, strictly to the conservative. The things you read in the paper, they may not be true. The directors of the Porcupine — they may be so many Mr. Pearsons!"

# THE CORNISH MYSTERY.

"The Cornish Mystery" was first published in *The Sketch* on November 28, 1923.

"Mrs. Pengelley," announced our landlady, and withdrew discreetly.

Many unlikely people came to consult Poirot, but to my mind, the woman who stood nervously just inside the door, fingering her feather boa, was the most unlikely of all. She was so extraordinarily commonplace—a thin, faded woman of about fifty, dressed in a braided coat and skirt, some gold jewellery at her neck, and with her grey hair surmounted by a singularly unbecoming hat. In a country town, you pass a hundred Mrs. Pengelleys in the street every day.

Poirot came forward and greeted her pleasantly, perceiving her obvious embarrassment.

"Madame! Take a chair, I beg of you. My colleague, Captain Hastings."

The lady sat down, murmuring uncertainly, "You are Monsieur Poirot, the detective?"

"At your service, Madame."

But our guest was still tongue-tied. She sighed, twisted her fingers, and grew steadily redder and redder.

"There is something I can do for you, eh, Madame?"

"Well, I thought — that is — you see —"

"Proceed, Madame, I beg of you — proceed."

Mrs. Pengelley, thus encouraged, took a grip on herself.

"It's this way, Mr. Poirot — I don't want to have anything to do with the police. No; I wouldn't go to the police for anything! But all the same, I'm sorely troubled about something. And yet I don't know if I ought —"

She stopped abruptly.

"Me, I have nothing to do with the police. My investigations are strictly private."

Mrs. Pengelley caught at the word.

"Private — that's what I want. I don't want any talk or fuss, or things in the papers. Wicked it is, the way they write things, until the family could never hold up their heads again. And it isn't as though I was even sure — it's just a dreadful idea that's come to me, and put it out of my head I can't." She paused for breath. "And all the time I may be wickedly wronging poor Edward. It's a terrible thought for any wife to have. But you do read of such dreadful things nowadays."

"Permit me — it is of your husband you speak?"

"Yes."

"And you suspect him of — what?"

"I don't like even to say it, Mr. Poirot. But you *do* read of such things happening — and the poor souls suspecting nothing."

I was beginning to despair of the lady's ever coming to the point, but Poirot's patience was equal to the demand made upon it.

"Speak without fear, Madame. Think what joy will be yours if we are able to prove your suspicions unfounded."

"That's true — anything's better than this wearing uncertainty. Oh, Mr. Poirot, I'm dreadfully afraid I'm being *poisoned*."

"What makes you think so?"

Mrs. Pengelley, her reticence leaving her, plunged into a full recital more suited to the ears of her medical attendant.

"Pain and sickness after food, eh?" said Poirot thoughtfully. "You have a doctor attending you, Madame? What does he say?"

"He says it's acute gastritis, Mr. Poirot. But I can see that he's puzzled and uneasy, and he's always altering the medicine, but nothing does any good."

"You have spoken of your — fears, to him?"

"No, indeed, Mr. Poirot. It might get about in the town. And perhaps it is gastritis. All the same, it's very odd that whenever Edward is away for the week-end, I'm quite all right again. Even Freda notices that — my niece, Mr. Poirot. And then there's that bottle of weed killer, never used, the gardener says, and yet it's half-empty."

She looked appealingly at Poirot. He smiled reassuringly at her, and reached for a pencil and notebook.

"Let us be businesslike, Madame. Now, then, you and your husband reside — where?"

"Polgarwith, a small market town in Cornwall."

"You have lived there long?"

"Fourteen years."

"And your household consists of you and your husband. Any children?"

"No."

"But a niece, I think you said?"

"Yes, Freda Stanton, the child of my husband's only sister. She has lived with us for the last eight years — that is, until a week ago."

"Oho, and what happened a week ago?"

"Things hadn't been very pleasant for some time — I don't know what had come over Freda. She was so rude and impertinent, and her temper something shocking, and in the end she flared up one day, and out she walked and took rooms of her own in the town. I've not seen her since. Better leave her to come to her senses, so Mr. Radnor says."

"Who is Mr. Radnor?"

Some of Mrs. Pengelley's initial embarrassment returned. "Oh, he's — he's just a friend. Very pleasant young fellow."

"Anything between him and your niece?"

"Nothing whatever," said Mrs. Pengelley emphatically.

Poirot shifted his ground.

"You and your husband are, I presume, in comfortable circumstances?"

"Yes, we're very nicely off."

"The money, is it yours or your husband's?"

"Oh, it's all Edward's. I've nothing of my own."

"You see, Madame, to be business-like, we must be brutal. We must seek for a motive. Your husband, he would not poison you just *pour passer le temps!* Do you know of any reason why he should wish you out of the way?"

"There's the yellow-haired hussy who works for him," said Mrs. Pengelley, with a flash of temper. "My husband's a dentist, Monsieur Poirot, and nothing would do but he must have a smart girl, as he said, with bobbed hair and a white overall, to make his appointments and mix his fillings for him. It's come to my ears that there have been fine goings-on, though of course he swears it's all right."

"This bottle of weed-killer, Madame, who ordered it?"

"My husband — about a year ago."

"Your niece, now, has she any money of her own?"

"About fifty pounds a year, I should say. She'd be glad enough to come back and keep house for Edward if I left him."

"You have contemplated leaving him, then?"

"I don't intend to let him have it all his own way. Women aren't the down-trodden slaves they were in the old days, Monsieur Poirot."

"I congratulate you on your independent spirit, Madame; but let us be practical. You return to Polgarwith to-day?"

"Yes, I came up by an excursion. Six this morning the train started, and the train goes back at five this afternoon."

"*Bien!* I have nothing of great moment on hand. I can devote myself to your little affair. To-morrow I shall be in Polgarwith. Shall we say that Hastings, here, is a distant relative of yours, the son of your second cousin? Me, I am his eccentric foreign friend. In the meantime, eat only what is prepared by your own hands, or under your eye. You have a maid whom you trust?"

"Jessie is a very good girl, I am sure."

"Till to-morrow then, Madame, and be of good courage."

Poirot bowed the lady out, and returned thoughtfully to his chair. His absorption was not so great, however, that he failed to see two minute strands of feather boa wrenched off by the lady's agitated fingers. He collected them carefully and consigned them to the waste-paper basket.

"What do you make of the case, Hastings?"

"A nasty business, I should say."

"Yes, if what the lady suspects be true. But is it? Woe betide any husband who orders a bottle of weed killer nowadays. If his wife suffers from gastritis, and is inclined to be of a hysterical temperament, the fat is in the fire."

"You think that is all there is to it?"

"Ah, *voilá*; I do not know, Hastings. But the case interests me—it interests me enormously! For, you see, it has positively *no* new features—hence the hysterical theory; and yet Mrs. Pengelley did not strike me as being a hysterical woman. Yes, if I mistake not, we have here a very poignant human drama. Tell me, Hastings, what do you consider Mrs. Pengelley's feelings towards her husband to be?"

"Loyalty struggling with fear," I suggested.

"Yet, ordinarily, a woman will accuse anyone in the world—but not her husband. She will stick to her belief in him through thick and thin."

"The 'other woman' complicates the matter."

"Yes, affection may turn to hate, under the stimulus of jealousy. But hate would take her to the police—not to me. She would want an outcry—a scandal. No, no; let us exercise our little grey cells. Why did she come to me? To have her suspicions proved wrong? Or—to have them proved *right*? Ah, we have here something I do not understand—an unknown factor. Is she a superb actress, our Mrs. Pengelley? No, she was genuine, I would swear that she was genuine, and therefore I am interested. Look up the trains to Polgarwith, I pray you."

The best train of the day was the 1:50 from Paddington which reached Polgarwith just after seven o'clock. The journey was uneventful, and I had to rouse myself from a pleasant nap to alight upon the platform of the bleak little station. We took our bags to the Duchy Hotel, and after a light meal, Poirot suggested our stepping round to pay an after-dinner call on my so-called cousin.

The Pengelleys' house stood a little way back from the road with an old-fashioned cottage garden in front. The smell of stocks and mignonette came sweetly wafted on the evening breeze. It seemed impossible to associate thoughts of violence with this Old World charm.

Poirot rang and knocked. As the summons was not answered, he rang again. This time, after a little pause, the door was opened by a disheveled-looking servant. Her eyes were red, and she was sniffing violently.

"We wish to see Mrs. Pengelley," explained Poirot. "May we enter?"

The maid stared. Then, with unusual directness, she answered: "Haven't you heard, then? She's dead. Died this evening — about half an hour ago."

We stood staring at her, stunned.

"What did she die of?" I asked at last.

"There's some as could tell." She gave a quick glance over her shoulder. "If it wasn't that somebody ought to be in the house with the missus, I'd pack my box and go tonight. But I'll not leave her dead with no one to watch by her. It's not my place to say anything, and I'm not going to say anything — but everybody knows. It's all over the town. And if Mr. Radnor don't write to the 'Ome Secretary, someone else will. The doctor may say what he likes. Didn't I see the master with my own eyes a-lifting down of the weed killer from the shelf this very evening? And didn't he jump when he turned round and saw me watching of him? And the missus' gruel there on the table, all ready to take to her? Not another bit of food passes my lips while I am in this house. Not if I dies for it."

"Where does the doctor live who attended your mistress?"

"Dr. Adams. Round the corner in High Street. The second house."

Poirot turned away abruptly. He was very pale.

"For a girl who was not going to say anything, that girl said a lot," I remarked dryly.

Poirot struck his clenched hand into his palm.

"An imbecile, a criminal imbecile, that is what I have been, Hastings. I have boasted of my little grey cells, and now I have lost a human life, a life that came to me to be saved. Never did I dream that anything would happen so soon. May the good God forgive me, but I never believed anything would happen at all. Her story seemed to me artificial. Here we are at the doctor's. Let us see what he can tell us."

Dr. Adams was the typical genial red-faced country doctor of fiction. He received us politely enough, but at a hint of our errand, his red face became purple.

"Damned nonsense! Damned nonsense, every word of it! Wasn't I in attendance on the case? Gastritis — gastritis pure and simple. This town's a hotbed of gossip — a lot of scandal-mongering old women get together and invent God knows what. They read these scurrilous rags of newspapers, and nothing will suit them but that someone in their town shall get poisoned too. They see a bottle of weed killer on a shelf — and hey, presto! — away goes their imagination with the bit between his teeth. I know Edward Pengelley — he wouldn't poison his grandmother's dog. And why should he poison his wife? Tell me that?"

"There is one thing, *Monsieur le Docteur*, that perhaps you do not know."

And, very briefly, Poirot outlined the main facts of Mrs. Pengelley's visit to him. No one could have been more astonished than Dr. Adams. His eyes almost started out of his head.

"God bless my soul!" he ejaculated. "The poor woman must have been mad. Why didn't she speak to me? That was the proper thing to do."

"And have her fears ridiculed?"

"Not at all, not at all. I hope I've got an open mind."

Poirot looked at him and smiled. The physician was evidently more perturbed than he cared to admit. As we left the house, Poirot broke into a laugh.

"He is as obstinate as a pig, that one. He has said it is gastritis; therefore it is gastritis! All the same, he has the mind uneasy."

"What's our next step?"

"A return to the inn, and a night of horror upon one of your English provincial beds, *mon ami*. It is a thing to make pity, the cheap English bed!"

"And to-morrow?"

"*Rien à faire*. We must return to town and await developments."

"That's very tame," I said, disappointed. "Suppose there are none?"

"There will be! I promise you that. Our old doctor may give as may certificates as he pleases. He cannot stop several hundred tongues from wagging. And they will wag to some purpose, I can tell you that."

Our train for town left at eleven the following morning. Before we started for the station, Poirot expressed a wish to see Miss Freda Stanton, the niece mentioned to us by the dead woman. We found the house where she was lodging easily enough. With her was a tall, dark young man whom she introduced in some confusion as Mr. Jacob Radnor.

Miss Freda Stanton was an extremely pretty girl of the old

Cornish type — dark hair and eyes and rosy cheeks. There was a flash in those same dark eyes which told of a temper that it would not be wise to provoke.

"Poor Auntie!" she said, when Poirot had introduced himself, and explained his business. "It's terribly sad! I've been wishing all the morning that I'd been kinder and more patient."

"You stood a great deal, Freda," interrupted Radnor.

"Yes, Jacob; but I've got a sharp temper, I know. After all, it was only silliness on Auntie's part. I ought to have just laughed and not minded. Of course, it's all nonsense her thinking that Uncle was poisoning her. She *was* worse after any food he gave her — but I'm sure it was only from thinking about it. She made up her mind she would be, and then she was."

"What was the actual cause of your disagreement, Mademoiselle?"

Miss Stanton hesitated, looking at Radnor. That young gentleman was quick to take the hint.

"I must be getting along, Freda. See you this evening. Good-bye, gentlemen; you're on your way to the station, I suppose?"

Poirot replied that we were, and Radnor departed.

"You are affianced, is it not so?" demanded Poirot, with a sly smile.

Freda Stanton blushed and admitted that such was the case.

"And that was really the whole trouble with Auntie," she added.

"She did not approve of the match for you?"

"Oh, it wasn't that so much. But you see, she …" The girl came to a stop.

"Yes?" encouraged Poirot gently.

"It seems rather a horrid thing to say about her — now she's dead. But you'll never understand unless I tell you. Auntie was absolutely infatuated with Jacob."

"Indeed?"

"Yes, wasn't it absurd? She was over fifty, and he's not quite thirty! But there it was. She was silly about him! I had to tell her at last that it was me he was after — and she carried on dreadfully. She wouldn't believe a word of it, and was so rude and insulting that it's no wonder I lost my temper. I talked it over with Jacob, and we agreed that the best thing to do was for me to clear out for a bit till she came to her senses. Poor Auntie — I suppose she was in a queer state altogether."

"It would certainly seem so. Thank you, Mademoiselle, for making things so clear to me."

A little to my surprise, Radnor was waiting for us in the street below.

"I can guess pretty well what Freda has been telling you," he remarked. "It was a most unfortunate thing to happen, and very awkward for me, as you can imagine. I need hardly say that it was none of my doing. I was pleased at first, because

I imagined the old woman was helping on things with Freda. The whole thing was absurd — but extremely unpleasant."

"When are you and Miss Stanton going to be married?"

"Soon, I hope. Now, Monsieur Poirot, I'm going to be candid with you. I know a bit more than Freda does. She believes her uncle to be innocent. I'm not so sure. But I can tell you one thing: I'm going to keep my mouth shut about what I do know. Let sleeping dogs lie. I don't want my wife's uncle tried and hanged for murder."

"Why do you tell me all this?"

"Because I've heard of you, and I know you're a clever man. It's quite possible that you might ferret out a case against him. But I put it to you — what good is that? The poor woman is past help — and she'd have been the last person to want a scandal — why, she'd turn in her grave at the mere thought of it."

"You are probably right there. You want me to — hush it up, then?"

"That's my idea. I'll admit frankly that I'm selfish about it. I've got my way to make — and I'm building up a good little business as a tailor and outfitter."

"Most of us are selfish, Mr. Radnor. Not all of us admit it so freely. I will do what you ask — but I tell you frankly you will not succeed in hushing it up."

"Why not?"

Poirot held up a finger. It was market day, and we were passing the market — a busy hum came from within.

"The voice of the people — that is why, Mr. Radnor. Ah, we must run, or we shall miss our train."

"Very interesting, is it not, Hastings?" said Poirot, as the train steamed out of the station.

He had taken out a small comb from his pocket, also a microscopic mirror, and was carefully arranging his moustache, the symmetry of which had become slightly impaired during our brisk run.

"You seem to find it so," I replied. "To me, it is all rather sordid and unpleasant. There's hardly any mystery about it."

"I agree with you; there is no mystery whatever."

"I suppose we can accept the girl's rather extraordinary story of her aunt's infatuation? That seemed the only fishy part to me. She was such a nice, respectable woman."

"There is nothing extraordinary about that — it is completely ordinary. If you read the papers carefully, you will find that many nice respectable women of that age leaves a husbands they have lived with for twenty years, and sometimes a whole family of children as well, in order to link their lives with that of a young man considerably their junior. You admire *les femmes*, Hastings; you prostrate yourself before all of them who are good-looking and have the good taste to smile upon you; but psychologically you know nothing whatever about them. In the autumn of a woman's life, there comes always one mad moment when she longs for romance, for adventure — before it is too late. It comes none the less surely to a woman because she is the wife of a respectable dentist in a country town!"

"And you think —?"

"That a clever man might take advantage of such a moment."

"I shouldn't call Pengelley so clever," I mused. "He's got the whole town by the ears. And yet I suppose you're right. The only two men who know anything, Radnor and the doctor — both want to hush it up. He's managed that somehow. I wish we'd seen the fellow."

"You can indulge your wish. Return by the next train and invent an aching molar."

I looked at him keenly.

"I wish I knew what you considered so interesting about the case?"

"My interest is very aptly summed up by a remark of yours, Hastings. After interviewing the maid, you observed that for someone who was not going to say a word, she had said a good deal."

"Oh!" I said doubtfully; then I harked back to my original criticism: "I wonder why you made no attempt to see Pengelley?"

"*Mom ami*, I give him just three months. Then I shall see him for as long as I please — in the dock."

For once I thought Poirot's prognostications were going to be proved wrong. The time went by, and nothing transpired as to our Cornish case. Other matters occupied us, and I had nearly forgotten the Pengelley tragedy when it was suddenly recalled to me by a short paragraph in the paper which stated that an order to exhume the body of Mrs. Pengelley had been obtained from the Home Secretary.

A few days later, and "The Cornish Mystery" was the topic of every paper. It seemed that gossip had never entirely died down, and when the engagement of the widower to Miss Marks, his secretary, was announced, the tongues burst out again louder than ever. Finally a petition was sent to the Home Secretary; the body was exhumed; large quantities of arsenic were discovered; and Mr. Pengelley was arrested and charged with the murder of his wife.

Poirot and I attended the preliminary proceedings. The evidence was much as might have been expected. Dr. Adams admitted that the symptoms of arsenical poisoning might easily be mistaken for those of gastritis. The Home Office expert gave his evidence; the maid, Jessie, poured out a flood of voluble information, most of which was rejected, but which certainly strengthened the case against the prisoner. Freda Stanton gave evidence as to her aunt's being worse whenever she ate food prepared by her husband. Jacob Radnor told how he had dropped in unexpectedly on the day of Mrs. Pengelley's death, and found Pengelley replacing the bottle of weed killer on the pantry shelf, Mrs. Pengelley's gruel being on the table close by. Then Miss Marks, the fair-haired secretary, was called, and wept and went into hysterics and admitted that there had been "passages" between her and her employer, and that he had promised to marry her in the event of anything happening to his wife. Pengelley reserved his defence and was sent for trial.

Radnor walked back with us to our lodgings.

"You see, Monsieur Radnor," said Poirot, "I was right. The voice of the people spoke—and with no uncertain voice. There was to be no hushing-up of this case."

"You were quite right," sighed Radnor. "Do you see any chance of his getting off?"

"Well, he has reserved his defence. He may have something—up the sleeve, as you English say. Come in with us, will you not?"

Radnor accepted the invitation. I ordered two whisky-and-sodas and a cup of chocolate. The last order caused consternation, and I much doubted whether it would ever put in an appearance.

"Of course," continued Poirot, "I have a good deal of experience in matters of this kind. And I see only one loophole of escape for our friend."

"What is it?"

"That you should sign this paper."

With the suddenness of a conjuror, he produced a sheet of paper covered with writing.

"What is it?"

"A confession that *you* murdered Mrs. Pengelley."

There was a moment's pause; then Radnor laughed.

"You must be mad!"

"No, no, my friend, I am not mad. You came here; you started a little business; you were short of money. Mr. Pengelley was a man very well-to-do. You met his niece; she was inclined to smile upon you. But the small allowance that Pengelley might have given her upon her marriage was not enough for you. You must get rid of both the uncle and the aunt—then the money would come to her, since she was the only relative. How cleverly you set about it! You made love to that plain middle-aged woman until she was your slave. You implanted in her doubts of her husband. She discovered first that he was deceiving her; then, under your guidance, that he was trying to poison her. You were often at the house; you had opportunities to introduce the arsenic into her food. But you were careful never to do so when her husband was away. Being a woman, she did not keep her suspicions to herself. She talked to her niece; doubtless she talked to other women friends. Your only difficulty was keeping up separate relations with the two women, and even that was not so difficult as it looked. You explained to the aunt that, to allay the suspicions of her husband, you had to pretend to pay court to the niece. And the younger lady needed little convincing — she would never seriously consider her aunt as a rival.

"But then Mrs. Pengelley made up her mind, without saying anything to you, to consult *me*. If she could be really assured, beyond any possible doubt, that her husband was trying to poison her, she would feel justified in leaving him, and linking her life with yours — which is what she imagined you wanted her to do. But that did not suit your book at all. You did not want a detective prying around. A favourable minute occurs. You are in the house when Mr. Pengelley is getting some gruel for his wife, and you introduce the fatal dose. The rest is easy. Apparently anxious to hush matters up, you secretly foment them. But you reckoned without Hercule Poirot, my intelligent young friend."

Radnor was deadly pale, but he still endeavoured to carry off matters with a high hand.

"Very interesting and ingenious; but why tell me all this?"

"Because, Monsieur, I represent — not the law, but Mrs. Pengelley. For her sake, I give you a chance of escape. Sign this paper, and you shall have twenty-four hours' start — twenty-four hours before I place it in the hands of the police."

Radnor hesitated.

"You can't prove anything."

"Can't I? I am Hercule Poirot. Look out of the window, Monsieur. There are two men in the street. They have orders not to lose sight of you."

Radnor strode across to the window and pulled aside the blind, then shrank back with an oath.

"You see, Monsieur? Sign — it is your best chance."

"What guarantee have I —"

"That I shall keep faith? The word of Hercule Poirot. You will sign? Good. Hastings, be so kind as to pull that left-hand blind half-way up. That is the signal that Mr. Radnor may leave unmolested."

White-faced, muttering oaths, Radnor hurried from the room. Poirot nodded gently.

"A coward. I always knew it."

"It seems to me, Poirot, that you've acted in a criminal manner!" I cried angrily. "You always preach against sentiment; and here you are letting a dangerous criminal escape out of sheer sentimentality."

"That was not sentiment — that was business," replied Poirot. "Do you not see, my friend, that we have no shadow of proof against him? Shall I get up and say to twelve stolid Cornishmen that *I*, Hercule Poirot, *know?* They would laugh at me. The only chance was to frighten him and get a confession that way. Those two loafers that I noticed outside came in very useful. Pull down the blind again, will you, Hastings. Not that there was any reason for raising it. It was part of our *mise en scène*.

"Well, well, we must keep our word. Twenty-four hours, did I say? So much longer for poor Mr. Pengelley — and it is not more than he deserves; for mark you, he deceived his wife. I am very strong on the family life, as you know. Ah, well, twenty-four hours — and then? I have great faith in Scotland Yard. They will get him, *mon ami* — they will get him."

# THE DOUBLE CLUE.

"The Double Clue" was first published in *The Sketch* on December 5, 1923.

"But above everything—no publicity," said Mr. Marcus Hardman for perhaps the fourteenth time.

The word "publicity" occurred throughout his conversation with the regularity of a *leitmotif* or the famous King Charles's head. Mr. Hardman was a small man, delicately plump, with exquisitely manicured hands and a plaintive tenor voice. H reminded me of a well-fed Persian cat. In his way, he was somewhat of a celebrity. In the lists of fashionable house-parties his name was almost sure to occur at the tail-end of the procession, following respectfully in the footsteps of the Dukes and Countesses. Almost unconsciously one came to expect the "...and Mr. Marcus Hardman" as the only fitting conclusion.

The fashionable life was Mr. Marcus Hardman's profession. He was rich, but not remarkably so, and he spent his money zealously in the pursuit of social pleasure. His hobby was collecting. He had the collector's soul. Old lace, old fans, antique jewellery — nothing crude or modern for Mr. Marcus Hardman.

Poirot and I, obeying an urgent summons, had arrived to find the little man writhing in an agony of indecision. Under the circumstances, to call in the police was abhorrent to him. On the other hand, not to call them in was to acquiesce in the loss of some of the gems of his collection. He hit upon Poirot as a compromise.

"My rubies, Monsieur Poirot, and the emerald necklace — said to have belonged to Catherine de' Medici. Oh, the emerald necklace!"

"If you will recount to me the circumstances of their disappearance?" suggested Poirot gently.

"I am endeavouring to do so. Yesterday afternoon I had a little tea party — quite an informal affair, some half-a-dozen people or so. I have given one or two of them during the season, and though, perhaps, I should not say so, they have been quite a success. Some good music — Nacora, the pianist, and Katherine Bird, the Australian contralto — in the big studio.

"Well, early in the afternoon, I was showing my guests my collection of mediæval jewels. I keep them in the small wall safe over there. It is arranged like a cabinet inside, with every coloured velvet background to display the stones. Afterwards we inspected the fans — in the case on the wall. Then we all went to the studio for music. It was not until after everyone had gone that I discovered the safe rifled. I must have failed to shut it properly, and someone had seized the opportunity to denude it of its contents. The rubies, Monsieur Poirot, the emerald necklace — the collection of a lifetime! What would I not give to recover them! But there must be no publicity! You fully understand that, do you not, Monsieur Poirot? My own guests, my personal friends. It would be a horrible scandal!"

"What about the servants?"

"I'm afraid it could not be Jevons," said Mr. Hardman in a melancholy voice. "He has been with me so many years, and has proved himself in so many ways. And the women servants never come to these rooms. No, no; I fear we must look elsewhere."

"Who was the last person to leave this room when you went to the studio?"

"Mr. Johnston. You may know him? The South African millionaire. He has just rented the Abbotburys' house in Park Lane. He lingered behind a few moments, I remember. But surely, oh, surely it could not be he!"

"Did any of your guests return to this room during the afternoon on any pretext?"

"I was prepared for that question, Monsieur Poirot. Three of them did so — Countess Vera Rossakoff, Mr. Bernard Parker, and Lady Runcorn."

"Let us hear about them."

"The Countess Rossakoff is a very charming Russian lady, a member of the old regime. She has recently escaped from the fury of the Bolsheviks to this country. She had bidden me good-bye, and I was therefore somewhat surprised to find her in this room, apparently gazing in rapture at my cabinet of fans. You know, Monsieur Poirot, the more I think of it, the more suspicious it seems to me. Don't you agree?"

"Extremely suspicious; but let us hear about the others."

"Well, Parker simply came here to fetch a case of miniatures that I was anxious to show to Lady Runcorn."

"And Lady Runcorn herself?"

"As I daresay you know, Lady Runcorn is a middle-aged woman of considerable force of character who devotes most of her time to various charitable committees. She simply returned to fetch a hand-bag she had laid down somewhere."

"*Bien*, Monsieur. So we have four possible suspects. The Russian countess, the English *grande dame*, the South African millionaire, and Mr. Bernard Parker. Who *is* Mr. Parker, by the way?"

The question appeared to embarrass Mr. Hardman considerably.

"He is — er — he is a young fellow. Well, in fact, a young fellow I know."

"I had already deduced as much," replied Poirot gravely. "What does he do, this Monsieur Parker?"

"He is a young man-about-town — not, perhaps, quite in the swim, if I may so express myself."

"How did he come to be a friend of yours, may I ask?"

"Well — er — on one or two occasions he has — performed certain little commissions for me."

"Continue, Monsieur," said Poirot.

Hardman looked piteously at him. Evidently the last thing he wanted to do was to continue. But as Poirot maintained an inexorable silence, he capitulated.

"You see, Monsieur Poirot — it is well-known that I am interested in antique jewels. Sometimes there is a family heirloom to be disposed of — which, mind you, would never be sold in the open market or to a dealer. But a private sale to me is a very different matter. Parker arranged the details of such things; he was in touch with both sides, and thus any little embarrassment is avoided. He brought anything of that kind to my notice. For instance, the Countess Rossakoff has brought some family jewels with her from Russia. She is anxious to sell them. Bernard Parker was to have arranged the transaction."

"I see," said Poirot thoughtfully. "And you trust him implicitly?"

"I have had no reason to do otherwise."

"Mr. Hardman, of these four people, whom do you yourself suspect?"

"Oh, Monsieur Poirot, what a question! They are my friends, as I told you. I suspect none of them — or all of them, whichever way you like to put it."

"I do not agree. You suspect one of those four. It is not Countess Rossakoff. It is not Mr. Parker. Is it Lady Runcorn or Mr. Johnston?"

"You drive me into a corner, Monsieur Poirot, you do indeed. I am most anxious to have no scandal. Lady Runcorn belongs to one of the oldest families in England; but it is true, it is most unfortunately true, that her aunt, Lady Caroline, suffered from a most melancholy affliction. It was understood, of course, by all her friends, and her maid returned the teaspoons, or whatever it was, as promptly as possible. You see my predicament?"

"So Lady Runcorn had an aunt who was a kleptomaniac? Very interesting. You permit that I examine the safe?"

Mr. Hardman assenting, Poirot pushed back the door of the safe and examined the interior. The empty velvet-lined shelves gaped at us.

"Even now the door does not shut properly," murmured Poirot, as he swung it to and fro. "I wonder why? Ah! What have we here? A glove, caught in the hinge. A man's glove."

He held it out to Mr. Hardman.

"That's not one of my gloves," the latter declared.

"Aha! Something more." Poirot bent deftly and picked up a small object from the floor of the safe. It was a flat cigarette case made of black moiré.

"My cigarette-case," cried Mr. Hardman.

"Yours? Surely not, Monsieur. Those are not your initials."

He pointed to an entwined monogram of two letters executed in platinum. Hardman took it in his hand.

"You are right," he declared. "It is very like mine, but the initials are different. A 'B' and a 'P.' Good heavens! Bernard Parker!"

"It would seem so," said Poirot. "A somewhat careless young man — especially if the glove is his also. That would be a double clue, would it not?"

"Bernard Parker!" murmured Hardman. "What a relief! Well, Monsieur Poirot, I leave it to you to recover the jewels. Place the matter in the hands of the police if you think fit — that is, if you are quite sure that it is he who is guilty."

"See you, my friend," said Poirot to me, as we left the house together, "he has one law for the titled, and another law for the plain, this Mr. Hardman. Me, I have not yet been ennobled, so I am on the side of the plain. I have sympathy for this young man. The whole thing was a little curious, was it not? There was Hardman suspecting Lady Runcorn; there was I, suspecting the Countess and Johnston; and all the time, the obscure Mr. Parker was our man."

"Why did you suspect the other two?"

"*Parbleu!* It is such a simple

thing to be a Russian refugee or a South African millionaire. Any woman can call herself a Russian countess; anyone can buy a house in Park Lane and call himself a South African millionaire! Who is going to contradict them? But I observe that we are passing through Bury Street. Our careless young friend lives here. Let us, as you say, strike while the iron is in the fire."

Mr. Bernard Parker was at home. We found him reclining on some cushions, clad in an amazing dressing gown of purple and orange. I have seldom taken a greater dislike to anyone than I did to this particular young man with his white, effeminate face and affected, lisping speech.

"Good-morning, Monsieur," said Poirot briskly. "I come from Monsieur Hardman. Yesterday, at the party, somebody has stolen all his jewels. Permit me to ask you, Monsieur, is this your glove?"

Mr. Parker's mental processes did not seem very rapid. He stared at the glove, as though gathering his wits together.

"Where did you find it?" he asked at last.

"Is it your glove, Monsieur?"

Mr. Parker appeared to make up his mind. "No, it isn't," he declared.

"And this cigarette case, is that yours?"

"Certainly not. I always carry a silver one."

"Very well, Monsieur. I go to put matters in the hands of the police."

"Oh, I say, I wouldn't do that if I were you," cried Mr. Parker in some concern. "Beastly unsympathetic people, the police. Wait a bit. I'll go round and see old Hardman. Look here — oh, stop a minute."

But Poirot beat a determined retreat.

"We have given him something to think about, have we not?" he chuckled. "To-morrow we will observe what has occurred."

But we were destined to have a reminder of the Hardman case that afternoon. Without the least warning the door flew open, and a whirlwind in human form invaded our privacy, bringing with her a swirl of sables (it was as cold as only an English June day can be) and a hat rampant with slaughtered ospreys. Countess Vera Rossakoff was a somewhat disturbing personality.

"You are Monsieur Poirot? What is this that you have done? You accuse that poor boy! It is infamous! It is scandalous! I know him. He is a chicken — a lamb — never would he steal. He has done everything for me. Will I stand by and see him martyred and butchered?"

"Tell me, Madame, is this his cigarette-case?" Poirot held out the black moiré case.

The Countess paused for a moment while she inspected it.

"Yes, it is his. I know it well. What of it? Did you find it in the room? We were all there; he dropped it then, I suppose. Ah, you policemen, you are worse than the Red Guards —"

"And is this his glove?"

"How should I know? One glove is like another. Do not try to stop me — he must be set free. His character must be cleared. You shall do it. I will sell my jewels and give you much money."

"Madame —"

"It is agreed, then? No, no, do not argue. The poor boy! He came to me, the tears in his eyes. 'I will save you,' I said. 'I will go to this man — this ogre, this monster! Leave it to Vera.' Now it is settled, I go."

With as little ceremony as she had come, she swept from the room, leaving an overpowering perfume of an exotic nature behind her.

"What a woman!" I exclaimed. "And what furs!"

"Ah, yes; *they* were genuine enough. Could a spurious countess have real furs? My little joke, Hastings .... No, she is truly Russian, I fancy. Well, well, so Master Bernard went bleating to her."

"The cigarette case is his. I wonder if the glove is also —"

With a smile Poirot drew from his pocket a second glove and placed it by the first. There was no doubt of their being a pair.

"Where did you get the second one, Poirot?"

"It was thrown down with a stick on the table in the hall in Bury Street. Truly, a very careless young man, *ce Monsieur Parker*. Well, well, *mon ami* — we must be thorough. Just for the form of the thing, I will make a little visit to Park Lane."

Needless to say, I accompanied my friend. Johnston was out, but we saw his private secretary. It transpired that Johnston had only recently arrived from South Africa. He had never been in England before.

"He is interested in precious stones, is he not?" hazarded Poirot.

"Gold-mining is nearer the mark," laughed the secretary.

Poirot came away from the interview thoughtful. Late that evening, to my utter surprise, I found him earnestly studying a Russian grammar.

"Good heavens, Poirot!" I cried. "Are you learning Russian in order to converse with the Countess in her own language?"

"She certainly would not listen to my English, my friend!"

"But surely, Poirot, well-born Russians invariably speak French?"

"You are a mine of information, Hastings! I will cease puzzling over the intricacies of the Russian alphabet."

He threw the book from him with a dramatic gesture. I was not entirely satisfied. There was a twinkle in his eye which I knew of old. It was an invariable sign that Hercule Poirot was pleased with himself.

"Perhaps," I said sapiently, "you doubt her being really a Russian. You are going to test her?"

"Ah, no, no; she is Russian all right. *Tout ce qu'il y a de plus Russe!*"

"Well, then —"

"If you really want to distinguish yourself over this case, Hastings, I recommend *First Steps in Russian* as an invaluable aid."

Then he laughed and would say no more. I picked up the book from the floor and dipped into it curiously, but could make neither head nor tail of Poirot's remarks. I concluded that he was merely pulling my leg.

The following morning brought us no news of any kind, but that did not seem to worry my little friend. At breakfast, he announced his intention of calling upon Mr. Hardman early in the day. We found the elderly social butterfly at home, and seemingly a little calmer than on the previous day.

"Well, Monsieur Poirot, any news?" he demanded eagerly.

Poirot handed him a slip of paper.

"That is the person who took the jewels, Monsieur. Shall I put matters in the hands of the police? Or would you prefer me to recover the jewels without bringing the police into the matter?"

Mr. Hardman was staring at the paper. At last he found his voice.

"Most astonishing. I should infinitely prefer to have no scandal in the matter. I give you *carte blanche*, Monsieur Poirot. I am sure you will be discreet."

Our next procedure was to hail a taxi, which Poirot ordered to drive to the Carlton. There he inquired for Countess Rossakoff. In a few minutes we were ushered up into the lady's suite. She came to meet us with outstretched hands, arrayed in a marvellous negligée of barbaric design.

"Monsieur Poirot!" she cried. "You have succeeded? You have cleared that poor infant?"

"*Madame la Comtesse*, your friend Mr. Parker is perfectly safe from arrest."

"Ah, but you are the clever little man! Superb! And so quickly too."

"On the other hand, I have promised Mr. Hardman that the jewels shall be returned to him to-day."

"So?"

"Therefore, Madame, I should be extremely obliged if you would place them in my hands without delay. I am sorry to hurry you, but I am keeping a taxi — in case it should be necessary for me to go on to Scotland Yard — and we Belgians, Madame, we practise the thrift."

The Countess had lit a cigarette. For some seconds she sat perfectly still, blowing smoke rings, and gazing steadily at Poirot. Then she burst into a laugh, and rose. She went across to the bureau, opened a drawer, and took out a black silk hand-bag. She tossed it lightly to Poirot. Her tone, when she spoke, was perfectly light and unmoved.

"We Russians, on the contrary, practise prodigality," she said. "And to do that, unfortunately, one must have money. You need not look inside. They are all there."

Poirot arose.

"I congratulate you, Madame, on your quick intelligence and your promptitude — "

"Ah! But since you were keeping your taxi waiting, what else could I do?"

"You are too amiable, Madame. You are remaining long in London?"

"I am afraid not … owing to you."

"Accept my apologies."

"We shall meet again elsewhere, perhaps."

"I hope so."

"And I — do not!" exclaimed the Countess with a laugh. "It is a great compliment that I pay you there — there are very few men in the world whom I fear. Good-bye, Monsieur Poirot."

"Good-bye, *Madame la Comtesse*. Ah — pardon me, I forgot! Allow me to return to you your cigarette case."

And with a bow he handed to her the little black moire case we had found in the safe. She accepted it without any change of expression — just a lifted eyebrow and a murmured: "I see!"

"What a woman!" cried Poirot enthusiastically, as we descended the stairs. "*Mon Dieu! quelle femme!* Not a word of argument — of protestation — of bluff! One quick glance, and she had sized up the position correctly. I tell you, Hastings, a woman who can accept defeat like that — with a careless smile — will go far! She is dangerous — she has the nerves of steel — she —" He tripped heavily.

"If you can manage to moderate your transports and look where you're going, it might be as well," I suggested. "When did you first suspect the Countess?"

"*Mon ami*, it was the glove *and* the cigarette-case — the double clue, shall we say — that worried me. Bernard Parker might easily have dropped one or the other — but hardly both. Ah, no, *par example,* that would have been *too* careless! In the same way, if someone else had placed them there to incriminate Parker, one would have been sufficient — the cigarette-case *or* the glove — again, not both. So I was forced to the conclusion that one of the two things did *not* belong to Parker. I imagined at first that the case was his, and that the glove was not. But when I discovered the fellow to the glove, I saw that it was the other way about. Whose, then, was the cigarette-case? Clearly, it could not belong to Lady Runcorn. The initials were wrong. Mr. Johnston? Only if he were here under a false name. I interviewed his secretary, and it was apparent at once that everything was clear and above-board. There was no reticence about Mr. Johnston's past. The Countess, then? She was supposed to have brought jewels with her from Russia;

she had only to take the stones from their settings, and it was extremely doubtful if they could ever be identified. What could be easier for her than to pick up one of Parker's gloves from the hall that day and thrust it into the safe? But, *bien sûr*, she did not intend to drop her own cigarette case."

"But if the case was hers, why had it got 'B.P.' on it? The Countess's initials are V.R."

Poirot smiled gently upon me.

"Exactly, *mon ami*; but in the Russian alphabet, B is V and P is R."

"Well, you couldn't expect me to guess that. I don't know Russian."

"Neither do I, Hastings. That is why I bought my little book — and urged it on your attention."

He sighed.

"A remarkable woman. I have a feeling, my friend — a very decided feeling — I shall meet her again. Where, I wonder?"

# THE ADVENTURE OF THE CHRISTMAS PUDDING.

"The Adventure of the Christmas Pudding" was first published in *The Sketch* on December 12, 1923.

I.

The big logs crackled merrily in the wide, open fireplace, and above their crackling rose the babel of six tongues all wagging industriously together. The house-party of young people were enjoying their Christmas.

Old Mrs. Endicott, known to most of those present as Aunt Emily, smiled indulgently on the clatter.

"Bet you can't eat six mince-pies, Jean."

"Yes, I can."

"No, you can't."

"You'll get the pig out of the trifle if you do."

"Yes, *and* three helps of trifle, *and* two helps of plum-pudding."

"I hope the pudding will be good," said Miss Endicott apprehensively. "But they were only made three days ago. Christmas puddings ought to be made a long time before Christmas. Why, I remember when I was a child, I thought the last Collect before Advent — 'stir up, O Lord, we beseech thee…' — referred in some way to stirring up the Christmas puddings!"

There was a polite pause while Miss Endicott was speaking. Not because any of the young people were in the least interested in her reminiscences of bygone days, but because they felt that some show of attention was due by good manners to their hostess. As soon as she stopped, the babel burst out again.

Miss Endicott sighed, and glanced towards the only member of the party whose years approached her own, as though in search of sympathy—a little man with a curious egg-shaped head and fierce up-standing moustaches. Young people were not what they were, reflected Miss Endicott. In olden days there would have been a mute, respectable circle, listening to the pearls of wisdom dropped by their elders. Instead of which there was all this nonsensical chatter, most of it utterly incomprehensible.

All the same, they were dear children! Her eyes softened as she passed them in review—tall, freckled Jean; little Nancy Cardell, with her dark, gypsy beauty; the two younger boys home from school, Johnnie and Eric, and their friend, Charlie Pease; and fair, beautiful Evelyn Haworth.... At thought of the last, her brow contracted little, and her eyes wandered to where her eldest nephew, Roger, sat morosely silent, taking no part in the fun, with his eyes fixed on the exquisite Northern fairness of the young girl.

"Isn't the snow ripping?" cried Johnnie, approaching the window. "Real Christmas weather. I say, let's have a snowball fight. There's lots of time before dinner, isn't there, aunt Emily?"

"Yes, my dear. We have it at two o'clock. That reminds me, I had better see to the table."

She hurried out of the room.

"I tell you what. We'll make a snowman!" screamed Jean.

"Yes, what fun! I know; we'll do a snow statue of Monsieur Poirot. Do you hear, Monsieur Poirot? The great detective, Hercule Poirot, modelled in snow, by six celebrated artists!"

The little man in the chair bowed his acknowledgments with a twinkling eye.

"Make him very handsome, my children," he urged. "I insist on that."

"Ra-ther!"

The troop disappeared like a whirlwind, colliding in the doorway with a stately butler who was entering with a note on a salver. The butler, his calm re-established, advanced towards Poirot.

Poirot took the note and tore it open. The butler departed. Twice the little man read the note through, then he folded it up and put it in his pocket. Not a muscle of his face had moved, and yet the contents of the note were sufficiently surprising. Scrawled in an illiterate hand were the words: "Don't eat any plum-pudding."

"Very interesting," murmured Monsieur Poirot to himself. "And quite unexpected."

He looked across to the fire-place. Evelyn Haworth had not gone out with the rest. She was sitting staring at the fire, absorbed in thought, nervously twisting a ring on the third finger of her left hand round and round.

"You are lost in a dream, Mademoiselle," said the little man at last. "And the dream is not a happy one, eh?"

She started, and looked across at him uncertainly. He nodded reassuringly.

"It is my business to know things. No, you are not happy. Me, too, I am not very happy. Shall we confide in each other? See you, I have the big sorrow because a friend of mine, a friend of many years, has gone away across the sea to the South America. Sometimes, when we were together, this friend made me impatient, his stupidity enraged me; but now that he is gone, I can remember only his good qualities. That is the way of life, is it not? And now, Mademoiselle, what is your trouble? You are not like me, old and alone — you are young and beautiful; and the man you love loves you — oh yes, it is so: I have been watching him for the last half-hour."

The girl's color rose.

"You mean Roger Endicott? Oh, but you have made a mistake; it is not Roger I am engaged to."

"No, you are engaged in Mr. Oscar Levering. I know that perfectly. But why are you engaged to him, since you love another man?"

The girl did not seem to resent his words; indeed, there was something in his manner which made that impossible. He spoke with a mixture of kindliness and authority that was irresistible.

"Tell me all about it," said Poirot gently; and he added the phrase he had used before, the sound of which was oddly comforting to the girl. "It is my business to know things."

"I am so miserable, Monsieur Poirot — so very miserable. You see, once we were very well off. I was supposed to be an heiress, and Roger was only a younger son; and — and although I'm sure he cared for me, he never said anything, but went off to Australia."

"It is droll, the way they arrange the marriages over here," interpolated Monsieur Poirot. "No order. No method. Everything left to chance."

Evelyn continued: "Then suddenly we lost all our money. My mother and I were left almost penniless. We moved into a tiny house, and we could just manage. But my mother became very ill. The only chance for her was to have a serious operation and go abroad to a warm climate. And we hadn't the money, Monsieur Poirot — we hadn't the money! It meant that she must die. Mr. Levering had proposed to me once or twice already. He again asked me to marry him, and promised to do everything that could be done for my mother. I said yes — what else could I do? He kept his word. The operation was performed by the greatest specialist of the day, and we went to Egypt for the winter. That was a year ago. My mother is well and strong again; and I—I am to marry Mr. Levering after Christmas."

"I see," said Monsieur Poirot; "and in the meantime, Monsieur Roger's elder brother has died, and he has come home—to find his dreams shattered. All the same, you are not yet married, Mademoiselle."

"A Haworth does not break her word, Monsieur Poirot," said the girl proudly."

Almost as she spoke, the door opened, and a big man with a rubicund face, narrow, crafty eyes, and a bald head stood on the threshold.

"What are you moping in here for, Evelyn? Come out for a stroll."

"Very well, Oscar."

She rose listlessly. Poirot rose also and demanded politely: "Mademoiselle Levering, she is still indisposed?"

"Yes, I'm sorry to say my sister is still in bed. Too bad, to be laid up on Christmas day."

"It is indeed," agreed the detective politely.

A few minutes sufficed for Evelyn to put on her snow-boots and some wraps, and she and her fiancé went out onto the snow-covered grounds. It was an ideal Christmas day, crisp and sunny. The rest of the house-party were busy with the erection of the snow-man. Levering and Evelyn paused to watch them.

"Love's young dream, yah!" cried Johnnie, and threw a snowball at them.

"What do you think of it, Evelyn?" cried Jean. "Monsieur Hercule Poirot, the great detective."

"Wait till the mustache goes on," said Eric. "Nancy's going to clip off a bit of her hair for it. *Vivent les brave Belges!* Pom, pom!"

"Fancy having a real live detective in the house!"—this from Charley—"I wish there could be a murder too."

"Oh, oh, oh!" cried Jean, dancing about. "I've got an idea. Let's get up a murder—a spoof one, I mean. And take him in. Oh do let's—it would be no end of a rag."

Five voices began to talk at once.

"How should we do it?"

"Awful groans!"

"No, you stupid, out here."

"Footprints in the snow, of course."

"Jean and her nightie."

"You do it with red paint."

"In your hand—and clap it to your head."

"I say, I wish we had a revolver."

"I tell you father and Aunt Em won't hear. Their rooms are on the other side of the house."

"No, he won't mind a bit; he's no end of a sport."

"Yes, but what kind of red paint? Enamel?"

"We could get some in the village."

"Fathead, not on Christmas day."

"No, water-color. Crimson lake."

"Jean can be it."

"Never mind if you *are* cold, it won't be for long."

"No, Nancy can be it. Nancy's got those posh pyjamas."

"Let's see if Graves knows where there's any paint."

A stampede to the house.

"In a brown study, Endicott?" said Levering, laughing disagreeably.

Roger roused himself abruptly. He had heard little of what had passed.

"I was just wondering," he said quietly.

"Wondering?"

"Wondering what Monsieur Poirot was doing down here at all."

Levering seemed taken aback; but at that moment the big gong pealed out, and everybody went in to Christmas dinner. The curtains were drawn in the dining room, and the lights on, illuminating the long table piled high with crackers and other decorations. It was a real old-fashioned Christmas dinner. At one end of the table was the Squire, red-faced and jovial; his sister faced him at the other. Monsieur Poirot, in honor of the occasion, had donned a red waistcoat, and his plumpness, and the way he carried his head on one side, reminded one irresistibly of a Robin redbreast.

The Squire carved rapidly, and everyone fell to on turkey. The carcasses of two turkeys were removed, and there fell a breathless hush. Then Graves, the butler, appeared in state, bearing the plum-pudding aloft — a gigantic pudding wreathed in flames. A hullabaloo broke out.

"Quick. Oh! My piece is going out. Buck up, Graves; unless it's still burning, I shan't get my wish."

Nobody had leisure to notice a curious expression on the face of Monsieur Poirot as he surveyed the portion of pudding on his plate. Nobody observed the lightning glances he sent round the table. With a faint, puzzled frown he began to eat his pudding. Everybody began to eat pudding. The conversation was more subdued.

Suddenly the Squire uttered an exclamation. His face became purple and his hand went to his mouth.

"Confound it, Emily!" he roared. "Why do you let the cook put glass in the puddings?"

"Glass?" cried Miss Endicott, astonished.

The Squire withdrew the offending substance from his mouth.

"Might have broken a tooth," he grumbled. "Or swallowed it and had appendicitis."

In front of each person was a small finger-bowl of water, designed to receive the sixpences and other matters found in the trifle. Mr. Endicott dropped the piece of glass into this, rinsed it, and held it up. "God bless my soul!" he ejaculated. "It's a red stone out of one of the cracker brooches."

"You permit?" Very deftly, Monsieur Poirot took it from his fingers and examined it attentively. As the Squire had said, it was a big red stone, the color of a ruby. The light gleamed from its facets as he turned it about.

"Gee!" cried Eric. "Suppose it's real."

"Silly boy!" said Jean scornfully. "A ruby that size would be worth thousands and thousands and thousands — wouldn't it, Monsieur Poirot?"

"Extraordinary how well they get up these cracker things," murmured Miss Endicott. *"But how did it get into the pudding?*

Undoubtedly that was the question of the hour. Every hypothesis was exhausted. Only Monsieur Poirot said nothing, but carelessly, as though thinking of something else, he dropped the stone into his pocket.

After dinner he paid a visit to the kitchen.

The cook was rather flustered. To be questioned by a member of the house-party, and the foreign gentleman too! But she did her best to answer his questions. The puddings had been made three days ago — "the day you arrived, Sir." Everyone had come out into the kitchen to have a stir and wish. An old custom — perhaps they didn't have it abroad? After that the puddings were boiled, and then they were put in a row on the top shelf in the larder. Was there anything special to distinguish this pudding from the others? No, she didn't think so. Except that it was in an aluminium pudding-basin, and the others were in china ones. Was it the pudding originally intended for Christmas day? It was funny that he should ask that. No, indeed! The Christmas pudding was always boiled in a big white china mould with a pattern of holly leaves. But this very morning (the cook's red face became wrathful) Gladys, the kitchen maid, sent to fetch it down for the final boiling, had managed to drop and break it. "And of course, seeing that there might be splinters in it, I wouldn't send it to table, but took the big aluminium one instead."

Monsieur Poirot thanked her for her information. He went out of the kitchen, smiling a little to himself, as though satisfied with the information he had obtained. And the fingers of his right hand played with something in his pocket.

## II.

"Monsieur Poirot! Monsieur Poirot! Do wake up! Something dreadful happened!"

Thus Johnnie in the early hours of the following morning. Monsieur Poirot sat up in bed. He wore a night-cap. The contrast between the dignity of his countenance and the rakish tilt of the night-cap was certainly droll; but its effect on Johnnie seemed disproportionate. But for his words, one might have fancied that the boy was violently amused about something. Curious sounds came from outside the door, too, suggesting soda-water siphons in difficulty.

"Come down at once, please," continued Johnnie, his voice shaking slightly. "Someone's been killed." He turned away.

"Aha, that is serious!" said Monsieur Poirot.

He arose, and, without unduly hurrying himself, made a partial toilet. Then he followed Johnnie down the stairs. The house-party was clustered around the door into the garden. Their countenances all expressed intense emotion. At the sight of him Eric was seized with a violent choking fit.

Jean came forward and laid her hand on Monsieur Poirot's arm.

"Look!" she said, and pointed dramatically through the open door.

"*Mon Dieu!*" ejaculated Monsieur Poirot. "It is like a scene on the stage."

His remark was not inapposite. More snow had fallen during the night, and the world looked white and ghostly in the faint light of the early dawn. The expansive white lay unbroken save for what looked like one splash of vivid scarlet.

Nancy Cardell lay motionless on the snow. She was clad in scarlet silk pajamas, her small feet were bare, her arms were spread wide. Her head was turned aside and hidden by the mass of her clustering black hair. Deadly still she lay, and from her left side rose up the hilt of a dagger, whilst on the snow there was an ever-widening patch of crimson.

Poirot went out into the snow. He did not go to where the girl's body lay, but kept to the path. Two sets of foot-marks, a man's and a woman's, led to where the tragedy had occurred. The man's foot-prints went away in the opposite direction alone. Poirot stood in the path, stroking his chin reflectively.

Suddenly Oscar Levering burst out of the house.

"Good God!" he cried. "What's this?"

His excitement was a contrast to the other's calm.

"It looks," said Monsieur Poirot thoughtfully, "like murder."

Eric had another violent attack of coughing.

"But we must do something," cried the other. "What shall we do?"

"There is only one thing to be done," said Monsieur Poirot. "Send for the police."

"Oh!" said everybody at once.

Monsieur Poirot looked inquiringly at them.

"Certainly," he said. "It is the only thing to be done. Who will go?"

There was a pause, then Johnnie came forward.

"Rag's over," he declared. "I say, Monsieur Poirot, I hope you won't be too mad with us. It's all a joke, you know — got up between us — just to pull your leg. Nancy's only shamming."

Monsieur Poirot regarded him without visible emotion, save that his eyes twinkled a moment.

"You mock yourselves at me, is

that it?" he inquired placidly.

"I say, I'm awfully sorry really. We shouldn't have done it. Beastly bad taste. I apologize, I really do."

"You need not apologize," said the other in a peculiar voice.

Johnnie turned.

"I say, Nancy, get up!" he cried. "Don't lie there all day."

But the figure on the ground did not move.

"Get up," cried Johnnie again.

Still Nancy did not move, and suddenly a feeling of nameless dread came over the boy. He turned to Poirot.

"What—what's the matter? Why doesn't she get up?"

"Come with me," said Poirot curtly.

He strode over the snow. He had waved the others back, and he was careful not to infringe on the other foot marks. The boy followed him, frightened and unbelieving. Poirot knelt down by the girl, then he signed to Johnnie.

"Feel her hand and pulse."

Wondering, the boy bent down, then started back with a cry. The hand and arm were stiff and cold and no vestige of a pulse was to be found.

"She's dead!" he gasped. "But how? Why?"

Monsieur Poirot passed over the first part of the question.

"Why?" he said musingly. "I wonder." Then, suddenly leaning across the dead girl's body, he unclasped her other hand, which was tightly clenched over something. Both he and the boy uttered an exclamation. In the palm of Nancy's hand was a red stone that winked and flashed forth fire.

"Aha!" cried Monsieur Poirot. Swift as a flash his hand flew to his pocket and came back empty.

"The cracker Ruby," said Johnnie wonderingly. Then, as his companion bent to examine the dagger, and the stained snow, he pointed out: "Surely it can't be blood, Monsieur Poirot. It's paint. It's only paint.

Poirot straightened himself.

"Yes," he said quietly, "you are right. It's only paint."

"Then how—" The boy broke off. Poirot finished the sentence for him.

"How was she killed? That we must find out. Did she eat or drink anything this morning?"

He was retracing his steps to the path where the others waited as he spoke. Johnnie was close behind him.

"She had a cup of tea," said the boy. "Mr. Levering made it for her. He's got a spirit-lamp in his room."

Johnnie's voice was loud and clear. Levering heard the words.

"Always take a spirit-lamp about with me," he declared. "Most handy thing in the world. My sister's been glad enough of it this visit—not liking to worry the servants all the time, you know."

Monsieur Poirot's eyes fell, almost apologetically as it seemed, to Mr. Levering's feet, which were encased in carpet slippers.

"You have changed your boots, I see," he murmured gently.

Levering stared at him.

"But, Monsieur Poirot," cried Jean, what are we to do?"

"There is only one thing to be done, as I said just now, Mademoiselle. Send for the police."

"I'll go," cried Levering. "It won't take me a minute to put on my boots. You people had better not stay out here in the cold."

He disappeared into the house.

"He is so thoughtful, that Monsieur Levering," murmured Poirot softly. "Shall we take his advice?"

"What about waking father—and everybody?"

"No," said Monsieur Poirot sharply. "It is quite unnecessary. Until the police come, nothing must be touched out here; so shall we go inside? To the library? I have a little history to recount to you which may distract your minds from this sad tragedy."

He led the way, and they followed him.

"The story is about a ruby," said Monsieur Poirot, ensconcing himself in a comfortable armchair. "A very celebrated ruby which belonged to a very celebrated man. I will not tell you his name—but he is one of the great ones of the earth. *Eh bien*, this great man, he arrived in London, incognito. And since, though a great man, he was also a young and a foolish man, he became entangled with a pretty young lady. The pretty young lady, she did not care much for the man, but she did care for his possessions—so much so that she disappeared one day with the historic ruby which had belonged to his house for generations. The poor young man, he was in a quandary. He is shortly to be married to a noble Princess and he does not want the scandal. Impossible to go to the police. He comes to me, Hercule Poirot, instead. 'Recover for me my ruby,' he says. *Eh bien*, I know something of this young lady. She has a brother, and between them they have put through many a clever *coup*. I happen to know where they are staying for Christmas. By the kindness of Monsieur Endicott, whom I chance to have met, I, too, become a guest. But when this pretty young lady hears that I am arriving, she is greatly alarmed. She is intelligent, and she knows that I am after the ruby. She must hide it immediately in a safe place; and figure to yourself where she hides it—in a plum-pudding! Yes, you may well say, oh! She is stirring with the rest, you see, and she pops it into a pudding-bowl of aluminium that is different from the others. By a strange chance, that pudding came to be used on Christmas day."

The tragedy forgotten for the moment, they stared at him open-mouthed.

"After that," continued the little man, "she took to her bed." He drew out his watch and looked at it. "The household is astir. Mr. Levering is a long time fetching the police, is he not? I fancy that his sister went with him."

Evelyn rose with a cry, her eyes fixed on Poirot.

"And I also fancy that they will not return. Oscar Levering has been sailing close to the wind for a long time, and this is the end. He and his sister will pursue their activities abroad for a time under a different name. I alternately tempted and frightened him this morning. By casting aside all pretense he could gain possession of the Ruby whilst we were in the house and he was supposed to be fetching the police. But it meant burning his boats. Still, with a case being built up against him for murder, flight seemed clearly indicated."

"Did he kill Nancy?" whispered Jean.

Poirot rose.

"Suppose we visit once more the scene of the crime," he suggested.

He led the way, and they followed him. But a simultaneous gasp broke from their lips as they passed outside the house. No trace of the tragedy remained; the snow was smooth and unbroken.

"Crikey!" said Eric, sinking down on the step. "It wasn't all a dream, was it?"

"Most extraordinary," said Monsieur Poirot. "The mystery of the disappearing body." His eyes twinkled gently.

Jean came up to him in sudden suspicion.

"Monsieur Poirot, you haven't—you aren't—I say, you haven't been spoofing us all the time, have you? Oh, I do believe you have!"

"It is true, my children. I knew about your little plot, you see, and I arranged a little counter-plot of my own. Ah, here is Mademoiselle Nancy—and none the worse, I hope, after her magnificent acting of the comedy."

It was indeed Nancy Cardell in the flesh, her eyes shining and her whole person exuberant with health and vigor.

"You have not caught cold? You drink the *tisane* I sent to your room?" demanded Poirot accusingly.

"I took one sip and that was enough. I'm all right. Did I do it well, Monsieur Poirot? Oh, my arm hurts after that tourniquet!"

"You were splendid, *petite*. But shall we explain to the others? They are still in the fog, I perceive. See you, *mes enfants*, I went to Mademoiselle Nancy, told her that I knew all about your little *complot*, and asked her if she would act a part for me. She did it very cleverly. She induced Mr. Levering to make her a cup of tea, and also managed that he should be the one chosen to leave footprints on the snow. So when the time came, and he thought that by some fatality she was really dead, I had all the materials to frighten him with. What happened after we went into the house, Mademoiselle?"

"He came down with his sister, snatched the ruby out of my hand,

and off they went post-haste."

"But I say, Monsieur Poirot, what about the ruby?" cried Eric. "Do you mean to say you've let them have that?"

Poirot's face fell, as he faced a circle of accusing eyes.

"I shall recover it yet," he said feebly; but he perceived that he had gone down in their estimation.

"Well, I do think!" began Johnnie. "To let them get away with the ruby—"

But Jean was sharper.

"He's spoofing us again!" she cried. "You are, aren't you?"

"Feel in my left-hand pocket, Mademoiselle."

Jean thrust in an eager hand, and drew it out again with a squeal of triumph. She held aloft the great ruby in its crimson splendor.

"You see," explained Poirot, "the other was a paste replica I brought with me from London."

"Isn't he clever?" demanded Jean ecstatically.

"There's one thing you haven't told us," said Johnnie suddenly. "How did you know about the rag? Did Nancy tell you?"

Poirot shook his head.

"Then how did you know?"

"It is my business to know things," said Monsieur Poirot, smiling a little as he watched Evelyn Haworth and Roger Endicott walking down the path together.

"Yes; but do tell us. Oh, do, please! *Dear* Monsieur Poirot, please tell us!"

He was surrounded by a circle of flushed, eager faces.

"You really wish that I should solve for you this mystery?"

"*Yes.*"

"I do not think I can."

"Why not?"

"*Ma foi*, you will be so disappointed."

"Oh, do tell us! How *did* you know?"

"Well, you see, I was in the library—"

"Yes?"

"And you are discussing your plans just outside—and the library window was open."

"Is that all?" said Eric in disgust. "How simple!"

"Is it not?" said Monsieur Poirot, smiling.

"At all events, we know everything now," said Jean in a satisfied voice.

"Do we?" muttered Monsieur Poirot to himself, as he went into the house. "*I* do not—I, whose business it is to know things."

And, for perhaps the twentieth time, he drew from his pocket a rather dirty piece of paper.

"Don't eat any plum-pudding—"

Monsieur Poirot shook his head in perplexity. At the same moment he became aware of a peculiar gasping sound very near his feet. He looked down and perceived a small creature in a print dress. In her left hand was a dustpan, and in the right a brush.

"And who may you be, *mon enfant?*" enquired Monsieur Poirot.

"Annie 'Icks, please, Sir. Between-maid."

Monsieur Poirot had an inspiration. He handed her the letter.

"Did you write that, Annie?"

"I didn't mean any 'arm, Sir."

He smiled at her.

"Of course you didn't. Suppose you tell me all about it?"

"It was them two, Sir — Mr. Levering and his sister. None of us can abide 'em; and she wasn't ill a bit — we could all tell that. So I thought something queer was going on, and I'll tell you straight, Sir, I listened at the door, and I heard him say as plain as plain, 'this fellow Poirot must be got out of the way as soon as possible.' And then he says to 'er, meaning-like, 'where did you put it?' And she answers, 'in the pudding.' And so I saw they meant to poison you in the Christmas pudding, and I didn't know what to do. Cook wouldn't listen to the likes of me. And then I thought of writing a warning, and I put it in the 'all where Mr. Graves would be sure to see it and take it to you."

Annie paused breathless. Poirot surveyed her greatly for some minutes.

"You read too many novelettes, Annie," he said at last. "But you have the good heart, and a certain amount of intelligence. When I return to London I will send you an excellent book upon *le ménage*, also the lives of the Saints, and a work upon the economic position of woman."

Leaving Annie gasping anew, he turned and crossed the hall. He had meant to go into the library, but through the open door he saw a dark head and a fair one very close together, and he paused where he stood.

Suddenly a pair of arms slipped around his neck.

"If you *will* stand just under the mistletoe!" said Jean.

"Me too," said Nancy.

Monsieur Poirot enjoyed it all — he enjoyed it very much indeed.

# THE LEMESURIER INHERITANCE.

"The Lemesurier Inheritance" was first published in *The Sketch* on December 18, 1923.

## I.

In company with Poirot, I have investigated many strange cases, but none, I think, to compare with that extraordinary series of events which held our interest over a period of many years, and which culminated in the ultimate problem brought to Poirot to solve.

Our attention was first drawn to the family history of the Lemesuriers one evening during the war. Poirot and I had but recently come together again, renewing the old days of our acquaintanceship in Belgium. He had been handling some little matter for the War Office—disposing of it to their entire satisfaction; and we had been dining at the Carlton with a Brass Hat who paid Poirot heavy compliments in the intervals of the meal. The Brass Hat had to rush away to keep an appointment with someone, and we finished our coffee in a leisurely fashion before following his example.

As we were leaving the room, I was hailed by a voice which struck a familiar note, and turned to see Captain Vincent Lemesurier, a young fellow whom I had known in France. He was with an older man whose likeness to him proclaimed him to be of the same family. Such proved to be the case, and he was introduced to us as Mr. Hugo Lemesurier, uncle of my young friend.

I did not really know Captain Lemesurier at all intimately, but he was a pleasant young fellow, somewhat dreamy in manner, and I remembered hearing that he belonged to an old and exclusive family with a property in Northumberland which dated from before the Reformation. Poirot and I were not in a hurry, and at the younger man's invitation, we sat down at the table with our two newfound friends, and chattered pleasantly enough on various matters. The elder Lemesurier was a man of about forty, with a touch of the scholar in his stooping shoulders; he was engaged at the moment upon some chemical research work for the Government, it appeared.

Our conversation was interrupted by a tall dark young man who strode up to the table, evidently labouring under some agitation of mind.

"Thank goodness I've found you both!" he exclaimed.

"What's the matter, Roger?"

"Your guv'nor, Vincent. Bad fall. Young horse..."The rest trailed off, as he drew the other aside.

In a few minutes our two friends had hurriedly taken leave of us. Vincent Lemesurier's father had had a serious accident while trying a young horse, and was not expected to live until morning. Vincent had gone deadly white, and appeared almost stunned by the news. In a way, I was surprised — for from the few words he had let fall on the subject while in France, I had gathered that he and his father were not on particularly friendly terms, and so his display of filial feeling now rather astonished me.

The dark young man, who had been introduced to us as a cousin, Mr. Roger Lemesurier, remained behind, and we three strolled out together.

"Rather a curious business, this," observed the young man. "It would interest Monsieur Poirot, perhaps. I've heard of you, you know, Monsieur Poirot — from Higginson." (Higginson was our Brass Hat friend.) "He says you're a whale on psychology."

"I study the psychology, yes," admitted my friend cautiously.

"Did you see my cousin's face? He was absolutely bowled over, wasn't he? Do you know why? A good old—fashioned family curse! Would you care to hear about it?"

"It would be most kind of you to recount it to me."

Roger Lemesurier looked at his watch.

"Lots of time. I'm meeting them at King's Cross. Well, Monsieur Poirot, the Lemesuriers are an old family. Way back in medieval times, a Lemesurier became suspicious of his wife. He found the lady in a compromising situation. She swore that she was innocent, but old Baron Hugo didn't listen. She had one child, a son — and he swore that the boy was no child of his and should never inherit. I forget what he did — some pleasing medieval fancy like walling up the mother and son alive; anyway, he killed them both, and she died protesting her innocence and solemnly cursing the Lemesuriers forever. No first-born son of a Lemesurier should ever inherit — so the curse ran. Well, time passed, and the lady's innocence was established beyond doubt. I believe that Hugo wore a hair shirt and ended up his days on his knees in a monk's cell. But the curious thing is that from that day to this, no first — born son ever has succeeded to the estate. It's gone to brothers, to nephews, to second sons — never to the eldest son. Vincent's father was the second of five sons, the eldest of whom died in infancy. Of course, all through the war, Vincent has been convinced that whoever else was doomed, he certainly was. But strangely enough, his two younger brothers have been killed, and he himself has remained unscathed."

"An interesting family history," said Poirot thoughtfully. "But now his father is dying, and he, as the eldest son, succeeds?"

"Exactly. A curse has gone rusty — unable to stand the strain of modern life."

Poirot shook his head, as though deprecating the other's jesting tone. Roger Lemesurier looked at his watch again, and declared that he must be off.

The sequel to the story came on the morrow, when we learned of the tragic death of Captain Vincent Lemesurier. He had been travelling north by the Scotch mail-train, and during the night must have opened the door of the compartment and jumped out on the line. The shock of his father's accident coming on top of the shell-shock was deemed to have caused temporary mental aberration. The curious superstition prevalent in the Lemesurier family was mentioned, in connection with the new heir, his father's brother, Ronald Lemesurier, whose only son had died on the Somme.

I suppose our accidental meeting with young Vincent on the last evening of his life quickened our interest in anything that pertained to the Lemesurier family, for we noted with some interest two years later the death of Ronald Lemesurier, who had been a confirmed invalid at the time of his succession to the family estates. His brother John succeeded him, a hale, hearty man with a boy at Eton.

Certainly an evil destiny overshadowed the Lemesuriers. On his very next holiday the boy managed to shoot himself fatally. His father's death, which occurred quite suddenly after being stung by a wasp, gave the estate over to the youngest brother of the five — Hugo, whom we remembered meeting on the fatal night at the Carlton.

Beyond commenting on the extraordinary series of misfortunes which befell the Lemesuriers, we had taken no personal interest in the matter, but the time was now close at hand when we were to take a more active part.

II.

One morning "Mrs. Lemesurier" was announced. She was a tall, active woman, possibly about thirty years of age, who conveyed by her demeanour a great deal of determination and strong common sense. She spoke with a faint transatlantic accent.

"Monsieur Poirot? I am pleased to meet you. My husband, Hugo Lemesurier, met you once many years ago, but you will hardly remember the fact."

"I recollect it perfectly, madame. It was at the Carlton."

"That's quite wonderful of you. Monsieur Poirot, I'm very worried."

"What about, Madame?"

"My elder boy — I've two boys, you know. Ronald's eight, and Gerald's six."

"Proceed, madame: why should you be worried about little Ronald?"

"Monsieur Poirot, within the last six months he has had three narrow escapes from death: once from drowning — when we were all down at Cornwall this summer; once when he fell from the nursery window; and once from ptomaine poisoning."

Perhaps Poirot's face expressed rather too eloquently what he thought, for Mrs. Lemesurier hurried on with hardly a moment's pause: "Of course I know you think I'm just a silly fool of a woman, making mountains out of molehills."

"No, indeed, madame. Any mother might be excused for being upset at such occurrences, but I hardly see where I can be of any assistance to you. I am not *le bon Dieu* to control the waves; for the nursery window I should suggest some iron bars; and for the food — what can equal a mother's care?"

"But why should these things happen to Ronald and not to Gerald?"

"The chance, madame — *le hasard!*"

"You think so?"

"What do you think, madame — you and your husband?"

A shadow crossed Mrs. Lemesurier's face.

"It's no good going to Hugo — he won't listen. As perhaps you may have heard, there's supposed to be a curse on the family — no eldest son can succeed. Hugo believes in it. He's wrapped up in the family history, and he's superstitious to the last degree. When I go to him with my fears, he just says it's the curse, and we can't escape it. But I'm from the States, Monsieur Poirot, and over there we don't believe much in curses.

We like them as belonging to a real high-toned old family—it gives a sort of cachet, don't you know. I was just a musical comedy actress in a small part when Hugo met me—and I thought his family curse was just too lovely for words. That kind of thing's all right for telling round the fire on a winter's evening, but when it comes to one's own children—I just adore my children, Monsieur Poirot. I'd do anything for them."

"So you decline to believe in the family legend, madame?"

"Can a legend saw through an ivy stem?"

"What is that you are saying, madame?" cried Poirot, an expression of great astonishment on his face.

"I said, can a legend—or a ghost, if you like to call it that—saw through an ivy stem? I'm not saying anything about Cornwall. Any boy might go out too far and get into difficulties—though Ronald could swim when he was four years old. But the ivy's different. Both the boys were very naughty. They'd discovered they could climb up and down by the ivy. They were always doing it. One day—Gerald was away at the time—Ronald did it once too often, and the ivy gave way and he fell. Fortunately he didn't damage himself seriously. But I went out and examined the ivy: it was cut through, Monsieur Poirot—deliberately cut through."

"It is very serious what you are telling me there, madame. You say your younger boy was away from home at the moment?"

"Yes."

"And at the time of the ptomaine poisoning, was he still away?"

"No, they were both there."

"Curious," murmured Poirot. "Now, madame, who are the inmates of your establishment?"

"Miss Saunders, the children's governess, and John Gardiner, my husband's secretary—"

Mrs. Lemesurier paused, as though slightly embarrassed.

"And who else, madame?"

"Major Roger Lemesurier, whom you also met on that night, I believe, stays with us a good deal."

"Ah, yes—he is a cousin, is he not?"

"A distant cousin. He does not belong to our branch of the family. Still, I suppose now he is my husband's nearest relative. He is a dear fellow, and we are all very fond of him. The boys are devoted to him."

"It was not he who taught them to climb up the ivy?"

"It might have been. He incites them to mischief often enough."

"Madame, I apologize for what I said to you earlier. The danger is real, and I believe that I can be of assistance. I propose that you should invite us both to stay with you. Your husband will not object?"

"Oh no. But he will believe it to be all of no use. It makes me furious the way he just sits around and expects the boy to die."

"Calm yourself, madame. Let us

make our arrangements methodically."

### III.

Our arrangements were duly made, and the following day saw us flying northward. Poirot was sunk in a reverie. He came out of it, to remark abruptly: "It was from a train such as this that Vincent Lemesurier fell?"

He put a slight accent on the "fell."

"You don't suspect foul play there, surely?" I asked.

"Has it struck you, Hastings, that some of the Lemesurier deaths were, shall we say, capable of being arranged? Take that of Vincent, for instance. Then the Eton boy—an accident with a gun is always ambiguous. Supposing this child had fallen from the nursery window and been dashed to death—what more natural and unsuspicious? But why only the one child, Hastings? Who profits by the death of the elder child? His younger brother, a child of seven? Absurd!"

"They mean to do away with the other later," I suggested, though with the vaguest ideas as to who "they" were.

Poirot shook his head as though dissatisfied.

"Ptomaine poisoning," he mused. "Atropine will produce much the same symptoms. Yes, there is need for our presence."

Mrs. Lemesurier welcomed us enthusiastically. Then she took us to her husband's study and left us with him. He had changed a good deal since I saw him last. His shoulders stooped more than ever, and his face had a curious pale grey tinge. He listened while Poirot explained our presence in the house.

"How exactly like Sadie's practical common sense!" he said at last. "Remain by all means, Monsieur Poirot, and I thank you for coming; but—what is written, is written. The way of the transgressor is hard. We Lemesuriers know—none of us can escape the doom."

Poirot mentioned the sawn-through ivy, but Hugo seemed very little impressed.

"Doubtless some careless gardener—yes, yes, there may be an instrument, but the purpose behind is plain; and I will tell you this, Monsieur Poirot, it cannot be long delayed."

Poirot looked at him attentively. "Why do you say that?"

"Because I myself am doomed. I went to a doctor last year. I am suffering from an incurable disease—the end cannot be much longer delayed; but before I die, Ronald will be taken. Gerald will inherit."

"And if anything were to happen to your second son also?"

"Nothing will happen to him; he is not threatened."

"But if it did?" persisted Poirot.

"My cousin Roger is the next heir."

We were interrupted. A tall man with a good figure and crispy curling auburn hair entered with a sheaf of papers.

"Never mind about those now, Gardiner," said Hugo Lemesurier, then he added: "My secretary, Mr. Gardiner."

The secretary bowed, uttered a few pleasant words and then went out. In spite of his good looks, there was something repellent about the man. I said so to Poirot shortly afterward when we were walking round the beautiful old grounds together, and rather to my surprise, he agreed.

"Yes, yes, Hastings, you are right. I do not like him. He is too good-looking. He would be one for the soft job always. Ah, here are the children."

Mrs. Lemesurier was advancing towards us, her two children beside her. They were fine-looking boys, the younger dark like his mother, the elder with auburn curls. They shook hands prettily enough, and were soon absolutely devoted to Poirot. We were next introduced to Miss Saunders, a nondescript female, who completed the party.

## IV.

For some days we had a pleasant, easy existence — ever vigilant, but without result. The boys led a happy normal life and nothing seemed to be amiss. On the fourth day after our arrival Major Roger Lemesurier came down to stay. He was little changed, still carefree and debonair as of old, with the same habit of treating all things lightly. He was evidently a great favourite with the boys, who greeted his arrival with shrieks of delight and immediately dragged him off to play wild Indians in the garden. I noticed that Poirot followed them unobtrusively.

## V.

On the following day we were all invited to tea, boys included, with Lady Claygate, whose place adjoined that of the Lemesuriers. Mrs. Lemesurier suggested that we also should come, but seemed rather relieved when Poirot refused and declared he would much prefer to remain at home.

Once everyone had started, Poirot got to work. He reminded me of an intelligent terrier. I believe that there was no corner of the house that he left unsearched; yet it was all done so quietly and methodically that no attention was directed to his movements. Clearly, at the end, he remained unsatisfied. We had tea on the terrace with Miss Saunders, who had not been included in the party.

"The boys will enjoy it," she murmured in her faded way, "though I hope they will behave nicely, an d not damage the flower beds, or go near the bees —"

Poirot paused in the very act of

drinking. He looked like a man who has seen a ghost.

"Bees?" he demanded in a voice of thunder.

"Yes, Monsieur Poirot, bees. Three hives. Lady Claygate is very proud of her bees—"

"Bees?" cried Poirot again. Then he sprang from the table and walked up and down the terrace with his hands to his head. I could not imagine why the little man should be so agitated at the mere mention of bees.

At that moment we heard the car returning. Poirot was on the doorstep as the party alighted.

"Ronald's been stung," cried Gerald excitedly.

"It's nothing," said Mrs. Lemesurier. "It hasn't even swollen. We put ammonia on it."

"Let me see, my little man," said Poirot. "Where was it?"

"Here, on the side of my neck," said Ronald importantly. "But it doesn't hurt. Father said: 'Keep still—there's a bee on you.' And I kept still, and he took it off, but it stung me first, though it didn't really hurt, only like a pin, and I didn't cry, because I'm so big and going to school next year."

Poirot examined the child's neck, then drew away again. He took me by the arm and murmured:

"Tonight, *mon ami*, tonight we have a little affair on! Say nothing—to anyone."

He refused to be more communicative, and I went through the evening devoured by curiosity. He retired early and I followed his example. As we went upstairs, he caught me by the arm and delivered his instructions:

"Do not undress. Wait a sufficient time, extinguish your light and join me here."

I obeyed, and found him waiting for me when the time came. He enjoined silence on me with a gesture, and we crept quietly along the nursery wing. Ronald occupied a small room of his own. We entered it and took up our position in the darkest corner. The child's breathing sounded heavy and undisturbed.

"Surely he is sleeping very heavily?" I whispered.

Poirot nodded.

"Drugged," he murmured.

"Why?"

"So that he should not cry out at—"

"At what?" I asked, as Poirot paused.

"At the prick of the hypodermic needle, *mon ami*! Hush, let us speak no more—not that I expect anything to happen for some time."

## VI.

But in this Poirot was wrong. Hardly ten minutes had elapsed before the door opened softly, and someone entered the room. I heard a sound of quick hurried breathing. Footsteps moved to the bed, and then there was a sudden click. The light of a little electric lantern fell on the sleeping child — the holder of it was still invisible in the shadow. The figure laid down the lantern. With the right hand it brought forth a syringe; with the left it touched the boy's neck —

Poirot and I sprang at the same minute. The lantern rolled to the floor, and we struggled with the intruder in the dark. His strength was extraordinary. At last we overcame him.

"The light, Hastings, I must see his face — though I fear I know only too well whose face it will be."

So did I, I thought as I groped for the lantern. For a moment I had suspected the secretary, egged on by my secret dislike of the man, but I felt assured by now that the man who stood to gain by the death of his two childish cousins was the monster we were tracking.

My foot struck against the lantern. I picked it up and switched on the light. It shone full on the face of — Hugo Lemesurier, the boy's father!

The lantern almost dropped from my hand. "Impossible," I murmured hoarsely. "Impossible!"

## VII.

Lemesurier was unconscious. Poirot and I between us carried him to his room and laid him on the bed. Poirot bent and gently extricated something from his right hand. He showed it to me. It was a hypodermic syringe. I shuddered.

"What is in it? Poison?"

"Formic acid, I fancy."

"Formic acid?"

"Yes. Probably obtained by distilling ants. He was a chemist, you remember. Death would have been attributed to the bee sting."

"My God," I muttered. "His own son! And you expected this?"

Poirot nodded gravely.

"Yes. He is insane, of course. I imagine that the family history has become a mania with him. His intense longing to succeed to the estate led him to commit the long series of crimes. Possibly the idea occurred to him first when travelling north that night with Vincent. He couldn't bear the prediction to be falsified. Ronald's son was already dead, and Ronald himself was a dying man — they are a weakly lot. He arranged the accident to the gun, and — which I did not suspect until now — contrived the death of his brother John by this same method of injecting formic acid into the jugular vein. His ambition was realized then, and he became the master of the family acres. But his triumph was short-lived — he found that he was suffering from an incurable disease. And he had the madman's fixed idea — the eldest son of a Lemesurier could not inherit. I suspect that the bathing accident was due to him — he encouraged the child to go out too far. That failing, he sawed through the ivy, and afterwards poisoned the child's food."

"Diabolical!" I murmured with a shiver. "And so cleverly planned!"

"Yes, *mon ami*, there is nothing more amazing than the extraordinary sanity of the insane! Unless it is the extraordinary eccentricity of the sane! I imagine that it is only lately that he has completely gone over the borderline, there was method in his madness to begin with."

"And to think that I suspected Roger — that splendid fellow."

"It was the natural assumption, *mon ami*. We knew that he also travelled north with Vincent that night. We knew, too, that he was the next heir after Hugo and Hugo's children. But our assumption was not borne out by the facts. The ivy was sawn through when only little Ronald was at home — but it would be to Roger's interest that both children should perish. In the same way, it was only Ronald's food that was poisoned. And today when they came home and I found that there was only his father's word for it that Ronald had been stung, I remembered the other death from a wasp sting — and I knew!"

## VIII.

Hugo Lemesurier died a few months later in the private asylum to which he was removed. His widow was remarried a year later to Mr. John Gardiner, the auburn haired secretary. Ronald inherited the broad acres of his father, and continues to flourish.

"Well, well," I remarked to Poirot. "Another illusion gone. You have disposed very successfully of the curse of the Lemesuriers."

"I wonder," said Poirot very thoughtfully. "I wonder very much indeed."

"What do you mean?"

"*Mon ami*, I will answer you with one significant word — red!"

"Blood?" I queried, dropping my voice to an awe-stricken whisper.

"Always you have the imagination melodramatic, Hastings! I refer to something much more prosaic — the colour of little Ronald Lemesurier's hair."

## With a Big Four of Beasties – Poirot's Creator.

**WITH THE RHODESIAN "ZOO" OF HER SUNNINGDALE HOME: MRS. AGATHA CHRISTIE, THE BRILLIANT WRITER OF DETECTIVE STORIES, AT SCOTSWOOD.**

"Sketch" readers, who are well acquainted with Hercule Poirot and the Big Four of crime, will be interested to see these portraits of his creator. Mrs. Christie and her husband, Colonel Archibald Christie, C.M.G., D.S.O., now live at Sunningdale, where she keeps her collection of wooden beasties brought from Rhodesia. Though Poirot's chase of the Big Four will shortly come to a conclusion, a new series of stories by the same writer will be published in the "Sketch" in the near future.

PHOTOGRAPHS BY STAGE PHOTO. CO., SPECIALLY TAKEN FOR "THE SKETCH."

*This photo spread on Agatha Christie was published in* The Sketch *in early 1924.*

# THE MAN WHO WAS NUMBER FOUR.

---

*The third series of short stories,*
*comprising a serial novel, published in*
**The Sketch: A Journal of Art and Actuality**
*from January to March 1924.*

# I.

# THE UNEXPECTED GUEST.

"The Unexpected Guest" was first published in *The Sketch* on January 2, 1924.

England once more! An indescribable wave of emotion swept over me as I watched the white chalk cliffs of Dover coming nearer and nearer. It was a year and a half since I had left England to try my fortunes on a ranch in the Argentine. I had prospered there, and my wife and I both enjoyed the free-and-easy life of the South American Continent. Nevertheless, it was with a lump in my throat that I approached the shores of my native land once more.

I had landed in France two days before, transacted some necessary business, and was now en route for London. I should be there some months—time enough to look up old friends, and one old friend in particular. A little man with an egg-shaped head and green eyes—Hercule Poirot! I proposed to take him completely by surprise. My last letter from the Argentine had given no hint of my intended voyage—indeed, that had been decided upon hurriedly as a result of certain business complications—and I spent many amused moments picturing to myself his delight and stupefaction on beholding me.

He, I knew, was not likely to be

far from his headquarters. He aimed more and more, as time went on, at being a "consulting detective"—as much a specialist as a Harley Street physician. No, there was little fear of finding Hercule Poirot far afield.

On arrival in London, I deposited my luggage at a hotel and drove straight on to the old address. What poignant memories it brought back to me! I hardly waited to greet my old landlady, but hurried up the stairs two at a time and rapped on Poirot's door.

"Enter then," cried a familiar voice from within. I strode in. Poirot stood facing me. In his arms he carried a small valise, which he dropped with a crash on beholding me:

"*Mon ami* Hastings!" he cried. "*Mon ami* Hastings!"

And, rushing forwards, he enveloped me in a capacious embrace.

Our conversation was incoherent and inconsequent. Ejaculations, eager questions, incomplete answers, messages from my wife, explanations as to my journey, were all jumbled up together.

"I suppose there is someone in my old rooms?" I asked at last, when we had calmed down somewhat. "I'd love to put up here again with you."

Poirot's face changed with startling suddenness.

"*Mon dieu!* But what a chance *épouvantable*. Regard around you, my friend."

For the first time I took note of my surroundings. Against the wall stood a vast ark of a trunk of prehistoric design. Near to it were placed a number of suit-cases arranged neatly in order of size from large to small. The inference was unmistakable.

"You are going away?"

"Yes."

"Where to?"

"South America."

"What?"

"Yes, it is a droll farce is it not? It is to Rio I go, and every day I say to myself I will write nothing in my letters—but oh! The surprise of the good Hastings when he beholds me!"

"But—but when are you going?"

Poirot looked at his watch.

"In an hour's time."

"I thought you always said nothing would induce you to make a long sea voyage?"

Poirot closed his eyes and shuddered.

"Speak not of it to me, my friend. My doctor, he assures me that one dies not of it—and it is for the one time only: you understand that never—never shall I return."

He pushed me into a chair.

"Come, I will tell you how it all came about. Do you know who is the richest man in the world? Richer even than Rockefeller? Abe Ryland."

"The American Soap King?"

"Precisely. One of his secretaries approached me. There is some very considerable, as you would call it, hocus-pocus going on in connection with a big company in Rio. He wished me to investigate matters on the spot. I refused. I told him that if the facts were laid before me, I would give him my expert opinion. But that he professed himself unable to do. I was to be put in possession of the facts only on my arrival out there. Normally that would have closed the matter. To dictate to Hercule Poirot is sheer impertinence. But the sum offered was so stupendous that for the first and last time in my life I was tempted by mere money. It was a competence — a fortune! And there was a second attraction — you, my friend. For this last year and a half I have been a very lonely old man. I thought to myself, why not? I am beginning to weary of this unending solving of foolish problems. I have achieved sufficient fame. Let me take this money and settle down somewhere near my old friend."

I was quite affected by this token of Poirot's regard.

"So I accepted," he continued, "and in an hour's time I must leave to catch the boat train. One of life's little ironies, is it not? But I will admit to you, Hastings, that had not the money offered been so big, I might have hesitated, for just lately I have begun a little investigation of my own. Tell me, what is commonly meant by the phrase, 'The Big Four'?"

"I suppose it had its origin at the Versailles conference, and then there is the famous 'Big Four' in the film world, and the term is used by hosts of smaller fry."

"I see," said Poirot thoughtfully. "I have come across the phrase, you understand, under certain circumstances where none of those explanations would apply. It seems to refer to a gang of international criminals or something of that kind; only —"

"Only what?" I asked as he hesitated.

"Only that I fancy that it is something on a large scale. Just a little idea of mine, nothing more. But I must complete my packing. The time advances."

"Don't go," I urged. "Cancel your passage and come out on the same boat with me."

Poirot drew himself up and glanced at me reproachfully.

"Ah, it is that you do not understand! I have passed my word, you comprehend — the word of Hercule Poirot. Nothing but a matter of life and death could detain me now."

"And that's not likely to occur," I murmured ruefully. "Unless at the eleventh hour 'the door opens and the unexpected guest comes in.'"

I quoted the old saw with a slight laugh and then in the pause that succeeded it we both started as a sound came from the inner room.

"What's that?" I cried.

"*Ma foi!*" retorted Poirot. "It sounds very like your 'unexpected guest' in my bed-room."

"But how can anyone be in there? There is no door except into this room."

"Your memory is excellent, Hastings. Now for the deductions."

"The window! But it's a burglar then? He must have had a stiff climb of it—I should say it was almost impossible."

I had risen to my feet and was striding in the direction of the door when the sound of a fumbling at the handle from the other side arrested me.

The door swung slowly open. Framed in the doorway stood a man. He was coated from head to foot with dust and mud; his face was thin and emaciated. He stared at us for a moment then swayed and fell. Poirot hurried to his side, then he looked up and spoke to me.

"Brandy—quickly."

I dashed some brandy into a glass and brought it. Poirot managed to administer a little, and together we raised him and carried him to the couch. In a few minutes he opened his eyes and looked around him with an almost vacant glance.

"What is it you want, Monsieur?" said Poirot.

The man opened his lips and spoke in a queer, mechanical voice.

"Monsieur Hercule Poirot, 14, Farraway Street."

"Yes, yes; I am he."

The man did not seem to understand, and merely repeated in exactly the same tone—

"Monsieur Hercule Poirot, 14, Farraway Street."

Poirot tried him with several questions. Sometimes the man did not answer at all; sometimes he repeated the same phrase. Poirot made a sign to me to ring up on the telephone.

"Get Dr. Ridgeway to come round."

The doctor was in, luckily; and as his house was only just round the corner, few minutes elapsed before he came bustling in.

"What's all this, eh?"

Poirot gave a brief explanation, and the doctor started examining our strange visitor, who seemed quite unconscious of his presence or ours.

"H'm!" said Dr. Ridgeway, when he had finished. "Curious case."

"Brain fever?" I suggested.

The doctor immediately snorted with contempt.

"Brain fever! Brain fever! No such thing as brain fever. An invention of novelists. No; the man's had a shock of some kind. He's come here under the force of a persistent idea—to find Monsieur Hercule Poirot, 14, Farraway Street—and he repeats those words mechanically without in the least knowing what they mean."

"Aphasia?" I said eagerly.

This suggestion did not cause the doctor to snort quite as violently as my last one had done. He made no answer, but handed the man a sheet of paper and a pencil.

"Let's see what he'll do with that," he remarked.

The man did nothing with it for some moments, then he suddenly began to write feverishly. With equal suddenness he stopped and let both paper and pencil fall to the ground. The doctor picked it up, and shook his head.

"Nothing here. Only the figure 4 scrawled a dozen times, each one bigger than the last. Wants to write 14, Farraway Street, I expect. It's an interesting case — very interesting. Can you possibly keep him here until this afternoon? I'm due at the hospital now, but I'll come back this afternoon and make all arrangements about him. It's too interesting a case to be lost sight of."

I explained Poirot's departure and the fact that I proposed to accompany him to Southampton.

"That's all right. Leave him here. He won't get into mischief. He is suffering from complete exhaustion. Will probably sleep for eight hours on end. I'll have a word with that excellent Mrs. Funnyface of yours and tell her to keep an eye on him."

And Dr. Ridgeway bustled out with his usual celerity. Poirot hastily completed his packing with one eye on the clock.

"The time, it marches with a rapidity unbelievable. Come now, Hastings, you cannot say that I have left you with nothing to do. A most sensational problem. The man from the unknown. Who is he? What is he? Ah, *sapristi*, but I would give two years of my life to have this boat go to-morrow instead of to-day. There is something here very curious — very interesting. But one must have time — time. It may be days — or even months — before he will be able to tell us what he came to tell."

"I'll do my best, Poirot," I assured him. "I'll try and be an efficient substitute."

"Ye-es."

His rejoinder struck me as being a shade doubtful. I picked up the sheet of paper.

"If I were writing a story," I said lightly, "I should weave this in with your latest idiosyncrasy and call it, 'the mystery of The Big Four.'" I tapped the pencilled figures as I spoke.

And then I started, for our invalid, roused suddenly from his stupor, sat up in his chair and said clearly and distinctly:

"Li Chang Yen."

He had the look of a man suddenly awakened from sleep. Poirot made a sign to me not to speak. The man went on. He spoke in a clear, high voice, and something in his enunciation made me feel that he was quoting from some written report or lecture.

"Li Chang Yen may be regarded as representing the brains of The Big Four. He is the controlling and motive force. I have designated him, therefore, as Number One. Number Two is seldom mentioned by name. He is represented by an 'S' with two lines through it — the sign for a dollar; also by two stripes and a star. It may be conjectured, therefore, that he is an American subject, and that he represents the power of wealth. There seems no doubt that Number Three is a woman, and her nationality French. It is possible that she may be one of the sirens of the demimonde but nothing is known definitely. Number Four —"

His voice faltered and broke. Poirot leant forward.

"Yes," he prompted eagerly. "Number Four?"

His eyes were fastened on the man's face. Some overmastering terror seemed to be gaining the day; the features were distorted and twisted.

"*The destroyer*," gasped the man. Then with a final convulsed movement, he fell back in a dead faint.

"*Mon dieu*," whispered Poirot, "I was right then. I was right."

"You think —?"

He interrupted me.

"Carry him on to the bed in my room. I have not a minute to lose if I would catch my train. Not that I want to catch it. Oh, that I could miss it with a clear conscience! But I gave my word. Come, Hastings."

Leaving our mysterious visitor in the charge of Mrs. Pearson, we drove away, and duly caught the train by the skin of our teeth. Poirot was alternately silent and loquacious. He would sit staring out of the window like a man lost in a dream, apparently not hearing a word that I said to him. Then, suddenly reverting to animation, he would shower injunctions and commands upon me, and urge the necessity of constant Marconigrams.

He had a long fit of silence just after we passed Woking. The train, of course, did not stop anywhere until Southampton; but just here it happened to be held up by a signal.

"Ah! *Sacre mille tonnerres!*" cried Poirot suddenly. "But I have been an imbecile. I see clearly at last. It is undoubtedly the blessed saints who stopped the train. Jump, Hastings, but jump, I tell you."

In an instant he had unfastened the carriage door and jumped out on the line.

"Throw out the suit-cases and jump yourself."

I obeyed him. Just in time. As I alighted beside him, the train moved on.

To all my questions and remonstrances Poirot paid no attention whatsoever. Not till we were safely ensconced in a car speeding back to London did he deign to satisfy my curiosity.

"You do not see? No more did I. But I see now. Hastings, *I was being got out of the way*."

"What?"

"Yes. Very cleverly. Both the place and the method were chosen with great knowledge and acumen. They were afraid of me."

"Who were?"

"Those four geniuses who have banded themselves together to work outside the law. A Chinaman, an American, a Frenchwoman, and — another. Pray the good God we arrive back in time, Hastings."

"You think there is danger to our visitor?"

"I am sure of it."

Mrs. Pearson greeted us on arrival. Brushing aside her ecstasies of astonishment on beholding Poirot, we asked for information. It was reassuring. No one had called, and our guest had not made any sign.

With a sigh of relief we went up to the rooms. Poirot crossed the outer one and went through to the inner one. Then he called to me, his voice strangely agitated.

"Hastings, he's dead."

I came running to join him. The man was lying as we had left him, but he was dead, and had been dead some time. I rushed out for a doctor. Ridgeway, I knew, would not have returned yet. I found one almost immediately, and brought him back with me.

"He's dead right enough, poor chap. Tramp you've been befriending, eh?"

"Something of the kind," said Poirot evasively. "What was the cause of death, doctor?"

"Hard to say. Might have been some kind of fit. There are signs of asphyxiation. No gas laid on, is there?"

"No, electric light — nothing else."

"And both windows wide open, too. Been dead about two hours, I should say. You will notify the proper people, won't you?"

He took his departure. Poirot did some necessary telephoning. Finally somewhat to my surprise, he rang up our old friend inspector Japp, and asked him if he could possibly come round.

No sooner were these proceedings completed than Mrs. Pearson appeared, her eyes as round as saucers.

"There is a man here from 'Anwell — from the 'sylum. Did you ever? Shall I show him up?"

We signified assent, and a big, burly man in uniform was ushered in.

"Morning, gentlemen," he said cheerily. "I've got reason to believe you've got one of my birds here. Escaped last night, he did."

"He was here," said Poirot quietly.

"Not got away again, has he?" asked the keeper, with some concern.

"He is dead."

The man looked more relieved than otherwise.

"You don't say so. Well, I daresay it's best for all parties."

"Was he — dangerous?"

"'Omicidal, d'you mean? Oh, no. 'Armless enough. Persecution mania very acute. Full of secret societies from China that had got him shut up. They're all the same."

I shuddered.

"How long had he been — shut up?" asked Poirot.

"A matter of two years now."

"I see," said Poirot quietly. "It never occurred to anybody that he might — be sane?"

The keeper permitted himself to laugh.

"If he was sane, what would he be doing in a lunatic asylum? They all say they're sane, you know."

Poirot said no more. He took the man in to see the body. He identified it immediately—"that's 'im, right enough"—and then went off to "make arrangements under the circumstances," as he put it.

Japp arrived almost immediately after his departure.

"Here I am, Moosior Poirot. What can I do for you? Thought you were off to the coral strands of somewhere or other to-day?"

"My good Japp, I want to know if you have ever seen this man before."

He led Japp into the bed-room. The inspector stared down at the figure on the bed with a puzzled face.

"Let me see now—he seems sort of familiar—and I pride myself on my memory, too. Why, God bless my soul, it's Mayerling!"

"And who is—or was—Mayerling?"

"Secret Service chap—not one of our people. Went to Russia five years ago. Never heard of again. Always thought the Bolshies had done him in."

"It all fits in," said Poirot, when Japp had taken his leave, "except for the fact that he seems to have died a natural death."

He stood looking down on the motionless figure with a dissatisfied frown. A puff of wind set the window curtains flying out, and he looked up sharply.

"I suppose you opened the windows when you laid him down on the bed, Hastings?"

"No, I didn't," I replied. "As far as I remember, they were shut."

Poirot lifted his head suddenly.

"Shut—and now they are open. What can that mean?"

"Somebody came in that way," I suggested.

"Possibly, since we know that this poor fellow managed it; but that is not the point. Why both windows?"

He hurried into the other room.

"The sitting-room window is open, too. That also we left shut. Ah!"

He bent over the dead man, examining the corners of the mouth minutely. Then he looked up suddenly.

"He has been gagged, Hastings. Gagged and then poisoned."

"Good heavens!" I exclaimed, shocked. "I suppose we shall find out all about it from the postmortem."

"We shall find out nothing. He was killed by inhaling strong prussic acid. It was jammed right under his nose. Then the murderer went out again, first opening all the windows. Hydrocyanic acid is exceedingly volatile, but it has a pronounced smell of bitter almonds. With no trace of the smell to guide them, and no suspicion of foul play, death would be put down to some natural cause by the doctors. So this man was in the Secret Service, Hastings.

And five years ago he disappeared in Russia."

"The last two years he's been in the asylum," I said. "But what of the three years before that?

Poirot shook his head, and then caught my arm.

"The clock, Hastings, look at the clock."

I followed his gaze to the mantelpiece. The clock had stopped at 4 o'clock.

"*Mon ami*, someone has tampered with it. It had still three days to run. It is an eight-day clock, you comprehend?"

"But what should they want to do that for? Some idea of a false sense by making the crime appear to have taken place at four o'clock?"

"No, no; rearrange your ideas, *mon ami*. Exercise your little grey cells. You are Mayerling. You hear something, perhaps — and you know well enough that your doom is sealed. You have just time to leave a sign. Four o'clock, Hastings. Number Four, *the destroyer*. Ah! an idea!"

He rushed into the other room and seized the telephone. He asked for Hanwell. A few minutes later he turned to me and hung up the receiver.

"You heard, Hastings? There has been no escape."

"But the man who came — the keeper?"

"I wonder — I very much wonder."

"You mean —?"

"Number Four — *the destroyer*."

"But we shall know him again anywhere, that's one thing. He was a man of very pronounced personality."

"Was he, *mon ami*? I think not. He was burly and bluff, and red-faced, with a thick moustache and a hoarse voice. He will be none of those things by this time; and for the rest, he has nondescript eyes, nondescript ears, and a perfect set of false teeth. Identification is not such an easy matter as you seem to think. Next time —"

"You think there will be a next time?" I interrupted.

Poirot's face grew very grave.

"It is a duel to the death, *mon ami*. You and I on the one side, The Big Four on the other. They have won the first trick; but they have failed in their plan to get me out of the way, and in the future they have to reckon with Hercule Poirot!"

# II.

## THE ADVENTURE OF THE DARTMOOR BUNGALOW.

"The Adventure of the Dartmoor Bungalow" was first published in *The Sketch* on January 9, 1924.

"But where are we going?" I inquired for about the tenth time.

Poirot loves being mysterious. He will never part with a piece of information until the last possible moment. In this instance, having taken successively a 'bus and two trains, and arrived in the neighbourhood of one of London's most depressing southern suburbs, he consented at last to explain matters.

"We go, Hastings, to see the one man in England who knows most of the underground life of China."

"Indeed? Who is he?"

"A man you have never heard of—a Mr. John Ingles. To all intents and purposes, he is a retired civil servant of mediocre intellect with a house full of Chinese curios with which he bores his friends and acquaintances. Nevertheless, I am assured by those who should know that the only man capable of giving me the information I seek is the same John Ingles."

A few moments more saw us ascending the steps of The Laurels, as Mr. Ingles' residence was called. Personally I did not notice a laurel bush of any kind, so deduced that it had been named according to the usual obscure nomenclature of the suburbs.

We were admitted by an impassive-faced Chinese servant and ushered into the presence of his master. Mr. Ingles was a squarely built man, somewhat yellow of countenance, with deep-set eyes that were oddly reflective in character. He rose to greet us, setting aside an open letter which he had held in his hand. He referred to it after his greeting.

"Sit down, won't you? Halsey tells me that you want some information and that I may be useful to you in the matter."

"That is so, Monsieur. I ask of you if you have any information of a man called Li Chang Yen."

"That's rum — very rum indeed. How did you come to hear about the man?"

"You know him, then?"

"I've met him once. And I know something of him — not quite as much as I should like to. But it surprises me that anyone else in England should even have heard of him. He's a great man in his way — Mandarin class and all that, you know — but that's not the crux of the matter. There is good reason to suppose that he is the man behind it all."

"Behind what?"

"Everything. The Republic, the various upheavals of China, all this last unrest. It's even suspected that he was at the bottom of the Russian trouble. Wherever you find the hand of China, there you will find Li Chang Yen behind it. What's his game? Nobody knows — but you can be sure of this, it's deep, and it's Oriental. That man is the controlling brain of the East to-day. We don't understand the East — we never shall; but Li Chang Yen is its moving spirit. Not that he comes out into the limelight — oh, not at all; never moves from his palace in Pekin. But he pulls strings — that's it, pull strings — and things happen far away."

"We have reason to believe that that is true," said Poirot quietly.

"Very odd, your knowing about him. Didn't fancy a soul in England had ever heard of him. I'd rather like to know how you did come to hear of him — if it's not indiscreet."

"Not in the least, Monsieur. A man took refuge in my rooms. He was suffering badly from shock, but he managed to tell us enough to interest us in this Li Chang Yen. He described four people — The Big Four — an organization hitherto undreamed of. Number One is Li Chang Yen, Number Two is an unknown American, Number Three an equally unknown Frenchwoman, Number Four may be called the executive of the organization — *The Destroyer*. My informant died. Tell me, Monsieur, is that phrase known to you at all? The Big Four."

"Not in connection with Lee Chang Yen. No, I can't say it is. But I've heard it, or read it, just lately — and in some unusual connection too.

Ah, I've got it."

He rose and went across to an inlaid lacquer cabinet — an exquisite thing, as even I could see. He returned with a letter in his hand.

"Here you are. Note from an old seafaring man I ran against once in Shanghai. Hoary old reprobate — maudlin with drink by now, I should say. I took this to be the ravings of alcoholism."

He read it aloud —

> *Dear Sir,* —
>
> *You may not remember me, but you did me a good turn once in Shanghai. Do me another now. I must have money to get out of the country. I'm well hidden here, I hope, but any day they may get me. The Big Four, I mean. It's life or death. I have plenty of money, but I daren't get at it, for fear of putting them wise. Send me a couple of hundred in notes. I'll repay it faithful — I swear to that.*
>
> — *Your servant, Sir,*
> *Jonathan WHALLEY.*

"Dated from Granite Bungalow, Hoppator, Dartmoor. I'm afraid I regarded it as rather a crude method of relieving me of a couple of hundred which I can ill spare. If it's any use to you —" He held it out.

"*Je vous remercie*, Monsieur. I start for Hoppator *á l'heure même*."

"Dear me, this is very interesting. Supposing I came along too? Any objection?"

"I should be charmed to have your company, but we must start at once. We shall not reach Dartmoor until close on nightfall, as it is."

John Ingles did not delay us more than a couple of minutes, and soon we were in the train moving out of Paddington bound for the West country. Hoppitor was a small village clustering in a hollow right on the fringe of the moorland. It was reached by a nine-mile drive from Moretonhamstead. It was about eight o'clock when we arrived; but, as the month was July, the daylight was still abundant.

We drove into the village and asked for the whereabouts of Granite Bungalow. A dozen willing hands pointed it out — a small grey cottage right in the center of the village.

"There be t'Bungalow. Do yee want to see t'Inspector? A shocking murder t'was, seemingly. Pools of blood, they do say."

We wasted no time in seeking out Inspector Meadows. Poirot introduced the magic name of Inspector Japp, and all was made easy for us.

"Yes, Sir; murdered this morning. A shocking business. They 'phoned to Moreton, and I came out at once. Looked a mysterious thing to begin with. The old man — he was about 70, you know, and fond of his glass, from all I hear — was lying on the floor of the living-room. There was a bruise on his head, and his throat was cut from ear to ear. Blood all over the place, as you can understand.

The woman who cooks for him, Betsy Andrews, she told us that her master had several little Chinese jade figures, that he told her were very valuable, and these had disappeared. That, of course, looked like assault and robbery; but there were all sorts of difficulties in the way of that solution. The old fellow had two people in the house: Betsy Andrews, who is a Hoppaton woman; and a rough kind of man-servant, Robert Grant. Grant had gone to the farm to fetch the milk, which he does every day, and Betsy had stepped out to have a chat with a neighbour. She was only away 20 minutes — between 10 and half past — and the crime must have been done then. Grant returned to the house first. He went in by the back door, which was open — no one locks up doors around here; not in broad daylight, at all events — put the milk in the larder, and went into his own room to read the paper and have a smoke. Had no idea anything unusual had occurred — at least that's what *he* says. Then Betsy comes in, goes into the living-room, sees what's happened, and lets out a screech to wake the dead. That's all fair and square. Someone got in whilst those two were out, and did the poor old man in. But it struck me at once that he must be a pretty cool customer. He'd have to come right up the village street, or creep through someone's backyard. Granite Bungalow has got houses all round it, as you can see. How was it that no one had seen him?"

The Inspector paused with a flourish.

"Aha, I perceive your point," said Poirot. "To continue?"

"Well, Sir, fishy, I said to myself — fishy. And I began to look about me. Those jade figures, now. Would a common tramp ever suspect that they were valuable? Anyway, it was madness to try such a thing in broad daylight. Suppose the old man had yelled for help?"

"I suppose, Inspector," said Mr. Ingles, "that the bruise on the head was inflicted before death?"

"Quite right, Sir. First knocked him silly, the murderer did, and then cut his throat. That's clear enough. But how the dickens did he come or go? They notice strangers quick enough in a little place like this. It came to me all at once — nobody did come. I took a good look round. It had rained the night before, and there were footprints clear enough going in and out of the kitchen. In the living room, there were two sets of footprints only (Betty Andrews' stopped at the door) — Mr. Whalley's (he was wearing carpet slippers) and another man's. The other man had stepped in the bloodstains, and I traced his bloody footprints — I beg your pardon, Sir."

"Not at all," said Mr. Ingles, with a faint smile; "the adjective is perfectly understood."

"I traced 'em to the kitchen — but not beyond. Point Number One. On the lintel of Robert Grant's door was a faint smear — a smear of blood.

That's point Number Two. Point Number Three was when I got hold of Grant's boots — which he had taken off — and fitted them to the marks. That settled it. It was an inside job. I warned Grant and took him into custody; and what do you think I found packed away in his portmanteau? The little jade figures and a ticket-of-leave. Robert Grant was also Abraham Biggs, convicted for felony and housebreaking five years ago."

The Inspector paused triumphantly.

"What do you think of that, gentlemen?"

"I think," said Poirot, "that it appears to be a very clear case — an almost singularly clear case, if I may say so. This Biggs, or Grant, must be a very foolish and uneducated man."

"Oh, he is that — a rough, common sort of fellow. No idea of what a footprint may mean."

"Clearly not a reader of detective fiction! Well, Inspector, I congratulate you. Any chance of our seeing the scene of the crime?"

"I'll take you there myself this minute. I'd like you to see those footprints."

"I, too, should like to see them. Yes, yes, very interesting, very ingenious."

We set out forthwith. Mr. Ingles and the Inspector forged ahead. I drew Poirot back a little so as to be able to speak to him out of the Inspector's hearing.

"What do you really think, Poirot? Is there more in this than meets the eye?"

"That is just the question, *mon ami*. Whalley says plainly enough in his letter that The Big Four are on his track, and we know from our own experience that The Big Four is no chimera of the imagination. Yet everything seems to point to the fact that this man Grant committed the crime. Why did he do so? For the sake of the little jade figures? Or is he an agent of The Big Four? I confess that the whole thing seems more credible on the latter hypothesis. However valuable the jade, a man of that class was not likely to realize the fact — at any rate, not to the point of committing murder for them. (That, *par example*, ought to have struck the Inspector.) He could have stolen the jade and made off with it instead of committing a brutal and quite purposeless murder. Ah, yes; I fear our Devonshire friend has not used his little grey cells. He has measured footprints and omitted to reflect and arrange his ideas with the necessary order and method."

The Inspector drew a key from his pocket and unlocked the door of Granite Bungalow. The day had been fine and dry, so our feet were not likely to leave any prints; nevertheless, we wiped them carefully on the mat before entering.

A woman came up out of the gloom and spoke to the Inspector, and he turned aside. Then he spoke over his shoulder.

"Have a good look round, Mr. Poirot, and see all there is to see. I'll be back in about five minutes. By the way here's Grant's boot. I brought it along with me for you to compare the impressions."

We went into the living-room, and the sound of the Inspector's footsteps died away outside. Ingles was attracted immediately by some Chinese curios on the table in the corner, and went over to examine them. He seemed to take no interest in Poirot's doings. I, on the other hand, watched him with breathless interest. The floor was covered with a dark green linoleum which was ideal for showing up footprints. A door at the farther end led into the small kitchen. From there another door led into the scullery (where the back room was situated), and another into the bed-room which had been occupied by Robert Grant. Having explored the ground, Poirot commented upon it in a low, running monologue.

"Here is where the body lay; that big, dark stain and the splashes all around mark the spot. Traces of carpet slippers and 'number nine' boots, you observe, but all very confused. Then two sets of tracks leading to and from the kitchen: whoever the murderer was, he came in that way. You have the boot, Hastings? Give it to me."

He compared it very carefully with the prints. "Yes, both made by the same man, Robert Grant. He came in that way, killed the old man, and went back to the kitchen. He had stepped in the blood: see the stains he left as he went out? Nothing to be seen in the kitchen — all the village has been walking about in it. He went into his own room — no, first he went back again to the scene of the crime — was that to get the little jade figures? Or had he forgotten something that might incriminate him?"

"Perhaps he killed the old man the second time he went in?" I suggested.

"*Mais non*, you do not observe. On one of the outgoing foot marks stained with blood there is superimposed an ingoing one. I wonder what he went back for — the little jade figures as an after-thought? It is all ridiculous — stupid."

"Well, he's given himself away pretty hopelessly."

"*N'est-ce pas?* I tell you, Hastings, it goes against reason. It offends my little grey cells. Let us go into his bed-room — ah, yes; there is the smear of blood on the lintel and just a trace of footmarks — blood-stained. Robert Grant's footmarks, and his only, near the body — Robert Grant the only man who went near the house. Yes, it must be so."

"What about the old woman?" I said suddenly. "She was in the house alone after Grant had gone for the milk. She might have killed him and then gone out. Her feet would leave no prints if she hadn't been outside."

"Very good, Hastings; I

wondered whether that hypothesis would occur to you. I had already thought of it and rejected it. Betsy Andrews is a local woman, well known hereabouts. She can have no connection with The Big Four; and besides, old Whalley was a powerful fellow, by all accounts. This is a man's work — not a woman's."

"I suppose The Big Four couldn't have had some diabolical contrivance concealed in the ceiling — something which descended automatically and cut the old man's throat and was afterwards drawn up again?"

"Like Jacob's ladder? I know, Hastings, that you have an imagination of the most fertile — but I implore of you to keep it within bounds."

I subsided, abashed. Poirot continued to wander about, poking into rooms and cupboards with a profoundly dissatisfied expression on his face. Suddenly he uttered an excited yelp reminiscent of a Pomeranian dog. I rushed to join him. He was standing in the larder in a dramatic attitude. In his hand he was brandishing a leg of mutton!

"My dear Poirot!" I cried. "What is the matter? Have you suddenly gone mad?"

"Regard, I pray you, this mutton. But regard it closely!"

I regarded it as closely as I could, but could see nothing unusual about it. It seemed to me a very ordinary leg of mutton. I said as much. Poirot threw me a withering glance.

"But do you not see this — and this — and this —"

He illustrated each "this" with a jab at the offending joint, dislodging small icicles as he did so.

Poirot had just accused me of being imaginative, but I now felt that he was far more wildly so than I had ever been. Did he seriously think these slivers of ice were crystals of a deadly poison? That was the only construction I could put upon his extraordinary agitation.

"It's frozen meat," I explained gently. "Imported, you know. New Zealand."

He stared at me for a moment or two and then broke into a strange laugh.

"How marvellous is my friend Hastings! He knows everything — but everything! How do they say — inquire within upon everything. That is my friend Hastings."

He flung down the leg of mutton onto its dish again and left the larder. Then he looked through the window.

"Here comes our friend the Inspector. It is well. I have seen all I want to see here." He drummed on the table absentmindedly, as though absorbed in calculation, and then asked suddenly, "What is the day of the week, *mon ami*?"

"Monday," I said, rather astonished. "What —"

"Ah! Monday, is it? A bad day of the week. To commit a murder on a Monday is a mistake."

Passing back to the living-room, he tapped the glass on the wall and glanced at the thermometer.

"Set fair, and 70°F. An Orthodox English summer's day."

Ingles was still examining various pieces of Chinese pottery.

"You do not take much interest in this inquiry, Monsieur?" said Poirot.

The other gave a slow smile.

"It's not my job, you see. I am a connoisseur of some things, but not of this. So I just stand back and keep out of the way. I've learnt patience in the east."

The Inspector came bustling in, apologizing for having been so long away. He insisted on taking us over most of the ground again, but finally we got away.

"I must appreciate your thousand politenesses, Inspector," said Poirot, as we were walking down the village street again. "There is just one more request I should like to put to you."

"You want to see the body, perhaps, Sir?"

"Oh, dear me, no! I have not the least interest in the body. I want to see Robert Grant."

"You'll have to drive back with me to Moreton to see him, Sir."

"Very well, I will do so. But I must see him and be able to speak to him alone."

The Inspector caressed his upper lip.

"Well, I don't know about that, Sir."

"I assure you that if you can get through to Scotland Yard you will receive full authority."

"I've heard of you, of course, Sir, and I know you've done us a good turn now and again. But it's very irregular."

"Nevertheless it is necessary," said Poirot calmly. "It is necessary for this reason — Grant is not the murderer."

"What? Who is, Then?"

"The murderer was, I should fancy, a youngish man. He drove up to Granite Bungalow in a trap, which he left outside. He went in, committed the murder, came out, and drove away again. He was bareheaded, and his clothing was slightly blood-stained."

"But — but the whole village would have seen him!"

"Not under certain circumstances."

"Not if it was dark, perhaps; the crime was committed in broad daylight."

Poirot merely smiled.

"And the horse and trap, Sir — how could you tell that? Any amount of wheeled vehicles may have passed along outside. There's no marks of one in particular to be seen."

"Not with the eyes of the body, perhaps; but with the eyes of the mind, yes."

The Inspector touched his forehead significantly with a grin at me. I was utterly bewildered, but I had faith in Poirot.

Further discussion ended in our all driving back to Moreton with the Inspector. Poirot and I were taken to Grant, but a constable was to be present during the interview.

Poirot went straight to the point.

"Grant, I know you to be innocent of this crime. Relate to me in your own words exactly what happened."

The prisoner was a man of medium height with a somewhat unpleasing cast of features. He looked a gaol-bird if ever a man did.

"Honest to God, I never did it," he whined. "Someone put those little glass figures amongst my traps. It was a frame-up, that's what it was. I went straight to my rooms when I came in, like I said. I never knew a thing till Betsy screeched out. S'welp me, God, I didn't."

Poirot rose.

"If you can't tell me the truth, that is the end of it."

"But, guv'nor —"

"You *did* go into the room — you *did* know your master was dead; and you were just preparing to make a bolt of it when the good Betsy made her terrible discovery."

The man stared at Poirot with a dropped jaw.

"Come now, is it not so? I tell you solemnly — on my word of honour — that to be frank now is your only chance."

"I'll risk it," said the man suddenly. "It was just as you say. I came in, and went straight to the master — and there he was, dead on the floor and blood all round. Then I got the wind up proper. They'd ferret out my record, and for a certainty they'd say it was me as had done him in. My only thought was to get away — at once — before he was found —"

"And the Jade figures?"

The man hesitated.

"You see —"

"You took them by a kind of reversion to instinct, as it were? You had heard your master say they were valuable, and you felt you might as well go the whole hog. That I understand. Now answer me this. Was it the second time you went into the room that you took the figures?"

"I didn't go in a second time. Once was enough for me."

"You are sure of that?"

"Absolutely certain."

"Good. Now, when did you come out of prison?"

"Two months ago."

"How did you obtain this job?"

"Through one of them Prisoners' Help Societies. Bloke met me when I came out."

"What was he like?"

"Not exactly a parson, but looked like one. The soft black hat and mincing way of talking. Got a broken front tooth. Spectacled chap. Saunders his name was. Said he hoped I was repentant, and that he'd find me a good post. I went to old Whalley on his recommendation."

Poirot rose once more.

"I thank you. I know all now. Have patience." He paused in the doorway and added: "Saunders gave you a pair of boots, didn't he?"

Grant looked very astonished.

"Why, yes, he did. But how did you know?"

"It is my business to know things," said Poirot gravely.

After a word or two to the Inspector, the three of us went to the White Hart and discussed eggs-and-bacon and Devonshire cider.

"Any elucidations yet?" asked Ingles with a smile.

"Yes, the case is clear enough now; but, see you, I shall have a good deal of difficulty in proving it. Whalley was killed by order of The Big Four — but not by Grant. A very clever man got Grant that post and deliberately planned to make him the scapegoat — an easy matter with Grant's prison record. He gave him a pair of boots, one of two duplicate pairs. The other he kept himself. It was all so simple. When Grant is out of the house, and Betsy is chatting in the village (which she probably did every day of her life), he drives up wearing the duplicate boots, enters the kitchen, goes through into the living room, fells the old man with a blow and then cuts his throat. Then he returns to the kitchen, removes the boots, puts on another pair, and, carrying the first pair, goes out to his trap and drives off again."

Ingles looked steadily at Poirot.

"There is a catch in it still. Why did nobody see him?"

"Ah! That is where the cleverness of Number Four — for it was Number Four, I am convinced — comes in. Everybody saw him — and yet nobody saw him. You see, he drove up in a butcher's cart!"

I uttered an exclamation.

"The leg of mutton?"

"Exactly, Hastings, the leg of mutton. Everybody swore that no one had been to Granite Bungalow that morning, but nevertheless I found in the larder a leg of mutton, still frozen. It was Monday, so the meat must have been delivered that morning; for if on Saturday, in this hot weather, it would not have remained frozen over Sunday. So someone *had* been to the bungalow, and a man on whom a trace of blood here and there would attract no attention."

"Damned ingenious!" cried Ingles approvingly.

"Yes, he is clever, Number Four."

"As clever as Hercule Poirot?" I murmured.

My friend threw me a glance of dignified reproach.

"There are some jests that you should not permit yourself, Hastings," he said sententiously. "Have I not saved an innocent man from being sent to the gallows? That is enough for one day."

# THE LADY ON THE STAIRS.

"The Lady on the Stairs" was first published in *The Sketch* on January 26, 1924.

"Good evening, Moosior," said our friend Inspector Japp. "Allow me to introduce Captain Kent, of the United States Secret Service."

Captain Kent was a tall, lean American, with a singularly impassive face which looked as though it had been carved out of wood.

"Pleased to meet you, gentlemen," he murmured, as he shook hands jerkily.

Poirot threw an extra log on the fire, and brought forward two more easy chairs. I brought out glasses and attended to the liquid refreshments. The captain took a deep draught, and expressed appreciation.

"Legislation in your country is still sound," he observed.

"And now to business," said Japp. "Moosior Poirot here made a certain request to me. He was interested in some concern that went by the name of The Big Four, and he asked me to let him know at any time if I came across a mention of it in my official line of business. I didn't take much stock in the matter, but I remembered what he said, and when the captain here came over with a rather curious story I said at once, 'We'll go round to Moosior Poirot's."

Poirot looked across at Captain Kent, and the American took up the tale.

"You may remember reading, Monsieur Poirot, that a number of torpedo-boats and destroyers were sunk by being dashed upon the rocks off the American coast. It was just after the Japanese earthquake, and the explanation given was that the disaster was the result of a tidal wave. Now a short time ago a round-up was made of certain crooks and gunmen, and with them were captured some papers which put an entirely new face upon the matter. They appeared to refer to some organization called The Big Four, and gave an incomplete description of some powerful wireless installation — a concentration of wireless energy far beyond anything so far attempted, and capable of focusing a beam of great intensity upon some given spot. The claims made for this invention seemed manifestly absurd, but I turned them in to headquarters for what they were worth, and one of our highbrow professors got busy on them. Now it appears that one of your British scientists read a paper upon the subject before the British Association. His colleagues didn't think great shakes of it, by all accounts — thought it far-fetched and fanciful; but your scientist stuck to his guns and declared that he himself was on the eve of success in his experiments."

"*Eh bien*?" demanded Poirot, with interest.

"It was suggested that I should come over here and get an interview with this gentleman. Quite a young fellow, he is — Halliday by name. He is the leading authority on the subject, and I was to get from him whether the thing suggested was in any way possible."

"And was it?" I asked eagerly.

"That's just what I don't know. I haven't seen Mr. Halliday — and I'm not likely to, by all accounts."

"The truth of the matter is," said Japp shortly, "Halliday's disappeared."

"When?"

"Two months ago."

"Was his disappearance reported?"

"Of course it was. His wife came to us in a great state. We did what we could, but I knew all along it would be no good."

"Why not?"

"Never is — when a man disappears that way." Japp winked.

"What way?"

"Paris."

"So Halliday disappeared in Paris?"

"Yes. Went over there on scientific work, so he *said*. Of course, he'd have to say something like that. But you know what it means when a man disappears over there. Either it's Apache work, and that's the end of it; or else it's voluntary disappearance — and that's a great deal the commoner of the two, I can tell you. Gay Paree and all that, you know. Sick of home life. Halliday and his wife had had a tiff before he started, which all helps to make it a pretty clear case."

"I wonder," said Poirot thoughtfully.

The American was looking at him curiously.

"Say, Mister," he drawled, "what's this Big Four idea?"

"The Big Four," said Poirot, "is an international organization which has at its head a Chinaman, who is known as Number One. Number Two is an American. Number Three is a Frenchwoman. Number Four, 'The Destroyer,' is an Englishman."

"A Frenchwoman, eh?" The American whistled. "And Halliday disappeared in France. Maybe there's something in this. What's her name?"

"I don't know. I know nothing about her."

"But it's a mighty big proposition, eh?" suggested the other.

Poirot nodded, as he arranged the glasses in a neat row on the tray. His love of order was as great as ever.

"What was the idea in sinking those boats? Are The Big Four a German stunt?"

"The Big Four are for themselves—and for themselves only, *Monsieur le Capitaine*. Their aim is world domination."

The American burst out laughing, but broke off at the sight of Poirot's serious face.

"You laugh, Monsieur," said Poirot, shaking a finger at him. "You reflect not—you use not the little grey cells of the brain. Who are these men who send a portion of your Navy to destruction simply as a trial of their power? For that was all it was, Monsieur—a test of this new force of magnetical attraction which they hold."

"Go on with you, Moosior!" said Japp good-humouredly. "I've read of Supermen many a time, but I've never come across them. Well, you've heard Captain Kent's story. Anything further I can do for you?"

"Yes, my good friend. You can give me the address of Mrs. Halliday—and also a few words of introduction to her if you will be so kind."

Thus it was that the following day saw us bound for Chetwynd Lodge, near the village of Chobham, in Surrey. Mrs. Halliday received us at once—a tall, fair woman, nervous and eager in manner. With her was her little girl, a beautiful child of five.

Poirot explained the purpose of our visit.

"Oh, Monsieur Poirot, I am so glad, so thankful! I have heard of you, of course. You will not be like the Scotland Yard people who will not listen or try to understand. And the French police are just as bad—worse, I think. They are all convinced that my husband has gone off with some other woman. But he wasn't like that! All he thought of in life was his work. Half our quarrels came from that. He cared for it more than he did for me."

"Englishmen, they are like that," said Poirot soothingly. "And if it is not work, it is the games, the sport. All these things they take *au grand sérieux*. Now, Madame, recount to me exactly, in detail and as methodically as you can, the exact circumstances of your husband's disappearance."

"My husband went to Paris on Thursday, July 20. He was to meet and visit various people there connected with his work, amongst them Madame Olivier."

Poirot nodded at the mention of the famous Frenchwoman chemist, who had eclipsed even Madame Curie in the brilliance of her achievements. She had been decorated by the French government, and was one of the most prominent personalities of the day.

"He arrived there in the evening, and went at once to the Hotel Castiglione in the Rue de Castiglione. On the following morning he had an appointment with Professor Bourgoneau, which he kept. His manner was normal and pleasant; the two men had a most interesting conversation, and it was arranged that he should witness some experiments in the professor's laboratory on the following day. He lunched alone at the Café Royal, went for a walk in the Bois, and then visited Madame Olivier at her house at Passy. There, also, his manner was perfectly normal. He left about six. Where he dined is not known — probably alone at some restaurant. He returned to the hotel about 11 o'clock and went straight up to his room, after inquiring if any letters had come for him. On the following morning he walked out of the hotel, and has not been seen again."

"At what time did he leave the hotel? At the hour when he would normally leave it to keep his appointment at Professor Bourgoneau's laboratory?"

"We do not know. He was not remarked leaving the hotel. But no *petit déjeuner* was served to him, which seems to indicate that he went out early."

"Or he might, in fact, have gone out again after he came in the night before?"

"I do not think so. His bed would have been slept in, and the night porter would have remembered anyone going out at that hour."

"A very just observation, Madame. We may take it, then, that he left early on the following morning — and that is reassuring from one point of view. He is not likely to have fallen victim to any Apache assault at that hour. His baggage, now, was it all left behind?"

Mrs. Halliday seemed rather reluctant to answer, but at last she said —

"No; he must have taken one small suitcase with him."

"Containing his washing things and a change of clothing, eh?"

"Yes," she replied unwillingly.

"And the French police doubtless regard that as proof positive that his disappearance was premeditated?"

She nodded. "Do not you?" she asked.

"I am bound to say, Madame, that I do. But I do not necessarily accept their view of the motive. With them it is always '*Cherchez la femme*.' Now, Madame, it is clear that something occurred the day before which impelled your husband to a complete change of plan. What was it? And when did it arise? At Madame Olivier's? During the evening? Or on returning to the hotel? You say he asked for letters before going up to bed. Did he receive any?"

"One only. And that must be the one I had written to him on the day he left England."

"H'm!" said Poirot thoughtfully. "I wonder where he was that evening. If we knew that, we should know a great deal. Whom did he meet? There lies the mystery, Madame — and to solve it I myself journey to Paris immediately."

"It is all a long time ago, Monsieur Poirot."

"Yes, yes. Nevertheless, it is there that we must seek. Tell me, Madame, do you ever remember your husband mentioning the phrase 'The Big Four'?"

"The Big Four," she repeated thoughtfully. "No, I can't say I do."

That was all that could be elicited from Mrs. Halliday. We hurried back to London, and the following day saw us *en route* for the Continent. With rather a rueful smile, Poirot observed —

"This Big Four, they make me to bestir myself, *mon ami*. I run up and down, all over the ground, like our old friend 'the human foxhound.'"

"Perhaps you'll meet him in Paris," I said, knowing that he referred to a certain Giraud, one of the most trusted detectives of the Sûreté, whom we had met on a previous occasion.

Poirot made a grimace. "I devoutly hope not. He loves me not, that one."

"Won't it be a very difficult task," I asked, "to find out what an unknown Englishman did on an evening two months ago?"

"Very difficult, *mon ami*. But, as you know well, difficulties rejoice the heart of Hercule Poirot."

"You think The Big Four kidnapped him?"

Poirot nodded.

Our inquiries necessarily went over old ground, and we learned little to add to what Mrs. Halliday had already told us. Poirot had a lengthy interview with Professor Bourgoneau, during which he sought to elicit whether Halliday had mentioned any plan of his own for the evening; but we drew a complete blank.

Our next source of information was the famous Madame Olivier. I was quite excited as we mounted the steps of her villa at Passy. It has always seemed to me so extraordinary that a woman should go so far in the scientific world. I should have thought a purely masculine brain was needed for such work.

The door was opened by a young lad of seventeen or thereabouts, who reminded me vaguely of an acolyte, so ritualistic was his manner. Poirot had taken the trouble to arrange our interview beforehand, as he knew that Madame Olivier never received anyone without an appointment, being immersed in research work most of the day.

We were shown into a small salon, and presently the mistress of the house came to us there. Madame Olivier was a very tall woman, her tallness accentuated by the long white overall she wore, and a coif like a nun's that shrouded her head. She had a long pale face, and wonderful dark eyes that burnt with a light almost fanatical. She looked more like a priestess of old then a modern Frenchwoman. One cheek was disfigured by a scar, and I remembered that her husband and co-worker had been killed in an explosion in the laboratory three years before, and that she herself had been terribly burned. Ever since then she had shut herself away from the world and plunged with fiery energy into the work of scientific research.

She received us with cold politeness.

"I have been interviewed by the police many times, Messieurs. I think it hardly likely that I can help you, since I have not been able to help them."

"Madame, it is possible that I shall not ask you quite the same questions. To begin with, of what did you talk together, you and Monsieur Halliday?"

She looked a trifle surprised.

"But of his work! His work, and also mine."

"Did he mention to you the theories he had embodied recently in his paper read before the British Association?"

"Certainly he did. It was chiefly of those we spoke."

"His ideas were somewhat fantastic, were they not?" asked Poirot carelessly.

"Some people thought so. I do not agree."

"You considered them practicable?"

"Perfectly practicable. My own line of research has been somewhat similar, though not undertaken with the same end in view. I have been investigating the *gamma* rays emitted by the substance usually known as Radium C., a product of radium emanation, and in doing so I have come across some very interesting magnetical phenomena. Indeed, I have a theory as to the actual nature of the force we call magnetism, but it is not yet time for my discoveries to be given to the world. Mr. Halliday's experiments and views were exceedingly interesting to me."

Poirot nodded. Then he asked

a question which surprised me.

"Madame, where did you converse on these topics? In here?"

"No, Monsieur. In the laboratory."

"May I see it?"

"Certainly."

She led the way to the door from which she had entered. It opened on a small passage. We passed through two doors and found ourselves in the big laboratory, with its array of beakers and crucibles, and a hundred appliances of which I did not even know the names. There were two occupants, both busy with some experiment. Madame Olivier introduced them.

"Mademoiselle Claude, one of my assistants." A tall, serious-faced young girl bowed to us. "Monsieur Henri, an old and trusted friend."

The young man, short and dark, bowed jerkily.

Poirot looked around him. There were two other doors besides the one by which we had entered. One, Madame explained, led into the garden; the other into a smaller chamber, also devoted to research. Poirot took all this in, then declared himself ready to return to the salon.

"Madame, were you alone with Monsieur Halliday during your interview?"

"Yes, Monsieur. My two assistants were in the smaller room next door."

"Could your conversation be overheard — by them or anyone else?"

Madame reflected, then shook her head.

"I do not think so. I am almost sure it could not. The doors were all shut."

"Could anyone have been concealed in the room?"

"There is the big cupboard in the corner — but the idea is absurd."

"*Pas tout à fait*, Madame. One thing more — did Monsieur Halliday make any mention of his plans for the evening?"

"He said nothing whatever, Monsieur."

"I think you, Madame, and I apologize for disturbing you. Pray do not trouble — we can find our way out."

We stepped out into the hall. A lady was just entering the front door as we did so. She ran quickly up the stairs, and I was left with the impression of heavy morning that denotes a French widow.

"A most unusual type of woman, that," remarked Poirot, as we walked away.

"Madame Olivier? Yes, she —"

"*Mais non*, not Madame Olivier. *Cela va sans dire*. There are not many geniuses of her stamp in the world. No, I referred to the other lady — the lady on the stairs."

"I didn't see her face," I said, staring. "And I hardly see how you could have done. She never looked at us."

"That is why I said she was an unusual type," said Poirot placidly. "A woman who enters her home — for I presume that it is her home since she entered with a key — and runs straight upstairs without even looking at two strange visitors in the hall to see who they are is a very unusual type of woman — quite unnatural in fact. *Mille tonnerres*, what is that?"

He dragged me back — just in time. A tree had crashed down onto the side-walk, just missing us. Poirot stared at it, pale and upset.

"It was a near thing, that! But clumsy, all the same, for I had no suspicion — at least, hardly any suspicion. Yes, but for my quick eyes, the eyes of a cat, Hercule Poirot might now be crushed out of existence — a terrible calamity for the world. And you too, *mon ami* — though that would not be such a national catastrophe."

"Thank you," I said coldly. "And what are we going to do now?"

"Do?" cried Poirot. "We are going to think. Yes, here and now, we are going to exercise our little grey cells. This Monsieur Halliday now, was he really in Paris? Yes, for Professor Bourgoneau, who knows him, saw and spoke to him."

"What on earth are you driving at?" I cried.

"That was Friday morning. He was last seen at eleven Friday night — but *was* he seen then?"

"The porter —"

"A night porter — who had not previously seen Halliday. A man comes in, sufficiently like Halliday — we may trust Number Four for that — asks for letters, goes upstairs, packs a small suit-case, and slips out the next morning. Nobody saw Halliday all that evening — no, because he was already in the hands of his enemies. Was it Halliday whom Madame Olivier received? Yes, for though she did not know him by sight, an impostor could hardly deceive her on her own special subject. He came here, he had his interview, he left. What happened next?"

Seizing me by the arm, Poirot was fairly dragging me back to the villa.

"Now, *mon ami*, imagine that it is the day after the disappearance, and that we are tracking footprints. You love footprints, do you not? See, here they go, a man's — Mr. Halliday's. He turns to the right, as we did; he walks briskly — ah, other footsteps following behind — very quickly — small footsteps, a woman's. See, she catches him up — a slim young woman in a widow's veil. 'Pardon Monsieur, Madame Olivier desires that I recall you.' He stops, he turns. Now where would the young woman take him? She does not wish to be seen walking with him. Is it coincidence that she catches up with him just where a narrow alley-way opens, dividing two gardens? She leads him down it. 'It is shorter this way, Monsieur.' On the right is the garden of Madame Olivier's villa — and from that garden, mark you, the tree fell. Garden doors from both open on the alley. The ambush is there. Men pour out, overpower him, and carry him into the strange villa."

"Good gracious, Poirot!" I cried. "Are you pretending to see all this?"

"I see it with the eyes of the mind, *mon ami*. So, and only so, could it have happened. Come, let us go back to the house."

"You want to see Madame Olivier again?"

Poirot gave a curious smile.

"No, Hastings; I want to see the face of the lady on the stairs."

"Who do you think she is — a relation of Madame Olivier's?"

"More probably a secretary — and a secretary engaged not very long ago."

The same gentle acolyte opened the door to us.

"Can you tell me," said Poirot, "the name of the lady, the widow lady, who came in just now?"

"Madame Veroneau? Madame's secretary?"

"That is the lady. Would you be so kind as to ask her to speak to us for a moment?"

The youth disappeared. He soon reappeared.

"I am sorry. Madame Veroneau must have gone out again."

"I think not," said Poirot quietly. "Will you give her my name, Monsieur Hercule Poirot, and say that it is important I should see her at once, as I am just going to the prefecture."

Again our messenger departed. This time the lady descended. She walked into the salon. We followed her. She turned and raised her veil. To my astonishment, I recognized our old antagonist, the Countess Rossakoff, a Russian countess who had engineered a particularly smart jewel robbery in London.

"As soon as I caught sight of you in the hall, I feared the worst," she observed plaintively.

"My dear Countess Rossakoff—"

She shook her head.

"Inez Veroneau now," she murmured. "A Spaniard, married to a Frenchman. What do you want of me, Monsieur Poirot? You are a terrible man. You hunted me from London. Now, I suppose, you will tell our wonderful Madame Olivier about me, and hunt me from Paris? We poor Russians — we must live, you know."

"It is more serious than that, Madame," said Poirot, watching her. "I propose to enter the villa next door and release Monsieur Halliday, if he is still alive. I know everything, you see."

I saw her sudden pallor. She bit her lip. Then she spoke with her usual decision.

"He is still alive — but he is not at the villa. Come, Monsieur, I will make a bargain with you. Freedom for me — and Monsieur Halliday, alive and well, for you."

"I accept," said Poirot. "I was about to propose the same bargain myself. By the way, are The Big Four your employers, Madame?"

Again I saw that deathly pallor

creep over her face, but she did not answer the question.

"You permit me to telephone?" She crossed to the instrument and asked for a number. "The number of the villa," she explained, "where our friend is now imprisoned. You may give it to the police — the nest will be empty when they arrive. Ah, I am through! Is that you, Andre? It is I, Inez. The little Belgian knows all. Send Halliday to the hotel, and clear out."

She replaced the receiver and came towards us, smiling.

"You will accompany us to the hotel, Madame."

"Naturally. I expected that."

I got a taxi, and we drove off together. I could see by Poirot's face that he was perplexed. The thing was almost too easy. We arrived at the hotel. The porter came up to us.

"A gentleman has arrived. He is in your rooms. He seems very ill. A nurse came with him, but she has left."

"That is all right," said Poirot; "he is a friend of mine."

We went upstairs together. Sitting in a chair by the window was a haggard young fellow who looked in the last stages of exhaustion. Poirot went over to him.

"Are you John Halliday?"

The man nodded.

"Show me your left arm. John Halliday has a mole just below the left elbow."

The man stretched out his arm. The mole was there. Poirot turned to the Countess, and she turned and left the room.

A glass of brandy revived Halliday somewhat.

"My God!" he muttered. "I have been through hell — hell.... Those fiends are devils incarnate. My wife, where is she? What does she think? They told me that she would believe — would believe —"

"She does not," said Poirot firmly. "Her faith in you has never wavered. She is waiting for you — she and the child."

"Thank God for that! I can hardly believe that I am free once more."

"Now that you are a little recovered, Monsieur, I should like to hear the whole story from the beginning.

Halliday looked at him with an indescribable expression.

"I remember — nothing," he said.

"What?"

"Have you ever heard of The Big Four?"

"Something of them," said Poirot dryly.

"You do not know what I know. They have unlimited power. If I remain silent I shall be safe; if I say one word — not only I but my nearest and dearest, will suffer unspeakable things. It is no good arguing with me. I *know*.... I remember — nothing."

And, getting up, he walked from the room.

Poirot's face wore a baffled expression.

"So it is like that, is it?" He muttered. "The Big Four win again. What is that you are holding in your hand, Hastings?"

I handed it to him.

"The Countess scribbled it before she left," I explained.

He read it.

" 'Au revoir. — I. V.' Signed with her initials — 'I. V.' Just a coincidence, perhaps, that they also stand for four. I wonder, Hastings, I wonder."

# IV.

## THE RADIUM THIEVES.

"The Radium Thieves" was first published in *The Sketch* on January 23, 1924.

It was the day after the sensational release of John Halliday from the hands of The Big Four. The scientist had departed for England, but Poirot and I had remained on in Paris. I was all for energetic proceedings of some kind or other, and Poirot's quiescence annoyed me.

"For heaven's sake, Poirot," I urged, "let us be up and at them!"

"Admirable, *mon ami*, admirable! Up where and at whom? Be precise, I beg of you."

"At The Big Four, of course."

"*Cela va sans dire*. But how would you set about it?"

"The police," I hazarded doubtfully.

Poirot smiled.

"They would accuse us of romancing. We have nothing to go upon — nothing whatever. We must wait."

"Wait for what?"

"Wait for them to make a move. See now, in England you all comprehend and adore *le boxe*. If one man does not make a move, the other must; and by permitting one's adversary to make the attack one learns something about him. That is our part — to let the other side make the attack."

"You think they will?" I said doubtfully.

"I have no doubt whatever of it. To begin with, see, they try to get me out of England. That fails. Then, in the Dartmoor affair, we step in and save their victim from the gallows. And yesterday, once again, we interfere with their plans. Assuredly, they will not leave the matter there."

As I reflected on this there was a knock on the door. Without waiting for a reply, a man stepped into the room and closed the door behind him. He was a tall, thin man, with a slightly hooked nose and a sallow complexion. He wore an overcoat buttoned up to his chin, and a soft hat pulled well down over his eyes.

"Excuse me, gentlemen, for my somewhat unceremonious entry," he said in a soft voice, "but my business is of a rather unorthodox nature."

Smiling, he advanced to the table and sat down by it. I was about to spring up, but Poirot restrained me with a gesture.

"As you say, Monsieur, your entry is somewhat unceremonious. Will you kindly state your business?"

"My dear Monsieur Poirot, it is very simple. You have been annoying my friends."

"In what way?"

"Come, come, Monsieur Poirot! You do not seriously ask me that? You know as well as I do."

"It depends, Monsieur, upon who these friends of yours are."

Without a word, the man drew from his pocket a cigarette-case, and, opening it, took out four cigarettes and tossed them on the table. Then he picked them up and returned them to his case, which he replaced in his pocket.

"Aha!" said Poirot. "So it is like that, is it? And what do your friends suggest?"

"They suggest, Monsieur, that you should employ your talents — your very considerable talents — in the detection of legitimate crime. Return to your former avocations and solve the problems of London society ladies."

"A peaceful programme," said Poirot. "And supposing I do not agree?"

The man made an eloquent gesture.

"We should regret it, of course, exceedingly," he said. "So would all the friends and admirers of the great Monsieur Hercule Poirot. But regrets, however poignant, do not bring a man to life again."

"Put very delicately," said Poirot, nodding his head. "And supposing I — accept?"

"In that case, I am empowered to offer you — compensation."

He drew out a pocket-book, and threw ten notes on the table. They were for 10,000 francs each.

"That is merely as a guarantee of our good faith," he said. "Ten times that amount will be paid you."

"Good God!" I cried, springing up. "You dare to think —"

"Sit down, Hastings," said Poirot autocratically. "Subdue your beautiful and honest nature and sit down. To you, Monsieur, I will say this. What is to prevent my ringing up the police and giving you into their custody, whilst my friend here prevents you from escaping?"

"By all means do so, if you think it advisable," said our visitor calmly.

"Oh, look here, Poirot," I cried, "I can't stand this! Ring up the police and have done with it."

Rising swiftly, I strode to the door and stood with my back against it.

"It seems the obvious course," murmured Poirot, as though debating with himself.

"But you distrust the obvious, eh?" said our visitor, smiling.

"Go on, Poirot," I urged.

"It will be your responsibility, *mon ami*."

As he lifted the receiver, the man made a sudden cat-like jump at me. I was ready for him. In another minute we were locked together, staggering round the room. Suddenly I felt him slip and falter. I pressed my advantage. He went down before me. And then, in the very flush of victory, an extraordinary thing happened. I felt myself flying forwards. Headfirst, I crashed into the wall in a complicated heap. I was up in a minute, but the door was already closing behind my late adversary. I rushed to it and shook it; it was locked on the outside. I seized the telephone from Poirot.

"Is that the Bureau? Stop a man who is coming out. A tall man, with a buttoned-up overcoat and a soft hat. He is wanted by the police."

Very few minutes elapsed before we heard a noise in the corridor outside. The key was turned and the door flung open. The manager himself stood in the doorway.

"The man—you have got him?" I cried.

"No, Monsieur. No one has descended."

"You must have passed him."

"We have passed no one, Monsieur. It is incredible that he can have escaped."

"You have passed someone, I think," said Poirot, in his gentle voice. "One of the hotel staff, perhaps?"

"Only a waiter carrying a tray, Monsieur."

"Ah!" said Poirot, in a tone that spoke infinities.

"So that was why he wore his overcoat buttoned up to his chin," mused Poirot, when we had finally got rid of the excited hotel officials.

"I'm awfully sorry, Poirot," I murmured, rather crestfallen. "I thought I'd downed him all right."

"Yes, that was a Japanese trick, I fancy. Do not distress yourself, *mon ami*. All went according to plan—his plan. That is what I wanted."

"What's this?" I cried, pouncing on a brown object that lay on the floor.

It was a slim pocket-book of brown leather, and had evidently fallen from our visitor's pocket during his struggle with me. It contained two receipted bills in the name of Monsieur Felix Laon, and a folded-up piece of paper which made my heart beat faster. It was a half-sheet of note paper on which a few words were scrawled in pencil, but they were words of supreme importance.

"The next meeting of the Council will be on Friday at 34, Rue des Echelles, at 11 a.m."

It was signed with a big figure "4."

And to-day was Friday, and the clock on the mantle piece showed the hour to be 10:30.

"My God, what a chance!" I cried. "Fate is playing into our hands. We must start at once, though. What stupendous luck."

"So that was why he came," murmured Poirot. "I see it all now."

"See what? Come on, Poirot, don't start day-dreaming there."

Poirot looked at me and slowly shook his head, smiling as he did so.

"'Will you walk into my parlour?' said the spider to the fly. That is your little English nursery rhyme, is it not? No, no — they are subtle — but not so subtle as Hercule Poirot."

"What on earth are you driving at, Poirot?"

"My friend, I have been asking myself the reason of this morning's visit. Did our visitor really hope to succeed in bribing me? Or, alternatively, in frightening me into abandoning my task? It seemed hardly credible. Why, then, did he come? And now I see the whole plan — very neat — very pretty: the ostensible reason to bribe or frighten me; the necessary struggle which he took no pains to avoid, and which should make the dropped pocket-book natural and reasonable; and, finally, the pitfall! Rue des Echelles, eleven a.m.? I think not, *mon ami!* One does not catch Hercule Poirot as easily as that."

"Good heavens!" I gasped.

Poirot was frowning to himself. "There is still one thing I do not understand."

"What is that?"

"The time, Hastings — the time. If they wanted to decoy me away, surely night-time would be better? Why this early hour? Is it possible that something is about to happen this morning? Something which they are anxious Hercule Poirot should not know about?"

He shook his head.

"We shall see. Here I sit, *mon ami.* We do not stir out this morning. We await events here."

It was at half past eleven exactly that the summons came. A *petit bleu.* Poirot tore it open, then handed it to me. It was from Madame Olivier, the world-famous scientist, whom we had visited yesterday in connection with the Halliday case. It asked us to come out to Passy at once.

We obeyed the summons without an instant's delay. Madame Olivier received us in the same small *salon*. I was struck anew with the wonderful power of this woman, with her long nun's face and burning eyes — this brilliant successor of Becquerel and the Curies.

She came to the point at once.

"Messieurs, you interviewed me yesterday about the disappearance of Monsieur Halliday. I now learn that you returned to the house and asked to see my secretary, Inez Veroneau. She left the house with you, and has not returned here since."

"Is that all, Madame?"

"No, Monsieur, it is not. Last night the laboratory was broken into, and several valuable papers and memoranda were stolen. The thieves had a try for something more precious still, but, luckily, they failed to open the big safe."

"Madame, these are the facts of the case. Your late secretary, Madame Veroneau, was really the countess Rossakoff, an expert thief, and it was she who was responsible for the disappearance of Monsieur Halliday. How long had she been with you?"

"Five months, Monsieur. What you say amazes me."

"It is true, nevertheless. These papers, were they easy to find? Or do you think an inside knowledge was shown?"

"It is rather curious that the thieves knew exactly where to look. You think Inez —"

"Yes, I have no doubt that it was upon her information that they acted. But what is this precious thing that the thieves failed to find? Jewels?"

Madame Olivier shook her head with a faint smile.

"Something much more precious than that, Monsieur." She looked round her, then bent forward, lowering her voice. "Radium, Monsieur."

"Radium?"

"Yes, Monsieur. I am now at the crux of my experiments. I possess a small portion of radium myself — more has been lent to me for the process I am at work upon. Small though the actual quantity is, it comprises a large amount of the world's stock and represents a value of millions of francs."

"And where is it?"

"In its leaden case in the big safe — the safe purposely appears to be of an old and worn-out pattern, but it is really a triumph of the safe-maker's art. That is probably why the thieves were unable to open it."

"How long are you keeping this radium in your possession?"

"Only for two days more, Monsieur. Then my experiments will be concluded."

Poirot's eyes brightened.

"And Inez Veroneau is aware of the fact? Good — then our friends will come back. Not a word of me to anyone, Madame. But rest assured, I will save your radium for you. You have a key of the door leading from the laboratory to the garden?"

"Yes, Monsieur. Here it is. I have a duplicate for myself. And here is the key of the garden door leading out into the alleyway between this villa and the next one."

"I thank you, Madame. To-night, go to bed as usual, have no fears, and leave all to me. But not a word to anyone—not to your two assistants—Mademoiselle Claude and Monsieur Henri, is it not?—Particularly not a word to them."

Poirot left the villa rubbing his hands in great satisfaction.

"What are we going to do now?" I asked.

"Now, Hastings, we are about to leave Paris—for England."

"What?"

"We will pack up our effects, have lunch, and drive to the Gare du Nord."

"But the radium?"

"I said we were going to leave for England; I did not say we were going to arrive there. Reflect a moment, Hastings. It is quite certain that we are being watched and followed. Our enemies must believe that we are going back to England, and they certainly will not believe that unless they see us get on board the train and start."

"Do you mean we are to slip off again at the last minute?"

"No, Hastings. Our enemies will be satisfied with nothing less than a bona-fide departure."

"But the train doesn't stop until Calais."

"It will stop if it is paid to do so."

"Oh, come now, Poirot—surely you can't pay an express to stop. They'd refuse."

"My dear friend, have you never remarked the little handle—the *signal d'arrêt*—penalty for improper use, 100 Francs, I think?"

"Oh, you are going to pull that?"

"Or rather a friend of mine, Pierre Combeau, will do so. Then, while he is arguing with the guard and making a big scene, and all the train is agog with interest, you and I will fade quietly away."

We duly carried out Poirot's plan. Pierre Combeau, an old crony of Poirot's, who evidently knew my little friend's methods pretty well, fell in with the arrangements. The communication cord was pulled just as we got to the outskirts of Paris. Combeau "made a scene" in the most approved French fashion, and Poirot and I were able to leave the train without anyone being interested in our departure.

Our first proceeding was to make a considerable change in our appearance. Poirot had brought the materials for this with him in a small case. Two loafers in dirty blue blouses were the result. We had dinner in an obscure hostelry, and started back to Paris afterwards.

It was close on eleven o'clock

when we found ourselves once more in the neighbourhood of Madame Olivier's villa. We looked up and down the road before slipping into the alley-way. The whole place appeared to be perfectly deserted. One thing we could be quite certain of — no one was following us.

"I do not expect them to be here yet," whispered Poirot to me. "Possibly they may not come until to-morrow night; but they know perfectly well that there are only two nights on which the radium will be there."

Very cautiously we turned the key in the garden door. It opened noiselessly, and we stepped into the garden.

And then, with complete unexpectedness, the blow fell. In a minute we were surrounded, gagged, and bound. At least ten men must have been waiting for us. Resistance was useless. Like two helpless bundles we were lifted up and carried along.

To my intense astonishment, they took us towards the house and not away from it. With the key, they opened the door into the laboratory and carried us into it. One of the men stooped down before the big safe. The door of it swung open. I felt an unpleasant sensation down my spine. Were they going to bundle us into it and leave us there to be asphyxiated slowly?

However, to my amazement, I saw that from the inside of the safe steps led down beneath the floor. We were thrust down this narrow way, and eventually came out into a big subterranean chamber. A woman stood there, tall and imposing, with a black velvet mask covering her face. She was clearly in command of the situation by her gestures of authority. The men slung us down on the floor and left us — alone with the mysterious creature in the mask. I had no doubt who she was. This was the unknown Frenchwoman — Number Three of The Big Four.

She knelt down beside us and removed the gags, but left us bound; then, rising and facing us, with a sudden swift gesture she removed her mask.

It was Madame Olivier!

"Monsieur Poirot," she said, in a low, mocking tone. "The great, the wonderful, the unique Monsieur Poirot! I sent a warning to you yesterday morning. You chose to disregard it — you thought you could pit your wits against us! And now, here you are!"

There was a cold malignity about her that froze me to the marrow. It was so at variance with the burning fire of her eyes. She was mad — mad — with the madness of genius!

Poirot said nothing. His jaw had dropped, and he was staring at her.

"Well," she said softly, "this is the end. We cannot permit our plans to be interfered with. Have you any last request to make?"

Never before or since have I felt so near death. Poirot was magnificent. He neither flinched nor paled—just stared at her with unabated interest.

"Your psychology interests me enormously, Madame," he said quietly. "It is a pity that I have so short a time to devote to studying it. Yes, I have a request to make. A condemned man is always allowed a last smoke, I believe. I have my cigarette-case on me. If you would permit —" He looked down at his bonds.

"Ah, yes!" she laughed. "You would like me to untie your hands, would you not? You are clever, Monsieur Hercule Poirot, I know that. I shall not untie your hands—but I will find you a cigarette."

She knelt down by him, extracted his cigarette-case, took out a cigarette, and placed it between his lips.

"And now a match," she said, rising.

"It is not necessary, Madame."

Something in his voice startled me. She, too, was arrested.

"Do not move, I pray of you, Madame. You will regret it if you do. Are you acquainted at all with the properties of curare? The South American Indians use it as an arrow poison. A scratch with it means death. Some tribes use a little blowpipe. I too have a little blowpipe—constructed so as to look exactly like a cigarette. I have only to blow.... ah, you start! Do not move, Madame. The mechanism of this cigarette is most ingenious. One blows—and a tiny dart resembling a fishbone flies through the air—to find its mark. You do not wish to die, Madame. Therefore, I beg of you, release my friend Hastings from his bonds. I cannot use my hands, but I can turn my head— so—you are still covered, Madame. Make no mistake, I beg of you."

Slowly, with shaking hands, and rage and hate convulsing her face, she bent down and did his bidding. I was free. Poirot's voice gave me instructions.

"Your bonds will now do for the lady, Hastings. That is right. Is she securely fastened? Then release me, I pray of you. It is a fortunate circumstance she sent away her henchmen. With a little luck we may hope to find the way out unobstructed."

In another minute, Poirot stood by my side. He bowed to the lady.

"Hercule Poirot is not killed so easily, Madame. I wish you good-night."

The gag prevented her from replying, but the murderous gleam in her eyes frightened me. I hoped devoutly that we should never fall into her power again.

Three minutes later we were outside the villa and hurriedly traversing the garden. The road outside was deserted, and we were soon clear of the neighbourhood.

Then Poirot broke out.

"I deserve all that that woman said to me. I am a triple imbecile, a miserable animal, thirty-six times an idiot! I was proud of myself for not falling into their trap. And it was not even meant as a trap — except exactly in the way in which I fell into it. They knew I would see through it — they counted on my seeing through it. This explains all — the ease with which they surrendered Halliday — everything. Madame Olivier was the ruling spirit — Vera Rossakoff only her lieutenant. Madame needed Halliday's ideas — she herself had the necessary genius to supply the gaps that perplexed him. Yes, Hastings, we know now who Number Three is — the woman who is probably the greatest scientist in the world! Think of it. The brain of the East, the science of the West — and two others whose identities we do not yet know. But we must find out. To-morrow we will return to London and set about it."

"You are not going to denounce Madame Olivier to the police?"

"I should not be believed. That woman is one of the idols of France. And we can prove nothing. We are lucky if she does not denounce us."

"What?"

"Think of it. We are found at night upon the premises with the keys in our possession which she will swear she never gave us. She surprises us at the safe, and we gag and bind her and make away. Have no illusions, Hastings. The boot is not upon the right leg — is that how you say it?"

# V.

# IN THE HOUSE OF THE ENEMY.

"In the House of the Enemy" was first published in *The Sketch* on January 30, 1924.

After our exciting adventure in the villa at Passy, we returned post-haste to London. Several letters were awaiting Poirot's return. He read one of them with a curious smile, and then handed it to me.

"Read this, *mon ami*."

I turned first to the signature, "Abe Ryland," and recalled Poirot's words: "the richest man in the world." Mr. Ryland's letter was curt and incisive. He expressed himself as profoundly dissatisfied with the reasons Poirot had given for withdrawing from the South American proposition at the last moment.

"This gives one furiously to think, does it not?" said Poirot.

"I suppose it's only natural he should be a bit ratty."

"No, no; you comprehend not. Remember the words of Mayorling, the man who took refuge here—only to die by the hands of his enemies. 'Number Two is represented by an S with two lines through it—the sign for a dollar; also by two stripes and a star. It may be conjectured, therefore, that he is an American subject, and that he represents the power of wealth.' Add to those words the fact that Ryland offered me a huge sum to tempt me out of

England—and—and what about it, Hastings?"

"You mean," I said, staring, "that you suspect Abe Ryland, the multi-millionaire, of being Number Two of The Big Four?"

"Your bright intellect has grasped the idea, Hastings. Yes, I do. The tone in which you said multi-millionaire was eloquent; but let me impress upon you one fact—this thing is being run by men at the top; and Mr. Ryland has the reputation of being no beauty in his business dealings. An able, unscrupulous man; a man who has all the wealth that he needs, and is out for unlimited power."

There was undoubtedly something to be said for Poirot's view. I asked him when he had made up his mind definitely upon the point.

"That is just it. I am not sure. I cannot be sure. *Mon ami*, I would give anything to know! Number One, Li Chang Yen, the man who moves the East; Number Three, Madame Olivier, the greatest woman scientist of the world; Number Four, an unknown Englishman, known as 'The Destroyer,' with an unparalleled gift of disguising himself. Let me but place Number Two definitely as Abe Ryland, and we draw nearer to our goal."

"He has just arrived in London, I see by this," I said, tapping the letter. "Shall you call upon him and make your apologies in person?"

"I might do so."

Two days later, Poirot returned to our rooms in a state of boundless excitement. He grasped me by both hands in his most impulsive manner.

"My friend, an occasion stupendous, unprecedented, never to be repeated, has presented itself! But there is danger—grave danger. I should not even ask you to attempt it."

If Poirot was trying to frighten me he was going the wrong way to work, and so I told him. Becoming less incoherent, he unfolded his plan.

It seemed that Ryland was looking for an English secretary, one with a good social manner and presence. It was Poirot's suggestion that I should apply for the post.

"I would do it myself, *mon ami*," he explained apologetically; "but, see you, it is almost impossible for me to disguise myself in the needful manner. I speak the English very well (except when I am excited), but hardly so as to deceive the ear; and even though I were to sacrifice my moustaches, I doubt not that I should still be recognizable as Hercule Poirot."

I doubted it not also, and declared myself ready and willing to take up the part and penetrate into Ryland's household.

"Ten to one he won't engage me, anyway," I remarked.

"Oh, yes, he will. I will arrange for you such testimonials as shall make him lick his lips. The Home

Secretary himself shall recommend you."

This seemed to be carrying things a bit far, but Poirot waved aside my remonstrances.

"Oh, yes, he will do it. I investigated for him a little matter which might have caused the grave scandal. All was resolved with discretion and delicacy; and now, as you would say, he perches upon my hand like the little bird, and pecks the crumbs."

Our first step was to engage the services of an artist in "make-up." He was a little man, with a quaint, bird-like turn of the head, not unlike Poirot's. He considered me some time in silence, and then fell to work.

When I looked at myself in the glass half-an-hour afterwards, I was amazed. Special shoes caused me to stand at least two inches taller, and the coat I wore was arranged so as to give me a long, lank, weedy look. My eyebrows had been cunningly altered, giving a totally different expression to my face; I wore pads in my cheeks; and the deep tan of my face was a thing of the past. My mustache had gone, and a gold tooth was prominent on one side of my mouth.

"Your name," said Poirot, "is Arthur Neville. God guard you my friend—for I fear that you go into perilous places."

It was with a beating heart that I presented myself at the Savoy, at an hour named by Mr. Ryland, and asked to see the great man.

After being kept waiting a minute or two, I was shown upstairs to his suite.

Ryland was sitting at a table. Spread out in front of him was a letter which I could see, out of the tail of my eye, was in the Home Secretary's handwriting. It was my first sight of the American millionaire, and, in spite of myself, I was impressed. He was tall and lean, with a jutting-out chin and a slightly hooked nose. His eyes glittered cold and grey behind pent-house brows. He had thick, grizzled hair; and a long black cigar (without which, I learned later, he was never seen) protruded rakily from the corner of his mouth.

"Siddown," he grunted.

I sat. He tapped the letter in front of him.

"According to this piece here, you are the goods all right, and I don't need to look further. Say, are you well up in the social matters?"

I said that I thought I could satisfy him in that respect.

"I mean to say, if I have a lot of dooks and earls and viscounts and such-like down to the country place I've gotten, you'll be able to sort them out all right and put them where they should be round the dining-table?"

"Oh, quite easily," I replied, smiling.

We exchanged a few more preliminaries, and then I found

myself engaged. What Mr. Ryland wanted was a secretary conversant with English society, as he already had an American secretary and the stenographer with him.

Two days later, I went down to Hatton Chase, the seat of the Duke of Loamshire, which the American millionaire had rented for a period of six months.

My duties gave me no difficulty whatever. At one period of my life I had been private secretary to a busy member of Parliament, so I was not called upon to assume a role unfamiliar to me. Mr. Ryland usually entertained a large party over the week-end, but the middle of the week was comparatively quiet. I saw very little of Mr. Appleby, the American secretary, but he seemed a pleasant, normal young American, very efficient in his work. Of Miss Martin, the stenographer, I saw rather more. She was a pretty girl of about twenty-three or -four, with auburn hair and brown eyes that could look mischievous enough upon occasion, though they were usually cast demurely down. I had an idea that she both disliked and distrusted her employer, though, of course, she was careful never to hint at anything of the kind; but the time came when I was unexpectedly taken into her confidence.

I had, of course, carefully scrutinized all the members of the household. One or two of the servants had been newly engaged: one of the footmen, I think, and some of the housemaids. The butler, the house-keeper, and the chef were the Duke's own staff, who had consented to remain in the establishment. The housemaids I dismissed as unimportant. I scrutinized James, the second footman, very carefully; but it was clear that he was an under-footman, and an under-footman only. He had, indeed, been engaged by the butler. A person of whom I was far more suspicious was Deaves, Ryland's valet, whom he had brought over from New York with him. An Englishman by birth, with an irreproachable manner, he yet excited vague suspicions in me.

I had been at Hatton Chase three weeks, and not an incident of any kind had arisen upon which I could lay my finger in support of our theory. There was no sign of the activities of The Big Four. Mr. Ryland was a man of overpowering force and personality, but I was coming to believe that Poirot had made a mistake when he associated him with that dread organization. I even heard him mention Poirot in a casual way at dinner one night.

"Wonderful little man, they say. But he's a quitter. How do I know? I put him on a deal, and he turned me down the last minute. I'm not taking any more of your Monsieur Hercule Poirot."

It was at moments such as these that I felt my cheek-pads most wearisome!

And then Miss Martin told me a rather curious story. Ryland had gone to London for the day, taking Appleby with him. Miss Martin and I were strolling together in the garden after tea. I liked the girl very much, she was so unaffected and so natural. I could see that there was something on her mind, and at last, out it came.

"Do you know, Major Neville," she said; "I am really thinking of resigning my post here."

I looked somewhat astonished, and she went on hurriedly.

"Oh, I know it's a wonderful job to have got, in a way. I suppose most people would think me a fool to throw it up. But I can't stand abuse, Major Neville. To be sworn at like a trooper is more than I can bear. No gentleman would do such a thing."

"Has Ryland been swearing at you?"

She nodded.

"Of course, he's always rather irritable and short-tempered. That one expects. It's all in the day's work. But to fly into such an absolute fury — over nothing at all. He really looked as though he could have murdered me! And, as I say, over nothing at all!"

"Tell me about it," I said, keenly interested.

"As you know, I open all Mr. Ryland's letters. Some I hand on to Mr. Appleby, others I deal with myself; but I do all the preliminary sorting. Now there are certain letters that come, written on blue paper, and with a tiny '4' written on the corner — I beg your pardon, did you speak?"

I had been unable to repress a stifled exclamation, but I hurriedly shook my head and begged her to continue.

"Well, as I was saying, these letters come, and there are strict orders that they are never to be opened, but to be handed over to Mr. Ryland intact. And, of course, I always do so. But there was an unusually heavy mail yesterday morning, and I was opening the letters in a terrific hurry. By mistake I opened one of these letters. As soon as I saw what I had done, I took it to Mr. Ryland and explained. To my utter amazement, he flew into the most awful rage. As I tell you, I was quite frightened."

"What was there in the letter, I wonder, to upset him so?"

"Absolutely nothing — that's just the curious part of it. I had read it before I discovered my mistake. It was quite short. I can still remember it word for word, and there was nothing in it that could possibly upset anyone."

"You can repeat it, you say?" I encouraged her.

"Yes." She paused a moment, and then repeated slowly, whilst I noted down the words unobtrusively, the following:

*Dear Sir, —*

*The essential thing now, I should*

> *say, is to see the property. If you insist on the quarry being included, then seventeen thousand seems reasonable; 11% commission too much, 4% is ample.*
>
> *—Yours truly,*
>
> *Arthur LEVERSHAM.*

Miss Martin went on: "Evidently about some property Mr. Ryland was thinking of buying. But, really, I do feel that a man who can get into a rage over such a trifle is—well—dangerous. What do you think I ought to do, Major Neville? You've more experience of the world than I have."

I soothed the girl down, pointed out to her that Mr. Ryland had probably been suffering from the enemy of his race—dyspepsia. In the end, I sent her away quite comforted. But I was not so easily satisfied myself. When the girl had gone, and I was alone, I took out my notebook and ran over the letter which I had jotted down. What did it mean—this apparently innocent-sounding missive? Did it concern some business deal which Ryland was undertaking, and was he anxious that no details about it should leak out until it was carried through? That was a possible explanation. But I remembered the small figure "4" with which the envelopes were marked, and I felt that at last I was on the track of the thing we were seeking.

I puzzled over the letter all that evening and most of the next day—and then, suddenly the solution came to me. It was so simple, too. The figure "4" was the clue. Read every fourth word in the letter and an entirely different message appeared. "Essential should see you quarry seventeen eleven four."

The solution of the figures was easy. Seventeen stood for the seventeenth of October—which was to-morrow—eleven was the time, and for was the signature—either referring to the mysterious number for himself, or else it was the "trademark," so to speak, of The Big Four. The quarry was also intelligible. There was a big, disused quarry on the estate about half a mile from the house—a lonely spot, ideal for a secret meeting.

For a moment or two I was tempted to run the show myself. It would be such a feather in my cap, for once, to have the pleasure of crowing over Poirot.

But in the end I overcame the temptation. This was a big business—I had no right to play a lone hand, and perhaps jeopardize our chances of success. For the first time we had stolen a march upon our enemies. We must make good this time—and, disguise the fact as I might, Poirot had the better brain of the two.

I wrote off post-haste to him, laying the facts before him, and explaining how urgent it was that we should overhear what went on at that interview. If he liked to leave it to me, well and good, but I gave him detailed instructions how to reach the quarry from the station, in case he should deem it wise to be present himself.

I took the letter down to the village and posted it myself. I had been able to communicate with Poirot throughout my stay, by the simple expedient of posting my letters myself; but we had agreed that he should not attempt to communicate with me, in case my letters should be tampered with.

I was in a glow of excitement the following evening. No guests were staying in the house, and I was busy with Mr. Ryland in his study all the evening. I had foreseen that this would be the case, which was why I had no hope of being able to meet Poirot at the station. I was, however, confident that my services would be dismissed well before eleven o'clock!

Sure enough, just after ten-thirty, Mr. Ryland glanced at the clock and announced that he was "through." I took the hint, and retired discreetly. I went upstairs as though going to bed, but slipped quietly down a side staircase and let myself out into the garden, having taken the precaution to don a dark overcoat to hide my white shirt-front.

I had gone some way down the garden when I chanced to look over my shoulder. Mr. Ryland was just stepping out from his study window into the garden. He was starting to keep the appointment. I redoubled my pace so as to get a clear start.

I arrived at the quarry somewhat out of breath. There seemed no one about, and I crawled into a thick tangle of bushes and awaited developments.

Ten minutes later, just on the stroke of eleven, Ryland stalked up, his hat over his eyes and the inevitable cigar in his mouth. He gave a quick look round and then plunged into the hollows of the quarry below. Presently I heard a low murmur of voices come up to me. Evidently the other man — or men — whoever they were, had arrived first at the rendezvous. I crawled cautiously out of the bushes, and, inch by inch, using the utmost precaution against noise, I wormed myself down the steep path.

Only a boulder now separated me from the talking men. Secure in the darkness I peeped round the edge of it, and found myself facing the muzzle of a black, murderous-looking automatic!

"Hands up!" said Mr. Ryland succinctly. "I've been waiting for you."

He was seated in the shadow of the rock, so that I could not see his face, but the menace in his voice was unpleasant. Then I felt a ring of cold steel on the back of my neck, and Ryland lowered his own automatic.

"That's right, George," he drawled. "March him around here."

Raging inwardly, I was conducted to a spot in the shadows, where the unseen George (whom I suspected of being the impeccable

Deaves) gagged me and bound me securely.

Ryland spoke again, in a tone which I had difficulty in recognizing, so cold and menacing was it.

"This is going to be the end of you two. You've gotten in the way of The Big Four once too often. Ever heard of landslides? There was one here about two years ago. There's going to be another tonight. I've fixed that good and square. Say, that friend of yours doesn't keep his dates very punctually."

A wave of horror swept over me. Poirot! In another minute he would walk straight into the trap. And I was powerless to warn him. I could only pray that he had elected to leave the matter in my hands and had remained in London. Surely if he had been coming he would have been here by now? With every minute that passed, my hopes rose.

Suddenly they were dashed to pieces. I heard footsteps — cautious footsteps, but footsteps nevertheless. I writhed in impotent agony. They came down the path, paused, and then Poirot himself appeared, his head a little on one side, peering into the shadows.

I heard the growl of satisfaction Ryland gave us he raised the big automatic and shouted, "Hands up!" Deaves sprang forward as he did so and took Poirot in the rear. The ambush was complete.

"Pleased to meet you, Mr. Hercule Poirot," said the American grimly.

Poirot's self-possession was marvelous. He did not turn a hair. But I saw his eyes searching in the shadows.

"My friend? He is here?"

"Yes; you are both in the trap — the trap of The Big Four."

He laughed.

"A trap?" queried Poirot.

"Say, haven't you tumbled to it yet?"

"I comprehend that there is a trap — yes," said Poirot gently, "but you are in error, Monsieur. It is *you* who are in it — not I and my friend."

"What?" Ryland raised the big automatic, but I saw his gaze falter.

"If you fire, you commit murder watched by ten pairs of eyes, and you will be hanged for it. This place is surrounded — has been for the last hour — by Scotland Yard men. It is checkmate, Mr. Abe Ryland."

He uttered a curious whistle, and, as though by magic, the place was alive with men. They seized Ryland and the valet, and disarmed them. After speaking a few words to the officer in charge, Poirot took me by the arm and led me away.

Once clear of the quarry, he embraced me with vigor.

"You are alive — you are unhurt. It is magnificent. Often have I blamed myself for letting you go."

"I'm perfectly all right," I said, disengaging myself. "But I'm just a bit fogged. You tumbled to their little scheme, did you?"

"But I was waiting for it! For what else did I permit you to go there? Your false name, your disguise, not for a moment was it intended to deceive!"

"What?" I cried. "You never told me."

"As I have frequently observed, Hastings, you have a nature so beautiful and so honest that, unless you are yourself deceived, it is impossible for you to carry conviction to others. Good then; you are spotted from the first, and they do what I had counted on their doing — a mathematical certainty to anyone who uses his grey cells properly — use you as a decoy. They set the girl on — by the way, *mon ami*, as an interesting fact psychologically, had she got red hair?"

"If you mean Miss Martin," I said coldly, "her hair is a delicate shade of auburn; but —"

"They are *épatant* — these people! They have even studied your psychology. Oh, yes, my friend; Miss Martin was in the plot — very much so. She repeats the letter to you, together with her tale of Mr. Ryland's wrath; you write it down, you puzzle your brains — the cipher is nicely arranged, difficult, but not too difficult — you solve it, and you send for me.

"But what they do not know is that I am waiting for just this very thing to happen. I go post-haste to Japp and arrange things. And so, as you see, all is triumph!"

I was not particularly pleased with Poirot, and I told him so. We went back to London on the milk-train in the early hours of the morning, and a most uncomfortable journey it was.

I was just out of my bath and indulging in pleasurable thoughts of breakfast when I heard Japp's voice in the sitting-room. I threw on a bath-robe and hurried in.

"A pretty mare's nest you've got us into this time," Japp was saying. "It's too bad of you, Monsieur Poirot. First time I've ever known you to take a toss."

Poirot's face was a study. Japp went on.

"There were we, taking all this Black Hand stuff seriously — and all the time it was the footman!"

"The footman?" I gasped.

"Yes. James, or whatever his name is. Seems he laid 'em a wager in the servants' hall that he could get taken for the old man by his nibs — that's you, Captain Hastings — and would hand him out a lot of spy stuff about a Big Four gang."

"Impossible!" I cried.

"Don't you believe it. I marched our gentlemen straight to Hatton Chase, and there was the real Ryland in bed and asleep, and the Butler and the cook and God knows how many of them to swear to the wager. Just a silly hoax — that's all it was — and the valet in with him."

"So that was why he kept in the shadow," murmured Poirot.

After Japp had gone we looked at each other.

"We know, Hastings," said

Poirot at last, "Number Two of The Big Four is Abe Ryland. The masquerading on the part of the footman was to ensure a way of retreat in case of emergencies. And the footman —"

"Yes," I breathed.

"*Number Four*," said Poirot gravely.

# VI.

## THE YELLOW JASMINE MYSTERY.

"The Yellow Jasmine Mystery" was first published in *The Sketch* on February 6, 1924.

"And what exactly is your opinion of the yellow Jasmine mystery?"

I did not reply at once to Poirot's question. I felt the need of going warily. We were alone in our compartment, whirling away from the dirt and smoke of London into the clean, peaceful country, bound for the little town of Market Handford in Worcestershire—the seat of the mystery.

That it must present unusual characters was certain, since it had actually tempted Poirot to abandon momentarily his investigations into the doings of The Big Four. It was the first outside case he had shown any interest in for months.

"It all seems so complicated," I said cautiously.

"Does it not?" said Poirot delightedly.

"I suppose our rushing off like this is a pretty clear sign that you consider Mr. Paynter's death to be murder—not suicide, or the result of accident?"

"No, no; you misunderstand me, Hastings. Granting that Mr. Paynter died as the result of a particularly terrible accident, there are still a number of mysterious circumstances to be explained."

"That was what I meant when I said it was all so complicated."

"Let us go over all the main facts quietly and methodically. Recount them to me, Hastings, in an orderly and lucid fashion."

I started forthwith, endeavoring to be as orderly and lucid as I could.

"We start," I said, "with Mr. Paynter. A man of fifty-five, rich, cultured, and somewhat of a globe-trotter. For the last twelve years he has been little in England; but suddenly, tiring of incessant travelling, he bought a small place in Worcestershire, near Market Handford, and prepared to settle down. His first action was to write to his only relative — a nephew, Gerald Paynter, the son of his youngest brother — and to suggest to him that he should come and make his home at Croftlands (as the place is called) with his uncle. Gerald Paynter, who is an impecunious young artist, was glad enough to fall in with this arrangement, and had been living with his uncle for about seven months when the tragedy occurred."

"Your narrative style is masterly," murmured Poirot. "I say to myself, 'It is a book that talks, not my friend Hastings.'"

Paying no attention to Poirot, I went on, warming to the story.

"Mr. Paynter kept a fair staff at Croftlands — six servants, as well as his own Chinese body-servant — Ah Ling."

"His Chinese servant, Ah Ling," murmured Poirot.

"On Tuesday last, Mr. Paynter complained of feeling unwell after dinner, and one of the servants was despatched to fetch the doctor. Mr. Paynter received him in his study, having refused to go to bed. What passed between them was not then known; but before Doctor Quentin left, he asked to see the housekeeper, and mentioned that he had given Mr. Paynter a hypodermic injection, as his heart was in a very weak state, recommending that he should not be disturbed, and then proceeded to ask some rather curious questions about the servants — how long they had been there, from whom they had come, etc. The housekeeper answered these questions as best she could, but was rather puzzled as to their purport.

"A terrible discovery was made on the following morning. One of the housemaids, descending, was met by a sickening odor of burned flesh which seemed to come from her master's study. She tried the door, but it was locked on the inside. With the assistance of Gerald Paynter and the Chinaman, that was soon broken in, but a terrible sight greeted them. Mr. Paynter had fallen forward into the gas-fire, and his face and head were charred beyond recognition.

"Of course, at the moment, no suspicion was aroused as to its being anything but a ghastly accident. If blame attached to anyone, it was to

Doctor Quentin for giving his patient a narcotic and leaving him in such a dangerous position. And then a rather curious discovery was made.

"There was a newspaper on the floor, lying where it had slipped from the old man's knees. On turning it over, words were found to be scrawled across it, feebly traced in ink. A writing-table stood close to the chair in which Mr. Paynter had been sitting, and the forefinger of the victim's right hand was ink stained up to the second joint. It was clear that, too weak to hold a pen, Mr. Paynter had dipped his finger in the ink-pot and managed to scroll these two words across the surface of the newspaper he held—but the words themselves seemed utterly fantastic: *Yellow Jasmine*—just that and nothing more.

"Croftlands has a large quantity of yellow jasmine growing up its walls, and it was thought that this dying message had some reference to it, showing that the poor old man's mind was wandering. Of course the newspapers, agog for anything out of the common, took up the story hotly, calling it the Mystery of the Yellow Jasmine—though in all probability the words are completely unimportant."

"They are unimportant, you say?" said Poirot. "Well, doubtless, since you say so, it must be so."

I regarded him dubiously, but I could detect no mockery in his eye.

"And then," I continued, "there came the excitements of the inquest."

"This is where you lick your lips, I perceive."

"There was a certain amount of feeling evidenced against Dr. Quentin. To begin with, he was not the regular doctor— only a *locum*, putting in a month's work whilst Dr. Bolitho was away on a well-earned holiday. Then it was felt that his carelessness was the direct cause of the accident. But his evidence was little short of sensational. Mr. Paynter had been ailing in health ever since his arrival at Croftlands. Dr. Bolitho had attended him for some time; but when Dr. Quentin first saw his patient he was mystified by some of the symptoms. He had only attended him once before the night when he was sent for after dinner. As soon as he was alone with Mr. Paynter, the latter had unfolded a surprising tale. To begin with, he was not feeling ill at all, he explained, but the taste of some curry that he had been eating at dinner had struck him as peculiar. Making an excuse to get rid of Ah Ling for a few minutes, he had turned the contents of his plate into a bowl, and he now handed it over to the doctor with injunctions for him to find out if there were really anything wrong with it.

"In spite of his statement that he was not feeling ill, the doctor noted that the shock of his suspicions had evidently affected him, and that his heart was feeling it.

Accordingly, he administered an injection — not of a narcotic, but of strychnine.

"That, I think, completes the case — except for the crux of the whole thing — the fact that the uneaten curry, duly analyzed, was found to contain enough powdered opium to kill two men!"

I paused.

"And your conclusions, Hastings?" asked Poirot quietly.

"It's difficult to say. It might be an accident — the fact that someone attempted to poison him the same night might be merely a coincidence."

"But you don't think so? You prefer to believe it — murder!"

"Don't you?"

"*Mon ami*, you and I do not reason in the same way. I am not trying to make up my mind between two opposite solutions, murder or accident — that will come when we have solved the other problem, the Mystery of the Yellow Jasmine. By the way, you have left out something there."

"You mean the two lines at right angles to each other faintly indicated under the words? I did not think they could be of any possible importance."

"What you think is always so important to yourself, Hastings. But let us pass from the Mystery of the Yellow Jasmine to the mystery of the curry."

"I know. Who poisoned it? Why? There are a hundred questions one can ask. Ah Ling, of course, prepared it. But why should he wish to kill his master? Is he a member of a *tong*, or something like that? One reads of such things. The *Tong* of the Yellow Jasmine, perhaps. Then there is Gerald Paynter."

I came to an abrupt pause.

"Yes," said Poirot, nodding his head. "There is Gerald Paynter, as you say. He is his uncle's heir. He was dining out that night, though."

"He might have got at some of the ingredients of the curry," I suggested. "And he would take care to be out, so as not to have to partake of the dish."

I think my reasoning rather impressed Poirot. He looked at me with a more respectful attention then he had given me so far.

"He returns late," I mused, pursuing a hypothetical case, "sees the light in his uncle's study, enters, and, finding his plan has failed, thrusts the old man down into the fire."

"Mr. Paynter, who was a fairly hearty man of fifty-five, would not permit himself to be burnt to death without a struggle, Hastings. Such a reconstruction is not feasible."

"Well, Poirot," I cried, "we're nearly there, I fancy. Let us hear what you think?"

Poirot threw me a smile, swelled out his chest, and began in a pompous manner:

"Assuming murder, the question once arises — why choose that particular method? I can think of only one reason — to confuse identity, the face being charred beyond recognition."

"What?" I cried. "You think —"

"A moment's patience, Hastings. I was going on to say that we examine that theory. Is there any ground for believing that the body found is not that of Mr. Paynter? Is there anyone else whose body it possibly could be? I examine these two questions, and finally I answer them both in the negative."

"Oh!" I said, rather disappointed. "And then?"

Poirot's eyes twinkled a little.

"And then I say to myself, 'since there is here something that I do not understand, it would be well that I should investigate the matter.' I must not permit myself to be wholly engrossed by The Big Four. Ah, we are just arriving. My little clothes-brush — where does it hide itself? Here it is. Brush me down, I pray you, my friend, and then I will perform the same service for you."

"Yes," said Poirot thoughtfully, as he put away the brush; "one must not permit oneself to be obsessed by one idea. I have been in danger of that. Figure to yourself, my friend, that even here, in this case, I am in danger of it. Those two lines you mentioned, a downstroke and a line at right angles to it — what are they but the beginning of a 4?"

"Good gracious, Poirot!" I cried, laughing.

"Is it not absurd? I see the hand of The Big Four everywhere. It is well to employ one's wits in a totally different milieu. Ah, there is Japp come to meet us!"

The Scotland Yard Inspector was, indeed, waiting on the platform, and greeted us warmly.

"Well, Moosior Poirot, this is good. Thought you'd like to be let in on this. Tip-top mystery, isn't it?"

I read this aright is showing Japp to be completely puzzled, and hoping to pick up a pointer from Poirot.

Japp had a car waiting, and we drove up in it to Croftlands. It was a square, white house, quite unpretentious, and covered with creepers, including the storied yellow jasmine. Japp looked up at it as we did.

"Must have been barmy to go writing that, poor old cove," he remarked. "Hallucinations, perhaps, and thought he was outside."

Poirot was smiling at him.

"Which was it, my good Japp?" he asked. "Accident or murder?"

The Inspector seemed a little embarrassed by the question.

"Well — if it weren't for that curry business, I'd be for accident every time. There's no sense in holding a live man's head in the fire — why, he'd scream the house down."

"Ah!" said Poirot in a low voice. "Fool that I have been. Triple imbecile. You are a cleverer man than I am, Japp."

Japp was rather taken aback by the compliment — Poirot being usually given to exclusive self-praise. He reddened and muttered something about there being a lot of doubt about that.

He led the way through most of the room where the tragedy had occurred — Mr. Paynter's study. It was a wide, low room, with book-lined walls and big leather armchairs.

Poirot looked across at once to the window, which gave upon a gravelled terrace.

"The window, it was unlatched?" he asked.

"That's the whole point, of course. When the doctor left this room, he merely closed the door behind him. The next morning, it was found locked. Who locked it? Mr. Paynter? Ah Ling declares that the window was closed and bolted. Dr. Quentin, on the other hand, has an impression that it was closed, but not fastened; but he won't swear either way. If he could, it would make a great difference. If the man was murdered, someone entered the room either through the door or the window. If through the door, it was an inside job; if through the window, it might have been anyone. First thing when they had broken the door down, they flung the window open, and the housemaid who did it thinks that it wasn't fastened; but she is a precious bad witness — will remember anything you ask her to!"

"What about the key?"

"There you are again. It was on the floor among the wreckage of the door. Might have fallen from the keyhole, might have been dropped there by one of the people who entered, might have been slipped underneath the door from the outside."

"In fact, everything is 'might have been'?"

"You hit it, Moosior Poirot. That's just what it is."

Poirot was looking round him, frowning unhappily.

"I cannot see light," he murmured. "Just now — yes — I got a gleam; but now, all is darkness once more. I have not the clue — the motive."

"Young Gerald Paynter had a pretty good motive," remarked Japp grimly. "He's been wild enough in his time, I can tell you. *And* extravagant. You know what artists are, too — no morals at all."

Poirot did not pay much attention to Japp's sweeping strictures on the artistic temperament. Instead, he smiled knowingly.

"My good Japp, is it possible that you throw the mud in my eyes? I know well enough that it is the Chinaman you suspect. But you are so artful. You want me to help you — and yet you drag the red kipper across the trail."

Japp burst out laughing.

"That's you all over, Mr. Poirot. Yes, I'd bet on the chink, I'll admit it now. It stands to reason that it was he who doctored the curry; and if he'd try once in an evening to get his master out of the way, he'd try twice."

"I wonder if he would," said Poirot softly.

"But it's the motive that beats

me. Some heathen revenge or other, I suppose."

"I wonder," said Poirot again. "There has been no robbery? Nothing has disappeared? No jewelry, or money, or papers?"

"No — that is, not exactly."

I picked up my years, and so did Poirot.

"There's been no robbery, I mean," explained Japp. "But the old boy was writing a book of some sort. We only knew about it this morning when there was a letter from the publishers asking about the manuscript. It was just completed, it seems. Young Paynter and I have searched high and low, but we can't find a trace of it — he must've hidden it away somewhere."

Poirot's eyes were shining with the green light I knew so well.

"How was it called, this book?" he asked.

" 'The hidden hand in China,' I think it was called."

"Aha!" said Poirot, with almost a gasp. Then he said quickly, "Let me see the Chinaman, Ah Ling."

The Chinaman was sent for and appeared, shuffling along, with his eyes cast down and his pig-tail swinging. His impassive face showed no trace of any kind of emotion.

"Ah Ling," said Poirot, "are you sorry your master is dead?"

"I welly sorry. He good master."

"You know who killed him?"

"I not know. I tell pleeceman if I know."

The questions and answers went on. With the same impassive face, Ah Ling described how he had made the curry. The cook had had nothing to do with it, he declared; no hand had touched it but his own. I wondered if he saw where his admission was leaving him. He stuck to it, too, that the window to the garden was bolted that evening. If it was open in the morning, his master must have opened it himself.

At last Poirot dismissed him. "That will do, Ah Ling."

Just as the Chinaman had got to the door, Poirot recalled him. "And you know nothing, you say, of the yellow jasmine?"

"No; what should I know?"

"Nor yet of the sign that was written underneath it?"

Poirot leaned forward as he spoke, and quickly traced something on the dust of a little table. I was near enough to see it before he rubbed it out. A downstroke, a line at right angles, and then a second line down which completed a big '4.'

The effect on the Chinaman was electrical. For one moment his face was a mask of terror; then, as suddenly, it was impassive again; and, repeating his grave disclaimer, he withdrew.

Japp departed in search of young Paynter, and Poirot and I were left alone together.

"The Big Four, Hastings," cried Poirot. "Once again The Big Four! Paynter was a great traveler. In his book there was doubtless some vital information concerning the doings of Number One, Li Chang Yen, the head and brains of The Big Four."

"But who — how —"

"Hush! Here they come."

Gerald Paynter was an amiable, rather weak-looking young man. He had a soft brown beard and a peculiar flowing tie. He answered Poirot's questions readily enough.

"I dined out with some neighbours of ours, the Wycherlys," he explained. "What time did I get home? Oh, about eleven. I had a latch-key, you know. All the servants had gone to bed, and I naturally thought my uncle had done the same. As a matter of fact, I did think I caught sight of that soft footed Chinese beggar, Ah Ling, just whisking round the corner of the hall; but I fancy I was mistaken."

"When did you last see your uncle, Mr. Paynter — I mean before you came to live with him?"

"Oh, not since I was a kid of 10. He and his brother — my father — quarreled, you know."

"But he found you again with very little trouble, did he not, in spite of all the years that had passed?"

"Yes; it was quite a bit of luck my seeing the lawyers' advertisement."

Poirot asked no more questions.

Our next move was to visit Dr. Quentin. His story was substantially the same as he had told at the inquest, and he had little to add to it. He received us in his surgery, having just come to the end of his consulting patients. He seemed an intelligent man. A certain primness of manner went well with his pince-nez, but I fancied that he would be thoroughly modern in his methods.

"I wish I could remember about the window," he said frankly. "But it's dangerous to think back — one becomes quite positive about something that never existed. That's psychology, isn't it, Monsieur Poirot? You see, I've read all about your methods, and I may say I'm an enormous admirer of yours. No, I suppose it's pretty certain that the Chinaman put the powdered opium in the curry; but he'll never admit it, and we shall never know why. But holding a man down in the fire — that's not in keeping with our Chinese friend's character, it seems to me."

I commented on this last point to Poirot as we walked down the main street of Market Handford.

"Do you think he let a confederate in?" I asked. "By the way, I suppose Japp can be trusted to keep an eye on him?" (The Inspector had passed into the police station on some business or other.) "The emissaries of The Big Four are pretty spry."

"Japp is keeping an eye on both of them," said Poirot grimly. "They have been closely shadowed ever since the body was discovered."

"Well, at any rate, we know that

Gerald Paynter had nothing to do with it."

"You always know so much more than I do, Hastings, that it becomes quite fatiguing."

"You old fox!" I laughed. "You never will commit yourself."

"To be honest, Hastings, the case is now quite clear to me — all but the words 'Yellow Jasmine' — and I am coming to agree with you that they have no bearing on the crime. In a case of this kind, you have got to make up your mind who is lying. I have done that. And yet —"

He suddenly darted from my side and entered an adjacent bookshop. He emerged a few minutes later, hugging a parcel. Then Japp rejoined us, and we all sought quarters at the inn.

I slept late the next morning. When I descended to the sitting-room reserved for us, I found Poirot already there, pacing up and down, his face contorted with agony.

"Do not converse with me," he cried, waving an agitated hand. "Not until I know that all is well — that the arrest is made. Ah, but my psychology has been weak. Hastings, if a man writes a dying message, it is because it is important. Everyone has said, 'yellow jasmine? There is yellow jasmine growing up the house — it means nothing.'"

"Well, what does it mean?" I said.

"Just what it says. Listen." He held up a little book he was carrying. "My friend, it struck me that it would be well to inquire into the subject. What exactly is yellow jasmine? This little book has told me. Listen."

He read —

"'*Gelsemii Radix.* Yellow Jasmine. Composition: Alkaloids *gelseminine* $C^{22}H^{26}N^{2}O^{3}$, a potent poison acting like conine; *gelsemine* $C^{12}H^{14}NO^{2}$, acting like strychnine; *gelsemic acid*, etc. Gelsemium is a powerful depressant to the central nervous system. At a late stage in its action it paralyzes the motor nerve endings, and in large doses causes giddiness and loss of muscular power. Death is due to paralysis of the respiratory centre.'

"You see, Hastings? At the beginning I had an inkling of the truth when Japp made his remark about a live man being forced into the fire. I realize then that it was a dead man who was burned."

"But why? What was the point?"

"My friend, if you were to shoot a man, or stab a man after he was dead, or even knock him on the head, it would be apparent that the injuries were inflicted after death. But with his head charred to a cinder, no one is going to hunt about for obscure causes of death; and a man who has apparently just escaped being poisoned at dinner is not likely to be poisoned just afterwards. *Who* is lying, that is always the question? I decided to believe Ah Ling —"

"What?" I exclaimed.

"You are surprised, Hastings? Ah Ling knew of the existence of

The Big Four, that was evident — so evident that it was clear he knew nothing of their association with the crime until that moment. Had he been the murderer, he would have been able to retain his impassive face perfectly. So I decided, then, to believe Ah Ling, and I fixed my suspicions on Gerald Paynter. It seemed to me that Number Four would have found an impersonation of a long-lost nephew very easy."

"What?" I cried. "Number Four?"

"No, Hastings; not Number Four. As soon as I had read up the subject of yellow Jasmine, I saw the truth. In fact, it leapt to the eye."

"As always," I said coldly, "it doesn't leap to mine."

"Because you will not use your little grey cells. Who had a chance to tamper with the curry?"

"Ah Ling. No one else."

"No one else. *What about the doctor?*"

"But that was *afterwards*."

"Of course it was afterwards. There was no trace of powdered opium in the curry served to Mr. Paynter; but, acting in obedience to the suspicions Dr. Quentin has aroused, the old man eats none of it, and preserves it to give to his medical attendant, whom he summons according to plan. Dr. Quentin arrives, takes charge of the curry, and *gives Mr. Paynter an injection*, not of strychnine, but of yellow jasmine — a poisonous dose. When the drug begins to take effect he departs, after unlatching the window. Then, in the night, he returns to the window, finds the manuscript, and shoves Mr. Paynter into the fire. He does not heed the newspaper that drops to the floor and is covered by the old man's body. Paynter knew what drug he had been given — possibly the doctor had taunted his helpless victim before departing — and strove to accuse The Big Four of his murder. It is easy for Quentin to mix powdered opium with the curry before handing it over to be analyzed. He gives his version of the conversation with the old man, and mentions the strychnine injection casually, in case the mark of the hypodermic needle is noticed. Suspicion at once is divided between accident and the guilt of Ah Ling owing to the poison in the curry."

"But Dr. Quentin cannot be Number Four?"

"I fancy he can. There is undoubtedly a real Dr. Quentin, who is probably abroad somewhere. Number Four has simply masqueraded as him for a short time. The arrangements with Dr. Bolitho were all carried out by correspondence, the man who was to do *locum* originally having been taken ill at the last minute."

At that moment Japp burst in, very red in the face.

"You have got him?" cried Poirot anxiously.

Japp shook his head, very out of breath.

"Bolitho came back from his holiday this morning — recalled by telegram. No one knows who sent it. The other man left last night. We'll catch him yet, though."

Poirot shook his head quietly.

"I think not," he said, and absentmindedly he drew a big 4 on the table with a fork.

# VII.

# THE CHESS PROBLEM.

"The Chess Problem" was first published in *The Sketch* on February 13, 1924.

Poirot and I often dined at a small restaurant in Soho. We were there one evening when we observed a friend at an adjacent table. It was Inspector Japp, and, as there was room at our table, he came and joined us. It was some time since either of us had seen him.

"Never do you drop in to see us nowadays," declared Poirot reproachfully. "Not since the affair of the Yellow Jasmine have we met, and that is nearly a month ago."

"I've been up north — that's why. How are things with you? Big Four still going strong — eh?"

Poirot shook a finger at him reproachfully.

"Ah, you mock yourself at me; but The Big Four — they exist."

"Oh, I don't doubt that — but they're not the hub of the universe, as you make them out."

"My friend, you are very much mistaken. The greatest power for evil in the world to-day is this Big Four. To what end they are tending no one knows, but there has never been another such criminal organization. The finest brain in China at the head of it, an American millionaire and a Frenchwoman scientist as members, and for the fourth —"

Japp interrupted.

"I know — I know. Regular bee in your bonnet over it all. It's becoming your little mania, Moosior Poirot. Let's talk of something else for a change. Take any interest in chess?"

"I have played it, yes."

"Did you see that curious business yesterday? Match between two players of worldwide reputation, and one died during the game?"

"I saw a mention of it. Dr. Savaronoff, the Russian champion, was one of the players; and the other, who succumbed to heart failure, was the brilliant young American, Gilmour Wilson."

"Quite right. Savaronoff beat Rubinstein and became Russian champion some years ago; Wilson is said to be a second Capablanca."

"A very curious occurrence," mused Poirot. "If I mistake not, you have a particular interest in the matter."

Japp gave a rather embarrassed laugh.

"You've hit it, Moosior Poirot. I'm puzzled. Wilson was sound as a bell — no trace of heart trouble. His death is quite inexplicable."

"You suspect Dr. Savaronoff of putting him out of the way?" I cried.

"Hardly that," said Japp dryly. "I don't think even a Russian would murder another man in order not to be beaten at chess; and anyway, from all I can make out, the boot was likely to be on the other leg. The doctor is supposed to be very hot stuff — second to Lasker, they say he is."

Poirot nodded thoughtfully.

"Then what exactly is your little idea?" he asked. "Why should Wilson be poisoned? For I assume, of course, that it is poison you suspect."

"Naturally. Heart failure means your heart stops beating — that's all there is to that. That's what a doctor says officially at the moment, but privately he tips us the wink that he's not satisfied."

"When is the autopsy to take place?"

"To-night. Wilson's death was extraordinarily sudden. He seemed quite as usual, and was actually moving one of the pieces when he suddenly fell forward — dead!"

"There are very few poisons that would act in such a fashion," objected Poirot.

"I know. The autopsy will help us, I expect. But why should anyone want Gilmour Wilson out of the way — that's what I'd like to know? Harmless, unassuming young fellow. Just come over here from the states, and apparently hadn't an enemy in the world."

"It seems incredible," I mused.

"Not at all," said Poirot, smiling. "Japp has his theory, I can see."

"I have, Moosior Poirot. I don't believe the poison was meant for Wilson — it was meant for the other man."

"Savaronoff?"

"Yes. Savaronoff fell afoul of the Bolsheviks at the outbreak of the revolution. He was even reported killed. In reality he escaped, and for three years endured incredible hardships in the wilds of Siberia. His sufferings were so great that he is now a changed man. His friends and acquaintances declare they would hardly have recognized him. His hair is white, and his whole aspect is that of a man terribly aged. He is a semi-invalid, and seldom goes out, living alone with a niece, Sonia Daviloff, and a Russian man-servant in a flat down Westminster way. It is possible that he still considers himself a marked man. Certainly he was very unwilling to agree to this chess contest. He refused several times point-blank, and it was only when the newspapers took it up and began making a fuss about the 'unsportsmanlike refusal' that he gave in. Gilmour Wilson had gone on challenging him with real Yankee pertinacity, and in the end he got his way. Now I ask you, Moosior Poirot, why wasn't he willing? Because he didn't want attention drawn to him. Didn't want somebody or other to get on his track. That's my solution — Gilmour Wilson got pipped by mistake."

"There is no one who has any private reason to gain by Savaronoff's death?"

"Well, his niece, I suppose. He's recently come into an immense fortune. Left him by Madame Gospoja, whose husband was a super-profiteer under the old regime. They had an affair together once, I believe, and she refused steadfastly to credit the reports of his death."

"Where did the match take place?"

"In Savaronoff's own flat. He's an invalid, as I told you."

"Many people there to watch it?"

"At least a dozen — probably more."

Poirot made an expressive grimace.

"My poor Japp, your task is not an easy one."

"Once I know definitely that Wilson was poisoned, I can get on."

"Has it occurred to you that, in the meantime, supposing your assumption that Savaronoff was the intended victim to be correct, the murderer may try again?"

"Of course it has. Two men are watching Savaronoff's flat."

"That will be very useful if anyone should call with a bomb under their arm," said Poirot dryly.

"You're getting interested, Moosior Poirot," said Japp, with a twinkle. "Care to come round to the mortuary and see Wilson's body before the doctors start on it? Who knows, his tie-pin may be askew, and that may give you a valuable clue that will solve the whole mystery."

"My dear Japp, all through dinner my fingers have been itching to rearrange your own tie-pin. You permit, yes? Ah, That is much more pleasing to the eye. Yes, by all means, let us go to the mortuary."

I could see that Poirot's attention was completely captivated by this new problem. It was so long since he had shown any interest in any outside case that I was quite rejoiced to see him back in his old form.

For my own part, I felt a deep pity as I looked down upon the motionless form and convulsed face of the hapless young American who had come to his death in such a strange way. Poirot examined the body attentively. There was no mark on it anywhere except a small scar on the left hand.

"And the doctor says that's a burn, not a cut," explained Japp.

Poirot's attention shifted to the contents of the dead man's pockets, which a constable spread out for our inspection. There was nothing much — a handkerchief, keys, note-case filled with notes, and some unimportant letters. But one object standing by itself filled Poirot with interest.

"A chess-man!" he exclaimed. "A white bishop. Was that in his pocket?"

"No; clasped in his hand. We had quite a difficulty to get it out of his fingers. It must be returned to Doctor Savaronoff sometime. It's part of a very beautiful set of carved ivory chest-men."

"Permit me to return it to him. It will make an excuse for my going there."

"Aha!" cried Japp. "So you want to come in on this case?"

"I admit it. So skillfully have you aroused my interest."

"That's fine. Get you away from your brooding. Captain Hastings is pleased, too, I can see."

"Quite right," I said, laughing.

Poirot turned back towards the body.

"No other little detail that you can tell me about — him?" he asked.

"I don't think so."

"Not even — that he was left-handed?"

"You're a wizard, Moosior Poirot. How did you know that? He *was* left-handed. Not that it's anything to do with the case."

"Nothing whatever," agreed Poirot hastily, seeing that Japp was slightly ruffled. "My little joke — that was all. I like to play you the trick, see you."

We went out upon an amicable understanding.

The following morning saw us wending our way to Dr. Savaronoff's flat in Westminster.

"Sonia Daviloff," I mused — "it's a pretty name."

Poirot stopped, and threw me a look of despair.

"Always looking for romance. You are incorrigible. It would serve you right if Sonia Daviloff turned out to be our friend and enemy the Countess Vera Rossakoff."

At the mention of the Countess, who was a prominent agent of The Big Four, my face clouded over.

"Surely, Poirot, you don't suspect —"

"But no, no — it was a joke. I have not The Big Four on the brain to that extent, whatever Japp may say."

The door of the flat was opened to us by a man-servant with a peculiarly wooden face. It seemed impossible to believe that that impassive countenance could ever display emotion.

Poirot presented a card on which Japp had scribbled a few words of introduction, and we were shown into a long, low room furnished with rich hangings and curios. One or two wonderful ikons hung upon the walls, and exquisite Persian rugs lay upon the floor. A samovar stood upon a table.

I was examining one of the ikons, which I judged to be of considerable value, and turned to see Poirot prone upon the floor. Beautiful as the rug was, it hardly seemed to me to necessitate such close attention.

"Is it such a very wonderful specimen? I asked.

"Eh? Oh, the rug? But no, it was not the rug I was remarking. But it *is* a beautiful specimen — far too beautiful to have a large nail wantonly driven through the middle of it. No, Hastings"— as I came forward — "the nail is not there now. But the hole remains."

A sudden sound behind us made me spin round, and Poirot sprang nimbly to his feet. A girl was standing in the doorway. Her eyes, full upon us, were dark with suspicion. She was of medium height, with a beautiful, rather sullen face, dark-blue eyes, and very black hair which was cut short. Her voice, when she spoke, was rich and sonorous, and completely un-English.

"I fear my uncle will be unable to see you. He is a great invalid."

"That is a pity; but perhaps you will kindly help me instead. You are Mademoiselle Daviloff, are you not?"

"Yes, I am Sonia Daviloff. What is it you want to know?"

"I am making some inquiries about that sad affair the night before last — the death of Monsieur Gilmore Wilson. What can you tell me about it?"

The girl's eyes opened wide.

"He died of heart failure — as he was playing chess."

"The police are not so sure that it was — heart failure, Mademoiselle."

The girl gave a terrified gesture.

"It was true, then," she cried. "Ivan was right."

"Who is Ivan; and why do you say 'he was right'?"

"It was Ivan who opened the door to you; and he has already said to me that in his opinion Gilmore Wilson did not die a natural death — that he was poisoned by mistake."

"By mistake?"

"Yes, the poison was meant for — my uncle."

She had quite forgotten her first distrust now, and was speaking eagerly.

"Why do you say that,

Mademoiselle? Who should wish to poison Dr. Savaronoff?"

She shook her head.

"I do not know. I am all in the dark. And my uncle, he will not trust me. It is natural, perhaps. You see, he hardly knows me. He saw me as a child, and not since till I came to live with him here in London. But this much I do know: he is in fear of something. We have many secret societies in Russia, and one day I overheard something which made me think it was of just such a society he went in fear. Tell me, Monsieur"— she came a step nearer and dropped her voice — "have you ever heard of a society called The Big Four?"

Poirot jumped nearly out of his skin. His eyes positively bulged with astonishment.

"Why do you — what do you know of The Big Four, Mademoiselle?"

"There is such an association, then? I overheard a reference to them, and asked my uncle about it afterwards. Never have I seen a man so afraid. He turned all white and shaking. He was in fear of them, Monsieur — in great fear, I am sure of it. And, by mistake, they killed the American, Wilson."

"The Big Four," murmured Poirot; "always The Big Four! An astonishing coincidence. Mademoiselle, your uncle is still in danger. I must save him. Now recount to me exactly the details of that fatal evening. Show me the chess-board, the table, how the two men sat — everything."

She went to the side of the room and brought out a small table. The top of it was exquisitely inlaid with squares of silver and black to represent a chess-board.

"This was sent to my uncle a few weeks ago as a present, with the request that he would use it in the next match he played. It was in the middle of the room — so."

Poirot examined the table with what seemed to me quite unnecessary attention. He was not conducting the inquiry at all as I should have done. Many of his questions seemed to me pointless, and upon really vital matters he appeared to have no questions to ask. I concluded that the unexpected mention of The Big Four had thrown him completely off his balance.

After a minute examination of the table in the exact position it had occupied, he asked to see the chess-men. Sonia Daviloff brought them to him in a box. He examined one or two of them in a perfunctory manner.

"An exquisite set," he murmured absent-mindedly.

Still not a question as to what refreshments there had been, or what people had been present. I cleared my throat significantly.

"Don't you think, Poirot, that —"

He interrupted me peremptorily.

"Do not think, my friend. Leave

all to me. Mademoiselle, is it quite impossible that I should see your uncle?"

A faint smile showed itself on her face.

"He will see you, yes. You understand, it is my part to interview all strangers first."

She disappeared. I heard a murmur of voices in the next room, and a minute later she came back and motioned us to pass into the adjoining room.

The man who lay there on the couch was an imposing figure. Very tall, gaunt, with huge bushy eyebrows and white beard, and a face haggard as the result of starvation and hardships, Dr. Savaronoff was a distinct personality. I noted the peculiar formation of his head, and its unusual height. A great chess-player must have a great brain, I knew. I could easily understand Dr. Savaronoff being the second greatest player in the world.

Poirot bowed.

"*Monsieur le docteur*, may I speak to you alone?"

Dr. Savaronoff turned to his niece.

"Leave us, Sonia."

She disappeared obediently.

"Now, Sir, what is it?"

"Dr. Savaronoff, you have recently come into an enormous fortune? If you should die — unexpectedly — who inherits it?"

"I have made a will leaving everything to my niece, Sonia Daviloff. You do not suggest —"

"I suggest nothing; but you have not seen your niece since she was a child. It would have been easy for anyone to impersonate her."

Savaronoff seemed thunderstruck by the suggestion. Poirot went on easily: "Enough as to that. I give you the word of warning, that is all. What I want you to do now is to describe to me the game of chess the other evening."

"How do you mean — describe it?"

"Well, I do not play the chess myself, but I understand that there are various regular ways of beginning — the gambit, do they not call it?"

Dr. Savaronoff smiled a little. "Ah, I comprehend you now. Wilson opened Ruy Lopez — one of the soundest openings, and one frequently adopted in tournaments and matches."

"And how long had you been playing when the tragedy happened?"

"It must have been about the third or fourth move when Wilson suddenly fell forward over the table, stone dead."

Poirot rose to depart. He flung out his last question as though it was of absolutely no importance, but I knew better.

"Had he had anything to eat or drink?"

"A whisky-and-soda, I think."

"Thank you, Dr. Savaronoff. I will disturb you no longer."

Ivan was in the hall to show us out. Poirot lingered on the threshold.

"The flat below this — do you know who lives there?"

"Sir Charles Kingwell, a member of Parliament, Sir. It has been let furnished lately, though."

"Thank you."

We went out into the bright winter sunlight.

"Well, really, Poirot," I burst out, "I don't think you've distinguished yourself this time. Surely your questions were very inadequate."

"You think so, Hastings?" Poirot looked at me appealingly. "I was *bouleversé*, yes. What would you have asked?"

I considered the question carefully, and then outlined my scheme to Poirot. He listened with what seemed to be close interest. My monologue lasted until we had nearly reached home.

"Very excellent, very searching, Hastings," said Poirot, as he inserted his key in the door and preceded me up the stairs; "but quite unnecessary."

"Unnecessary?" I cried, amazed. "If the man was poisoned —"

"Aha!" cried Poirot, pouncing upon a note which lay on the table. "From Japp. Just as I thought." He flung it over to me.

It was brief and to the point. No traces of poison had been found, and there was nothing to show how the man came by his death.

"You see," said Poirot, "your questions would have been quite unnecessary."

"You guessed this before hand?"

" 'Forecast the probable result of the deal,' " quoted Poirot from a recent bridge problem on which I had spent much time. "*Mon ami*, when you do that successfully, you do not call it guessing."

"Don't let split hairs," I said, impatiently. "You foresaw this?"

"I did."

"Why?"

Poirot put his hand into his pocket and pulled out — a white bishop.

"Why," I cried, "you forgot to give it back to Dr. Savaronoff."

"You are in error, my friend. That bishop still reposes in my left-hand pocket. I took its fellow from the box of chess-men Mademoiselle Daviloff kindly permitted me to examine. The plural of one bishop is two bishops."

He sounded the final "S" with a great hiss. But I was completely mystified.

"But why did you take it?"

"Parbleu, I wanted to see if they were exactly alike."

He stood them on the table side by side.

"Well, they are, of course," I said. "Exactly alike."

Poirot looked at them with his head on one side. "They seem so, I admit. But one should take no fact for granted until it is approved. Bring me, I pray you, my little scales."

With infinite care he weighed the two chess-men, then turned to me with a face alight with triumph. "I was right. See you, I was right.

Impossible to deceive Hercule Poirot!"

He rushed to the telephone — waited impatiently. "Is that Japp? Ah, Japp, it is you. Hercule Poirot speaks. Watch the man-servant, Ivan. On no account let him slip through your fingers. Yes, yes; it is as I say."

He dashed down the receiver and turned to me. "You see it not, Hastings? I will explain. Wilson was not poisoned; he was electrocuted. A thin metal rod passes up the middle of one of those chessmen. The table was prepared before hand and set upon a certain spot on the floor. When the bishop was placed upon one of the silver squares the current pass through Wilson's body, killing him instantly. The only mark was the electric burn upon his hand — his left hand because he was left-handed. The "special table" was an extremely cunning piece of mechanism. The table I examined was a duplicate, perfectly innocent. It was substituted for the other immediately after the murder. The thing was worked from the flat below, which, if you remember, was let furnished. But one accomplice at least was in Savaronoff's flat. The girl is an agent of The Big Four, working to inherit Savaronoff's money."

"And Ivan?"

"I strongly suspect that Ivan is none other than the famous Number Four!"

"*What?*"

"Yes. The man is a marvelous character actor. He can assume any part he pleases."

I thought back over past adventures: the lunatic-asylum keeper, the butcher's young man, the suave doctor — all the same man, and all totally unlike each other.

"It's amazing," I said at last. "Everything fits in. Savaronoff had an inkling of the plot, and that's why he was so averse from playing the match."

Poirot looked at me without speaking. Then he turned abruptly away and began pacing up and down.

"Have you a book on chess by any chance, *mon ami*?" he asked suddenly.

"I believe I have somewhere."

It took me some time to ferret it out, but I found it at last, and brought it to Poirot, who sank down in a chair and started reading it with the greatest attention.

In about a quarter of an hour the telephone rang. I answered it. It was Japp. Ivan had left the flat, carrying a large bundle. He had sprung into a waiting taxi, and the chase had begun. He was evidently trying to lose his pursuers. In the end he seemed to fancy that he had done so, and had then driven to a big empty house at Hempstead. The house was surrounded.

I recounted all this to Poirot. He merely stared at me as though he scarcely took in what I was saying. He held out the chess-book.

"Listen to this, my friend. This is the Ruy Lopez opening — 1. P to

K 4th, P to K 4th; 2. Kt to K B 3rd, Kt to Q B 3rd; 3. B to Kt 5th. Then there comes a question as to Black's best third move. He has the choice of various defenses. It was White's third move that killed Gilmore Wilson. 3. B to Kt 5th. Only the third move — does that say nothing to you?"

I hadn't the least idea what he meant, and told him so.

"Suppose, Hastings, that while you were sitting in this chair you heard the front door being opened and shut, what would you think?"

"I should think someone had gone out, I suppose."

"Yes; but there are always two ways of looking at things. Someone gone out, someone come *in* — two totally different things, Hastings. But, if you assume the wrong one, presently some little discrepancy would creep in and show you that you were on the wrong track."

"What does all this mean, Poirot?"

Poirot sprang to his feet with sudden energy.

"It means that I have been a triple imbecile. Quick, quick, to the flat in Westminster. We may yet be in time."

We tore off in a taxi. Poirot returned no answer to my excited questions. We raced up the stairs. Repeated rings and knocks brought no reply, but, listening closely, I could distinguish a hollow groan coming from within.

The hall porter proved to have a master key, and after a few difficulties he consented to use it.

Poirot went straight to the inner room. A whiff of chloroform met us. On the floor was Sonia Daviloff, gagged and bound, with a great wad of saturated cotton-wool over her nose and mouth. Poirot tore it off and began to take measures to restore her. Presently a doctor arrived, and Poirot handed her over to his charge and drew aside with me. There was no sign of Dr. Savaronoff.

"What does it all mean?" I asked, bewildered.

"It means that before two equal deductions I chose the wrong one. You heard me say that it would be easy for anyone to impersonate Sonia Daviloff because her uncle had not seen her for so many years?"

"Yes."

"Well, precisely the opposite held good also. It was equally easy for anyone to impersonate the uncle."

"What?"

"Savaronoff *did* die at the outbreak of the revolution. The man who pretended to have escaped with such terrible hardships, the man so changed 'that his own friends could hardly recognize him,' the man who successfully laid claim to an enormous fortune —"

"Yes. Who was he?"

"*Number Four.* No wonder he was frightened when Sonja let him know she had overheard one of his private conversations about The Big Four. Again he has slipped through my fingers. He guessed I should get on the right track in the end, so he sent off the honest Ivan on a tortuous wild-goose chase, chloroformed the girl, and got out, having by now doubtless realized most of the securities left him by Madame Gospoja."

"But — but who tried to kill him, then?"

"Nobody tried to kill him. Wilson was the intended victim all along."

"But why?"

"My friend, Savaronoff was the second greatest chess-player in the world. In all probability, Number Four did not even know the rudiments of the game. Certainly he could not sustain the fiction of a match. He tried all he knew to avoid the contest. When that failed, Wilson's doom was sealed. At all costs he must be prevented from discovering that the great Savaronoff did not know how to play chess. Wilson was fond of the Ruy Lopez opening, and was certain to use it. Number Four arranged for death to come with the third move, before any complications of defense set in."

Poirot paused and then added —

"But one thing I swear to you, Hastings. Number Four and I will meet again — many times perhaps, but in the end Hercule Poirot will be victorious. It must be so."

# VIII.

# THE BAITED TRAP.

"The Baited Trap" was first published in *The Sketch* on February 20, 1924.

It was mid-January—a typical English winter day in London, damp and dirty. Poirot and I were sitting in two chairs well drawn up to the fire. I was aware of my friend looking at me with a quizzical smile, the meaning of which I could not fathom.

"A penny for your thoughts," I said lightly.

"I was thinking, my friend, that at midsummer, when you first arrived, you told me that you proposed to be in this country for a couple of months only."

"Did I say that?" I asked, rather awkwardly. "I don't remember."

Poirot's smile broadened. "You did, *mon ami*. Since then, you have changed your mind, is it not so?"

"Er—yes, I have."

"And why is that?"

"Dash it all, Poirot, you don't think I'm going to leave you all alone when you're up against a thing like The Big Four—do you?"

Poirot nodded gently. "Just as I thought. You are a staunch friend, Hastings. It is to serve me that you remain on here. And your wife—little Cinderella, as you call her—what does she say?"

"I haven't gone into details, of course; but she understands. She be the last one to wish me to turn my back on a pal."

"Yes, yes; she, too, is a loyal friend. But it is going to be a long business, perhaps."

I nodded, rather discouraged. "Six months already," I mused, "and where are we? You know, Poirot, I can't help thinking that we ought to — well, to do something."

"Always so energetic, Hastings! And what precisely would you have me do?"

This was somewhat of a poser; but I was not going to withdraw from my position. "We ought to take the offensive," I urged. "What have we done all this time?"

"More than you think, my friend. We have learned that the head of this organization is the Chinaman, Li Chang Yen; that the man designated as Number Two is the American millionaire, Abe Ryland — the richest man in the world. We have discovered also the identity of Number Three: Madam Olivier, the world-famous scientist. And we have learned a little — not much, but a little — of the methods and ways of the mysterious Number Four."

I brightened up a little. As Poirot put it, things didn't sound so bad.

"Oh, yes, Hastings; we have done a great deal. It is true that I am not in a position to accuse either Ryland or Madame Olivier — who would believe me? You remember once when I thought I had Ryland successfully cornered? Nevertheless, I have made my suspicions known in certain quarters — the highest. Lord Alloway, who enlisted my help in the matter of the stolen submarine plans, is fully cognizant of all my information respecting The Big Four — and while others may doubt, he believes. Ryland and Madame Olivier, and Li Chang Yen himself may go their ways; but there is a searchlight turned on all their movements."

"And Number Four?" I asked.

"As I said just now — I am beginning to know and understand his methods. You may smile, Hastings; but to penetrate a man's personality, to know exactly what he will do under any given circumstances — that is the beginning of success. It is a duel between us; and whilst he is constantly giving away his mentality to me, I endeavor to let him know little or nothing of mine. He is in the light, I in the shade. I tell you, Hastings, that every day they fear me the more for my chosen inactivity."

"They've let us alone, anyway," I observed. "There have been no more attempts on your life, and no ambushes of any kind."

"No," said Poirot thoughtfully. "On the whole, that rather surprises me. Especially as there are one or two fairly obvious ways of getting at us which I should have thought certain to have occurred to them. You catch my meaning, perhaps?"

"An infernal machine of some kind?" I hazarded.

Poirot made a sharp click with his tongue, expressive of impatience.

"But no! I appeal to your imagination, and you can suggest nothing more subtle than bombs in the fireplace. Well, well; I have need of some matches. I will promenade myself despite the weather. Pardon, my friend, but is it possible that you read *The Future of the Argentine*, *A Mirror of Society*, *Cattle Breeding*, *The Clue of Crimson*, and *Sport in the Rockies* at one and the same time?"

I laughed, and admitted that *The Clue of Crimson* was at present engaging my sole attention. Poirot shook his head sadly.

"But replace then the others in the book-shelf! Never, never shall I see you embrace the order and the method. *Mon Dieu!* What then is a book-shelf for?"

I apologized humbly, and Poirot, after replacing the offending volumes, each in its appointed place, went out and left me to uninterrupted enjoyment of my selected book. I must admit, however, that I was half asleep when Mrs. Pearson's knock at the door aroused me.

"A telegram for you, Captain."

I tore the orange envelope open without much interest. Then I sat as though turned to stone. It was a cable from Bronsen, my manager out at the South American ranch; and it ran as follows:

"Mrs. Hastings disappeared yesterday feared been kidnapped some gang calling itself Big Four cable instructions have notified police but no clue as yet Bronsen."

I waved Mrs. Pearson out of the room, and sat as though stunned, reading the words over and over again. Cinderella — kidnapped! In the hands of the infamous Big Four! God! What could I do? Poirot! I must have Poirot. He would advise me. He would checkmate them somehow. In a few minutes now he would be back. I must wait patiently until then. But Cinderella — in the hands of The Big Four!

Another knock. Mrs. Pearson put her head in once more.

"A note for you, Captain — brought by a heathen Chinaman. He's a-waiting downstairs."

I seized it from her. It was brief and to the point. "If you ever wish to see your wife again, go with the bearer of this note immediately. Leave no message for your friend or she will suffer." It was signed with a big "4."

What ought I to have done? What would you who read have done in my place?

I had no time to think. I saw only one thing — Cinderella in the power of those devils. I must obey — I dare not risk a hair of her head. I must go with this Chinaman and follow whither he led. It was a trap, yes, and it meant certain capture and possible death; but it was baited with the person dearest to me in the whole world, and I dared not hesitate.

What irked me most was to

leave no word for Poirot. Once set him on my track and all might yet be well. Dare I risk it? Apparently I was under no supervision, but yet I hesitated. It would have been so easy for the Chinaman to come up and assure himself that I was keeping to the letter of the command. Why didn't he? His very abstention made me more suspicious. I had seen so much of the omnipotence of The Big Four that I credited them with almost superhuman powers. For all I knew, even the little bedraggled servant girl might be one of their agents.

No, I dared not risk it. But one thing I could do—leave the telegram. He would know then that Cinderella had disappeared, and who was responsible for her disappearance.

All this passed through my head in less time than it takes to tell, and I had clamped on my hat and was descending the stairs to where my guide waited in a little over a minute.

The bearer of the message was a tall, impassive Chinaman, neatly but rather shabbily dressed. He bowed and spoke to me. His English was perfect, but he spoke with a slight sing-song intonation.

"You Captain Hastings?"

"Yes," I said.

"You give me note, please."

I had foreseen the request, and handed him over the scrap of paper without a word. But that was not all.

"You have telegram to-day—yes? Come along just now? From South America—yes?"

I realized anew the excellence of their espionage system— or it may have been a shrewd guess. Bronsen was bound to cable me. They would wait until the cable was delivered and would strike hard upon it. No good could come of denying what was palpably true.

"Yes," I said; "I did get a telegram."

"You fetch him—yes? Fetch him now."

I ground my teeth, but what could I do? I ran upstairs again. As I did so, I thought of confiding in Mrs. Pearson, at any rate as far as Cinderella's disappearance went. She was on the landing; but close behind her was the little maid-servant, and I hesitated. If she was a spy? The words of the note danced before my eyes—"... She will suffer.... " I passed into the sitting-room without speaking.

I took up the telegram and was about to pass out again when an idea struck me. Could I not leave some sign which would mean nothing to my enemies, but which Poirot himself would find significant? I hurried across to the bookcase and tumbled out four books onto the floor. No fear of Poirot's not seeing them. They would outrage his eyes immediately—and, coming on top of his little lecture, surely they would be thought unusual? Next I put a shovelful of coal on the fire and managed to spill four knobs into the grate. I had done all I could—pray heaven Poirot would read the sign aright.

I hurried down again. The Chinaman took the telegram from me, read it, then placed it in his pocket, and with a nod beckoned me to follow him.

It was a long, weary march that he led me. Once we took a 'bus, and once we went for some considerable way in a tram, and always our route led us steadily eastward. We went through strange districts, the existence of which I had never dreamed of. We were down by the docks now, I knew, and I realized that I was being taken into the heart of Chinatown. In spite of myself I shivered. Still my guide plodded on, turning and twisting through mean streets and byways, until at last he stopped at a dilapidated house and rapped four times upon the door.

It was opened immediately by another Chinaman, who stood aside to let us pass in. The clanging-to of the door behind me was the knell of my last hopes. I was indeed in the hands of the enemy.

I was now handed over to the second Chinaman. He led me down some rickety stairs and into a cellar which was filled with bales and casks, and which exhaled a pungent odor as of eastern spices. I felt wrapped all round with the atmosphere of the East—tortuous, cunning, sinister....

Suddenly my guide rolled aside two of the casks, and I saw a low tunnel-like opening in the wall. He motioned me to go ahead. The tunnel was of some length and it was just too low for me to stand upright. At last, however, it broadened out into a passage, and a few minutes later we stood in another cellar.

My Chinaman went forward and rapped four times on one of the walls. To my amazement, a whole section of the wall swung out, leaving a narrow doorway. I passed through and, to my utter astonishment, found myself in a kind of Arabian Nights palace—a low, long, subterranean chamber hung with rich Oriental silks, brilliantly lighted, and fragrant with perfumes and spices. There were five or six silk-covered divans, and exquisite carpets of Chinese workmanship covered the ground. At the end of the room was a curtained recess. From behind these curtains came a voice—

"You have brought our honoured guest?"

"Excellency, he is here," replied my guide.

"Let our guest enter," was the answer.

At the same moment the curtains were drawn aside by an unseen hand, and I was facing an immense cushioned divan on which sat a tall, thin Oriental, dressed in wonderfully embroidered robes, and clearly, by the length of his finger-nails, a great man.

"Be seated, I pray you, Captain Hastings," he said, with a wave of his hand. "You acceded to my request to come immediately, I am glad to see you."

"Who are you?" I asked. "Li Chang Yen?"

"Indeed no; I am but the humblest of the Master's servants. I carry out his behests, that is all, as do other of his servants in other countries — in South America, for instance."

I advanced a step. "Where is she? What have you done with her out there?"

"She is in a place of safety — where none will find her. As yet, she is unharmed. You observe that I say — *as yet!*"

Cold shivers ran down my spine as I confronted the smiling devil. "What do you want?" I cried. "Money?"

"My dear Captain Hastings, we have no designs on your small savings, I can assure you. Not — pardon me — a very intelligent suggestion on your part. Your colleague would not have made it, I fancy."

"I suppose," I said heavily, "you wanted to get me into your toils. Well, you have succeeded. I have come here with my eyes open. Do what you like with me, and let her go. She knows nothing, and she can be of no possible use to you. You've used her to get hold of me — you've got me all right, and that settles it."

The smiling Oriental caressed his smooth cheek, watching me obliquely out of his narrow eyes.

"You go too fast," he said purringly. "That does not quite — settle it. In fact, to 'get hold of you,' as you express it, is not really our objective. But through you, we hope to get hold of your friend, Monsieur Hercule Poirot."

"I'm afraid you won't do that," I said, with a short laugh.

"What I suggest is this," continued the other, his words running on as though he had not heard me. "You will write Monsieur Hercule Poirot a letter, such a letter as will induce him to hasten hither and join you."

"I shall do no such thing," I said angrily.

"The consequences of refusal will be disagreeable."

"Damn your consequences."

"The alternative might be death!"

A nasty shiver ran down my spine; but I endeavored to put a bold face upon it.

"It's no good threatening me and bullying me. Keep your threats for Chinese cowards."

"My threats are very real ones, Captain Hastings. I ask you again, will you write this letter?"

"I will not, and what's more, you daren't kill me. You'd have the police on your tracks in no time."

My interlocutor clapped his hands swiftly. Immediately two Chinese attendance appeared, as it were, out of the blue, and pinioned me. Their master said something rapidly to them in Chinese, and they dragged me across the floor to a spot in one corner of the big chamber. One of them stooped, and suddenly, without the least warning, the flooring gave beneath my feet. But for the restraining hand of the other man, I should have gone down the yawning gap beneath me. It was inky black, and I could hear the rushing of water.

"The river," said my questioner from his place on the divan. "Think well, Captain Hastings. If you refuse again, you go headlong to eternity, to meet your death in the dark waters below. For the last time, will you write that letter?"

I'm not braver than most men. I will admit frankly that I was scared to death and in a blue funk. That Chinese devil meant business, I was sure of that. It was goodbye to the good old world. In spite of myself, my voice wobbled a little as I answered.

"For the last time, no! To hell with your letter!"

Then, involuntarily, I closed my eyes and breathed a short prayer. But, to my astonishment, a low laugh fell on my ears. I opened my eyes in surprise. Obeying a sign from the man on the divan, my two gaolers un-pinioned me and brought me back to my old seat facing him.

"You are a brave man, Captain Hastings," he said. "We of the East appreciate bravery. I may say that I expected you to act as you have done. That brings us to the appointed second act of our little drama. Death for yourself you have faced — will you face death for another?"

"What do you mean?" I asked hoarsely, a horrible fear creeping over me.

"Surely you have not forgotten the lady who is in our power — the Rose of the Garden."

I stared at him in dumb agony.

"I think, Captain Hastings, that you will write that letter. See, I have a cable form here. The message I shall write on it depends on you, and means life or death for your wife."

The sweat broke out on my brow. My tormentor continued, smiling amiably and speaking with perfect *sangfroid.*

"There, Captain, the pen is ready to your hand. You have only to write. If not —"

"If not?" I echoed.

"If not, that lady that you love dies — and dies slowly. My master, Li Chang Yen, amuses himself in his spare hours by devising new and ingenious methods of torture —"

"My God!" I cried. "You fiend! Not that — you wouldn't do that —"

"Shall I recount to you some of his devices?"

Without heeding my cry of protest, his speech flowed on — evenly, serenely — till, with a cry of horror, I clapped my hands to my ears.

"It is enough, I see. Take up the pen and write."

"You would not dare —"

"Your speech is foolishness, and you know it. Take up the pen and write."

"If I do?"

"Your wife goes free. The cable shall be dispatched immediately."

"How do I know that you will keep faith with me?"

"I swear it to you on the sacred tombs of my ancestors. Moreover, judge for yourself—why should I wish to do her harm? Her detention will have answered its purpose."

"And—and Poirot?"

"We will keep him in safe custody until we have concluded our operations. Then we will let him go."

"Will you swear that also on the tombs of your ancestors?"

"I have sworn one oath to you. That should be sufficient."

My heart sank. I was betraying my friend—to what? For a moment I hesitated; then the terrible alternative arose like a nightmare before my eyes. Cinderella—in the hands of these Chinese devils, dying by slow torture.

A groan rose to my lips. I seized the pen. Perhaps by careful wording of the letter, I could convey a warning, and Poirot would be enabled to avoid the trap. It was the only hope. But even that hope was not to remain. The Chinaman's voice rose, suave and courteous.

"Permit me to dictate to you."

He paused, consulted a sheaf of notes that lay by his side, and then dictated as follows.

> *Dear Poirot,—*
>
> *I think I'm on track of Number Four. A Chinaman came this afternoon and lured me down here with a bogus message. Luckily, I saw through his little game in time and gave him the slip. Then I turned the tables on him, and managed to do a bit of shadowing on my own account—rather neatly too, I flatter myself. I'm getting a bright young lad to carry this to you. Give him half-a-crown, will you? That's what I promised him if it was delivered safely. I'm watching the house, and daren't leave. I shall wait for you until six o'clock, and if you haven't come then I'll have a try at getting into the house on my own. It's too good a chance to miss, and, of course, the boy mightn't find you. But if he does, get him to bring you down here right away. And cover up those precious moustaches of yours, in case anyone's watching out from the house, and might recognize you.*
>
> *—Yours in haste,*
>
> *A. H.*

Every word that I wrote plunged me deeper in despair. The thing was diabolically clever. I realized how closely every detail of our life must be known. It was just such an epistle as I might have penned myself. The acknowledgment that the Chinaman who had called that afternoon had endeavored to "lure me away" discounted any good I might have done by leaving my "sign" of four books. It had been a trap, and I had seen through it: that was what Poirot would think. The time, too, was cleverly planned. Poirot, on receiving the note, would have just time to rush off with his innocent-looking guide;

and that he would do so I knew. My determination to make my way into the house would bring him post-haste. He always displayed a ridiculous distrust of my capacities. He would be convinced that I was running into danger without being equal to the situation, and would rush down to take command.

But there was nothing to be done. I wrote as bidden. My captor took the note from me, read it, then nodded his head approvingly and handed it to one of the silent attendants, who disappeared with it behind one of the silken hangings on the wall which masked the doorway.

With a smile the man opposite of me picked up a cable form and wrote. He handed it to me.

It read: "Release the white bird with all despatch."

I gave a sigh of relief. "You will send it at once?" I urged.

He smiled, and shook his head.

"When Monsieur Hercule Poirot is in my hands it shall be sent. Not until then."

"But you promised —"

"If this device fails, I may have need of our white bird — to persuade you to further efforts."

I grew white with anger. "My God! If you —"

He waved a long, slim yellow hand. "Be reassured. I do not think it will fail. And the moment Monsieur Poirot is in our hands, I will keep my oath."

"If you play me false —"

"I have sworn it by my honoured ancestors. Have no fear. Rest here a while. My servants will see to your needs whilst I am absent."

I was left alone in this strange underground nest of luxury. The second Chinese attendant had reappeared. One of them brought food and drink and offered them to me, but I waved them aside. I was sick — sick at heart.

And then, suddenly, the master reappeared. Tall and stately in his silken robes, he directed operations. By his orders I was hustled back through the cellar and tunnel into the original house I had entered. There they took me into a ground-floor room. The windows were shuttered, but one could see through the cracks into the street. An old, ragged man was shuffling along the opposite side of the road, and when I saw him make a sign to the window I understood that he was one of the gang on watch.

"It is well," said my Chinese friend. "Hercule Poirot has fallen into the trap. He approaches now — and alone, except for the boy who guides him. Now, Captain Hastings, you have still one more part to play. Unless you show yourself, he will not enter the house. When he arrives opposite, you must go out on the step and beckon him in."

"What?" I cried, revolted.

"You play that part alone. Remember the price of failure. If

Hercule Poirot suspects anything is amiss and does not enter the house, your wife dies by the 70 lingering deaths! — Ah! here he is."

With a beating heart, and a feeling of deathly sickness, I looked through the crack in the shutters. In the figure walking along the opposite side of the street I recognize my friend at once, though his coat collar was turned up, and an immense yellow muffler hid the bottom part of his face. But there was no mistaking that walk and the poise of that egg-shaped head. It was Poirot, coming to my aid in all good faith, suspecting nothing amiss. By his side ran a typical London urchin, grimy of face and ragged of apparel.

Poirot paused looking across at the house, whilst the boy spoke to him eagerly and pointed. It was time for me to act. I went out in the hall. At a sign from the tall Chinaman, one of the servants unlatched the door.

"Remember the price of failure," said my enemy in a low voice.

I was outside on the steps. I beckoned to Poirot. He hastened across.

"Aha! So all is well with you, my friend. I was beginning to be anxious. You managed to get inside? Is the house empty, then?"

"Yes," I said, in a voice I strove to make natural. "There must be a secret way out of it somewhere. Come in and let us look for it."

I stepped back across the threshold. In all innocence Poirot prepared to follow me.

And then something seemed to snap in my head. I saw only too clearly the part I was playing — the part of Judas.

"Back, Poirot!" I cried. "Back for your life. It's a trap. Never mind me. Get away at once."

Even as I spoke — or, rather, shouted — my warning hands gripped me like a vice. One of the Chinese servants sprang past me to grab Poirot. I saw the latter spring back, his arm raised; then, suddenly, a dense volume of smoke was rising around me, choking me — killing me.... I felt myself falling — suffocating — this was death.

I came to myself slowly and painfully — all my senses dazed. The first thing I saw was Poirot's face. He was sitting opposite me, watching me anxiously. He gave a cry of joy when he saw me looking at him.

"Ah! You revive — you return to yourself. All is well! My friend — my poor friend!"

"Where am I?" I said painfully.

"Where? But *chez vous!*"

I looked around me. True enough, I was in the old familiar surroundings. And in the grate were the identical four knobs of coal I had carefully spilled there. Poirot had followed my glance.

"But yes, that was a famous idea of yours — that and the books. See you, if they should say to me at any time, 'That friend of yours, that

Hastings, he has not the great brain, is it not so?' I shall reply to them, 'You are in error.' It was an idea magnificent and superb that occurred to you there."

"You understood their meaning, then?"

"Am I an imbecile? Of course I understood. It gave me just the warning I needed, and the time to mature my plans. Somehow or other The Big Four had carried you off. With what object? Clearly not for your *beaux yeux*, equally clearly not because they fear you and wanted to get you out of the way. No, their object was plain. You would be used as a decoy to get the great Hercule Poirot into their clutches. I have long been prepared for something of the kind. I make my little preparations, and presently, sure enough, the messenger arrives, such an innocent little street urchin. Me, I swallow everything, and hasten away with him, and, very fortunately, they permit you to come out on the doorstep. That was my one fear, that I should have to dispose of them before I had reached the place where you were concealed, and that I should have to search for you, perhaps in vain, afterwards."

"Dispose of them, did you say?" I asked feebly. "Single-handed."

"Oh, there is nothing very clever about that. If one is prepared in advance, all is simple — the motto of the Boy Scout, is it not? And a very fine one. Me, I was prepared. Not so long ago, I rendered the service to a very famous chemist, who did a lot of work in connection with poison gas during the war. He devised for me a little bomb, simple and easy to carry about, one has but to throw it and *poof*, the smoke, and then the unconsciousness. Immediately I blow a little whistle and straightaway some of Japp's clever fellows who were watching the house here long before the boy arrived, and who managed to follow us all the way to Limehouse, came flying up and took charge of the situation."

"But how was it you weren't unconscious too?"

"Another piece of luck. Our friend Number Four (who certainly composed that ingenious letter) permitted himself a little jest at my moustaches, which rendered it extremely easy for me to adjust my respirator under the guise of a yellow muffler."

"I remember," I cried eagerly, and then with the word "remember" all the ghastly horror that I had temporarily forgotten came back to me. Cinderella! I fell back with a groan.

I must have lost consciousness again for a minute or two. I awoke to find Poirot forcing some brandy between my lips.

"What is it, *mon ami?* But what is it, then? Tell me."

Word by word, I got the thing told, shuddering as I did so. Poirot uttered a cry.

"My friend! My friend! But what

you must have suffered! And I who knew nothing of all this! But reassure yourself! All is well!"

"You will find her, you mean? But she is in South America. And by the time we get there, long before, she will be dead, and God knows how and in what horrible way she will have died."

"No, no, you do not understand. She is safe and well. She has never been in their hands for one instant."

"But I got a cable from Bronsen?"

"No, no, you did not. You may have got a cable from South America signed Bronsen — that is a very different matter. Tell me, has it never occurred to you that an organization of this kind, with ramifications all over the world, might easily strike at us through the little girl, Cinderella, whom you love so well?"

"No, never," I replied.

"Well, it did to me. I said nothing to you because I did not want to upset you unnecessarily, but I took measures of my own. Your wife's letters all seem to have been written from the ranch, but in reality she has been in a place of safety devised by me for over three months."

I looked at him for a long time.

"You are sure of that?"

"*Parbleu!* I know it. They tortured you with a lie!"

I turned my head aside. Poirot put his hand on my shoulder. There was something in his voice that I had never heard there before.

"You like not that I should embrace you or display the emotion, I know well. I will be very British. I will say nothing, but nothing at all. Only this, that in this last adventure of ours, the honours are all with you, and happy is the man who has such a friend as I have!"

# IX.

## THE PEROXIDE BLONDE.

"The Peroxide Blonde" was first published in *The Sketch* on February 27, 1924.

It must sometimes seem as though our whole time was spent in circumventing the activities of the Four. In a sense this was so. Never, for one instant, did Poirot lose sight of the fact that he was up against the biggest thing he had ever tackled. Nevertheless, two or three months sometimes would elapse without a sign or hint of our opponents.

In the meantime, of course, cases were continually being brought to Poirot to solve. Some of these were interesting, presenting unusual and piquant features which at another time I should have enjoyed chronicling—but the shadow of the Four obscured all else. And although Poirot displayed his usual acumen, his heart was not in the business. All work, other than the Big Work, was irksome to him.

Some months now had passed since we had seen or heard anything more of the Four. Madame Olivier, the French scientist, was mentioned now and then in the newspapers as concluding some experiment. The American, Abe Ryland, the richest man in the world, had returned to New York, and the American newspapers kept us fully informed as to his movements. Of Number One, the obscure Chinaman, Li Chang Yen, the head and controlling genius of the organization, no mention was ever made in any journal. Nevertheless there were a select few — Englishmen who really knew their China — who realized the powerful personality that moved the levers of the Asiatic world.

"'To know, is to be prepared,'" said Poirot. Of late this was a favorite axiom of his, quoted so frequently that I had begun to hate the sound of it.

"We know something, Hastings," he continued. "Yes, we know something — and that is to the good — but we do not know nearly enough. We must know more."

"In what way?" I queried.

Poirot settled himself back in his chair, straightened the box of matches which I had thrown carelessly down on the table, and assumed an attitude that I knew only too well. I saw that he was prepared to hold forth at some length.

"See you, Hastings, we have to contend against four adversaries — that is, against four different personalities. With Number One we have never come into personal contact; we know him, as it were, only by the impress of his mind — and in passing, Hastings, I will tell you that I begin to understand that mind very well, a mind most subtle and Oriental; every scheme and plot that we have encountered has emanated from the brain of Li Chang Yen. Number Two and Number Three are so powerful, so high up, that they are for the present immune from our attacks. Nevertheless what is their safeguard is, by a perverse chance, our safeguard also. They are so much in the limelight that their movements must be carefully ordered. And so we come to the last member of the gang — we come to the man known as Number Four."

Poirot's voice altered a little.

"Number Two and Number Three are able to succeed, to go on their way unscathed, owing to their notoriety and their assured position. Number Four succeeds for the opposite reason — he succeeds by the way of obscurity. How many times have we seen him, you and I? Five times, is it not? And could either of us be sure of recognizing him again?"

I was forced to shake my head, as I ran back in my mind over those five different people who, incredible as it seemed, were one and the same man. The burly lunatic-asylum keeper, the man in the buttoned-up overcoat in Paris, James the footman, the quiet young medical man in the Yellow Jasmine case, and the Russian professor — in no way did any two of these people resemble each other.

"No," I said hopelessly. "We've nothing to go by whatsoever."

Poirot smiled.

"Do not, I pray of you, give way to such enthusiastic despair. We know one or two things."

"What things?" I asked sceptically.

"We know that he is a man of

medium height, and of medium or fair coloring. If he were a tall man of swarthy complexion he could never have passed himself off as the fair, stocky doctor. It is child's play, of course, to put on an additional inch or so for the part of James, or the professor. In the same way he must have a short, straight nose. Additions can be built onto a nose by skillful make-up, but a large nose cannot be successfully reduced at a moment's notice. Then again, he must be a fairly young man, certainly not over thirty-five. You see, we are getting somewhere. A man between thirty and thirty-five, of medium height and coloring, and adept in the art of make-up, and with very few, if any, teeth of his own."

"What?"

"Surely, Hastings! As the keeper, his teeth were broken and discolored, in Paris they were even and white, as the doctor they protruded slightly, and as Savaronoff they had unusually long canines. Nothing alters the face so completely as a different set of teeth. You see where all this leads?"

"Not exactly," I said cautiously.

"A man carries his profession written in his face, they say, Hastings. Do you not see that the man is, or has been, at one time or another, an actor?"

"An actor?"

"But certainly. He has the whole technique at his finger-tips. Among that class it is that we must look for our Number Four. He is a supreme artist in the way he sinks himself completely in each part he plays."

I was growing interested. "So you fancy you may be able to trace his identity through his connection with the stage?" I questioned.

"Your reasoning is always brilliant, Hastings."

"It might have been better," I said coldly, "if the idea had come to you sooner. We have wasted a lot of time."

"You are in error, *mon ami.* No more time has been wasted than was unavoidable. For some months now my agents have been engaged on the task. Joseph Aarons is one of them. You remember him? They have compiled a list for me of men fulfilling the necessary qualifications—young men round about the age of thirty, of more or less nondescript appearance, and with a gift for playing character parts—men, moreover, who have definitely left the stage within the last three years."

"Well?" I said, deeply interested.

"The list was, necessarily, rather a long one. For some time now, we have been engaged on the task of elimination. And finally we have boiled the whole thing down to four names. Here they are, my friend."

He tossed me over a sheet of paper. I read its contents aloud:

"Ernest Luttrell. Son of a North Country parson. Public school education. Went on stage at age of twenty-three."

(There followed a list of parts he had played, with dates and places.)

"Addicted to drugs. Supposed to have gone to Australia four years ago. Cannot be traced after leaving England. Age thirty-two, height five feet, ten and one-half inches, clean-shaven, hair brown, nose straight, complexion fair, eyes grey.

"JOHN ST. MAUR. Assumed name; real name not known. Believed to be of Cockney extraction. On stage since quite a child. Did music-hall impersonations. Not been heard of for three years. Age, about thirty-three, height five feet, ten inches, slim build, blue eyes, fair coloring.

"AUSTEN LEE. Assumed name; real name Austen Foly. Good family. Always had taste for acting and distinguished himself in that way at Oxford. Brilliant war record. Acted in —" (the usual list followed.) "An enthusiast on criminology. Had bad nervous breakdown as the result of a motor accident three and one-half years ago, and has not appeared on the stage since. No clue to his present whereabouts. Age thirty-five, height five feet, nine and one-half inches, complexion fair, eyes blue, hair brown.

"CLAUD DARRELL. Supposed to be real name. Some mystery about his origin. Played at music-halls, and also in repertory plays. Seems to have had no intimate friends. Was in China in 1919. Returned by way of America. Played a few parts in New York. Did not appear on the stage one night, and has never been heard of since. New York police say most mysterious disappearance. Age about thirty-three, hair brown, fair complexion, grey eyes. Height, five feet, ten and one-half inches."

"Most interesting," I said, as I laid down the paper. "And so this is the result of the investigation of months — these four names? Which of them are you inclined to suspect?"

Poirot made an eloquent gesture.

"*Mon ami*, for the moment it is an open question. I would just point out to you that Claud Darrell has been in China and America — a fact not without significance, perhaps, but we must not allow ourselves to be unduly biased by that point. It may be a mere coincidence."

"And the next step?" I asked eagerly.

"Affairs are already in train. Every day cautiously worded advertisements will appear. Friends and relatives of one or the others will be asked to communicate with my solicitor at his office. Even to-day we might — aha, the telephone! Probably it is, as usual, the wrong number, and they will regret to have troubled us, but it may be — yes, it may be — that something has arisen."

I crossed the room, took up the receiver. "Captain Hastings speaking.... Oh! It's you, Mr. McNeil!" (McNeil and Hodgson were Poirot's solicitors.) "I'll tell him.... Yes, we'll come round at once."

I replaced the receiver and turned to Poirot, my eyes dancing with excitement.

"I say, Poirot, there's a woman there. Friend of Claud Darrell's—Miss Flossie Monro! McNeil wants you to come round."

"At the instant!" cried Poirot, disappearing into his bed-room, and reappearing with a hat.

A taxi soon took us to our destination, and we were ushered into Mr. McNeil's private office. Sitting in the armchair facing the solicitor was a somewhat lurid-looking lady no longer in her first youth. Her hair, of an impossible yellow, was prolific in curls over each ear, her eyelids were heavily blackened, and she had by no means forgotten the rouge and the lip-salve.

"Ah! Here is Monsieur Poirot," said Mr. McNeil. "Monsieur Poirot, this is Miss—er—Monro, who has very kindly called to give us some information."

"Ah! But that is indeed most kind!" cried Poirot, heartily.

He came forward with great *empressement*, and shook the lady warmly by the hand.

"Mademoiselle blooms like a flower, in this dry-as-dust old office," he added, superbly careless of the feelings of Mr. McNeil.

This outrageous flattery was not without effect. Miss Monro blushed and simpered.

"Oh, go on now, Mr. Poirot!" she exclaimed. "I know what you Frenchmen are like!"

"Mademoiselle, we are not mute like Englishmen before beauty. Not that I am a Frenchman—I am a Belgian, you see."

"I've been to Ostend myself," said Miss Monro.

The whole affair, as Poirot would have said, was marching splendidly.

"And so you can tell us something about Mr. Claud Darrell?" queried Poirot.

"I knew Mr. Darrell very well at one time," explained the lady. "And when I saw your advertisement, being out of the shop for the moment, and my time being my own, I said to myself: 'there, they want to know about poor old Claudie—lawyers, too! Maybe it's a fortune looking for the rightful heir. I'd better go round at once.'"

Mr. McNeil rose.

"Well, Monsieur Poirot, shall I leave you for a little conversation with Miss Monro?"

"You are too amiable. But stay—a little idea presents itself to me. The hour of the *déjeuner* approaches. Mademoiselle will perhaps honour me by coming out to luncheon with me?"

Miss Monro's eyes glistened. It struck me that she was in exceedingly low water, and that the chance of a square meal was probably not to be despised.

A few minutes later saw us all in a taxi, bound for one of London's most expensive restaurants. Once arrived there, Poirot ordered a most delectable lunch, and then turned to his guest.

"And for wine, Mademoiselle? What do you say to champagne?"

The meal started pleasantly. Poirot replenished the lady's glass with thoughtful assiduity, and gradually slid into the topic nearest his heart.

"The poor Mr. Darrell! What a pity he is not with us!"

"Yes, indeed," sighed Miss Monro. "Poor boy, I do wonder what's become of him."

"It is a long time since you have seen him, yes?"

"Simply ages — not since the war. He was a funny boy, Claudie — very close about things, never told you a word about himself. But of course that all fits in if he's a missing heir. Is it a title, Mr. Poirot?"

"Alas, a mere heritage," said Poirot unblushingly. "But you see, it may be a question of identification. That is why it is necessary for us to find someone who knew him very well indeed. You knew him very well, did you not, Mademoiselle?"

"I don't mind telling you, Mr. Poirot. You're a gentleman. You know how to order lunch for a lady — which is more than some of these young whippersnappers do nowadays. Downright mean, I call it. As I was saying, you, being a Frenchman, won't be shocked. Ah, you Frenchmen! Naughty, naughty!" She wagged her finger at him in an excess of archness.

"Well, there it was, me and Claudie, two young things — what else could you expect? And I've still a kindly feeling for him. Though, mind you, he didn't treat me well — no, he didn't — he didn't treat me well at all; not as a lady should be treated. They're all the same when it comes to a question of money."

"No, no, Mademoiselle, do not say that," protested Poirot, filling up her glass once more. "Could you now describe this Mr. Darrell to me?"

"He wasn't anything so very much to look at," said Flossie Monro dreamily. "Neither tall nor short, you know, but quite well-set-up. Spruce-looking. Eyes a sort of blue-grey. And more or less fair-haired, I suppose. But oh, what an artist! I never saw anyone to touch him in the profession! He'd have made his name before now if it hadn't been for jealousy. Ah, Mr. Poirot, jealousy — you wouldn't believe it, you really wouldn't, what we artists have to suffer through jealousy! Why, I remember once at Manchester —"

We displayed what patience we could in listening to a long, complicated story about a pantomime, and the infamous conduct of the principal boy. Then Poirot led her gently back to the subject of Claud Darrell.

"It is very interesting, all of this that you are able to tell us, Mademoiselle, about Mr. Darrell. Women are such wonderful observers — they see everything, they notice the little detail that escapes the mere man. I have seen a woman identify one man out of a dozen others — and why, do you think? She had observed that he had a trick of stroking his nose when he was agitated! Now would a man ever have thought of noticing a thing like that?"

"Did you ever!" cried Miss Monro. "I suppose we do notice things. I remember Claudie, now I come to think of it, always fiddling with his bread at the table. He'd get a little piece between his fingers and then dab it round to pick up crumbs. I've seen him do it a hundred times. Why, I'd know him anywhere by that one trick."

"Is not that just what I say? The marvelous observation of a woman! And did you ever speak to him about this little habit of his, Mademoiselle?"

"No, I didn't, Mr. Poirot. You know what men are — they don't like you to notice things, especially if it should seem you were telling them off about it. I never said a word — but many's the time I smiled to myself. Bless you, he never knew he was doing it even."

Poirot nodded gently. I noticed that his hand was shaking a little as he stretched it out to his glass.

"Then there is always hand-writing as a means of establishing identity," he remarked. "Without doubt you have preserved a letter written by Mr. Darrell?"

Flossie Monro shook her head.

"He was never one for writing. Never wrote me a line in his life."

"That is a pity," said Poirot.

"I tell you what, though," said Miss Monro suddenly. "I've got a photograph — if that would be any good."

"You have a photograph?" Poirot almost sprang from his seat with excitement.

"It's quite an old one — eight years old, at least."

"*Ça ne fait rien!* No matter how old and faded! Ah, *ma foi*, but what stupendous luck! You will permit me to inspect that photograph, Mademoiselle?"

"Why, of course!"

"Perhaps you will even allow me to have a copy made? It would not take long."

"Certainly, if you like." And she rose.

"Well, I must run away," she declared archly. "Very glad to have met you and your friend, Mr. Poirot."

"And the photograph? When may I have it?"

"I'll look it out tonight. I think I know where to lay my hand upon it. And I'll send it to you right away."

"A thousand thanks, Mademoiselle. You are all that is of the most amiable. I hope that we shall soon be able to arrange another little lunch together."

"As soon as you like," said Miss Monro. "I'm willing."

"Let me see — I do not think that I have your address?"

With a grand air, Miss Monro drew a card from her handbag, and handed it to him. It was a somewhat dirty card, and the original address had been scratched out and another substituted in pencil.

Then, with a good many bows and gesticulations on Poirot's part, we bade farewell to the lady and got away.

"Do you really think this photograph so important?" I asked Poirot.

"Yes, *mon ami.* The camera does not lie. One can magnify a photograph, seize salient points that otherwise would remain unnoticed. And then there are a thousand details — such as the structure of the ears, which no one could ever describe to you in words. Ah, yes, it is a great chance, this, which is come our way! That is why I propose to take precautions."

He went across to the telephone as he finished speaking, and gave a number which I knew to be that of a private detective agency which he sometimes employed. His instructions were clear and definite. Two men were to go to the address he gave, and, in general terms, were to watch over the safety of Miss Monro. They were to follow her wherever she went.

Poirot hung up the receiver and came back to me.

"Do you really think that necessary, Poirot?" I asked.

"It may be. There is no doubt that we are watched, you and I, and since that is so, they will soon know with whom we were lunching to-day. And it is possible that Number Four will scent danger."

About twenty minutes later the telephone-bell rang. I answered it. A curt voice spoke into the phone.

"Is that Mr. Poirot? St. James Hospital speaking. A young woman was brought in ten minutes ago. Street accident. Miss Flossie Monro. She is asking very urgently for Mr. Poirot. But he must come at once. She can't possibly last long."

I repeated the words to Poirot. His face went white.

"Quick, Hastings! We must go like the wind!"

A taxi took us to the hospital in less than ten minutes. We asked for Miss Monro, and were taken immediately to the accident ward. A white-capped nurse met us in the doorway.

Poirot read the news in her face.

"It is over, eh?"

"She died six minutes ago."

Poirot stood as though stunned. The nurse, mistaking his emotion, said gently:

"She did not suffer, and she was unconscious toward the last. She was run over by a motor, you know — and the driver of the car did not even stop. Wicked, isn't it? I hope someone took the number."

"The stars fight against us," said Poirot, in a low voice.

"You would like to see her?"

The nurse led the way, and we followed.

Poor Flossie Monro, with her rouge and her dyed hair! She lay there very peacefully, a little smile on her lips.

"Yes," murmured Poirot. "The stars fight against us — but is it the stars?"

He lifted his head as though struck by a sudden idea. "If it is not — I swear to you, my friend, standing here by this poor woman's body, that I will have no mercy when the time comes!"

"What do you mean?" I asked.

But Poirot had turned to the nurse and was eagerly demanding information. A list of the articles found in her handbag was finally obtained. Poirot gave a suppressed cry as he read it over.

"You see, Hastings, you see?"

"See what?"

"There is no mention of the latch-key. But she must have had a latch-key with her. No, she was run down in cold blood, and the first person who bent over her took the key from her bag. But we may yet be in time. He may not have been able to find at once what he sought."

Another taxi took us to the address Flossie Monro had given us, a squalid block of "mansions" in an unsavory neighbourhood. It was some time before we could gain admission to Miss Monro's flat, but we had at least the satisfaction of knowing that no one could leave it while we were on guard outside.

Eventually we got in. But it was plain that someone had been there before us. The contents of drawers and cupboards were strewn all over the floor. Locks had been forced, and small articles of furniture had been overthrown, so violent had been the searcher's haste.

Poirot began to hunt through the debris. Suddenly he stood erect with a cry, holding out something. It was an old-fashioned photograph frame — empty.

He turned it slowly over. Affixed to the back was a small round label — a price label.

"It cost four shillings," I commented, absently.

"*Mon Dieu!* Hastings, use your eyes! That is a new clean label! It was stuck there by the man who took out the photograph, the man who was here before us, but knew that we should come, and so left this for us — Claude Darrell — alias Number Four!"

# X.

## THE TERRIBLE CATASTROPHE.

"The Terrible Catastrophe" was first published in *The Sketch* on March 5, 1924.

It was after the tragic death of Miss Flossie Monro that I began to be aware of a change in Poirot. Up to now, his invincible confidence in himself had stood the test. But it seemed as though, at last, the long strain was beginning to tell. His manner was grave and brooding and his nerves were on edge. In these days he was as jumpy as a cat. He avoided all discussion of The Big Four as far as possible, and seemed to throw himself into his ordinary work with almost his old ardour.

Nevertheless, I knew that he was secretly active in the big matter. Extraordinary-looking Slavs were constantly calling to see him; and though he vouchsafed no explanation as to these mysterious activities, I realised that he was building some new defense or weapon of opposition with the help of these somewhat repulsive-looking foreigners. Once, purely by chance, I happened to see the entries in his pass-book (he had asked me to verify some small item), and I noticed the paying-out of a huge sum — a huge sum even for Poirot, who was coining money nowadays — to some Russian with apparently every letter of the alphabet in his name.

But he gave me no clue as to the line on which he proposed to operate. Only over and over he gave utterance to one phrase. "It is the greatest mistake to underestimate your adversary. Remember that, *mon ami*." And I realized that that was the pitfall he was striving at all costs to avoid.

So matters went on until the end of March, and then, one morning, Poirot made a remark which startled me considerably.

"This morning, my friend, I should recommend the best suit. We go to call upon the Home Secretary."

"Indeed? That is very exciting. He has called you in to take up a case?"

"Not exactly. The interview is of my seeking. You may remember my saying that I once did him some small service? He is inclined to be foolishly enthusiastic over my capabilities in consequence, and I am about to trade on this attitude of his. As you know, the French premier, Monsieur Desjardeaux, is over in London, and, at my request, the Home Secretary has arranged for him to be present at our little conference this morning."

The Right Honorable Sydney Crowther, His Majesty's Secretary of State for Home Affairs, was a well-known and popular figure. A man of some fifty years of age, with a quizzical expression and shrewd grey eyes, he received us with that delightful *bonhomie* of manner which was well known to be one of his principal assets.

Standing with his back to the fireplace was a tall, thin man with a pointed black beard and a sensitive face.

"Monsieur Desjardeaux," said Crowther, "allow me to introduce to you Monsieur Hercule Poirot, of whom you may, perhaps, already have heard."

The Frenchman bowed and shook hands.

"I have indeed heard of Monsieur Hercule Poirot," he said pleasantly. "Who has not?"

"You are too amiable, Monsieur," said Poirot, bowing, but his face flushed with pleasure.

"Any word for an old friend?" asked a quiet voice, and a man came forward from a corner by a tall bookcase.

It was our old acquaintance, Mr. Ingles.

"And now, Monsieur Poirot," said Crowther, "we are at your service. I understood you to say that you had a communication of the utmost importance to make to us?"

"That is so, Monsieur. There is in the world to-day a vast organization — an organization of crime. It is controlled by four individuals who are known and spoken of as The Big Four. Number One is a Chinaman, Li Chang Yen; Number Two is the American multi-millionaire, Abe Ryland; Number Three is a

Frenchwoman; Number Four, I have every reason to believe, is an obscure English actor called Claude Darrell. These four are banded together to destroy the existing social order, and to replace it with an anarchy in which they would reign as dictators."

"Incredible," muttered the Frenchman. "Ryland mixed up with a thing of that kind? Surely the idea is too fantastic."

"Listen, Monsieur, whilst I recount to you some of the doings of this Big Four."

It was an enthralling narrative which Poirot unfolded. Familiar as I was with all the details, I was thrilled anew as I heard the bald recital of our adventures and escapes.

Monsieur Desjardeaux looked mutely at Mr. Crowther as Poirot finished. The other answered the look.

"Yes, Monsieur Desjardeaux, I think we must admit the existence of The Big Four. Scotland Yard was inclined to jeer at first; but they have been forced to admit that Monsieur Poirot was right in many of his claims. The only question is the extent of its aims. I cannot but feel that Monsieur Poirot — er — exaggerates a little."

For answer Poirot set forth ten salient points. I have been asked not to give them to the public even now, and so I refrain from doing so, but they included the extraordinary disasters to submarines which occurred in a certain month, and also a series of aeroplane accidents and forced landings. According to Poirot, these were all the work of The Big Four, and bore witness to the fact that they were in possession of various scientific secrets unknown to the world at large.

This brought us straight to the question which I had been waiting for the French premier to ask.

"You say that the third member of this organization is a Frenchwoman. Have you any idea of her name?"

"It is a well-known name, Monsieur — an honoured name. Number Three is no less than the celebrated Madame Olivier."

At the mention of the world-famous scientist, successor to the Curies, Monsieur Desjardeaux positively bounded from his chair, his face purple with emotion.

"Madame Olivier? Impossible! Absurd! It is an insult what you say there!"

Poirot shook his head gently, but made no answer.

Desjardeaux looked at him in stupefaction for some moments. Then his face cleared, and he glanced at the Home Secretary and tapped his forehead significantly.

"Monsieur Poirot is a great man," he observed. "But even the great man — sometimes he has his little mania, does he not; and seeks in high places for fancied conspiracies? It is well known. You agree with me, do you not, Mr. Crowther?"

The Home Secretary did not

answer for some minutes. Then he spoke slowly and heavily.

"Upon my soul, I don't know," he said at last. "I have always had, and still have, the utmost belief in Monsieur Poirot; but — well, this takes a bit of believing."

"This Li Chang Yen, too," continued Monsieur Desjardeaux; "who has ever heard of him?"

"I have," said the unexpected voice of Mr. Ingles.

The Frenchman stared at him, and he stared placidly back again, looking more like a Chinese idol than ever.

"Mr. Ingles," explained the Home Secretary, "is the greatest authority we have on the interior of China."

"And you have heard of this Li Chang Yen?"

"Until Monsieur Poirot here came to me, I imagined that I was the only man in England who had. Make no mistake, Monsieur Desjardeaux, there is only one man in China who counts to-day — Li Chang Yen. He has, perhaps (I only say perhaps), the finest brain in the world at the present time."

Monsieur Desjardeaux sat as though stunned. Presently, however, he rallied.

"There may be something in what you say, Monsieur Poirot," he said coldly. "But as regards Madame Olivier you are most certainly mistaken. She is a true daughter of France and devoted solely to the cause of science."

Poirot shrugged his shoulders and did not answer.

There was a minute or two's pause, and then my little friend rose to his feet, with an air of dignity that sat rather oddly upon his quaint personality.

"That is all I have to say, Messieurs — to warn you. I thought it likely that I should not be believed. But, at least, you will be on your guard. My words will sink in, and each fresh event that comes along will confirm your wavering faith. It was necessary for me to speak now — later, I may not be able to do so."

"You mean — ?" asked Crowther, impressed, in spite of himself, by the gravity of Poirot's tone.

"I mean, Monsieur, that since I have penetrated the identity of Number Four, my life is not worth an hour's purchase. He will seek to destroy me at all costs — and not for nothing is he named The Destroyer. Messieurs, I salute you. To you, Monsieur Crowther, I deliver this key and this sealed envelope. I have got together all my notes on the case, and my ideas as to how best to meet the menace that any day may break upon the world, and have placed them in a certain safe deposit. In the event of my death, Monsieur Crowther, I authorize you to take charge of those papers and make what use you can of them. And now, Messieurs, I wish you good day."

Desjardeaux merely bowed

coldly, but Crowther sprang up and held out his hand.

"You have converted me, Monsieur Poirot. Fantastic as the whole thing seems, I believe utterly in the truth of what you have told us."

Ingles left at the same time as we did.

"I am not disappointed with the interview," said Poirot, as we walked along. "I did not expect to convince Desjardeaux; but I have at least ensured that if I die my knowledge does not die with me. And I have made one or two converts. *Pas si mal!*"

"I'm with you, as you know," said Ingles. "By the way, I'm going out to China as soon as I can get off."

"Is that wise?"

"No," said Ingles dryly; "but it's necessary. One must do what one can."

"Ah, you are a brave man," cried Poirot with emotion. "If we were not in the street I would embrace you."

I fancied that Ingles looked rather relieved.

"I don't suppose that I shall be in any more danger in China than you are in London," he growled.

"That is possibly true enough," admitted Poirot. "I hope that they will not succeed in massacring Hastings also, that is all. That would annoy me greatly."

I interrupted this cheerful conversation to remark that I had no intention of letting myself be massacred and shortly afterwards Ingles parted from us

For some time we went along in silence, which Poirot at length broke by uttering a totally unexpected remark.

"I think — I really think — that I shall have to bring my brother into this."

"Your brother?" I cried, astonished. "I never knew you had a brother."

"You surprise me, Hastings. Do you not know that all celebrated detectives have brothers who would be even more celebrated than they are were it not for constitutional indolence?

Poirot employs a peculiar manner sometimes which makes it well-nigh impossible to know whether he is jesting or in earnest. That manner was very evident at the moment.

"What is your brother's name?" I asked, trying to adjust myself to this new idea.

"Achille Poirot," replied Poirot gravely. "He lives near Spa, in Belgium."

"What does he do?" I asked with some curiosity, putting aside a half-formed wonder as to the character and disposition of the late Madame Poirot and her classical taste in Christian names.

"He does nothing. He is, as I tell you, of a singularly indolent disposition. But his abilities are hardly less than my own — which is saying a great deal."

"Is he like you to look at?"

"Not unlike. But not nearly so

handsome. And he wears no moustaches."

"Is he older than you, or younger?"

"He happens to have been born on the same day."

"A twin," I cried.

"Exactly, Hastings. You jump to the right conclusion with unfailing accuracy. But here we are at home again. Let us at once get to work on that little affair of the Duchess's necklace."

But the Duchess's necklace was doomed to wait a while. A case of quite another description was waiting for us.

Our landlady, Mrs. Pearson, at once informed us that a hospital nurse had called and was waiting to see Poirot.

We found her sitting in the big arm-chair facing the window—a pleasant-faced woman of middle age, in a dark-blue uniform. She was a little reluctant to come to the point, but Poirot soon put her at her ease, and she embarked upon her story.

"You see, Monsieur Poirot, I've never come across anything of the kind before. I was sent for, from the Lark sisterhood, to go down to a case in Hertfordshire. An old gentleman it is, Mr. Templeton. Quite a pleasant house, and quite pleasant people. The wife, Mrs. Templeton, is much younger than her husband, and he has a son by his first marriage who lives there. I don't know that the young man and the stepmother always get on together. He is not quite what you'd call normal—not 'wanting' exactly, but decidedly dull in the intellect. Well, this illness of Mr. Templeton's seemed to me from the first to be very mysterious. At times there appears to be really nothing the matter with him, and then he suddenly has one of these gastric attacks with pain and vomiting. But the doctor seemed quite satisfied, and it wasn't for me to say anything. But I couldn't help thinking about it. And then—"

She paused, and became rather red.

"Something happened which aroused your suspicions?" suggested Poirot.

"Yes."

But she still seemed to find it difficult to go on.

"I found the servants were passing remarks too."

"About Mr. Templeton's illness?"

"Oh, no! About—about this other thing—"

"Mrs. Templeton?"

"Yes."

"Mrs. Templeton and the doctor, perhaps?"

Poirot has an uncanny flair in these things. The nurse threw him a grateful glance and went on.

"They were passing remarks. And then one day I happened to see them together myself—in the garden—"

It was left at that. Our client was in such an agony of outraged propriety that no one could feel it necessary to ask exactly what she had seen in the garden. She had evidently seen quite enough to make up her own mind on the situation.

"The attacks got worse and worse. Doctor Treves said it was all perfectly natural and to be expected, and that Mr. Templeton could not possibly live long; but I've never seen anything like it before myself— not in all my long experience of nursing. It seemed to me much more like some form of —"

She paused, hesitating.

"Arsenical poisoning?" said Poirot helpfully.

She nodded.

"And then, too, he — the patient, I mean — said something queer: 'they'll do for me, the four of them. They'll do for me yet.'"

"Eh?" said Poirot quickly.

"Those were his very words, Monsieur Poirot. He was in great pain at the time, of course, and hardly knew what he was saying."

"'They'll do for me, the four of them,'" repeated Poirot thoughtfully. "What did he mean by 'the four of them,' do you think?"

"That I can't say, Monsieur Poirot. I thought perhaps he meant his wife and son and the doctor, and perhaps Miss Clark, Mrs. Templeton's companion. That would make four, wouldn't it? He might think they were all in league against him."

"Quite so, quite so," said Poirot in a preoccupied voice. "What about food? Could you take no precautions about that?"

"I'm always doing what I can. But, of course, sometimes Mrs. Templeton insists on bringing him his food herself, and then there are the times when I am off duty."

"Exactly. And you are not sure enough of your ground to go to the police?"

The nurse's face showed her horror at the mere idea.

"What I have done, Monsieur Poirot, is this. Mr. Templeton had a very bad attack after partaking of a bowl of soup. I took a little from the bottom of the bowl afterwards, and have brought it up with me. I have been spared for the day to visit a sick mother, as Mr. Templeton was well enough to be left."

She drew out a little bottle of dark fluid and handed it to Poirot.

"Excellent, Mademoiselle. We will have this analyzed immediately. If you will return here in, say, an hour's time, I think that we shall be able to dispose of your suspicions one way or another."

First extracting from our visitor her name and qualifications, he ushered her out. Then he wrote a note and sent it off together with the bottle of soup. Whilst we waited to hear the results, Poirot amused himself by verifying the nurse's credentials, somewhat to my surprise.

"No, no, my friend," he declared; "I do well to be careful. Do not forget The Big Four is on our track."

However, he soon elicited the information that a nurse of the name of Mabel Palmer was a member of the Lark Institute and had been sent to the case in question.

"So far, so good," he said, with a twinkle. "And now here comes Nurse Palmer back again; and here, also, is our analyst's report."

Both the nurse and I waited anxiously whilst Poirot read the analyst's report.

"Is there arsenic in it?" she asked breathlessly.

Poirot shook his head, re-folding the paper. "No."

We were both immeasurably surprised.

"There is no arsenic in it," continued Poirot. "But there is antimony. And, that being the case, we will start immediately for Hertfordshire. Pray heaven that we are not too late."

It was decided that the simplest plan was for Poirot to represent himself truly as a detective; but that the ostensible reason of his visit should be to question Mrs. Templeton about a servant formerly in her employment whose name he obtained from nurse Palmer, and whom he could represent as being concerned in a jewel robbery.

It was late when we arrived at Elmstead, as the house was called. We had allowed nurse Palmer to precede us by about twenty minutes, so that there should be no question of our all arriving together.

Mrs. Templeton received us; a tall, dark woman, with sinuous movements and uneasy eyes. I noticed that as Poirot announced his profession, she drew in her breath with a sudden hiss, as though badly startled; but she answered his questions about the maid-servant readily enough. And then, to test her, Poirot embarked upon a long history of a poisoning case in which the guilty wife had figured. His eyes never left her face as he talked, and, try as she would, she could hardly conceal her rising agitation.

Suddenly, with an incoherent word of excuse, she hurried from the room.

We were not long left alone. A squarely-built man with a small red mustache and pince-nez came in.

"Doctor Treves," he introduced himself. "Mrs. Templeton asked me to make her excuses to you. She's in a very bad state, you know. Nervous strain. Worry over her husband, and all that. I've prescribed bed and bromide. But she hopes you will stay and take potluck, and I'm to do host. We've heard of you down here, Monsieur Poirot, and we mean to make the most of you. Ah! Here's Micky."

A shambling young man entered the room. He had a very round face and foolish looking eyebrows, raised as though in perpetual surprise. He grinned awkwardly as he shook hands. This was clearly the "wanting" son.

Presently we all went in to dinner. Doctor Treves left the room — to open some wine, I think — and suddenly the boy's physiognomy underwent a startling change.

"You've come about father," he said, nodding his head. "I know. I know lots of things — but nobody thinks I do. Mother will be glad when father's dead and she can marry Doctor Treves. She isn't my own mother, you know. I don't like her. She wants father to die."

It was all rather horrible. Luckily, before Poirot had time to reply, the doctor came back, and we had to carry on a forced conversation.

Suddenly, Poirot lay back in his chair with a hollow groan. His face was contorted with pain.

"My dear Sir, what's the matter?" cried the doctor.

"A sudden spasm. I am used to them. No, no; I require no assistance from you, doctor. If I might lie down upstairs."

His request was instantly acceded to, and I accompanied him upstairs, where he collapsed on the bed, groaning heavily.

For the first minute or two I had been taken in; but I had quickly realized that Poirot was — as he would have put it — playing the comedy, and that his object was to be left alone upstairs near the patient's room.

Hence I was quite prepared when, the instant we were alone, he sprang up.

"Quick, Hastings, the window. There is ivy outside. We can climb down before they begin to suspect."

"Climb down?"

"Yes, we must get out of this house at once. You saw him at dinner?"

"The doctor?"

"No, young Templeton. His trick with his bread. Do you remember what Flossie Munro told us before she died? That Claude Darrell had a habit of dabbing his bread on the table to pick up crumbs. Hastings, this is a vast plot, and that vacant looking young man is our arch-enemy — Number Four! Hurry!"

I did not wait to argue. Incredible as the whole thing seemed, it was wiser not to delay. We scrambled down the ivy as quietly as we could, and made a bee-line for the small town and the railway station. We were just able to catch the last train — the 8.34 — which would land us in town about eleven o'clock.

"A plot," said Poirot thoughtfully. "How many of them were in it, I wonder? I suspect that the whole Templeton family are just so many agents of The Big Four. Did they simply want to decoy us down there? Or was it more subtle than that? Did they intend to play the comedy down there and keep me interested until they had time to do — what? I wonder now."

He remained very thoughtful.

Arrived at our lodgings, he restrained me at the door of the sitting room.

"Attention, Hastings. I have my suspicions. Let me enter first."

He did so, and, to my slight amusement, took the precaution to press on the electric switch with an old golosh. Then he went around the room like a strange cat, cautiously, delicately, on the alert for danger. I watched him for some time, remaining obediently where I had been put by the wall.

"It's all right, Poirot," I said impatiently.

"It seems so, *mon ami*—it seems so. But let us make sure."

"Rot!" I said. "I shall light the fire, anyway, and have a pipe. I've caught you out for once. You had the matches last, and you didn't put them back in the holder as usual—the very thing you're always cursing me for not doing."

I stretched out my hand. I heard Poirot's warning cry—saw him leaping towards me—my hand touched the match-box.

Then—a flash of blue flame—an ear-rending crash—and darkness....

I came to myself to find the familiar face of our old friend Dr. Ridgeway bending over me. An expression of relief passed over his features.

"Keep still," he said soothingly. "You're all right. There's been an accident, you know."

"Poirot?" I murmured.

"You're in my digs. Everything is quite all right."

A cold fear clutched at my heart. His evasion woke a horrible dread.

"Poirot?" I reiterated. "What of Poirot?"

He saw that I had to know, and that further evasions were useless.

"By a miracle you escaped. Poirot—did not!"

A cry burst from my lips.

"Not dead? Not dead?"

Ridgeway bowed his head, his features working with emotion.

With desperate energy I pulled myself to a sitting position.

"Poirot may be dead," I said weakly; "but his spirit lives on. I will carry on his work! Death to The Big Four!"

Then I fell back, fainting.

# XI.

# THE DYING CHINAMAN.

"The Dying Chinaman" was first published in *The Sketch* on March 12, 1924.

Even now I can hardly bear to write of those days in March. Poirot—the unique, the inimitable Hercule Poirot—dead! Killed by the explosion so cunningly arranged in our rooms during our absence in Hertfordshire. There was a particularly diabolical touch in the disarranged match-box which was certain to catch Poirot's eye, and which he would hasten to rearrange—and thereby touch off the explosion. That, as a matter of fact, it was I who actually precipitated the catastrophe never ceased to fill me with unavailing remorse. It was, as Doctor Ridgeway said, a perfect miracle that I had not been killed, but had escaped with a slight concussion.

Although it had seemed to me as though I regained consciousness almost immediately, it was, in reality, over twenty-four hours before I came back to life. It was not until the evening of the day following that I was able to stagger feebly into an adjoining room, and view with deep emotion the plain elm coffin which held the remains of one of the most marvelous men this world has ever known.

From the very first moment of

regaining consciousness, I had only one purpose in mind — to avenge Poirot's death and to hunt down The Big Four remorselessly.

I had thought that Ridgeway would be of one mind with me about this; but, to my surprise, the good doctor seemed unaccountably lukewarm.

"Get back to South America," was his advice, tendered on every occasion. "Why attempt the impossible?" Put as delicately as possible, his opinion amounted to this. If Poirot, the unique Poirot, had failed, was it likely that I should succeed?

But I was obstinate. Putting aside any question as to whether I had the necessary qualifications for the task (and I may say, in passing, that I did not entirely agree with his views on this point. I had worked so long with Poirot that I knew his methods by heart, and felt fully capable of taking up the work where he had laid it down), it was, with me, a question of feeling. My friend had been thoroughly murdered. Was I to go tamely back to South America without an effort to bring his murderers to justice?

I said all this and more to Ridgeway, who listened attentively enough.

"All the same," he said, when I had finished, "my advice does not vary. I am earnestly convinced that Poirot himself, if he were here, would urge you to return. In his name, I beg of you, Hastings, abandon these wild ideas and go back to your ranch."

To that only one answer was possible; and, shaking his head sadly, he said no more.

It was a month before I was fully restored to health. Toward the end of April, I sought, and obtained, an interview with the Home Secretary.

Mr. Crowther's manner was reminiscent of that of Doctor Ridgeway. It was soothing and negative. Whilst appreciating the offer of my services, he gently and considerately declined them. The papers referred to by Poirot had passed into his keeping, and he assured me that all possible steps were being taken to deal with the approaching menace.

With that cold comfort I was forced to be satisfied. Mr. Crowther ended the interview by urging me to return to South America. I found the whole thing profoundly unsatisfactory.

I should, I suppose, in its proper place, have described Poirot's funeral. It was a solemn and moving ceremony; and the extraordinary number of floral tributes passed belief. They came from high and low alike, and bore a striking testimony to the place my friend had made for himself in the country of his adoption. For myself, I was frankly overcome by emotion as I stood by the graveside and thought of all our varied experiences and the happy days we had passed together.

By the beginning of May I had mapped out a plan of campaign. I felt that I could not do better than keep to Poirot's scheme of advertising for any information respecting Claude Darrell. I had an advertisement to this effect inserted in a number of morning newspapers. I was sitting in a small restaurant in Soho, and judging of the effect of the advertisement, when a small paragraph in another part of the paper gave me a nasty shock.

Very briefly, it reported the mysterious disappearance of Mr. John Ingles, from the *S.S. Shanghai*, shortly after the latter had left Marseilles. Although the weather was perfectly smooth, it was feared that the unfortunate gentleman must have fallen overboard. The paragraph ended with a brief reference to Mr. Ingles' long and distinguished service in China.

The news was unpleasant. I read into Ingles' death a sinister motive. Not for one moment that I believe the theory of an accident. Ingles had been murdered; and his death was only too clearly the handiwork of that accursed Big Four.

As I sat there, stunned by the blow, and turning the whole matter over in my mind, I was startled by the remarkable behavior of the man sitting opposite me. So far, I had not paid much attention to him. He was a thin, dark man of middle age, sallow of complexion, with a small pointed beard. He had sat down opposite me so quietly that I had hardly noticed his arrival.

But his actions now were decidedly peculiar, to say the least of them. Leaning forward, he deliberately helped me to salt, putting it in four little heaps around the edge of my plate.

"You will excuse me," he said, in a melancholy voice. "To help a stranger to salt is to help him to sorrow, they say. That may be an unavoidable necessity. I hope not, though. I hope that you will be reasonable."

Then, with a certain significance, he repeated his operations with the salt on his own plate.

The symbol "4" was too plain to be missed. I looked at him searchingly. In no way that I could see did he resemble young Templeton, or James the footman, or any of the other various personalities we had come across. Nevertheless, I was convinced that I had to do with no less than the redoubtable Number Four himself. In his voice there was certainly a faint resemblance to the buttoned-up stranger who had called upon us in Paris.

I looked round, undecided as to my course of action. Reading my thoughts, he smiled and gently shook his head. "I should not advise it," he remarked. "Remember what came of your hasty action in Paris. Let me tell you that my way of retreat is well assured. Your ideas are inclined to be a little crude, Captain Hastings, if I may say so."

"You devil!" I said, choking with rage; "you incarnate devil!"

"Heated—just a trifle heated. Your late lamented friend would have told you that a man who keeps calm has always a great advantage."

"You dare to speak of him!" I cried — "the man you murdered so foully! And you come here —"

He interrupted me. "I came here for an excellent and peaceful purpose. To advise you to return at once to South America. If you do so, that is the end of the matter as far as The Big Four are concerned. You and yours will not be molested in any way. I give you my word as to that."

I laughed scornfully.

"And if I refuse to obey your autocratic command?"

"It is hardly a command. Shall we say that it is — a warning?"

There was a cold menace in his tone.

"The first warning," he said softly. "You will be well advised not to disregard it."

Then, before I had any hint of his intention, he rose and slipped quickly away towards the door. I sprang to my feet and was after him in a second; but by bad luck, I cannoned straight into an enormously fat man, who blocked the way between me and the next table. By the time I had disentangled myself, my quarry was just passing through the doorway, and the next delay was from a waiter carrying a huge pile of plates who crashed into me without the least warning. By the time I got to the door, there was no sign of the thin man with the dark beard.

The waiter was fulsome in apologies; the fat man was sitting placidly at a table ordering his lunch. There was nothing to show that both occurrences had not been a pure accident. Nevertheless, I had my own opinion as to that. I knew well enough that the agents of The Big Four were everywhere.

Needless to say, I paid no heed to the warning given me. I would do or die in the good cause. I received in all only two answers to the advertisements. Neither of them gave me any information of value. They were both from actors who had played with Claude Darrell at one time or another. Neither of them knew him at all intimately, and no new light was thrown upon the problem of his identity and present whereabouts.

No further sign came from The Big Four until about ten days later. I was crossing Hyde Park, lost in thought, when a voice, rich with a persuasive foreign inflection, hailed me.

"Captain Hastings, is it not?"

A big limousine had just drawn up by the pavement. A woman was leaning out. Exquisitely dressed in black with wonderful pearls, she was the lady first known to us as Countess Vera Rossakoff, and afterwards under a different alias as an agent of The Big Four. Poirot, for some reason or other, had always had a sneaking fondness for the Countess. Something in her very flamboyance attracted the little man. She was, he was wont to declare in moments of enthusiasm, a woman in a thousand. That she was arrayed against us, on the side of our bitterest enemies, never seem to weigh in his judgment.

"Ah, do not pass on!" said the Countess. "I have something most important to say to you. And do not try to have me arrested, either, for that would be stupid. You were always a little stupid — yes, yes; it is so. You are stupid now, when you persist in disregarding the warning we sent you. It is the second warning I bring you. Leave England at once. You can do no good here — I tell you that frankly. You will never accomplish anything."

"In that case," I said stiffly, "it seems rather extraordinary that you are all so anxious to get me out of the country."

The Countess shrugged her shoulders — magnificent shoulders and a magnificent gesture.

"For my part, I think that too stupid. I would leave you here to play about happily. But the Chiefs, you see, are fearful that some word of yours may give great help to those more intelligent than yourself. Hence — you are to be banished."

The Countess appeared to have a flattering idea of my abilities. I concealed my annoyance. Doubtless this attitude of hers was assumed expressly to annoy me, and to give me the idea that I was unimportant.

"It would, of course, be quite easy to — remove you," she continued; "but I am quite sentimental sometimes. I pleaded for you. You have a nice little wife somewhere, have you not? And it would please the poor little man who is dead to know that you were not to be killed. I always liked him, you know. He was clever — but clever! Had it not been a case of four against one, I honestly believe he might have been too much for us. I confess it frankly — he was my master! I sent a wreath to the funeral as a token of my admiration — an enormous one of crimson roses. Crimson roses express my temperament."

I listened in silence and a growing distaste.

"You have the look of a mule when it puts its ears back and kicks. Well, I have delivered my warning. Remember this, the third warning will come by the hand of The Destroyer —"

She made a sign, and the car whirled away rapidly. I noted the number mechanically but without the hope that it would lead to anything. The Big Four were not apt to be careless in details.

I went home a little sobered. One fact had emerged from the Countess's flood of volubility. I was in real danger of my life. Though I had no intention of abandoning the struggle, I saw that it behoved me to walk warily and adopt every possible precaution.

Whilst I was reviewing all these facts, and seeking for the best line of action, the telephone bell rang. I crossed the room and picked up the receiver.

"Yes. Hullo. Who's speaking?"

A crisp voice answered me. "This is Saint Giles Hospital. We have a Chinaman here, knifed in the street and brought in. He can't last long. We rang you up because we found in his pocket a piece of paper with your name and address on it."

I was very much astonished. Nevertheless, after a moment's reflection I said that I would come down at once. Saint Giles Hospital was, I knew, down by the docks, and it occurred to me that the Chinaman might have just come off some ship.

It was on my way down there that a sudden suspicion shot into my mind. Was the whole thing a trap? Wherever a Chinaman was, there might be the hand of Li Chang Yen. I remembered the Adventure of the Baited Trap. Was the whole thing a ruse on the part of my enemies?

A little reflection convinced me that at any rate a visit to the hospital would do no harm It was probable that the thing was not so much a plot as what is vulgarly known as a "plant."The dying Chinaman would make some revelation to me upon which I should act, and this would have the result of leading me into the hands of The Big Four. The thing to do was to preserve an open mind and whilst feigning credulity, to be secretly on my guard.

On arriving at Saint Giles Hospital and making my business known, I was taken at once to the accident ward, to the bedside of the man in question. He lay absolutely still, his eyelids closed; and only a very faint movement of the chest showed that he still breathed. A doctor stood by the bed, his fingers on the Chinaman's pulse.

"He's almost gone," he whispered to me. "You know him, eh?"

I shook my head. "I've never seen him before."

"Then what was he doing with your name and address in his pocket? You are Captain Hastings, aren't you?"

"Yes; but I can't explain it any more than you can."

"Curious thing. From his papers he seems to have been the servant of a man called Ingles — a retired civil servant. — Ah! You know *him*, do you?" he added quickly, as I started at the name.

Ingles servant! Then I had seen him before. Not that I had ever succeeded in being able to distinguish one Chinaman from another. He must have been with Ingles on his way to China, and after the catastrophe he had returned to England with a message for me. It was vital, imperative that I should hear that message.

"Is he conscious?" I asked. "Can he speak? Mr. Ingles was an old friend of mine, and I think it possible that this poor fellow has brought me a message from him. Mr. Ingles is believed to have gone overboard about ten days ago."

"He's just conscious, but I doubt if he has the force to speak. He lost a terrible lot of blood, you know. I can administer a stimulant, of course; but we've already done nearly all that is possible in that direction."

Nevertheless, he administered a hypodermic injection, and I stayed by the bed, hoping against hope for a word — a sign — that might be of the utmost value to me in my work.

But the minutes sped on, and no sign came.

And suddenly a baleful idea shot across my mind. Was I not already falling into the trap? Suppose that this Chinaman had merely assumed the part of Ingles' servant — that he was in reality an agent of The Big Four? Had I not once read that certain Chinese priests were capable of simulating death? Or, to go further still, Li Chang Yen might command a little band of fanatics who would welcome death itself if it came at the command of their master. I must be on my guard.

Even as these thoughts flashed across my mind, the man in the bed stirred. His eyes opened. He murmured something incoherently. Then I saw his glance fasten upon me. He made no sign of recognition, but I was at once aware that he was trying to speak to me.

Be he friend or foe, I must hear what he had to say. I leaned over the bed; but the broken sounds conveyed no sort of meaning to me. I thought I caught the word "hand," but in what connection it was used I could not tell. Then it came again, and this time I heard another word, the word "Largo." I stared in amazement, as the possible juxtaposition of the two suggested itself to me.

"Handel's Largo?" I queried.

The Chinaman's eyelids flickered rapidly, as though in assent, and he added another Italian word, the word *carrozza*. Two or three more words of murmured Italian came to my ears, and then he fell back abruptly.

The doctor pushed me aside. It was all over. The man was dead. I went out into the air again, thoroughly bewildered.

"Handel's Largo," and a *carrozza*. If I remembered rightly, a *carrozza* was a carriage. What possible meaning could lie behind those simple words? The man was a Chinaman, not an Italian; why should he speak in Italian? Surely, if he were indeed Ingles' servant, he must know English?

The whole thing was profoundly mystifying. I puzzled over it all the way home. Oh, if only Poirot had been there to solve the problem with his lightning ingenuity!

I let myself in with my latch-key, and went slowly up to my room. A letter was lying on the table, and I tore it open carelessly enough. But in a minute I stood rooted to the ground whilst I read. It was a communication from a firm of solicitors.

"Dear Sir (it ran),—As instructed by our late client, Monsieur Hercule Poirot, we forward you the enclosed letter. This letter was placed in our hands a week before his death, with instructions that in the event of his demise it should be sent to you at a certain date after his death.—Yours faithfully, etc."

I turned the enclosed missive over and over. It was undoubtedly from Poirot. I knew that familiar writing only too well. With a heavy heart, yet a certain eagerness, I tore it open.

*Mon cher ami—*

*When you receive this I shall be no more. Do not shed tears about me, but follow my orders. Immediately upon receipt of this, return to South America. Do not be pig-headed about this. It is not for sentimental reasons that I bid you undertake the journey. It is necessary. It is part of the plan of Hercule Poirot! To say more is unnecessary to anyone who has the acute intelligence of my friend Hastings.*

*À bas The Big Four! I salute you, my friend, from beyond the grave.*

*—Ever thine,*

*Hercule POIROT.*

I read and re-read this astonishing communication. One thing was evident. This amazing man had so provided for every eventuality that even his own death did not upset the sequence of his plans! Mine was to be the active part—his the directing genius. Doubtless I should find full instructions awaiting me beyond the seas. In the meantime my enemies, convinced that I was obeying their warning, would cease to trouble their heads about me. I could return, unsuspected, and work havoc in their midst.

There was now nothing to hinder my immediate departure. I sent off cables, booked my passage, and one week later found me embarking on the *Anconia en route* for Buenos Aires.

Just as the boat left the quay, a steward brought me a note. It had been given him, so he explained, by a big gentleman in a fur coat, who had left the boat last thing before the gangway planks were lifted.

I opened it. It was terse and to the point.

"You are wise," it ran. It was signed with a big figure 4.

I could afford to smile to myself.

The sea was not too choppy. I enjoyed a passable dinner, made up my mind as to the majority of my fellow-passengers, and had a rubber or two of bridge. Then I turned in and slept like a log, as I always do on board ship.

I was awakened by feeling myself persistently shaken. Dazed and bewildered, I saw that one of the ship's officers was standing over me. He gave a sigh of relief as I sat up.

"Thank the Lord I've got you

awake at last. I've had no end of a job. Do you always sleep like that?"

"What's the matter?" I asked, still bewildered and not fully awake. "Is there anything wrong with the ship?"

"I expect you know what's the matter better than I do," he replied dryly. "Special instructions from the Admiralty. There is a destroyer waiting to take you off."

"What?" I cried. "In mid-ocean?"

"It seems a most mysterious affair, but that's not my business. They've sent a young fellow aboard who is to take your place, and we are all sworn to secrecy. Will you get up and dress?"

Utterly unable to conceal my amazement, I did as I was told. A boat was lowered, and I was conveyed aboard the destroyer. There I was received courteously, but got no further information. The commander's instructions were to land me in a certain spot on the Belgian coast. There his knowledge and responsibility ended.

The whole thing was like a dream. The one idea I held to firmly was that all this must be part of Poirot's plan. I must simply go forward blindly, trusting in my dead friend.

I was duly landed at the spot indicated. There a motor was waiting, and soon I was rapidly whirling across the Flemish plains. I slept that night at a small hotel in Brussels. The next day we went on again. The country became wooded and hilly. I realized that we were penetrating into the Ardennes, and I suddenly remembered Poirot saying that he had a brother who lived at Spa.

But we did not go to Spa itself. We left the main road and wound into the leafy fastnesses of the hills, until we reached a little hamlet and an isolated white villa high on the hillside. Here the car stopped in front of the green door of the villa.

The door opened as I alighted. An elderly man-servant stood in the doorway bowing.

"*Monsieur le Capitaine* Hastings?" he said in French. "*Monsieur le capitaine* is expected. If he will follow me."

He led the way across the hall, and flung open the door at the back, standing aside to let me pass in.

I blinked a little, for the room faced west, and the afternoon sun was pouring in. Then my vision cleared, and I saw a figure waiting to welcome me with outstretched hands.

It was — oh, impossible! It couldn't be — but yes!

"Poirot!" I cried, and for once did not attempt to evade the embrace with which he overwhelmed me.

"But yes, but yes, it is indeed I! Not so easy to kill Hercule Poirot!"

"But, Poirot — *why*?"

"A *ruse de guerre*, my friend, a *ruse de guerre*. All is now ready for our grand *coup*."

"But you might have told *me*!"

"No, Hastings, I could not. Never, never, in a thousand years, could you have acted your part at the funeral! As it was, it was perfect. It could not fail to carry conviction to The Big Four."

"But what I've been through —"

"Do not think me too unfeeling. I carried out the deception partly for your sake. I was willing to risk my own life, but I had qualms about continually risking yours. So, after the explosion, I had an idea of great brilliancy. The good Ridgeway, he enables me to carry it out. I am dead; you will return to South America. But, *mon ami*, that is just what you would not do. In the end I have to arrange a solicitor's letter and a long rigmarole. But, at all events, here you are — that is the great thing. And now we lie here — *perdu* — till the moment comes for the last grand coup — *the final overthrowing of The Big Four!*"

# XII.

## THE CRAG IN THE DOLOMITES.

"The Crag in the Dolomites" was first published in *The Sketch* on March 19, 1924.

From our quiet retreat in the Ardennes we watched the progress of affairs in the great world. We were plentifully supplied with newspapers, and every day Poirot received a bulky envelope, evidently containing some kind of report. He never showed these reports to me, but I could usually tell from his manner whether their contents had been satisfactory or otherwise. He never wavered in his belief that our present plan was the only one likely to be crowned by success.

"As a minor point, Hastings," he remarked one day—"I was in continual fear of your death lying at my door. And that rendered me nervous—like a cat upon the jumps, as you say. But now I am well satisfied. Even if they discover that the Captain Hastings who landed in South America was an impostor (and I do not think they will discover it, as they are not likely to send an agent out there who knows you personally), they will only believe that you are trying to circumvent them in some clever manner of your own, and will pay no serious attention to discovering your whereabouts. Of the one vital fact, my supposed death, they are thoroughly convinced. They will go ahead and mature their plans."

"And then?" I asked eagerly.

"And then, *mon ami*, grand resurrection of Hercule Poirot! At the eleventh hour, I reappear, throw all into confusion, and achieve the supreme victory in my own unique manner!"

I realized that Poirot's vanity was of the case-hardened variety which could withstand all attacks. I reminded him that once or twice the honours of the game had lain with our adversaries. But I might have known that it was impossible to diminish Hercule Poirot's enthusiasm for his own methods.

"See you, Hastings, it is like the little trick that you play with the cards. You have seen it, without doubt? You take the four names, you divide them, one on top of the pack, one underneath, and so on — you cut and you shuffle, and there they are, all together again! That is my object. So far, I have been contending, now against one of The Big Four, now against another. But let me get them all together, like the four names in the pack of cards, and then, with one *coup*, I destroy them all!"

"And how do you propose to get them all together?" I asked.

"By awaiting the supreme moment. By lying *perdu* until they are ready to strike."

"That may mean a long wait," I grumbled.

"Always impatient, the good Hastings! But, no; it will not be so long. The one man they were afraid of — myself — is out of the way. I give them two or three months at most."

His speaking of someone being got out of the way reminded me of Ingles and his tragic death; and I remembered that I had never told Poirot about the dying Chinaman in Saint Giles hospital.

He listened with keen attention to my story.

"Ingles' servant, eh? And the few words he uttered were in Italian? Curious."

"That's why I suspected it might have been a plant on the part of The Big Four."

"Your reasoning is at fault, Hastings. Employ the little grey cells. If your enemies wish to deceive you, they would assuredly have seen to it that the Chinaman spoke in intelligible pidgin-English. No; the message was genuine. Tell me again all that you heard?"

"First of all, he made a reference to Handel's Largo, and then he said something that sounded like 'Carrozza' — that's a carriage, isn't it?"

"Nothing else?"

"Well, just at the end he murmured something like 'Cara' somebody or other — some woman's name. Zia, I think. But I don't suppose that that had any bearing on the rest of it."

"You would not suppose so, Hastings! Cara Zia is very important, very important indeed."

"I don't see —"

"My dear friend, you never see — and anyway, the English know no geography."

"Geography?" I cried. "What has geography got to do with it?"

"I daresay Monsieur Thomas Cook would be more to the point."

As usual, Poirot refused to say anything more — a most irritating trick of his. But I noticed that his manner became extremely cheerful, as though he had scored some point or other.

The days went on, pleasant, if a trifle monotonous. There were plenty of books in the villa, and delightful rambles all around; but I chafed sometimes at the forced inactivity of our life, and marveled at Poirot's state of placid content. Nothing occurred to ruffle our quiet existence; and it was not until the end of June, well within the limit that Poirot had given them, that we had our news of The Big Four.

A car drove up to the villa early one morning — such an unusual event in that peaceful spot that I hurried down to satisfy my curiosity. I found Poirot talking to a pleasant-faced young fellow of about my own age. He introduced me.

"This is Captain Harvey, Hastings, one of the most famous members of your intelligence service."

"Not famous at all, I'm afraid," said the young man, laughing pleasantly.

"Not famous, except to those in the know, I should have said. Most of Captain Harvey's friends and acquaintances consider him an amiable but brainless young man — devoted only to the trot of the fox, or whatever the dance is called."

We both laughed.

"Well, well, to business," said Poirot. "You are of opinion the time has come, then?"

"We are sure of it, Sir. China was isolated politically yesterday. What is going on out there, nobody knows. No news of any kind, wireless or otherwise, has come through: just a complete break — and silence!"

"Li Chang Yen has shown his hand. And the others?"

"Abe Ryland arrived in England a week ago, and left for the continent yesterday."

"And Madame Olivier?"

"Madame Olivier left Paris last night."

"For Italy?"

"For Italy, Sir. As far as we can judge, they are both making for the resort you indicated — though how you knew that —"

"Ah, that is not the cap with the feather for me. That was the work of Hastings here. He conceals his intelligence, you comprehend, but it is profound, for all that."

Harvey looked at me with due appreciation, and I felt rather uncomfortable.

"All is in train, then," said Poirot. He was pale now, and completely serious. "The time has come. The arrangements are all made?"

"Everything you ordered has been carried out. The governments of Italy, France, and England are behind you, and are all working harmoniously together."

"It is, in fact, a new Entente," observed Poirot dryly. "I am glad that Desjardeaux is convinced at last. *Eh bien*, then, we will start — or, rather, I will start. You, Hastings, will remain here — yes, I pray of you. In verity, my friend, I am serious."

I believed him, but it was not likely that I should consent to being left behind in that fashion. Our argument was short, but decisive. It was not until we were in the train, speeding towards Paris, that he admitted that he was secretly glad of my decision.

"For you have a part to play, Hastings. An important part! Without you, I might well fail. Nevertheless, I felt that it was my duty to urge you to remain behind."

"There is danger, then?"

"*Mon ami*, where The Big Four are there is always danger."

On arrival in Paris, we drove across to the Gare de l'Est, and Poirot at last announced our destination. We were bound for Bolzano and the Italian Tyrol. During Harvey's absence from our carriage, I took the opportunity of asking Poirot why he had said that the discovery of the rendezvous was my work.

"Because it was, my friend. How Ingles managed to get hold of the information I do not know; but he did, and he sent his servant to us primed with the knowledge. We are bound, *mon ami*, for Karersee, the new Italian name for which is Lago di Carezza. You see now where your 'Cara Zia' comes in, and also your 'carrozza' and 'Largo' — the 'Handel' was supplied by your own imagination. Possibly some reference to the information coming from the 'hand' of Mr. Ingles started the train of association."

"Karersee?" I queried. "I never heard of it.

"I always tell you that the English know no geography. But, as a matter of fact, it is a well-known and very beautiful summer resort, four thousand feet up, in the heart of the Dolomites."

"And it is in this out-of-the-way spot that The Big Four have their rendezvous?"

"Say, rather, their headquarters. The signal has been given, and it is their intention to disappear from the world and issue orders from their mountain fastness. I have made the inquiries — a lot of quarrying of stone and mineral deposits is done there, and the company, apparently a small Italian firm, is in reality controlled by Abe Ryland. I am prepared to swear that a vast subterranean dwelling has been hollowed out in the very heart of the mountain, secret and inaccessible. From there the leaders of the organization will issue by wireless their orders to their followers, who are numbered by the thousands in every country. And from that crag in the Dolomites the dictators of the world will emerge. That is to say, they would emerge, were it not for Hercule Poirot!"

"Do you seriously believe all this, Poirot? What about the armies and general machinery of civilization?"

"What about it in Russia, Hastings? This will be Russia only on an infinitely larger scale; and with this additional menace — that Madame Olivier's experiments have proceeded farther than she has ever given out. I believe that she has to a certain extent succeeded in liberating atomic energy and harnessing it to her purpose. Her experiments with the nitrogen of the air have been very remarkable; and she has also experimented in the concentration of wireless energy, so that a beam of great intensity can be focused upon some given spot. Exactly how far she has progressed, nobody knows, but it is certain that it is much farther than has ever been given out. She is a genius, that woman — the Curies were as nothing to her. Add to her genius the power of Ryland's almost unlimited wealth, and with the brain of Li Chang Yen (the finest criminal brain ever known) to direct and plan — *eh bien*, it will not be, as you say, all jam for civilization."

His words made me very thoughtful. Although Poirot was given at times to exaggeration of language, he was not really an alarmist. For the first time I realized what a desperate struggle it was upon which we were engaged.

Harvey soon rejoined us, and no more was said.

We arrived at Bolzano about midday. From there the journey on was by motor. Several big blue motor-cars were waiting in the central square of the town, and we three got into one of them. Poirot, notwithstanding the heat of the day, was muffled to the eyes in great-coat and scarf. His eyes and the tips of his ears were all that could be seen of him. I did not know whether this was due to precaution — or merely his exaggerated fear of catching a chill.

The motor journey took a couple of hours. It was a really wonderful drive. For the first part of the way we wound in and out of huge cliffs, with a trickling waterfall on one hand. Then we emerged into a fertile valley which continued for some miles; and then, still winding steadily upwards, the bare rocky peaks began to show, with dense, clustering pine-woods at their base. The whole place was wild and lovely. Finally there was a series of abrupt curves, with the road running through the pine-woods on either side, and we came suddenly upon a big hotel, and found that we had arrived.

Our rooms had been reserved for us, and under Harvey's guidance we went straight up to them. They looked out over the rocky peaks and the long slopes of pine-woods leading up to them. Poirot made a gesture towards them.

"It is there?" he asked in a low voice.

"Yes," replied Harvey. "There is a place called the Felsenlabyrinth — all big boulders piled about in a most fantastic way; a path winds through them. The quarrying is to the right of that, but we think that the entrance is probably in the Felsenlabyrinth."

Poirot nodded.

"Come, *mon ami*," he said to me, "let us go down and sit upon the terrace and enjoy the sunlight."

"You think that wise?" I asked.

He shrugged his shoulders.

The sunlight was marvelous — in fact, the glare was almost too great for me. We had some creamy coffee instead of tea, then went upstairs and unpacked our few belongings. Poirot was in his most unapproachable mood, lost in a kind of reverie. Once or twice he shook his head and sighed.

I had been rather intrigued by a man who had gone out of our train at Bolzano and had been met by a private car. He was a small man, about the size of Poirot, and the thing about him that had attracted my attention was that he was almost as much muffled up as Poirot had been. More so, indeed, for, in addition to great-coat and muffler, he was wearing huge blue spectacles. I was convinced that here we had an emissary of The Big Four. Poirot did not seem very impressed by my idea; but when, leaning out of my bed-room window, I reported that the man in question was strolling about in the vicinity of the hotel, he admitted reluctantly that there might be something in it.

I urged my friend not to go down to dinner, but he insisted on doing so. We entered the dining-room rather late, and were shown to a table by the window. As we sat down, our attention was attracted by an exclamation and a crash of falling china. A dish of *haricots verts* had been upset over a man who was sitting at the table next to ours. The head waiter came up and was vociferous in apologies.

Presently, when the offending waiter was serving us with soup, Poirot spoke to him.

"An unfortunate accident that; but it was not your fault."

"Monsieur saw that? No indeed, it was not my fault. The gentleman half-sprang up from his chair — I thought he was going to have an attack of some kind. I could not save the catastrophe."

I saw Poirot's eyes shining with the green light I knew so well, and as the waiter departed he said to me in a low voice —

"You see, Hastings, the effect of Hercule Poirot — alive and in the flesh?"

"You think —"

I had not time to continue. I felt Poirot's hand on my knee, as he whispered excitedly—

"Look, Hastings, look! *His trick with the bread!* Number Four!"

Sure enough, the man at the next table to ours, his face unusually pale, was dabbing a small piece of bread mechanically about the table. This little trick, of which he himself was quite unaware, was our only means of identifying Number Four. Indeed I would have sworn readily enough that the man sitting there was a complete stranger to me.

"He has recognized you," I murmured. "You should not have come down."

"My excellent Hastings, I have feigned death for three months for this one purpose."

"To startle Number Four?"

"To startle him at a moment when he must act quickly or not it all. And when we have this great advantage—he does not know that we recognize him. He thinks that he is safe in his new disguise. How I bless Flossie Monro for telling us of that little habit of his with the bread."

"What will happen now?" I asked.

"What can happen? He recognizes the only man he fears, miraculously resurrected from the dead, at the very moment when the plans of The Big Four are in the balance. Madame Olivier and Abe Ryland lunched here to-day, I find, and it is thought that they went on to Cortina. We only are aware that they have secretly retired to their prepared hiding place. How much do we know? That is what Number Four is asking himself at this minute. He dares take no risks. I must be suppressed at all costs. *Eh bien*, let him try to suppress Hercule Poirot! I shall be ready for him."

As he finished speaking the man at the next table got up and went out.

"He has gone to make his little arrangements," said Poirot placidly. "Shall we have our coffee on the terrace, my friend? It would be pleasanter, I think. I will just go up and get a coat."

I went out on the terrace a little disturbed in mind. Poirot's assurance did not quite content me. However, so long as we were on our guard, nothing could happen to us. I resolved to keep thoroughly on the alert.

It was quite five minutes before Poirot joined me. With his usual precautions against cold, he was muffled up to the ears. He sat down beside me, and sipped his coffee appreciatively.

"Only in England is the coffee so atrocious," he remarked. "On the continent, they understand how important it is for the digestion that it should be properly made."

As he finished speaking, the man from the next table suddenly appeared on the terrace. Without any hesitation he came over and drew up a third chair to our table.

"You do not mind my joining you, I hope?" he said in English.

"Not at all, Monsieur," said Poirot.

I felt vaguely uneasy. It is true that we were on the terrace of the hotel, with people all around us; but, nevertheless, I was not satisfied. I sensed the presence of danger.

Meanwhile, Number Four chatted away in a perfectly natural manner. It seemed impossible to believe that he was anything but a bona-fide tourist. He described excursions and motor trips, and posed as quite an authority on the neighbourhood.

He took a pipe from his pocket and began to light it. Poirot drew out his case of tiny cigarettes. As he placed one between his lips, the stranger leaned forward with the match.

"Let me give you a light."

As he spoke, without the least warning all the lights went out. There was a clink of glass and something pungent under my nose, suffocating me....

I could not have been unconscious more than a minute. When I came to myself I was being hustled along between two men. They had me under each arm, supporting my weight, and there was a gag in my mouth. It was pitch-dark, but I gathered that we were not outside, but passing through the hotel. All around I could hear people shouting and demanding in every known language what had happened to the lights.

My captors swung me down some stairs. We passed along the basement passage, then through a door and out into the open again through a glass door at the back of the hotel. In another moment we had gained the shelter of the pine-trees.

I had caught a glimpse of another figure in a similar plight to myself, and realized that Poirot, too, was a victim of this bold coup.

By sheer audacity, Number Four had won the day. He had employed, I gathered, an instant anesthetic, probably ethyl-chloride — breaking two small bulbs of it under our noses. Then, in the confusion of the darkness, his accomplices, who had probably been guests sitting at the next table, had thrust gags in our mouths and hurried us away, taking us through the hotel to baffle pursuit.

I cannot describe the hour that followed. We were hurried through the woods at a breakneck pace, going uphill the whole time. At last we emerged in the open, on the mountainside, and I saw just in front of us an extraordinary conglomeration of fantastic rocks and boulders. This must be the Felsenlabyrinth of which Harvey had spoken. Soon we were winding in and out of its recesses. The place was like a maze devised by some evil genie.

Suddenly we stopped. An enormous rock barred our path. One of the men stooped and seemed to push on something, when, without a sound, the huge mass of rock turned on itself and disclosed a small tunnel-like opening leading into the mountain-side. Into this we were hurried.

For some time the tunnel was narrow, but presently it widened, and before very long we came out into a wide, rocky chamber lighted by electricity. There the gags were removed. At a sign from Number Four, who stood before us with mocking triumph in his face, we were searched, and every article was removed from our pockets, including Poirot's little automatic pistol.

A pang smote me as it was tossed down on the table. We were defeated — hopelessly defeated and outnumbered. It was the end.

"Welcome to the headquarters of The Big Four, Monsieur Hercule Poirot," said Number Four, in a mocking tone. "To meet you again is an unexpected pleasure. But was it worthwhile returning from the grave only for this?"

Poirot did not reply. I dared not look at him.

"Come this way," continued Number Four. "Your arrival will be somewhat of a surprise to my colleagues."

He indicated a narrow doorway in the wall. We passed through and found ourselves in another chamber. At the very end of it was a table behind which four chairs were placed. The end chair was empty, but was draped with a mandarin's cape. On the second, smoking a cigar, sat Mr. Abe Ryland. Leaning back on the third chair, with her burning eyes and her nun's face, was Madame Olivier. Number Four took his seat on the fourth chair.

We were in the presence of The Big Four. Never had I felt so fully the reality and the presence of Li Chang Yen as I did now when confronting his empty seat. Far away in China, he yet controlled and directed this malign organization.

Madame Olivier gave a faint cry on seeing us. Ryland, more self-controlled, only shifted his cigar and raised his grizzled eyebrows.

"Mr. Hercule Poirot," said Ryland slowly. "This is a pleasant surprise. You put it over on us all right. We thought you were good and buried. No matter, the game is up now."

There was a ring as of steel in his voice. Madame Olivier said nothing; but her eyes burned, and I disliked the slow way she smiled.

"*Madame et messieurs*, I wish you good evening," said Poirot quietly.

Something unexpected, something I had not been prepared to hear in his voice, made me look at him. He seemed quite composed. Yet there was something about his whole appearance that was different.

"You have not your cigarette-case this time, Monsieur Poirot," said Madame Olivier, in her slow, measured voice.

"My cigarette-case? Ah, no, Madame."

For the moment it seemed as though he did not understand the significance of her allusion.

"You fool," said Number Four—"to pit yourself against—us! I warned you in Paris."

"True," said Poirot. "True."

I was puzzled. There was something about Poirot that I could not understand at all. Then there was a stir of draperies behind us, and the Countess Vera Rossakoff came in.

"Ah!" said Number Four. "Our valued and trusted lieutenant. An old friend of yours is here, my dear lady."

The Countess whirled round with her usual vehemence of movement.

"God in heaven!" she cried. "It is the little man! But he has the nine lives of the cat! Oh, little man, little man! Why did you mix yourself up in this?"

"Madame," said Poirot, with a bow, "me, like the great Napoleon, I am on the side of the big battalions."

As he spoke, I saw a sudden suspicion flash into her eyes, and at the same moment I knew the truth which subconsciously I had already sensed. The man beside me was not Hercule Poirot!

He was very like him—extraordinarily like him. There was the same egg-shaped head, the same strutting figure, delicately plump. But the voice was different, and the eyes, instead of being green, were dark; and surely the moustaches—those famous moustaches—?

My reflections were cut short by the Countess's voice. She stepped forward, her voice ringing with excitement.

"You have been deceived. That man is not Hercule Poirot!"

Number Four uttered an incredulous exclamation; but the Countess leaned forward and snatched at Poirot's moustaches. They came off in her hand, and then indeed the truth was plain, for this man's upper lip was disfigured by a small scar which completely altered the expression of the face.

"Not Hercule Poirot," muttered Number Four. "But who can he be then?"

"I know," I cried suddenly, and then stopped dead, afraid I had ruined everything.

But the man I will still refer to as Poirot had turned to me encouragingly.

"Say it if you will. It makes no matter now. The trick has succeeded."

"This is Achille Poirot," I said slowly—"Hercule Poirot's twin brother."

"Impossible," said Ryland sharply; but he was shaken.

"Hercule's plan has succeeded to a marvel," said Achille placidly.

Number Four leapt forward, his voice harsh and menacing.

"Succeeded, has it?" he snarled. "Do you realize that before many minutes have passed you will be dead—dead?"

"Yes," said Achille Poirot gravely,

"I realize that. It is you who do not realize that a man may be willing to purchase success by his life. There were men who laid down their lives for their country in the war. I am prepared to lay down my life in the same way for the world."

It struck me just then that, although perfectly willing to lay down my life, I might have been consulted in the matter! Then I remembered how Poirot had urged me to stay behind, and I felt slightly appeased.

"And in what way will your laying down your life benefit the world?" asked Ryland sardonically.

"I see that you do not perceive the true inwardness of Hercule's plan. To begin with, your place of retreat was known some months ago, and practically all the visitors, hotel assistants, and others are detectives or Secret Service men. A cordon has been drawn round the mountain. You may have more than one means of egress; but even so, you cannot escape. Poirot himself is directing the operations outside. Before I came down to the terrace in my brother's place, my boots were smeared with a preparation of aniseed tonight, and hounds are following the trail. It will lead them infallibly to the rock in the Felsenlabyrinth where the entrance is situated. You see, do what you will to *us*, the net is drawn tightly around *you*. You cannot escape."

Madame Olivier laughed suddenly.

"You are wrong. There is one way we can escape, and, like Samson of old, destroy our enemies at the same time. What do you say, my friends?"

Ryland was staring at Achille Poirot. "Suppose he's lying," he said hoarsely.

The other shrugged his shoulders. "In an hour it will be dawn. Then you can see for yourself the truth of my words. Already they should have traced me to the entrance in the Felsenlabyrinth."

Even as he spoke, there was a far-off reverberation, and a man ran in shouting incoherently. Ryland sprang up and went out. Madame Olivier moved to the end of the room and opened a door that I had not noticed. Inside I caught a glimpse of a perfectly equipped laboratory, which reminded me of the one in Paris. Number Four also sprang up and left the room for a minute. He returned with Poirot's revolver, which he gave to the Countess.

"There is no danger of their escaping," he said grimly. "But still, you had better have this."

Then he went out again. The Countess came over to us and surveyed my companion attentively for some time. Suddenly she laughed.

"You are very clever, Monsieur Achille Poirot," she said mockingly.

"Madame, let us talk business. It is fortunate that they have left us alone together. What is your price?"

"I do not understand. What price?"

"You can aid us to escape. You know the secret ways out of this retreat. I ask you, what is your price?"

She laughed again. "More than you could pay, little man! Why, all the money in the world would not buy me!"

"Madame, I did not speak of money. I am a man of intelligence. Nevertheless, this is a true fact — *everyone has his price!* In exchange for life and liberty I offer you your heart's desire."

"So you are a magician?"

"You can call me so if you like."

The Countess suddenly dropped her jesting manner. She spoke with passionate bitterness.

"Fool! My heart's desire! Can you give me revenge upon my enemies? Can you give me back youth and beauty and a gay heart? Can you bring the dead to life again?"

Achille Poirot was watching her very curiously. "Which of the three, Madame? Make your choice."

She laughed sardonically.

"You will sell me the elixir of life, perhaps? Come, I will make a bargain with you. Once, I had a child ... find my child for me — and you shall go free."

"Madame, I agree. It is a bargain. Your child shall be restored to you. On the faith of — on the faith of Hercule Poirot himself!"

Again that strange woman laughed — this time long and unrestrainedly.

"My dear Monsieur Poirot, I am afraid I laid a little trap for you! It is very kind of you to promise to find my child for me; but, you see, I happen to know that you would not succeed; and so that would be a very one-sided bargain, would it not?"

"Madame, I swear to you by the holy angels that I will restore your child to you."

"I asked you before, Monsieur Poirot, could you restore the dead to life?"

"Then the child is —"

"Dead? Yes."

He stepped forward and took her wrist.

"Madame, I — I who speak to you — swear once more. I will bring the dead to life."

She stared at him as though fascinated.

"You do not believe me. I will prove my words. Get my pocket-book which they took from me."

She went out of the room, and returned with it in her hand. Throughout all, she retained her grip on the revolver. I felt that Achille Poirot's chances of bluffing her were very slight. The Countess Vera Rossakoff was no fool.

"Open it, Madame. The flap on the left-hand side. That is right. Now take out that photograph and look at it."

Wonderingly, she took out what seemed to be a small snapshot. No sooner had she looked at it then she uttered a cry and swayed as though about to fall. Then she almost flew at my companion.

"Where? Where? You shall tell me. Where?"

"Remember your bargain, Madame."

"Yes, yes; I will trust you. Quick, before they come back."

Catching him by the hand, she drew him quickly and silently out of the room. I followed. From the outer room, she led us into the tunnel by which we had first entered; but a short way along, this forked, and she turned off to the right. Again and again the passage divided; but she led us along, never faltering or seeming to doubt her way, and with increasing speed.

"If only we are in time," she panted. "We must be out in the open before the explosion occurs."

Still we went on. I understood that this tunnel led right through the mountain, and that we should finally emerge on the other side, facing a different valley. The sweat streamed down my face, but I raced on.

And then, far away, I saw a gleam of daylight. Nearer and nearer it came. I saw green bushes growing. We forced them aside — pushed our way through. We were in the open again, with the faint light of dawn making everything rosy. Poirot's cordon was a reality. Even as we emerged, three men fell upon us, but released us again with a cry of astonishment.

"Quick!" cried my companion. "Quick! — there is no time to lose —"

But he was not destined to finish. The earth shook and trembled under our feet, there was a terrific roar, and the whole mountain seemed to dissolve. We were flung headlong through the air.

I came to myself at last. I was in a strange bed and a strange room. Someone was standing by the window. He turned and came and stood by me.

It was Achille Poirot — or, stay, was it?

The well-known ironical voice dispelled any doubts I might have had.

"But yes, my friend, it is I. Brother Achille has gone home again — to the land of myths. It was I all the time. It is not only Number Four who can act a part! Belladonna in the eyes, the sacrifice of my moustaches, and a real scar — the inflicting of which caused me much pain two months ago; but I could not risk a fake beneath the eagle eyes of Number Four. And the final touch, your own knowledge and belief that there was such a person as Achille Poirot! It was invaluable, the assistance you rendered me; half the success of the coup is due to you! The whole crux of the affair was to make them believe that Hercule Poirot was still at large directing operations. Otherwise, everything was true — the aniseed, the cordon, etc."

"But why not really send a substitute?"

"And let you go into danger without me by your side? You have a pretty idea of me there! Besides, I always had a hope of finding a way out through the Countess."

"How on earth did you manage to convince her? It was a pretty thin story to make her swallow — all that about a dead child."

"The Countess has a great deal more perspicacity than you have, my dear Hastings. She was taken in at first by my disguise; but she soon saw through it. When she said, 'You are very clever, Monsieur Achille Poirot,' I knew that she had guessed the truth. It was then or never to play my trump-card."

"All that rigmarole about bringing the dead to life?"

"Exactly — but then, you see, I had the child all along."

"What?"

"But yes! You know my motto — be prepared. As soon as I found out that the Countess Rossakoff was mixed up with The Big Four, I had every possible inquiry made as to her antecedents. I learned that she had had a child who was reported to have been killed, and I also found that there were discrepancies in the story which led me to wonder whether it might not, after all, be alive. In the end, I succeeded in tracing the boy, and by paying out a large sum, I obtained possession of the child's person. The poor little fellow was nearly dead of starvation. I placed him in a safe place, with kindly people, and took a snapshot of him and his new surroundings. And so, when the time came, I had my little *coup de théâtre* all ready!"

"You are wonderful, Poirot; absolutely wonderful!"

"I was glad to do it, too. For I have always admired the Countess. I should have been sorry if she had perished in the explosion."

"I've been half afraid to ask you — what of The Big Four?"

"All the bodies have now been recovered. That of Number Four was quite unrecognizable — the head blown to pieces. I wish — I rather wish it had not been so. I should have liked to be sure — but no more of that. Look at this."

He handed me a newspaper in which a paragraph was marked. It reported the death by suicide of Li Chang Yen, who had engineered the recent revolution which had failed so disastrously.

"My great opponent," said Poirot gravely. "It was fated that he and I should never meet in the flesh. When he received the news of the disaster here, he took the simplest way out. A great brain, my friend, a great brain. But I wish I had seen the face of the man who was Number Four.... Supposing that, after all — but I romance. He is dead. Yes, *mon ami*, together we have faced and routed The Big Four; and now you will return to your charming wife, and I — I shall retire. The great case of my life is over. Anything else will seem tame after this. No, I shall retire. Possibly I shall grow vegetable marrows! I might even marry and range myself!"

He laughed heartily at the idea, but with a touch of embarrassment. I hope … small men always admire big, flamboyant women ….

"Marry and range myself," he said again. "Who knows?"

www.ingramcontent.com/pod-product-compliance
Lightning Source LLC
Chambersburg PA
CBHW081137020726
47504CB00009B/1893
*9781635916621*